The Lime Walk

The Lime Walk

a Norfolk romance

J.A. Noble

Matador
5 Weir Road
Kibworth Beauchamp
Leicester LE8 0LQ, UK
Tel: (+44) 116 279 2299
Fax: (+44) 116 279 2277
Email: books@troubador.co.uk
Web: www.troubador.co.uk/matador

ISBN 978 1848764 446

British Library Cataloguing in Publication Data.
A catalogue record for this book is available from the British Library.

Typeset in 11pt Bembo by Troubador Publishing Ltd, Leicester, UK
Printed and bound in Great Britain by TJI Digital, Padstow, Cornwall

Matador is an imprint of Troubador Publishing Ltd

This book is dedicated to my children,
Dale Noble and Claire Tierque
for their love, support and encouragement.

CHARACTERS

Thomas Roberts Challiss. Gardener, soldier. *Moat Farm,* and *Lyndon Manor,* (East Norfolk); Waterloo, (Belgium); Escalles (France) and Uppham St Mary, (West Norfolk).

George Challiss. Soldier. Master of *Uppham House* and estate, Uppham St Mary; Waterloo; Escalles; Ontario (Upper Canada).

Miss Mary Emma Kay. *Lyndon Manor;* Welthrop (Lincolnshire); *Uppham House,* Uppham St Mary.

Josiah Kay. Miss Kay's uncle/ guardian. Owner of *Lyndon Manor.*

Miss Jane Peters, Mary Emma's governess and companion. *Lyndon Manor;* Welthrop. Scarborough, (Yorkshire).

Adam (Adie) Brook. Gardener. *Lyndon Manor;* Welthrop; and *Church House,* Uppham St Mary.

Dulcibella Brook, Adam's wife. Their family: Burton, Agnes, John, Ann, Fanny, Dovey, Zeb, Noah.

Miss Garnet Brown. Trained nurse. Waterloo (Belgium); Fakenham.

Daniel Jones. Attorney-at-law. Fakenham.

Antoine d'Escalles. Merchant. *Les Flamants,* Pas-de-Calais (France). Honorine, his wife, and their children: Aimée, Phillipe, Edouard.

Alain, Le Comte de Briouze-Gournay, St Amand-Montrond, (France) Aimée d'Escalles' fiancé.

Lord and Lady Vyvyan of *Passendean,* Isle of Axholme, (Lincolnshire). Their children. Woodruff, Lady Vyvyan's personal maid. Servants.

Giles Ingleby, *alias* Ollander & c., London, Welthrop, (Lincs.) and Uppham St Mary, (West Norfolk).

Joseph Aldrich of *Uppham Lodge*, steward and estate manager.

Miss Ruth Vale, trained nurse, resident in Downham.

The Reverend John Wood, M.A., Vicar of St Mary's Church.

Ned Rudge, Barty Peckover, Maddy, Bob, Mrs Rudge, Miss Nevett and the Looret sisters: house servants at *Uppham House*.

Dr. Barnes of Downham. Miss Ruth Vale, trained nurse, Downham.

Lambert Jardine of *Lyndon Manor*. Mrs Esther Mawby, cook at *Lyndon Manor*. Wade Southwood, head gardener at *Lyndon Manor*.

The Reverend Edward Fieldgate, MA., Vicar of St Mary's Church, his wife, Catherine and their children: Robert and Frances.

Sir Everard Belmaine of *Martlets*, magistrate. Son, Percival Belmaine. Everett Pawl, illegitimate son of Bessie Pawl, once servant at *Martlets*.

Kit Warrender, Jem Webster, David Deacon, Clem Rix, Will Wright, Ben Wright: servants employed about the Uppham estate.

The above represent the major players in *The Lime Walk* saga.

Prologue
Waterloo. June 18th 1815
7.00 p.m. . . . or thereabouts . . .

The Foot Guards hide themselves among the corn. They wait behind the hill's rim in a ditch, near a wall, out of sight of the French cavalry. Tom Roberts crouches and fights down the cough triggered by the day's rain and battlesmoke. In a synchronous lull in the bombardment his empty stomach growls. Conscious of the glare thrown his way from black browed Sergeant Mylotte he grins but continues to stare ahead as if that rumble has nothing to do with him. Waiting to engage in another bloody battle tests his courage. Last night's congress with willing Léa and later, Julie, has relieved tension. Now, as Wellington's army waits in silence, the sounds of enemy cavalry ascending the hill are terrifying. The duke's injunction to "Stand firm, men!" is all very well. Tom intends to do just that if only his bowels will hold tight. Twenty's too young to die. He's not ready. He doesn't want his eyes to close on life under these leaden skies. After almost forty hours of misery he thanks God when the rain ceases. He's not seen much of the glory trumpeted by warmongers. Wet stinking clothes, damp muddy boots, lice, bolted scanty rations, shitting in the rain with his comrades, marching, asleep on his feet. As a Foot Guard attached to Maitland's Brigade he's part of a fighting machine, trained to fight to the death. He tries not to think about it.

The battlesmoke thins for an instant. A sliver of blue rends the pall of umber cloud that has covered the sky since morning. *Could be an omen.* Tom resolves that, should he be doomed to die in the next few minutes, he'll mind it less under a sky akin to a Norfolk summer blue. Just such a sky is spreading now above this god-forsaken ditch. *That Norfolk summer leaving sweet Mary Emma Kay. . .* Tom's reverie of Mary Emma amid yellowing corn, smiling at him from the shade of her leghorn bonnet, blue frock and ribbons fluttering in a soft breeze, is rudely shattered.

Wellington stands in his stirrups. "Now, Maitland! Now's your time!" Sergeant Mylotte signals his men. Hoofbeats. Exploding muskets. Horses neigh, rear, baulk. Blue sky. Helmets dazzle, sabres slice. Men fall. Screams shots smoke shouts stink shit slime. A blow. Pain head. Corn, mud. Someone cries: "Mary Emma!". . .

Chapter One

"Lie still, Roberts, if you want to live." Sergeant Mylotte's reassuring brogue penetrated the fallen soldier's returning consciousness. "It's nothing more than a hefty knock on the head." After the confusion and noise of battle the quiet was profound.

Eyes closed against the painful lights from the sergeant's dark lanterns – two lanterns? Tom lay back again. So night had fallen since he'd felt the world descend on his head. In the interval between the blow to his temple and returning consciousness he had been prey to jumbled dreams. It was true what the men said: your whole life does pass before you in moments of near death.

Himself as a solitary small boy weeding his grandparents' vegetable plot. Older, as an apprentice sieving soil for the master gardener at Lyndon Manor and playing with little Miss Mary Emma in the lime walk –

His empty stomach clenched painfully, folded and unfolded and he brought up a white froth that did nothing to alleviate the overwhelming nausea that assailed him.

"That's it, me boy." Joseph Mylotte passed a dampened cloth across Tom Roberts' pounding brow. "'Twas a nasty bump the falling horse gave ye. Ye have the concussion and the only remedy I know of for that is to lie still and be quiet."

Two sergeants swam before Tom's eyes. He was full of questions; but if he so much as stirred nausea returned. The dull pain in his right temple overrode every other sensation, swamped him. He lost consciousness once more…

"I won't tell you again, boy! You're Thomas Roberts", his Grandfather Roberts boomed. Tiny Tom, at three years old barely able to comprehend what the big man with the red face said to him, knew better than not to listen. Not to listen when spoken to by his yeoman grandfather was invariably followed by a walloping. "You'll do as I tell you! Your mama's gone, see? 'Tis no matter what she told you. Do you hear? As for your father –"

"Leave the child alone, Henry!" His grandmother intervened, and stooped to gather the small boy to her ample bosom. "Whatever sins others have committed, Tommy is innocent; though he'll bear the stigma of their folly for the whole of his life." Safe against the starched white bib of his grandmother's voluminous apron he breathed in her

special smell. Her plump arms surrounded him and pressed him to her pillowy breast. He knew Grandmother Roberts loved him because she was always telling him so and kissing him when Grandfather wasn't looking as well as showing it in countless other ways. He snuggled up to the comforting bosom – and awoke to find himself burrowing into the rough folds of an army blanket. Stars twinkled through the open flap of the tent in which he lay. They seemed to him exceptionally clear.

"Awake, are ye?" Sergeant Mylotte sat nearby smoking a short clay pipe.

"Aye, sergeant." Tom was relieved to be looking at only one brawny Irishman.

"You've slept away a night and a day and almost a second night. Look here! How many fingers d'ye see?" A single blunt digit was just discernible in the lamplight.

"One."

"Ye're on the mend!" This was said with immense satisfaction. "I won't deny ye gave me an awful fright when first I found ye. I thought we was both done for."

"I owe you my life then, Sergeant." A sobering thought. . . *Both?*

"Now; I wouldn't go so far as that, me boy." Mylotte looked embarrassed, cleared his throat and tapped his pipe against his large fist. "To be perfectly truthful, 'twas Captain Challiss found ye was still breathin'. To me everlastin' shame, I told him ye'd joined the angels. But 'twas himself saw that ye still had a spark o' life left in ye. The captain has kept an eye on ye from a distance, so to speak. Asked me to keep watch over ye, unbeknownst like. That's why I was always so down on ye, d'ye see?"

Tom smiled wanly. "Not exactly, Sergeant. I thought I simply irritated you."

The big Mayo man shook with suppressed laughter. "'Twas all I could do, at times, to keep it up. But, ye see. It was the only way I could think of keepin' ye skin whole! To drill ye and drill ye until ye became one o' the best of me platoon. And, by God!, ye was that soft a molly when ye first joined us I was in pure despair of ever makin' a fightin' man o' ye. 'Twas only the size of ye gave me any hope."

Gingerly, so as to disturb his injured head as little as possible, Tom stretched himself to his full six feet. It was true. The majority of the men were no more than five-and-a-half feet in height. But the Foot Guards were an elite body of men who, when seen in formation, presented a formidable fighting force made up of giants.

★

Something the sergeant had said nagged at Tom. *Challiss!* "You said

Captain Challiss asked you to watch over me. Why should he have done that?"

The sergeant tossed him a quizzical look and drew on his replenished pipe before replying. "Ye'll have noticed the captain's somewhat unusual colouring, Roberts? The dark red hair and grey eyes? Have ye studied his gait? Apart from which there's his build. 'Tis remarkably similar to your own, I'd say; wouldn't you? Does that tell ye nothing?"

"Of course I've noticed all that. But red hair's common enough especially among you Irish and for that matter so are grey eyes. I suppose it's possible that we had a common ancestor way back."

"Way back, my arse!" The sergeant voiced his disgust. "Sure, 'tis no mystery. Ye can't be his son, unless he fathered ye when himself was still in skirts. But the resemblance is too close to put the blame for it on *distant* ancestors. I'd say one generation would be more like. Why – aren't ye noses as alike as two peas, now?"

Tom was becoming interested. If only his head would stop hurting. "So?"

"Why, ye fool; don't ye see? Ye must be brothers!" The sergeant's broad face split into a smile. "Why else would one o' the quality be takin' such an interest in ye?"

Of course, it was nonsense. Tom had no brother. How he had longed for one when growing up! Yet the Challiss name had meant something special to him from his first hearing of Captain George Challiss. When he'd met the man he had been astonished at the similiarity to himself: it had intrigued him. Then training took over.

"It happens all the time in the old country," Sergeant Mylotte rambled on. "Aye; come to that, it happens all over and always has. A bit o' fun. A tumble in the hay. A lord taken with a pretty maid's face. If we did but know it, we're all of us descended from the aristocracy and they from the likes o' you an' me, like it or not! You've a look o' the quality about ye. Did it not occur to ye that ye're *half*-brothers?"

With the abruptness of a shaken kaleidoscope stilled, order was brought out of chaos as the disparate fragments of his earlier life coalesced. Everything made sense at last. He wasn't a Roberts at all – well, his *maternal* half was – he was a Challiss! He must seek permission to speak to Captain Challiss at the earliest opportunity.

★

"Tell me more about Uppham, sir," Tom said eagerly. His head was spinning and not from the after-effects of concussion this time. The two men were seated in a ramshackle outbuilding of a farm that had been caught up in the battle around Château de Hougoumont. Formalities had been dropped and the two men sat at ease with each other. Captain Challiss had confirmed the sergeant's theory. The Captain and Tom were indeed half-brothers and the officer seemed more than friendly to boot.

"You can drop the 'sir'." George Challiss smiled, revealing an amazingly sound set of even white teeth. Tom's own teeth were strong and fairly even but he couldn't help wondering how George, as he must learn to think of this vastly superior being, kept them so white. "I referred to our father as pater and mostly managed to avoid sirring him. As to Uppham – what can I say? It's a smallish house surrounded by the usual acreage one expects a gentleman to possess. How it has fared in my absence I cannot imagine. The care of it has been left in the hands of a friend who agreed, for a financial arrangement, to oversee the management and repairs of it. I have no love for the place. Too flat... Mylotte tells me you yourself are a Norfolk man, Tom."

"From east Norfolk, s– George. A little town near the north east coast called Felixton. I lived there on my Roberts grandparents' farm. It's not far from a great house with a large estate where I worked as a gardener before joining the army. Perhaps you've heard of Lyndon Manor, sir?"

George wagged an admonitory finger at Tom's slip, uncoiled his length from the chair on which he'd been sitting and strode over to a folding table supporting bottles and empty glasses. Tom saw that his brother was taller than himself by a good four inches but of a lighter frame. George poured something amber-coloured into two glasses and handed one to Tom. He reseated himself, supported his booted right ankle on his well-made left thigh and swallowed half the measure. "Drink up, man; it's demned good whiskey," his handsome brother chivied.

Tom sniffed the contents of his glass. "I never had whiskey before," he marvelled and took an injudicious gulp. The next instant he thought might be his last as fire burned his throat and tore through his vital organs like a living flame. Choking, eyes streaming, face burning, he felt an enormous thump on his back.

George was vastly amused by Tom's reaction and proffered him a tumbler of water. "Here, drink this." When Tom peered suspiciously at the liquid he urged: "Go on! It'll cool you down." As his brother swallowed the quenching liquid George, chuckling, said: "I see that whiskey isn't your tipple. What d'ye usually drink?"

Tom managed a barely audible: "Ale." As the water mixed with the whiskey he began to feel better and recalled his brother to the topic of conversation.

"Lyndon Manor? No. I think I never heard of it." Although George Challiss affected the careless drawl fashionable among those of his station Tom wouldn't have labelled him a fop. There was about him a hard grittiness, a certain look in his full grey eyes that commanded respect. "Where d'ye say it was situated?"

"Midway between Felixton and Cromer." And will I ever see it again? Tom wondered.

"No. Means absolutely nothing. How many acres, d'ye estimate? Is it a sizeable spread?"

"It's the grandest house in those parts," Tom said defensively. "And I don't know how many acres: but the lands are too vast to be encompassed by the naked eye, that I do know!"

"You don't say so? Anyway; enough of that. 'Tis Uppham you were asking of. I mean to be shot of the place −"

Tom heard him with dismay.

"− as soon as is practicable. I mean to try my luck in one of the colonies; I fancy Canada. Uppham will never be anything but a millstone around anybody's neck. As far as money goes the place is a bottomless pit and I mean to free myself of it before its demands on my income see me declared a bankrupt."

Warily sipping his whiskey and surprised that he was, after all, able to tolerate it, Tom spoke his thoughts aloud. "I had hoped, sir, to see the place where my mother worked. Where... our father lived. When mother was sent away from the farm I was too young to understand all that she had told me of her life at Uppham. But I could tell that she had loved the place and its people. Her voice softened whenever she mentioned anything to do with it. She said that I should go there when I was a man and ask for Mr Thomas Challiss. I suppose she meant your... our father, sir."

"And she took care to name you after him, eh?" George got up and poured himself a second drink, smiling his understanding when Tom declined. He settled himself and leaned towards this newly found brother. "Now that the war's over what are your plans, Tom?"

"Plans? I never got as far as making any. To tell you the truth, I never expected to come through it."

"What? That's no way for a Challiss to talk! Never look on the black side,

Tom. Fortune may be fickle but ye shouldn't offer her a helping hand."

Tom laughed. "Such as foiling her dastardly plans by not waiting to be made bankrupt, you mean. I suppose I'll go back to Norfolk and find employment as a gardener. That and farming are all I know."

George frowned and bit his lower lip in thought. Then he burst out: "Dash it all, I hate to think of such a grand young fellah hobbling himself to such a narrow outlook. There must be something else to be done."

"I've picked up a bit of an education." Tom recalled the lessons shared with Mary Emma Kay, their secret meetings, reading her books together in the bothy.

"I assumed that. You're obviously no fool. You strike me as the sort of man who observes closely and learns quickly. You are nine-tenths Challiss, I think."

Tom's heart swelled at this favourable account of his character. "If I might ask, sir —"

"Not so formal. Ask away!"

"How soon do you intend to sell Uppham? Is there any chance that I might see it before you put it on the market?"

"Much good may it do you!" George seemed preoccupied. "Tell you what. On the way back to England I intend to visit a branch of our family that live in the Pas-de-Calais. Sort of distant cousins. Go by the name of d'Escalles. They run an import-export business. If you agree, I'll take the opportunity to introduce you to them. There may be something there to occupy you while you decide on your future."

This was exciting news! A whole new world seemed to be opening up before him. Tom was on the point of thanking George for his consideration when the latter said: "But before we get started I still have much to do here. I suggest you occupy your time during the interim by writing down your history in the form of a letter to me."

Tom's euphoria crumbled into dismay. He'd always found putting quill to paper to be a tedious, messy exercise at which he had never excelled. "I hardly think—"

"You'll oblige me by doing as I ask, Tom," George said quietly, his expression adamant as he handed to him a sheaf of paper, a few quills and an inkhorn. "You may use my quarters. You'll find this table adequate, I think," he said, carrying away bottles and glasses to a handy shelf.

Appalled by the prospect of attempting to undertake such a daunting task, Tom decided to resist the imposition. "Well, *George* – in the first place I wouldn't know where to start. And then I shouldn't know how to go on. So you can stuff your pen and paper!"

The captain smiled and shrugged disdainfully. "So you were not serious when you said you desired to visit Uppham?"

"Oh yes, I was!" Tom was confused. He'd thought that was out of the question.

"Obviously, I haven't expressed myself clearly," George said. "Let's strike a bargain. Your history, in some detail, mind, as a passport to Uppham. Oh! And you might try by beginning at the beginning and continuing in sequence. Just tell your tale as it happened to you from your earliest memories to date, year by year. Have no fear. I won't be hard on your handwriting, spelling or grammar. Consider it a favour to me, there's a good fellah." That said, he strode out of the war-damaged barn to attend to his numerous duties leaving Tom with the beginnings of a headache.

He stared at the pile of blank paper with distaste. Heaving a huge sigh of resignation he drew a sheet towards him, sharpened a quill, unscrewed the inkhorn, dipped the chiselled nib into the ink and laboriously began to write.

★

Chapter Two

Waterloo, Belgium. The 21st Day of June 1815.

To George Challiss
I write here my life story believing it to be the truth as I know it.

'I was born of sin in the year 1795 at Uppham House, Norfolk. How that came about belongs to my mother's story of which I know something. My mother, Ann Roberts, was employed as lady's maid to Mrs Challiss. She was Lavinia, the ailing wife of the owner of Uppham House who was Mr Thomas Ralph Challiss. For many years I knew nothing of these things and it was not until my Grandmother Roberts told me of some of the details surrounding my birth that I began to understand my rightful place in the world.

My mother, the aforesaid Ann Roberts, was the only child of her parents, Henry Roberts and his wife Hannah. My Grandfather Henry Roberts was a yeoman farmer who owned land near the town of Felixton. His forebears had inhabited that place for many centuries and, should there be any doubt as to this assertion, their histories can be traced in the parish records. My Grandfather's farm is called Moat Farm, there once having been a keep and a moat nearby. Being the sole child of comparatively wealthy parents my mother spent a happy and indulged childhood. She was encouraged to help in lighter duties around the farm and to assist her mother in the work of the farmhouse. My Grandparents kept servants and laborers for the heavy work, although my Grandfather Roberts was always to be found among his men doing his share of the rough work.

Ann Roberts, my mother, attended a school in Felixton and could read, write, cipher and do fine needlework. When she reached the age of thirteen she begged her parents to allow her to go as a needlewoman to a fine house on the west side of the county of Norfolk. This was known as Uppham House. A schoolfriend of my mother's was a servant at Uppham. When a vacancy occurred for a good needlewoman, on account of the present one being about to leave in order to get married, she wrote of the post to my mother. The Challisses were considered respectable so my mother was allowed to go there as needlewoman on the understanding that she would return home if she disliked *anything about her new position. She wrote back to say that Uppham House was the most beautiful place she had ever seen, that Mr and Mrs Challiss were elegant, respectable and kind. They had one child, a son called George, who at the time of her writing, was a pretty boy and still in skirts. But the birth of this child had left Mrs Challiss a permanent invalid. At the time of my mother's going there Mrs Challiss was still able to walk abroad. As time passed she got about by driving a small dogcart around the grounds.*

By all accounts my mother was extremely happy in her place. Mrs Challiss took to her for, according to my Grandmother, Ann Roberts was a very pretty child who grew into a lovely young woman with a kind nature. Soon Mrs Challiss would ask for Ann to accompany her wherever she went and as the years passed my mother became her mistress's constant companion.

By the time Ann had reached her nineteenth year Mrs Challiss had been completely bedridden for over a year. My mother's master, Mr Thomas Ralph Challiss, was in the prime of life and a very handsome man. His son, George Challiss, was away at school. It was natural that Ann Roberts and Thomas Challiss should be thrown together in the evenings when Mrs Challiss was sleeping, heavily drugged with opium against the increasing pain of her malady. They would play chess together and by degrees their intimacy grew.

Their relationship changed. My mother became Mr Challiss's mistress and before many months had passed she was carrying Mr Challiss's child, in other words, myself.

My mother was brought to bed in the summer of 1795 and I was born on the fourth day of July. My Grandmother understood that from the moment of my entering the world I had the Challiss hair. My mother's disgrace was a dreadful blow to her parents. She had sullied the name of Roberts by presenting to the world her bastard child.

My Grandfather came to fetch us away from Uppham when I was one month old. My mother and I went home to Moat Farm where we lived under the stern daily rebuke of my Grandfather Roberts for the next three years. Even so, I consider that time to be the happiest in my life. My Grandmother saw that there would never be peace at the farm again while my mother was under the same roof as her father. One night I heard shouting and my mother sobbing. Next morning I was told that my mother had run away and was going to try to get back to Uppham. Some months later, in my fourth year, her body was found in a ditch. Ann Roberts was only recognizable by the fragments of clothing that clung to her corpse. And that was how my poor mother had met her untimely end. Her remains are buried in a pauper's grave at Cromer, I believe.

I was inconsolable for many months for I could not believe that my loving mother had willingly abandoned me. After that sad time I began to forget my mother's face and, as children will, I transferred my affections to the one who gave me the most love: my Grandmother Roberts. She was a kind old lady and very affectionate towards me. She protected me from my Grandfather's wrath. She taught me to read and write and to say my prayers and to fear God. It was because of my Grandmother that I became interested in natural history and gardening. She taught me the names of the wild flowers, the birds, trees and insects as we worked about the farm and tended her bit of garden near the farmhouse. I earned my keep in any way I could at Moat Farm. I was never allowed to idle away my time.

When I reached ten years old my Grandfather decided it was time for me to earn my own living. He had heard that a Gardener's Boy was wanted at Lyndon Manor and took me there to see if I would suit. Apparently I was considered suitable for I was taken on at once. Right after the Head Gardener and my Grandfather had come to an agreement I was surprised to see my Grandfather mount his horse – for we had ridden pillion to Lyndon Manor – and ride off without a farewell or a backward glance. That was my last sight of him.

"How goes the autobiography?" George Challiss's cheerful voice intruded on Tom's labours. He came up to the desk and peered over Tom's shoulder. "Good! Good! That's the ticket! Keep plugging away at it. I'll have an orderly bring you something to eat later on. Er – You'll forgive my mentioning it, old fellah, but I'd say it was time to mend your pen. Those blots and spatters are as thick as Boney's artillery fire!" Without waiting for any comment he wheeled about and was gone.

This interruption to his labours was decidedly offputting to Tom who had just got into the swing of his narrative. He might manage to complete the thing if only he were left alone. Irritably conceding that his brother was right, he cut a new point to his quill and collected his thoughts... *my last sight of him.* Perplexed, Tom scratched his head with the tip of the goose feather and tried to stir his sluggish memory... *my last sight of him.* What happened next? Ah! Of course. Adam!

To my joy and surprise I found the work congenial. It was less arduous and, to me, far more interesting than my work had been at Moat Farm. But the best thing about my move to Lyndon was meeting Mary Emma Kay.

Mary Emma was seven years old when I first saw her. Nobody could know her and not be enchanted by such a beautiful, sweet-natured child. Her heart-shaped face dimpled whenever she spoke, laughed or sang, while carmine tints played across her animated fair-skinned features. Her glossy black hair was cut into a fringe across the forehead with long shining ringlets cascading down her back. She seemed to me, then a rough boy of ten years old, dainty as a fairy; running about, dancing, skipping, putting her pony, Dandy, through its paces and, marvellous to me, she always looked so clean. Her voice was like a silver bell and when she laughed the bell tinkled. To look into those large, smiling blue eyes was to be captivated for life. And I was, as this account will reveal in time; for you say I must set down things in their right order.

But as far as I was concerned Mary Emma was forbidden. This was made quite clear to me on my first day at Lyndon by the Under Gardener, a young married man who spoke broad Norfolk and who told me his name was Adie, or Adam, Brook. "Though," he said, " you will always address me as MISTER Brook. Got that? I'm your Master and you answer to me." Then, seeing my eye stray to the little girl clad in a blue velvet habit, riding sidesaddle and trotting her chestnut pony across the paddock, he added: "And you can keep your eyes to yourself. That there's Miss Kay and not for the likes of you. Do you hear? No matter what she has to say, you stay dumb, boy. You'll only find yourself in trouble if you try and ape your betters."

For two whole days I obeyed Mister Brook. There was plenty for me to learn and do and I had no time to think of Mary Emma during the day. It was in the evenings that I wished I could get to know her better. I decided that if Mary Emma should take it into her head to speak to me I would speak up, as I had been taught to do by my Grandmother Roberts. Three days after my setting foot on the place we came face to face. I had been set to weed one of the flowerbeds in front of the Manor and Mary Emma came skipping around the corner. At the sight of me bareheaded and in my shirtsleeves she stopped dead in her tracks. "What a lovely colour your hair is in the sun," she said. "You must be Mr Brook's new Boy. What's your name, boy?"

The reference to my red hair had sent the blood rushing to my face so I kept my head bent over my work. "My name is Thomas Roberts, miss," I said.

She laughed. "How funny! That's like having two Christian names," she said, dimpling. "Have you no other?"

"No. Only two, miss. What's yours?"

"Don't you know? I suppose that's because you are new. I am Miss Mary Emma Kay of Lyndon Manor. I am my uncle's ward. He is Mr Josiah Kay and he owns everything around here. Tell me, Thomas Roberts. Do you like to play?"

I looked at her. "Play, miss? I'm not sure I know what you mean."

"Well, I could teach you, you know. It will be so much more fun, having someone to play with." Her large blue eyes stared into mine. I stared back. "I shall ask Miss

Peters; she's my governess," she said. "And I'll ask Miss Peters if you may come to the schoolroom and share my lessons. I'm sure you may, if I ask her nicely. It will be such fun! You'd like that, wouldn't you, Thomas Roberts? I know I should!"

Before I could reply Mister Brook came marching up. He raised his hat. "'Morning, Miss Kay. Has this boy been making a nuisance of himself, miss?"

"Good Morning, Mister Brook. No, he hasn't. Thomas Roberts has been very respectful. He would not have spoken to me had I not spoken to him first." She screwed up her face in sympathy. "He has to work very hard, doesn't he, poor boy."

Brooks mumbled: "Don' t know about that, miss." (I should say at this point that I find it impossible to translate Adam Brook's Norfolk accent into writing so I have not attempted it.)

Mary Emma's face rearranged itself into a mischievous smile as she asked Adam: "When does Roberts play, please, Mister Brook?"

"He don't, miss. He's a working boy, see, and too old to be skywannicking."

I said nothing. Nobody had ever weeded so assiduously before.

"Well I think that's a great pity," Mary Emma said, "especially as I was hoping he would be able to play with me sometimes. I shall ask Uncle Josiah about it."

"Aye, miss; you do that," Brook muttered as the little girl skipped away. "Now, listen, me lad. You stick to what I tell you and you and me will get along famously. Little miss likes her own way, see? But you and her's like chalk and cheese. You don't mix. Got it?" He spoke with firmness as a master should, not as a bully, and I took no exception to it. But I had my own ideas about what the little mistress proposed; so I kept quiet, worked hard, and waited to see how things would develop.

"Your vittles, sir; Captain Challiss's compliments." The orderly stood before Tom, a loaded tray poised on his right hand. "Where would you like it, sir?" the young soldier asked, staring pointedly at the littered table.

Dragging himself back to the present was something of a mental effort for Tom. Writing about his early days at Lyndon Manor had brought everything vividly before his eyes. He had become lost, reliving those times. He swept a glance around the wreck of a building. "Anywhere will do; please yourself. And cut out that sirring nonsense. I'm not an officer. No need to address me as if I were, Private."

"Used to be a waiter at 'Olborn, sir. It's an 'abit," the cheerful cockney smirked, wasting no breath on aitches. "This do yer, sir?" He'd contrived a table out of an up-ended barrel that had retained enough of its original form to be of some use.

"Admirably – Thank you – I'm much obliged – Now – If you don't mind –"

"Beggin' yer pardon, sir. I don't mean ter contradict yer, sir. Captain Challiss said I was ter stay long enough to see you swaller food an' drink, sir. Them's orders."

Tom realised that, if he wished to be rid of the man, he must comply with his brother's terms. Irritably, he threw down his pen, jumped up, stretched his cramped limbs and approached the steaming tray. It wasn't until he'd sunk his teeth into a leg of roast chicken that he realised how famished he was. How on earth had his brother managed to acquire such a feast? There was even a tumbler of ale with which to wash it down! Satisfied that his duty had been carried out, the orderly left him to finish his picnic in peace.

With a sense of well-being he hadn't felt for many days, Tom wandered round to the back of the building to relieve himself before settling down to his task with renewed vigour. As he sliced away once more at the frayed nib he spoke aloud to himself. "I shall have to cut short this account of my past or I'll be here until Domesday. Now; where was I?" No longer daunted by the prospect before him, he discovered that he was beginning to enjoy this re-examination of his past.

Dear Brother George. I am slow with my pen for writing does not come naturally to me. If I am to write this account of my life in only a few hours it is necessary to cut out too much detail. To continue in brief then:

Such were Miss Mary Emma's powers of persuasion over her guardian, Mr Josiah Kay, and Miss Peters, her governess, that it seemed they could forbid her nothing. It was arranged that I should share Emma Kay's afternoon lessons providing I rose an hour earlier than the other servants and got through the work Adie Brook (for so I called him in my mind) had set for me to do, before I was free. Scrubbing flowerpots by lamplight in the dark of a frosty autumn morning seemed to me a small price to pay for the sound education I was receiving at the hands of Miss Peters.

The governess was a small woman of about forty-five years. Some would have called her plainfaced but her warm nature and happy spirit shone through her hazel eyes and her face was transformed when she smiled. We took to each other at once. She loved to teach and I was hungry to learn and so I made swift progress. I had soon overtaken little Mary Emma, who was prone to daydreaming. Miss Peters insisted we go out into the grounds for daily exercise, even in the rain, providing we were well wrapped up. Mr Brook looked the other way when Mary Emma and I took our afternoon break and I discovered what was meant by play. What with good regular meals and plenty of fresh air and exertion, I had soon outgrown my clothes.

"I will speak to Mr Kay and see what might be done about providing you with new garments and boots," Miss Peters said one day, after I had bent down to retrieve my fallen quill and the seam of my tight trousers had split with a loud report. Mary Emma had tinkled with laughter as Miss Peters had remarked: "Oh, dear!" Yet the governess had been unable to keep her countenance as she had inspected the damage.

"But I have no money to pay for new clothes, Miss Peters," I'd said, tears of embarrassment springing to my eyes as I sat down to hide my exposed nether regions.

"We shall see," was all that Miss Peters said to that. "Now. We must go on with our work. Your handwriting is improving, Tom, but you must try not to get so much ink where it doesn't belong!" (I haven't mastered that fault yet, as you see.)

The very next morning two new suits of clothing appeared with two pairs of boots to go with them, for I was given new work clothes as well as a buff-coloured suit to change into for my lessons and for church attendance. I soon discovered that I was expected to forfeit part of my wages towards the replacement of my clothing. But that pleased me well, for I had no wish to be the object of anybody's charity.

The years passed in great happiness for me. I was passionately fond of my work and the more I learned about horticulture the more I wished to find out. My superiors were kind and didn't keep too many secrets to themselves relating to methods of propagation, the best recipes for weed control, or the mysteries of producing for the Manor dining table luscious tropical fruits in the severest of winter weather. I was allowed to see anything and to listen to what the gardeners discussed. I had never seen Mr Josiah Kay or any company about the place; he seemed content to leave the care of his niece to Miss Peters and the servants. So Mary Emma and I were often alone together. We shared books, vied for academic excellence and invented games to play in Lyndon's park. I was allowed to ride Dandy until we both outgrew him. The filly, Star, bought for Mary Emma's twelfth birthday, I never rode.

Our favourite haunt was the lime walk. Twice times fifty majestic limes paralleled the carriage drive which led through the park to the courtyard and the porte-cochère at the front of the house. We raced each other along the avenue, the loser's forfeit: a kiss. Marvelling at leaf-patterns cast by the sun on our slates, we outlined them in chalk, tried to catch subtle hues in paintings, cavorted through piles of russet leaves that accumulated in autumn and in winter sketched the skeletons of the naked trees. Since that time the lime has been my favourite tree. I have but to scent its perfumed buds to be transported to Lyndon Manor. Mary Emma and I became inseparable and grew as close as brother and sister. Though I lived in two worlds and took my meals with the servants the arrangement worked well and I was able to adapt myself to both stations with ease. That was a happy time for us all at Lyndon.

One day I observed a very old man climbing into a carriage and was surprised to be told that he was Mr Josiah Kay of Lyndon Manor. To me – I was then in my seventeenth year and had reached my full height – he looked more like a grandfather than an uncle; for the man must surely have been in his late seventies.

My darling Mary Emma had grown into a tall and beautiful girl of thirteen and, despite my good fortune, I looked into our future with despair. Recently, I had become aware that my feelings towards her were changing. Yet she seemed to me as unattainable as the stars. Months passed. Had I known then how soon my perfect bubble of happiness was to be pricked I should have prepared myself more adequately for the onset of disaster.

The corn had just been declared fit for harvesting when we all learned that Mr Josiah Kay had died during the night from a heart attack. Selfishly, all I could think of was how his death would affect my prospects as a future suitor for the hand of Mary Emma. The timing of the old man's death was most unlucky for me. I had spoken no words of love to Mary Emma who was still but a child. I had been content to wait until the time when she became a woman, when I hoped she would come to me of her own free will, though it might take years. Such a prize was worth waiting for. My immediate thought was: who will be responsible for Mary Emma now that she is without a guardian? We were not kept in suspense for long.

Lyndon Manor and its entire estate had been left to a Mr Lambert Jardine, a distant relative of Mr Kay's. He was some sort of nephew. We understood that he had inherited everything, with the proviso that he was to support Mary Emma Kay and Miss Peters who was to remain with her charge, first as governess and eventually as companion, until the occasion of Mary Emma Kay's marriage. There was to be no change at present to staffing arrangements. This was all the news we had been able to glean as to our immediate future. But as soon as Lambert Jardine took possession he began to make changes that were to affect us all.

"Hallo there, Tom! Gad! What are you doing writing in the gloom?" George fetched a lamp, removed its chimney and lit the wick from the glowing tip of his cigar. "There! That's better." He surveyed the scattered, ink-blotted papers that surrounded the legs of the writer's chair, bent down, picked up a sheet and read a few lines. "I say, this is jolly good, me boy. Reads just like a story. I suppose that isn't what it is by any chance?"

Angrily, Tom snatched the paper from George's hand. "Give it here, if you please. To read anything out of context gives but a superficial idea of the whole. If you'll just wait until I have finished—"

"Steady on, old fellah," George laughed. "I merely wish to show an interest in your labours. How much more is there to come? You've got through a devil of a quantity of paper and ink."

"If people wouldn't keep interrupting me I should get on a great deal better," Tom grumbled. "There isn't much more. By the way, that was a delicious meal you sent. My thanks, George. How on earth did you manage to assemble such a feast?"

"Aha! My secret, old fellah. But Mort Aris, the orderly who delivered it, has a nose for the very best ingredients to be found – wherever we happen to bivouac. How he acquires them I never ask and he never tells. But he is a valuable man to have at hand in a battle, eh?"

"Indeed. Now, George, am I in your way here or shall I try to finish this damned epistle somewhere else?"

"I'm away to Leuven for a night's relaxation, old fellah. Expect to be back at first light. By which time I hope to find your work done and you tucked up in my apology for a bed. Help yourself to whiskey," his eyes twinkled mischievously, "or anything else that take's ye fancy. No women available, I fear. Which is one reason for my temporary defection. À bientôt!"

Tom selected a new quill, trimmed the nib, took up the inkspattered half-written sheet, sighed wearily and marshalled his thoughts. "Oh, God," he groaned, as memories returned to haunt him. This was going to be difficult indeed.

The year was 1812. News of our victories in the Peninsular Wars had reached even the tranquil corner of Norfolk in which Lyndon Manor was situated. The steep rise in the price of corn had caused Bread Riots the year before. The riots had spread north to Yorkshire, Lancashire and Derbyshire. A rioting band of Luddites were shot, their leaders caught. After a trial the latter were hanged or transported. Wheat prices continued to soar until they reached an unheard of £30 a ton. Land-owners grew even richer, the poor could not afford bread and the Luddites, or their disciples, continued to wreak havoc. War was declared on the English by the Americans and the next we heard was that recruiting sergeants were busy at Cromer and Lynn.

This unrest throughout the world hardly impinged on my consciousness for it was becomingly increasingly obvious to me that the easy way of life formerly enjoyed by all of us living at Lyndon Manor would soon be changed for the worse. What happened was beyond my worst imaginings.

Lambert Jardine, unlike the former owner of Lyndon, was in evidence everywhere, questioning the established way of doing things. He must, by my reckoning, have been enormously rich; yet he began to pare away expenditure almost at once. Long-serving staff were unceremoniously dismissed with an extra week's wages as if their years of loyal servitude were of no consequence. Nor were they to Jardine. He was no true gentleman and his colonial drawl offended the men's lugs. They called him 'Coddy' Jardine behind his back, by which they meant he was full of false pride.

A whitefaced Adam Brook came to me at the end of a busy Friday to tell me that he had lost his place for no good reason. Apparently, I was now Under Gardener. On being told by Jardine that his wage would have to be reduced Brook had reminded his employer that he had a large family to support and another child on the way. It was exactly the excuse Jardine had been seeking. He accused Adie of disrespect and told him to be out of Gardener's Cottage within a fortnight. I wasn't around the place much longer and never discovered what became of poor Adie, his pretty wife, Dulcie, and their numerous children.

As Under Gardener I now took my orders from the Head Gardener, Mr Wade Southwood. Jardine had realised that Southwood was irreplaceable. Mr Southwood's position was unassailable because the whole of the estate's yield was dependent upon his vast experience and accumulated knowledge of horticulture. I was safe for the moment because my wage would be a great deal lower than that Adam Brook had been receiving after years of working his way up the ladder.

Now it comes to it! I have reached the point in my life story that I would willingly omit but which I must face if I wish to call myself an honest man.

Lambert Jardine, who was a well-made man in his late twenties, was evidently much taken with budding Mary Emma's charms. One morning he sent for me. Apparently he wished to discuss a matter that concerned my position at Lyndon. Naturally, I assumed it had to do with my duties as Under Gardener and speculated as to what misdemeanour he could justly accuse me of committing. But I was never one to meet trouble halfway and despite being in my working clothes took myself to Jardine's study via the servants' entrance. As I approached his door I heard a scream followed by a man's cry and the sound of heavy furniture crashing to the floor. The door was wrenched open and flung back on its hinges against the study wall with a thud as a dishevelled Mary Emma sped from the room and up the stairs. She was so distraught that she hadn't noticed my approach from the gloomy narrow corridor that led from the servants' entrance into the living rooms.

"What's happening here?" I demanded of Jardine on entering the study. "What has upset Miss Kay?"

Jardine's face was distorted with fury. He was dabbing his handkerchief at four long scratches that marred one olive cheek. Scarlet drops beaded from the wounds as soon as he tried to staunch them and his white silk handkerchief had become a blood-stained rag. "It would seem that the kitten has very sharp claws, Roberts," he said, in an attempt at regaining his composure. "Come in! It's about the little vixen that I wish to talk to you."

My hackles rose. "If by that base description you mean Miss Mary Emma Kay I have nothing to say to you, sir."

"Ah, but I think you have, Roberts," he sneered. "Don't think I haven't observed you and that minx cavorting in the lime avenue. I'm not blind; and I had no objection to the little madam being petted, within limits. I've met coves of your honourable breed before and can well imagine that both you and the girl are a pair of intact virgins. But I sent for you to tell you that your furtive assignations in the lime walk will cease from now on. I have just proposed that the spirited Miss Kay become affianced to me with a view to our nuptials taking place in say two or three years' time, perhaps on her sixteenth birthday. I assure you: things will be arranged as I intend. Our alliance will bring together Lyndon and the fortune left her in that part of her guardian's will that must remain untouched until she is married. The hoity-toity Miss Kay will do as she is told! She has no choice in the matter for I can turn her out of Lyndon without a penny and she knows it."

"That's not true!" I burst out. "Her guardian's will stipulates that you are honour bound to provide a home for Miss Kay and Miss Peters."

Jardine raised his eyebrows above the pad of the bloodsoaked handkerchief which he kept pressed to the injured cheek. "So you are privy to that, are you? Have you forgotten the rest of it? 'Until she marries' or some such phrase. That is my intention and I mean to see it carried out. It seems to me that you are a dangerous young fellow to have loose about the place, Roberts. Once I send you packing there'll be nobody left to thwart my desires—"

"You're forgetting Miss Peters!" I interjected loudly. "She'll never allow you to…"

"So you don't know everything!" He gave a harsh laugh. "Miss Peters, is it? Most amusing. Did it never occur to you that the governess is Mary Emma's mother, you idiot? And that the frequently-absent Mr Josiah Kay was the girl's father! And who's to say how many other brats he's spawned in his travels. Dear, dear! What a sheltered life you've led, Roberts." He watched for my reaction to his revelations.

I strove to keep my temper in check. "If Miss Peters – or whatever her name is – is indeed Mary Emma's true mother she will fight you tooth and nail before she'll sanction her daughter's marriage to one such as you!"

Jardine studied the blood drying on his soiled handkerchief. The parallel welts that ploughed his cheek had congealed. He was an ugly sight. Indicating his torn face, he *said softly: "I shall see that the little witch pays handsomely for this. I'll enjoy breaking that haughty spirit. And, mark you, I shall do it. She shall become my creature. I'll soon have her hungrily begging for my attentions. The only thing to be decided is when to begin. By which I mean before or after we are officially man and wife."*

I sprang at him. I remember shouting something. It might have been: "Shut your filthy mouth, you dog!" as my clenched fist met his chin with a mighty thwack. I shall never forget the look of surprise on his face as he fell backwards. He tried to right himself, failed, and in falling must have caught his head on the corner of his desk. I prodded the prone body with the toe of my thick muddy boot. After such a hullaballoo the room seemed unnaturally quiet and still, dust motes dancing in a slanted sunbeam. He didn't stir! Had I committed murder? Murder! A hanging offence, even were there mitigating circumstances and I had none to offer. The horror of my position has haunted me from that day to this. I dared not wait around to see whether Lambert Jardine were dead or not. I was damned either way. If he survived, he had the power to ruin me, perhaps be the cause of my death for attempted murder or, at least, to see me transported for my crime. Call it cowardice, if you will, but I felt I had no alternative. I had to leave Lyndon Manor immediately; but before I quitted the place for good I had to see Mary Emma one last time.

Tom flung down his quill. He felt unwell. The recollected horror returned: the crack as his own fist had connected with Jardine's chin, the man's surprised face, the falling body followed by the bright stillness of the study. It crushed him with the suddenness of a vicious blow from a lurking enemy. He staggered out into the starry night and lost most of the splendid meal he'd eaten earlier. Head hammering, face clammy, he found his way back inside with the uncertain steps of an old man and sluiced his face with cold water that he found in the bottom of a bucket. The row of bottles caught his eye. Brandy! He poured himself a small measure, swallowed it down and waited. Better! He sat himself down before his uncompleted task and wondered how he was to find the strength of will to finish it.

He dozed off and awoke as dawn streaked the horizon. Marvellously refreshed, he looked at his timepiece and saw that he'd slept for less than two hours. At the noise of carrion crows flapping about, cawing and squabbling, he poked his muzzy head out of the doorway and shuddered on seeing their yellow beaks tearing away at the staring eyes and bloody remnants of the battle's corpses. He sluiced his face again and rinsed his furry mouth. Ravenous, his empty stomach growling after the loss of Mort Aris's feast of the previous evening, he foraged among the shelves and found a hunk of bread wrapped in a cloth. Thanking God, he tore away great chunks of the stale loaf and bolted them half chewed. His hunger appeased, he downed a couple of glasses of rough red wine. The end of his task in sight, he gathered his writing materials about him and recommenced the account of his life with renewed vigour.

Mary Emma had fled from Lambert Jardine's study to the sanctuary of Miss Peters' room. I discovered them staring with apprehension at the opening door, evidently fearing that the intruder was Jardine. "Don't be alarmed!" I cried. "Jardine won't harm you any more, if what I believe is true." My legs gave way beneath me and, regardless of my soiled gardening clothes, I sank onto the snowy counterpane.

As Mary Emma sobbed against Miss Peters' breast, the woman's hazel eyes were riveted on the bloodied knuckles of my right hand. "What have you done, Tom? What is it you believe?" Mary Emma continued to sob as I met the eye of the governess. (I hesitate to use the term 'mother', George, for I had only Jardine's word as to the truth of that assertion.)

"I believe that I might have killed that man downstairs; Lambert Jardine."

"You've killed him?" The sun seemed to shine from Mary Emma's tearstained face as she broke free from Miss Peters' arms. "Oh, Tom! He was such a wicked man… Ah! … But now they'll come for you! They'll take you away and hang you!"

"That's what I came to say," I broke in. Every second was of the greatest urgency, it seemed to me. "I must leave here at once and … disappear, I suppose."

The moments following are painful to me still. Miss Peters was all efficiency while Mary Emma and I made our hurried farewells. Soon my former governess was pressing a bag of coins into my hand, had packed food for my immediate needs and had tied up a bundle of clothing, saying as she hurried to and fro: "God go with you, dear Thomas. You are a good young man: certainly, you meant Mr Jardine no lasting harm. Always believe well of yourself. We will remember you in our nightly prayers."

"Oh, yes: God keep you safe, dear Tom." Mary Emma caught up my damaged hand and pressed it to her lips. "But where will you go?" she said, her blue eyes wild with concern for my safety.

If I had loved her before, I now felt as if my full heart would burst; for the thought of leaving her behind was unbearable to me. "To Moat Farm, to begin with: though God alone knows what I shall find there after seven long years' absence and so few letters between us. The last I heard was that my Grandmother was unwell."

"And then?" Miss Peters urged. "The farm will be the first place they'll look!"

I shook my head in bewilderment. None of this should be happening. Everything was going wrong for us. "There's always the army, I suppose," I said, more for something to say than from any belief that I should ever be induced to follow that path. The afternoon sun had lost its brightness and the shadows in the room slanted at new angles. Hating to leave Mary Emma and Miss Peters, I said: "I must be off before Jardine's discovered."

Recovered a little from the insult perpetrated by one supposed to be her guardian, Mary Emma said: "You must go now. I'll meet you in the lime walk. Wait for me there. I'll come as quickly as I can without being seen. Hurry, Tom!"

They kept watch as I left the house by the servants' entrance and sprinted towards the safety of the shrubbery surrounding the manor. Once in its shadows, I looked back at the windows but saw only the pallid disc of Miss Peters' kind face. A flash of blue travelling fast towards the lime walk attracted my eye. With a desperate dash I followed, and my dear girl and I met for the last time beneath the green canopy. The pendulous lime flowers had outlived their honeyed scent of July and the air was filled with that faintly unpleasant perfume of dying blooms. We stood facing one another, our shoes speckled with the amber dust of the withered lime blossoms of late summer, and gazed at one another in silence for what seemed an eternity; and I knew then, though she spoke no word of it, that my darling returned my love. There was no time for a kiss. We left the park surrounding Lyndon Manor by the field gate and raced along the path through the ripe cornfield. And that was where I left my sweet darling girl, a slender figure in a narrow blue dress of some thin stuff, with its high waist emphasising her budding curves. Framed by yellow corn she made just such a picture as might have been painted by the late George Romney himself. "I'll never forget you, Tom dear," she called, smiling at me from the shade of her leghorn bonnet: hair, dress and ribbons buffeted by the late afternoon breeze.

"Nor I you, sweet Mary Emma," I called back. "Never! Well ... I must be off." I sprinted a short distance along the path that would eventually bring me to the Felixton road. Then I ran back and kissed her swiftly on the lips. Before she could utter a word I had hurried off again, turning once to shout back: "Wait for me, Mary Emma! Promise you'll wait! I'll come for you one day, my darling, I swear it."

Tears of emotion gathered in the soldier's eyes as he reread his last sentences. Three years had passed since he had spoken those words and yet he was no nearer keeping his promise to Mary Emma; nor was there any likelihood of his being able to do so in the immediate future as far as he could see. He began to write once more.

When I reached Moat Farm it was to find strangers inhabiting the farmhouse. A laborer I had known as a boy recognized me, despite the physical changes the intervening years had wrought in me. He told me that my grandparents were both dead and that Moat Farm, that had been owned by a Roberts for generations and that might once have been my own, had new owners. My heart being heavy at finding things so greatly altered, it never occurred to me to wonder what had happened to the money raised from the sale of the house and the vast acres of rich Norfolk farmland that surrounded it. I took myself away from such a painful experience.

From there I travelled by cart with a vegetable farmer on his way to Cromer with a load of fresh produce. My money was dwindling alarmingly so I next signed on as a hand on a coaster. That was a bad mistake for I was seasick much of the time and earned little for my pains. I thought it best to disembark as soon as the vessel reached King's Lynn. My plight became desperate and I feared every day to feel a restraining hand on my shoulder and to find myself arrested for an attempt on my employer's life or, even more frightening, for his actual murder. A whaler was on the point of leaving for Greenland and, despite possessing a poor constitution for a sailor, I signed on as a member of the crew. The discomfort, disgust and horror of those months at sea, imprisoned with the stench and slime of whaleblood and whalemeat, determined my next course of action. Oddly enough, my seasickness had been overcome. Even so, I had had more than enough of the sea and its terrors and have been barely able to stand the smell of an oil lamp since. The hard work on the whaler had developed my physique so that I now possessed an iron muscular frame and stood over six feet without boots. So when we docked again at King's Lynn, after six hard months at sea, I sought out the nearest recruiting office and signed on as an infantryman in Wellington's army and was soon on my way to Spain.

My adventures as one of Wellington's men took me from the Duke's successful campaign in north-east Spain, where I was first attached to the British army, to the Battle of Bordeaux in France. From there we swept through Arcis-sur-Aube to La Fère-Champenoise. With our Allies, we stormed Montmartre and entered Paris at the end of March 1814. Napoleon abdicated less than a fortnight later.

Many men were lost in the fighting, among them those I had loved as brothers. Yet we were glad to fight for the liberation of the peoples who had suffered the cruelties of Bonaparte's armies and to release the French from the tyranny of a self-proclaimed emperor. It was a just war. To have survived the Battle of Waterloo is cause for thanksgiving. To know that a simple Gardener from Norfolk was there and played his small part in the victory for Justice, and survived to tell of it when so many gave their lives, is humbling. Napoleon returned. The remainder of my story is so recent that you must already know most of it. Thomas Roberts Challiss,
late Maitland's Brigade attached to His Majesty's Imperial Foot Guard.

And then, without bothering to tidy the evidence of his long labour, Tom threw himself fully clothed onto his brother's makeshift bed and fell into the first deep and dreamless sleep that he had had for many months.

★

Chapter Three

The clatter of cutlery dropping onto the wooden table awoke Tom from a profound sleep. "Beggin' yer pardon, Guardsman Roberts, sir." Private Aris stood before him, a linen cloth draped over his left forearm as if he was still in employment as a waiter at Furnival's Inn Coffee House and Hotel. "Captain Challiss sends 'is compliments. 'E says you're to 'ave a turn hin 'is tub, swaller yer breakfast an' be ready to leave wivvin the hour. We're leavin' at noon. An' 'e's got a moun' for yer, an' all."

Still barely awake, Tom asked Aris to repeat the list of instructions, which the late resident of Holborn did verbatim. "Where do I find the tub?" he asked as he threw back the few covers.

"It's 'ere. I've added a drop of 'ot water to the Captain's. It 'ad got a bit cold, like; so yer should be awrigh', sir."

Still clad in his nightshirt, Tom waited for Aris to leave. "Er–"

Mort Aris grinned. "Don' you mind me, sir! I'll busy meself wiv yer breakfast an' it'll be ready to eat by the time you're aht o' the tub. After all, there ain't nuffin interestin' ter see, now is there, sir? It's not as if you was a young lady, sir, is it?"

Tom stripped and said with studied nonchalance as he stepped into the tub of tepid water: "I haven't ridden for many years," seeing Emma Mary's pony Dandy in his mind's eye. "You said Captain Challiss has a horse for me? I trust I shall not disgrace him with my poor horsemanship."

"Well. 'E said a *moun'*, sir. As ter what kind o' beast it is, I couldn' say. 'Ow d'yer like yer heggs done, Guardsman Roberts?"

"Any way that gives you the least trouble, Private Aris." Tom had not had such a feeling of absolute well-being for as long as he could remember. To be really clean was a luxury after many months of living in squalor. With a harsh brush and a jar of soft, green soap he scrubbed at his grimy skin. He paid particular attention to thoroughly ridding his body hair of its unwelcome inhabitants, and tried to think back to his last proper bath. He failed. He recalled river-dipping, swimming in lakes or pools and immersions in salt water which left his skin sticky to the touch. Now his body glowed from its vigorous attack. He stood up and experienced the forgotten wonder of dirty water draining from immaculately clean skin, taking with it a legion of drowned parasites. As he rubbed himself dry with a clean rag Tom reflected how, on many occasions during his life as a soldier, he and his comrades had had to make do with downpours of rain as the sole means of cleansing themselves. He shrugged. Rainwater was at least an effective diluent of the humiliating stench that accompanied each man like an alter ego. The stink came from their closely fitting woollen uniforms, especially during the hot summer months. Caused by contamination with each man's own unwashed body, the smell was inescapable. It disgusted Tom. It nauseated him. He turned to scowl at the offending garments. He was both surprised and cheered to see that mud and bloodstains had been sponged away as far as was possible and the tunic brushed. Nearby lay a small pile of fresh, precisely-folded linen. Inspecting it, he was overjoyed to discover clean underdrawers, hose and – astonishing – a fine cambric shirt. The latter was such a dazzling white that it could only belong to his brother. The pleasure he derived from donning the sweet-smelling garments outmatched any sensation he'd had so far. Including, he thought with a dash of insight as he fastened the shirt buttons, recent amatory liaisons, which drew from him a response of an entirely different nature. What was that, then? Mere animalism? Surely n–

"I'll leave yer breakfast 'ere, sir. It's pipin' 'ot an' there's a pot o' coffee. If you'll excuse me, sir, I'll leave yer to it. 'S all go, this mornin', an' no mistake!"

"My thanks, Private Aris. This looks splendid." Aris commandeered a passing volunteer to assist him in the removal of the tubful of bathwater and they staggered off with it. Tom sniffed the tantalizing aromas of fresh bread, egg and bacon, poured himself a cup of good coffee and set about clearing his plate. That accomplished, he felt like a new man and ready for anything that Fate might throw at him.

His mind still preoccupied with the remembrance of the unexpected gift of cleanliness, he recalled how he'd been taught to respect his body and to keep it clean as a ritual second only to godliness. As a boy, each morning, before he was allowed to eat a morsel of breakfast, his Grandmother Roberts had inspected his hands, neck and ears to ensure that they were well-washed. Not until she was sufficiently satisfied had he been allowed to sit down to eat. And so the habit of hygiene had been caught early and fixed for life. Even as a gardener he had meticulously scrubbed himself free of dirt and sweat at the end of each day's exertions. And he had bathed his body every Saturday night in preparation for the Sabbath in the knowledge that Miss Kay and her guardian, Mr Lambert Jardine, would be among the congregation. If they and he should meet face to face he hoped to be looking his best and free from giving offence by being associated with unpleasant odours of a personal nature.

Mary Emma's fastidious habits, allied to an appearance of robust health, had inspired him to emulate her routine. Almost. As he had been in the case of his brother's teeth, Tom had been mystified as to how Mary Emma had managed to keep her pretty teeth so white. His own were dingy despite his rubbing them with a rag dipped in salt every morning. He resolved to ask George to enlighten him.

Finding himself rid of months of accumulated filth brought back pleasant memories of the loving care and attention bestowed on him by his grandmother. It was to her regime that he owed his own good health. He wished now that he had demonstrated more love and appreciation. But he'd had nothing and nobody with whom to compare her. Childlike, he had taken for granted the hours spent by her in caring for his every need: in teaching him not only his letters and numbers, but also to love nature, to sing folk songs and to care for growing things. He had mistakenly thought that his being obedient to her will was enough of a return. But all that was in the past. Thoughts of those days, of his return to Moat Farm as he fled from Lyndon, reminded him of the unsolved riddle of the money raised by the sale of the farm. Once back in Norfolk, he would take a trip to Felixton to see what he could find out about that business. He made up his mind. Despite the threat of danger from the consequences of his last meeting with Lambert Jardine he would definitely risk a visit. There was no reason for Jardine to know that he was in the area.

Sounds of marshalling troops impinged on his reverie. The appetizing meal now a thing of the past, he took the plate and utensils outside, found a patch of dried earth and scoured them clean. Then he went in search of his brother. Thoughts of a long ride ahead of him on the back of an unspecified animal worried him.

Sergeant Mylotte detached himself from the mustering crowd and came over to Tom. "My! Don't ye look the regular dandy, Tom, me boy. 'Tis a fine animal they've acquired for ye," he cried, as excited as a schoolboy about to begin his holidays. "Follow me."

Laughing at the man's high good humour, Tom fell into step beside the large Irishman. "I was telling Aris earlier that it's years since I've ridden anything at all – not since I was a boy when I had the chance to ride heavy work horses and a pony."

"Aha! Have ye not? Wait till ye set eyes on this grand fellah." Mylotte whistled. A fine stallion cantered across the field and up to the retaining fence. The head of the bright-eyed animal tossed above the rail. "Will ye just look at the divine creature? He's a regular Pegasus now, don't ye agree? A battlefield casualty, so to speak."

Sorrow clouded Tom's face when he learned that the noble animal had been injured during the recent battle. Looking him over, he said: "I don't see any damage."

Mylotte guffawed as he patted the stallion's strong neck. "There's not so much as a flea bite puncturin' his magnificent chestnut hide. He's a Trakenher that finds himself an orphan… Don't ye, me poor boy… Approachin' sixteen hands, or I'm no judge. You'll not find a finer cavalry horse on this earth." He caressed the animal's nose with his large blunt-fingered hand. "No. 'Tis just that he's riderless at present, owin' to the fact that his master don't require his services no more, if ye foller me. This splendid bit o' horseflesh is a legacy left ye by a late Prussian officer, me boy."

"This is my mount? What a huge piece of luck! Where will I find a saddle?" As soon as saddle and bridle had been found Tom mounted the spirited horse, only to find himself immediately tumbled to the ground by a haughty equine rebuff. Discomforted by the laughter of the gathering crowd of onlookers, he remounted, took the reins firmly in his hands, jigged his unspurred heels into the stallion's sides and was borne away on the wind. As yet unaware of what a valuable treasure carried him over the blurred pasture, what little knowledge he had of horseflesh told him that this was one of the finest horses of its breed. "I must give him a name," he thought, his heart in his mouth as the pair of them effortlessly sailed over hedge and ditch.

"He appears to be capable of managing him, Joe," George Challiss remarked as he stood beside the sergeant watching Tom's deft handling of the lively Trakenher. No sooner had horse and rider vanished over the horizon than the observers heard the thunder of approaching hooves as the route was retraced. With a firm pull on the reins the young guardsman brought the stallion to a halt alongside the rails of the fence. Cheeks flushed from the exhilarating gallop, he bent forward and patted the horse's moist neck. "Good boy," he said quietly, and thrilled as he felt the animal's quivering response beneath him. He dismounted with an athletic spring and, the reins still in his hand, gave George and Mylotte a broad smile. "I agree with Sergeant Mylotte. There couldn't possibly be a better horse on earth! He's magnificent!"

George threw down the stump of a cigar. "You took to him like a duck to water," he commented. "Well done, Tom. Get one of the lads to give him a rub down before we set out; that's in about fifteen minutes. Look sharp." After which piece of advice he hurried away before Tom could express a word of gratitude.

"Here, Runciman!" the sergeant yelled. "At the double! I've a little job for ye." A tow-headed youngster, possibly no more than thirteen, came running. "Look lively, now. Give this horse a good rub down and report back to me in ten minutes."

"Sarge." The boy smartly caught hold of the reins and trotted the stallion away.

"Have ye thought of a name for him?" Mylotte enquired as the two of them walked back to George's quarters. " 'Twill have to be something befittin' his stature."

"I'll put my mind to it," Tom promised. "Now it's time I got my belongings together." He was about to depart when a sickening thought struck him. The letter, left scattered about the floor, where he'd dropped each page as soon as it was filled, had been missing when he'd bathed! And after the hours of sustained effort that had gone into its writing, Tom agonized. "Did you, Sergeant, or Aris, take away the letter I wrote to Captain Challiss? It's no longer where I left it last night when I retired."

"A letter, you say? Now what would I be knowin' of any letter, me boy?"

"Never mind, Sergeant. Thank you for nursing me along after my bump on the head. I'm very grateful to you. Think no more about the letter; it's sure to turn up." After which exchange the two soldiers went to prepare for the long ride to the coast.

★

George and Tom swung themselves up into their saddles. There was no sign of either Sergeant Mylotte or of Mort Aris, both of whom had agreed to accompany them on the homeward journey. "What the devil's keeping 'em?" George was plainly impatient to be off.

Tom, as eager as his brother to quit the scene of recent carnage, said: "If they don't come soon I vote we start for Ath without them. They have a copy of the route, haven't they?"

For answer, George turned his horse's head towards the north-west and set off at a smart trot. Tom followed and caught him up to ride abreast of him.

"Isn't that Aris over there?" He indicated a distant figure bending over one of the mass of unburied corpses. "What's he up to?"

"Pulling good sets of teeth for resale in London, by the look of it."

"Good God! I've seen the aftermath of battles before; watched the women and soldiers stripping the bodies of anything of the slightest value. But I've not seen anybody pulling dead men's teeth, until now." Tom was glad to be leaving Waterloo. "Reminds me of those crows hovering above the battlefield. See? There! That flock awaiting the opportunity to descend and pluck out the eyes of the dead and dying."

"And at night the rats swarm over the unburied bodies and feast themselves on our late brothers-in-arms," George said sombrely. "'Tis a common enough scene. But some soldiers are engaged in honourable work, collecting the identities and mementos of the fallen to be sent home to their next of kin. Yet, 'twould be against human nature not to pocket the odd bag of coins, any rings or trinkets, that might fetch a price. One never knows what might have befallen one's home and family while away."

Mary Emma leapt into Tom's mind. How had she fared in his absence? "I had no idea Aris was so cold-blooded," he said. "He struck me as a mild-mannered cove."

"And so he is," said George. "But he's a fly cockney with an eye to the main chance. There's many a fortune been made from battlefield corpses, Tom." With a quizzically raised right eyebrow, he added: "I suppose you're aware, my dear brother, that at this very moment you're sitting on your own battlefield nest egg?"

Tom laughed at the bizarre association of ideas. "But I'll never sell *him*," he said.

"Who said anything about selling the beast? I watched you give him his head when you first sat him. You've the makings of a fine racehorse there, if I'm any judge. I've spent many hours at Newmarket studying the sport of kings, Tom. As soon as we reach open country we must match your Prussian against Quicksilver." Irritably, he twisted in the saddle to scan the road they had travelled. "No sign of them! We've a ride of twenty miles ahead of us. Well, they must catch up as best they can. Come on, Quicksilver! Show Waterloo the undersides of your hooves." And spurring the grey Thoroughbred, he streaked away in the direction of the small Belgian town of Ath, leaving a surprised Tom determined to match his pace and, if possible, to overtake him. The impromptu race ended in a tie accompanied by the brothers' uproarious laughter.

★

They reached Ath by late afternoon and decided to put up for the night at an inn, leaving their horses at the rough and ready livery stables attached to the main building. "I suppose they'll be safe enough?" Tom said, anxious at the idea of letting his newly acquired stallion out of his sight.

"One takes one's chances, Tom," George said. "But if anybody lays hands on Quicksilver they'll have my pistol to reckon with and I shall make demned sure the varmints know it." He was as good as his boast, placing his pistol on the table in front of him with a clatter. They seated themselves and ordered platters of the savoury suckling pig with trimmings which was being served to other customers.

The innkeeper, impressed by the aristocratic bearing of the tall English *milords* mumbled something understood by neither brother into the ear of his weary-looking wife before he himself brought them two goblets and a flagon of wine. The Flemish couple seemed unduly pleased by the Englishmen's hearty attack on the improvised savoury mess. A sardonic smile flitted across the woman's haggard face: why grieve for a barking dog when his stewed bones brought gold chinking into their coffers?

In the room Tom and George had hired for the night, the men washed away some of the dust picked up on the road. "Have you had a chance to read the letter you insisted I write you?" Tom began. "It caused me much time and trouble—" He was silenced as he took in his brother's fatigued figure, the shadows beneath his eyes.

"Letter?" George paused in the act of removing his left boot. "Oh, *that* letter; I intend to peruse its contents this very night as a matter of fact." He struggled with the obstinate piece of footwear. "Looking... forward to... reading it." The boot flew off rather suddenly and dropped with a thud on the uncarpeted floor. "Haven't had a chance before... this," he added, as the right boot followed its mate.

Tom realised then how preoccupied he'd been with his own problems, had been so engrossed with the writing of the letter that he had not appreciated that the cause of George's long absences was due to all that his brother had had to attend to.

He was reminded of the sense of anticlimax that invariably accompanied cessation of conflict even if it ended in victory. Patriotism and unquestioning obedience to orders, allied to mercilessly rigorous training in the art of warfare, turned men into precise fighting machines. It tried each man to his limit and brought out feats of daring and courage he would never have known he possessed had he not gone to war. The brief sense of euphoria experienced in the knowledge that he had survived a difficult and dangerous undertaking evaporated all too quickly. When he was no longer an unthinking cog in a vast destructive machine, but was allowed for a time to become a man again, the sheer futility of warfare deflated Tom. Once the thrill of combat was removed, he realized that, because he had survived, the whole stressful pantomime must be undergone repeatedly until either death or demobilization ended it. In addition to obvious physical injury, he was convinced that war took an additional toll of survivors. Some veterans lived in a constant nightmare.

Tom later discovered that George had been responsible for that gruesome business following the aftermath of any conflict of arms: the Burial Detail. He'd had the difficult task of writing to the next of kin of battle casualties. It was his responsibility to ensure that small parcels of the personal effects of the fallen were returned as keepsakes via the bi-weekly penny postal service that had come into operation the previous April. These sobering thoughts put Tom's own epistolary efforts into perspective. He had no doubt that there were many other aspects of George's duties as an officer of which he was ignorant and regretted his peevish and childish remark.

"You must be dog tired," he said, as George stifled a yawn. "Get some rest: the letter will keep until some other time."

"No, no. I'd rather read it tonight. It'll help me to blot out some of the sights I've seen in the last few days. Distract me from things I'd rather forget."

Subdued by the aura of misery that filled the dingy chamber, Tom said: "Then I'll leave you to your labours, George. Goodnight."

Before sleep overtook him, he watched his brother unroll a thick sheaf of papers, which he assumed must be his own letter, move the candlestick to a table beside his chair and settle himself down to read. Shadows cast by the candlelight illumined his brother's haggard face. Tom was surprised to see it filled with sadness. By this time, he thought, George must have become hardened to the obscenities of war. As he turned away from the light, Tom could only imagine that something more personal had got him down.

★

Chapter Four

George's bed was empty. Hurriedly, Tom began to dress and was immediately aware of excruciating pain in his buttocks. He sat down on the edge of the bed and groaned as he thought of the day's hard riding ahead of him. A commotion below drew him to the small uncurtained window that overlooked the yard of the inn. The thickset innkeeper had a struggling boy by the scruff of the neck and was clubbing him about the head with his closed fist.

Before he'd had time to react, Tom heard George command: "Leave him be!" which, when the innkeeper failed to obey, he repeated in French. Tom watched his brother, who was stripped to the waist, his red hair darkened by a session under the pump, forcefully separate man and boy with his bare hands. He kept a firm grip on the boy, who had stopped struggling as soon as he heard the familiar voice, and cried: "Captain Challiss, sir! I'm right glad to see you, sir!"

"Quiet!" George thundered. He turned to the scowling innkeeper, addressing him in French. "What has he done?" Tom now recognized the boy as Mark Runciman. The innkeeper replied in halting French. "He is a thief! I found him in the stables. He slept. I fear for your horses."

Tom, partially dressed, hastened downstairs and was in time to catch his brother's rejoinder. "I know this boy. He is no thief. He is a stable boy late of the Duke of Wellington's Army of Alliance. He is a good boy. He was responsible for the care of the two horses now resting in the stables there."

"But – There are more 'orses since you arrive," the man growled, still eyeing Mark Runciman with suspicion.

Tom had money with him and tried his French. "Here, m'sieur. Breakfast for three, if you please." George smiled his approval of this tactic while Mark's bruised face split into a wide smile; but the boy wisely held his tongue.

Mollified, the man nodded agreement and returned to the inn where, from within, they heard him ranting in his unintelligible tongue.

"Run your head under the pump, Runciman," George said. "It'll take down the swelling and prevent further bruising. Looks like a wash wouldn't go amiss, anyhow."

Mark grinned. "Thought he was gonna kill me, sir, the way he was leathering into me. Didn't half clout me head, sir! And I hadn't even done nothing," he said in an aggrieved tone, " 'less you count taking a kip on his straw without asking first."

While the boy made a half-hearted visit to the pump, Tom and George went upstairs to finish dressing. Tom found a bowl and a pitcher of cold water in the room and set about making a hasty toilet. He poured a few drops of water into the bowl, shook a few salt crystals into it, swished the solution with a forefinger and was about to dip his tooth rag into it.

"Wait!" George produced a small tin and opened the hinged lid. It contained a white powder. He measured a quantity with a small horn spoon, added it to Tom's saline solution and stirred. It effervesced. "Try it now," he said, his eyes twinkling.

"Ugh!" Tom shuddered. "What the devil is it?" He spat the foul-tasting mixture into a handy cup.

George laughed at his expression of disgust. "One soon gets used to it," he chuckled. "Bicarbonate of soda, old fellah. Me old nurse swore by it as a receipt for keeping the teeth and gums in a healthy condition. You'll notice the difference in a day or two, I assure you."

"Hmm! Hope you're right. I should think that's how a rabid dog's mouth tastes." He ran his tongue over his teeth and was pleasantly surprised by the silkiness the mixture had produced on their surfaces. His mouth had never felt so clean. "It might be worth a few seconds' agony each morning, after all," he acceded.

"I find this little fellah useful, too." George held up a small, bristle-headed wooden brush for Tom's inspection.

"Where did you find that?"

"Got a Parisian brushmaker to make it for me."

Tom filed that information away for future reference. What a Frenchman could do any Englishman could equal, he thought, as he went to find Runciman.

★

Rested and breakfasted, the three soon set out for Lille. During the meal it had emerged that Mark Runciman was attempting to return to Essex; so Tom had suggested he ride pillion on the Trakenher. Mark's gratitude shone in his freckled face and he managed to drag out: "Cor! Thanks, sir," before climbing up behind him.

Tom was relieved to have left behind him the piles of fly-covered dead that had littered the road to Ath. The highway to Lille was busy with redundant fighting men, each making the journey home as best he could. Most would cover the almost one-hundred mile journey from the battlefield to the coast on foot and, accustomed as they were to route marching at a given pace, appeared content enough with their lot. They had survived. They sang or whistled as they marched. A smaller number, mostly wounded relics, rode in the heavy carts that transported artillery. A fortunate few had claimed riderless horses on the battlefield, some of them excellent specimens of horseflesh. Nobody appeared envious of anybody else. Camaraderie blossomed under the summer sky. Everyone had a common goal: home and loved ones. At no time since leaving Lyndon had Tom been so desperately homesick.

And as they rode in silence through the level countryside which, thought Tom, had some of Norfolk's topographical features but nothing to rival its lushness, he became prey to his own thoughts and memories. The monotony of the northern landscape was relieved by a bright patchwork of summer crops, meandering rivers, canals and cornfields. Corn. The scent of ripe cornfields had become inextricably woven into the pattern of his life. But these cornfields only depressed him now, reminded him of his last sight of a slim girl in a blue dress. Perhaps that vision was never to be exorcised. His heart ached with the longing to be with Mary Emma once more. As the sun climbed higher the day grew uncomfortably warm. The heat accompanied by the steady rhythm of his horse's hooves set him daydreaming...

One of his earliest memories is of himself as a small boy, short legs splayed across the wide dappled grey back of Magnus, his Grandfather Roberts' huge Shire, as he draws the sail-reaper. His small fingers are tangled in Magnus's rough mane. He recalls the thrill of fear that he might fall off, how he clings on for dear life while the patient animal toils up and down the golden wheatfields of Moat Farm; how far below him the sea of corn waves about, shining and rustling under the hot sun. He recollects the joyful years of growing up with Mary Emma, his long days out harvesting in the cornfields of Lyndon Manor in the time before Lambert Jardine became Master. He wishes he could erase the memory of that sickening sensation of slowly tumbling to earth and losing consciousness amid the trampled corn at Hougoumont.

The blow to his head has left no visible sign. But his small part in that decisive battle has left an indelible scar on his memory; and the final evening's momentous events re-enact themselves without conscious prompting.

He rides automatically and sees nothing of his present surroundings.

Unbidden, an image of a group of dejected figures – the peasants who live on the outer rim of the concave battleground – flashes onto Tom's inner eye...

Once more, the English and Dutch troops overrun the fields surrounding the Château of Hougoumont. The presence of the allied army draws the noisy and bloody conflict up towards their part of the ridge. The Duke stands in his stirrups, issues his command to Major Maitland, letting loose hell. Fierce fighting takes place in the fields adjacent to the château. Tom fully expects his own death within the next few moments as his battalion of the First Foot Guards hide themselves among the corn. In that eerie lull, Tom hears the peasants muttering curses. They anathematize the redfaced Anglais in their green and scarlet tunics, les homards *who hide among the ripening corn and ruin it. They curse their own countrymen, the wasted months of hard toil. They spit on all those who would disregard the bounty of the land with their warring.*

Tom floats above the battlefield and as the smoke clears sees below him a horrifying panorama of the effects of war. A scene of carnage. The screams of mutilated horses. Thousands of men lie dead or in the throes of dying. The cries of mortally wounded and maimed young men rend the heart. They call for their mothers, wives and sweethearts – call on their God to help them – in English, French, German, Dutch. Vulturine women – camp followers – are at their pilfering, picking away, rifling the dead and dying. The sombre peasant family – two women, an old man and a boy – stand, as if transfixed, gazing at their ruined crops which, only a week or two before this 18th of June, had held the promise of a bumper harvest! ...

Tom jolted out of his reverie. How could he have seen that? He'd been unconscious at that time. His injury must have been more serious than he'd realised. Nothing's fair in war, he thought. Each casualty leaves a long line of mourners in his wake. His mother, his sisters, his brothers; perhaps a sweetheart or a wife; his children, his friends... Death is a stone thrown into the pool of life: rings encircle the spot where it fells its quarry and spread outward to infinity. And during this campaign thousands, most of them men in the flower of their youth, have died before their time. In the end nobody wins.

"Penny for them," George said, coming abreast of Tom's chestnut as it carried its double burden. "You were miles away."

"What? Oh! Just thinking about getting home. How I long to be back on English soil, George. No. On my own soil: Norfolk." Tom was relieved to see that his brother seemed more like his old self after his adverse reaction to the battle the previous night – if that had been the cause of his low spirits. "Did you finish reading the letter?"

"I did." George dropped back. "How are you finding the ride, young Mark?"

"To tell you the truth, Captain Challiss, sir, I wouldn't say no to resting me bum: it's been hurting something shocking for miles now. He's a lovely horse, aint he, sir. Not that I'm not grateful to Guardsman Roberts for giving me a ride, like. Do you think he'd mind very much if I was to walk for a bit, sir?" Listening Tom smiled.

"Help him down, Tom. We'll meet you at the next inn, Runciman. Got that?"

"Sir!"

Tom dismounted and caught the boy as he slid from the horse. "And we won't wait more than an hour. Right?" Tom said. "On your own head be it if you're late."

But Mark's attention had been drawn to a pair of soldiers dragging a travois on which lay a boy of about Mark's age. "Blimey!" he exclaimed as he ran towards the litter. "It's Billy Courtenay! I thought you was a goner, mate."

The two young soldiers who had been pulling the makeshift conveyance, lowered it gently, got out their pipes and wandered away into a nearby field. One called over his shoulder: "Back in a minute, Billy."

"He'll be all right," George said, eyeing Mark. The brothers grinned at each other, amused by the Essex boy's vivacity.

As he remounted, Tom heard the injured boy's lusty yell as he caught sight of Mark. "Runcie! Where'd you spring from?"

As the brothers trotted away Tom heard his own name being called and slowed his horse to a halt. Mark caught him up and held aloft a small bag, saying: "Sergeant Mylotte asked me to give you this, Guardsman Roberts, sir. Said it was a going away present. Hopes it'll give you a good start in life when you leave the army, sir."

Puzzled, Tom reached down and took hold of a drawstring bag made of chamois. "Where is Sergeant Mylotte?" he said, scanning the thronged road as he stuffed the bag into his tunic.

"He ain't *here*, sir." Mark said pityingly, in a tone not quite as respectful as it should have been. "Sergeant Mylotte told me to tell you that he and Private Aris have volunteered for pit-digging. They're burying the dead 'uns back at Waterloo. They was going on to Paris after that, he said." Blowing out his cheeks as he tried to recover his spent wind, Mark added excitedly: "Me friend Billy's bin shot in the foot. But they think he's gonna be all right. Thanks again for the ride, sir!" he cried, as he ran back to his friend. "See you at the wotcher-me-call-it."

★

Chapter Five

They came to an inn on the outskirts of Lille and the heat was becoming troublesome. As it was nearing noon they decided they might as well stop for something to eat.

"Besides," George said as they dismounted, "there are several things we have to discuss." A glance at his face showed Tom that his brother had something serious on his mind. Leaving their horses with an ostler, they entered the low-ceilinged building.

Addressing their host, George said: "A private room, if you have one, landlord. Bring us something to eat and drink, if you please, and make sure we are not disturbed."

Tom admired the ease with which George managed people. He appeared to have a natural aptitude for it. "Why a private room?" he wanted to know.

"I don't want us to be overheard, that's all. There's no mystery." A servant showed them into a cubicle opening off the main room where they seated themselves in a booth. As the man busied himself in preparing the table he asked if they would like the window open or closed. "Leave it!" George said testily. "Now fetch our meal and bring a bottle of good wine to complement it. None of your dregs, man." He waited for the servant to depart, then said: "It won't have escaped your notice that I've been out of sorts the last few days. I apologize if I seem to have behaved towards you in an offhand manner but I had good reason. It's about that I wish to talk to you first."

Tom shrugged. "I don't know you well enough yet to be able comment on your various moods–"

"The fact is– This is dashed difficult–" He extricated himself from the confines of the table that separated them and paced the small space like a caged panther. He stopped suddenly. "Dash it all… there's no other way but to say it straight out. I'm sorry to have to tell you that our father is dead."

This was a blow. "No!" Tom had been looking forward to meeting the man who had sired him. "Sad news for us both, George. But for you who knew him it is infinitely worse. I... I don't know what to say... my condolences, of course."

"Good of you. Can't say it hasn't hit me for six, old fellah." He reseated himself. "Fact is, I'd counted on the pater running Uppham for several more years."

"What happened? When did he die?"

"Only got the letter on the 17th. Day before Waterloo. Bally bad timing, that was. Just when a fellah needs to have his wits about him. Demned unsettlin'." A polite knock at the door interrupted him. "Enter."

A savoury aroma preceded the manservant carrying two plates full of appetizing-looking food. "Thank you. Leave the bottle. We shan't require your services further." The man bowed himself out, closing the door quietly.

"Pater fell ill soon after Christmas with a severe chill," George resumed as they set about eating. "I knew that already. Aldrich, one of our men, wrote me a few lines then – Help yourself to wine. Tom – But I'd heard nothing further until this week."

Tom said: "I never heard of anybody dying from a chill before."

"Couldn't shift it. Settled on his chest. Turned to pneumonia. All over in a few days. Last day of May." A silence followed in which the only sounds were of the two men making a hearty meal.

His plate cleared, Tom helped George to more wine before filling his own glass. "So we've missed the funeral. Was our father a great age? I always thought of him as being little older than my mother."

"Nor was he! That's just it!" George complained. "In his early fifties. I'd counted on him to run the place for the next half-dozen years, at least."

Recalling what little his brother had told him of Uppham, Tom said: "But you should look on the bright side. As his only legal heir you stand to inherit everything."

"Exactly!" George gave a cynical laugh. "Everything. Shall I tell you what everything is? A decaying house, neglected gardens, fields overrun with brambles and weeds, the herd depleted, sheep – nil. As for staff to run the place..." he waved away the smoke from his cigar with a long slender hand, "died off, gone to war, too old or plain lazy. The place is a shambles."

As his brother had been talking, Tom had been forming a plan in his mind that would restore Uppham to its former glory. "You paint a gloomy picture, George. But it presents a challenge." He hesitated before his next words. "If you think I might be of help. . ."

George shook his head. "It would cost a fortune, old fellah. But thanks for the offer. The demned place has been nothing but a white elephant for most of me life. Can't wait to be shot of it."

"But it's been your family home for years," Tom protested.

"A mere sixty-eight, to be precise. Won by my grandfather on a turn of the cards halfway through the last century."

"From what you said I had imagined a much older house."

"That's the trouble with the place. Much of the house dates back to the seventeenth century. Only the façade is modern. But the place had been neglected for years before it became the Challiss seat." He stubbed out his cigar. "No, Tom. You can forget any ideas of restoring Uppham."

That's easier said than done, thought Tom.

George consulted his timepiece. "Where the devil's Runciman? Time's up. If he's not here—"

There was a rhythmic rap on the door. It opened and Runciman's grubby face appeared in the crack. "Ain't late, am I, Captain Challiss, sir? Guardsman Roberts?"

"Just as we thought we'd got rid of him," Tom said with mock seriousness.

"Cor, sir. Wait till you hear what Billy told me! You know, Billy Courtenay, sir. Him with the foot. Me and him run away from the workus to enlist as stable boys."

"And the Board was jolly glad to be shot of you both, I dare say," George said severely. "Well, come on, lad. Look lively. Over to the stables and fetch us our mounts. We've a good few miles to cover before dark."

"Sir!" The boy saluted and, properly subdued, ran off to carry out his orders.

"Rather hard on the boy, weren't you George? The war's over, you know."

"Keep 'em in their place, Tom; they'll be nothing but trouble otherwise."

Tom wasn't so certain of that. It hadn't worked that way with himself, he thought, as he swung into the saddle. "How's your behind, Mark? Any better?"

"Dunno 'til I sits on a horse again, sir," he said as he scrambled up behind Tom. "But the pain's eased off a bit. That Billy, though! The terrible things he said!"

"Such as what?" Tom said over his right shoulder as they trotted along at an easy pace.

George, obviously out of patience with Mark's non-stop prattling and their sedate progress, had galloped ahead. They'd skirted Lille and were now following the Hazebrouck road. By that means they hoped to avoid marauding survivors of the defeated French army. The brothers were sufficiently aware of themselves as targets for revenge and plunder, for their splendid horses had attracted unwanted attention as they traversed each highway. So they had decided on the the Hazebrouck route.

"Such as what?" Tom said in answer to Mark's mock outrage at his friend's disclosures.

"Well… Such as – When he went to the surgeon's house at Monsy John."

"And?"

"First, the surgeon geezer poured whiskey into the bullet hole in Billy's foot – he said it hurt like blue blazes but he didn't make a sound. There was a sergeant in there who'd just had his shattered arm cut off. Billy said this sergeant didn't make so much as a whimper not even when they tarred the stump. Gawd! Stood there with his own left arm tucked underneath his right arm like a French loaf. Anyway, Billy thought to himself: 'Poor bugger! If he can keep quiet so can I.' Then he had a horrible thought. P'raps his own foot would have to come off! And he said to me, ashamed like, that he did shed a silent tear over that. The surgeon saw he was upset and told him he was lucky. But Billy thought: 'I can do without any more of this kind of luck, thanks very much!' Anyway, the surgeon goes on to say: 'The bullet went clean through the – what was it he called it? – dor something."

"Dorsum," Tom said, grateful to Miss Peters for her Anatomy of Drawing lessons. "Thassit! It'd gone clean through the dorsum of his right foot. What's he mean, sir?"

"What you or I would call the front of our foot; between the ankle and the toes." Tom hoped the poor boy would be able to walk again. He was a spry little tike.

Mark was silent. They jogged on. "Right, sir. I was just looking at me own foot. I can see what your're on about, now. Billy showed me his wound. It looks horrible. He said it hurts him like the devil. Keeps him awake these hot nights."

Gangrene? God, I hope not, Tom thought. "Where d'you leave him, Mark?"

Catching a note of alarm in the guardsman's voice, the boy sounded frightened as he said: "Back on the Lille road. You know, sir, where we first saw him."

"Was he going into the town?"

"I dunno, sir."

"Think! It could be a matter of life or death for Billy."

Mark sobbed. "I can't think. I dunno, sir. Didn't tell me where he was going. But he won't have got far on that dragged bit of fence. Will he?"

"We must try to find him," Tom said, turning his horse about. "Sounds to me like that wound needs immediate attention." Worried by the fact that George was by this time out of sight he felt he had no option but to go back to the inn where he and his brother had dined at midday. Perhaps they would find Billy there. They set off.

Once arrived, by using a combination of bad French and gesture, Tom did his best to make the landlord understand that they were looking for a boy with an injured foot. It was no use. The man either couldn't or wouldn't understand him but kept winking at Tom. Tom raked the dining room seeking help from one of his own kind. No sign of a British uniform in the room. Except his own! What a fool he was to have returned here! Clearly, Wellington's dispersed army had departed the place long since.

"*Excusez-moi*, Johnny." A dark-eyed Frenchman lounged back in his chair and regarded Tom over the rim of his wine glass. His brown eyes slid from Tom and Mark to the men seated around his table and back to the two English. "I speak a little *anglais, mon ami*. I 'elp you, yes?"

"Don't tell him nothing, sir," whispered Mark. "Let's scarper!"

"Oo-la-la! '*Sir*', is it? *Mes amis*, we 'ave 'ere an English milor'!" He cast a swaggering grin around the group of onlookers and mockingly raised his glass to Tom.

Affecting not to notice the insult, Tom said blandly: "Ah! Well. Then I shall trouble you no further. If, as you say, you have no idea where the boy is—"

The Frenchman raised his shoulders and asked softly: "Did I say zat?" He turned down his mouth and appealed to those sitting and drinking around the table.

Before Tom could utter another word, Mark propelled himself at the surprised speaker, knocked him off his chair and had him by the throat.

"You cocky little bastard! You tell me where Billy is or I'll kill you with me own hands, you – you Frog you!" Despite his youth Mark matched the Frenchman in height if not weight. The Frenchman's comrades muttered and began to stir.

Seeing no other option, Tom darted forward, intending to prise the boy away. He shouted at the struggling bundle of limbs on the floor. "That's enough, Mark! Here. Behind me." Through the darkening window lightning flashed.

Mark yelled: "Watch it, sir! He's got a knife!" A clap of thunder rolled overhead almost obscuring another report.

The fracas ceased immediately as dusty fragments drifted down in the wake of a shot that had been fired into the ceiling. The weapon's destructive powers were amply demonstrated by the extensive damage caused by the single shot. In the doorway stood the rotund figure of the landlord. He stepped into the room wielding a blunderbuss, its flared muzzle pointed in their direction. Waving the barrel and with a display of anger he motioned Tom and Mark towards the open door.

"Get out, you English dogs!" he shouted in French, adding softly in English, "You'll find your little cripple with his lobster friends on the road into town." And again in audible French: "Out! Out!" He held the party of angry Frenchmen at bay until he heard the sound of the chestnut Trakenher and its double burden galloping away.

The first large drops of a thunderstorm fell as they sped towards Lille. They had covered no more than a mile or two when the heavens opened and Mark yelled in protest: "I'm getting drownded back here, Guardsman Roberts, sir." Tom looked around for cover. Through the surrounding gloom he spied a shack that looked as if it might serve as shelter until the rain eased. He twitched his horse. To the accompaniment of a vivid flash followed by the explosion of a stricken tree, he shouted to Mark to duck his head, ducked his own and the three of them dashed into the lowbeamed structure. The sudden entry of so large an animal into the confined space caused a howl of protest from its occupant followed by a rich stream of oaths.

Though the hut was not large it was impossible to see into its farthest corners. Tom was tired. The last thing he wanted now was to have to defend himself against attack from an unknown number of enemies. If only I had a light, he thought. As if in answer, somebody struck a flint into a tinderbox and a brief flame leapt upwards from a twist of dry straw. The shortlived illumination had been enough to show that the occupants – for there were two – were none other than George Challiss and Billy. In the semi-darkness once more the four greeted each other with relief.

Their being crowded into the flimsy shack with two large horses, no light and little food did nothing to detract from the feeling of companionship. Even so, George's first words were scarcely welcoming. "Where the devil have ye been, Tom?" he said. "One minute I could've sworn you were following me; the next time I looked round the road was empty."

"We went to look for Billy," Tom explained.

"We had an adventure, an' all," Mark added, for Billy's benefit.

"Quiet, Runciman!" George snapped. "What d'you mean? That you took off on a wild goose chase in search of this boy here? He was never lost!"

Embarrassed at being dressed down in front of the two boys, Tom felt his own temper rising. "How were we to know that? As far as I knew, Billy was in danger of losing his foot—"

"No I ain't, sir. Me foot's better since Captain Challiss found me at the side of the road. He carried me in here as the storm blew up and poured whiskey over me wound. It still pains me—"

"Quiet, Courtenay!" Tom heard his brother's exasperated sigh. "Those two mollies abandoned him, Tom. Left him to God knows what fate. They deserve to be shot."

"No they don't, Captain Challiss," Billy said defiantly. "They dragged me for miles, until the gate fell apart. I told 'em to leave me. I was sure somebody would turn up sooner or later."

"Oh were you? And suppose it had been the French?"

"But the war's over, sir. They wouldn't do nothing to me now. Would they?"

Tom laughed at the boy's simple reasoning. "Oh, yes, Billy. The war is over. But some of our French brothers in arms don't seem to know it! Still. All's well that ends well." He had an overwhelming desire for sleep. "No sign of the storm abating." His noisy yawn was eclipsed by a clap of thunder directly overhead. "I shall try to sleep." The others agreed that it was a good idea and, not for the first time in their lives, lay down to sleep supperless. Before he drifted off, Tom mumbled: "I shall call him Rufus." And the horse whinnied softly and stamped a hoof as if he understood and was relieved to have a new name at last.

★

Chapter Six

Rain fell steadily on the unsound roof of the shack and Tom was awakened by cold drops falling on his face. The others slept on. He rose as quietly as he was able to under such cramped conditions, led Rufus and Quicksilver outside and tethered them loosely so that they could nibble the grass verge. Ravenously hungry himself, he returned to the shack and set about rummaging through his saddlebags for something to eat. At the bottom of one of the bags he came upon the little chamois drawstring which Mark had said contained Sergeant Mylotte's going away present. Curiosity temporarily banished hunger. Using the leather saddlebag as a stable surface, he shook out the contents and immediately recoiled in disgust. Teeth! Perfect, strong white teeth. He counted them. Thirty-two. He arranged them into a complete set of uppers and lowers. Despite his initial reaction he studied the teeth individually. No cavities, no sign of the French disease: he'd seen plenty of notched teeth among the rank and file soldiers and knew the signs well. But what would he do with them? Mylotte had obviously thought them of value. How was he to find out? Unable to solve the problem, he gathered up the strangely sad spoils of war − for, thought Tom, some young casualty had undergone the final mutilation of having his beautiful teeth drawn − and was about to dribble them back into the chamois sac when his fingers detected something else within the lining of the bag. Surely not more teeth? On turning the receptacle inside out he saw that a seam had been opened and that whatever was hidden there had been deposited between the outer and inner skins. Then the seam had been resewn so that only a close inspection of the work revealed any tampering. The others slept on. He'd carried a needle and thread since his seafaring days and now took out the needle and proceeded to unpick the stitches that held the seam together. Ten small stitches had been undone. In the resulting aperture something gleamed dully. Please, God; not more teeth! It was tightly fixed and difficult to dislodge. He worked the leather backwards and forwards between finger and thumb until a stone popped out and shot away into the debris that covered the floor of the shack. "Damn!"

George sprang up at once, his hand on his pistol. "What's happening?" He was outside and back again in a few long strides. "I don't see anybody about.

What's Quicksilver doing out there. Ah! Grazing. Good." The boys stirred.

On his hands and knees, searching the filthy floor for the dropped stone, Tom said: "Oh, you're awake at last."

Billy rubbed his eyes and forgetting his injured foot started to rise only to sink back immediately with an indrawn breath. "Can't so much as take a leak because of this bally foot," he grumbled, looking around the space as if he might relieve himself there and then – until he caught George's eye.

"We'll both go," Mark said, stifling a yawn. "Come on, mate. Ups-a-daisy!" and the two hobbled out of the shack in unison. "Not raining, *still*," he said in disgust as the rain drove into their sleepy faces.

"Just what are you doing, crawling about on your hands and knees," George said as he took a small bowl from his saddlebag and stood it outside to catch rain.

Tom told him.

"What kind of stone? Describe it."

"As far as I can remember, as like to a piece of seawashed broken bottle as anything. I only had time for the briefest glimpse before it shot out of my fingers."

George showed interest at once. "In which direction did it fly?"

Tom sat back on his haunches. "Well! If I knew that I'd have picked it up by now, wouldn't I."

George grinned. "You're going about it in entirely the wrong way, old fellah.One must be methodical, you know. Have you any idea which part of the floor you have searched?"

Tom waved a hand about. "I've looked this bit over fairly thoroughly."

"Where exactly were you when you dropped it?" Tom indicated the spot. "In that case I suggest we each take a quarter of the space once the boys are back. That will divide the search."

"We are back," Billy said more cheerfully now that he was comfortable. "What's lost then?"

A plan of action was decided upon and each of them took a quarter of the hut to search from right to left in inch deep rows. In next to no time George had found the drab-looking stone. "Here!" He flourished it aloft.

The boys looked at each other as if the other two were mad. "Is that it?" Mark said, plainly wondering what all the fuss had been about.

"It is," said George, indicating by a glance at his brother that he should say nothing more about it.

Obviously disappointed by the apparently time-wasting exercise, Mark said: "I don't suppose anyone's got anything to eat."

"Have you?" George said, right eyebrow raised.

Discomforted by the captain's haughty stare, the boy mumbled: "No, sir."

"What makes you think that others should provide for you?" George said sharply. "If the army has taught you nothing else, it should have shown you that one must be self-sufficient. Self-reliance is a cardinal virtue and you should try to cultivate it, my boy. Suppose I were to ask you for sustenance? I should fare very badly."

"Whatever it is, I ain't got none, anyway," Mark mumbled.

Tom couldn't help smiling to himself. "Well," he said, "it's no feast; but I happen to have some stale bread and a hunk of cheese, if that's any good to anybody. It was fresh two days since."

Remembering Captain Challiss's recent homily, Mark said humbly: "If you could spare a bit for Billy and me we'd be ever so grateful, sir. Me stomach's rumbling something awful."

Observing that the boy had been thoroughly chastened George relented by adding four young carrots to the pool, saying; "We must make do with Adam's ale until we can find something better."

Billy's eyes lit up. "Never had ale before, sir," he smiled.

"Course you have, daft!" laughed Mark. "It's only another name for water!"

Both boys were suitably impressed when George retrieved the basin from outside. The amount of liquid collected was small but the captain allowed each of them a swallow. When it came to his own turn they were amazed when he produced a small brush which he dipped into the water, brushed his teeth vigorously with it several times, held it out in the rain, shook off as much water as possible and carefully wrapped it into a cloth before returning it to his saddlebag.

Mark and Billy exchanged meaningful glances at the apparent madness of the upper classes.

"I suggest, Tom, that we stow our shakoes and tunics out of sight. Might be safer as we travel across our recent enemy's country. It really would be like taunting a bull with a red rag. Eh?" He laughed. "I had Sergeant Mylotte pack a late Dutchman's waterproof cape for you; that roll, there. Good disguise and it'll keep you dry." While talking he had donned a redingote and a large-brimmed hat.

Tom looked the boys over. "Have we anything these fellows might wear to keep out the rain?" he asked.

Surprised, George said: "Such as what?"

"That's all right, Guardsman Roberts, sir. Billy and me are used to the wet and it ain't nearly so bad as yesterday's storm. But what about Billy's foot, sir?"

As he was walking out of the shack, George turned to smile at Mark. "Nice to know you're thinking about somebody other than yourself, Runciman. He'll ride pillion with me. That's of course."

"Crikey! On Quicksilver? Thank you, Captain Challiss, sir. Quicksilver and me's real pals, as you know. I've always wondered what it'd be like feel him under me for a proper long ride. Never thought I would, though," Billy marvelled.

"Stop prattling, boy!" George said, though less severely than was customary. "You'll give him a hand up Tom, will you?" he said as they left the shelter. "Wait until I've mounted and have brought Quicksilver back here."

The song of a thrush rent the moist air. The sun broke through, a rainbow formed and the rain gradually ceased, to leave a blue sky. The odd-looking group set out on the return journey to Hazebrouck and refreshment. Once there, the brothers sought the luxury of soap and water, a shave and clean clothes. But Mark and Billy, exhausted by the long ride, were ready for sleep as soon as they'd eaten. The night was spent at a crowded inn and early next morning they took the road to St Omer.

They had travelled half the distance to their destination, about seven miles, when Mark complained that his behind was becoming troublesome once more. "Sorry, Captain. I'll have to walk for a bit, sir. Feels as if me arse's clamped in a vice!"

"You're a damned nuisance, Runciman," George said, though mildly for him. "Makes one wish one had left you to your fate at the hands of the innkeeper at Ath. I suppose you'll have to get down, then. We could all do with a short respite. The horses, too."

As he helped Mark descend Tom said to anyone who cared to take note: "I've called him Rufus." The others approved his choice by a variety of responses.

Once off Rufus, Mark searched their surroundings for the short whatever-it-was the captain had said they could all do with; but, not knowing what the thing looked like, gave up worrying about it. "Hope he means vittles," he whispered to Billy as he helped his friend along. "Me belly thinks me throat's bin cut." They had devised hopping as the best means of travel for Billy while his foot was out of action, Mark's shoulder serving as a crutch.

The Challiss brothers soon left the others behind. The privacy gave them a chance to speak of matters they were reluctant to discuss before the boys.

Immediately they were out of earshot, George said, "Of course, Tom, you know that Mylotte's stone is an uncut diamond?"

Tom stood stock still, facing his brother. "How could I have known? I've never set eyes on one before today! It scarcely seems possible. Why, it's as dull as a pebble."

"But what a size! Big as a wren's egg! It must be worth tens of thousands of pounds." They walked on slowly beside their mounts, the reins loose in their hands.

Tom was sceptical. "Well... I'm not going to get my hopes up, George. There's a set of teeth, too. But I must say, it was uncommonly kind of the sergeant to think of me. I understood he had a large family to support back in county Mayo?"

"Good old Joe Mylotte! He had ten children, at the last count, I believe. But you may rest assured that he'd not have parted with that stone had he not found a quantity of them on some poor Dutchman stretched out on the battlefield. And the teeth are more likely to be a present from Mort Aris. Teeth-pulling's not in Joe's line. You must've made a favourable impression on both men, old fellah."

This changes everything, Tom thought. He fought down a sense of rising elation. He tried not to think about what such a sum of money might mean in his attempt to win Mary Emma's hand. The fact that now he would be perceived by Lambert Jardine as a man of means could be a powerful factor in altering that money-grabbing man's opinion of him. Immediately, Tom's hopes plummeted. What a fool he was! How could he have forgotten? Were Jardine alive, Tom's attack on him would be a case for prosecution. Were he dead, that would alter the case considerably. For who was there to say how Jardine had come by his accident? As far as he himself knew, there had been no witnesses to the quarrel.

"Perhaps our uncle d'Escalles will know of a diamond merchant to advise you," George said as a result of his own train of thought.

"What concerns me is how I'm to separate Miss Kay from her loathsome guardian, Mr Lambert Jardine, should he be alive," Tom said gloomily. "Whatever the case, I don't think I want to go through life with his death on my conscience. Whatever his injuries, I shall have to face the consequences of what I've done if I'm ever to be at peace with myself."

"There you go! Meeting trouble half-way. I understood from your letter that it was something you didn't do. Suppose you find yourself sentenced to transportation for life? What then?"

"But you must see, George, that I have to clear up this business if I'm ever to hold up my head?"

"Yes, I do see. I should act in the same way myself. But anything might have happened in the three years you've been away from Lyndon. Don't go throwing yourself headlong into trouble before spying out the land, old fellah."

"Oh, I shall take care, for Mary Emma's sake rather than merely to save my skin. What I dread is that he's managed to force her into marriage against her will!"

"You're at it again! You must have patience. Wait until we're back at Uppham. Then we shall see what's to be done." George laid a hand on his brother's shoulder. "Remember this: you're no longer alone. Whatever I can do to help you out of your difficulties I will do, Tom. You can be as sure of that as you are sure that there will be a new day tomorrow. There's a lot to discuss, arising from your letter to me. For now, though, I suggest we get on our way. If I know anything at all about boys it is that they're constantly hungry! Time to do some foraging and get those lads washed."

Tom shouted and beckoned to Mark and Billy. The boys joined them. The remainder of the journey to St Omer was uneventful and the boys lapsed into silence after a few miles of steady riding. All four were relieved to see the city rising above surrounding marshland with the Basilica of Notre Dame dominating the low horizon. George, having visited the town before, identified the ancient edifice. He then led the way to the east side of the city where he halted in front of a large rooming house which had been built in the shadow of the ruins of the Abbey of St Berthin.

Rooms were found easily and so cheaply that George paid for two adjoining each other. This would allow the men the luxury of a night free of the company of the normally loquacious stable boys. That Mark and Billy were also glad to be left to themselves was apparent by their happy faces when told of the arrangement. But their euphoria wasn't to last very long.

Once they had eaten and drunk their fill, George supervised a sluice under the pump for the two boys. Despite their vociferous protests he succeeded, with Tom's assistance, in getting their verminous heads washed with lye soap. Mark's objections reached a terrible pitch full of Essex expletives when the solution got into his partially-healed cuts and bruises. Next, George encouraged the boys to strip naked behind a screen of drying bedsheets and then bullied them into scrubbing every inch and every nook and cranny of their thin, grimy white bodies.

"It ain't decent!" Mark raged. "Parading us mother-naked in a public place. You're worse than the workus matron!"

This remark amused George who smiled. "I take that as a compliment, Runciman," he laughed, as he emptied the contents of a wooden bucket over each boy in turn, "and I might point out that if cleanliness is indeed next to godliness then your souls must be as black as the devil's coat. It'd do you both good to attend church every day for a month!"

As if to prove his point, they shouted back obscenities while he inspected their fingernails and toenails and peered into their ears. Finally, ignoring their howls of protest, he threw their filthy clothes into the brimming horse trough with an injunction to the boys to pound them as clean as they could with what was left of the soap. And he and Tom stood over them until they were satisfied that they were as clean as it was possible for them to be.

Despite the early hour, the boys were wrapped in blankets and sent up to their room while their pitifully ragged clothes were spread to dry in the afternoon sun. Mark and Billy, looking like two strangers without their coating of grime and with their hair trimmed by a motherly serving woman, seemed none the worse for their recent ordeal. The boys soon recovered their usual high spirits when Tom brought them a game of draughts he'd found in the other room. So by the time their clothes were dry they'd become quite creditable tacticians in the deployment of black and white counters across a chequered board. So addicted to the game's stratagems did they become that they preferred to stay where they were rather than to hobble about in tandem under the late afternoon sun.

Tom and George, at last with enough time to think of their own matters, had a bottle of brandy brought up to their room and settled themselves down to talk.

"My first thought on finishing the letter, Tom, was that you come of a more ancient stock than my own. The Robertses are indeed a distinguished family. I have no need to inspect any parish records to verify that fact. Now that we have the freedom to talk at leisure I want to shake you by the hand and tell you how very glad I am to have found such a fine specimen for a brother!" And he put down his glass, took Tom's right hand in a firm grip and shook it up and down as he spoke. "Wouldn't have been quite the thing to have called attention to ourselves in public, old fellah. But I do think it dashed bad luck that we couldn't have known one another years ago."

Much moved by his austere brother's obvious demonstration of genuine affection, Tom said: "What wouldn't I have given to know you when I was a boy! Still, no doubt the disparity in our ages would have been a stumbling block to close intimacy. At that age a difference of nine years is like coming from another generation."

"Not a bit of it!" George argued, as he struck a flint into his tinder box and lighted a cigar. "Had you known what a desert Uppham was you would say no such thing. My mother an invalid, my father a frustrated man whose whole life was wrapped up in trying to restore the estate. My early years were spent with a nurse and a tutor. I was kept quite separate until I was considered old enough, at the age of eight, to be sent away to school. I seldom saw my parents and Ann Roberts was allowed nowhere near my part of the house then." His expression was bitter. "The first bright spark I can remember was coming home from school at the end of my first Michaelmas term away and finding Ann Roberts in the house. The gloomy old place seemed suddenly filled with sunshine."

Tom was astonished. "You knew my mother?" He shook his head rapidly from side to side as he tried to sieve the idea into his brain. "What was she like? How do you remember her?"

"Much as you describe her in the letter. Full of the vitality of vigorous youth, gay and light and graceful of movement. Beautiful, to me. We spent hours together–"

A pang of jealousy shot through Tom. "But my grandmother told me you were away at school, that our father and my mother met in the evenings. It hadn't occurred to me to wonder how her daytime hours were spent," he said doubtingly.

"Hadn't it?" He blew a cloud of fragrant smoke across the room where it tangled with a sunshaft in a slow, sinuous dance. "Of course, your mother and I were often together in the daytime during the holidays, Tom. From what you wrote, your grandmother was a kind woman. I suspect she tried to spare you unnecessary distress. By that age I was developing a mind of my own. My mother became increasingly confined to bed, my father was preoccupied with the affairs of Uppham. Of course Ann and I sought each other's company during the day." He seemed to be having trouble with something in his throat that prevented him from continuing. He jumped up and strode about the room with averted face.

Tom waited for him to go on. He sipped the fiery liquid and followed his brother's peregrinations with puzzled eyes.

George noisily cleared his throat and said with forced brightness: "You know, I thought you might have named your horse Peregrine after old Brigadier-Major Maitland. Rufus is a dog's name." He reseated himself. "Forgive me. I'm not given to emotional nonsense, as a rule. Where was I?"

"No idea Maitland had a Christian name," Tom said. Then, seriously, "You were finding it incredibly difficult to talk about my mother – Ann Roberts, I believe."

George studied his fingernails as if they were of tremendous importance. "Dashed difficult to put it into words, old fellah. Never tried before. But Ann – I beg your pardon – your mother was the first person ever to show me any love. It was she who wrapped me in her arms when she found me sobbing in my bedroom: I forget what had occasioned that. It was she who ran with me in the wild meadows in summer, took me for brisk walks in autumn and winter. She played with me in the snow. To me, she was a mother-sister figure; a true friend. And I'll confess to you now, while I've got the nerve to say it, that reading of her horrible lonely death brought the tears to my eyes. Reading of it only days after receiving news of our father's death was a tremendous blow. How she must have suffered, poor girl. And so young! I was never told why she went away. At the time I was eleven years old. I only know that something died in me with her going. Perhaps it was the ability to show any feeling of true affection until finding you – the cause of her leaving Uppham."

Accutely embarrassed by his brother's candour, Tom didn't know what to say to this personal revelation. He was spared the necessity by a knock on the door. He opened it. The motherly serving woman who had volunteered to trim the boys' unkempt hair stood there. She bore a pile of boys' clothing on her outstretched arms. In rapid French she began to explain. Desperately, Tom grabbed at a word here and there in an attempt to make sense of the unpunctuated string of sounds. "*Excusez-moi, m'sieur. . . donnez. . . mes garçons. . . culottes. . . chemises. . . bans. . . pour les pauvres gamins anglais*—"

Tom held up his hand. "*Arrêtez, s'il vous plait*! George! I can't make out—"

"*Merci beaucoup, madame*," George said, bowing his head and smiling as he accepted the clothing and closed the door. "For Mark and Billy," he explained. "Clothes that her own sons have outgrown." He placed the garments on a chair. "They'll come in jolly useful, for the boys' clothes are in tatters."

"So they're in luck. Shouldn't we offer her some payment?" Tom suggested, remembering Miss Peters' provision of new clothing when he was a boy and how wonderful it had made him feel to pay for them.

"Not unless you would offend the woman. The clothes are a gift, old fellah." He returned to his chair. "I've been cogitatin' about what to do with the lads after we leave here. We can't take them with us to our people at Escalles: it's out of the question."

Billy's incapacity immediately sprang to Tom's mind. "We can't abandon them now!" he said hotly. "What about Billy's foot? He still can't walk a step unaided."

"He isn't likely to be unaided, is he," said George, reasonably. "Mark is quite capable of looking after Billy until—"

"But they're only boys, George!"

"— Mark will look after him until they reach the coast. I shall arrange for them to be conveyed by cart for the rest of the journey," said George, disregarding Tom's interruption. "With sufficient money for their passage—"

"What about food?"

"—With sufficient money they'll buy their own food, and any other necessities, on the journey. Good God! They've wits enough to get themselves back to Essex, haven't they, Tom? They're a sharp pair of young coves."

Though Tom was not happy with the arrangements he decided to hold his tongue. It was true, he reasoned, both lads were sharp-witted enough; yet they had looked so vulnerable as they stood naked in the yard of the inn. Recalling Mark's ferocious attack on the Frenchman, he smiled to himself. George was probably right. After all, Mark and Billy had survived a harsher upbringing than his own; one that made his own early life seem idyllic by contrast. And yet—

"Well?" said George, obviously irritated. "What now? You're still not satisfied!"

"I was thinking. How would it be if we were to take them as far as Escalles—"

"Now, look here, Tom—"

"No! Please hear me out, George. I understood you to say that your – our uncle is a merchant. Yes? Well, he must be able to find the boys passage to England on one of the ships they own or charter. If not—"

George frowned. "It's hardly likely they would be concerned with trade to the British Isles any more. Uncle Antoine wrote in − 1808 I believe it was − I took little notice at the time. After the British blockade of the sugar beet and indigo imports into France from Britain, although the French beet industry flourished, uncle predicted the eventual replacement of beet with cane. As far as I recall, d'Escalles et Fils now deal in cane sugar and tobacco imported from the Americas. Anyway, their trade is across the Atlantic, not with the English any longer."

"Still, there must be other vessels plying between Escalles and the English coast."

"Dammit! I'm sure you're right. Just leave our uncle out of your plans, eh? It wouldn't do to offend him, now, would it? Especially if you're considering a position with the company, old fellah." He lighted a cigar and expelled an aromatic cloud of smoke. "Right! We're agreed, then. Mark and Billy travel with us as far as the coast. Once there, I shall make it my personal responsibility to see the scallywags aboard the first craft crossing the Channel. And I can't say I shall be sorry to be rid of them!" Dismissively, with a long forefinger, he tapped the loose ash from his cigar.

Tom was thankful to hear no more of George's proposal for his finding employment in the merchant's house. Nothing would induce him to follow that course. He had other plans: for his future lay not in Pas-de-Calais but in Norfolk.

★

Chapter Seven

Mark and Billy, barely recognizable in their improved appearance – from shining heads of neatly trimmed hair to serviceable sabots (though Billy was able to wear only one at present) – had been taken aboard an English fishing trawler. The *Seagull*, returning on the night tide to Dymchurch with a consignment of tobacco, brandy, silks and laces, looked seaworthy. Her mate was an affable Kentish man who cheerfully welcomed the boys aboard. He pocketed the gold coins that George had counted into his hand and promised to set the boys ashore at Dymchurch at first light. As they fearlessly crossed the springy narrow gangplank, his friend's hand on his shoulder for support, Mark innocently remarked on the trim condition of the vessel and hopping Billy loudly approved the absence of any fishy smell. The two crewmen sullenly eyed the boys as, silently, they made the small boat ready.

Tom had said good-bye to the boys with a feeling of misgiving; but they had seemed happy enough to be on their way home to Essex at last. Tom gave Mark a piece of paper on which he'd written the word Uppham and told him to contact him should he ever find himself in need of work, that Norfolk was only a step from Essex.

"We can do nothing more for them," George said, as they remounted. "I doubt they've ever been so molly-coddled in their lives. Now to introduce ourselves to Uncle Antoine and his ménage before dark. We could both do with a good meal." They turned their backs on the sea and set off at a smart canter uphill to the town of Escalles. "It's several years since I was at *Les Flamants*," he added, "but I think you'll find it interesting. And the place certainly has pleasant memories for me." He lapsed into silence as they approached the high gates of a large stonebuilt house. At the pull of a bell a man soon emerged and let them in and led away their horses.

A dark-eyed girl wearing a bouffant muslin cap, together with a long, frilled apron over a blue gown, appeared at the open front door. Tom was astonished by the girl's prettiness and he and the maid exchanged glances of mutual interest. She asked them what business brought them at so late an hour. George explained to the maid, who was new to him. While he was in the process of introducing Tom and himself, stating their business to the girl, a tall man emerged from an upper room and looked over the balustrade: "Is it George Challiss? But, no! It's not possible. From where did you spring?" Napkin in hand, the man waved away the inquisitive maid and waited for the two young men to ascend the curving staircase. Tom glanced after the girl's retreating figure and blushed to the roots of his hair when he found her looking back at him with a bold and mischievous grin on her enchanting face.

On the landing, Antoine d'Escalles held his arms wide and George Challiss stepped into his uncle's waiting embrace. The two men exchanged kisses – left, right, left, right, bouncing apart as cheeks were changed with a nimble avoidance of banged noses. Tom's astonishment must have been apparent and Antoine, sensing his chill reserve, turned to this other visitor and surveyed him coolly. "Well, my friend; you must be *anglais*. I see that you are also a Challiss. But from where?"

"Uncle, may I be allowed to present my younger brother, Thomas Roberts Challiss? Tom, our Uncle Antoine." The two strangers bowed formally. "Perhaps I'd better explain, uncle," George began as they followed an obviously surprised Antoine back into the room he had quitted on their arrival.

"If you have no objection, George," Tom broke in, "I would rather tell M'sieur d'Escalles my own history – in brief, of course," he smiled, remembering his lengthy written version. "I must apologise for my ignorance of the French tongue, m'sieur."

"Have no fear of that, young man," laughed Antoine, revealing strong tobacco- stained teeth. "As you have heard already, I comprehend English and also speak it – after a fashion. But first, you must have something to eat. Is it not so?" He fired a string of rapidly muttered instructions at a deferential manservant and gestured to George and Tom to join those already in the process of dining. "*Ma chère*," he said, addressing a plump woman who was seated at the far end of the table, "we are honoured by two of my English relatives. George, of course, you remember. This young man – a mystery awaiting further explanation – is his younger brother, Thomas. Some wine for the gentlemen," he ordered the returned manservant.

Tom became aware of being the object of scrutiny from several pairs of eyes. The piercing brown pair belonged to Madame, a handsome woman in her late thirties, Tom guessed. Two pairs of full grey orbs, similar to his own and George's, belonged to a pair of youths, obviously brothers. A pair of startling violet-blue eyes stared at him from beneath straight black brows, soft dark hair piled high above an ivory forehead. These belonged to a young lady of about his own age.

"*Enchantée*, Meester Challiss." Madame d'Escalles inclined her elegant head. "Permit me to introduce our sons. On the left is Phillipe, the elder; and Edouard, my *bébé*." The youths dipped their heads in recognition. "And this is our lovely daughter, Aimée, who is affianced to Monsieur Le Comte de Briouze-Gournay."

That's got that out of the way then, thought Tom, as he smiled at the soignée young beauty. Definitely hands off! Though she was young she seemed to him very stately. He had difficulty keeping his eyes averted from her majestic bust which filled to overflowing the decolleté bodice of a gown whose clinging white satin set off her colouring to perfection. When conversation resumed he darted a look in her direction and saw that she had eyes only for George, who was in conversation with her father.

The next moment various appetizing dishes arrived and soon the brothers were attacking them with a relish sharpened by hunger. It was the signal for the rest of the family to recommence their interrupted repast and the meal progressed amid politely animated conversation. Somehow, Tom got his history told and was amused to find himself an object of romantic interest to the younger d'Escalles. Bastardy was taken philosophically by the French, it seemed.

"So now we 'ave another Challiss cousin!" young Edouard said, raising his glass. "I give you a toast, everybody. To our new cousin, Thomas Roberts Challiss!"

The toast was joined with a display of such genuine cordiality that it warmed Tom's heart. He noticed that Aimée, too, her glass raised in salute, was turned in his direction. Her dazzling smile left him so weak with longing to fondle those magnificent breasts that he was glad to be sitting down. When he met George's raised eyebrow he knew that his brother had observed the exchange and understood.

The meal ended, the two women and the youths rose and left the three men to their brandy and cigars. It was then that George broached the subject of the possibility of a position for his brother being found in their uncle's merchant business.

"Before any more is said on the subject," Tom said energetically, "I'd like to say that, honoured as I have been to meet my uncle and his splendid family, I have no wish to become a clerk, or anything else, in his enterprise." Antoine d'Escalles' brow darkened; but before he could speak, Tom pressed on. "I mean to cast no slur on your affairs, m'sieur; but my heart would not be in it. Sorry, George," he said, "but I have plans of my own. I must return to Norfolk as soon as it is practicable."

George seemed to smoulder with repressed anger. "Norfolk? There's nothing there for you, ye young fool! Forget the girl. There are plenty more fish in the sea. Anyway; I dare say she's married and in the family way by this time." He stood abruptly and carrying his brandy balloon and cigar together in his right hand stalked to the far end of the room.

To Tom's surprise, his uncle was more sympathetic. "It's true, Tom," he said, "women are to be found everywhere. But you, I think, 'ave found The One, 'ave you not? I understand. There is no contest between a dreary business 'ouse in Pas-de-Calais and one's life partner, even if she does 'ave the bad taste to live in the Norfolk that George here so despises. It's true, I myself was never there; but I think it cannot be so bad, eh?"

Tom opened his heart and divulged to his uncle all that Mary Emma and his special part of East Anglia meant to him. He hadn't noticed that George had returned and was sitting listening beyond the ring of light thrown by the chandelier. His voice startled the others when he said softly: "You've inhabited a different Norfolk from the one I've known, Tom. Of course, you'll never be parted from the land belonging to your Roberts ancestors; I see that now. Your roots are there. But I fear, old fellah, that you're in for a deal of hardship as well as heartache if that's the life ye choose to follow."

Antoine d'Escalles shrugged his shoulders, turned out his hands and stood up. "There is nothing more to be said on the matter, I think," he said. "Shall we join the ladies?"

The following morning was fine and Phillipe, who was a keen horseman and rode superbly, proposed that George and Tom join the young d'Escalles in a ride before breakfast. Aimée appeared in a severely cut black riding habit that showed off her Junoesque figure to great advantage. The groom assisted her into the sidesaddle and Aimée arranged her skirts decorously over her booted legs. Everyone declared themselves ready and the little party trotted away in the direction of Cap Blanc Nez. They passed through a verdant valley that opened on to a beach and, led by Phillipe, the company gave the horses their heads as they galloped along the lacy edge of the dredging surf. It was an exhilarating ride. The sea sparkled beneath the summer sun. Clouds floated high above the hazy horizon and seabirds called as they wheeled and dived.

"Come on!" Phillipe called, signalling with raised arm from his position in the lead. The others were content to follow as he turned his mount away from the sea and galloped inland. Up, up, Tom and Edouard raced after him until they topped the mount and clustered in a hard-breathing, laughing group with Phillipe.

Though Aimée was a superb horsewoman she and George lagged behind and soon dismounted. Cheeks aglow, eyes sparkling, tendrils of smoky curls had escaped the net that held her hair in place and now fluttered about her face in the breeze.

George gazed at her openmouthed. "God! Aimée," he cried, battling the buffeting wind and insistent clamour of sea-sounds, "you're an absolute vision! It's enough to drive a man insane! When is it you marry your count What's-'is-name?"

A captivating low throaty laugh escaped her. "My count — as you say in your rough English way — is Alain, Le Comte de Briouze-Gournay, sir!" Suddenly serious, she said: "We are to be married on the first day of September. He is a little old but a very good match for me." Ahead of them, the others had also dismounted and were carefully leading their horses along the narrow coast path.

"But you don't love 'im, do you," George whispered, his arm stealing around her slender waist. "We know whom you do love, *ma belle cousine*, don't we."

Gently disengaging his hand, she led her horse to the cliff's edge and stood gazing out towards the invisible Dover cliffs. Leading Quicksilver, he followed her.

"What good does it do to talk of such things?" She sighed. "It is my destiny."

"Destiny? Fiddlesticks! It's a money match. Tell me different if you dare." His voice sounded harsh, bitter, as he said: "I would have given you everything, Aimée."

She wore a wintry smile. "But, Georges, your *everything* is too little, *mon cher*."

"Does true love count for nothing with you, then?" he whispered angrily.

She shrugged. "Love? What is that? A brief madness... a feverish rapture that lasts a few years, if one is lucky. Things change when the children come. Love can die very quickly if there is insufficient money to provide for—"

He grasped her arm and pulled her close. "Deny that you love me!"

"But we both know that you are my natural mate. Why should I deny it? But I am not a cat, Georges. Me, I am not one to cohabit only where my lust leads me. Ah! Don't look so unhappy, *mon cher*. Come to my room tonight. My marriage day is only a few weeks away; there is little danger. Besides, I have a *préservatif* for you."

He glanced around to ensure that they were unobserved, snatched up her free hand, peeled back the cuff of her riding gauntlet and kissed the soft skin of her inner wrist.

"*Arrête, tu es méchant!*" she chided playfully. "Come. You are becoming too dangerous! We must catch up with the others. Until tonight, *mon amour*."

Tom, looking back along the path, had surmised much of what he had observed occurring between his brother and their voluptuous cousin and thought: unless I'm mistaken, the lucky dog has made an assignation.

"I'm famished," Edouard complained as the laggards joined them. The thought of food soon had everyone remounted and cantering back the way they had come. No sooner had they breakfasted than a storm blew up and they agreed that Edouard's keen appetite had saved them a soaking. "Well, I'm not averse to staying indoors for a few hours," said George. "Might I have the use of your library, Uncle?"

"But of course, dear boy, please do. My home is yours for as long as you wish."

The knowledge that no definite period had been put on the length of their uninvited stay irked Tom. Impatient as he was to get home his irritation was instantly curbed as George, leading the way, opened the door to the library. Tom's eyes were assailed by the sight of a magnificent, lofty room, every wall of which was lined with shelves of books that reached from floor to ceiling. He'd never seen such a fine collection. The library at Lyndon Manor paled by comparison. What must it be like to be the proud owner of such a library as this! He'd seen nothing like it in his life but his spirits plummeted when he read a few titles and discovered that, naturally, the volumes were in French; books he was unable to read for himself. At a loose end, he said: "No wonder you wanted to return to this place; its library alone would be a strong inducement to a well-educated man."

George looked up from his book. "Indeed," he agreed. "And I had hoped to be able to read in peace. Can't you find something among the shelves to amuse you, old fellah?"

Easier said than done, thought Tom. He noticed how ladders attached to overhead rails made it easy for one to search the shelves by gliding around the curving walls. One entire wall was filled with leatherbound books in as many shades of green as could be found in any English garden in late spring. On all sides, bound volumes sang with colour: from sets covered in cream vellum, through to amber and red calfskin or blue suede, all tooled in gold leaf which softly caught the light. There were tables large enough to accept oversize books on art or architecture, plans and maps; but Tom found his store of Latin inadequate in assisting his translation of the motto below the curious device that had been tooled into the spines below each and every title. "Before you get too engrossed," he said, "can you tell me what this means?"

With a short sigh of exasperation, George jumped up from his comfortable chair and strode to the place where Tom had his index finger placed below the motto.

"*Sursum Deorsum*? Refers to the name d'Escalles. It means 'up and down'; look, a device of a chalice and a ladder." He returned to his chair and picked up his book.

"Er... sorry to bother you again—"

George slammed his book onto a small table. "What?"

"Are you certain? It seems an odd thing to place on the spine of a book."

"God save us! Your education has been sadder than I thought. The chalice refers to a female who married into the family in the twelfth century. The ladder is the emblem of rising and falling: hence 'up and down'. The French line. It's a reminder of the first fellah to bear the name, apparently a tiler, who took a tumble from a high roof. And before you ask — It's a warning that our family fortunes will always tend to fluctuate." He laughed. "You couldn't have sunk much lower than that muddy ditch at Waterloo. I should say your fortunes are about to rise. As for mine: I've been up at the top for most of my life. It's time for a tumble, I imagine."

Tom was reminded of a few lines of John Bunyan's that he'd learned from Miss Peters. 'He that is down need fear no fall,/ He that is low no pride,/ He that is humble ever shall/ Have God to be his guide.' He remembered that it was called *The Shepherd Boy's Song* and he and Mary Emma had memorised the quatrain. He said: "You'll have the worst of it, George. I've known nothing but being at the bottom of society. I stepped up a rung when I went to work at Lyndon Manor and climbed a rung or two higher in the army. I haven't far to tumble. I know what to expect. Whereas you—"

"Whereas I must expect it to come as a devil of a shock to my pampered system? The army's knocked a good deal of my pampered life out of me, old fellah. I can rough it without whimpering, along with the toughest of my men."

"And what about your infernal pride?" smiled Tom. "*That* has a way of rearing its ugly head from time to time, whatever you may say. Nobody in his right mind would ever describe George Challiss as *humble*."

"Then it's a bally good thing I'm not a clergyman, ain't it?" George smiled. "I happen to believe that God's not nearly so discriminatin' as pious John Bunyan! Now. If you don't mind–"

"Positively my last interruption, I swear," Tom said. "What about the diamond?"

"Ah, yes! We'll sound out Uncle Antoine this evening. He should be able to help." That said, he turned his back on Tom, reopened his book and began to read.

Left to his own devices, Tom took down a book of garden designs and opened it on one of the tables. The plans were easy to follow, apart from the annotations which were all in French, and he was engrossed in exploring the details of a plan for the formal gardens of a *château* in the Loire when there was a knock at the library door. It opened inwards and the pert maid of the previous evening poked her pretty little head through the opening.

"*Excusez-moi, messieurs.* M'sieur d'Escalles… 'e wish to see M'sieur Thomas Challiss. Come, *s'il vous plaît.*"

Tom, surprised to hear his own name, quitted the library at once. Indicating silence, the maid drew him into the shadow of the stairwell. "Shh!" she said, finger to her lips. To Tom's amazement, she stood on tiptoe, pulled down his head and kissed him hungrily on the lips. "Oh… *m'sieur*," she breathed. "*Je t'aime.*" Kiss. "*Je t'aime!*" Kiss, kiss. "*Ça a été le coup de foudre!*"

"What the devil?" He'd heard all about the *coup de foudre* – love at first sight – and could guess the rest of her amorous outburst. He grabbed the girl's upper arms and held her away from him and said: "That's enough of that, m'girl!"

The girl wrenched herself from his restraining grasp, only to fly back at him, once free, as a pin to a magnet. "Oh… m'sieur!"

"Whoa! Er… *Arrête!*" Tom tried hard not to smile as he held her off again with one hand and wagged a finger at her with the other. Despite his best efforts at self-control a giggle escaped him.

The little minx fastened her hands behind her back and smiled up at him, her dark eyes full of mischief. Her muslin cap awry, she said: "Thomas. It is a nice English name. No?" He found her accented English utterly delightful.

"And yours, you baggage?"

She bobbed a curtsey. "*Je m'appelle* Ghislaine."

"Well, Ghislaine, my little beauty, somebody should take you in hand. You're a dangerous little thing!"

She pouted and looked up at him from beneath long lashes. "But I love you very much," she sulked. "*En* France, we love, and so we – 'ow you say? – kiss. It's natural. No?"

"*No! Well, that is – Yes.* But your mother should have taught you—"

She affected great sadness. "I nevaire 'ave no muzzer, *m'sieur.*" She raised soulful eyes to his and he was chagrined to observe a large tear roll down her cheek.

Somebody called – "Ghislaine! Ghislaine!" – followed by an unmistakeable imprecation shouted in robust French. With a swirl of narrow petticoats, the maid fled in the direction of the angry voice.

Tom followed her disappearing figure with speculating eyes. "I wonder?" he muttered; before dismissing the idea. "She's no more than a foolish little girl," he said to himself. Yet he had to acknowledge that Ghislaine had almost caused him to make a fool of himself. A few minutes more of her amorous games and he might well have committed an indiscretion that would have brought disgrace upon himself and George and, moreover, cost the girl her place. He laughed softly. What a little liar! Uncle Antoine had not sent for him at all. Though he had to admit that her kisses had been as sweet as her breath. Her scarlet lips had tasted of strawberries. He smiled at the memory of the firm softness of her breasts as she'd thrown herself at him. Despite his best intentions, he couldn't help wondering how far she might go…

Edouard was beside him waving a pack of cards. "You play piquet, Tom?"

"Sorry, Edouard. I know nothing at all about card games."

"No matter. I teach you," the youth said eagerly. "Piquet is very amusing. Come." He led the way to a withdrawing room that was tastefully arranged with spindly-looking furniture, made from blond wood, that had been upholstered in sky blue and cream brocade, reminding Tom of a sunny day trapped in a room.

The chairs appeared so delicate that Tom feared to sit on one and lowered his bulk warily. Thanks to his young cousin's patience, he'd soon got the hang of the game and Edouard's whooping every time he beat Tom grew increasingly loud. Phillipe and Aimée, waging a chess battle at the far end of the room found their younger brother's enthusiasm for the card game irritating and frowned their displeasure.

Phillipe said tetchily: "Must you bray in that fashion, Edouard? Cannot you find something quieter with which to occupy your time?" His sweeping scowl had included Tom in the rebuke.

Tom took umbrage. He'd done nothing but reluctantly partner Edouard in his silly card game. Mastering his anger, Tom said softly: "Although it's still overcast I do believe the rain is easing. Perhaps you'd like to show me the grounds, Edouard?"

His cousin seemed reluctant. "It rains, Tom. But we will carry umbrellas. Yes?"

Tom disliked the idea of holding a foppish parasol over his head. "My hat will be sufficient, thank you, Edouard," he said, as they left the house by a side door.

Tom was enchanted by the design of the formal garden. Almost unconsciously, he was taking mental note of details with an eye to transforming Uppham's grounds should he ever be given the chance. As he and Edouard traversed the gravel paths that meandered among the flowerbeds and shrubs they rounded a corner and Tom was brought to a standstill by the scene before him.

A small rectangular courtyard had been laid out with the ubiquitous gravel paths around its perimeter. But it was the arrangement of the rose bushes filling the interior rectangle that had stopped Tom in his tracks. Quite accustomed to seeing rambling roses arranged over metal supports shaped like umbrellas, he marvelled now at seeing that idea literally turned on its head. Instead of using as supports umbrellas covered with rambling roses, frames fashioned as cups were filled to the brim with roses of every colour except red. Repeated rows of cups filled the space, the curved sides of the frames rendered invisible by pruned sprays of blooms. They made a fine spectacle and Tom, viewing them with his gardener's eye, was enormously impressed.

Edouard beamed at his cousin's obvious appreciation and said: "This garden represents the name of an ancestress. A *calembour* 'ow you say? – a pun on 'er name. See? Many chalices!" He laughed. "*C'est drôle, n'est-ce-pas?* And that arrangement over there represents our family name: d'Escalles." Ornamental ladders had been affixed at intervals against a high wall of russet-coloured brick, each ladder covered with cascades of alternating cream or apricot-coloured climbing roses.

"Tell me what you think of my little garden, Thomas," his aunt called from the doorway of the summerhouse in which she stood. "It is I 'ave made this, you must know. Come! What do you think of it?"

"Good-day, Aunt Honorine!" Tom lifted his hat. "I missed you at breakfast. A miracle: I never saw anything so lovely in my life. It's wonderful! And the perfume!"

Edouard smiled up at Tom. "*Maman*, she is an artiste, very creative," he said, smiling at his mother, in turn. "That's why she miss breakfast—"

"*Ce n'est ne plus un secret maintenant!*" Madame d'Escalles said, following the words with a guilty laugh. "I must confess, Thomas: I love to paint. I've been out 'ere since long before you set off on your ride. This wretched rain will spoil my blooms. There! More sunder. And 'ere comes anozzer shower. In 'ere, before you get soaked."

Savagely, the torrent drummed on the roof, liquid rods barred the door of the summerhouse, trapping them within. Lightning, thunder. The sky blackened further.

Honorine's paints, pots and palette lay on a table and a rush seated chair stood before an easel. Tom, not wishing to be thought impertinent, kept his eyes from his aunt's work in progress, until she said: "Please, Thomas, look at it, if you wish."

He was pleasantly surprised by what he saw yet unable to think why. Honorine had not made a slavishly realistic copy of the low bowl of roses which had been set up at a distance from her easel. The representation seemed … out of focus… blurred, the image seen through a frosted window. She had caught the play of light wonderfully. "It is a sensitive interpretation, Aunt Honorine. My congratulations."

"Ah! *Merci*, Thomas. You 'ave the eye of a painter! 'Ave you seen the work of your Joseph Turner? No? It is 'is work I try to emulate; but I fall short, I fear."

Madame d'Escalles covered her palette with a large upturned baking dish and cleaned her brushes. "Enough for today," she said, draping a cloth over her canvas.

The rain ceased as abruptly as if God had turned off a tap. Thunder distanced itself, light filled the sky and the sun burst forth in its full mid-day summer brilliance. The drenched garden was transformed before their eyes as every surface glittered with reflected light. Rivulets of dispersing rain ran down the central vein of each leaf until they reached the tips where clinging droplets formed twinkling prisms of light. Each upturned bloom held a dazzling meniscus at its centre and the scent of roses, wet earth and vegetation filled the steaming air of the enclosed garden.

Madame d'Escalles inhaled deeply. "You see?" she said with a smile, her arms spread wide as if to embrace the whole garden, "there is reason in everysing. Wizzout the storm we should not 'ave caught this glimpse of Paradise!" Among the weather-beaten trees drabbled birds shook themselves dry, flinging aside cloaks of iridescent raindrops, filling the dripping, gurgling garden with song. After a while the charm was broken by the sound of a girl singing in the distant house. Tom sighed with regret.

Edouard remarked: "Ghislaine is happy – for the moment."

Madame d'Escalles drew the ends of her white silk shawl over her majestic bosom. "Ah! Ghislaine, that *bête à bon Dieu! Elle est une coquette incorrigible!*"

Luncheon was imminent and there was barely time to tidy themselves before M. d'Escalles joined them. Eaten outside in fine weather, *déjeuner* was a festive meal; and it was today, although the capricious weather made it necessary to dine indoors. Ghislaine flew about competently serving the family members with a selection of cold dishes. Monsieur poured the wine with his own hand and toasted his English guests. So far, the subject of the decisive battle in the Napoleonic Wars, after so many weary years of conflict on land and at sea, had not arisen. Nor did it now; as if, thought Tom, everybody was heartily sick of the topic. He was determined that he should not be the one to introduce it at table. Yet he was impatient to be on his way to Norfolk and was most anxious to speak to his uncle about the rough diamond given him by Sergeant Mylotte. He made up his mind to tackle the subject as soon as the coffee cups had been removed but, to his annoyance, no opportunity presented itself.

"Come, *ma cherie*," M. d'Escalles said warmly, extending his hand to his wife. "Let us take a little *sieste* together before the business of commerce drags me away."

"*Bien sûr, mon cher*," Madame replied, her expression that of a cat promised cream. After bowing and smiling graciously to the assembled company, they went out of the room, M. d'Escalles with his arm entwining his wife's tightly corseted waist.

Tom mentally raised an eyebrow and wondered what George had made of it but thought it best to avoid his brother's eye. He saw that any discussion about the diamond must be ruled out until the evening. Frustrated, at a loose end, he snatched up his hat and was halfway to the stables when he heard George calling him. "Hang on, Tom!" he shouted; and as he caught him up: "I'll keep you company – unless you'd rather be alone?"

"I'd welcome your company. I was hoping to ask Uncle Antoine about the diamond. Time's passing. I've half a mind to fling the bally thing over a cliff."

George laughed and shrugged his shoulders. "But ye won't be such a demned fool. If it's worth anything at all, uncle will soon find it out, one way or another. You're going to need every penny you can get hold of now that you've turned down any chance of a position in the export-import business."

"I don't think you fully appreciate just how urgently I want to get home," Tom said angrily as he threw the saddle onto Rufus' back. His voice rose. "Just how much longer are we going to be stuck here?" He tightened the girth with unnecessary force. "Oh, it's all right for you! It's obvious that you're besotted with Aimée."

"I'd be very careful what I say next, if I were you!"

Tom leered. "Tell me George, is it tonight you hope to share our cousin's bed?" He found himself on the stable floor, amid the straw and dung, nursing a sore jaw.

George glared, reached down and pulled his brother to his feet. "I did warn you. It isn't done to mention a lady in those terms, old fellah. Bear that in mind."

Tom was furious. Giving his brother a baleful look, he swung himself up into the saddle, turned Rufus with a jerk of the reins and sped away from *Les Flamants*.

George, riding Quicksilver in pursuit, caught him up. "Slow down, you fool!"

Ignoring him, Tom flew across the fields without any thought of direction, his one idea to distance himself from his brother as quickly as possible. They approached a straggling hedge. Tom urged his horse on, timing the jump. George and Quicksilver thundered alongside. In unison, the two beautiful animals sailed over the obstruction but, on landing, a fallen log caused Rufus to stumble and buck. Tom was thrown. George glanced back, swiftly dismounted and ran to where his brother lay silent and immobile while Rufus, reins trailing, placidly cropped the grass nearby.

Casting about him for assistance, George became aware of the sound of running water somewhere in the vicinity. He snatched off his hat and followed the sound but could find no stream or river to account for it. The rhythmic trickle taunted him, drew him on. Beyond a fringe of trees he discovered a gate set into a wall. The sound of water, and of voices, grew louder once he'd opened the gate. He passed through it, found himself in a cemetery and saw that the voices belonged to a man and woman who were walking among the graves. In answer to his request for water, they indicated a fountain, the source of the trickling. George thanked them, filled his linen hat – which proved a poor receptacle for his purpose – at the fountain and, clutching the precious liquid in his sodden hat and cupped hands, ran back to the spot where he'd left Tom. Quicksilver nickered as George neared him; but Tom and Rufus were no longer where he had left them.

★

Chapter Eight

Nobody at *Les Flamants* had set eyes on Tom since the early afternoon. George had returned fully expecting to find his brother there before him. On the return ride it had occurred to him that a second blow to Tom's head so soon after the first couldn't have done him much good. Perhaps the fall from his horse had brought on amnesia? Cursing himself for leaving Tom when he was unconscious, he paced his uncle's library floor in consternation. His thoughts were interrupted by a polite knock at the door. It opened and the manservant, who's name he'd discovered was Bonar, stood on the threshold. "Ah! Mr Challiss. Excuse me, sir. Madame requests that you join her in the blue withdrawing room, if you please."

What now? George thought moodily as he followed the man up the curving staircase.

He saw at once that his aunt was not present. "My mother has been called away, Georges," Aimée said by way of explanation. "She wishes me to say that we are all very concerned about the disappearance of Thomas. Where do you think he could have gone?"

"To the devil, I hope!" George said petulantly. "I beg your pardon, Aimée. Forgive my rudeness. But that young man is enough to try the patience of a saint!"

She smiled and raised her eyebrows. "Then you are quite safe, *mon cher*." She patted the space beside her on the sofa. He was beside her in two strides. "Was there anything on his mind, do you know?"

George thought it best to say nothing about the diamond. "He's devilish impatient to get back to Norfolk. I'm sick of hearing about it. Why anyone in his right mind who'd got away from the place should want to go back is beyond me."

"Do you think that's where he's gone, then?"

George got up and began to prowl about the room. "Unlikely, I should say. But he's had another knock on his head – he was injured at Waterloo, you know – and who knows how it's affected him?" He resumed his seat beside Aimée and lifted her hand to his lips. "Forget my pest of a brother, darling. We have so little time left." He took her, unresisting, in his arms and found her mouth with his own. She drew away. "Be patient, *mon amour*. We have the whole of tonight, at least. After that, I don't know. Only the good God can say if we will find further happiness together."

"How can you think of spending the rest of your life with a man you confess you don't love? If you knew how much I loved you, you'd swoon," he said.

A tiny frown briefly marred the marble smoothness of her forehead. "Let us not go over that again, Georges. What is the point? I am to marry Alain and let that be an end to it. No. I don't love him the way I love you—"

"There is no other way—"

"You speak like a spoiled child deprived of sweets. I told you: such a passion as you and I feel for each other would soon burn itself out. Alain and I are suited. We have the same religion and that, to me, is very important. He loves me very much; a slow smouldering love that can flare and abate, yet not die; constant. I know that. He is kind and gentle and will make the best of fathers. Above all, he has my respect. I shall do my best to become a dutiful and loving wife. My mother tells me that a deep and abiding love can grow from such a liaison. She speaks from experience."

Bitterly, George said: "You left out of the list of his virtues the fact that he is titled and enormously wealthy. The idea of you conjoined with him sickens me."

Now she found his hand and covered it with kisses. "Oh, Georges! Let's not spend what little time we have left in bitter quarrelling. We must make the best of what we have now. We can feed on it for the rest of our lives, *mon amour*."

Someone was approaching, heels tapping across the uncarpeted portions of parquet. The door opened and Madame d'Escalles swept in. "What news, Georges?"

The couple had separated and George, now at the window, turned around. "None, Aunt Honorine."

"If I find that he is taking his pleasure with that little alley-cat—"

"He was in no state for that kind of exercise, Aunt," George said sternly. "If he has not returned within the next half hour I'll begin a search for him, I promise."

"But why do you delay? He is my guest. I am responsible for his welfare. It is too bad of him to absent himself in this way." She sank onto a delicate upright chair which creaked faintly in protest. "Oh, *mon Dieu!*" She rose swiftly and tugged at the bellpull. "I shall send for Antoine directly. He will know what to do." As she hurried from the room they heard her calling in her own tongue: "Ghislaine! Ghislaine! Come here at once!" and George was relieved to hear the sound of the girl's answer as she came running upstairs.

Silhouetted against the window George stood and regarded Aimée. "And what about my need of you? Must I wait until tonight?" he implored. "Surely, my love—"

"You really should go and search for your brother at once, you know," she admonished him playfully. "But perhaps one kiss before—"

In three strides he had her in his arms. Barely able to control his passion he edged her towards the sofa and was pressing her down onto it when the door flew open and Ghislaine stood in the doorway, her eyes enormous. "Oh! Excuse me!" she cried in confusion, nevertherless, taking her leave tardily, closing the door very slowly. Aimée extricated herself from their tangled embrace and laughed softly. "God works in his mysterious ways, *mon amour*. I was ready to succumb."

"Damn the girl!" said George, turning away to hide his embarrassment. "Damn! Damn! Damn!" Then he too realised what a ridiculous spectacle they must have presented to the maid and collapsed beside Aimée in a rare fit of laughter. His ardour cooled, he gave her a swift peck on the cheek and said with resignation: "I might as well go and look for Tom. At least it will remove me from temptation."

Returning his kiss with a chaste one of her own she smiled into his eyes. "That's a good boy." She caressed his shaven cheek. "Go and look for your brother; but be sure to be back by dinner-time to fortify yourself. You will need all your strength for what is to follow – and I don't refer to brandy and cigars. Go!"

It was hot and humid under the mid-afternoon sun and the last thing George would have chosen to do was to ride around on what he was sure was a useless quest. He retraced the route they had taken on the pre-breakfast ride and found no trace of Tom. Despite his show of sanguinity before the d'Escalles he was beginning to feel anxious on his brother's account. Where the devil had he got to? Hot and thirsty from riding about in the sticky heat, he was glad to encounter an *auberge*. He dismounted and entered the dark, cool, fruity atmosphere with relief. He ordered beer and while awaiting its arrival bent his mind to the problem of Tom's disappearance. As he sat pondering their recent conversations two subjects emerged, both sources of irritation to his brother. He was frantic to get back to Norfolk but not before he had discovered the value of the diamond. The diamond! Tom had been on tenterhooks about not being able to speak to their uncle about it. George's beer arrived and he paid the man. So? Even if his brother was mad enough to go into the town in order to try to visit their uncle's business, what then? As the long draught of cool liquid bathed his throat a thought occurred to him. He hailed the passing waiter and asked if any strangers had passed that way earlier in the day. When the man affirmed that there had indeed been a tall foreigner, with no French, very much like monsieur to look at, George felt a huge weight lift from his shoulders. Using the French tongue he asked: "Did you see which way he went?"

"*La direction de Calais, m'sieur.*" The man inclined his head in response as he picked up the extra coin which George tossed onto the table. "*Merci, m'sieur.*"

With a ride of ten kilometers before him and the sky blackening by the second George did not relish negotiating the coast road to Calais. When the heavens opened just as he got into a rural wilderness he sheltered in an open barn and unrolled his redingote. Replacing his linen hat with one of felt, which he kept in his saddlebag for just such an emergency, he felt better equipped to face the coming storm. He patted Quicksilver's neck and fed him a handful of oats which was followed by a drink from a pond outside the barn. Thus refreshed, they left their humble shelter and set forth, this time with more to go on and a better hope of finding Tom. If anything, the ferocity of the storm was greater than it had been that morning. It was as if God was hurling everything he could at man and beast in order to obstruct them in their search. The rain drove into George's face with stinging ferocity. Visibilty was so poor that he dared go no faster than a gentle trot. It would scarcely help matters were we to shoot over the cliff's edge, he thought. Alive to the danger of lightning in an open space, he looked around in vain for shelter. Flash after livid flash embrued the gloomy sky with a lurid red glow and the thunder caused even battle-hardened Quicksilver to balk. "This had better not turn out to be a wild goose chase," George muttered angrily as rain trickled down the back of his neck and dripped off the end of his nose.

A few kilometers out of Escalles he was relieved when the rain abated and finally stopped. Clouds rolled away and the hot sun came out at once. Uncomfortable in his long, sodden coat and felt hat, he stopped at the side of the road to discard them. While his horse cropped the juicy grass verge George spent a few moments taking in the scene around him. Under the dazzling light, the wet vegetation blazed emerald green. What had Phillipe said the peasants called the countryside around Escalles? Some fanciful name. George racked his brain. What was it? Something about a green pearl. "A fair description, on such a day as this," George said to Quicksilver, giving his neck an affectionate pat while turning in his saddle to take another look around him at the delightful panorama. They resumed the journey to Calais with George feeling a lot happier travelling under a cloudless blue sky.

Just as the outskirts of Calais became visible George was conscious of a horseman approaching from the opposite direction. He urged Quicksilver off the highway into the sheltering wall of a cowshed and waited. Horse and rider sped past in a chestnut blur. In an instant George saw that it was Tom on Rufus and set Quicksilver after them in pursuit. "Hallo! Tom!" he yelled as he strove to catch them. Tom reined in his horse and, turning, was amazed to find that his pursuer was his own brother. He brought Rufus to a halt and jumped down in surprise. "What are you doing here, of all places?" he asked with a laugh.

George dismounted. The Challiss brothers walked side by side, leading their horses. To their right the sea glittered. Squabbling gulls screamed in the early evening sun. "You have the temerity to ask me that?" George said angrily. "I've half a mind to knock you down, you demned nuisance. What were you doing in Calais?"

"Knock me down?" Tom laughed. "Again? What on earth for?" He seemed genuinely puzzled.

George heaved a huge sigh, indicative of immense irritation. "Don't tell me that your recent fall has erased all memory of the last few hours? We jumped a hedge, your horse landed awkwardly and you were thrown. You were knocked out. I left you only a few minutes while I went in search of water to bring you round. When I got back there was no trace of you or Rufus. I was sick with worry, I can tell you."

Tom frowned. "But I was never unconscious; only winded." He regarded his brother in dismay. "We had quarrelled, you remember? I soon recovered from my toss and found myself alone. Naturally, I thought you'd ridden off."

"You're an idiot. As if I would have left you–"

"Well, what does it matter now? There's been no harm done, after all."

"A lot you know about it!" George snapped. "The whole house has been in an uproar because you chose to ride off without telling anybody where you were going!"

Tom halted and faced his brother squarely. "Now, you just wait a minute–"

"I'll be demned if I will!" George's eyes, so like his own, glittered dangerously. "Aunt Honorine was as near swooning as I've ever seen anybody. And I had to leave her and Aimée in order to come and look for you."

Tom laughed sarcastically. "Oh, *well*. Now I understand why you're so upset! But I wasn't lost, George. No. I rode into Escalles. I was determined to speak to Uncle Antoine about the diamond–"

"Curse Joe Mylotte for his ever having thought to give it you!"

"Uncle gave me the address of a diamond merchant at Calais. Then he wrote two notes. One I was to give to the merchant as an introduction. The other was despatched by messenger to *Les Flamants* to inform the household that I would not be back until after dinner was underway." He was puzzled. "But it must have reached the house well before you left."

Oh, God! Ghislaine's ill-timed interruption! Cursing himself for a blathering idiot George saw it all in a flash. Much as he disliked humble pie, he said: "I beg your pardon, Tom. I'm afraid the muddle is of my own making," and went on to explain most of what had occurred in Tom's absence. "But what news of the diamond?"

Tom's face lit up. "The diamond merchant sent me to an expert in the judgement of rough stones. To my dismay, he scratched the surface of my stone with a tool which was, he said, diamond-tipped. Then he nodded and smiled at me. Apparently, we were right in our estimation. It's of the first water – and pale yellow!"

They remounted and George asked, dubiously: "Is that good?" The horses picked their way carefully along the chalky cliff path. "Never heard of a yeller diamond in m' life."

Tom smiled. "No more had I. But it seems that there are diamonds of many colours. As well as colourless or white, a diamond can be yellow, orange, blue, brown or black, according to its impurities, I was told. Apparently, mine's a fine gemstone, the expert said. He showed me one of a similar size that had been polished and cut into many facets. I cannot think when I have seen any jewel of such beauty: as if the sun had trapped rainbows of splintered light within itself."

Throwing him a sceptical glance, George said tetchily; "That's all well and good, Tom. But what is it *worth* – in monetary terms? Will it make ye a rich man?"

"Assuredly!" he said with enthusiasm. "And not only that, George. It will be divided so that six smaller diamonds can be cut from it in fashioning the large stone. I intend to have them set into a ring to form a girandole in imitation of a lime flower – five diamonds set around a central diamond. It will be my gift to Mary Emma; a promise of our marriage."

George said nothing as to that. "And the diamond? Where is it now?"

"With Monsieur Fleury, the merchant. And before you start to explode: I have a receipt for the stone describing it in detail together with its weight, its dimensions and its estimated worth."

George frowned. "Hmm. I suppose the fellah's to be trusted. Yet, I'd hate to think you might be swindled. You have only Fleury's word as to its worth."

"Uncle Antoine would not have recommended a swindler, George. Of that you may be certain." Nevertheless, his brother's doubts had sown seeds of mistrust in Tom's own mind and he wanted nothing more now than to get back to *Les Flamants*. They began the descent from the cliff path. "Come on!" he cried and Rufus suddenly surged ahead of Quicksilver. "Race you back to the stables!"

Dinner had reached the stage of dessert when they appeared in the dining room after a hasty toilet and a hurried explanation of the afternoon's events, some inkling of which had been carried home by their uncle. Monsieur d'Escalles summoned Bonar, and the brothers had soon blunted their appetites with delicious food and wine. Tom noted that Aimée had avoided George's eye throughout what remained of the meal. When she and Madame d'Escalles had left the men, George turned to his uncle to question him as to the trustworthiness of the diamond merchant.

Monsieur d'Escalles brow darkened. "What would you 'ave, *messieurs*? How can one know whether or not a man is honest? Me, I am not a diamond merchant. I know nothing of diamonds other than that they sparkle brilliantly and are greatly prized by women." He shrugged. "As to their value, I know no more than do you. I 'ave no means of telling whether you will be cheated, or not. But *men* I do know. I trust Monsieur Fleury to give you a fair price for your stone. But you are at liberty to take it elsewhere if you think you are being cheated," he added with an air of offence.

Embarrassed by the tone of the conversation, Tom took out the receipt and passed it to his uncle. "Does this seem fair to you, m'sieur?"

Antoine scanned the slip of paper. "'Ow can one say, Thomas? But it is a great deal of money promised… and also *une bague* 'ow you say? – a ring of, what is it? – 'six yellow diamonds set in a girandole'. For why? For whom?"

"A ring intended as a marriage gift, uncle," Tom said, blushing with self-consciousness. "I really do have a young lady waiting in England. In Norfolk."

Antoine smiled. "So? You are the dark horse, young Tom! *Félicitations*!"

George shifted irritably in his seat, leaned forward and stubbed out his cigar. "As you say, uncle, one would have to be an expert in the valuation of diamonds oneself, in order to avoid being exploited by an unscrupulous buyer. We are in M'sieur Fleury's hands. I thank you, on Tom's behalf, for your thoughtfulness and help in the matter." That seemed to close the subject and they went to join the ladies.

★

Chapter Nine

The evening passed in music-making. Madame d'Escalles possessed a beautiful contralto voice of professional standard, though she had never displayed her talents in front of a public audience for material gain. While still scarcely more than a girl, aware that she had been endowed with a unique talent, she had made her choice and had chosen marriage to Antoine d'Escalles in preference to the life of an opera singer. He had persuaded her that she would be at liberty to perform every evening, if she so wished, before an invited audience and in the comfort of her own magnificent salon. Antoine had sealed the bargain with the gift of a wonderful giraffe piano. As it had turned out, the small communities that populated the Escalles environs consisted mainly of peasant families who had no liking for opera – Honorine d'Escalles' preferred repertoire – so the promised soirées had been few and far between. Now, to have a captive audience of two handsome young Englishmen as well as the local priest, doctor and notary – her faithful and adoring band – gave to this particular evening an added glamour. Aunt Honorine was a passionate woman who knew how to project her sexuality to each male member of her little audience, whatever his age.

It was a revelation. As soon as she began to sing, the figure of the merchant's heavy wife was momentarily forgotten. The modest matron George and Tom had come to know seemed to disappear and in her place the audience beheld Gluck's ravaged Orfeo. Madame, as the hero, was amazing. Her enactment of Orfeo's stupefied grief at bringing about Euridice's death, because of his great love for her, gripped her audience. Tom sensed the electric current that passed between George and Aimée as the sensuous melody unfurled. Orfeo's repeated cries for his dead wife struck a chill into the heart of each listener as Honorine's passionate dark tones filled the candlelit salon with misery.

As with so many physicians, Doctor Girardet was a talented musician. Madame's accompanist, he performed on her Dutch giraffe pianoforte with wonderful proficiency. If Madame d'Escalles' voice sent shivers down the listeners' spines, Girardet's dramatic and sensitive rendition of the piano reduction of Gluck's orchestral score only added to the illusion that an opera was being performed before their eyes. The spontaneous applause that followed the dying vibration of the last chord was loud and sincere and included Doctor Girardet's important part in the performance.

Honorine basked in her moment of glory then said warmly: "Now somebody else must take a turn. Thomas? Georges?" When they demurred she looked at the others in despair. "Antoine?" She held out her arms to him in entreaty. "You will not desert me, *mon cher*?" Dramatically, she crossed her arms on her bosom.

Monsieur d'Escalles smiled warmly at his wife. "'Ow could anyone 'ere follow such a performance, *ma chère*? You 'ave eclipsed us all!" Then, as she made a moue and affected great unhappiness, he relented and said: "Ah, well! If I must – But it 'as been a long while since I dared to perform. I warn you all!"

Madame, though plump, ran lightly to the piano. Extracting a volume of music from a shelf she opened it at a certain page and placed it before Doctor Girardet's startled, bespectacled eyes. He peered at the plethora of notes that covered the score, which looked as if the composer had sneezed snuff across the staves, sent Madame a look of mock despair over the rim of his spectacles and began to play the introduction. Stéphane Dreux, the notary, smiled and nodded, obviously pleased.

"Rossini!" Monsieur d'Escalles cried with a rapturous look at his wife.

Girardet's eyes twinkled. He stopped playing, his hands suspended above the keys in readiness for Madame's summons to resume.

"'*L'Italiana*', *mon amour*!" she replied, blowing him a two-handed kiss. "It is the love duet between Isabella and 'er lover, Lindoro," she explained, chiefly for the benefit of George and Tom. They thanked her politely. Girardet waited patiently, his hands now resting upon his knees. Phillipe and Edouard exchanged sly grins.

Their mother coaxed her coy husband: "Come now, Antoine; you know this very well indeed."

"If you are quite sure, *chérie*," Monsieur said, loudly clearing his throat.

"But, of course! Ready, *mon amour*?" she asked her husband solicitously.

"Ready!" he replied bravely, taking an operatic stance.

Madame signalled that the doctor might now begin. His long fingers met the keys and before long the duet was underway.

Tom was surprised, after his uncle's protestations, to hear that he possessed a lyrical tenor that was adequate as a foil and support to Madame d'Escalles' rich contralto. The singers' voices matched the considerable difficulty of the demands on their technique in scale passages and embellishments, and Doctor Girardet's piano accompaniment enhanced their performance. Monsieur d'Escalles had made a brave attempt at the hero's exceptionally high notes and the effect had not been too much marred by his strangulated delivery. The appreciation of the audience made itself felt. Tom, to his surprise, thought it altogether delightful. George managed to hide a yawn in a cough. Aimée saw through his subterfuge and smiled at him enigmatically from behind her fan. Edouard yawned openly and apologised profusely. Phillipe stood up and begged to be excused as he, too, was feeling sleepy.

"Of course, Phillipe, *mon chou-chou; aussi* Edouard. Off to bed. They are tired, poor things," Honorine apologised with an indulgent smile at her offspring. "Pay your respects to Père Matthieu, Monsieur Dreux and Docteur Girardet." They performed the ceremony with a good grace, despite their ages. "Away with you!" she said, clasping to her bosom each of her sons in turn and planting kisses on their cheeks, grown as they were. Tom thought it as good as a play and couldn't hide his smile.

The youngsters gone, a light supper was followed by the continuation of the *soirée* for another hour in which Aimée, who displayed a talent for piano duets, was partnered by Doctor Girardet. With their backs to the audience the duettists drew sounds from the bizarre and flamboyant instrument the like of which neither George nor Tom had heard before coming from a pianoforte: a loud and spirited display.

But George was beside himself with irritation and could scarcely hide his impatience as piece after piece and song after song followed one another. It was as if the assembled company's love of music-making was insatiable. Tom was enthralled by everything he heard and saw and was oblivious to his brother's *ennui*.

The clock on the mantlepiece tinkled out a string of bell-like melodies which were followed by eleven strokes. Madame d'Escalles heaved a sigh and smiled at her guests. "Ah! Time to stop, I fear, my friends. Thank you all for giving me such a delightful evening," she said, her eyes moist. "I have enjoyed myself enormously and I hope Antoine and I have not made you suffer too greatly! And you, Doctor! A thousand thanks for your beautiful playing. Where should we all be without you?" And so on, and so forth, as the party gradually dispersed into the night, leaving the d'Escalles and their guests to share a nightcap before retiring to their rooms.

It was an evening that George and Tom would remember for the rest of their lives, though for different reasons. The brothers took their candles to light themselves to bed and paused on the upper landing before going to their rooms. These were at the back of the house and were separated from the family's bedrooms by a long passage. Their aunt and uncle slept in a sumptuously-appointed bedchamber on the other side of the building and Aimée and her brothers had their rooms along a passage, similar to that where the Challiss brothers slept, but running in a different direction. The servants slept on the floor above.

"Thank God that's over, at last!" George whispered with feeling. "I don't know when I spent a more tedious evening in my life."

Surprised by his brother's verdict on the evening's entertainment, Tom cautioned him. "Quiet, old fellow! Suppose someone should hear you? I thought it all rather splendid, myself. What a voice Aunt Honorine has! She certainly is a loss to the opera houses of Europe."

George yawned. "I dare say you're right, Tom. But she did go on rather longer than I cared for. As for Uncle Antoine's top notes – I feared he would injure himself permanently!" He stifled a laugh as he recalled the performance. "Well, good-night, old fellah. Sleep well."

"And you," Tom replied, knowing full well that his brother had no intention of doing any such thing. The two rings of candlelight separated and receded as each took himself off to his own room.

Tom placed his candlestick on the chest inside the door and, stifling a yawn, quickly undressed. He blew out the candle and felt his way to the bed, pulled aside the curtains and climbed in only to recoil in horror. Something warm and smooth occupied the centre of the bed. "What the–!" The thing stirred.

"Ah, M'sieur Tommy! At last you are 'ere."

He fetched the candle, relighted it and bent over the supine figure. A mass of dark curls spread across the pillow. "Ghislaine?"

The girl giggled and wriggled across to the edge of the bed. "I wait a long time for you, Tommy." Languidly, she stretched up her arms and caught his startled face between her soft warm hands. "We make love. No?"

Astonished, abashed, thrilled, in turn, Tom set the candlestick down on a bedside cabinet. "What? What are you thinking of?"

She giggled. "I think of love, Tommy. *L'amour.*" She turned back the covers and revealed herself as naked as the day she was born. "You like?"

He needed no second invitation and threw himself on her at once, only to have his ardour dampened when she wriggled free of his weight. "You little tease!"

"Ah, no! *Tu es méchant!* First, you wear the *capote anglaise, mon ami*. Always. M'sieur d'Escalles, he say, one must protect oneself against becoming *enceinte* and also against the *maladie*."

Angry at finding himself frustrated, Tom said: "What the devil are you gabbling about, girl? *Je ne comprends pas*." He rolled away from her.

Before he knew what was happening, she had jumped out of bed, opened a drawer in the cabinet and taken from it a small packet. "*Voila!*" She opened it up.

"Ah…" He knew the French for the little package. "*Un préservatif!*" … And then the fun began…

George smiled sardonically as he passed his brother's door. Muffled sounds of amorous frolic came from within, and he thought: The young whelp! Never mentioned a word to me about his plans for rounding off the evening's delights. The moon had risen and the passage was as bright as day. Cautiously, keeping close to the wall and flitting from shadow to shadow, he scooted across the upper landing, into the other passage and found Aimée's room. Softly, he tapped on the door with his fingernails. Nothing. Again he tapped. Again no response; he turned the doorhandle and silently pushed the door inwards. Snores? He crept towards the bed and had just lifted his hand to open the bedcurtains when he became conscious of somebody moving behind him. Turning, afraid of what he might find, he was startled to see Aimée's beautiful ripe body silhouetted against the open door, her diaphanous nightgown a useless preserver of modesty, had that been her intention. A finger to her lips, she took hold of George's hand and led him towards the open doorway. His eyes questioning proceedings, he allowed himself to be withdrawn from the bedroom into the passageway. Noiselessly, Aimée closed the bedroom door, her finger still to her lips. She led him along the passage to the next door, opened it and they entered.

Inside, the door fastened, they fell upon one another, each disrobing the other, their mouths joined, jealous of wasting a single moment of the night. George swept Aimée into his arms and carried her to the bed. Enclosed in the private world of Aimée's heavily-baldaquined bed, the curtains drawn about them, slowly they took their pleasure of one another. Words were unnecessary. They made love repeatedly as the night wore away and at the pinnacle of each union melted into the stars.

★

Les Flamants was in uproar. The place was alive with the noise of scurrying feet, of raised voices, of doors opening and closing, of Madame sobbing, of Monsieur curtly issuing orders, of Ghislaine's shrill responses and of horses galloping away from the house.

Tom thought he must be having a waking nightmare. His head hurt from the quantity of wine he had drunk the night before. He hurt in other places too private for him to dwell on. Ghislaine! Everything came back with a resounding wallop. The *soirée*, the nightcap, he and George in the passage outside his room. The girl in his bed – He smiled contentedly. He had to admit that he hadn't enjoyed himself so much for a long time. In fact, he couldn't recall having had such a good time – ever! Ignoring the chaos going on all around him, he continued to smile as he recalled Ghislaine's shameless abandonment. How or where one as young as she had acquired such a lexicon of titillating tricks he was unable to fathom. Yet he was disinclined to condemn the winsome little creature. Madame had called her an alley-cat and a *coquette*. He preferred the French word because it seemed less ugly and he didn't quite understand its meaning. He sighed and snuggled down in the bed. He was just thinking what a delightful little thing Ghislaine was and looking forward to further shenanigans that very night when someone began pounding on his door.

"Monsieur Thomas! Are you awake, m'sieur? Monsieur Thomas!" The door reverberated with repeated battering.

Tom was out of bed immediately. Something of the urgency that had stirred the disrupted household to a hornets' nest of frenzy began to penetrate his sluggish brain. He wrenched open the door to confront an ashen-faced Bonar. "I beg your pardon, m'sieur – My master must speak with you urgently. Hurry, if you please. Your robe will suffice, m'sieur," he said, helping Tom into his uncle's expensive gift.

Thrusting bare feet into slippers as he fastened his robe, Tom hurried after the manservant to his uncle's bureau. Bonar knocked, opened the door in response to Monsieur d'Escalles' invitation to enter, ushered Tom into his presence, and bowed before discreetly retiring from the confrontation.

Discomforted by presenting himself in undress before his impeccably-attired relative, Tom was near to quaking in his slippers when he met his uncle's fierce gaze.

"I will be brief, Thomas," he began. "Your brother, 'e 'as eloped with

Aimée." His voice trembled as he uttered the words. Tom opened his mouth to speak but was stopped from doing so by his uncle's obvious suffering. "'E left you this," he said, giving Tom a sealed paper folded into four. Invariably polite, the merchant moved to the window and affected to find great interest in looking out at the beautiful day.

Tom broke the brittle seal. Disregarding the crimson wax flakes that fell to the floor he unfolded the sheet of stiff paper and read:

'*Dear Tom,*

By the time you read this Aimée and I will be on our way to Calais. Of course, you will have heard everything by now. We find we are unable to live without each other. Because of Aimée's impending marriage we have been forced to take this drastic step. Try not to think too badly of me. Though we have no intention of going there, you may reach me by writing to Uppham House, West Norfolk, c/o Joseph Aldrich. Once we have a settled address he will forward any post to me. I will be in touch soon.

Your affectionate brother, George Wretham Challiss

Hardly knowing what to say to him, Tom joined his uncle at the window. "I am so sorry, Uncle Antoine. I had no idea—"

His uncle turned on him with ferocity: "Oh, really? You 'ad none, you say? Hmm!" He went to his desk, sat down and picked up a lethal-looking paper knife. Toying with the dagger in repressed silence for some time, he made Tom jump out of his skin by suddenly shouting: "It is not the action of a gentleman! Nor of a guest!"

"Er… No, uncle it is not," Tom said, keeping a close eye on the knife. "Had he and Aimée—"

"I forbid you to speak of them in the same breath!" d'Escalles thundered: and suddenly seemed to crumple. "The shame of it," he moaned. Tom was relieved to see him replace the paper knife in its sheath. "What can have possessed my daughter?"

Tom was embarrassed and knew not what to say; so he said the only thing that he could think of under the circumstances: "I suppose there's no hope of catching them before they reach Calais?"

His uncle's expression brightened. "Perhaps. A slight one, to be sure. Le Comte de Briouze-Gournay has gone after them. His coach had a team of four so—" He slumped forward and sank his head onto his arms where they lay across the desk.

Tom pitied the man from the bottom of his heart. Daringly, he placed a comforting hand on his uncle's bowed shoulder and was surprised when a strong hand reached up and clasped his own. " *Merci, Thomas. Tu es très gentil, très sympatique, mon garçon.*" He patted the hand that rested below his own. "*Merci. Merci.*" He raised his head then stood up, batting the air and releasing a long sigh. "*Eh, bien!*"

Grasping only the sentiments expressed by the fact that his uncle was now calm and regarding him with kindness, Tom said: "Well, Uncle Antoine... If there's nothing more I can do at present I think I had better get myself dressed. Oh! I should have thanked you before for the gift of clothing," he plucked at the skirt of the robe by way of example, "this, and all the other garments – shirts, drawers, cravats."

"It's nothing. Go now and dress. This is not an 'appy 'ouse this morning but that's no reason to go about in an unseemly fashion. And thank you, my boy. You 'ave 'elped me much. Now. If you can find 'er, send that little witch Ghislaine to me."

Tom met her on the stairs, cap awry and curls spilling as she ran up the flight. "Oo-la-la!" she cried as they paused halfway. " *Madame est éperdue... elle est folle—*"

Conscious of his state of undress, he spoke more sharply than he intended. "For God's sake, girl, speak English!"

"She is like a mad zing! *Elle souffre beaucoup. Pardon.* She suffers terrible."

"Your master is asking for you," Tom said, becoming suspicious when she reached up to tweak her cap straight and started busily tucking in the errant curls. When she pinched her cheeks to make them pinker he was no longer suspicious, he knew. Taking hold of her by the upper arm, he asked: "Why does he want you?"

She shook herself free. "Why?" She shrugged, eyebrows raised, mouth turned down. "'Ow should I know, M'sieur Tommy. But I can guess," she said, her heart-shaped little face suddenly all dimples. " Each monz, when Madame is *indisposée—*"

"Stop! I don't want to hear any more!" Tom whispered, acutely embarrassed by her candour.

She formed her lips into a rosebud and said with a saucy twinkle: "But you asked. No?" Before he knew what was happening her hand was inside the skirt of his robe, her fingers squeezing. "Tonight, *mon amour,*" she laughed. "Zen it will be your turn." With that she ran up the remaining stairs to her master's door, knocked lightly on the panelling and soon disappeared inside her master's study.

Tom gulped and looked about him hoping to find himself unobserved. Bonar's stiff back was receding along the passage that led to the kitchen. Had he seen them? There's nothing I can do about it now even if he did, thought Tom, and went to dress.

★

Just after midday the sound of an approaching coach and horses was heard. Those within *Les Flamants* ran to the nearest windows and looked down onto the drive that fronted the house. Monsieur d'Escalles was the first to speak. "It's Alain's coach-and-four." A groom came running, opened the door of the coach and pulled down the steps. "But as yet I am unable to see who? *Mon Dieu!*" the merchant breathed, as an elegantly-shod slender foot appeared on the top step. "It's Aimée!"

"Aimée?" Madame swooned and Ghislaine ran to her side with the smelling salts.

From his place at the window, Tom waited impatiently to see who were the other occupants of the coach. The groom, having assisted Aimée's descent, ran around to the other side of the vehicle, opened that door, pulled down the steps and deferentially stood back. So this is the famous Comte de Briouze-Gournai, thought Tom, much intrigued. From his elevated point of view it was difficult to see the man's face clearly but Tom was disappointed by his sober dress. He looked much as any other Frenchman dressed in the height of fashion – a yellowish-green frock coat with turn down collar and double-notch lapels, buff breeches, and black boots with brown tops. On his head he sported an elegant black top hat and, although the day was very warm, he wore gloves. Above average in height, Tom estimated, he held himself well but not too stiffly and walked purposefully, without a swagger. But where was George? Tom began to feel anxious on his brother's behalf.

Aimée, on her fiancé's arm, entered the house and they were lost to his view. Voices drifted upwards from the hall as the new arrivals divested themselves of their outer garments. Monsieur d'Escalles called over the balustrade: "Come up! Come up, Alain, and tell us all about it." He deliberately disregarded his daughter.

Madame d'Escalles had recovered from her recent swoon. "Where is my precious Aimée?" she cried in tragic tones. Seeing her in the hall below she ran swiftly down to her and crushed her to her bosom. Alain bowed to his future mother-in-law in passing and ascended the curving staircase. Monsieur d'Escalles took him by the elbow, and Tom heard him invite the Count into his bureau and the door close.

Tom felt left out of it, demoted to the status of Phillipe and Edouard. All three were agog to know what had taken place. How had Aimée been prevailed upon to return? Would she be punished for her disgraceful conduct? What had become of George? And Quicksilver? Had George taken his horse? Well . . . at least he could find the answer to that last question for himself. He descended to the hall and discovered that mother and daughter had escaped into the garden. They were deep in serious conversation and approaching Madame's summerhouse. As Tom watched, they went in and closed the door.

He walked to the stables and his enquiries revealed that Quicksilver was gone.

Everything seemed to have gone wrong. It was difficult to believe that only last night almost everyone had been so happily enjoying Madame d'Escalles' *soirée*. It had been obvious that George hadn't been among them; but Tom had had no idea that within so short a time their little world would have been turned upside down with his brother its instigator.

Everybody at *Les Flamants* got through the difficult day as best they could. But lunch was a strange affair with Madame d'Escalles absent and a wan Aimée picking at the food placed before her. Monsieur had said no word to his daughter since her return and throughout the meal he carried on a falsely cheerful conversation with Alain, Tom, Phillipe and Edouard which excluded her. Tom found the whole atmosphere unbearable and longed to follow George's example by quitting the place. Even the prospect of sleeping with Ghislaine had lost some of its allure for he still ached from her ministrations of the previous night.

After the disastrous lunch Aimée retired to her room, the boys elected to go riding and Tom took himself to his uncle's library. He wanted to be alone to think about what he should do for the best. If only he knew what had befallen George he might have been able to remain calm. As things were, he was becoming more and more agitated. Problems associated with the diamond prevented him from taking his leave of the d'Escalles. He was compelled to wait until Mary Emma's ring was ready and how many days it would be until then it was impossible to know. He felt he couldn't worry his uncle with his own affairs and his Aunt Honorine was apparently prostrated by Aimée's attempted elopement.

Le Comte de Briouze-Gournay was staying for the remainder of the day and overnight. Tom was curious to know how things stood between him and his wayward fiancée. He hadn't long to wait before his curiosity on that point was satisfied. The library door opened and Alain entered. His first words betrayed the fact that he obviously expected to find the room deserted.

"Oh! Please excuse me, Monsieur Challiss," he exclaimed in faultless English. "Had I known you wished for privacy I would have taken myself elsewhere."

While he was speaking, Tom studied the man and was favourably impressed by what he'd seen and heard so far. The comte was, it seemed, a true-bred aristocrat; one to whom the ease of conversing amicably with those from social spheres other than his own was a source of enjoyment. Tom took an immediate liking to him. Though he could not be described as handsome, he possessed remarkable dark-lashed hazel eyes; but his nose, though well-shaped was a little too long to be deemed classical. His beautifully-moulded mouth was his chief attraction. Tom imagined that most young ladies would have found it so and wondered if Aimée was among them.

As Alain prepared to vacate the library, Tom said: "Please don't leave on my account, sir. Though I have no right to expect you to wish to remain in the company of the brother of one who has injured you."

The comte sighed and took a seat near to Tom's. "As to injury... I cannot blame either of them. Aimée has never given me to understand that she was in love with me; whereas I do believe her to be deeply infatuated, perhaps even truly in love, with your brother."

Tom was astonished, both at the comte's candour and his generosity. "Then you didn't call him out?" he said, feeling heartily relieved. "Naturally, I assumed–"

"One should not assume, my dear sir," the comte said with a charming smile. "Though I think no one would call me a coward, I have always thought that to put one's life in unnecessary jeopardy is rather a stupid thing to do. Nor should I wish to take any man's life; especially if I thought he was justified in acting in the way he did without malice."

Tom began to like this sensible man more and more. "But you and Aimée are betrothed. You must condemn the behaviour of a man who would suborn an affianced woman!"

"The heart knows nothing of such matters, Monsieur Challiss," the comte said philosophically. "I know I cannot hope to set Aimée on fire in the same way as your brother has done. Perhaps she and I will never take flight to the stars – as she claims she and George have done – but..." He shrugged. "All will be made right now. *Père* Matthieu will give us the benefit of his guidance when he calls this afternoon."

So. They'd called in the priest. "I hope so, sir. I hope you and Aimée will find lasting happiness once this unfortunate episode has been put behind you."

"As we are to be related by marriage, it would please me very much to have you call me by my first name," Alain said.

The treacherous thought flitted through Tom's mind that Aimée would be better off by agreeing to become the wife of this gentleman than if the elopement had succeeded and she had undertaken an uncertain future with irascible George. "Thank you," he said. "I hope you will find it equally easy to call me Tom." They shook hands on it. "Fancy a stroll around the grounds?" he said. And when Alain concurred, added: "Have you seen my aunt's rose garden yet this year? It's a picture."

On their way to the scented courtyard they encountered Madame d'Escalles and Aimée. Madame left her daughter's side at once and moved swiftly towards Alain. Taking his face between her pretty, plump hands she kissed him warmly on both lean cheeks and said: "Bless you, Alain! You are too good."

Aimée, witnessing the little scene, waited in apparent calm for her mother to return to her side. She and Alain's eyes met briefly and the comte bowed deferentially to his future bride. Neither spoke a word, which surprised Tom immensely: it seemed so unnatural. The women turned towards the direction of the house. The men continued to take the air in the pleasant grounds that surrounded *Les Flamants* and, as their acquaintance grew, found themselves in sympathy with one another. Indeed, thought Tom, it would be almost impossible to find a more pleasant, even-tempered man than Alain, Comte de Briouze-Gournai.

After wandering about the grounds and shrubberies for some time, the two men returned to the rose garden and seated themselves in view of the extraordinary chalice-shaped rose trees. Tom found himself talking of his plans for Uppham and was overjoyed to discover that Alain had a keen interest in horticulture. The Frenchman seemed genuinely interested to hear of Tom's life in farming, gardening and afterwards. He sighed. "Your life has been so different, so full of interest and adventure, in comparison to my own narrow existence. A title brings with it many obligations. One is not free to follow one's heart when one is rich any more than when one is poor. The constraints can be just as onerous. The great difference is that a rich man may be miserable in comfort while the poor man has to suffer hardship as well as thwarted ambitions. I am inclined to think that a little hardship is a necessary ingredient in every man's upbringing. I believe that your great public schools share this view?"

"So I'm told. There you have me, Alain," Tom said with a smile. "But George could tell you all about–" He broke off in embarrassment at the realisation that he'd named the cause of all the recent upset.

Alain patted his arm reassuringly. "I dare say he could, and may well do so on some future occasion, Tom." He leaned towards him and said earnestly: "Please. Don't feel that you may never mention his name to me. Any unpleasantness that has been between George and me has been amicably resolved. It is forgotten by me."

Tom could only look his surprise at this liberal outlook on one's enemies. For God's sake! he thought. George has almost robbed this man of his future wife, not to mention the sin he's committed repeatedly before that! "I must say, you're taking it all very calmly," he remarked.

"And why not?" Alain smiled. "Why waste time in bitter recriminations? Life is too short, Tom. One day one is twenty with all the world before one. Suddenly one is thirty and the years have vanished without trace in one trivial pursuit after another. A man must live his life in the knowledge that he is not immortal. I long for sons, if the good God wills it. But I will be content with daughters, if that is to be my fate. What I fear is to lead a life of self-gratification in an empty *château* that should ring with the laughter of children. Do you understand?"

Admiration shone from Tom's eyes. "Oh! I do indeed. What else is there if a man has no family to work for? Everything else seems meaningless to me. I can't wait to begin a family. I think that's because I had such a lonely childhood before I went to Lyndon Manor. It's a cruel fate for a child to be abandoned at the age of ten but I was lucky to spend the next seven years growing up with my darling Mary Emma."

"And you plan to marry and begin your family soon, Tom?"

"Mary Emma is not yet seventeen and my future is uncertain," Tom explained. "Were things different I would marry her tomorrow. I believe and hope she would marry me just as swiftly." Always supposing her feelings have not changed towards me, he thought.

Before either of them had time to say more Bonar had come up with the request that the comte's presence was required within. Père Matthieu had arrived and he and Monsieur d'Escalles wished to speak to Monsieur le Comte de Briouze-Gournai on an urgent matter. If Monsieur le Comte would be so good as to accompany him, he would conduct him to his master's *bureau*.

Tom was left alone in the rose garden to think over all that had been said. Yet, after all, what had he learned of the actual confrontation between George and Alain? As to what had taken place on the quayside at Calais he was none the wiser. But the impression made on him by Alain lingered and he was aware of having been in the company of a rare human being.

After drowsing in the afternoon sunshine for half-an-hour or so, he was roused from his musings by the sound of the coach-and-four driving off. He thought that seemed very odd. Hoping to discover more he returned to the house and found it empty of family members. He caught sight of Ghislaine's skirts as they whisked around the jamb of a door and followed her into the room. "Where is everybody, Ghislaine?" he asked.

"Oh!" She let out a startled shriek. "M'sieur Tommy! Why are you 'ere? Everyone has gone to *l'église*... 'ow you say? ... church. Mademoiselle Aimée et le comte are being married *à deux heures de l'aprés-midi*." She giggled. "It is best. Is it not? Before she become *enceinte* and p'raps people count on the fingers."

"That's enough, Ghislaine!" Tom said firmly. "Which way is it to the church?"

He followed her directions easily enough having seen the church on their ride of the previous day. Rufus was brought in from the paddock, quickly saddled and bridled and Tom was away before a quarter-hour had elapsed since the coach's departure. He felt rather peeved at not having been asked to witness the nuptials but supposed the d'Escalles' had good reason for the omission. He tethered his horse to the bar in front of the austere twelfth-century church and went inside. It took a while for his eyes to become accustomed to the interior gloom. He found a place at the rear of the shadowy church to demonstrate that he had no wish to intrude upon a private ceremony. As his pupils adjusted themselves to the gloom, he became aware that his Aunt Honorine had turned around in her pew at the front of the almost empty church and was regarding him with anything but pleasure. She stared at him with disdain for a second before presenting him with her broad back. Discomforted by her evident animosity, he assumed that the family's anger towards George had spread to encompass himself. Hostility seemed to bristle from the backs of those assembled in front of the altar steps.

The priest's sing-song voice, punctuated by the tinkle of bells and the swinging of the smoking thurible, droned on monotonously in doleful echoes which rebounded from the beamed ceiling to the stone floor of the church. An acolyte assisted throughout the ceremony.

The sickly smell of incense made Tom's head ache and the bell-ringing kept startling him awake just as he was beginning to drowse; besides which, he was hardly able to understand a word of what was being said. As far as he could see, there was no obvious joy in the tedious ritual. It seemed to him as dull as tombs and he cursed himself for a fool. What had he gained by imposing himself upon what was obviously meant to be a family affair? He wished himself back drowsing in the rose garden . . .

It was over. Alain raised Aimée's veil and his lips met hers in a chaste salute. Wearing a simple gown of cream muslin with embroidered hem, her lovely face enclosed within a bonnet trimmed with Valenciennes, Aimée evinced inner contentment. Tom thought his beautiful cousin looked as if she had recently recovered from a malevolent fever and was returned to full health at last. Incense perfumed the air and beside the altar steps the flames of a hundred candles flared in the breeze that entered the sombre church through its recently opened doorway.

Aimée placed her gloved hand on Alain's arm. After a gaze of frank adoration he placed his gloved hand on hers. No music accompanied their progress along the short aisle as they began the first journey of their married life. They emerged into sunlight where solemnity was banished by excited clamour as the others joined them.

★

Chapter Ten

"Thomas!" In the process of untethering his horse, in order to swiftly ride away from the embarrassing situation into which he'd got himself, Tom paused. Conscious that he was the object of interest of everybody in the marriage party, he cursed himself for not making his escape in time. His uncle had left the group and was coming over. Sounding short of breath, Antoine hurried forward and taking hold of both of Tom's hands said, "Thomas. My dear boy! In the dimness of the church we mistook you for George! Where did you get to? We sent Ghislaine and Bonar in search of you but neither was successful."

Greatly relieved at finding himself still in favour, Tom surmised that Ghislaine had deliberately failed to find him. He imagined she'd had in mind spending the afternoon in bed with him without the prior formality of a religious ceremony. "My apologies, Uncle Antoine," he said. "I was wandering the grounds of the house and only discovered the family's absence after you'd left for the church." It was near enough to the truth.

Monsieur d'Escalles had taken him by the arm and was leading him over to the waiting group. He basked in a battery of smiles. Everyone seemed relieved at finding the unpleasantness in the church to have been a misunderstanding.

Tom went immediately to Aimée and gave her a cousinly kiss. "I wish you every happiness, Madame La Comtesse de Briouze-Gournay," he said, making her a deferential bow. She responded with a radiant smile and seemed genuinely happy at the way things had turned out. He shook Alain by the hand and was surprised to find himself clasped in a brotherly hug and the recipient of a double salute.

On being released, he said: "I wish you joy, Alain. I confess I understood little of the ceremony but I was glad to have witnessed it all the same."

Aunt Honorine gathered him to her scented bosom and planted a warm kiss on each of his cheeks. "Please forgive my nasty frown. But I thought you were your brother come to make trouble. But now all is well!" she cried, her face bright with a happy smile while a tear sparkled in her eye.

Père Matthieu beamed on the happy couple and, clasping their joined hands between his own soft and gracile pair, blessed them all over again, calling them his children. That much Tom did understand.

While the comte and comtesse, Aimée's parents and the priest travelled the short distance to *Les Flamants* by coach, Tom accompanied them on Rufus. He failed to understand why everybody concerned with the recent ceremony, including Aimée, was behaving as though she was a virgin bride. Yet he was glad that things had turned out so well and could only marvel again at Alain's forbearance and his willingness to unite himself with a sullied bride. He must love her a great deal, he thought, to have found it possible to overlook such wanton depravity. It must have something to do with their religion, he reasoned. What was it he'd heard? The forgiveness of sins? ... Forgive the sinner but not the sin? It all seemed very convenient, he thought, as they rode into the courtyard of *Les Flamants*.

Nobody would have thought it possible that such a terrible morning could turn into an afternoon and evening of such happiness. Bonar and Ghislaine had been at great pains to provide a delicious wedding breakfast. The girl had even gone to the trouble, and by doing so had risked her mistress's wrath, of making swags of living roses and greenery with which to decorate the long table. Silver and crystal glittered, the late afternoon sun shone through the glasses of red wine, and the room buzzed with animated and happy voices. Tom experienced a sudden pang at the thought that George might by this time have been Aimée's bridegroom himself had things turned out differently. But again, he had to acknowledge that Alain was eminently more suitable as a husband.

Phillipe and Edouard had evidently known of their sister's impending marriage and had been deliberately excluded from the ceremony. They seemed not to resent the fact but had returned with healthy appetites in good time to partake of the feast.

Monsieur d'Escalles, all smiles and forgiveness, appeared to have suddenly remembered that he had a daughter and was even now engaged in re-filling her glass.

The feast cleared away, Tom was surprised when, as the clock struck eight, the newly-weds bid everyone good evening and took themselves off to seal their union.

Madame d'Escalles wept openly as Antoine d'Escalles warmly embraced his lovely daughter. *Père* Matthieu blessed the the young couple's consummation while Phillipe and Edouard looked hard at one another and Tom made a pretence of studying the toes of his boots. Ghislaine, Tom saw with annoyance, had slipped her hand into one of Bonar's and was looking up at the imperturbable manservant with an oddly serious expression on her face, as if she'd like nothing better than to give him something to be perturbed about. What dismayed Tom more was that Bonar, while he appeared to ignore the girl, had not only allowed Ghislaine's hand to remain in his, but had curled his own fingers possessively about hers.

The evening wore away with music-making and cards, though Tom had felt no inclination for either. The thought that Alain and Aimée were by now indulging in connubial bliss made him impatient for bedtime and Ghislaine's company. He hardly expected the Briouze-Gournay to reappear before breakfast of the following morning. So he alone, apparently, was more than a little surprised when they returned to the salon seeking something to eat. Aimée clung to her husband's arm as if afraid to let him out of her sight. Her lovely eyes scarcely left his face. My God!, thought Tom, she's besotted with him, the lucky dog! He only wished he had the temerity to ask Alain if they had taken flight after all. He hoped they had. Alain deserved it. Le Comte de Briouze-Gournay was transformed; he looked positively handsome as he returned his wife's adoring gaze with an ardent one of his own. The couple were the centre of attention and Tom's aunt and uncle behaved as if it was entirely their doing that the lasting happiness of the couple had been achieved.

But it was plain to Tom that something had upset Ghislaine. The girl's soft mouth was uncharacteristically turned down and she looked as if she had recently been crying. She brought in the supper tray and thumped it down so hard upon a side table that tailed beads of milk flew up in a ring, sprang out of the jug and landed on the freshly-laundered tray cloth. She stomped rather than walked and seemed to smoulder with repressed anger. Stranger still, she studiously avoided Tom's gaze.

At last people began to yawn, to bid each other goodnight and take up their candles. Tom's spirits rose as he anticipated the night ahead of him in Ghislaine's sweet company. He undressed and washed, sprang into bed and lay with the bed-curtains tied back, waiting for her to join him and the fun to begin. As he gazed up at the moonlit ceiling time seemed to pass very slowly. The chimes of the musical clock in the salon struck twelve. He sat up. Damn the girl! Where was she? She had been acting strangely ever since the wedding party's return from the church. Anger tore through him as he saw again in his mind's eye Ghislaine's hand steal into Bonar's and the manservant's fingers enclose her own. Everything became clear in a flash.

He jumped out of bed and pulled on his nightshirt furiously; robe was followed by slippers. Stealthily, he opened the door of his room, made certain the passage was empty and cautiously crept up the stairs in the moonlight. Uncertain of who slept where, he stole along the cramped space under the eaves and stopped before the first door he came to. No sound came from within. He moved to the next, paused to listen and was about to move on when a stifled cry arrested him. Recognizing Ghislaine's voice he was unable to move and found himself eavesdropping against his will. She seemed to be pleading with someone, probably Bonar, he thought, and jealousy engulfed him like a physical pain.

Hating himself for listening, he listened, nevertheless. Bonar said something that to Tom was unintelligible. Ghislaine gave a tearful affirmative. He understood that much. Next, Tom was shocked to hear the sound of somebody being whipped followed by muffled cries. Then, it seemed, Ghislaine was pleading with Bonar to forgive her. Tom couldn't make it out. What followed, however, was abundantly clear. In disgust at what he thought he'd heard he slunk back to bed; and after tossing and turning for long hours punctuated by the chiming clock, he fell into an uneasy sleep.

★

The morning was chill and overcast. Tom awoke to the sound of his aunt ranting at Ghislaine who, it seemed, had displeased her mistress. And she's not the only one, thought Tom. He tossed back the covers and got out of bed to make his morning ablutions only to find that there was no water in his ewer. Furious, out of all proportion to the omission, he donned his robe and slippers and, picking up the empty ewer, went in search of hot water. He encountered Bonar on the staircase. He carried a steaming jug of water. "Ah! Monsieur Thomas. I have here your water. Please excuse its lateness. There is a little trouble in the kitchen this morning."

Tom thanked the man, took the ewer and returned with it to his room. It had taken great self-control not to confront the manservant; but he'd be unable to say anything about what he'd heard last night because he would have been unable to justify his presence outside the servants' bedrooms.

Breakfast was almost normal. Guardedly, Tom watched Ghislaine as she attended to the family's needs. The girl seemed none the worse for her encounter with Bonar. If anything, she seemed less giddy and went about her duties with a smug expression that he found maddening. God damn it! She owed him an explanation and before the day was much older he intended to exact it from her.

Aimée and her husband were incandescent. They had eyes for nobody but themselves. It was plain for all to see that the consummation of their marriage had not been a light commitment but was already so deeply rooted that it presaged a happy and contented life together. Tom wondered how Aimée could have switched her affections from George to Alain so effortlessly. The men were so very different and perhaps that was the reason, he thought. Even so, it continued to puzzle him.

Monsieur d'Escalles was about to leave for business at the warehouse when he met the postman in the drive and relieved him of several letters. Sorting the delivery and finding two letters addressed to Tom, he retraced his steps and gave them to him. By now familiar with George's handwriting, Tom was relieved to see that one of the letters was from him. The other bore a Calais address on the reverse and could only be concerned with the diamond. Excusing himself, he took himself off to the summerhouse, glad to find himself alone. He unfolded George's letter. It was quite short and contained nothing that explained Aimée's change of heart. He read that George, together with Quicksilver, had taken the packet boat for Dover and from there he would be travelling in easy stages to Newmarket to try his luck on the horses. He would return to Uppham in time for Michaelmas which, Tom recalled, was the twenty-ninth of September. He guessed George had it in mind to hire servants at the autumn fair to run the place. Tom approved his plan but was aware that he himself might very well arrive at Uppham before his brother. He would consider the implications of that later. He picked up the letter from Calais and had just broken the seal when he spied Ghislaine on her way to the kitchen garden. He leapt up and was in time to open the door, grab her by the wrist, yank her inside the summerhouse and slam the door shut before she knew what was happening. Tom's grip was vicelike. No matter how much she struggled she was unable to free herself. He'd been impressed that her struggle had been made in silence and he was soon to know why.

Ghislaine became still and, facing him said with considerable spirit: "If you please, Monsieur Thomas, be a good boy and loose me!" He released her at once.

"What's happened to 'Tommy', Ghislaine?" he said, aware that something had changed in their relationship. "I want an explanation. What happened? Why didn't you come to me last night?"

She sighed and sat down on Aunt Honorine's painting chair. "Ah, *oui*. Last night." She ran the tip of her tongue over her top lip and said: "I couldn't come."

He shook his head. "I'm afraid that won't do, my sweet. You'll have to tell me why; *exactly* why," he said, leaning towards her.

Her eyes darted to his and away again. "Monsieur. You should know that I am affianced to Etienne… Etienne Bonar. Since yesterday afternoon when 'e… and I–"

"Yes, yes!" Tom said abruptly, hiding his surprise. "I can guess what happened while the house was empty. Go on, " he insisted.

"Etienne, 'e 'as love me for a long time, you must know."

Tom laughed but not unkindly. "How old are you, Ghislaine? Sixteen?"

She pouted. Then, as if the sun had come out, she smiled and said happily: "I shall be seventeen *le quatorze juillet*. Etienne, 'e ask Monsieur d'Escalles for permission to marry me on zat day and my master, 'e agree to it! Oh, Tommy! I am so 'appy. Etienne 'e is strict with me. 'E saw what I do to you on ze stairs and 'e was very angry. *Oo-la-la, terrible!*" Her eyes widened dramatically.

Remembering what he had overheard last night, Tom was concerned. "Tell me, Ghislaine. Did Etienne hurt you?"

She hung her head. "'E ask me to confess all zer bad sing I do. I tell 'im everysing. I tell 'im about Monsieur d'Escalles, and all zer uzzer men I like zat come to ze 'ouse. 'E is so angry, Tommy! 'E say, if I really want to marry 'im I must be punish for all zer bad thing I do. I say: 'What will you do to me?' Zen I remember: my farzer, 'e beat my muzzer when she do bad thing. So I say: '*Cher* Etienne, me you must beat.' *Mais*, Etienne, 'e no like. I say: 'You must'. 'E say: 'Zere is no need. Confess your sin to *Père* Matthieu.' *Quelle horreur!* I cannot. I tell 'im I rarzer 'e beat me. I cry. I beg 'im. So 'e do it and zen 'e cry, *mon pauvre* Etienne. Zen 'e break zer rod in two and say: *jamais plus!*" She shivered and added: "*Ensuite, nous faisons l'amour.* "

Tom caught the gist of this diatribe. "And what of your visits to your master?"

"Etienne, 'e go to 'im and say it must stop, *tout de suite*. 'E is brave. Non?"

"*Et m'sieur?*" prompted Tom, unaware that he'd slipped into the French tongue and wondering just how much he could believe her. So now she had a mother!

"My master, 'e look very – 'ow you say–?"

"Angry?"

"Non! … Very —"

"Unhappy?"

" *Non-non-non-non-non!* … Very – as if 'e small boy and steal *les gâteaux*."

"Oh! Very ashamed." He mimed it: hung his head, rubbed his eyes with his fists.

"Ashamed? Ah! *Honteux*! Très." Ghislaine smiled with relief. "*Oui! C'est ça!*"

There being nothing more to be said, Tom opened the door and allowed her to escape. He found it amusing that she hadn't flirted with him once during the whole of their encounter. He smiled thoughtfully at the way he'd got the wrong end of the stick by what he'd overheard passing between Ghislaine and Bonar and vowed not to jump so easily to conclusions in the future. If only he understood their lingo!

The letter from Calais lay unread on a small table and Tom now picked it up and unfolded it only to be disappointed when he found it written in French. He thought he might manage to read it if he picked out those words he seemed to have heard spoken and then try to fill in the sentences with the words he didn't understand. But it was a hopeless exercise and he thought he might as well go in search of somebody in the house who not only was able to read the letter but also to speak good enough English for him to understand the meaning of its content. Alain sprang to mind as perfect for the task, being fully conversant with both languages and, moreover, discreet.

Aunt Honorine met him on his way into the house and, on Tom's enquiry, told him that Alain had gone to Paris on business. When Tom explained his problem with the letter, his aunt told him that Aimée was about the house somewhere and suggested that she would certainly be able to help him.

He found Aimée in the library poring over a huge map of France. "Ah, Tom!" she said. "Good. Perhaps you will have better luck than I. I have been trying to find Alain's *chateâu* in the Berry but it doesn't seem to be marked on this map. At least, I cannot find it anywhere." It was the longest speech his newly-found cousin had ever made to him and he was surprised to find her so cordial.

Joining her and bending over the map he asked: "Where is it supposed to be in the Berry? Have you any other details that might pinpoint its location?"

She made room for him, indicating with a beautifully manicured fingernail the area in which she'd supposed the *chateâu* might be found. "I thought Alain said somewhere about here."

"What's the nearest large town?" Tom said, stirred by the lemon scent of verveine emanating from her body as they bent over the map together.

"I think Vierzon was mentioned. Quite close to Châteauroux. Ah! *Voila!*

Saint- Amand-Montrond! South of there, Alain said but I don't see any *chateâu* marked."

"The scale, even of this large map, is probably too small to show its exact location but it appears to be situated in a beautiful part of France, Aimée."

"*Merci*, Tom. It is said to be." She closed the huge atlas. "I shall have to curb my impatience until tomorrow evening when Alain returns from Paris."

"Sorry I was unable to be of help," Tom said. "But I wonder if you would do me a favour?"

"Of course, if I can," she smiled at him graciously, as they seated themselves. "What is it you want?"

He produced the letter from Monsieur Fleury and explained the problem he had with reading it.

Aimée read it slowly, translating it sentence by sentence for Tom's benefit. "But how did a diamond of such quality come into your possession, Tom?"

Realising that by this time the whole family must be aware of his good fortune he told the story of how he'd benefited from the spoils of war.

"You are indeed most fortunate," his cousin said coolly. "It says in your letter that Monsieur Fleury will be available to see you tomorrow morning. I hope that once you have your money and your ring you will not be taking your leave of us too soon? Alain and I will ourselves be leaving very soon for Saint-Amand-Montrond, of course. But I know that papa, *maman* and my brothers have greatly enjoyed your company. They will be sorry to see you go, Tom."

With a surge of elation, Tom realised that only a few days separated him from his return to Norfolk. He hardly knew how to get through the remaining interval, such was his impatience to be off to Calais. "Kind as you have all been to one who was so recently unknown to you, I fear that I must get back to England as soon as possible," he said. "Thank you for helping me with my letter, Aimée. But as soon as I have the ring for Mary Emma – and the money for the larger part of the diamond, of course – I shall be on my way. If all goes well tomorrow with Monsieur Fleury it's possible I shall be leaving the next day." It seemed that the day after tomorrow, God willing, he would be on his way to England, to Norfolk and to Mary Emma.

Something made him hesitate before asking a question and Aimée forestalled him, saying: "You wish to know what happened at Calais yesterday morning to make me change my mind? Of course. I will tell you. Even before we had travelled a kilometre I knew I had made a grave mistake. In the light of day I saw that what I had thought to be love was nothing more than a mad infatuation for Georges. It was like a terrible drug: the more I had of it the more I craved. It was depraved. Whether I would have sailed with Georges to England I cannot say. At first, it seemed possible. But I knew that in the end he couldn't give me what I need."

"What couldn't he give you?" Tom asked, suddenly eager for his cousin's reply.

"What every woman needs in her marriage but not all find, Tom: security, confidence in herself, friendship and love in that order. *Père* Matthieu says that the constant gratification of one's lust should not be mistaken for true love," she said gravely, "which, to be fully experienced, must include a spiritual element. True love gives the beloved so much more than the assuagement of mere lust, does not it? How does one define it? It's a mixture of deep feeling, sexual attraction, desire and a shared faith. Above all, respect for the loved one. Tom, I almost lost all that! But I thank the good God for taking pity on me and sending me my Alain to prevent it."

Tom wasn't altogether satisfied. "I simply can't imagine George agreeing to give you up without a fight. I would have sworn on the Bible that he loved you, Aimée."

She hung her head, twisted her bright wedding ring and said softly: "Yes. I know. But he wanted only my happiness. It was because his love for me was genuine that Georges had the will to give me up." When she raised her head her eyes sparkled with unshed tears and she added: "But mine was not. I did not really love him. I was a weak fool. But I have performed my penance and the good *Père* Matthieu has absolved me of my sins."

As if her wicked past might be brushed away just as easily, she stood up and smoothed her narrow-skirted gown. "It is as if I have been reborn! Oh, Tom! I pray that you make your Mary Emma as ecstatically happy as Alain has made me. He and I have found the joy of heaven in one another!"

So presumably they did fly to the stars. Tom felt an overwhelming pity for George but amid the flood of sympathy floated the buoyant thought that his brother had had a very narrow escape. Aimée and he would never have been truly happy.

★

Chapter Eleven

Tom watched as the coast of Calais receded and finally disappeared over the horizon. Mid-Channel, he paced the deck of the packet boat and strained his eyes towards England as if by that means he could speed the crossing. Though the sea was choppy the day was fair and passengers strolled the deck or sat in the shelter of the boat's canopy out of the blustery wind. Some were engaged in lively conversation while, in the lee of the wind, others lay sunning themselves on long chairs. As he went about his work, a sailor sang *The Keys of My Heart*, a Norfolk folk song. It warmed Tom's heart. He smiled to himself and joined in singing the last two lines of each verse:

It was so good just to be alive and he was so happy that he could scarcely contain himself. Who would have thought that his joining Wellington's army would have led to such adventures and surprises? First, having the luck to have survived the battles and diseases. His selection from the Infantry to the Foot Guards. The bonus of his splendid chestnut, Rufus. The gift of Sergeant Mylotte's wonderful yellow diamond and Mort Aris's present of a full set of teeth. It seemed incredible to him that, after having been alone for so many years, he had found not only his brother, George, but also a warm family who had taken him in as if they had known him from birth. To finish up with the d'Escalles had been good fortune beyond his wildest dreams! True, the bloodline had been diluted somewhat but nobody could deny that the French family were his kin folk. And generous Ghislaine! If ever a girl deserved lasting happiness it was she and he wished her and Etienne a long and happy life. Tom had little doubt that they would create their own dynasty in double quick time.

The crossing passed swiftly. As the white cliffs neared he became chilled by the thought that now he must face the problem of his fate at the hands of Lambert Jardine. The boat docked and before long he and Rufus stepped ashore onto English soil.

★

Tom had forgotten just how warm and friendly the majority of the English are. The dockside at Dover was thronged with men from many walks of life all going about their business in a calm, businesslike way. The few women to be seen, whilst nobody could accuse them of shyness, seemed to him open and guileless after his witnessing similar dockyard scenes on the continent of Europe. It was good to be back in the right place, whatever the future might hold in store. And he made a secret vow to himself that he would never again leave England voluntarily.

He decided to avoid London and its allurements. At one time he'd thought to call on Mort Aris at Holborn. But, as far as he knew, the cockney waiter was still enjoying the many and varied delights that the French capital had to offer to former soldiers who had money to spend.

One of the first things Tom bought was *The London Times*. He blessed good Miss Peters for making him persevere with his reading! His immediate reaction was relief at being able to read the words with ease after his struggles with the French tongue. Yet, as he began to comprehend those words something like alarm took hold of him. What a fool he'd been to imagine, that, because Wellington's Allied Army had won a resounding and decisive victory and exiled Bonaparte for good, everything in a peaceful England would be to rights. As his eyes flew over the news columns it seemed clear that, after twenty years of war, the country was far from right. It was in an economic mess. As he read, unknown to him, the first of many frowns knit his formerly unclouded brow and parallel furrows began to delve it. Aghast, he sought peace and quiet in order to be able read the devastating news with proper attention.

He stopped at the *Ship* inn, handed over Rufus to an ostler to feed and water and carried his saddlebags away with him. Next he ordered bread and cheese with a tankard of ale and settled down to read the news-sheet thoroughly. What looked like a gloomy future was partly alleviated in his case by the *louis d'or* – each golden coin worth twenty French francs – that weighed heavily in his saddlebags along with bundles of notes. Carrying such a large amount of money about with him made him nervous.

A group of rough-looking individuals — returning soldiers from the Peninsular Wars Tom imagined from the items of uniform each of them wore — seemed to be taking rather too much of an interest in him for his liking. The saddlebags were in full view on the table where he sat taking refreshment and he cursed himself for being guilty of such carelessness. His repast finished, he drained the tankard, paid the innkeeper and took his leave. In his hurry he left the unread *Times* lying on the table.

He had noticed a sign advertising the services of J.M.Fector, Esq., *Banker*, as he rode up to the *Ship* inn. Having collected Rufus, he made haste to retrace his route back into that part of Dover town and had soon located the place.

In response to the bell-pull the door was opened by an angular man dressed in an antiquated black suit, stockings and pumps. When Tom asked to see Mr Fector in person, the man replied: "And so you do, sir. I am Inigo Fector, proprietor of this bank." Inside, Tom glanced around him with some misgivings. What he saw hardly inspired him with confidence and he half wished he had not acted so rashly but had tried to find another banking house. The room, like its occupant, was outmoded and lacked adornment. But closer inspection revealed that boxes and ledgers were clearly labelled and everything exceptionally neat and clean. The oak desk, a relic from the previous century, bore a serviceable inkstand rather than one of any value or of an opulence Tom would have expected a banker to exhibit in order to impress his clients.

The recent arrival not having opened his mouth since entering the room, Mr Fector asked in a dry-as-dust voice: "What is the nature of your business with me, young man?"

Tom agonized. His whole fortune was at stake. It had been impossible to gain an insight into the banker's character on so short an acquaintance. But he must say something. How did he know he could he trust this man? Before giving himself time to think, he blurted out: "I have a quantity of money I must deposit in a secure place immediately, sir."

Inigo Fector allowed the sides of his eyes to crinkle. "Then you have shown admirable wisdom in choosing to place it in a bank," he said. "I am greatly honoured that you have chosen mine for the purpose." He inclined his head politely. "Might I enquire how much you wish to deposit?"

Heaving the two leather saddlebags onto Mr Fector's desktop, he said: "The contents of these. French gold and banknotes." Tom felt decidedly queasy at the thought that he might be handing over his entire fortune, never to see it again.

Displeasure showed plainly on Mr Fector's countenance. He allowed his watery blue eyes to linger on Tom's face for a second before speaking. "Before we come to business, Mr—?"

"Roberts... I mean, Challiss!"

Inigo Fector sat back in his chair, his expression very severe. "Which do you care to be known by, sir?"

What a damned mess he was making of it, Tom chided himself. He said with an apologetic laugh which did nothing to alter Mr Fector's judgemental expression: "You must forgive my confusion, sir. I have only lately adopted the name of Challiss." Oh, God! Worse and worse.

"As I had suspected," the banker said in acid tones. "Might I ask how you came by this seemingly vast amount of capital, Mr. . . shall we agree on Challiss?"

"By all means," Tom said in some relief. "But it'll sound rather far-fetched, sir, I'm afraid." This was too complicated! "Perhaps I should take my business elsewhere—"

"Suppose you allow me to decide that for myself, young man," Mr Fector said. "My fee is one guinea per hour, Mr Challiss. I hope that is agreeable to you? As it happens, I have no other business this afternoon and am at your complete disposal until—" He brought out from an inner pocket of his frock coat a heavy silver timepiece and waited for the second hand to complete its orbit. "–until... one hour from now!" Saying which, he placed the watch on the desk in front of him and well within sight of both banker and client so that they might be certain how quickly Tom's guinea-worth of time was flying away.

The gesture impressed Tom and inspired confidence. He recited the pertinent part of his tale to Mr Fector and was uninterrupted by the banker for its entirety.

By the time Tom had finished accounting for the vast fortune that lay on Mr Fector's desk half a guinea's worth of time had flown in the telling. Mr Fector unfastened the bags, lifted the flaps and pursed his narrow lips at what he beheld. He said nothing for a space but he looked very grave indeed. "This is a great deal of money, Mr Challiss," he said at length. "How do you know that I am to be trusted with such a fortune? Why! I might run off to France with it as soon as you've turned your back!"

Tom laughed. "I doubt you would be telling me your plans if that were really your intention, Mr Fector, sir."

The banker covered his mouth with his left hand as if pondering how to act for the best. Suddenly placing his clasped hands before him on the desk, he asked: "You understand, my dear sir, that this is a great responsibility?"

"Oh! I appreciate that, sir," Tom agreed. "I had no idea that a fortune could be so much of a mixed blessing, almost a millstone in a way, one might say."

"Hmm." The banker's left hand was back over his mouth.

Tom was becoming worried. If Fector wouldn't agree to bank the contents of the saddlebags he'd be back in the vulnerable position he'd been in before he sought the man's help.

The banker, having freed his mouth once more, said: "I don't think we established your place of residence, Mr Challiss. Do you reside in Dover?"

Another ten minutes ticked by as Tom gave his address and further outlined his immediate plans.

"Excuse me," Inigo Fector said, rising abruptly and going to a door that had gone unnoticed by Tom until now. Opening the door, the banker said to somebody within: "Just step into my office for a moment, Mr Gravener, if you'd be so good. I need a witness to a transaction of some magnitude."

A chair scraped back, footsteps crossed uncarpeted boards and a stocky man in early middle age entered the room saying: "What can I do for you, Mr Fector?"

The banker explained. A document was written, signed and witnessed by Mr Gravener who, it transpired, was an attorney. Tom read the document slowly and thoroughly until he was satisfied that he wasn't being cheated. Mr Fector thanked Mr Gravener, who said affably: "Anything to oblige, my dear sir," before retreating to his own office, only to reappear and add diffidently: "Half a guinea should settle it."

Tom produced the lawyer's fee. Mr Gravener, smiled, bowed and pocketed the ten shillings and sixpence. And Tom thought that it wasn't a bad business to be in if so much money was to be made as easily as that.

"Out of time!" announced Mr Fector, snapping his watch closed and accepting Tom's guinea. "Much obliged, Mr Challiss. I shall, of course, await your further instructions. You may depend on me, my dear sir. Meanwhile, your money will be placed in my vault under lock and key." And with that assurance Tom was shown out.

Glad to be rid of the responsibility of carrying about with him so much loose money he, nevertheless, couldn't help wondering if he'd done the right thing. Suppose both the banker and the attorney were charlatans? He felt so sick with worry that he actually began to retrace his steps only to think better of it. What is to be will be, he thought. One must trust *somebody* and I feel in my bones that Fector is an honest man. Oh, God! I hope so.

Dover had been left behind and Tom was well along the road on the sixteen-mile ride to Canterbury where he'd decided to spend the night. Deep in thought about the fortune he had entrusted to a casual acquaintance, he entered a treelined stretch of highway without noticing the fact. Three ruffians ran out. That they meant mischief was obvious and they had seized Rufus' bridle and pulled Tom down into the dust before he was fully aware of what was happening. Before he could get his hand to his pistol, somebody had given him a blow to the head from behind and he sank into unconsciousness. . .

★

Shivering with cold, he sat up and looked around. Night had fallen and the moon was obscured by clouds. The wind soughed through the treetops and an owl hooted. He had never felt so alone in all his life. At first, still feeling groggy from the blow, he couldn't understand why he should feel so cold. It didn't take him long to discover that almost all of his clothing had been peeled off him, including his boots. They'd left him his trousers, his stockings and his hat. His hat! Hurriedly, he ran his fingers around the inside expecting the worst. So when he found the reverse to be true he felt that nothing else mattered. Mary Emma's ring was safe! Before quitting Escalles he'd stitched it into the lining of his hat as a precaution. Aris's present – the set of teeth – he'd sewn into the bottom of the pocket of his trousers and the robbers hadn't found them; or if they had, they must have thought them worthless. But Rufus, it seemed, had been taken. He whistled. There was no answering whicker from his horse. Tom felt that loss more keenly than any other.

He sat at the side of the road in the dewy grass, knees drawn up, head in hands, and tried to think what to do next. Money was needed. He guessed he looked a sorry sight without a shirt to his back, barefoot and stripped of almost everything of value. But not quite! He still had the set of perfect teeth and they were saleable.

Having no idea how far he was from Canterbury, he'd just made up his mind to walk it in his stockinged feet when he heard the sound of singing. It was coming from some way back along the road but growing stronger by the second. Tom sat down again and patiently awaited the approach of the raucous nightingale.

As the singer neared the spot on which Tom sat, his eyes made out the dim beam of a lantern and the bulk of an animal. The rhythm of the beast's hooves betrayed great weariness as it plodded steadily along the dark road. Now the animal and its musical burden were almost upon him and he stood up to confront them.

"Whoa, Dainty!" slurred a gruff voice, followed by a loud belch. "What have we here, my darling?" The speaker slid off the back of the animal, lurched over to Tom and held up the lantern. "Lor' love us! Ain't you a pretty thing," the woman slurred, staggering slightly and pawing Tom's chest in an effort to regain her balance. "What you doing out here at thish time o' night, young man?"

Gently disengaging her wandering hands and holding them captive to prevent further violation of his scantily-clad person, Tom laughed and said: "What time of night is it, my friend?"

The woman hiccupped violently and turned to address the animal. "D'ye hear that, Dainty, my love? Called me hish friend." She turned back and said fumily: "*Like* to be your friend, dearie, that I would. Can't shee mush in thish light but you've a good pair o' thighs on ye, boy!" Whether the woman's mount took exception to its mistress bestowing her affections on another Tom couldn't say; but, suddenly, all hell was let loose. A loud bellow, accompanied by a furious pawing sound, was followed by a loud, breathy snort that rent the night air.

Tom remembered the sounds of an angry bull only too well and darted behind the trunk of a nearby tree. If only he were able to see the thing! He suddenly burst out laughing at the sheer absurdity of his predicament. The woman joined in the laughter in a slightly puzzled way. It was as if she couldn't see the joke, Tom thought. That set him off in another gale of laughter – it being so damned dark that even the keenest-eyed of night owls would have had the devil of a job to see the trees and avoid crashing into them. His ribs ached from the fit of laughter and he'd forgotten all about the threat posed by the belligerent bull.

When he'd recovered from his laughing fit, he said to the woman: "I was set upon by robbers, madam. Stole almost everything I owned, including my valuable horse. Suppose they thought they'd left me for dead after whacking me over the head, the dogs. I wonder if I could prevail upon you to direct me to the nearest inn?" No reply. But he distinctly heard the bull breathing heavily; or perhaps it was the woman? Then where? . . .

Thundering hooves were coming his way but he was unable to see from which direction. Sheer fear rapidly drove him up the nearest tree by feel. He had scarcely reached the safety of the lowest limb when the tree was shaken to its roots by an almighty thud. The silence that followed was so profound that it was as if the whole world had been placed under a bell jar.

Warily, Tom left his perch and tried to investigate the outcome of Dainty's charge. A heap of animal blacker than the surrounding night lay piled at the foot of the tree which Tom had lately vacated. The bull was so still that Tom, recalling the force of its collision with the stout tree trunk, assumed that it must be dead.

Out of the night a voice slurred: "That you, Dainty, my love?"

Tom prowled about until he found the drunken woman where she'd fallen at the roadside. He shook her by the shoulder until she was finally roused to an "Eh?"

"Wake up!" he implored her, shivering with cold. "I think your bull is dead."

"What's that you say?" In an instant she was sober. "Dead? *Never!* Where?" The moon sailed out from behind a cloud and the intense blackness of the last hour paled to a penetrable grey. As they searched the fringe of trees for Tom's saviour oak, at the foot of which the stunned beast should still be crumpled, he saw that the woman was middle-aged and less sluttish that he had imagined from the few clues he'd been given. For one thing, she was respectably dressed in a decent black and white gown. A light woollen shawl was draped over her shoulders and bosom, and her feet were stoutly shod. He could discern that at one time she must have been handsome. An excess of drinking and the unkindness of a life spent out of doors had coarsened and wrinkled her complexion. What had been blonde hair had faded to a dirty grey and a smart new straw leghorn, tied with blue ribbons beneath a double chin and pushed sideways by her sleep upon the ground, looked faintly ludicrous. Her blousy face, which was by no means unattractive in a raddled way, wore an unruffled expression as she turned this way and that looking for the lost bull.

"He can't 've gone far, can he?" she said to Tom, smiling when she saw for the first time the state the young man was in. "He'd 've bin fair dazed, poor boy." She took off her shawl and silently handed it to Tom as she called softly:

"Dainty... Dainty, my love." Tom covered his naked torso in the garment while the woman cooed: "Come to mother, there's a good boy. He's only a baby, you know," she explained. There was a loud report of trampled undergrowth being pulverised. Amid a flurry of stripped foliage the huge beast appeared a short distance from where they stood. Amiably, he trotted up to his mistress who patted his enormous, undamaged head.

"There!" she said proudly. "What did I tell you? Take more 'n a tap on his noddle to do my Dainty in. Eh, boy?" She caressed the bull's ears and the beast looked foolish and became docile under the spell woven by her rough fingers. "He's in for a rare treat, aren't you boy? Taking him to service the herd on my son's farm, outside Canterbury." She suddenly burst out laughing as she took in Tom's comical appearance. "Don't mean to be rude, young man; but you should see yourself!"

Tom stared down at his muddy, stockinged feet and examined the points of the shawl of which he had hold. "I'm hardly fit for company," he laughed. "Thank you for the loan of the shawl, Mrs—?"

"Henshaw; but a nice-looking fellow like you may call me Hannah," she said, invitingly. Her wide smile revealed appallingly blackened teeth that reversed his former opinion of her looks. If ever anybody could do with a new set of teeth it was this poor creature. She couldn't have been much over forty. He thought of the little chamois bag residing in his trouser pocket and wondered if he should make her a gift of the beautiful teeth. Reluctantly, he decided he needed the money that they would undoubtedly fetch.

"Tom Challiss," he said, with a slight bow. "Mrs Henshaw... Hannah... I was wondering–"

She cast up at him a slanting glance of understanding. "What was that, dearie?"

"– if your son might be able to sell me some clothing. I can hardly face civilised people in this state!"

"Oh." The sunshine left her face. "You're a big strapping lad," she said, suddenly practical. "My Jim's a well-made young fellow but shorter than you by about six inches. Still, you come along o' me and we'll see if we can't manage something."

★

Seated comfortably inside the Mail Coach en route to Canterbury, Tom, respectably clad in Jim Henshaw's black Sunday best, was musing over his recent experiences. Once more, his luck had turned for the better. He was beginning to get the hang of this sursum deorsum thing that George had said foretold the way destiny treated the Challiss dynasty. It certainly seemed to be working out in his own case, he thought with amusement. No sooner had he been a rich man up on top of the ladder, so to speak, than he'd been dragged from his horse into the dust of the road, hit over the head and robbed. Not only down and out but right off the bottom rung, as one might say. Still, again as George had advised, he had given fortune a helping hand by banking the bulk of his money. He only hoped he would live to see it again.

Things had turned out very well at Priory Farm, Jim Henshaw's thriving homestead. Tom had been warmly welcomed by the young farmer who, aware of his mother's weakness for gin, thanked him for his part in seeing Dainty safely to his door and refused to hear Tom's protestations of it being the other way around. It had needed little persuasion on Hannah Henshaw's part to get her son to hand over his suit of best broadcloth. Tom had insisted on reimbursing the farmer with the bag of teeth. Mrs Henshaw had pounced on them as if they had been diamonds, declaring to her son, his wife and young family: 'Didn't I always say that the Lord works in His mysterious ways? If these teeth ain't a wonder I don't know what is!"

The whole family was laughing and didn't seem in the least put out by the sight of the gruesome ivories scattered over their breakfast table. "Mother's been on at me for months to give her the money for a new set of teeth," Henshaw said by way of corroborating his parent's assertion as to miracles. As Tom had done before him, he placed the uppers and lowers into the usual arrangement and counted them. "Exactly thirty-one," he said, smiling. "You'll manage well enough minus one. Eh, Ma?"

One of his small sons had dived beneath the table and now poked his head out from beneath the tablecloth. He held up a molar. "Thirty-two!" he piped up proudly.

"A full set's worth a deal more than a suit of worn clothes," said Mrs Henshaw the Younger in awe. "Right, Jim?" His mother studied Jim's face but kept quiet.

"I were thinking that myself, Peg," he said to his buxom young wife. "I hope sir, you'll accept these five golden guineas that I've had put by for this very purpose."

Humbled, Tom thought: How kind these people are. "My thanks, Farmer Henshaw; but I must protest! You are being far too generous, sir. You forget: the teeth have yet to be made up by a mechanic. That will cost you as much again."

"That it will, Mr Challiss, sir. Which is why–" He placed ten golden guineas on the tablecloth amid the breakfast crockery in two equal piles of five coins each and stood back, arms akimbo, while they told their own tale. All but one beamed at this. Hannah Henshaw was in tears. She sniffed, wiped her eyes with the corner of her white apron and bobbed a curtsey at Tom. "Oh, sir!" she said, "you can't know how much this means to me. I used to have such lovely teeth until last year. God bless you, sir! I hope you'll forgive my being so familiar in the dark afore I knew you was a gentleman." She gathered up the dirty dishes and took them away to wash them.

★

Chapter Twelve

Tom spent the night at Canterbury and was much taken by what he was able to see of the beauty of the cathedral city. Before applying for a room at the *Sun* inn he asked directions to the nearest pawnbroker's shop. He bought some old trousers and a good suit of clothes and, wearing the latter, soon emerged feeling much more comfortable. While the secondhand suit of clothes that he had purchased in exchange for Jim's suit, plus a further two guineas, was not fashionable, it looked as if it had once belonged to a gentleman and the trousers were long enough in the leg. Tom reflected, not for the first time, that too much respect was given, or not, because of the way a person was dressed. But realising that first impressions were important, he was too young or too cowardly, or both, to disregard those twin tyrants: Fashion and Class. He had been wise, for he had been given a comfortable room at the *Sun*.

He breakfasted early and took the carrier cart to Whitstable. The fare cost him a florin which left him one guinea of the five given him by Jim Henshaw for the teeth. After a slow journey of six or seven miles the cart rolled into the fishing village at ten.

Carrying nothing but the pair of old canvas slops, intended for working in, Tom crossed the pebbled shore to look for work aboard one of the vessels still at anchor. Before long, having related to the sceptical master his previous experiences as a seaman and convinced him that he knew what would be expected of him, he was engaged as a hand aboard a lugger that was to sail on the afternoon tide. The square rigged working boat was the first of a series of small vessels to carry him north, mostly within sight of the varied and interesting east coast of England. He worked his passage from the end of July into the third week of August 1815. He disembarked at Cromer and was overjoyed to set foot in his own county of Norfolk once more.

The Lyndon Manor estate lay only a few miles inland from the coast. To be so near his own darling thrilled him. She would be a little woman by now! He imagined Mary Emma clasped close to his heart, his wife, and trembled with suppressed passion. And yet – How could he go to her with a slur against his name? Misery filled him. He could not possibly offer her marriage while this Sword of Damocles hung over him? Unable to rest until he had faced the consequences of his impetuous act of three years earlier, Tom went to the expense of hiring a fly for the short journey. Well aware that Lambert Jardine would show him no mercy, he dreaded the forthcoming encounter and wanted to know the worst as soon as possible. The vehicle drew up before the imposing gates of Lyndon Manor and he paid the man off.

Closer to, the gates evinced signs of neglect. A rusted chain padlocked the massive handles. Chipped and peeling paintwork and patches of absent gold leaf filled him with alarm. Some catastrophe must have overtaken the estate if this was how it presented itself to the outer world.

With the suddenness of a thunderbolt, Tom saw that he must have indeed been the cause of Jardine's death and had unwittingly set in train a series of events that had led to this obvious dereliction. Fear gripped him. He was a murderer! He must hang! A sudden sense of loss doused his fear. The thought that he would never now marry Mary Emma, never father her children, not share her life, was unbearable. Sadly, he wondered how the aftermath of his crime had affected her fate.

By peering through the ornate wrought ironwork of one of the gates he was able to see that the gravel was weedstrewn, the shrubs that lined the drive overgrown. Certainly, no carriages had rolled over that surface for many months. Uncertain of what to do next, he had more or less decided to force a way into the grounds when he was hailed from one of the windows in the lodge which stood a few yards inside the locked gates.

"Be orf with yew!" a woman shrilled while shaking her fist at him. "Get away, afore I set the dawgs on yew. This be private property."

Tom was filled with relief as he recognized the familiar face and tones of Esther Mawby, former assistant cook at the manor. "Good-day to you, Mrs Mawby!" Tom called. "'Tis Thomas Roberts, under gardener to Mr Southwood. I'd like a word with you, if I may."

"Roberts, is it?"

Tom whipped off his hat to reveal his coppery hair. "I might have changed–"

"Wait there," she said, banging the window shut. Very shortly, the front door of the lodge opened and the woman herself appeared. "I'd know that noddle anywhere," she said affably. "Wait while I unfasten the side gate, Roberts. I'm 'ere on me own and 'ave ter be careful oo I let in." Allowing him through a narrow iron gate set into the high wall that bounded the estate she re-locked it at once. "I'll tell yer this fer nothin', young man," the stout woman said as she puffed ahead of him along the brick path that led to the front door of the lodge, "I was never ser glad ter see anybody as yerself in all me life! My! 'Ow yew've growed. Come in! Come in!"

Over a fresh pot of tea, and newly-baked scones liberally spread with butter and topped with homemade strawberry jam, she began her tale, and Tom was only too happy to sit, to eat and sup, and to drink in the sorely-missed Norfolk dialect.

"We all thought yew was dead, Roberts, and that's the truth. Nobody knowed where yew'd vanished to after the barney atwin you an t' maister. Dint surprise none of us in the 'ouse when yer did. Such a nasty biggoty-botty man, 'e were, tew. Us 'eard 'im, more'n once, puttin' on 'is parts with young mistress Mary Emma. But 'twere Wade Southwood 'eared yer bumbaistin' t' maister that day! 'E come inter the kitchen full of it. I never see 'is long face look so 'appy all the years I knowed 'im! Fair 'ated Jardine, did Mr Southwood. Couldn't wait ter git away from Lyndon, and 'im thought ter be gardener 'ere fer the rest of 'is days." She folded her hands across her high stomach and smiled with satisfaction as she added: "'Twere Southwood's goin' that done fer Mr Lambert Jardine."

Hating to interrupt, but aware that such knowledge might be of use in the future, Tom had to ask: "Where did Mr Southwood go? Which part of the country?"

"Kep' on writin' away after one position an another – without lettin' on ter Mr Jardine, acourse – 'til 'e landed 'isself maister gard'ner of a big noo estate in Cornwall. Fergit what it were called. But very grand, an miles bigger'n Lyndon Manor, 'e said."

"Go on, Mrs Mawby," Tom said, cheered to hear that Jardine had been 'done fer' and anxious to hear how and whether his demise was permanent. "Sorry I interrupted."

"'Elp yerself tew another scone, bor," the woman said, proffering the diminishing pile. "Now… Where was I?"

"Mr Southwood's new position," Tom said, before biting into his third scone.

"Oh, ah! Southwood's goin' left Jardine in the lurch good an proper!" Mrs Mawby confided. "'E could've run the Lyndon estate with 'is eyes closed, could Mr Southwood."

She tapped her skull. "Wade 'ad it all in 'is 'ead, yer see, though I dew know 'e kept notebooks an all. But 'e weren't givin' Jardine a sight o' them, no fear! Well... It so 'appened that Wade 'eard 'e got the Cornwall position by that mornin's post and was on 'is way ter Mr Jardine ter give 'im 'is notice when 'e 'eared a lumberin' inside. 'E looked in the side winder an' saw yew an maister 'ack-slaverin'. When 'e told us 'ow yer give Mr 'Igh-an-Mighty a lovely custard on the chin the ole fule – Southwood, I mean – laughed so loud 'e showed 'ow many teeth 'e'd lorst! An 'e tells us that Jardine dew stagger back an ding 'is 'ead on the corner of 'is desk."

Translated into the King's English, it was just as Tom remembered it. So Southwood had witnessed everything! Once more his future looked bleak. "Did Mr Southwood see me leave?" he asked.

"Not only that: he saw Jardine pick 'isself up orf the floor a minute or tew later. An Wade Southwood threatened to choke 'isself with laughin' as 'e tried ter tell us the best bit." Mrs Mawby chuckled at the memory. "T'maister went straight ter the lookin'-glass and fingered 'is bunny eye. It promised ter be a right Swarston winder, an' it were by next mornin'." A raucous guffaw fought its way up from the depths of her pigeon chest and exploded into a horrible sound that infected Tom by its sheer ugliness.

He laughed in sympathy with Mrs Mawby as well as from his relief at discovering that he had done the man no permanent injury. But no doubt he had dented Jardine's pride and the price for that injury would be high. "And where is Mr Jardine now?" Tom forced himself to ask the question while dreading the answer.

The former assistant cook turned lodgekeeper eyed Tom sympathetically. "Yew can breathe easy as ter that, Roberts," were her wonderful words. "Though, 'ad yew 'ung about 'e would 'ave seen yer transported, for sure. 'E were a spiteful man. Yew was right tew disappear yerself. But where did yew go, lad?"

Not wanting to go into detail, Tom said blandly: "I went for a swoddy – a soldier – in Wellington's army and finished up by fighting at the Battle of Waterloo."

Esther Mawby's eyes widened with admiration. "Never! Yew'll 'ave a lot ter tell yer grandchildren, bor, an no mistake. Fancy yew bein' there on the same bit o' ground as that monster Boney. Yew dew your country and Norfolk credit, Roberts, yew really dew! And ter think yer come through it all without a scratch! I got my niece to read me the papers so I know what 'orrors yew must've seen. 'Tis a marvel!" Each was aware that the other was thinking the same thought: that there were many who had not been so lucky.

Throughout Mrs Mawby's encomium Tom had been anxious to continue their discussion as to the fate of Lambert Jardine and he reopened the subject as soon as she had finished speaking. "What happened to Mr Jardine after Mr Southwood gave his notice, Mrs Mawby?"

"Hmmph!" she snorted, lifting her shoulders and grimacing. "What happened? Why, nothin' ter begin with. 'E jist carried on livin' orf the fat o' the land as if Mr Southwood's goin' weren't gonna make no difference ter nothin' nor nobody." Heaving herself from her chair she went to the singing kettle on the trivet beside the open fire and refilled the teapot. "'Elp yerself, now, Roberts. Big lads the likes o' yew needs a deal o' feedin', I knows." She poured each of them another cup of tea. "Yer can't treat Norfolk folk like that an 'ope ter git away with it," she said darkly. "There 'e was, livin' orf the fat o' the land, like I says, while some of 'is people was fair clammed wi' 'unger an 'avin ter make dew with chates as was only fit for pigs."

Tom felt his anger rising as he heard this. "And then?"

"Ter cut a long story short – yer knows as 'ow I always was one for yarmanderin' whenever I gits the chance – things went from bad ter worse until the 'ole place was run down somethin' shockin'. Jardine 'ad turned orf so many that there wasn't enough servants ter look after the 'ouse nor the estate neither. Then, one fierce windy night in October 1813 someone set fire ter one o' the barns and while everyone was tryin' ter put that'n out the manor was torched – must've bin more'n one person involved, 'cause fires sprung up in sev'ral rooms, upstairs an' down. There was plenty 'ad a grudge agin t'maister, as well yew know. Because we was all out tryin' to quench the fire in the barn, there weren't no-one ter save the 'ouse an', what with the wind an' so many fires, an' it bein' so old an' dry like, the 'ole lot burned ter the ground. There weren't even time ter save any o' the pictures or furniture or other old treasures; the 'ole lot wen' up in smoke. All we could dew was stand an watch it. Any'ow, Mr Jardine, 'e must've 'ad an inklin' that there was gonna be trouble 'cause 'e moved down 'ere, *the day afore the fires started*, ter this very lodge, an ax me along ter keep 'ouse for 'im. The rest 'ad ter fend for 'emselves, poor souls."

Tom's anger had been fanned to boiling point by the events Mrs Mawby had related. He burst out: "How could he have behaved in such a callous way to those who relied on him for their bread?"

Esther Mawby looked at him pityingly. "Yew've bin away a long time, Roberts. Things in these parts – an' all over England – 'ave changed fer the worse, as yew'll see fer yerself as yer go about the countryside. The long an' the short of it is, that a week after the fire Mr Jardine ordered the carriage ter take 'im ter Lynn. Said 'e were goin' ter see 'is lawyer, an' I've no doubt 'e did! What 'e didn't tell *me*, nor anyone else neither, was that 'e were leavin' Lyndon fer good. As far as I noo, 'e just disappeared. A week after that, a letter comes. I never 'ad no schoolin', as yew know, lad; so I had ter wait 'til me niece called ter read it ter me. 'Twere from Jardine's lawyer. 'Jardine's gone back ter 'Stralia', it says. It says more. I'm ter stay in this lodge an' consider it mine for life, providin' I keeps an eye on oo comes an goes. What's ter become o' the place devil knows. But I'm not grumblin'. I'm just glad ter 'ave a roof over me 'ead an me veg'table patch at the back. So I don't starve. I dew all right compared ter some." She'd talked herself to a standstill, it seemed to Tom.

"Was Mary – Miss Kay – still living here at the time of the fire, Mrs Mawby?"

Twisting her mouth into a wry smile, the woman replied: "I thought yew was never goin' ter mention 'er name, pore liddle thing. An' yew an' 'er so close afore."

Tom's heart thumped painfully. "Why? What do you mean?"

"She an Miss Peters run orf the day after yew left in 1812 and no-one's 'eard a word from either of 'em since. Vanished inter thin air, yer might say."

The ticking of the clock seemed unnaturally loud in the minutes following their talk. Coals shifted and settled as the silence lengthened. Mrs Mawby had closed her eyes and appeared to be cogitating. Tom was startled when she broke the silence and said with certainty: "Only one person might know something." As if they were giving her pain, she started to rub the knobbly knuckles of her right hand, passing her left back and forth over it.

He leaned forward in his chair. "Who?"

"Wade Southwood, if 'e's still alive." Though the day was warm by Tom's reckoning, she stopped rubbing her gnarled hands, leaned over the fire and held her palms towards the glow. "'E 'd know, if anybody would." Her brow furrowed and she screwed up her face as she wrestled with the insoluble problem. "Dang it! The name's on the tip o' me tongue," she cried in frustration. "I knows it's *Cornwall*. But I can't, fer the life o' me, remember the name o' the big 'ouse. 'Tis no good. Sorry, Roberts."

Tom laid his hand gently on her arm. "You've been more than kind enough already, Mrs Mawby. I must thank you for taking the time to put my mind at rest with regard to Mr Jardine." He smiled. "I don't suppose you have any idea what a tremendous relief it is to me to know that he is at the opposite end of the globe?"

She patted his hand as it lay on her arm. "Oh, I think I can just about imagine that, bor," she said with a wry smile. "Wait! . . . Dang it! I almost 'ad it then. Shh!"

Her eyes closed while she looked inside her head. She opened them again. "Ah!"

"You've remembered?" Tom willed.

"There! Now it's gorn agin," she said testily. "Did you 'ave ter speak just then?"

Tom apologised.

"Well. . . ," she sighed, "it's gorn right outa me 'ead now! Except − Yes! Wade said it were in *South* Cornwall; 'cause I remember thinkin' 'ow funny it were that 'e was Mr *South*wood an 'e were orf ter South Cornwall. If I 'ear any word concernin' Miss Kay, I'll git me niece ter write, if yew'll tell me where."

Tom scribbled the name Uppham House onto a piece of paper, saying that he would take it kindly if her niece would send any communications to that address. Leaving a shilling towards paper and postage, he thanked her again. There being nothing further to detain him he took his leave and set out to walk to Felixton.

★

The town had changed little in the three years since he'd paid his hurried visit to the farm on the day of his running away from Lyndon Manor.

Before quitting the area for good, it was Tom's intention to try to find out what had become of the money that had been paid for his grandfather's farm. It was his by right. The money from the sale of Moat Farm would not be negligble. If George's description of the condition of Uppham was anything like as bad as Tom imagined, it would take even more than his considerable fortune to restore the place to its former glory. He was going to need every bit of capital he could lay his hands on.

Moat Farm was situated on the other side of Felixton. He had reached the farm's outer fields by late afternoon and there remained several hours of daylight left in which to accomplish his investigations.

Hereabouts, the land was pleasantly undulating, unlike the environs of Uppham, according to George's description of it. His brother had disparaged the fen country; but Tom had no sympathy with his objections to the gentle Norfolk landscape. As far as he was able to tell, George despised Norfolk merely because he considered it too flat.

Pity George had not seen the lands around Moat Farm. Flat? How well he remembered this high-banked, steep and twisting lane! Grandmother Roberts had called the lane sometimes a *grundle*, sometimes a *loke*. As dust rising from the sun-dried earth beneath his tramping feet, the old words rose in a cloud from his childhood days! Even as a boy, Tom had known every hedgerow tree flanking the lane by its country name. He delighted now in being able to name each one as he descended to Home Field and it was like greeting old friends. In memory's eye, he pictured each wild flower in its season and where it grew beneath the hedge and on the sloping banks of the lane.

When he first began to work as gardener's boy at Lyndon Manor he'd been amazed to discover that almost every plant or bird he knew by sight bore a different name, a proper Latin name, from that taught him by his countrified grandmother.

The rough music of her Norfolk dialect sounded again in his ears and something dragged at his heart as he thought of the kind and loving woman who had reared him to the age of ten. What wouldn't he give to be able to be back in the comfort and safety of her strong, tender embrace once more!

Mixed feelings of sadness, loneliness and nostalgia accompanied his steps across well-remembered Home Field where men laboured in the long summer daylight. Many days had passed without female comfort and the need to remedy the situation had been mounting steadily. His plight had worsened since the moment he had imagined Mary Emma pressed to him. He longed for solace in the arms of a warmhearted and willing maid. So it seemed he might be in luck when a heavy-featured girl drifted across from the back door of the farmhouse towards the wicket. As she narrowed the space between them he saw that, though not downright ugly, she was cursed with a more than plain face and wall-eyed, to boot.

But after all, he reasoned to himself, he wasn't seeking romance, merely company and physical release. He'd used women before this without looking them in the eye; though he had to admit that it had usually been when under the influence of strong liquor and he had known no better.

The girl, or young woman he supposed as she neared him and he saw the well-filled bib of her apron, demanded to know his business at the farm.

"Good-day to you, young lady," Tom said, removing his hat with a bright smile, while not quite sure how he should address her. "I wonder if I might buy a cooling drink? I've walked from beyond Felixton and the day is hot and dusty."

As far as he was able to follow, she eyed him up and down. "Yew must've knowed that afore yew set out," she responded tartly. "I've some paigle wine in the spring room. 'Tis nice an' cool. Would that suit – at... twopence a glass?"

She's no fool, he observed, thinking the price steep. Obviously, she took him for a real gentleman. He'd forgotten what paigle wine was but assuming it must be drinkable said cheerfully: "That will suit admirably, my dear."

"Don' yew let my 'usban 'ear yew *my-dearin'* me," she laughed. "Lucky fer yew 'e be out in Far Field!" She poured wine from a glass pitcher into two glasses and sipped from one and gave the other to Tom. "Could yer fancy a slice of fape pie? Made yisty for the men's noonin'."

"I haven't tasted gooseberry pie for over three years," he replied, glad that fape had produced an intantaneous image in his visual memory. "Thank you, Mrs–?"

"Roberts. Where yew bin, then, if you int 'ad a decent fape pie in all that time?"

He enlightened her; and, taking a sip of the paigle wine, he had it: cowslip!

"See'd yew was strong-docked, sir, like a swoddy might be," she said, her eyes on his thighs. "Yew puts in me in mind of our stallion, Blaze." She sipped her wine and looked approximately in his direction.

Promising, Tom thought, as he bit into the melting crust of the pie.

"Nice teeth, maister," Mrs Roberts said, running the tip of her tongue across her top lip and observing: "Yew look as if yew could dew with a lie down, bor."

"Oddly enough," Tom said, while quite understanding her meaning, "my own name is Roberts." Why try to go into the intracacies of the Challiss connection?

"There's a coincidence!" she said. "Where yew from, if I may make so bold?"

Let's see how she takes this, thought Tom. "Moat Farm was my home for a number of years," he said quietly.

"Yew wouldn' be any relation to ol' Farmer Roberts, by any chance?" she said, her eyes narrowing.

"His only grandson – and rightful heir to this farm," Tom replied bitterly.

Shaking her head from left to right she averred: "You've got that wrong, Mr Roberts, sir."

"No, I have not!" Tom stared her in her right eye, the one that kept still long enough to be stared into. "By rights, this is my farm."

She was by his side in an instant. "You'll find yerself mistaken in that, sir. My 'usband, Mr 'Enry Roberts Junior, was his father's sole heir. 'E were 'is only son. There weren't nobody contested the will. Nor could there be," she added with certainty, "cause 'is only other chile were a daughter oo died years ago." Her hand was on his arm. "Yew'm mistaken, bor," she said kindly. "My 'usband 'as all the papers to prove it. 'Tis all legal an above board." Her hand slid between his thighs and began a slow journey. "Per'aps I can 'elp make up fer yer disappointment, sir."

Needing her services desperately, as she could see by the evidence of her own eyes, he felt he must not let such an opportunity pass before establishing the truth of her assertion.

"Might I see these papers that you say prove that your husband is the legal heir to Moat Farm?" he said with difficulty.

Bringing him to fever pitch, she spoke one word: "Afterwards." Firmly taking him by the hand, she drew him towards the spring room and closed the door so that they were in total darkness.

Three people would be made happy by their brief encounter. Tom was eased of his pain and discomfort. Mrs Roberts experienced an orgasm for the first time in her life. And Farmer Henry Roberts Junior would become father to the child he had longed for. His two marriages had proved fruitless so far. But a pretty red-haired daughter, delivered of wall-eyed Mrs Roberts in the spring of 1816, was to be the firstborn of his family of ten children. Nine boys followed: all brown-haired and plain.

Tom took the fact that Henry Roberts Junior was indeed his grandparents' son, his own uncle, philosophically. Legal papers proved the legitimacy. That nobody had thought to mention his existence while Tom lived with his grandparents at Moat Farm did not seem so unlikely. No doubt Grandfather Roberts had forbidden his son's name to be spoken after a quarrel that led to an irreparable breach. But a son is a son, thought Tom, and the old man had loved his progeny in his own stern way; enough to leave him the farm and with it the continuity of the Roberts line.

I was only ever half a Roberts anyway, born out of wedlock, sired by a Challiss, Tom mused. The sire is the dominant partner in any breeding and the bloodline stems from him. Therefore, he reasoned, I am more Challiss than Roberts, after all. My place is at Uppham with George who needs my help.

From there I will try to – I *must* – find Mary Emma. With that resolve, he set out to walk back to Felixton. As he covered the miles, he decided to take the earliest form of transport that would carry him west, to Fakenham : one more stage on his long journey to Uppham House.

★

Chapter Thirteen

A coach rolled over the rutted road towards the sinking sun. The landscape through which the coach travelled was seven-eighths sky. From horizon to firmament the heavens blazed with the glow cast by a fiery orb enclosed by a ring of cerise. Glimpses of the celestial spectacle flashed past the vehicle's side window with the monotonous regularity of a hypnotist's watch. Lulled by the rhythm of the coach's wheels and the stuffiness of the confined space Thomas Roberts Challiss soon grew weary of staring at the dazzling display. Gradually, his head began to droop, drowsiness overtook him and he slept.

Light had not quite drained from the sky when he awoke. Looking out across the landscape he noticed mist swirling about darkening hollows. Autumn would soon be upon him and he had yet to discover how much needed to be done at Uppham.

Tom sat wedged against the right hand window of the coach, facing forward. He studied his fellow travellers. A plump woman, her boy, and various bundles and baggages occupied the opposite seat, travelling backwards. A stocky gentleman dressed in clerical black relieved by touches of spotless linen was seated at Tom's left and, in the left corner, a young woman did her best to make herself inconspicuous. Nobody spoke. Not a word had passed between the four adults occupying the seats. The plump woman's small boy had been overcome with shyness at the heavy silence that prevailed. He had stared out of enormous blue eyes at the three people opposite him until his lids had drooped and he had been overpowered by sleep. His mother knitted busily at a child's stocking and Tom was surprised to see how much it had lengthened in the interval beween his falling asleep and his waking.

Tom addressed the man on his left. "I beg your pardon, sir," he began. "Thomas Roberts Challiss," he said by way of introduction. "I have no timepiece. I'd be be obliged if could you tell me how long it might be before we reach Fakenham."

The man took out a fine gold watch from his waistcoat pocket, clicked open the lid and said: "We should be drawing into the yard of the *Crown* within the space of a few minutes, sir." He snapped his watch closed and replaced it in his pocket.

The plump woman, having shown no sign that she had been listening to the conversation, packed away her knitting needles and half-knitted stocking into a basket and began to gather her other belongings together. The boy slept on, oblivious to his surroundings. The young woman checked to see that her all-concealing veil had not come adrift and smoothed the fingers of her gloves one by one. The man in black sat with his hands resting upon his knees and Tom gazed idly out of the swiftly darkening window at the first pale stars.

The coach lurched violently. Suddenly the passengers were in a tangled heap on the coach floor amid the soiled straw in the footspace between the bench seats. Simultaneously, a loud voice: "Stand and Deliver!" A pistol shot.

    the coach swaying dangerously to a halt,

    the small boy awaking with a startled cry and beginning to bawl,

    the young woman still seated but clutching her veil about her face,

    the plump woman banging her head on the opposite seat,

    the man in black grazing his nose on the handle of the plump woman's basket, and

Tom gashing the little finger of his right hand in trying to save himself. "Everybody out!" a deep voice bellowed. "Now! And smart about it!" The occupants of the coach's interior stumbled out of the narrow doorway. The boy began to snivel and his mother did her best to quiet him. The veiled young woman was shaking like a leaf, her teeth chattering as if with fright. By the light of the coach's lanthorn Tom saw that the man in black was white-faced and tight-lipped with suppressed outrage as he dabbed at his blooded nose.

Blood trickled from the tip of his finger as Tom tried to take in as many details as he could concerning the robber and his horse. The animal, an Arab stallion, was as black as everything belonging to his master seemed to be. Despite the warmth of the night the highwayman wore a long black cloak that effectively concealed his figure and clothing. A wide-brimmed black hat was pulled down over his eyes and a scarf covered most of his face. Pistols at the ready, he confronted the alarmed passengers. "Good-evening, ladies and gentlemen," said the rogue with mock affability.

London accent, Tom noted, his eyes busy studying the man's boots.

"I'll thank you to place your valuables in this bag," he said, giving it to the fractious boy and levelling one of his brace of pistols at the infant's head. "No funny business, anybody, or the brat gets it! Turn out your pockets and, ladies, remove your gloves, if you please. Take off your rings and brooches, ear-bobs and any fancy shoebuckles – unless you'd care to have me search you myself.

Much as I'd enjoy it, I haven't the time. Off you go, boy, and collect all those shiny, pretty things for me." He prodded the reluctant boy in the back to help him on his way along the line.

"Oh, sir," the plump woman begged. "Please don't hurt him. Let me collect the things instead." Tears stood in her eyes.

"Hold yer tongue, woman," bellowed the highwayman.

His mind working feverishly to devise some action that would bring this outrageous liberty to an end without anybody being killed or injured, Tom became aware of movement behind him. Out of the corner of his eye he saw that the coachdriver, creeping toward the robber, had almost reached him. The highwayman didn't take his eyes off the line of terrified victims. He rested his long-barrelled pistol across his left arm, aimed behind him at random and brought down the driver. The man lay in a huddled heap where he'd fallen and groaned in agony.

Taking the bag of trinkets from the boy the robber thanked him and stuffed it into a larger bag beneath his cloak. Fearful of the man's presence, the child cried for his mother. Defiantly, she held out her arms and her frightened son ran into them.

"Now I'll thank you to remove your hats one by one, if you please."

Frantic at the thought that Mary Emma's ring might be discovered, Tom was still wondering what to do when the man appeared before him and held his pistol at the centre of his forehead. "Hand it over, if you please," the man said quietly.

After a brief show of reluctance, Tom whipped off his hat, flung it at the man's eyes and dived to the ground as a bullet whistled over his head and lodged itself in the panelling of the coach. Expecting death in the next instant, he was surprised when a report came from the direction of the passengers.

The bullet missed the robber but it was enough to decide him against further risk. Scooping up Tom's hat, he was on his horse in a running jump and away with a clatter of hooves, his cloak billowing out behind him as if he were a winged Devil.

It was with some satisfaction that Tom had noticed the highwayman's unusual silver spurs for he was certain he knew to whom they belonged.

★

In the immediate aftermath of the robbery everyone had begun to talk at once except the young woman. Now hatless, she knelt beside the injured coachman and supported his head upon her lap. Tom had observed the young woman's exquisite profile and she had aroused his interest. Why cover such loveliness, he wondered?

The moon had risen above the low horizon and shed its cold light over the scene as if illuminating characters in a tableau. The black-garbed gentleman was inspecting the horses and the coach. The boy stood sucking his thumb and watching the man. The plump woman had resurrected her child's half-finished stocking and, seated on a box that had dislodged itself from the coach roof in the late disturbance, sat knitting as contentedly as if she were at home in her own parlour.

"Pray excuse me, ma'am," Tom said to the plump lady with whom he had been talking and who had introduced herself to him as Mrs Polly Pryer. "The young lady needs some assistance, I think." As he walked over to where she cradled the coachman's head in her lap her figure seemed to stiffen. She reached up and unbound her hair. Released, it cascaded in vivid luxuriance around her face and down her back and provided a living screen as effective as her thick veil had been.

"Is he much injured, madam?" Tom asked.

She answered him in a sweet musical voice: "He has taken a bullet in his right shoulder, it seems. He's lost quite a lot of blood and it's caused him to swoon, which is a mercy, for he's in pain. He needs to see a doctor or a surgeon urgently, sir."

How lovely she is! So self-possessed and calm at the sight of so much blood, Tom marvelled. Her travelling dress was quite spoiled by the horrible stain across its front. "I see," he said. "Are you able to stay as you are at present for a while longer?"

"It is not I with whom you should concern yourself, sir," she said in a low voice. "This man will live only if aid can be given in time. He is growing very weak."

Needing no further encouragement, Tom ran to the coach and horses to see whether they were fit to continue the short distance to Fakenham. "Is the vehicle roadworthy, d'ye think?" he asked the man in black who had introduced himself as Mr Daniel Jones, an attorney.

"I'm happy to say it is, as far as I am able to judge, Mr Challiss," the lawyer replied, adding: "And the horses seem to have escaped harm."

"Good! Then we must convey the injured coachman to the *Crown* with all speed," said Tom. "He's losing blood fast and in urgent need of medical assistance."

Despite his lack of inches – he was barely five-and-a-half feet in height – Jones was a man of dignity. He said in measured tones: "But who is to drive the coach?"

"I will!" said Tom, astonishing himself by climbing up onto the box, hoping to manage it without getting them all killed. "I've driven only farm waggons before this but I think I can handle the team," he said, with a greater confidence than he felt. "Might I ask you to assist the young lady, sir – I didn't catch her name – in getting the man into the coach?" He had no need to entreat the attorney further for the man had run off to carry out his errand almost before Tom had finished speaking.

Mrs Pryer, being of a stronger build than the younger woman, insisted on helping Mr Jones to carry the wounded, now conscious, man to the coach.

The coachman reclined on the seat lately vacated by Mrs Pryer and her son, Anthony. The reticent young woman, Attorney Daniel Jones and Mrs Polly Pryer with her son on her lap, were squeezed into the seat opposite the casualty. Out of sight, out of mind. Only one of the passengers gave a thought to Tom as he wrestled with the four-horse team, so smooth was the remainder of their interrupted journey.

John Heath, M.D., happened to be supping a quiet drink in the saloon bar of the inn. He was attending the coachman within minutes of his arrival and very shortly the haemorrhage had been stemmed. A florid-complexioned man in his early fifties, the doctor reappeared in the saloon wiping his hands on a cloth and, before rolling down his shirtsleeves reached for Tom's hand, shook it heartily, and declared so that all could hear: "You've saved this man's life!" Adding: "Well done, young man!"

Where was the mysterious young woman? Tom knew that it was her swift action that had saved the man, not his. He had merely followed her instructions. He blushed at the mistakenly-attributed accolade but had said nothing to put the matter right until it became too late to alter his undeserved moment of glory. But where could the true heroine of the hour have vanished to? Tom was puzzled.

Daniel Jones' was a familiar face among the regulars who patronized the *Crown*. The small band of unfortunate travellers became aware by the numerous greetings directed at him that he invariably used the hostelry as he travelled to and from Felixton in the course of his profession. In the event, as soon as their sorry plight became known to him, the landlord was only too happy to accommodate the Felixton passengers on the recommendation of the respected attorney.

At least I am assured of one night's food and rest, thought Tom gratefully, but what then? Once more he was reduced to utter penury but this time he had neither diamond nor teeth to sell. All he had was what he stood up in: a secondhand suit of clothes and some less than perfect boots. He was hatless and – worse! – he'd lost Mary Emma's pretty limeflower ring.

Starting on a series of *if onlys* was a fruitless exercise.

Just let me set eyes on that buck, Jake Reville, and his flashy silver spurs! Tom fumed. What a fool! he thought derisively What a damned fool: to have hung on to those gew-gaws.

Tom recalled Reville removing the fancy spurs from a dead Spaniard's boots after the combined forces of Britain and Spain had routed the French at Vitoria. Always a robber, thought Tom. He and Reville had met and fought alongside each other when they were infantrymen at the Battle of Vitoria, Spain, in June 1813. They had never become true friends, merely wary comrades-in-arms. It had sickened Tom to see Reville and other predators picking over the corpses as soon as hostilities ceased. Jake Reville must have recognized Tom when the former had robbed the coach passengers but had thought himself safe from recognition.

Jones was speaking. "… he'll hang before long. It's only a matter of time," the dark-eyed attorney assured his audience. "He'll make a fundamental mistake one day and that will end his short career as a gentleman of the road." Had he been a spitting man he would have done so then. Instead he said scornfully: "Gentleman, indeed! To hold a pistol to an infant's head in front of the boy's mother, the cur! He's robbed me of my late father's watch and the women have lost their jewellery." He turned to Tom. "Did you lose anything of great value, Mr Challiss?"

Tom was conscious that somebody had looked in his direction the instant his name had been mentioned. He turned to survey the saloon but nobody was conspicuous to his probing eye. "Indeed I did, sir," Tom replied in answer to Jones' query. "'Twas sewn into the lining of my hat! I had thought it safe from everything but an earthquake; which goes to show how wrong one can be!"

"I'm intrigued, Challiss," the attorney said, with a smile that set his brown eyes twinkling. "What could you possibly have had sewn into a hat? It defies imagination!"

Turning his back to thwart any would-be eavesdroppers or lip-readers, Tom whispered: "An engagement ring of great value," and he went on to describe it in minute detail. "I'm resigned to the fact that I shall never see it again. 'Tis a great loss to me."

"I can guess that it would be," Daniel Jones said, looking thoughtful. "And you, Mrs Pryer. Did you have very much taken?"

"Everything of value I was wearing," was the poor woman's reply. She suddenly burst out laughing. "But my little Anthony was carrying all our money and my best bits of jewellery in his pocket, weren't you, my dove, just in case." Chuckling over the way she had tricked the highwayman, she added: "I was always a prudent woman, sir, and know all about the dangers of keeping all my eggs in a single basket!" The saloon filled with laughter at hearing of her clever ruse.

It grew late. The room began to clear and little Anthony Pryer had fallen asleep beside the damped down fire which the landlord kept going winter and summer, no matter how hot the weather.

Two rooms had been made ready for the coach party: Tom and Daniel Jones were to share one and Mrs Pryer, Anthony and the young woman were assigned the other. But nobody had seen the younger woman since Tom had driven the coach into the inn yard. He found himself worrying about her and decided to go outside to see if she could be found.

She was seated on the stump of a tree, away from the inn's lights, in the shadow of an apple tree whose ripening fruit Tom would always afterwards associate with this night. "Because of the unusual events of the past hour or two somebody forgot to introduce us," he said as he approached her; "therefore I must take the liberty of introducing myself; Thomas Roberts Challiss, madam." He inclined his head.

No answer. The moon had climbed up the sky and the inn yard and its orchard was a study in black and silver. The silence lengthened. "I don't wish to appear rude, but might I ask why are you hiding yourself away like this?" Tom said at last.

"A gentleman would not have asked a lady such a question," she replied. "I was mistaken in thinking you one. One hides because one wishes to avoid company."

Affronted by the inference that he was no gentleman even though he had never thought of himself as one, he considered her remark unwarranted. He said frostily: "You have eaten nothing, madam, and must be in need of sustenance." He had heard George use the word and thought it rather a good choice to add dignity to his speech. "I certainly had no wish to disturb your privacy. I was merely concerned for your well-being. At least allow me to bring you something to eat if you would rather not go inside."

Though nothing of her face was visible behind the curtain of her hair she, nevertheless, kept her head averted and said in a gentler tone: "You must forgive my bad temper, Mr Challiss. I have been ill for some months and have lost the art of going among strangers and making myself pleasant company. Forgive my rudeness, please." Taking care to remain on the dark side of the apple tree she extended a gloved hand and said: "My name is Brown... Garnet Brown... *Miss* Garnet Brown."

"My dear Miss Brown," Tom said warmly, having finally breached her reserve, "Won't you please allow me to fetch you something? If not to eat, then something to drink. You must be very thirsty."

To his surprise she laughed, a low soft chuckle and he imagined her smiling to herself in the dark. "Must I?" she said.

"I don't mean to be impertinent–"

"Then don't!" she said firmly. Again she sighed. "I suppose everybody has been wondering what has become of me," she said in a subdued voice. "And you, I suppose, are owed an explanation of sorts. I was impressed by your quick thinking, Mr Challiss, and the courage you showed when you offered to drive the coach."

Shamed by the praise heaped upon him by the one truly deserving recognition, Tom said: "'Twas your level head that spurred me on, Miss Brown. How did you come by such medical knowledge, might I ask?"

"I see that nothing I say will turn you from your inquisition," she said affably. "'Tis no great mystery, sir. Any one of a number of women could have done as much; but none, I think, would have found it as easy to drive a coach-and-four as you did."

"You are too modest, Miss Brown. I suspect you have led an adventurous life."

"I see you are determined to know all about me," she said. "Well... I can't promise to tell you all. What I will say is that, before my illness, I was a nurse."

"But you are a lady!"

"A woman first," she insisted. "Gentle birth does not preclude pity, Mr Challiss. When my brother John, who is a surgeon, joined Wellington's army in Spain I refused to be left behind," she explained. "The only way I could become involved in assisting him and still retain my honour was to accompany him as a surgical nurse under his protection. It was John who taught me how to care for casualties. I learned for myself how to comfort and ease the passing of the mortally wounded. Women are particularly well-suited to nursing, sir. They have a greater store of patience than men."

Now here's an extraordinary young woman, thought Tom. He had no difficulty in believing that her pleasant voice had soothed many injured and dying men on the battlefield. The idea of this lovely creature in surroundings of such horror and amid scenes of carnage appalled him. "You have my wholehearted admiration, Miss Brown," he said warmly.

"Thank you, sir. But you mustn't set me up for a saint." She gave a short laugh. "I must confess that I wasn't being entirely unselfish and altruistic in my desire to accompany my brother to Spain. Have you any idea how tedious the life of a well-bred young lady can be? I wanted adventure! Apart from which, I suffer from a serious affliction that has made my life reclusive. Naturally, when I saw the the opportunity that presented itself as a means to an alternative way of life, I seized the chance to fly my cage and followed the army."

Having seen the kind of women who followed the camps, Tom was horrified by her last words. "But it was hardly fitting work for a gentlewoman," he repeated. "D'ye mean to tell me that you attended men who were completely – er – unclothed?"

"Yes, Mr Challiss, I do," Miss Brown said seriously. "And why not, pray?"

"'Tis usual for male orderlies to attend the wounded, madam," he said. "What possessed your brother to have allowed you to follow such a course?"

Keeping in shadow, she stood up. "He was concerned for the suffering men to whom I might minister, sir," she said hotly. "And who are you to question the wisdom of one as brave as he? John never spared himself in his fight to save the injured from an untimely death. Where many surgeons would have given up on a case, he persevered until he seemed almost to bring back from the dead some of his patients. How dare you presume to imply that he had no proper consideration for my reputation?"

"Forgive me," Tom said. "You are, of course, right. I did presume. But you must know that women who follow the regiments from camp to camp are held in the lowest esteem?"

"And why is that, Mr Challiss?" was Garnet Brown's startling question.

Tom was dumfounded. It was impossible for him to pursue the subject of prostitution with a gentlewoman. "I allude to their morals, Miss Brown," he finally got out with difficulty.

It seemed she would not spare him when she said: "I'm afraid I do not understand your allusion, sir. What of their morals?"

He cleared his constricted throat. "Why... The women are drabs, ma'am, if you understand the term."

To his surprise, she stepped from the shadows into the day-bright moonlight. "Oh, yes, Mr Challiss," she said bitterly, "I do. And do you consider that men have any part to play in the stratum of society to which these poor women are consigned?"

"I fail to understand—"

"—what *men* have to do with the subject under discussion?" she said, her voice full of scorn. "Might *I* presume, Mr Challiss, that you have had occasion to avail yourself of... shall we stick to your choice of word? ... a *drab*, on occasion?"

"Well, yes," Tom said, growing hot under the collar. "But that was an entirely different matter. The women of whom we are speaking blatantly sell themselves."

"I think you have demonstrated that you know precious little about the women who follow the camps, sir," she said severely. "A fair number of those women are the legal wives of the soldiers. Others are those recently widowed who had accompanied their husbands. They are only too well aware that their lot is one of abject poverty unless they can persuade some man to take pity on their plight and offer to make them so-called *honest* women. And, of course, they are alive to the fact that such a marriage is likely to be of short duration, especially if the woman marries an infantrymen. And then what are they expected to do to keep themselves?"

Tom's conscience was plaguing him as he recalled several casual liaisons during his spell in the army. And then there had been Ghislaine... He hadn't given the women a thought other than that they were a convenient means of easement. But – damn it all! – they had *enjoyed* the coupling as much as he had. Hadn't they? "I hadn't thought about it before in quite that light," he said.

"I wonder what you would think of me now were I to tell you that I have lain with a man – out of wedlock?" She tossed back her mane of hair. Her eyes sparkled.

"I should not believe you," he said with conviction.

"Why not? Simply because I speak and behave as you think a lady should? You would be mistaken, Mr Challiss. Tell me: have you a relative by the name of George Challiss?"

What the devil– ? "He is my brother, madam," Tom said, wondering what was coming next.

"I had thought so," Garnet Brown said. "You are very much alike – but only in appearance. Your characters are very different, I think."

"Am I given to understand that you know George, Miss Brown?"

"Yes," she said, "very well indeed. Once upon a time he and I were lovers."

"George and you–?" Lovely as she was, Tom found the idea hard to grasp.

"Would you care to hear about it, Mr Challiss? I'm sorry, if I've shocked you: I took you for a man of the world." Her large eyes glittered in the moonlight.

A man of the world! thought Tom; it seems I've a lot to learn. For he *had* been shocked. He'd had no idea that gentlewomen could sink so low. "When was it?"

"When did it begin? Ah…" A shuddering sigh escaped her. "My brother had trained other women, mostly young widows, in the art of nursing by the summer of 1812. Your brother and I met quite by chance in July of that year, at Salamanca. He had sustained a superficial wound and it happened to fall to my lot to tend him. We nurses attended casualties as they were brought in, according to urgency, and George was assigned to me." Her voice had sunk almost to a whisper. She suddenly burst out: "Oh! Mr Challiss! I had thought I was over it at last; but I don't think I shall ever be over it. You must excuse me." Her hands covered her face as a sob escaped her.

He wished he knew what to do. He dare not touch her, so he said: "Please don't distress yourself, Miss Brown, I beg you. It might be better if we postpone this conversation unt—"

Her hands flew from her face as she interrupted forcefully: "No! It is preferable that you know everything now." Her next words were spoken calmly. "Then… when next you see George, you will be able to tell him what I am going to tell you. I think it only right that he should know."

"Perhaps the time will come when you will be able to tell him it yourself," said Tom, not very convincingly.

A bitter laugh escaped her. "I can tell you now, Mr Challiss – that time will never come. You had far better keep quiet and pay heed to my story. It is a common enough tale and quite short, sir."

"As you wish, " Tom said reluctantly. "You're certain you want to share such personal details with a stranger?"

"Oh, yes!" she said. "Now. Please have the goodness not to interrupt until I have done. You cannot know what a terrible burden this secret has been and how much I have longed to share it with someone."

Tom said, " I really think we should find a more suitable place first. The coach is standing empty. Suppose we use that?"

"An excellent idea!" she said, instantly crossing the inn yard to where the shadowed coach stood outside the stables. As she opened the door and they followed one another into the confined dark space she remarked: "Yes. What could be better? Clever Mr Challiss! This gloomy place, though 'tis a trifle evil-smelling, will make a suitable confessional and is dark enough to spare my blushes into the bargain."

Wishing himself a thousand miles away, Tom said: "But I am no priest, Miss Brown."

"Do not upset yourself, Mr Challiss," she said, "I won't hold it against you, sir."

★

Chapter Fourteen

They sat opposite each other, Miss Brown on the seat lately occupied by Mrs Pryer, her son Anthony and her numerous packages. Tom's eyes had adjusted to the dark interior of the coach but the young woman's outline remained vague. Intensely interested in what the former nurse had to tell him, Tom relaxed into his seat and prepared himself to listen.

"I found the work of caring for the wounded congenial," Garnet Brown began, "although the reality of it was a jolt. My first sight of a man's naked body in the flesh shocked me, for until I became a nurse I had seen only classical illustrations. Then I reasoned that if the man had the courage to bear the pain of mutilation, even minor wounds—and they were *so* brave, Mr Challiss! – the least I could do was to look on one of God's creatures with compassion. My own feelings were of no account: I was there to do a job. After a while I became immune to the sight of the male member until it offended my sight no more than did a man's thumb."

Tom heard her with distaste and was unable to stifle a sharp intake of breath.

"I'm sorry if hearing me speak plainly offends you, sir. By the time Captain Challiss was carried into my tent as a casualty the sight of a naked man had become no more shocking to me than it does to an artist. I viewed each man with clinical detachment, concentrating on his wounds or lacerations, how best I could treat them with the means at hand. But of all the men I had nursed up to that moment, I had not seen such a glorious body as that belonging to George Challiss as he lay stripped on the casualty table. I do not wish to sound depraved, Mr Challiss; but the sight of such a classically proportioned man took my breath away.

"Your brother was lightly wounded: a nick from a sabre taken high on the inner left thigh and deep enough to warrant stitches. He was not in great pain from the wound but after I had swabbed the gash with alcohol and inserted the curved needle to make the first stitch – John had taught me how and I had become so adept that I was able to inflict as little pain as possible on my patients – your brother let out a yell and cursed me roundly in language best kept for the battlefield."

"Of course, I suspended my needle and thread, merely raising my eyebrows as I awaited his permission to proceed. I had not spoken a word up to that moment. With a bad grace, Captain Challiss bade me get on with my clumsy needlework and that I'd better make a tidy job of it or I'd have him to deal with."

I don't doubt the veracity of that for a moment, thought Tom, highly amused. How like his irascible brother it sounded.

"Keeping a straight face, as we nurses had been trained to do by my brother, I said: 'Have I your permission to proceed then, Captain?' Something in the tone of my voice at once wrought a change in his demeanour. He told me to carry on with my devilish work and be quick about it. And then he smiled. My heart was captured in that instant, Mr Challiss: I had not known that a kind smile could be used as a weapon, a snare. One rarely sees such even, white teeth. One grows used to rotted gums and blackened stumps, to evil-smelling breath, the stench of diseased and unwashed bodies, to verminous body hair and uniforms, and every kind of vile excretion. George Challiss smelled wholesome and was so different from the run of the mill, a veritable Adonis. Although I tried to keep hold of my wits I was powerless to resist his magnetism and I believe he knew it from that instant. I finished the stitches, swabbed the area with more alcohol and dressed the wound with a yarrow compound. I said: 'The soreness will abate in a day or two and your leg will be as good as new, sir. Keep the wound clean and there should be no lasting damage.'

"He smiled again and said he'd be back to complain to the surgeon if my promise did not hold good. Whereupon I told him that the surgeon was my brother and very skilled in using a scalpel. He laughed outright at my saucy remark and asked would I do him the honour of dining with him the next evening. By this time he had donned his uniform and looked so splendid that my heart was a-flutter and I was ready to swoon at his feet. However, I did not. I am not given to such missish behaviour as a rule and could not understand what had happened to make me behave in such a silly, unladylike fashion. I promised him I would seek my brother's permission to absent myself from the field hospital, as we called our collection of tents, and would send an answer if he would tell me where he was billeted.

"The next evening we dined at a *posada* and I could not remember eating so well for months past. George had been plainly surprised when I appeared in full evening dress. Admiration shone from his eyes. I knew I looked well:

even John had remarked it, telling me that I looked too splendid to spend the evening with a mere captain in Wellington's army; that I should be taking supper with an *hildalgo* at the very least. When George gave me his arm to take me in to dine, I trembled like an autumn leaf that is ready to fall. He looked down into my eyes with his own, so dark that they were almost black, and I knew at once that I would obey his every wish."

Her story was having a disastrous effect upon Tom's self-command. Not that he was about to ravish Miss Brown; but he doubted he would be able to contain himself for much longer. His agitation caused him to shift in his seat.

"Not much longer, Mr Challiss," she said. "Have patience, sir, for I am coming to that part of my story that I would have you carry to your brother. Your mind has leapt ahead, I am sure, and I have no need to burden you with detail. That I loved – love – George with all my heart and body you will have understood. My mistake was in believing my love reciprocated. I truly thought he loved me. I gave myself to George deliriously, repeatedly and with abandon. The outcome of my madness was that I bore him a child, a daughter. I have call—"

"Does he know?" Astonished by her revelation, Tom could not keep silent.

"He will know," she said, "when you tell him of it. Tell him our child has red-gold hair the colour of sunrise and is two years old. Little Aurora is the most beautiful child I have ever seen. She is also a constant reminder of an unrequited love affair. When next you see your brother, tell him I have called our child Aurora Challiss Brown. You will do that, Mr Challiss? Thank you. Now, shall we join the others?" She opened the coach door. "You have been a good listener, sir."

Following her across the moonlit yard, he said: "You mentioned an affliction, Miss Brown. As yet I have seen no sign of anything amiss."

"Wait," she said, as they entered the quiet inn. The lamps had been dimmed and it seemed that all the guests, except themselves, had retired for the night. Deliberately, Garnet Brown walked over to one of the lamps, turned up its flame and held it up so that the left side of her face was illuminated.

At first, Tom noticed nothing. Involuntarily, he gasped as he saw that her lovely face was disfigured by a pale stain, a faded port wine mark that reached from her left ear to halfway across her ivory cheek.

Her tone bitter, she said: "I see that you, too, are repelled by my birthmark."

Tom protested: "No! 'Twas such a surprise, that was all, I assure you."

"Some people find it repulsive," she said in a low, weary voice. "To make matters worse, my mother, by naming me Garnet, ensured that I would never for a moment forget my disfigurement. How I detest the name!" Replacing the lamp and lowering its wick, she let her hair fall so that the rosy stain was hidden once more. "You must agree that such a defect might be termed an affliction, sir?"

"But it's of so little significance—"

"Not to me, sir, not to *me*," she said tragically. "It was because of it that my brother took up the study of medicine. In the zeal of youth he imagined that he would find a cure for such birthmarks, or devise a way of removing them without endangering the patient. 'Twas that led him to study surgery. But I despair of a cure being found in my lifetime. No doubt my disfigurement revolted your brother."

Unconsciously, Tom shook his head in denial. He pitied her with all his heart. Yet, surely, George must have been drawn to such a fine woman, one who had been so generous with her love, enough to ignore such a slight imperfection? To change the subject, he said: "Any idea who it was fired the shot at the highwayman?"

"It was I," she said calmly. "I have carried a small pistol since I began battle-field nursing, as a precaution. Not that I ever had occasion to use it before tonight."

Tom was astonished at her temerity. What a fool George had been to cast away such a spirited prize, he thought, gazing at Miss Brown with open admiration.

She smiled. "Good-night, Mr Challiss," she said, taking up a candlestick and lighting her unlit candle from the flame of one nearby, kept alight for the purpose.

He watched her ascend the stairs and thought that, had he not met his own darling Mary Emma Kay first, he would have made Garnet Brown his wife most gladly and taken George's daughter under his wing into the bargain.

★

Seated at a small table, Daniel Jones was writing rapidly and – if the pile of finished pages was any indication – looked as if he had been at it for some hours. As Tom entered the cramped room the attorney flung down his quill and spun round to face him. "You keep late hours, Mr Challiss," he said.

Annoyed at finding him still up, Tom said: "Yes. I have been engaged on a private matter." Affecting a yawn he studied the beds. "Which is mine, sir?"

"It is immaterial," Jones replied, "take your pick. Having inspected them I shall use neither. I value my hide too much to risk it. I would guess that both beds are already occupied and that you'll share space with bugs as well as the usual vermin." He gave an exaggerated shudder. "Look at that filthy, stained linen."

Tom had seen worse. "Where do you intend to spend the night then, sir?"

"Here; at this table." Jones' brown eyes twinkled. He certainly looked as if he were in no need of sleep. "I trust my busy pen will not disturb you too much, Mr Challiss. I intend to write all night. At cock crow, I shall take myself off to my office in the High Street." Having resumed his writing, he faced Tom again and, quill in hand, said: "You are welcome to join me, sir. Unless you have other plans?"

"No. I have no other plans," Tom said, ruefully. "I am in no position to plan anything beyond the next moment, Mr Jones. I am destitute."

"Nonsense," smiled Daniel Jones. "If you've discovered nothing else about me, I hope, sir, that you feel you know me well enough to apply to me for a small loan to tide you over in these exceptional circumstances?"

"I'm obliged to you, sir," Tom said, his relief plain. "Well. . . in that case—"

"Good! Then it's settled." The lawyer's expression changed to one of anxiety. "But I trust you will take my advice and eschew the beds, Mr Challiss? I cannot risk vermin being carried into my establishment, you understand. Forgive me for robbing you of your rest." He looked around the chamber. "You might manage to doze in that chair. But I have no right to inconvenience you so. You're a dashed big fellow—"

"Might I take this opportunity, Mr Jones," Tom said, unaware that he'd interrupted the man's apology, "to speak to you on a matter concerning myself?"

"What is it?"

Tom began: "I have money deposited with Fector's bank at Dover."

"What made you choose to leave it with Fector?" the attorney asked suavely.

Alarmed and surprised by his response, Tom said, "You know of him, then. Was it an unwise decision?"

"By no means, my dear sir; you could hardly have chosen more wisely," Jones said affably. "Such a dry stick Fector, but honest and trustworthy. Your money's as safe as houses with him, sir. Though in these turbulent, inflammatory times I might have chosen a more apt simile. In what way may I be of service to you, Mr Challiss?"

Greatly relieved, Tom said: "I wish to have my money, or a banker's draft to the amount, sent to my forwarding address. It is Uppham House, Uppham St Mary, Norfolk." The lawyer wrote down the address. "'Tis a matter of some urgency, Mr Jones. But I thank my lucky stars that I had the foresight to deposit it with Mr Fector. This highway robbery tonight was the second attack on my person since I left Dover."

"Most unfortunate, Mr Chaliss. Did you lose a great deal in the first robbery?"

"Almost everything, including a valuable horse, sir. I'd congratulated myself on escaping with my life," Tom said. "I was fortunate that time to have hung onto the lime flower ring. I feel really bitter about the loss of that, sir, more than I can say."

"Don't despair too soon, my dear sir! All may not be lost as to that."

Barely daring to hope, Tom said eagerly: "You think my ring might be returned?"

Daniel Jones picked up the top sheet from the pile of writing. "Read that." On the sheet he handed to Tom had been written a detailed description of the highwayman and his Arabian horse. The huge sum of ten pounds was offered as a reward for information leading to the apprehension of the thief. The address of Daniel Jones, Attorney, was given at the foot of the page as that to which the informant should apply for recompense. "'Twas a thousand pities nobody was able to get a good look at the rogue's face," said Jones in a regretful tone.

Whereupon, Tom told him of sighting the incriminating spurs and of having known Jake Reville in Spain.

"What? It was Reville! You don't say so," Jones said excitedly. "It was supposed that he'd returned to London. Well, well! Jake Reville. 'Twould be feathers in our caps if we were to land that gallows-bait. Eh, sir? There's a price on his head."

The image of Jake Reville suspended from a gallows did not appeal to Tom. "Much as I dislike the man, Mr Jones, I would not wish to see him – or, indeed, any man, woman or child – dispatched in such a barbarous way," Tom said.

"Tch! You're too soft, sir," Jones admonished him. "D'ye think he would care a snap of his fingers had he killed that inoffensive coachman instead of maiming him? Reville's killed many times in the pursuit of his evil calling – all in the name of greed. No. I will show no mercy to such scoundrels as that fellow. We'll be well rid of him."

"I suppose you are right," Tom said abstractedly. "Though I think it probable that he's left the district by this time. I'm sure he recognized me from our army days."

Annoyed, the attorney said: "You may well be right. Nevertheless, I shall hand a sheaf of these to every driver of mail coaches and post coaches, as well as to the carters, to be displayed at every inn in Norfolk and all the way to London. Ten pounds reward will prove too great a prize for many of that fraternity. One of his own kind will betray him before long." He was scribbling idly on one of the notices.

"Yet I don't see how that will bring back Mary Emma's ring," said Tom dolefully. "Reville would have been sure to have disposed of it at the first opportunity. Would it help, perhaps, were I to sketch its design on the reward notices?"

Daniel Jones laughed and pointed to a badly drawn image of a ring, which might have been taken for a poor attempt at a pigeon's nest, in the margin of the page. It was unrecognizable as the beautiful jewel Tom had lost. "I am no artist, sir, as you can see," he said good-naturedly, handing the quill to him. "You had better try."

The attorney was impressed by Tom's clearly-drawn pictures of the ring, one in profile and another showing the arrangement of the diamonds into a lime flower. And so they passed the few remaining hours of the eventful night: Daniel Jones writing furiously, covering a pile of reward notices to be distributed immediately; and Tom, lovingly drawing the images of the ring with such care that each representation was an improvement on the former. At the end of their combined labours, Tom yawned, stretched his stiff body and flexed his cramped right hand. Mary Emma and Miss Peters had been in his thoughts throughout his task. Where were they at this moment?

"You seem to be able to draw, Mr Challiss," observed Jones as he collected his papers. "It would assist in the rogue's capture were you to sketch his likeness. Posters could be printed from it. D'you think you might try?"

"I suppose I might," Tom said evincing great reluctance for the task. "Though I think any portrait that I produce will be more likely to assist Reville in *avoiding* capture than the reverse. I have studied the ring so well that recalling every detail of it came easily. A likeness is a different prospect altogether."

"Suppose you try, anyway," Jones urged.

Damn the man! thought Tom. "To be perfectly honest with you, Mr Jones, I have no liking for the exercise. Jake and I fought together as soldiers and one does not forget camaraderie so easily. You must excuse me."

"As you wish, sir," Jones said, all warmth gone from his manner. "But I must say, I think your unwillingness to rid the roads of a public menace ignores your duties as a citizen. Morally, you have no choice in the matter." A clean sheet of paper and pencil were placed on the table that Jones had vacated. "One can but try, sir," the lawyer said encouragingly.

Seating himself with a scowl at his oppressor, Tom made up his mind to deliberately botch his effort at a true likeness of Jake Reville. As these things will, the rudimentary portrait that he had effortlessly conjured from his pencil produced a good likeness of the highwayman by force of its sheer simplicity. "Here," he said ungraciously, thrusting it to Jones behind his back without turning around.

As he rolled the poster into a cylinder Jones had an inkling of what the effort had cost Tom in the matter of scruples, and said: "It's really very good and I am certain will help bring the fellow to justice. I'm indebted to you, Mr Challiss."

Day was dawning and a cock crowed in the vicinity of the inn. To Tom's ears the bird's jerky strangling cry seemed to accuse him of deliberate betrayal.

★

The poster carrying Tom's hand drawn likenesss of Jake Reville was taken to a local printing shop where Daniel Jones ordered two hundred copies to be made. The legend accompanying the highwayman's visage described him in most unflattering terms and promised a substantial reward of one hundred pounds for his being delivered – dead or alive. Tom loathed everything about the poster.

Early on the morning following the robbery, Daniel Jones and his new acquaintance, Thomas Roberts Challiss, were to be seen entering the front door of the lawyer's comfortable abode in Fakenham High Street. Passing through his place of business on the ground floor of the premises, they ascended a wide staircase which led to the attorney's living quarters. Everything was of good quality and in the best of taste. Tom hadn't been in such well-appointed rooms since his stay at *Les Flamants*. He could understand why Daniel had been so particular about keeping his rooms free of vermin.

The two young men were beginning to understand one another. Soon, they had become such firm friends that they were on Christian name terms. During the few days that Tom spent at the attorney's home, he learned something of the small histories of the other participants in the fateful coach ride.

"You remember Mrs Pryer, Tom?" Daniel said, as they sat eating breakfast one morning. "That woman has her wits about her. She told me – while you were otherwise engaged with the delectable Miss Brown – that she and her small son were on their way to take up residence at the Reverend Septimus Skrimshire's Academy for Young Gentlemen. She's a schoolmaster's widow and has taken the post of matron at the Academy. I know the place well. It has an excellent reputation. Mrs Pryer has dropped into a busy but rewarding and comfortable life, and young Anthony will receive a first-class education into the bargain, gratis."

"I'm glad," said Tom, helping himself to a second mutton chop. "A widow's life can be a hard one, particularly if one has offspring to support." He was reminded of what Garnet Brown had told him of soldiers' widows. "Any news of Miss Garnet Brown? I had no chance to bid her farewell in a proper manner."

Daniel regarded Tom quizzically over his raised tea cup. "I should have thought you had said all that you had to say that first night," he said, "you were absent long enough! Well... Remember the business I had to attend to at Dereham? I called in at the *Crown* on the way home and learned that Miss Brown had boarded the Cambridge coach next morning, after we'd left; though not before she had enquired after the condition of the wounded coachman – goes by the name of Pegrum, I believe." He buttered a slice of toast. "Apparently, Miss Brown told Pegrum she was going to stay with an aunt, or some other female, at Wisbech."

Tom tucked this information away for future reference. He'd conceived an ambition: to bring George face to face with Garnet and their daughter, Aurora. Just how he would go about it was still only a vague plan. But, somehow, he meant to achieve a meeting between two people who had become very important to him.

Tom's stay with the Fakenham attorney came to an abrupt end when Daniel was called away to attend an important case at Norwich which would necessitate his absence for several days. Having no reason to linger at Fakenham, Tom left as well.

Once more he was on the road, this time a passenger on the crowded coach to Lynn. He'd elected to travel outside and was glad that he had done so. This countryside is going to be mine for the remainder of my days, he thought, as the coach bowled along under immense skies. This bit of Norfolk with its few rises among wide sweeps of fenland is almost like a foreign country to me, quite different from the Felixton and Lyndon area. Excitement mounted at the thought that he would soon see Uppham House and its estate for himself and he would be able to put into action the plans he had for the place.

The busy port of Lynn was reached in time for him to snatch refreshment before boarding the coach to Downham. After a short journey, the coach drew into the market town and, using money loaned him by Daniel, he took a room for one night at the *Queen's Head*. With time to spare before dining, he decided to spend the interval in exploring the small town, which happened to be the nearest place of any size to the village of Uppham St Mary and therefore of great interest to Tom.

His exploration of Downham revealed gangs of silent, uncouth men thronging the streets. They resembled each other in appearance: gaunt, disgruntled-looking, ill-kempt and clad in threadbare garments. Their bowed heads signified resignation. Yet if Tom should encounter the frank stares of any of these men their angry eyes spat forth the same message: *desperation*. He'd recognized ex-soldiers and former sailors by the remnants of their uniforms and anger had surged through him. But the majority of idlers looked as if they had once worked on the land and were now redundant agricultural labourers. After Tom had questioned one or two of the fuming men in exchange for a much-needed shilling or two, a terrible story emerged of wrongs piled upon injustice.

Unaccountably, Tom felt ashamed to have witnessed such abject poverty. Again, a burning anger swept through him as he recalled the images he'd seen during his early evening stroll. His anger was directed towards those in a society which would deprive men, already barely able to subsist, of a fair wage for unremitting labour when in employ.

He had learned that mechanisation had cut the numbers of labourers needed to run the farms, the chief culprit being the threshing machine where agricultural labourers were concerned. It deprived the men of work during the twenty-nine week winter when most of that period had, previous to the introduction of the machines, ensured indoor employment during the harshest weather and, although wages were less in winter than in summer or harvest, there had been some payment for work done. Now there was no work and no money for food.

One wool spinner, concerned that the 'gennelman' heard his own tale of woe, complained to Tom about unemployment resulting from the introduction of the Spinning Jenny.

"This diabolical noo-fangled invention fills the noo *manufactories*. Just one o' their danged machine can do the work of several men yer see, sir. So now 'undreds of we spinners and weavers are called *redundant*, even though our work is of a much bedder quality than anything a danged machine can prodoos," lamented the man. "We've larst not only our liveli'ood but some of us 'ave larst our 'omes an all! I dunno what's ter become of us all; but I ain't goin' in no workus, that I *dew* know."

The unemployed, their numbers swelled by ex-servicemen returning from the Peninsular Wars, milled about the streets of Downham in enforced idleness, without prospect of mitigation of their dire circumstances. To Tom, it was no wonder that the men were desperate.

What had happened to his country in the three years that he'd been away fighting Napoleon's armies? Mrs Mawby, Lambert Jardine's erstwhile cook-housekeeper, had mentioned a change for the worse in the country's economy; but Tom had scarcely paid attention. Selfishly, he'd been so wrapped up in his own affairs that he'd failed to notice signs indicating a failing economy. With the exception of deserted Lyndon Manor, everything had seemed to him perfectly normal in the north-eastern coastal area of Norfolk.

Now it was obvious that things were coming to a head in west Norfolk, as well as in the country: that the boil of discontent, which had begun to form with the rise in the price of corn, was ripe for bursting. While Tom didn't yet fully understand the cause, he was determined to find out what had gone so wrong that the working men of Downham seethed with resentment. From what he'd observed, those desperate men were at flash-point and the camel's back of their discontent was about to be broken. What form would the last straw take? Tom wondered, as he made his way back to the inn.

Light and warmth spilled out of the *Queen's Head* as he pushed open the door. The inn was crammed. The reek of sawdust mixed with spilled drink, tobacco smoke, unwashed bodies and animal manure invaded his nostrils. Among the boisterous company a group of men were conspicuous by their comparative sobriety. Each sat with a pot of ale before him yet drank from it sparingly. It appeared to Tom that those gathered about the table in a shadowy corner were engaged in some sort of meeting. Voices were kept low, heads nodded for or against a proposition, expressions were grim.

Counterpointing the general hubbub, the quavering voice of an old man impinged upon Tom's consciousness. Searching the room for its source, he made out a bent figure seated on a settle and crouched over the low fire. To Tom, after his vigorous ramble about the town, the room was stifling; but it seemed that the old man would never be warm, however close to the embers he bent his twisted body. An incessant whine issued from the old man's sunken lips as he repeated his threnody without pause. Unable to make sense of the thin dribble of gibberish, Tom drew nearer to its source.

His white-locked head shaking from side to side, the man was moaning: "They ploughed up the common and me wennel Bu"ercup died. An so me chile died and then me 'ooman died. They all on 'em died cos they ploughed up the common. Me wennel Bu"ercup died. An so me chile died an then me 'ooman died. All cos they ploughed up the common. . ."

Tom leaned towards the pitiful creature. "Can I buy you a pint of ale, sir?"

"He's already bosky, sir," a red-faced man of middle-age said helpfully. "Allus goos on like that when he's bosky, does ol' Joe; though 'is troubles 'appened more'n twenty-five year agoo. Turned 'is 'ead, it did, see. Pore ol' bugger. 'Twas one o' the cruellest things the gentry done to the workin' man: inclosin' the land an' ploughin' up the free grazin'. Aye." He spat into the fire. " 'Twere the beginning' o' the end fer the likes of us, that were. Look at 'im, pore ol' sod. Joe ain't got nothing now 'cept his rheumatics. Yew buy 'im a pint anyway, sir. Good luck ter yer honour. That's mighty civil of yer, sir," he added in response to Tom's offer of a pint of ale for himself.

What's the world coming to, thought Tom angrily, when a poor man is separated from what few possessions he has and his family's wiped out by starvation and disease? Why had he known nothing of these things before? He thought back to his last days at Lyndon Manor and remembered that Jardine had started to turn off the labouring servants as soon as he took possession of the place. Tom saw now that he had been walking around with blinkered eyes.

He bought Joe and his champion their pints and ordered his own dinner; but his appetite had been blunted by the sorry sequence of events falling from old Joe's shrivelled lips and what the other labourer had added to the background of the old man's history. It was as if the country was inhabited by two groups of Englishmen.

There had been the vastly larger number of poor men, the peasants, who had owned very little, or nothing at all, but who had enjoyed the life-sustaining bonus of free common grazing land, as of right, for as long as they could remember.

And there had been, and continued to be, a tiny group of individuals – the aristocracy and the gentry and a few wealthy landowning farmers – who had systematically robbed the peasants by enclosing the common land and taking it into their own hands to form part of their already huge estates.

Tom's sympathy for the labourers grew when he joined the few who haunted the table in the dimmest corner of the *Queen's Head*. They aired their grievances over additional pints which were paid for by Tom out of the dwindling number of coins remaining from Daniel's generous loan.

"Once the commons was gone, there wasn't nowhere ter graze a cow, or sheep or pig, 'cept grass sprung at the side o' the road. Then dang me if those rich bastards dint go an' plough *them* up, an all! Then there weren't *no* place ter keep livestock. We was thrown off our small bits o' land, yer see, cos we couldn't pay the rents, cos of the fixed wage them judges said we must 'ave, so we 'ad to goo ter market fer milk an bu"er an cheese. Only our wages was so low they wouldn't stretch to it, see."

The men seated around the shadowy table nodded their heads vigorously in agreement.

"Tell the gennelman 'as 'ow we campaigned for lower food prices, Jem," urged another of the hollow-eyed men. The others mumbled among themselves, their seamed faces further distorted with suppressed fury and disgust.

Jem, who it seemed to Tom had been elected by them to speak on the men's behalf, first spat into the sawdust to vent his spleen, then continued: "The buggers wouldn' 'ear of it. We tried lobbyin' the Parlymint man an' even godda lawyer on our side. All we got fer our pains was a loada toffee-mouthed blather. Well, they've 'ad their turn," he said with a grim look at his smouldering-eyed fellow labourers. "Now they must take the consequences! Eh, bors? There's some things no man will stand fer ever. Arter all, they c'n only 'ang us fer it, at the worst. At least, 'anging's a merciful quick death which is more'n c'n be said fer starvation," he finished bitterly. Tom caught the murmured words: " 'E watched 'is youngist die o' want, did Jem, pore sod." And thought again that it was no wonder the men were so incensed.

As the men dragged their feet from the cheerful interior of the inn and went off to their various haunts, Tom's previous elation gave way to a mixture of pity and alarm. The fierce resolve that had masked every man's prematurely-aged face meant trouble. Provoked beyond endurance, it would not be many months, he felt certain, before the burning resentment of those men ended in a spontaneous combustion that would harm their oppressors where it hurt most: in the destruction of their property.

★

Chapter Fifteen

"Beg pardon, Mr Challiss, sir; but would yew be wantin' to hire a hack?" The stout innkeeper of the *Queen's Head* had just set down a plate of succulent lamb chops garnished with apricots, the postlude to a magnificent breakfast.

Tom, who had that moment swallowed the last of a dish of fried eggs, was in the process of dabbing his mouth with his napkin. He shook his head against the suggestion.

"Mebbe yew'd prefer a gig, then, sir?"

"Thank you, Mr. Beswick. I shall require neither. I intend to go by shanks's pony to Uppham St. Mary. It's no more than a couple of miles, I think you said?"

An expression of alarm crossed the man's florid, usually bland face. "That wouldn't be wise, sir: not with the bad feelin' there is in the town. The men's in an ugly mood an'– beggin' yer pardon, Mr Chaliss– yew'm likely to stick out like a sore thumb in that garb."

"But–" Tom smiled in disbelief at such an idea. "Why should my clothes cause you to worry, Mr Beswick?"

"You saw the men in 'ere last night, sir. Most of 'em have got ter the stage where coverin' their nakedness is about as much as they can 'ope ter do with the ragged state of 'em after months out o' work, sir."

"I still don't see how that affects me," Tom said, applying himself assiduously to another chop.

"Well, sir. Don't say I didn't warn yer! Yew set out ter walk through the town dressed like yew are an' yew'll soon find yerself in bother," Beswick said as he cleared the dirty dishes. "I could lend yew an old coat, Mr Challiss, sir, if I might make so bold."

Tom swallowed the last of his ale and stood up, towering over the inkeeper. "I appreciate your concern, Mr Beswick, but I assure you that I am perfectly able to take care of myself. Three years in the army has taught me the ways of men. Now, how much do I owe you?"

The bill settled, he drew on his gloves, tapped in place the new topper purchased during his peregrinations of the previous evening, and left the inn to set out on the final stage of his journey.

His first meeting with George at Waterloo had set him on this long journey that had led him to Uppham. He mused over the small adventures he'd encountered on the way, dwelling for some time on Sergeant Mylotte's gift of the diamond; the teeth, their stay at *Les Flamants*, on Ghislaine and Garnet; and the recently lost ring.

He became so engrossed in his own thoughts that he was unaware of the hostile glances and mutterings that he was attracting. He was rudely brought back to the present by an accurately hurled stone which sent his new topper flying. The sight of it lying in the dust and muck of the highway infuriated him. After picking it up and brushing it off as best he could, he turned towards the direction from which he surmised the missile must have been flung. Several men returned his angry stare with theirs, which were just as angry, and which left him in no doubt that, as far as they were concerned, he was a pariah. When he started across the rutted road to where they were gathered his fearless action seemed to surprise one or two of them who lowered their eyes to blot out the sparks that seemed to spurt from 'the gennelman's' own.

"Good-morning, friends," Tom began affably.

"We ain't no friends o' the likes o' yew!" a hollow-cheeked, sandy-headed young man said, aiming a gob of spit at the spot immediately in front of Tom's boots. The others shuffled uncomfortably but said nothing.

Tom glanced from the ring of damp dirt that had absorbed the globule of saliva straight into the young man's green eyes. "Your spitting isn't as accurate as your ability at flinging stones, it seems," he said quietly and unsmilingly.

Refusing to be cowed by his adversary's accent, which carried unpleasant associations for him as belonging to one of the ruling classes, the sandy-haired youth replied defiantly: "No it ain't. It landed just zactly where I mennit tew."

Tom gazed briefly at the drying spot of moisture and back again to the hot-headed young man, saying: "Well done, then." As he turned his back on the group and began to walk on he heard the same man say softly: "Come on, men! Let's 'ave 'im!"

Before any of them could translate words into actions a loud voice called out: "Stow it, Clem!", and Tom saw, approaching at a run, the figure of the tall leader of the radical group from last evening's impromptu meeting. What was his name, now?

"Stay out of it, Jem," the angry young man shouted. "We ain't got no quarrel with yew."

Others had drifted up, perhaps to see what the fuss was about, perhaps as a diversion from enforced idleness. Uncomfortably aware of his being the object of unwelcome attention, Tom acknowledged, belatedly, that his host at the *Queen's Head* had been right to warn him of trouble. Panting for breath, Jem joined the growing crowd and pushed his way into the centre where he confronted the hothead.

"Now, just yew calm down, Clem Rix," said Jem, puffed and short of breath. "I'd say yew was in enough trouble already without addin' tew it. What's your quarrel with this gennelman?"

The young man seemed to sag as if to demonstrate that even a balloon as emaciated as himself might be pricked with a pin. He could only bring himself to utter a mumbled accusation. "Well… 'E's one o' *them*, ainnee! Look at 'is togs! A right dandy, an all. La-di-dah, toffee-nosed bugger."

Whosoever 'one o' them' might be, Tom exploded with laughter at this description of himself. Some of the crowd were infected by his ringing laugh and one or two titters of amusement followed. Nevertheless, he had the sense to keep quiet.

"But, I mean," Jem urged patiently, "what's he done tew yew ter make yer pick on 'im?"

Clem could no longer meet Jem's eye but affected to find of great interest the pattern he was describing in the dust with the toe of his split boot.

"Nothin more ter say, then?" Jem said and, lifting his voice so that everybody could hear him, added: "Show's over, friends. Nothin' but a leaky bag o' wind. Best scatter 'fore we draw the wrong sort of attention tew ourselves, everyone." And as the crowd dispersed and the knot of angry men took themselves to a different corner, leaving Jem and Tom suddenly alone, the former said: "I'd best accompany yer ter wherever you're goin', sir. It'll be safer fer yer and cause less trouble in the long run. The men know better'n ter pick on me or anyone in me company."

Chastened, Tom said: "There really is no need, you know. I'm perfectly capable of finding my own way to Uppham. But I thank you, nevertheless. Thomas Challiss, by the way."

Jem threw a quizzical look at the affable younger man. "Oh, ah," he said agreeably, nodding wisely and adding: "I've just seen 'ow good y'are at takin' care o' yerself." Without further words the two unlikely companions walked on in silence.

Though his mind still surged with the threatening images of his late encounter with the inhabitants of Downham, Tom's mood began to lift as he took in the picturesque and quaint architecture of the place. Eventually his curiosity got the better of him and he broke out: "I've not come across any other town like this for such a diversity of handsome buildings. Tell me: what material is it that many of the houses are built from? For instance, this one." He'd paused before a small but exceptionally pretty villa that appeared to glow a buttery yellow in the morning sun.

Jem had had some difficulty in adjusting his ear to Tom's accent. Before answering his enquiry he said: "You're not from these parts, sir, or I'm no judge. Be yer from Lunnon, then?"

"I'm a Norfolk man and proud of it," Tom answered. "Why do you ask?"

"Well, sir; beggin yer pardon, but yer lingo ain' zactly Norfolk, as I understand it."

Tom smiled. "What's the saying? 'East is east and west is west', et cetera. I grew up in East Norfolk, Jem – may I call you that as I know no other name? It's been a job, attuning my ears to your West Norfolk dialect." Jem looked at Tom in surprise. "But – what does accent matter? – we're both Norfolk men, both *Englishmen*. I'd guess we have a lot more in common than not. Don't you agree – Mr...?"

"James Webster, carpenter," the man said, scowling, "but most people call me Jem. We'd 'ardly be took fer brothers though, sir, if yer don't mind my pointin' it out," he added, indicating Tom's secondhand clothes and then plucking at the worn fabric of his own. "I'd say yew was born with a silver spoon in yer mouth, from yer looks an yer fancy talk. I *might* call yer proud – even arrogant."

"Then you'd be quite wrong, Jem!" Tom smiled. "What would you say if I told you I was brought up by my grandparents on their farm?"

"I'd say yew 'ad rich grandparents, sir; prob'ly yeoman stock. Eh? Am I right?"

Here's a man with his head screwed on, thought Tom. "You are. I've had my share of good luck, it's true. But I've also been a common soldier in Wellington's army."

A new respect crept into the other man's eyes. E's not run-o-the-mill gentry, then, thought Jem, an' I like 'im all the better for it. Maybe — "You was askin' about that yeller 'ouse. Made from carrstone, wi' grey limestone dressin's. Takes all shades, does carrstone, dependin' on weatherin' and the direction the buildin' faces." He pointed to the house next to it. "Now, thattens built outa carrstone an' all. But yer see how it's took on a greenish-brown colour cause o' the way it faces north? That's damp, that is. The orange bricks is all mossy-like and the two colours mixin' make it out ter be brown. Oh – you'll see every shade an colour of carrstone in this town. I've 'eard 'em called *gingerbread* 'ouses. Bit fanciful that, ter my mind."

Tom compared the two houses, noticing the thin evenness of the brickwork façade. The brick tiles appeared to be piled on top of one another without the benefit of mortar. Odd, that. "Where does the stone come from?" asked Tom. "Is it local?"

"There's a quarry out near Bexwell church, two miles to the east of Downham. An' there's others hereabouts." Lips screwed up, eyes closed in concentration, Jem cogitated. His eyes opened. "There's a big'n out near Shouldham, I do know. Why?"

"No particular reason," said Tom. "But I've seen nothing to compare with these houses in East Norfolk." They walked on. "I'm making for Uppham House. Know it?"

"Oh-ah." O' course! Challisses. Same red 'air an' build. Dang it! 'E *is* gentry, after all! Cast down by the thought that Challiss was not likely to be on the side of the workers, Jem kept pace beside the puzzling young man who seemed to be first one thing and then another but didn't at all fit his established idea of the gentry.

They continued for some time in silence making their way out of Downham by the London Road. Soon, it became obvious that they were passing an important estate whose high, enclosing stone wall stretched around the curving highway until it was lost to sight. No shortage of money there, thought Tom. "Who's place is that?"

As the carpenter followed Tom's eyes, his own darkened, and his mouth, generous in repose, became mutinous. "Belongs to Sir Everard Belmaine – God rot 'im! The place is called Martlets, whatever that means. 'E's not done a real day's work in 'is life! An a greater criminal never walked the earth."

This is dangerous talk: slanderous, thought Tom. Men have been transported, even hanged, for less. "Take care, my friend," he said in a low voice, "anybody might hear you. Even though you might have good grounds for such a low opinion of the man, you would do well to remember his powers."

"Good grounds!" cried the carpenter, almost beside himself with rage. "A fat lot yew know about it. Belmaine as good as murdered my little Essie."

To his own discomfort, Tom saw tears well up in Jem's hazel eyes. "Have yew ever watched a child die of starvation, Mr Challiss? Bad enough. But if that child's yer own flesh an blood that's bin loved an nurtured—" He was overcome with grief.

I must *do* something!, thought Tom looking around wildly, alarmed that they would both be compromised by Jem's wild talk. For someone totally uninterested in politics he seemed to have stepped into a hornets' nest of political unrest. The wall of the Martlets estate still mocked them on their left although they had been walking steadily for almost half an hour and had left the last straggling houses of Downham a while back. To his immense relief they came to a fork in the road at once and a fingerpost in the form of a white-gloved hand pointed the way to the village of Uppham St Mary which was, apparently, but a quarter of a mile down the lane into which they now turned.

The stricken carpenter had managed by a huge effort to recover himself and said: "You're almost there, now, Mr Challiss. I won't impose meself upon yew any further; there'll be no trouble now." He looked down in sudden embarrassment. "The least thing sets me orf, try as I might tew 'old it in. Essie was such a pretty li'l thing! I 'ope yew'll be kind enough tew overlook a grievin' father's weakness, sir. I ain't proud of it; but I can't seem to 'elp it. But Belmaine'll get 'is deserts one day, if there's ever ter be any justice fer the workin' men of England."

They had paused beneath a horse chestnut. Overhead green fanlike leaves had begun to turn yellow at the edges; at their feet remnants of yellowing split husks and newly-fallen shiny horse chestnuts, the colour of burnt sienna, littered the grass. Tom removed the glove from his right hand and grasped Jem's brown one, feeling the callouses across the carpenter's palm. "My dear fellow! Let's say no more about it. You've had much to bear." He paused, then said earnestly: "I'd like to try to understand just what are the troubles in these parts that make men fly at each other's throats so."

Jem's mouth fell open as his hand dropped to his side. "Where yew bin 'idin'? 'Taint only in Downham there's trouble. 'Tis all over the country. 'Specially bad in the north." He searched Tom's face and seemed to reach a decision. "If yew'm serious about wantin' ter know about the workin' man's justifiable grievances, Mr Challiss, yew can find us in the *Queen's 'Ead* in the usual corner any Fridey night. Ah. Yew come along an listen tew us talkin' an make up yer own mind." They shook hands and Jem took himself back towards the town. He turned once and raised his right hand in salute. As Tom watched his spare, upright figure striding away, he experienced a guilty pang as he remembered the greedy breakfast he'd consumed that morning and the hungry faces of the men who had accompanied Clem Rix. "It would have fed every one of those starving men, and more," he said aloud and, remembering young Clem Rix's gaunt face and emaciated body, was disgusted by his own gluttony. He walked slowly along the lane, oblivious to the loveliness of the August day, totally preoccupied with thoughts that were quite new to him.

He was taken unawares when his progress was barred by a pair of wrought iron gates set in a high wall and flanked by sandstone pillars in which two words, separated by the gates and indistinct at first, were chiselled deep into the stone. Tom's heart gave a tremendous lurch as he drew near enough to decipher UPPHAM HOUSE. As he was savouring the euphoric moment a man came out of a nearby lodge which had escaped Tom's notice, it having been obscured by mature hollies which grew on the inside of the high wall.

"Good-day to you, sir! You must be the expected Mr Thomas Challiss," the swarthy man called in a bass voice that issued from a large head supported on a small wiry body. They met and the two men shook hands. To Tom's embarrassment, the other bowed. Tom guessed him to be between thirty and thirty-five and that he must be the Joseph Aldrich of whom George had spoken. A plentiful thatch of black hair, bushy eyebrows and an overall hirsuteness lent the man a forbidding appearance. In repose, Aldrich's visage was severe, melancholy, ugly even.

"Good-day, sir," said Tom, forcing down the urge to start off up the long drive that he guessed must lead to the house and which he was enormously curious to see. "And you must be Mr Joseph Aldrich, unless I'm mistaken."

"The same, Mr Challiss." The disproportionate man gave him a smile that transformed his plain face; so that Tom's mind was instantly changed for the better as to his disposition. He was not, it seemed, the brooding gnome that on first acquaintance he appeared to be; merely an affable man with many cares. Time and sorrow had engraved deep furrows from the sides of his nose to the corners of his mouth and what Tom had mistaken for melancholy was, he now saw, sadness.

"Mr George has been expecting your arrival for the past week, sir," said Aldrich. "If you will allow me—" he swept a bow and kept his right arm extended to indicate the direction "it will give me great pleasure to accompany you to the house."

Tom was struck by his mellifluous tone of voice which was at odds with his appearance.

"By all means, Mr Aldrich," he said. "I must confess that I am most anxious to see it, having heard so much about it from my mother and my half-brother." They had already started to walk beneath the tunnel of trees planted on both sides of the drive and whose leafy canopies met and mingled overhead. Tom vowed to remember that first morning's walk for as long as he lived; for the place had taken on a magical aspect. Sunlight filtered through the various species of leaf-lit trees and shrubs and dappled the gravelled path; and he glimpsed patches of shaved emerald turf sparkling with heavy dew that the morning sun had not yet dried off. "This is beautiful!" he burst out.

Aldrich smiled broadly, revealing crooked teeth. "You think so?" he said, at the same time observing with inward surprise the younger man's obvious delight in tamed nature. "Sadly, your brother does not share your enthusiasm, Mr Thomas. Uppham has no charms for him." He had spoken bitterly and immediately looked abashed. "Forgive me, my dear sir! I have expressed myself too freely. I forget myself. It is not my place to comment on the actions, foibles or opinions of my betters. Yet I must defend myself on the grounds that I was surprised – nay, delighted – to hear that your appreciation of natural beauty is so congenial to one who has had to curb his own enthusiasm for the attractions that Uppham and its grounds afford the truly discerning."

How antiquated his mode of expression is! thought Tom. "Er – think nothing of it, Mr Aldrich, I beg you. It's forgotten, as far as I'm concerned."

They had been traversing the long snaking drive for a good quarter-of-an-hour and Tom reckoned they must have covered a mile. Comparing the drive to that at Lyndon Manor, to break the silence that had followed Aldrich's lapse he asked if it were much further.

"I fear so," the man said in his incongruously deep voice. "The grandeur of Uppham is enhanced by its long and varied approach. The drive has been constructed with twists and turns, undulations and harmonious occlusions, with the sole purpose of making the eventual revelation of the mansion more dramatic. I almost envy you the sight of Uppham for the first time, my dear sir. I fear we have another mile to go before you will have that pleasure, Mr Challiss."

At last the drive issued from its green tunnel into parkland amid which stood a number of old trees as well as many that had been planted within the last three decades. Around the next curve the land swept gently upwards. With a swift intake of breath, as he caught sight of the mansion, Tom stood stock still.

Alongside him, Joseph Aldrich observed his reaction with obvious pleasure. "Well, Mr Challiss? What do you think of Uppham House?"

How was he to put his thoughts and emotions into plain words. "I— It's overwhelming!" breathed Tom, awestruck. This was to be his home? Incredible! "I don't know how to express— It's beautiful! Magnificent! I had no idea—"

Aldrich seemed well-pleased by his reaction. "Compared to Martlets, Sir Everard Belmaine's seat on the fringes of Downham – you passed it on your way here, by the way – Uppham House, with its park and farms, is of inferior rank," Aldrich remarked. "Uppham's lands cover not much over a thousand acres. But for sheer beauty of setting and proportion there is no *mansion* in West Norfolk to match Uppham." Had he been speaking of a beloved woman, thought Tom, his honeyed tones could not have expressed his admiration and love of the place more clearly. "But of late – due to the war, you understand – both house and grounds have been somewhat neglected."

As they ascended the steps that led to the entrance to Uppham House, Aldrich said: "Mr George has guests, sir. The party has been in progress for a week now. It was originally intended to be held in honour of your homecoming. However. . ." His words trailed away as they approached the front portico. "I shall leave you here, if you are quite happy for me to do so, Mr Challiss. I have urgent business at Home Farm and was just about to go to it when your arrival interrupted me. If you'll forgive my abrupt departure, I must bid you good-day." As they shook hands again Aldrich smiled warmly, his frank brown eyes meeting Tom's. "I shall look forward to our next meeting, sir. Until that time." He turned on his heel, ran nimbly down the flight of steps and round to the side of the house, after which Tom lost sight of him.

Left standing at the partially open door without anyone to introduce him, he had no option but to let himself in. Once inside he became aware of music, loud male laughter and the strong smell of cigar smoke and spirits that drifted down from upstairs. Guessing that George must be entertaining his guests up there, Tom took the stairs two at a time and, having gained the upper floor, was outside the noisy room in two strides. As he was about to knock, the door opened inwards and he stood face to face with his brother George who looked somewhat the worse for drink.

"By Gad!" he shouted back into the room, "it's me young brother, Tom!"

and, turning back: "where'd you spring from, old fellah? Bin expectin' you for a week. What kept you?" Tom, almost overpowered by the strong smell of whiskey and cigar fumes, found himself clasped in his brother's sinewy arms. "Let's look at you." George stepped back. "Hmm... *Disgustin'* suit o' clothes! Welcome to Uppham House."

★

The majority of George's guests had departed by the morning of the third day after Tom's unannounced arrival. Of those who remained two – an attorney named John Danderson and Edward Manby, a surgeon, both men from Lynn – seemed to be inveterate gamblers. George was in thrall to the other two. It had not taken Tom long to discover that his brother was recklessly gambling away his inheritance before Tom's very eyes. He wondered if it were this that accounted for the misery so apparent in Joseph Aldrich's face. He himself was alarmed by the profligacy with which coins, notes, jewellery and other valuable items from the Uppham estate found their way onto the gaming table, to be lost on thrown dice or turned card and pocketed by Manby or Danderson, who seemed to lose only trifling sums and rarely. Being so lately come to Uppham at the generous invitation of his half-brother, Tom wouldn't interfere. But one evening, after some spectacular losses, he realised he could no longer sit idly by looking on while Uppham's fortune was squandered. Tom had wanted no part of gambling and had sought George's permission to borrow his Thoroughbred, Quicksilver, that he might explore the estate in company with Aldrich each morning before the others were up. George had found the request amusing, remarking as he readily gave his permission that "there's nothing worth seeing. And as for Aldrich – most grateful to you, old fellah, for getting him out of my hair." Their excursions had been a revelation to Tom and had sparked off ideas for improving the land which had delighted Aldrich. But he had to tackle the thorny problem of George's gambling before everything was thrown away. He must speak.

"George. I wonder if you could spare me a moment in private?" he began, one morning directly after a very late breakfast had been taken by the three gamblers and the few other remaining guests, for the company was departing on a daily basis now.

"*Private*, eh? Of course. Forgive me, ladies and gentlemen. My brother has spoken and I must obey!" He made a theatrical bow to the assembled company and followed Tom out of the dining room, trailing a cloud of laughter in his wake.

As if a shutter had come down on his clowning George, looking tired and debauched, slumped onto a couch and growled: "Well? I sincerely hope this is not going to be a brotherly lecture, Tom. I tell ye frankly; I won't wear it."

"Two things need to be said," Tom began, drawing up a chair. "I hope you're ready for the first which will come as something of a surprise."

Suddenly alert, George sat up. "Eh? What's this?"

"I've tried more than once to tell you about the hold-up of the coach just outside Fakenham."

"Oh, that!"

"I'd be grateful, George, if you will refrain from interrupting. I'm finding this devilish hard to get out as it is." George lay back again without another word. "One of the travellers in the coach was a Miss Brown—"

This time George shot up onto his feet and towered over his brother. "Garnet? You've seen her?"

"I've seen her and spoken to her, George;" I will say it! Tom thought, after all, he can do no worse than kill me: "and I think she has been cruelly wronged by you."

"Thank your stars you're my brother," George said fiercely. "If anyone else had accused me—"

"Has been cruelly wronged by you," Tom reiterated, rubbing salt into the wound, "as has your daughter, Aurora Challiss Brown."

George sank onto a chair and whispered in disbelief: "I have a daughter?" Suddenly finding his voice: "How do I know the child is mine? What proof is there?"

Tom got up and placed a hand on his brother's shoulder. "The child herself. According to her mother, not only is the child beautiful but she is also, incontrovertibly, a Challiss. Apparently she has our colouring and, though but two years old, the bearing that is our inheritance from our father and all those Challisses who preceded him."

"Garnet," George murmured, as if he were alone. A sudden thought caused him to burst out: "Where is she now? Is she here? At Downham?"

Tom racked his brain. "I last heard that she'd gone to live with an aunt at Wisbech. That is all I can tell you. It is all I know. Why?"

"Oh! . . . Why did she say nothing to me of this?" George said, prowling about the room. "I tell you frankly, Tom: Garnet Brown is the only woman I ever loved. That affair with Aimée d'Escalles was nothing more than mad lust, or what you will; certainly nothing so binding as true love – mere solace. Any other woman whose charms could effectively blot out the memory of Garnet once I'd lost touch with her would have done just as well. I'll find her! As soon as I'm shot of these hangers-on, I'll be off to Wisbech; I'll not return until I've found Garnet and the child."

"Since I came back, you've shown precious little interest in my affairs," said Tom. "For one thing, I've had no word about Mary Emma Kay for three years."

Contrition crossed George's face. "Do forgive me, old fellah. Well. . . I suppose that's an end to it, Tom." He shrugged his shoulders and sighed. "'Tis a great pity. But if she's as lovely as you say, she'll have been snapped up long ago. No doubt she's married by this time." He made a sympathetic grimace. "How old is she now?"

Angered by his brother's cursory dismissal of something that meant the whole world to himself, Tom retorted: "Seventeen! If you really care. And I won't believe that she would go back on her promise. She wouldn't! You don't know her."

George laughed softly. "By Gad, old fellah! A sensitive subject indeed. What measures have you taken to discover her whereabouts?"

"None, yet. But there's much I have to tell you. Lyndon Manor, Mary Emma's home, is burned down and Lambert Jardine has returned to Australia, thank God!"

"So you're out of danger from that quarter," George said vaguely. "While I hate to divert you from your subject, Tom, I have guests to consider. What was the other burning issue you wished to discuss?"

Plunging in, Tom said: "It's about these nightly gambling parties—"

"Now just you stop right there!" George thundered, pointing a long, menacing forefinger at him. "I will not be dictated to by anybody in my own home, least of all a younger half-brother who's no more than a bastard, to boot!"

Tom had known that his interference would be unacceptable to George but the vindictive violence of his brother's reaction to his hint of criticism surprised him.

After striding angrily up and down the broad passage, in which their confrontation now took place, he stationed himself in front of Tom and said softly: "You demned fool! D'ye think I don't know what Danderson and Manby are up to? I mean to let them have Uppham so that we can be rid of it once and for all." He threw himself down onto the couch again. "Don't you see?" He cast his eyes up at the ornately-plastered ceiling which was sorely in need of a coat of fresh paint. "This demned house is nothing but a money pit. I saw what it did to my father. I'd shoot myself in the head this instant if I thought I'd be doomed to the same fate!"

Unable to contain himself, Tom burst out: "But you as good as promised that we would share the burden of running the estate; that I would farm–"

"I own as much," George cut in calmly. He left the couch, hunted about on a nearby table for a cigar, resumed his seat and lighted up with a series of short puffs, until the tip of the narcotic glowed to his satisfaction. "But you must see that if we're to have any kind of a decent life it isn't to be had here. My sole motive in this is to spare us both a life of misery. Uppham's gone to the dogs while I've been away." He expelled a cloud of aromatic smoke, waved it away. "Oh! Aldrich has done his best; but it's gone too far downhill – has been goin' downhill since my grandfather's time. Believe me, my dear Tom, you'll be better off carvin' out a future for yourself almost anywhere else. Have you considered settlin' in the colonies, for instance?"

Seething with anger since the first hint of the broken promise, furious at his brother's calm dismissal of his own share in the estate, Tom found himself trembling as he said: "No, damn you, I haven't! Nor will I. All my plans for the future are centred on this place; and what you're doing is hardly fair. Rather than sift it away into the hands of those two rogues why not allow me, at least, to try to recover its fortunes through the application of modern agricultural methods? I know farming; it's in my blood! I've ridden all over Uppham's acres and I find that the soil is fertile. I know I can succeed here. Moreover, any profits I can make from the land will be poured into the restoration of the house. You have to give me a chance."

George's full grey eyes surveyed him with aristocratic disdain. "I have to do no such thing, old fellah," he said, pausing to inhale. He blew a smoke ring and in a moment's silence they both watched it float up to the ceiling. "However, I will make you a proposition. What say you to a turn of the cards?" Seeing that Tom was about to protest he warded off any objection with a raised hand. "Hear me out, old fellah. Are ye willin' to trust to the Challiss luck? *Sorsum Deorsum* – y'know. Will you climb or fall on a flick of the wrist? Everything you covet dependin' on a single card? 'Twill make an interestin' wager; such a prize at stake, eh? Should I win, I dispose of the Uppham estate as I think fit. And have no illusions – it'll all be over so demned quick your head will spin! Should fate decree that you become the next master of

Uppham then I'll abide by it, whatever the outcome. And just to prove to you that I aint the dastardly blackguard you seem to make me out to be, I'll have Danderson draw up the papers; papers that will uphold your legal rights, in any court in the land, to the undisputed possession of the mansion, its lands, farms, cottages and every jot and tittle of the accursed place. If you're willin' to accept these conditions the game will take place this evenin' after a late supper. Well, what d'ye say?"

★

Chapter Sixteen

A ground bass supplied by the ticking of the longcase clock was punctuated by the running counterpoint of wings beating against the chimney of the burning lamp. An acute listener would also have detected the regular breathing issuing from the four men who were seated around the card table in the library of Uppham House. The illuminated pool of green baize bathed the men's faces in a sickly light as George Challiss added a third splash of sound to the rhythm of clock and moth; he had unwrapped a new deck of playing cards and now placed it decisively in the centre of the table.

"Will you toss a coin, Danderson?"

The tension was momentarily lightened as Manby said: "What! Are you so low in funds that you cannot even provide a ha'penny for the call?"

The others laughed at the man's wit as Danderson produced half a sovereign and asked: "How will you call?"

Without hesitation, George called: "Heads!"

"Then I suppose I must call 'Tails', " Tom said ruefully, thinking it hardly fair.

The moth, which Tom saw was a buff tip, circled the hot glass of the lamp's chimney. Manby waved it away but it flew back almost at once. "Demned insect," George muttered. "Get on with it, Danderson. Ignore the thing. 'Tis of no consequence." Nevertheless, the ping of the moth's wings against the hot glass heightened the tension as the two brothers waited for the coin to be tossed.

"Wait!" George cried, rising. "We need more light. A moment, gentlemen." He fetched down two candelabra from the mantlepiece and soon had the six candles lighted. "Now we shall be able to see where the coin falls without having to fumble about in the half dark," he said with a meaningful look in Danderson's direction. He reseated himself and in the brightened room bade the proceedings continue.

Right-handed, Danderson balances the coin on his thumbnail around which his forefinger curls protectively and poises it to be flicked into the air. "Ready?"

The brothers nod assent. The coin spins upwards in a shining parabola, is deftly caught by Danderson's right hand, clapped onto the back of his left, is covered. The clock ticks on, the moth gradually cooks itself as it circles the mesmerising lamp, batters its wings into dusty tatters: "Call," says the lawyer.

"Heads," George calls firmly.

Danderson discloses the half-sovereign and lowers his wrist so that the lamplight shines on the obverse of the coin. "Heads it is, George."

Manby smiles with satisfaction. "Lucky dog! Now, if only you can pull off a double – I'll give the pack a good shuffle." He does so with dazzling dexterity.

Tom's heart is in his boots; he looks without seeing as the moth's wings kiss the hot chimney of the lamp with a zizz. The lifeless insect plummets to the green baize cloth and lies there on its back with its six legs pointing to the ceiling.

"Demned thing!" George curses softly. Aware that the falling moth might be a portent, he is uncharacteristically clumsy with his drink. A crimson drop spills onto his shirtfront and spreads into a circular stain. Ignoring it, he stretches forth his right hand, slides a pliant card from the top of the pack, furtively reads his future in the pattern of its pips, and holds the rectangle of card close to his chest.

Tom, too, has taken the falling buff tip to be an omen. But for whom? The card he is about to take could make him master of Uppham! Is it possible that the others are unaware that his heart is racing with a mixture of excitement and dread?

George fidgets in his chair. "For God's sake, take a card Tom! The suspense is killing us!" He sips his claret and studies the men's faces across the rim of his glass.

Tom is suspicious; he disliked Manby's slick manipulation of the new deck and has rapidly evolved a plan to thwart any cheating on the surgeon's part. "George: just set me straight. I don't necessarily have to take the top card, do I? I may choose any card from the pack?"

"Of course!" snaps George. "Just so long as you get on with it."

Danderson and Manby look surprised at the turn of events.

Taking care to keep the cards face down, Tom divides the pack by removing the top half of the deck and placing it alongside the bottom. Only then does he make his selection. How easily the new-milled piece of thin board slips from the middle of the pack, thinks Tom, as he cradles his right hand about the card, curved in his left hand secure from prying eyes.

A brief hiatus, in which the longcase clock ticks on, claret is sipped and

Tom is near fainting with the strain of the suspense of waiting to see the cards laid side by side. He gives George a look of appeal, hoping for a hint of how to proceed.

"You first, Tom, old fellah. I want none of your demned surprises. If I'm to be homeless I want time to get used to it." He joins in the laughter his words provoke.

Scarcely daring to breathe, Tom lays the Ace of Diamonds on the green cloth, its red design startlingly bright beneath lamplight radiantly intensified by candlepower.

George shrugs his shoulders and places the Queen of Hearts alongside Tom's card, saying with manifest sincerity and warmth: "Congratulations, Tom. Fate has decreed that you are to be the master of Uppham. I know it's what you want more than anything."

The contest over and decided, his brother drains his glass and looks relieved, Tom thinks, as George adds: "Knew destiny wasn't on my side as soon as that demned moth fried itself and fell."

Manby and Danderson looked disappointed at the outcome but hooted sycophantically at George's lepidopterous quip as their host refilled their glasses.

"Gentlemen," he said amid a babble of commiserations and congratulations, "a toast! To Tom, the new master of Uppham!" Lawyer and surgeon raised their glasses. "And may he have joy of the crumbling old pile; which is more than I ever did! By the way, my friends," said George, buttonholing Manby and Danderson, "my brother is not a gambling man – as a rule. This seems to have been his lucky day."

"It was clear from his arrival that your brother had his eye on your neglected acres, George!" John Danderson said good-naturedly. "Well, Mr Thomas Challiss," the attorney shook him warmly by the hand, "I wish you prosperity and all good fortune! This is yours, sir; I think you'll find everything in order." The lawyer placed a signed and witnessed document before Tom, who sat at the table in a euphoric daze, unable to grasp the fact that he was truly master of everything he surveyed.

"He isn't likely to find much prosperity here," George said wryly, sweeping his arm around the room to demonstrate the truth of his assertion. Tom had to agree with his brother that, at present, the damp-stained walls of what at one time must have been a handsome library hardly indicated success or wealth.

But Tom also viewed the dereliction around him as a challenge, as one of many projects that seethed in his brain for restoring to the mansion something of its former glory. Evidence abounded which would aid restoration. Mary Emma would know what had to be done for she had been reared in just such a house. Now that he had a home to offer her in which it was possible for them to share their lives, thought Tom, his next task must be to try to discover what had become of her. He had no idea where he would begin the search; but he determined that tomorrow should see the start of it.

★

The last of the guests had gone. The house seemed unnaturally quiet and Tom became aware for the first time since his arrival of the servants, almost unseen, who had been ensuring his every comfort. He didn't like the discovery. It seemed to him in some way immoral that he should have been waited on hand and foot and that those doing the waiting hadn't had so much as a smile or (surely not!) a simple "Thank you" in response to their labours on his behalf. So when a trim little housemaid, having first tapped politely on the drawing room door, entered the room and made a neat bob, Tom made it his business to look at her, not as a housemaid but as a person in her own right. He waited expectantly for the girl to speak.

As if she detected a change in his attitude, the girl — who, Tom surmised, was probably about thirteen — hesitated and visibly lost some of her self-possession.

Tom's smiled encouragement seemed to make matters worse; so he said: "Yes? What is it?"

The sound of his voice restored the realisation of her position in the hierarchy of society. She spoke up in a soft Norfolk accent. "If yew please, Mr Challiss, sir; there's a messenger on 'orseback askin' fer yew by name. Master says will yer please ter come downstairs an' see what it is 'e wants."

"Thank you — What is your name?"

The girl dropped a curtsey. "Maddy, sir."

"Well, Maddy, ask the man to wait, please. I'll follow you down directly."

Something he'd said had caused her to widen her eyes; but she said no more and whisked herself away.

Wondering what a messenger could want, Tom straightened his cravat and followed Maddy downstairs and out of the front door to where the man waited. "I am Thomas Challiss. You have something for me?"

"I was asked ter deliver this tew yew with all speed, sir," the messenger said as he placed a small package into Tom's outstretched hand.

Tom saw by the state of his horse that the young man hadn't wasted any time. "Thank you, messenger," he said, and dug into his waistcoat pocket for a half sovereign which he gave to the agreeably-surprised messenger.

After thanking Tom profusely, the young horseman vaulted onto his lively stallion, touched his cocked hat and galloped away at top speed to his next destination.

George hadn't been seen since the previous evening and was obviously preoccupied with his own affairs.

Tom took the hymnal-sized package into the library. The dilapidated state of the room was even more apparent in the light of day. Seating himself at the baize table, he took out his pocket knife and cut the string that tied the rectangular parcel, which also carried a stamped seal. On examining the blob of shellac, Tom managed to decipher the initials 'D.J.' embedded in the wax. From Daniel Jones! Hastily, he tore away the wrapping and discovered that the parcel consisted of a small box, wrapped around which was a brief letter from the attorney himself. It was dated that very day and read:

> *Dear Tom,*
>
> *An extraordinary piece of good luck has come your way and I am delighted to be the means of sending it to you. Your limeflower ring dropped through my letterbox some time during the night before last. It was from an actress calling herself Diana Parys. The ring was wrapped in a paper in which Parys says she is the paramour of that dastardly highwayman Jake Reville who made her a present of the ring. She claims to be an expert in lipreading and read yours at the inn at Fakenham as you faced the looking-glass over the bar. In her note she claims to have felt sorry for you and 'your intended'. Seems to have a sentimental streak. Glad it ends well for you. No sign of my gold watch!*
>
> *Kindest Regards*
>
> *Dan.*
>
> *P.S. Reville has been apprehended in Whitechapel. Due to be hanged. D.J.*

The box was much too large for the size of the ring and Daniel had padded it about with a quantity of black darning wool which caused Tom some amusement. Nestling in the midst of the dark fibres was the ring. He took it out, removing soft black filaments that clung to its setting as he did so. He had forgotten how very beautiful the ring was! How Mary Emma would love it.

The return of the ring was another spur to the urgency of finding her and, replacing the ring in its unlikely repository, re-wrapping it in Daniel's letter, Tom determined to place it in a very safe place before going in search of George to share his good news.

He found him in the bedchamber of his suite of rooms which were situated in the west wing of the house. Clothes were strewn across the bed in great disorder and trunks and portmanteaux stood gaping open ready to receive George's entire wardrobe, it seemed. A manservant was grappling manfully in an attempt to bring order out of chaos without bringing himself to his irascible master's attention.

"Not that one, you demned fool!" George snatched a fancy waistcoat from the patient servant's white-gloved hands. "Even you must be able to see that the thing's not fit for a gentleman to wear. Here," he flung it at the man. "Do what you like with the rag."

"Packing, George?" said Tom, stating the obvious.

His brother whirled round. "Oh! It's you, Tom. Packing! The place looks like a demned rummage sale. I can't think what to take and what to leave behind; for as soon as I decide I can do without something I shall be sure to need it."

The manservant had the temerity to speak without his master's invitation. "Shall I return later, sir? It will give you time to deliberate—"

George spun round and said haughtily: "What? Where did you learn such a word as 'deliberate' ?" He faced his brother again, his voice rising. "Did you ever hear the like of that, Tom?"

Astonished by his brother's arrogance, he replied softly: "No, George, I never did. But then you must remember that I was not brought up to be waited upon by servants and so I know no better. One must make allowances for the lower orders."

"Eh?" Unsure of the exact meaning of Tom's words, he had an uncomfortable feeling that they carried an implied criticism. Irritated beyond measure with his brother, the manservant and himself, he barked at the docile servant: "Oh! … Get out of my sight! I can get on all the better without your meddlin'."

Tom cast an encompassing glance at the chaos that had been caused by every article of George's clothing being strewn about the room and across the bed. Clothes drooped from their pegs half in and half out of the clothes press and boots and pumps littered the floor. "This place is in the devil of a state,

George," he said. "How did you manage it?" Before his brother could draw breath he continued: "If you'll send – what's his name? – back here, you can take yourself off for a smoke or a ride or something while we restore some kind of order."

George roared with laughter. "By Gad! I do believe I'm witnessin' the new master of Uppham goin' about his business! Well done, old fellah! That's put me in me place right enough. I can see you're already considerin' me a troublesome guest so I'll take up your suggestion and go for a gallop on Quicksilver."

"Give me an hour," Tom shouted after him, chuckling to himself as his mercurial brother ran down the stairs like a schoolboy released from the schoolroom.

★

The manservant's name was Ned Rudge, Tom soon discovered, known at Uppham simply as Rudge. Between them they returned the scattered garments to their original places in a very short time. Next, they laid piles of clothes upon the bed that would enable even the most fastidious gentleman to be decently dressed for a year – providing he had a good manservant to take care of his every need. All was ready long before an hour had elapsed and Rudge was astonished when Tom suggested they carry the baggage downstairs. Word had spread among the servants that Uppham had changed owners but Rudge had been unprepared for so drastic a change as the humane treatment of menials which the young master had adopted. He feared that some of the servants would think him soft and so take advantage of his leniency.

Tom spent the short period before luncheon deliberating on how best to begin his quest for Mary Emma. Another problem was his need for ready money. He was surprised that Daniel had sent no word of the transfer of it by draft from Fector's bank. What he should do if his fortune had gone astray didn't bear thinking about.

As they sat eating in the vast gloomily decorated dining-room, placed at each end of the long table, with a single footman hurrying the length of it each time a wineglass needed filling, Tom vowed that the pretentious nonsense would come to an end with his brother's departure.

"I'll be orf as soon as we've finished here," George said, holding up his glass to be refilled. The footman accommodated him and returned to his station where he affected to be part of the faded wallpaper and could neither hear what was said nor see what was done.

"I wish I had a destination to search," Tom said dolefully. "I haven't a notion where to begin. How would you go about it, George?"

The footman was on the trot again, this time with cigars that had been summoned with a snap of George's fingers. Tom waited while the man bent over his brother with a lighted taper which he applied to the cigar's tip. Once it was smouldering, George banished the man to his wallpapery existence. "Well..." he expelled a cloud of bluish smoke and plucked a speck from his tongue. "I should return to the place that you know was last inhabited by her. Always proceed from the known to the unknown, old fellah."

Tom kept calm. "But I told you: Lyndon Manor was burned down. That's the last address I had for her. Wait! There was a cook! A Mrs Mawby. She had a niece—"

"—and Uncle Tom Cobbley and all," George sang as, beating time with his cigar, he rose to his full height. "Well, Tom, good luck," he said, striding towards him and dismissing the footman with a cursory nod on the way, "I must be orf."

The brothers embraced and Tom followed George out to the stables where a waggon and two horses had been hired for the conveyance of George's luggage to the port of Lynn. Quicksilver was to be ridden by a groom who would have to find his own way back to Uppham if he wanted to keep his post there. George had decided that from the port of Lynn he and his trappings would be carried round the coast and up the River Nene by boat the eighteen miles to Wisbech. "You can reach me at the *Vine* inn for the next week," he said. "I'll take a room there as a starting point."

Tom wished that his own plans were so precise.

"Good luck, old fellah," George said somewhat gruffly. "Look after the old place. Though I'm heartily glad it's you who are stayin' and me that's goin'! I'll send word as soon as I have anything worth writing you."

With a lump in his own throat Tom watched his kind bully of a brother bowl along the drive and disappear into the green tunnel that he and Joseph Aldrich had walked up only a few days before. Feeling suddenly downcast, he hurried back into the mansion, ran upstairs to the room he'd been allocated and started to pack. He would set out for Esther Mawby's lodge first thing tomorrow morning and nothing would be allowed to stop him.

★

He'd done no more than find a bag in which to carry a spare shirt and his smalls when Rudge appeared at the open door to say that Joseph Aldrich was waiting to speak to him. "I've shown him into the library, sir."

Repressing an expletive, Tom ushered Rudge out of the room and followed him downstairs. At the sound of their footfalls Aldrich emerged from the library.

"Ah! Mr Challiss, sir. I do apologise for disturbing you; but I have just discovered that congratulations are in order. That is, if you don't consider my felicitations a presumption—"

Tom was in no mood for Aldrich's long-winded speeches. "Not at all, Mr Aldrich. It's good of you to take the trouble. You must excuse me just now if I seem discourteous. I am in rather a hurry."

Aldrich's face fell into sombre lines. "I beg your pardon, sir, for being a nuisance. Will you please accept my congratulations on becoming master of Uppham. Everybody here is delighted. We wish you well and will serve you as best we can."

Now why couldn't he have just said that in the first place? Aware that he had offended the steward, Tom softened his tone. "Thank you, Mr Aldrich; it's very good of you. Please convey my thanks to the rest of the staff."

Aldrich bowed and began to walk away but returned as Tom said: "However, there is something I wish you to take care of for me." It gave him pleasure to see the effect his few words had on the man. His face positively lit up.

"I shall be most happy to carry out any commission—"

"I have to go away for a week or two, perhaps longer." The steward's face fell. "It's impossible to be precise. But I want you to know that I have every confidence in your abilities to look after the estate. I know what a good job you've done while my brother was absent for so long—"

"Forgive me for interrupting, sir; but running the estate singlehanded has been a great burden to me." Aldrich looked ill. "I was hoping that now Uppham has come into your possession you would be available to assist me in its management—"

"And I intend to!" Tom said warmly, taking hold of Aldrich's upper arm in order to reassure the man. "Have no fear, Joseph – may I call you that? – I am anxious to take up my responsibilities as soon as it is possible. But I must go. There isn't time to go into my motives at this point."

Aldrich's face cleared. "Thank you, Mr Challiss, sir. You have quelled my fears. I'm sorry I interrupted you; please give me your instructions."

"Do you happen to know a Downham man called James or Jem Webster?"

Aldrich looked surprised. "I do, sir. We were at dame school together."

"Capital! I want you to speak to him on my behalf. Ask him to coppice the hazels in the top wood and make me twenty strong hurdles six by six feet. Tell him I'll pay him four shillings a hurdle."

Aldrich had produced a notebook and was writing down Tom's instructions. "Very good, Mr Challiss, sir." Pencil poised, all attention, he waited to be dismissed.

Tom knew what the person looked like but just couldn't recall his name. "There's another Downham man – Jem Webster will know him – an out-of-work shepherd; gaunt-looking fellow with sandy hair and green eyes. Tell Jem to ask the shepherd to select a hundred Southdown ewes and two fine rams. The vendor will have to make do with a note of hand until I return. Make it clear that there's a permanent job for both men if they care to work for me — Oh! And Joseph; make sure you have my signature on the draft letter for the purchase of the flock before I leave at first light tomorrow morning."

"Of course, Mr Challiss," Aldrich murmured as he scribbled away like fury.

"Oh! And can you think of any place on the estate where a lodger would not be too inconvenient? The shepherd will need somewhere to lay his head, a place to find hot victuals at those times when he'll not be needed in the pastures. Is there a shepherd's hut for the lambing season? If not, acquire one as soon as you can. I think that will be more than enough to keep you busy for the time being, don't you?"

When he had placed a full stop at the end of the list, Aldrich bestowed on Tom a look of utter worship from a pair of shining eyes. "I believe old Mrs Hignell would take the shepherd in, Mr Challiss. She's recently widowed and is probably feeling lonely. Shall I sound her out?"

"Yes, yes! I leave everything to you. Now, I really must get on. I'll not be away a moment longer than is absolutely necessary, Joseph, I promise you."

The two men went their separate ways, Tom into the house to finish packing, Joseph Aldrich to the stables to collect Barbary, his strawberry roan gelding, and begin the business of carrying out his master's orders.

Before sunset that day the steward had drafted the note of hand to Tom's satisfaction, which he duly signed for authorisation. Despite his own preoccupations, he was amused to note a new spring in Aldrich's step and that he held himself differently, more erect, as if his confidence in his own abilities had been restored.

★

Chapter Seventeen

"Well I never! Speak o' the devil an' 'e is sure tew appear!" Mrs Mawby's eyes had almost popped out of her head at the sight of Tom. "I were just this minute sayin' ter me niece, Patsy-as-is-Mrs-Frith: 'Yew must write a note to young Roberts at his new place.' And then if I aint gone an' lorst the bit o' paper yew wrote down your address on. We've looked everywhere! I dunno what I've done with it. But what must yew be thinkin'? Come in, come in!"

Smiling at the garrulous woman's exuberence, Tom ducked his head and followed her into her cosy kitchen where, despite the mildness of the day, a coal fire burned in the grate of the open fire and a kettle sang on the hob. "What dew yew think, Patsy? This is the very young man I was tellin' yew about: Tom Roberts. Fancy that, now! This is me sister's girl, Patsy-as-is-Mrs-Frith. Sit yerself down, young man. We was just about to 'ave a bite tew eat an' a cup 'o tea. You'll join us, o' course."

Tom and Patsy-as-is-Mrs-Frith had introduced themselves by nods, signs and smiles, so far not having been able to get a word in edgeways. But while Esther Mawby busied herself with making tea, fetching a third cup, saucer and plate for Tom, and opening a large tin of what Tom was delighted to discover was some of Esther's day-old gingerbread, they managed to converse.

"How d'yer dew, Mr Roberts." Patsy Frith began without preamble. "I believe yew wanted Mr Southwood's address. I've just written it out agin for yew. Me an Auntie was just wonderin' how we was goin' to get it ter yew when you popped up out o' nowhere." She opened her reticule and produced a piece of paper which had been folded into four and which she gave to Tom. "Funny how things turn out, innit."

"It certainly is, Mrs Frith," Tom said with a light laugh.

Mrs Frith had looked at him with astonishment as soon as he spoke. "Lor! Auntie Esther; yew dint tell me 'e were a gennelman," she said, in some embarrassment. "I dew beg yer pardon, sir."

"'E ain't no gennelman are yer Roberts – e's a gardner," a note of doubt crept into her voice, "ain't yer?"

"Yes. Your aunt's quite right; I am a gardener," Tom said, hoping to keep the matter uncomplicated.

"I dint notice afore," Mrs Mawby said as she handed round the cups of tea, "but yew dew talk kind o' funny, Roberts." She swallowed a mouthful of tea, carefully replaced her cup in its saucer, looked up at him and asked: "Did yew ever find your Miss Kay that yew was lookin' for?"

"Not yet," Tom said, breathing in a crumb and succumbing to a coughing fit. Esther Mawby put down her cup and saucer and came over to his chair. She gave him a hefty thump between the shoulder blades, his coughing ceased. She returned to her seat, picked up her cup of tea and said: "Never fails! I've known a good wallop on the back to dislodge all sorts o' things that've bin introduced inter the windpipe. Yew remember that young boy who swallered a pea an' it went down the wrong way an 'e was turnin' blew?" she reminded her niece. "I saved 'is life by wallopin' him on the back; an' that time I turned 'im upside-down an all! 'Is Ma was ever so grateful."

Tom smiled. But now that he had Wade Southwood's address he was impatient to be off on his quest. He stayed until it was time for Patsy-as-is-Mrs-Frith to take her leave and then said that he too must be on his way. He thanked Mrs Mawby for her hospitality and her niece for the address, aware that it was unlikely that they would ever see each other again. That night he wrote to Wade Southwood. He next booked an outside seat as a passenger on the post coach to Fakenham where he called at Daniel Jones's comfortable premises in the High Street. The draft from Fector's Bank at Dover had arrived at Daniel's address a couple of days earlier and, subsequently, had been sent on to Uppham House by the attorney's clerk.

Daniel was delighted to see Tom again and pressed him to stay a day or two. Tom demurred. Daniel only acceded to his promise to stay with him for a single night on the condition that Tom came for a longer stay in the spring.

"I can't promise you that, Dan," Tom said. "Farming's a different kettle of fish from the law. A farmer is at the mercy of nature and her whims. But if I get the chance I'll be only too glad to renew our acquaintance."

They parted company the following morning and Tom returned to Uppham to wait for an answer to his letter to Wade Southwood. Not knowing how to proceed in the hunt for Mary Emma he had no option but to be on hand for any clue to her whereabouts that Southwood's letter might contain.

★

Joseph Aldrich happened to be at home when Tom, mounted on a fine-looking black stallion hunter, rode up to the gate. He came out of the lodge to meet him. His new master was full of surprises, the man thought, and life was certainly not going to be dull now that he had the running of the estate.

"We hadn't expected you back so soon, Mr Challiss; but I, for one am delighted to see you." Aldrich said cheerfully. "That's a very fine animal, sir."

"Thank you, Joseph." He patted the horse's strong neck. "He is a find, I think. Spotted him for sale at a horse-dealer's on my way to the Fakenham post coach. We seemed to take to each other at once so I decided to cancel the seat I'd booked and to ride him home instead. Goes like the wind. Shouldn't be surprised if there wasn't some Arab in him." He kept to himself the fact that he'd had to borrow the money – no light sum – for the purchase of the horse from his friend Daniel Brown. "Anything of note to report?" he asked, almost as an afterthought, so besotted was he with his new steed. He'd renamed the stallion Saladin considering it more fitting than Black Knight, which was the name under which he'd purchased him.

"I spoke to Jem Webster about cutting the hazels and weaving the hurdles, as you directed, sir. He was overjoyed. Jem's a steady man and will be all the steadier for having his days occupied with something worthwhile to do, other than hang about the streets of Downham."

Tom noticed that Aldrich was managing to converse in straightforward English.

"As for young Rix, I have my doubts." He moved away from the fidgety horse.

"Oh? In what way? Steady Saladin, good boy! Was the young man difficult?"

"Not exactly difficult as much as. . . resistant to your generous offer; he actually told me to go and stuff myself!"

Tom laughed, imagining what an affront to Aldrich's dignity such an earthy remark must have been. "Clem Rix can be hot-headed and has no love of anybody he thinks inhabits a station even a millimetre higher than his own. Did you manage to persuade him to accept, eventually?"

"Between us, Jem and I made him see what a grand opportunity he was dismissing on account of his silly prejudice. He was persuaded, albeit reluctantly, in the end, and is at this very moment engaged on the business of acquiring the flock."

"Good!" The stallion was becoming restive and was obviously impatient to be off. "We'll talk more this evening, Joseph. Come and dine with me, will you!" he called back over his shoulder as he galloped away.

How good it was to emerge from the treelined drive and into the park!

Tom felt his heart swell at the prospect before him, sadly neglected at present but one which he could envisage brought to order and harmony. He trotted Saladin around the last bend of the drive and reined him in to a halt. He was unconscious of what a graceful pair he and the horse made as both stood motionless facing the mansion.

George, thoroughly bored by Tom's enthusiasm, had told him that the original house had been built around 1685. It had been a less imposing building than the one that now topped the rise above the ornamental lake, he'd told him, more of a large farmhouse. Their grandfather had followed the fashion of his day and modernised the original façade with one that imitated John Nash's *picturesque* style. This, George had remarked sourly, was when expense had overtaken income; a state of affairs that their father had done his best to remedy, but which he had been unable to reverse before death had claimed him.

Their discussion of the matter recurred to Tom now as he gazed at the handsomely-proportioned house in its rustic setting. The mansion was considered small by some but Tom would not have changed a single detail. To him it looked so right, at one with its location, beautiful – and it was his for as long as he could hang on to it. He clicked his teeth and the horse started forward; and as they neared Uppham House he made a vow that it would remain in his possession, God willing, for the rest of his life and, moreover, the lives of his children and grandchildren.

When he appeared in the stable block astride Saladin they made such an imposing pair that the stable lad goggled. "Take good care of him, Bob," said Tom, dismounting and tossing him the reins. "His name's Saladin. Give him a rub down and a good feed. Thank you."

As soon as he entered the house he was conscious that everything was not as it should be. There was no sign of Rudge or, indeed, any other servant. Tom stood in the entrance hall listening. Laughter rose from the servants' quarters and he decided to investigate its cause.

Not having explored the rooms situated on the lower ground floor he navigated his way by the direction from which the noise was coming until he found himself before a broad door containing glazed panels in its upper half. He turned the handle and walked into the room. It was a few moments before his presence was felt by all the revellers. When they were aware that their master had mysteriously returned over a week early from what they had been assured would be a two-week absence they stood and gazed at him in frozen horror. Maddy attempted to slide a half-empty wineglass containing a red liquid behind an earthenware jar.

"Stand still, Maddy!" Tom thundered. The girl jumped out of her skin and the glass fell to the floor where it shattered and the red fluid spoiled the scrubbed flags.

Rudge stepped forward at once.

"Would you care to explain just what has been going on here, Mr. Rudge?"

Maddy tittered nervously, presumably at the use of the title bestowed on the manservant. "It's cook's birthday, sir," said Rudge in answer to Tom's question. "We – I thought it would do no harm to mark her sixtieth year. Forty-eight of those years have been spent in the bowels of this house, Mr Challiss." Maddy tittered at the mention of 'bowels'. "I take upon myself full responsibility for this disruption," Rudge continued. "It was entirely my own idea, sir. We had just toasted Mrs. Rudge's health in raspberry cordial when you appeared out of nowhere, it seemed."

"I see," Tom said slowly, his head bowed as he wrestled with conflicting emotions in order to find the best way in which to deal with this innocent-sounding explanation without seeming too lenient. So the cook was Rudge's mother! He looked up and smiled at the jolly-looking woman. "Congratulations, Mrs Rudge!" he surprised them by saying. "I'm glad I happened to stumble upon such a happy occasion. D'you think I might have a measure of your raspberry cordial; that is, if young Maddy has left me a glass to drink it out of."

"Here y'are, Mr Challiss, sir!" The running footman, who had lately lived a wallpapery existence, Tom soon discovered was called Barty Peckover and came from Diss. He had found another glass, which Tom hoped was clean, and soon had it filled to within a quarter inch from its brim.

"I would like to propose a toast. Do the honours, Barty." Tom said, raising his glass towards the cook who had been overtaken by a crippling shyness as soon as the footman began to charge the company's glasses. She covered her glowing cheeks by throwing her voluminous white apron over her face.

"Come on, Auntie Bee," Maddy said coaxingly. "Let's see yer phizog, dew, or we'll find ourselves toastin' an apron!" Whereupon the cook lowered her visor and looked Tom boldly in the eye. Everyone agreed that Mrs Rudge made the best raspberry cordial for miles around and while they sipped Norfolk nectar the cook cut wedges from a frosted cake she'd made for herself to celebrate the occasion of her birthday.

Having ascertained that the company were, at last, ready to toast the cook and that the cook had kept her head unwrapped so that she could receive it, Tom said: "To our cook, Mrs Rudge. A happy birthday!" The others echoed the toast, and tears of joy trickled down the cook's smooth vermilion cheeks while she smiled and said: "Thank you, all; I don't remember when I had a nicer birthday. Thank you, all."

Whether he'd made a fool of himself Tom was unable to decide; but he had done what he had thought to be right in the circumstances. Time would tell.

When Joseph Aldrich came to the house that evening, Tom described the birthday celebration, and asked Aldrich if he'd known that the cook was Rudge's mother and Maddy's aunt.

Aldrich emitted one of his rare laughs. "One of my duties has been the hiring of servants, Mr Challiss. The relationships are not quite what you have supposed. Mrs Beatrice Rudge is aunt to the manservant Edward Rudge and also to Madeleine Smith, the parlourmaid. Bartholomew Peckover is no relation – as far as I am aware. Er – I have here a letter for you which came by messenger and which I intercepted at the gates on account of your being absent. I was doubtful of the man leaving it at the house as you had intended being away for some time, sir. I hope I did right?"

"Certainly. Thank you for your thoughtfulness, Joseph." Tom took possession of the sealed and folded parchment with rising good spirits as he spotted the familiar DJ stamped into the seal. The banker's draft! He pocketed the letter, got up and poured glasses of sherry, carried them over to a wine table which had been conveniently placed near their armchairs, and raised his glass. "Will you join me in a toast, Joseph? To the future of Uppham!" Their glasses clinked and they drank the toast.

"If I may, sir?" Aldrich said raising his glass to Tom who had recharged their bumpers: "To the the master of Uppham! Success and long life to him!"

Tom was astonished by Aldrich's confident tone. "With your invaluable knowledge of the estate, Joseph, and our combined hard work we should be able to make something worthwhile of Uppham, both the house and its acres, wouldn't you say?"

The steward's eyes positively beamed. "I ask no better reward for my labours, Mr Challiss, sir. If you knew..."

"If I knew what?" Tom said, intrigued.

"No matter. Suffice it to say that Uppham is now in good hands. I shall do everything in my power to serve you faithfully, sir. You may depend on my loyalty."

Whether it was the sherry that sent a glow through his veins, Tom couldn't have said. Joseph's warm little speech had given him immense pleasure and had sealed the bond of friendship between them. "Well put, sir!" he said with a broad smile. The knowledge that he wouldn't have to wrestle singlehanded with the multitude of problems that would certainly present themselves in the immediate future invested Tom with the courage necessary to the success of his plans. The dinner-gong reverberated. They drained their glasses and went in to dine. Tom caused a scandal below stairs by suggesting that he and Aldrich sit near one another at one end of the long table, and his dismissal of Barty Peckover's ministrations during the meal, once the main course and fruit had been served, fuelled kitchen gossip for days.

★

A period of four days had elapsed and still no word had come in response to Tom's letter to Wade Southwood. The former Head Gardener was the only person likely to be able to tell Tom where he might seek Mary Emma Kay and her governess and companion, Miss Peters. His frustration had grown when Barty Peckover returned from his daily trips to collect from the Post Office at Downham the letters for Uppham House and Tom had found no letter from Cornwall among them.

On the forenoon of the fifth day after the return from his trip to Lyndon Manor Lodge and his short stay with Daniel Jones at Fakenham he was aroused by the sound of bleating, whistling and the barking of a dog. Being occupied upstairs in assessing water damage to the ceiling of the drawing room that overlooked the park, he walked over to the window and his spirits lifted for the first time in days. A veritable tide of sheep poured across the park like milk from an upset churn. As he watched the fascinating spectacle, an Old English sheepdog ambled into sight, padded around wayward sheep, nipped at their legs and barked obedience until every animal was brought to a standstill. Having nothing better to do, the animals began nibbling the long grass, inching towards the house almost imperceptibly. A besmocked Clem Rix brought up the rear. Wearing a soft broad-brimmed hat that hid his bright hair, to Tom's delight the youth carried a shepherd's crook as if it were his badge of office and he Black Rod. The change in the truculent young man's demeanour was striking. Even from this fair distance Tom saw that he held himself more erect and walked with an assurance that boded well for their meeting. What struck the master most forcibly, as he studied his new shepherd, was that Clem was in his element.

Aldrich galloped up in the wake of the herd and Tom looked up at the marked ceiling with an exasperated sigh before descending to meet him.

"Are you content to allow them to pasture here, Mr Challiss?" Aldrich began. "Or shall I ask Rix to drive them away to the West Field? There's a windbreak there which will provide good shelter; it's also where Jem Webster's stacked the hurdles."

"They'll do well enough here for the present, I think," Tom said. "But we must look to fencing the grass nearest the house for I want to reserve that for an ornamental garden. Besides, we don't want the stink of sheep too near the windows or their turds sullying our boots." The excitement of seeing his theoretical plan translated into reality was making him giddy! "To be on the safe side, why not consult young Rix? He's the shepherd, after all."

"As you wish, sir," Aldrich said stiffly; and as he rode away to carry out the suggestion, Tom realised that his steward did not relish speaking with the young shepherd as man to man. He hoped that there wasn't going to be trouble between the two now that things had got off to a promising start. Aldrich's curt response irritated Tom. Too bad if he doesn't like it, he thought; he'll just have to rise above his prejudices. Later in the day, he galloped Saladin over to the West Field to see for himself what progress Jem was making with the hurdles. Jem was busy and smiled broadly as Tom galloped up. "Fine 'orse y'ave there, Mr Challiss. A might fancy for farmwork though, ain't 'e?"

"Good-day, Jem," Tom said, lowering his head and patting Saladin's neck to hide the anger that Jem's words had aroused. "Saladin will not be used on the farm, Jem," he said evenly, "he's a hunter."

Jem, who had been tying hurdles together so that they would be ready to make into folds as soon as required, carried on with his work and only said: "Oh-ah." He worked on in a silence that Tom found more infuriating than if the carpenter had spewed a string of oaths. Then Jem stopped, stretched, looked Tom in the eye, and said: "Oh! yer reckon you're gonna 'ave time ter jaunt orf 'untin' then, dew yer, sir?"

"It was the animal I bought, not a way of life!" Tom said, provoked, wondering why he felt compelled to justify his actions. "There's enough land on Uppham to allow Saladin to stretch his legs as often as he wants without following the hunt."

Returning to his labours, Jem repeated in his irritating way: "Oh, ah."

The two silly syllables sounded like a criticism to Tom's ears; as though Jem were saying: "We'm a righ' green 'orn 'ere." He thinks I'm not serious about farming, Tom fumed. Why should I care what he thinks? And yet he did care; and it rankled. With a huge effort, Tom forced himself to say: "You're doing fine work here, Jem."

As he trotted away he was conscious that things were not turning out as well as he'd imagined. He hadn't taken into consideration each man's individuality and, for the first time he saw that if one wished to lead men one had to listen to what they had to say; must try to see things from their point of view. Not for the first time, he saw that George possessed a natural ability in dealing with men; a native arrogance that men of a lower rank had been bred to defer to; a personality that others were willing to respect without his having to lift a finger to earn it. He had been born into the ruling class. Whereas, he himself, Tom began to see, would have to earn the respect of the men and women who worked for him. It wasn't enough to try to make people like you, though to be popular was an asset Tom acknowledged with a wry smile as he trotted across the fields on the back of his black stallion; he would have to demonstrate that he was willing to work as hard as any one of them.

The very idea that Jem Webster had him pegged as merely playing at being a farmer continued to rankle for the remainder of that day and as he slid between the sheets he swore to himself that he would revise the carpenter's low estimate of his abilities. And again, he wondered to himself drowsily, what it was about Jem that led Tom to court his good opinion. As he was dropping off his eyes flew open with the revelation that the mysterious hold Jem had over himself was that the carpenter had earned his master's respect; but that it was not yet fully reciprocated.

★

Chapter Eighteen

After a restless night during which the heat had made sleep impossible and his mind had refused to relax, he left his bed and dressed in open-necked shirt, breeches and boots as soon as the sky lightened. Part of his restlessness and irascibility was his need of female company. He'd not lain with a woman since he'd been accommodated by wall-eyed Mrs Roberts in the spring room of his grandfather's farm and that bizarre coupling seemed so long ago that it might never have taken place. But he had no intention of going in search of a willing maid. Saladin whinnied softly as Tom led him from his stall and a sleepy-eyed Bob emerged from the empty compartment that served as his bedroom with cornstalks sticking out of his tousled hair. "Where yew takin' him, Mr Challiss, sir?"

"Not that it's any of your business, lad; but I need a hard ride. Couldn't sleep for the heat. But I see it didn't bother you."

The boy smiled. "I c'n sleep anywhere, Mr Challiss; just give me the chance!"

His remark made Tom scrutinise him. He observed that Bob was at that age when the young begin to shoot up, all arms and legs. A good deal of Bob's anatomy protruded from an old jerkin that was far too small for him. "Tell me Bob," he began tentatively as he threw the saddle onto Saladin's back, "Do you get plenty to eat?"

The boy pulled a wry face. "Well. . . I wouldn't be tellin' the truth if I answered yes to that, sir; but I'm a lot better orf 'ere than if I was livin' at 'ome. Afore I got this job we was livin' orf turnip soup an spring water 'alf the time."

As he mounted his horse, Tom looked down at the gangling stableboy. "Go up to the kitchen. As soon as cook's about tell her I said you're to be given a breakfast each day of bacon, eggs and kidneys and something to bring back here to eat later."

His sleepiness banished by this good news, Bob's eyes shone with gratitude. "Yes, Mr Challiss, sir! Thank yer, sir." Openmouthed, he watched his master until he had cantered out of sight and only then went to dabble his face and hands in the horse trough before drying them on a bundle of hay. He thought he was in heaven.

★

Tom rode the stallion hard. The heat increased as the sun spread its brassy glow across the flat fields. Tom's shirt was soaked with sweat, his hair darkened by it. Following a lengthy and punishing gallop across three large fields, that had included hedges to jump and ditches to avoid, Tom slowed the quivering animal to a walk and dismounted. Leading him by the bridle to a brook, whose banks revealed by how much the water had dwindled during the dry summer months, he tethered him loosely to the branch of an alder and left him to take his fill. Screened by a convenient holly he relieved himself before wading into the stream and sluicing the cool water over himself; clothes, boots and all. Saladin turned his head to look at Tom and nickered.

Though he had grown to love the magnificent beast he admitted to himself that Jem Webster had been right to scoff at his pretentions. Saladin had no place on a working farm; he belonged in the stable of a wealthy man whose chief concern was to hunt more than once a week.

Churchbells sounded from across the fields and it occurred to him that he hadn't been inside a church on a Sunday since his days at Lyndon Manor. Moreover, he hadn't so much as peeped at the village of Uppham St Mary, which he'd learned was little more than a hamlet made up of a few isolated dwellings that were clustered about the mansion's perimeter wall. Determined to remedy his lapse, he spurred Saladin to a canter back to the stables where a happy-looking Bob pulled his forelock with one hand as he caught the reins that Tom tossed to him with the other.

Back in his bedroom he was pleased to see that a ewer of hot water had recently been put there and, having poured a quantity of it into a basin, began to shave himself with unusual care. He washed his hair and rinsed it and laid out fresh smalls on the end of his rumpled bed. Only then did he pause. His top clothes were decidedly the worse for wear, wrinkled, spotted and sour-smelling, after constant wear since purchased weeks ago at Canterbury. Tom realised he had two alternatives: he could appear for the first time among the villagers in the secondhand suit; or he could rummage among the clothes in George's press to see if there was anything more salubrious to wear to church.

Making his way to what had been his brother's suite of rooms in the west wing of the mansion he noticed that this part of the house was in much better repair and more recently decorated than the rest of the place. Why hadn't he thought of moving into George's rooms before this? He'd have it seen to immediately he returned from church.

It didn't take him long to discover a respectable pair of cream-coloured pantaloons, a fresh shirt with a scarcely-noticeable darn in its sleeve that his fastidious brother had discarded as unworthy to adorn his person, and a dark blue cutaway with velvet lapels made from a lightweight fabric whose name Tom didn't know. Though shorter than his brother by at least two inches the clothes fitted him well enough. Indeed, thought Tom as he surveyed the effect of the borrowed plumes, he'd not seen as good an image of himself as the one reflected in the long glass since his army days. Satisfied that he would not disgrace his Challiss forebears, he caught up a pair of doeskin gloves and went down to breakfast.

"Lor'! You give me a terrible fright, Mr Challiss, sir," Maddy said, forgetting to curtsey. "I thought it was Mr George Challiss come back! Beg pardon, sir," she added, making a belated bob. "Cook says," she cast up her eyes in order to recall the exact words, "will yew 'ave coffee, tea or ale to drink with yer breakfast, sir?"

★

Tom had just tethered Saladin to the hitching rail alongside St Mary's church when he was assailed by the haughtiest and most mangled voice his ears had ever received. "I say; that's a demned fine animal you hev there, sir! I believe I hev the honour of addressin' Mr Challiss of Uppham House? You Challisses are as alike as peas in a pod!" The man seemed cordial enough and was effetely handsome. "You are our nearest neighbours of any account in this demned hole. Allow me to introduce m'self: Percival Belmaine. How d'ye do, sir." He extended his right hand.

So. This aristocrat was a Belmaine. "How d'ye do, sir," Tom echoed, taking Belmaine's gloved hand in his. "Thomas Challiss. Yes. I've taken over the running of the Uppham estate and have been there – on and off – for a few days now. My brother has departed for Cambridgeshire for the foreseeable future."

"Heard the beggar 'ad taken himself orf," Belmaine said as they walked up to the church porch. "We shell miss 'im at Martlets. Demned good sport, old George; a first-rater at cards." He dropped his voice as they entered the church. "Might I hev a word about your stallion after the service, old fellah? Looks a first-rate bit o' horse flesh, or I'm no judge. Demned good breedin' stock if the way he's hung is anythin' to go by!" He wandered away to the crested Belmaine pew in which sat a gentleman who looked as if he'd been dressed with an ironing board left down the back of his shirt. He stirred not a jot as Percival Belmaine entered the elevated box and sat down.

Tom was conscious of being an object of interest to the rest of the congregation, who numbered perhaps two dozen, so he seated himself in the body of the church and tried to make himself less conspicuous; but his unusual height, even when seated, made that an impossibility. The wavering organ music ceased, the worshippers settled, and a very elderly clergyman climbed laboriously into the pulpit.

The Reverend John Wood's sermon was dull and tedious, and Tom repressed a sigh of relief when it was over. Reverend Wood came to meet his parishioners as more reedy organ music spiralled up to the rafters only to cease rather abruptly in mid-phrase. As the congregation shuffled towards the exit Tom heard a woman whisper: "E's done it agin! Fell asleep, when 'e's meant ter be pumpin'!" After a brief interval, in which a dull, scuffling thud followed by a distinct yelp of: "Ow!" was emitted from the organ loft, the music continued while the Reverend Wood shook hands with his flock, interspersing a few words to the more prosperous, of whom there were few. The bent old man graciously welcomed Tom to his church.

Percival Belmaine, having been the second person to leave the church at the end of the service, was waiting for Tom when he emerged. "Well, Challiss? Given the matter any thought during Wood's interminable mumblin'?"

"You're referring to my stallion? Why, no. Dull as the sermon was I did try to give my attention to it. Though I'll confess I had difficulty in following him half the time."

Belmaine drew him out of earshot of the departing worshippers. "Look here, Challiss. I'm not one fer beatin' about the bush. I like the look of your Arab. Ever thought of sellin' him, old fellah?"

To his own surprise Tom heard himself say: "As a matter of fact I was considering that very thing only this morning. I'm not really a hunting man. Haven't the time."

"Don't hunt, m'dear fellah?" Belmaine said, his face alight with happy surprise at Tom's answer. "What the devil d'ye do with yerself all day in this God-forsaken hole?" He frowned. "I suppose there's nothin' untoward concernin' the brute? He aint lame or sterile, fer instance?" He ran his hands over Saladin's legs.

"As to the first, he goes like the wind for miles without tiring and, for a stallion, is sweet-tempered. As to his abilities as a stud I'm unable to help you." As he spoke Tom was rapidly calculating what reasonable price he could expect in exchange for this horse, for which he himself had borrowed a thousand guineas from Daniel Jones.

Belmaine said: " I'll make ye an offer of two thousand guineas and throw in a nag, to boot. What say you?"

He was astonished to hear Belmaine name such a fortune without turning a hair. Playing for time, Tom appeared to consider the offer.

"Oh, come on, old fellah! You aint goin' ter haggle about it. Are you?" the young man said wheedlingly. "Tell yer what. I'll send a kerridge up ter the house about noon termorrer. Come and take luncheon with me and afterwards we'll look at my string. I promise you, sir: you shall hev any demned nag that takes yer fancy. Is it a bargain?"

Dazed by the munificence of the offer, Tom was delighted to accept such terms. "I shall be happy to accommodate you, Mr Belmaine, sir," he said, shaking the other's hand to seal the bargain before swinging up into the saddle. "Until tomorrow!" he cried as he trotted away. Once clear of the churchyard he gave Saladin his head.

★

The sight of the haughty footman, plus the Belmaine Arms displayed on the doors of the closed carriage that stood before the entrance to Uppham House on the following day, drew Mrs Rudge, Peckover and Maddy to the basement window. They dwelt on the various merits of the splendid equipage for days and felt that everybody connected with Uppham House had been elevated by its mere presence.

Tom took luncheon at Martlets; he'd never set foot inside such a grand house before and did his best not to be overawed by its opulence. Sir Everard remained aloof while his scourge of a son entertained the commoner.

Tom was astonished at the magnificence of the stable block whose stalls lined three sides of a square. His eye had been caught by a reliable Irish hack, Mulderrig, almost full-grown, and who promised well. Having walked along the splendid collection of horseflesh more than once, he had chosen the sturdy chestnut workhorse as most fitting for his requirements. He returned home overjoyed with the transaction for he had already formed an idea of how he would spend the thousand-guinea profit he'd made by the exchange of animals. Furthermore, he'd made a firm friend of The Honourable Percival Belmaine; though nothing could have been further from his intention. He disliked the fop; he'd have as little to do with him as was possible.

He was met in front of the house by Barty Peckover who had been on the lookout for his master. He surveyed the hack with open disapproval, and was depressed at seeing Mr Challiss so soon come down in the world. But, knowing his place, he mutely accepted the reins that were tossed to him as his master dismounted.

Barty had made his daily perambulation to Downham post office to collect the Uppham post. Every servant was aware that their master was champing at the bit for the arrival of a letter from a Mr Southwood. So when Barty had discovered a letter carrying a return address to *W. Southwood, Esq.* among that day's collection he wanted to be the first to witness the reaction the long-awaited letter would provoke in his young master. He had expected greater animation and was disappointed when Tom merely thanked him for such important news; but, nevertheless, the young footman noted with satisfaction a look of such happiness light up his master's features that he correctly surmised that there must be a young woman at the bottom of the impatient wait for news from the west country. It would all come out in good time, he told himself as he led the workaday horse to the stall so lately inhabited by the magnificent hunter. "Ain a patch on Saladin," he sniffed, as he handed him over to Bob.

Tom had broken the seal and torn open the letter from Southwood before he'd reached the topmost of the flight of the front steps. His hand trembled with anticipation and excitement as he rapidly scanned Wade Southwood's well-remembered copperplate. If a man's true character could be read in his handwriting Southwood's was an excellent indication of it: open, upright and well-formed.

My dear Mr Challiss, the letter began,

I had some trouble at first in placing you as young Tom Roberts, Under Gardener at Lyndon Manor. Such a lot has happened here in the three years since I last saw you. Allow me to congratulate you on your great good fortune. You are a very young man to have had so much responsibility thrust upon you. I trust you will use your inheritance to good effect. The success of an estate depends largely on good leadership and management and the careful selection of those who form the workforce for its maintenance. As to the farms and gardens ~ you might try to persuade Adam Brook to accept the position of Head Gardener, that is, if you are able to promise him suitable remuneration. He will not come cheap ~ but a good man at the top will save you more than his wages over the years. I cannot recommend Brook too highly. ~

As to the other matter: Miss Kay and Miss Peters have been lodging with the Brookses since they left Lyndon. The last address I have for Adam is at the Isle of Axholme in Lincolnshire. He has made a success of a Market Garden in the village of Welthrop. Whether he remains there I cannot say, since I have not heard from him for more than a year and have been too preoccupied with my own affairs to take up my pen to write him.

I wish you well with your inheritance. Hard work and ~ determination have much to do with success. You must decide what it is you want to do and then become very good at it. It is as simple as that. I wish you joy of your intended marriage to Miss Kay

and Remain

Yours Truly, Wade Southwood.

Tom's eyes flew back to that part of the letter that gave Adie Brook's address. His heart had given a great lurch on the first reading and he had scarcely been able to take it in. At last he knew where to begin the search for his darling. Good old Wade!

He had to share his wonderful news with somebody. As he erupted from the library he almost knocked the tea things out of Maddy's hands. "Excuse me, Maddy; I'm in a tearing hurry and can't stop to drink tea. Sit down and pour yourself some and help yourself to a slice of Mrs Rudge's delicious-looking fruitcake. Tell anyone who cares to ask that I gave you permission. I must dash!"

"But Mr Challiss, sir—" She found herself addressing air.

Sprinting to the stables, he and Bob between them had Mulderrig saddled in a trice and man and horse were away like the wind. As he galloped across the park and into the mouth of the tunnel of trees, at the end of which was Aldrich's lodge, he was sure that his choice of the sturdy animal had been absolutely right.

Belmaine had said Mulderrig meant 'red chief' which he'd thought something of a misnomer for such a plebeian brute. "Glad ter be shot of the ugly devil, old fellah," Belmaine had assured him. "Disgrace ter me stables – won 'im on a wager."

But Tom decided that the name was apt and would certainly do, even though he considered it a bit of a mouthful.

His disappointment was huge when he found the lodge deserted and Aldrich was nowhere to be found. He tethered his horse to the post in front of the lodge and went in search of the steward. Tom had not noticed before how deep the building was, a really splendid house in its own right. The hollies gave it a degree of privacy and the gardens that surrounded the lodge were well-stocked with flowers, trees and shrubs. Tom saw they were tended by one who possessed a knowledge of horticulture.

Frustrated at being compelled by Aldrich's absence to contain his good news, he took the liberty of turning the handle of the garden door. It yielded under his hand and he soon found himself in a conservatory which was stocked with ferns and a riot of hothouse blooms. He stood gazing around him in amazement. He'd had no idea that his steward possessed so green a thumb, or the wherewithal, with which to indulge his obvious passion. He traversed the flagged floor of the indoor garden and passed from it through an archway into a splendid day room, aware that his feet were now silenced by an immense Turkey rug that stretched over the whole of the planked floor, except for a two-foot border of time-darkened oak. Graceful furniture had been lavishly upholstered in the best of taste. Glowing damask and finest muslin drapery hung beside the large windows. Tom had not seen anywhere so beautifully appointed since Lyndon Manor. By comparison, the grandiose apartments of Martlets seemed to him ostentatious and pompous and Uppham itself a wreck.

Growing angry at the rightness of every piece of Wedgwood, the Venetian looking-glass – he cast his gaze over the pristine order about him and couldn't help but compare it to the dilapidated state of the mansion.

How had all this quiet splendour come about? Tom very much doubted if Aldrich had received any regular wages during the years George had been away fighting; and by the state Uppham house and lands were in there could have been little to spare to pay him anything since. It certainly was a mystery.

The noise of a key turning the lock of the front door drew Tom out into the entrance hall. "Forgive my intrusion, Aldrich," he said coldly; "I took the liberty of letting myself into your house by the conservatory door, which I found unlocked."

Tom's unfriendly manner chilled the steward, who said: "Good." Aldrich's response surprised Tom. "I've wanted to invite you here ever since your arrival; but circumstances had been against it. However, now that you are here, do let me show you the rest of the house."

"Before we go into that," Tom said, "you must put my mind at ease over something I find – puzzling."

Forestalling him, Aldrich said, "I think I have an idea. You were wondering how my own home comes to be so lavishly furnished and the fabric of the building in such excellent repair, when the mansion has been so neglected. Am I right?"

Taken aback by his openness, Tom nodded agreement. "Go on."

"Did you imagine I'd diverted Uppham's income to my own ends? The explanation is very simple, really. But before I tell you about the lodge may I offer you some tea, Mr Challiss?"

Pressed for time, Tom was about to decline the steward's offer when he realised that he had a monstrous thirst. "You haven't any ale?"

"If you prefer it; a moment while I fetch it. As you see, I live here alone with no servant to call upon. Please; take a seat and make yourself comfortable." He soon returned with two full tankards on a tray and offered one to Tom. Seating himself opposite his uninvited guest, Aldrich began: "I don't suppose anyone has thought to tell you that I was once married and that my wife died?"

Shocked by Aldrich's revelation, Tom said: "My dear fellow! I had no idea. When was this?" If he was honest, Tom had the man down as a confirmed bachelor.

"Oh. . . It all happened a long time ago – It'll be fourteen years this Christmas. I was twenty-two and my dear wife, Lucy, was not much more than a girl. She was eighteen when she died after giving birth to our stillborn son."

No wonder the man wore such a sad face most of the time, Tom thought. A cold hand had seemed to clutch at his heart as Joseph Aldrich had stated the bald facts in his deep voice. What if Mary Emma should be dead already? If not that, and their marriage took place, suppose childbirth were to take its toll of his young wife? "You have had much to bear, Joseph; but did you never think of marrying again after some years had elapsed?"

"For many years I could not think of it; I had loved Lucy very deeply, you see. Lately, I have thought that I would take a second wife, should fate cause my path to cross that of a congenial and willing companion. Life is very lonely on one's own; but there is so much demand on my time in the summer that I have little time to regret my single state. It is harder to bear in winter when the long dark days and evenings seem interminable." His voice had grown very mournful in the telling of his woes.

Guilt stabbed Tom. He'd been so wrapped up in his own exciting affairs that it hadn't occurred to him that his steward might be finding life so hard to bear. He put down his ale, strode to the man's chair and took his free hand in his own.

"Forgive me, Joseph. I've been selfish and I've treated you unsympathetically sometimes. Let me say now; you will no longer spend your winters here in isolation. Whether I am at home or abroad you will always have access to my drawing-room, and my library is at your disposal. I will instruct the servants to that effect."

Joseph's eyes shone. "Bless you, Mr Challiss! You are very kind. But I wouldn't want to impose—"

"Let's hear no more about it. But to return to your explanation about all this." He'd resumed his chair and waved his half-empty tankard in a lateral arc to indicate the handsomely furnished room.

"My wife was the only child of her widowed father and brought with her a generous dowry," Joseph said. "A nuptial agreement was drawn up that expressly forbade that any part of Lucy's fortune, once it passed into my hands, be spent other than on Lucy and myself and any children that might follow. Her father worried about his child's future with one who, though in a secure position, was neither wealthy nor handsome. But his daughter's wishes overcame all objections; for it was obvious to him that we were head over heels in love with each other. In the year prior to our marriage, Mr Brown – Lucy's father – had this place renovated from top to bottom, retaining the better features, and furnished it in such a way that, when complete, it was a residence fit for a princess."

"But you said that your wife died fourteen years ago," Tom said, thinking that Aldrich's tale did not take into account the pristine condition of the place.

"This lodge is my shrine to Lucy and our dead son," the man said. "I have no need of any salary; my fortune is something of an embarrassment to me. My work is all-important and it is my dearest wish to see Uppham restored to its former glory. Oh . . . the mansion had been a lost cause since long before my time; the house needs a fortune spent on it. But I had known the splendid gardens when I was a younger man and still living in Downham. Ever since I became steward I have dreamed of returning the weedcovered beds and borders to their former loveliness."

"What stopped you? Surely not my father, or George?"

"Lack of time. The upkeep of the estate squanders it all, Mr Challiss. Some of the farmhouses and their labourers' cottages are in bad repair and manpower has always been lacking. I could have achieved much had there been the skilled men to set to work. I have it in my power to direct others, sir; but I would be the last to claim such practical skills as tiling, carpentry or the work of a farrier or a wheelwright."

Somewhere in the house a clock tinkled a melody prior to the striking of the hour. Astonished to discover how the time had flown, Tom said: "Thank you for taking me into your confidence, Joseph. I'm sorry; I must go immediately. Much as I dislike leaving you to run Uppham singlehanded again so soon, I have no option but to journey into Lincolnshire. I'm told I'll probably find my future wife living there."

Alarm showed on Aldrich's face. That his master was proposing to leave, having been returned only a few days from his last jaunt seemed most unfair. "Mr Challiss— sir, I must protest! I have come near breaking point over the last three years, trying to juggle the affairs of Uppham without any help or, indeed, anyone to turn to for consultation; or how best to solve the multitude of problems that occur about the estate daily. If I am left to manage on my own again, I fear for my reason."

Tom believed him; Joseph looked almost demented and had begun to speak in the convoluted sentences that had characterised his speech on Tom's arrival. Nevertheless, Tom would not be put off any longer from fetching home Mary Emma and Miss Peters, since he now had their address. What was to be done? "Suppose I were to make Jem Webster foreman under your direction?" he proposed. "He's an able and reliable man and skilled in the handling of men. D'ye think, with his help, you could manage for a few weeks?" He was relieved to see Aldrich take command of himself. "Speak to Jem about my proposal," Tom said. "If he's willing, give him the position for as long as he wants it. Oh – one other thing, of great importance." Bringing out his pocket book he drew forth the banker's draft. "I want you to deposit this with Bagg and Bacon's bank at Lynn. I will feel happier if you'll see to it; I don't want to risk losing it. Give it a week for arrangements to be made for any withdrawals you might need to make. I have enclosed a letter to that effect naming a finite sum beyond which you are not authorised to draw further funds without my written permission. Mr Bagg will keep everything in order and, as long as he is in agreement, you have *carte blanche* to draw on the bank."

Fully restored now, Aldrich enquired calmly: "I am deeply honoured to have such trust placed in my hands, Mr Challiss; you may depend on me. Are there any special instructions concerning the servants, or preparations for your return? For instance, sir; should I see to the cleaning of the suite of rooms in the west wing? Those are the most habitable, I think. A fresh lick of paint? And, perhaps the dining-room—"

"Yes! Yes! Use your initiative, Joseph!" Tom snapped. "'Tis a pity there's no housekeeper . . . But that can wait " . . . until Mary Emma is here to hire her own women. He left abruptly, mounted Mulderrig and cantered up the drive to the house. He packed in a hurry, selecting a variety of clothing for every climate and enough to see him through a prolonged absence. He'd heard warnings about Lincolnshire's withering winds.

This time he would make no promise about the length of time he would be away. He would absent himself for as long as it took him to find his dear girl and to deal with anything else that might arise from his journey into Lincolnshire, such as persuading Adie Brook to accept the position of Head Gardener at Uppham. He hoped to be able to accomplish everything he had in mind within a few weeks. If it took a year, then so be it.

★

Chapter Nineteen

The panniers hanging on either side of Mulderrig's strong back contained everything Tom considered necessary for what promised to be a lengthy journey. Close behind his saddle he'd strapped a rolled, ankle-length mackintosh cloak. Hessians had been left behind and a stout pair of George's black leather riding boots covered his legs to the knees. Over these he wore a triple-caped redingote and large-brimmed hat. As he was leaving the house, he'd caught sight of his reflection in the glass of an inner door and thought he looked even more of a highwayman than the felon, Jake Reville.

Ned Rudge and the other servants had waved him off with a "God speed, Mr Challiss, sir!" and his last words with Joseph Aldrich had allayed any misgivings he might have had about leaving the steward in charge of the estate. He passed through the gates of Uppham House and his heart gave a great leap of joy. A mere matter of days – weeks at the most – separated him from Mary Emma. His journey had begun!

Once on the road to Lynn he began to leave behind the silent groups of ragged, starving men and gaunt women comforting their whimpering children, who had edged the streets of Downham. Elated though he was by the thought of what soon lay ahead for himself, his joy was overshadowed by images of the dispossessed that haunted him for miles. For a considerable time he wracked his brain as to what he himself could do to alleviate their desperate plight. He thrashed the problem about inside his head but came to no useful conclusion and was almost glad to have something else to think about when the heavens opened and a savage storm forced him to seek shelter in the lee of a hayfilled open-sided barn.

Away from the sheeting rain the sheltered air was heavy with the scent of sun-filled meadows. Although he was a only a couple of miles short of Lynn he had ridden his mount hard and without respite or refreshment. Taking advantage of the enforced rest, Tom emptied his bladder into the field of mayweed and stubble and then fed Mulderrig a handful of corn. He rummaged in one of the panniers for something to eat and had just pulled in two one of Mrs Rudge's freshly-baked loaves when the hairs on the back of his neck rose as he sensed that he was not alone.

Between gusty squalls he heard rustlings close by. He had two alternatives: he could leave right away and journey on; or he could investigate the cause of his uneasiness. Temporarily forgotten, the broken loaf lay on a pile of hay.

One of Tom's weaknesses was the possession of an insatiable curiosity. He had to know who or what was hidden in the barn; but as soon as he shifted, every sound other than the rain and wind ceased. Rain drumming on the shingled roof of the barn made his ears useless in detecting the hiding place so, as soon as a slight lull in the turmoil occurred, he shouted: "Hallo, there! Where are you?" No response. Tom distinctly heard a muffled sneeze; but from which direction had it come? "Damn and blast this rain!" he muttered.

Mulderrig stamped about on the edge of the barn and whinnied. Turning to quiet him with more feed, Tom was just quick enough to see, disappearing into the hay, a small hand clutching a hunk of his bread. With a leap, he tore a large hole in the banked wall and found himself looking into the terror-filled brown eyes of a bedraggled little girl. She had dropped the stolen bread and seemed dumbstruck at the suddenness of her discovery. Tom thought she could be no more than ten years old and saw that she wasn't alone in the cave that had been fashioned out of the hay.

Visible only from the waist up, the lower half of her body concealed beneath a coverlet of hay, a woman lay stretched out on the floor of the barn. Though her large grey eyes stared up at the rafters of the roof that covered the hay crop Tom saw at once that she was no longer living. The well-remembered stench of death was present — and a sweeter smell that he was unable to identify. The child remained frozen in the attitude resulting from the terror that had so overwhelmed her; she was unable to tremble or cry out.

His finger to his lips, Tom backed away from the hole. "Don't be afraid," he said softly, "I mean you no harm, child." She didn't move. He remembered that one of the panniers contained a small spiced ham that Mrs Rudge had packed for his travels. In no time, he had cut from it two thick slices, laid the spicy meat on some pieces of bread and was holding it near enough for the girl to catch its aroma. She remained crouched on her knees, wide brown eyes gazing into his as if mesmerised. Unable to think what more he could do that would not terrorise her further, he set the tempting fare on some clean-looking hay, turned his back on the child and settled down to eat his own portion.

After a while, small sounds told him that the girl had regained her powers of motion, that she had taken up the little meal and was frantically cramming it into her mouth. She choked and cried out. Tom turned as he heard her retching and vomiting. His heart went out to the child. "Let me help you," he said, catching up his water bottle and stepping over the flimsy barrier of hay that separated them before she had time to resist.

The damp air was sour, sickly-smelling where the child sat among her own vomit; but Tom had smelled worse smells; much worse. Moaning with misery, tears spilling from her eyes the girl cleared her throat and spoke for the first time. "Ma's dead, i'nt she," she croaked, stating a fact. "I knoo she was but pretended she wasn't. She was ollerin and ollerin in the dark for ages. I must've fell asleep, 'cause when I woke up it was all quiet; it were so quiet I thought the 'ole world 'ad stopped. I was no good to 'er," the tears coursed down the pale cheeks as she spoke, "I dint know what t'do for 'er when she was ollerin an then she went an died when I was asleep—"

Resisting the impulse to take the folorn youngster in his arms and comfort her, Tom held his flask to her lips and said: "There was nothing you could have done for your poor mother. Nobody will blame you for falling asleep, you poor child."

Regarding the stranger with her wide brown eyes, the girl said: "You're very good, mister. Not many folks is kind to our sort. What'll I do now, though? What's to become o' me?"

Tom had been asking himself the same question. "What's your name," he said.

"Eppie, short fer Epzibah – out the Bible."

"Well, Eppie," Tom said, "I must fetch help. Will you stay here, or would you rather come with me? There's nothing more to be done for your poor mother, God rest her soul."

"What you gonna do with me?" Eppie said, with a worried look. "I ain goin' in no workus orphnidge!"

"We'll hope it won't come to that," said Tom, though he very much feared it would. For what else was to be done with her? The rain and wind not having diminished, he removed his hat, unrolled his long waterproof cape and drew it over his head. "You must ride inside my cape, Eppie. Do you mind that?"

She eyed him with suspicion. "Ow do I know you wont get up to nasty tricks?" she queried, suddenly looking much older as she waited for his reply.

Taken aback, Tom said: "You don't; except that I give you my word that I have no wish to molest you. But . . . if you'd rather I left you here—"

"'Old on! I dint say that, did I?" Suddenly ashamed, she mumbled: "There's those that wouldn't think twice about it, mister. But p'raps you're diff'rent. You seem it; but I know that don't mean nothing. Anyway, I'll have ter trust yer, won't I."

He knew that the girl's fears were justified; that some men would have seen her helplessness as an opportunity to satisfy their lust. Saddened by her knowledge of the evils even a child might encounter, he said no more but swung up into the saddle and, leaning down, offered Eppie his arm.

★

On entering Lynn they made a single corpulent figure and the oddly-shaped rider on his hack drew the attention of the few people braving the storm. At his wits' end as to what course of action to take, yet aware that it should be undertaken speedily, Tom accosted a cross-looking clergyman who was standing at the open door of his chapel surveying the weather. Shouting in an effort to make himself heard against the forces of nature, Tom called out: "Good-day to you, sir!"

Before he had time to utter another syllable the man surveyed the skies with an exaggerated motion of his head and shouted back: "I see precious little good about the day, sir."

Despite the damnable weather and his predicament Tom laughed at the man's neat riposte. "I wonder if I might ask your assistance, sir."

"Nobody else seems to think it worth their while to brave the storm, sir," the clergyman laughed, "and you look as if you are in need of shelter. By all means. Enter. Be sure to tie your horse to the rail first, of course."

Extricating Eppie from the confines of his cape proved difficult and Tom was amused by the surprised expression that fastened itself to the clergyman's face as the scruffy-looking bundle that slid from beneath his waterproof to the ground underwent a metamorphosis and became a child. "Bless me!" the clergyman exclaimed, as Eppie, keeping her eyes on Tom, darted to the shelter of the porch.

The man introduced himself as Philip Westwood. "Come in out of this inclement weather, my dear sir," he said, dubiously, as soon as he saw the rags that barely covered the barefoot girl, "your *daughter*, too, of course." The cheerless chapel seemed to Tom a positive haven in contrast to the tempest that continued to rage outside.

"My thanks, sir. My name is Thomas Challiss. It is about this child – no daughter of mine – known to me as Eppie or Epzibah, who until this morning was a stranger to me, that I wish to speak to you, sir."

The man's face fell. "Oh, I can have nothing to do with charity cases, my good sir," he said in a rush, with a shake of his head. "Oh, dear me, no; nothing whatever."

"I was not aware that I'd mentioned any such thing," Tom said, anger rising.

"True, true. But the circumstances speak for themselves, sir. Do they not?"

Keeping his temper in check for Eppie's sake, Tom said reasonably: "Please do me the courtesy of hearing me out before making any rash assumptions, sir."

Plainly put out by the predicament which he'd brought upon himself, Westwood said: "By all means; so long as you keep it short, my dear sir. The luncheon hour draws near. Shall we sit down?"

Seated in the front pew with Eppie beside him, Tom faced Mr Westwood who had acquired a chair from somewhere. As briefly as he could, he made Westwood acquainted with the facts and ended by saying: "So you see, Mr Westwood. Something must be done about Eppie's mother whom we've left lying dead in the hay barn. Would you do me the kindness of directing me to the nearest undertaker?"

Westwood looked worried. "The chapel can spare no funds to meet any unexpected outlay—"

"You misunderstand me, sir!" Tom thundered, sounding more like his brother than he knew. "I shall, of course, meet any costs arising from that source. As for Eppie—" He sighed. "What arrangements are there in the town for the accommodation of an indigent orphan?" He turned to speak to Eppie. At the mention of the word 'orphan' she had slipped off the pew and had streaked out of the chapel before either man could stop her. Tom noted Westwood's enormous relief at the turn of events. A search of the locality proved fruitless. Eppie was lost; was gone to ground.

Depressed by the outcome of his morning's work, Tom sought out the undertaker, obtained his services for the required fee and escorted him the two miles back out of town to the barn. On lifting Eppie's mother to place her body into the plain coffin a further horror was uncovered in the form of a perfectly-formed dead baby boy which the undertaker and his assistant found lying among the bloodsoaked hay beneath his mother's skeletal body.

God forgive me, thought Tom, while the men hammered down the lid to the white deal coffin; but I do believe that newborn boy is more fortunate than poor little Eppie. What will become of her now? He hoped Westwood's luncheon choked him. Oh, he groaned inwardly, that such suffering can go on in modern England. The pity of it all! Yet he felt himself powerless to do anything about it. It wasn't until the undertaker asked what name should be chalked onto the coffin lid that Tom realised he hadn't a name for the dead woman. He laid his hand on the rough-planed wood. "Write 'Mother of Epzibah, and infant son' and today's date. I know no other details."

★

Let that little adventure be a lesson to you, my son, Tom admonished himself as he gave a silver sixpence to the boy who had taken care of his horse. As he untethered Mulderrig from the rail outside *The Globe* he thought of Eppie's mother and her little son sealed in their coffin which, by this time, must have reached the pauper burial ground. They, at least, were spared further misery. By association, he imagined Eppie begging her way about the dangerous waterfront at Lynn, of her probable fate, and raged that he was impotent to prevent her inevitable descent into crime and squalor – that is, if she managed to survive the coming winter.

The rain had ceased at last. A blistering sun appeared and was busy sucking up the morning's moisture; roofs, walls and vegetation resembling a Turkish bath. A stifling heat followed and Tom was glad he'd stopped to dine at the inn for he was about to begin the journey that would take him into Lincolnshire. A study of the map of that county, in an old atlas he'd unearthed among a higgledy-piggledy pile of dilapidated oversized volumes in Uppham's damp library, had revealed that he would have to traverse almost the whole of Lincolnshire from south to north, taking a westerly bearing in a roughly diagonal line; a journey approaching ninety miles.

Eppie had bequeathed to Tom some of the multitude of lice that had found in even her meagre body a fertile breeding ground. He had hoped to press on to Spalding and avoid Holbeach; but his crawling guests were troubling him with bites in intimate places and he wanted nothing more than to rid himself of the parasites. He was in need of a thorough de-lousing if he could find the means to procure it. It would not do to turn up at the Brooks residence bringing with him an infestation. Besides, the very thought that he might contaminate Mary Emma decided him. So he made for the mail road that led westward from Lynn to Cross Keys Wash and into Lincolnshire.

By the end of the afternoon's ride he had booked himself into a comfortable room at *The King's Head* at Holbeach where he divulged his predicament to the landlord who immediately, and with discretion, ordered hot water and a large tub to be carried up to Tom's room. His verminous clothes were dropped into a large barrel of oily water and his outer clothing taken outside and hung in the garden of the inn. On the advice of the admirable landlord, for a nominal fee an Italian gentleman was engaged who, he said, would rid Tom of vermin in no time. It sounded too good to be true. Nobody got free of lice that easily, nits especially. Still . . .

Signor Marrone turned out to be one of those knowledgeable individuals with a special interest in herbal medicine. What he was doing working in a provincial inn Tom failed to guess; but as soon as Marrone opened his mouth to speak it was evident that he had lived in London for many years. Almost nothing of his native lyricism had been retained among the cockney vowels of the metropolis. He alarmed Tom by telling him that he would add to his bath a few drops of oil made from the poisonous seeds of a parasiticide called lousewort. "Heard of it, sir? No? Sometimes called stavesacre. Same thing. Kills off these little buggers in no time. But dangerous stuff in the wrong hands. Not for novices."

Eyeing him warily, Tom said: "Hope y'know what you're doing," as he lowered himself into the hot water.

The small, olive-skinned man smiled reassuringly. "Everything will go well enough provided you do not open your mouth or try to speak when I pour the oily water over your head, sir. Should you swallow any of the oil by accident it would make you very ill."

Tom didn't like the sound of that at all. "Look here, Signor Morrone," he began, rising from the tub only to find himself pressed back into the water by the firm hand of the Italian.

"No more talk, if you please. I am going to douse your head in the lousewort oil. But first—" Tom first felt something being stuffed into his ears. Next, a pair of goggles were fastened over his eyes and hooked onto his ears. Lastly, through the crude lenses he saw something in Morrone's hands and realised that it was a wax seal intended for his mouth. He wanted to cry out, to jump out of the tub and escape his ordeal. Too late, he thought, with resignation as warmed wax was painted over his lips, allowed to cool and to form a waterproof seal. A pitcher of liquid was emptied over his head. He waited for an adverse reaction. Nothing untoward happened. Just as he was feeling relief that his torment was over a second dose of the parasiticide deluged his head and he was glad that Morrone had taken all the necessary precautions for his safety. He waited.

"Not much longer, sir," Signor Morrone shouted. "Just you stay put for a while and give the lousewort oil time to kill 'em off." He laughed. "You'll find all that discomfort was worthwhile when you look at the number of dead bodies floating on the tubwater." Time passed; and again Morrone shouted close to Tom's ear: "Right-o! I'm going to pour a quantity of clean water over your head now, sir, then you'll be free to step out of the tub." It was over. Wrapped in a clean bathsheet, Tom felt the stuffing being removed from his ears, the goggles unhooked and the plaster peeled from his lips. "Take a look at that, sir," said Morrone, indicating the tubwater. A scum had formed on the surface of the cooling liquid and the sight of the floating bodies of dead vermin mixed with oil was horrible. Eppie must have been crawling with lice from head to toe! "I cannot thank you enough, Signor Morrone," Tom said. "You've performed a miracle, my dear sir. Why isn't the cure more widely known?"

The little man shrugged his wide shoulders. "Why, indeed. It is very well-known in France and in my own country. I work from an ancient recipe of my grandmother's. But the Greeks and Romans knew of it and Pliny has described its use. For some unknown reason it was forgotten by many some time in the Middle Ages."

"D'you really think I'm completely free of the vermin now, Signor Morrone?"

The Italian held out a small container to Tom. "If not, you can smite any that linger about your person with this. It's an ointment that is as efficacious and as deadly – if not used with great care – as the oil. Take it, my dear sir, with my compliments. Always wash your hands well after applying it. The little devils are particularly tenacious under the armpits and around the genital area. It's possible they might linger in those parts which are damp and moist, where the light cannot reach, and you might find occasion to use the ointment."

"I'm eternally grateful for your assistance, Signor. But I still find it strange that such a potent remedy against lice is so little known. Perhaps the reason it died out as a cure was because of the dangers it posed if it came into the wrong hands," Tom offered as he finished dressing himself in fresh clothing and began combing his damp hair.

"Perhaps," Morrone said with a shrug. "One last thing. Should you have the misfortune to contract the itch, a decoction of the boiled seeds may be applied to the affected part with a linen rag, with good results.. Now I must leave you, my dear sir. I wish you good luck. It has been a pleasure to be of service to you. No. Pray don't come down. I'm used to coming and going here as I please. Good-evening to you."

★

While Tom had been enjoying a meal of roast partridge complete with all the usual accompaniments, his belongings had been removed from the room he'd engaged and taken out to the stables. The landlord, mindful of his hostelry's excellent reputation, had ordered Tom's vacated room to be fumigated before further occupation. A different room was allocated where he spent the night in greater comfort than he had anticipated a few hours before.

Yesterday's storm had cleared the air and after a substantial breakfast Tom left Holbeach with the firm intention of allowing nothing further to deflect him from his purpose. One of the panniers held his deloused clothes; but his hat, redingote and cape he purposely left behind hoping to find replacements at Spalding or Sleaford. Mulderrig was fresh and frisky, keen to be off, as was his master who, in turn, was relieved to be under clear skies and a temperate sun for his journey across the fens.

★

They made good progress. A new waterproof cape had been purchased at Sleaford and had already been put to use on more than one occasion. He'd seen nothing good enough in the way of a redingote that had tempted him to part with his money until he reached the beautiful cathedral city of Lincoln. A splendid ready-made garment had been obtained at Plumb's in the High Street and the tailor had directed him along the street to the establishment of Robert Reynolds, hatter, who was able to satisfy him with a wide-brimmed hat. He left Mulderrig at the livery stables in the hands of an ostler while he stretched his own legs with a wander around the quaint streets that led down from the cathedral to the canal bank, and returned by a different route. Uphill again, he entered the towered landmark and was over-awed both by its size and its architectural beauty. As he collected his hack and they left the city behind them, to descend once more into the flat lands that surround the cathedral, he carried away in his mind's eye the image of the glowing rose window, the cathedral's own eye, with its myriad fragments of coloured glass that had been fashioned and fitted into the ornate masonry by men long dead and forgotten.

From Lincoln to Fillingham, where he spent the night, and from there onward to the small town of Kirton-in-Lindsey. From Kirton, his pleasant westerly ride to Scotton was but a morning's jaunt. His enquiries there for directions to Welthrop had the Scotton man sucking in his breath with a doubtful shake of the head. "'Tis a wet ride. 'Tis all fen atween 'ere an Welthrop, sir. You must go south for a bit till you come to a large manor 'ouse set at the fork of the road." He used his gnarled hands to illustrate the lie of the land. "Take the right hand fork." The palm of the man's right hand slid across the palm of his left and glanced off obliquely into unknown realms where it came to rest at the end of his outstretched arm. "Foller the road to Scotton Common – anyone'll tell yer the way – 'til yer come to Jerry's Bog. It aint called that fer nothing. You keep your 'orse to the road and you'll come to no 'arm." His right hand was active again; it came up by the side of his nose and oscillated between his face and another unknown realm far ahead from where they stood, back and forth, back and forth his lower arm went. "Keep straight on along that road, with Jerry's Bog on your left." His left arm swung out in line with his shoulder and he held it there while his right arm continued to point straight ahead. "Now. If you've tacken 'eed of my instructions, young man, you'll see before you the Ferry. That's the only way you'll get acrorst the Trent, in these parts, short o' swimmin' it." He laughed at his own jest, showing a remarkable deficiency in serviceable teeth.

Tom thanked the man, offered him a shilling, which was politely refused, and set off to act upon the semaphored directions before they faded from his memory.

The immense skies over the fens were settling into a uniform glow as he led Mulderrig from the ferry and they took the road to the north-west which would carry them to Welthrop. In the Isle of Axholme at last, the few miles that separated him from Mary Emma could be covered before sunset. He tried to imagine her as she might be now: no longer a girl but blossomed into womanhood; and the lonely road seemed to him interminable, no matter how hard he rode Mulderrig. When the sun dipped behind the fringe of trees far away across the flat landscape and still there was no sign of the town he became anxious and wondered if he had taken the wrong road.

Suddenly, as if rising from a black sea, he saw the first dim lights of the town and was surprised to see that he was nearer to it than he'd imagined. Somebody carrying a dark lantern on the road ahead of him turned around at the sound of the approaching horseman and stood waiting for the rider to come alongside. In answer to Tom's enquiry, the youth said: "Brook? That's me own name: Burton Brook."

Tom dismounted and with Mulderrig in tow accompanied the lanky lad on foot. He asked the youth if he were anything to do with the family of

Adam Brook; upon which the boy stopped dead and held the lantern up to Tom's face. "What's it to you, sir, if I might ask? I don't know you."

"Forgive the abruptness of my manner, Mr Brook. My name is Thomas Roberts Challiss. Your father and I once worked together at Lyndon Manor in east Norfolk. He was Under Gardener there when I was no more than a Gardener's Boy."

"I'm sorry if I seemed uncivil," Burton Brook responded with more warmth in his voice. "We've had our troubles, sir, and have to be careful what we say to strangers." Tom's hand was clasped and shaken. "My father's often mentioned your name when talking of the old days, Mr – I thought your name was Thomas Roberts?" By the time Tom had enlightened him on that point they had reached the gates of a barely discernible rambling thatched house. A lighted candle that had been placed in a small window beside the front door shed its dim rays along a pathway.

"I'll take your horse to the stables, Mr Rob -er- Challiss, shall I? The house door's always left open until we're all in bed. Let yourself in. Just give a knock first. Shan't be a tick." Youth and horse were soon swallowed up in the darkness, their progress visible only by the bobbing lantern whose fitful beams eventually died away. Loath to burst in unannounced, Tom's rap on the door immediately brought someone to open it. The lighted candle was taken out of the small window; the door opened a crack and holding the candlestick aloft a girl of perhaps fifteen years old peered out into the darkness. His business explained, he gained admission at once. Adam Brook himself appeared at the sound of a stranger's voice and as soon as Tom removed his hat his former taskmaster knew him.

"Why, it's Roberts!" he exclaimed, taking Tom's hand in his firm grip and shaking it. "We'd given you up for dead long since, bor." Observing the pain his words had caused, he swiftly added : "Not havin' had a word from you since the day you ran orf — Well, what with the casualty lists, an all, an so many of our men bein' killed daily . . . Mary Emma – beggin' her pardon, Miss Kay, had begun to give up hope since the war ended and still no word. She'll be beside herself with joy when she learns you're safe."

Tom broke in. "Miss Kay isn't here, then?"

"Well, she is an' she isn't, as you might say," Adam said, maddeningly, ushering him into a large and comfortable room. "She works as governess up at Passendean, the big house. Since Miss Peters went, Mary Emma comes home on Friday evenin' to Welthrop to spend her Saturdays an' Sundays with us. She's grown right fond of the children and is just like one o' the family now."

While Adam had been explaining Mary Emma's absence Tom, who had been struggling to try to remember what day of the week it was, came up with the idea that it was Wednesday; but was far from certain. He caught Adam's last few words and was filled with alarm. "You mean she lives at Passendean?" A fine house, no doubt, and perhaps young gentlemen in the family.

Adam Brook shot him a look of amusement. "Come down to earth, Roberts!" he laughed. "You'll see her soon enough, bor. Tomorrow's Thursday; you'll only have a couple o' days to wait." He walked over to a cupboard as young Brook came in.

"I gave your hack a rub down, Mr Challiss, and he's stalled for the night. The weather's fine enough for him to be in the pasture, but I didn't know how soon you'd want to be on your way so I judged it best to keep him near the house. Anything to eat, Pa?" He was answered simultaneously by both men.

"Thank you, Burton – if I may call you that," said Tom.

"Your mother's left you something in the kitchen." Adam Brook turned his puzzled gaze from one to the other. "What's all this nonsense about 'Mr Challiss', Burt?"

"I'll explain," Tom said to the young man who was already halfway out of the door. The tale he told impressed Adam Brook a great deal.

"So, Mr Thomas Roberts Challiss, you've not only come into your own property but are comfortably orf inter the bargain. You've become quite a swell." He smiled good-naturedly as he provided him with a supper of bread and cheese and a tankard of ale. "And how old are you?"

"I know," Tom laughed. "It does sound too good to be true, doesn't it? But believe me: I mean to use my luck to some good." He swallowed some ale and broke off a portion of bread and cheese and raised it to his mouth but put it down, untasted. "Which seems a good time to ask you to do me a great favour, Mr Brook."

Adam Brook looked both surprised and offended. "And what it is you think I could do for you, *sir*, as I suppose I must call you now? Haven't you enough already?"

"I meant no offence, Adie," said Tom, slipping into familiarity. "Of course, I expect no such deference from you. Why – it was you and Wade Southwood who taught me everything I know about growing plants . . . And it's about that I want to talk to you." He saw that Brook, despite his initial hostility, was becoming interested. "We've had no chance to discuss your affairs—"

"—Which are my own concern, Mr Challiss."

"Exactly," Tom concurred. "But, whatever they are – however successful your market garden is—"

"That died a death over a year ago, after the drought."

Tom was irritated by his interruptions. "Please hear me out before making further comment," he said. "I'm finding this difficult enough as it is. I know I have no right to ask anything of you. In a way, it's more of a proposition. I've described the Uppham estate to you and I know what I'm about to say is presumptuous– Dash it all, Adam! I need a Head Gardener-cum-Farm Manager; you have the knowledge and I have a neglected estate that's gone to rubbidge and beggary. It will benefit from your experience and attention. I need your help. Will you do me the great honour of accepting the position if I make it worth your while to do so?"

Brook had sat bolt upright in his chair as Tom disclosed his offer. "Well! Yew floored me with that," said Brook lapsing into his own dialect. "I'm so surprised I 'ardly know what ter say; 'tis so sudden, like. But let me be honest with yew, Tom. Things've not bin goin' ser well lately. Me an Mrs Brook 'ave eight children ter bring up; our Noah's over a year old but does nuthin' but blar an' is always so gallus-droply 'cause 'e won't use the guzunder. Dulcie spoils 'im: I dunno why; she was sensible with t'others. Maybe it's her time o' life. But the market failed in the drought an I tried sev'ral crops: flax, hemp, rape – even turnip. I dunno; we barely scraped by after workin' from dawn 'til dusk, sometimes 'til Bull's Moon. So now I'm tryin' me 'and at geese. I've put everything I 'ad into this flock. The Lincolnshire farmers tell me that a goose is treasure in disguise: 'tis good to eat, so they say; an it's feathers are a prime source of revenue; yew know: quills to make pens, breast feathers for stuffin' pillers; and then there's whole goose wings to be sold to rich men with libr'ies whose housekeepers use 'em to dust their books. Leastways, that's what they say. But can a Norfolk man trust what a Lincolnshire man says, Tom? Yew know 'ow 'tis with furriners. 'Tis tew soon ter know if what they say is trew; but livin' like this, from 'and ter mouth, is a might risky when a man has so many mouths ter feed."

"'Night, Pa. 'Night, Mr Challiss," Burt Brook said as he went through with his candle to light himself upstairs. Tom was favourably impressed with the young man's demeanour; he was polite, seemed level-headed and promised well. Tom and Adam bade him goodnight and continued talking into the early hours. By the time an agreement had been reached a newly-broached bottle of madeira stood empty.

A strong inducement had been offered to Adam Brook: a large house would be provided and, in addition, the promise of a generous salary would be paid, unusually, on the first day of each calendar month, rather than by the quarter. A month's grace was given, after which time the offer would be withdrawn. If things failed to improve at Adam's smallholding – the erstwhile market garden – he promised he would seriously consider Tom's offer. Both men realised that uprooting his family once again was a big step for Brook to contemplate. But the good news that Lambert Jardine was out of their lives for good made the offer very tempting.

★

How Tom got through the intervening hours until Friday evening he never was quite able to remember. On Thursday morning, as soon as the early September sun rose, the house began to throb with life. Baby Noah had usurped the cockerel's duties by beginning to bawl before first light and Mrs Brook was already astir in the kitchen. Savoury smells wafted up to the landing where Tom lay dozing on a makeshift bed. Burt hurtled past him with a hasty apology for tripping over his foot and could be heard clumping down the wooden stairs, followed by his father's more measured tread. Five tousled children in various stages of undress tumbled out of one bedroom after being roused by their older sister, Agnes, who had emerged from another, and whom Tom remembered as the girl who had opened the door to him the night before. After that, all seemed a kind of ordered chaos which left his woozy head throbbing but impressed him by its almost military precision. By the time breakfast was over and the rooms straightened the house seemed to shrink as a fretful peace settled over it. Adam Brook had gone to tend the geese and Burton had set out to walk the two miles to Passendean where he worked in the formal gardens, Mrs Brook told Tom. Baby Noah, glutted with milk and porridge, had mercifully drifted off to sleep in his cot beside the open casement window, his exceptionally powerful lungs at rest. The four youngest sat around one end of the kitchen table, its grain raised by daily scrubbing, with their slates before them, while Agnes drew letters of the alphabet for her little brother, three year old Zeb, and their five year old sister, Dovey, to copy. Eleven year old John, nine year old Ann and Fanny, seven, were toiling over sums that Agnes had prepared for them the night before. Mrs Brook was at the other end of the large table kneading bread while the kettle sang on the hob and the cat sat before the fire; and Tom thought he'd never seen a lovelier sight than the whole family so profitably occupied.

That pang he'd thought gone for ever returned to stab him in the heart as he recalled his solitary, harsh upbringing; it brought home to him, as nothing before had, the loss he had suffered by not possessing loving, caring parents; of not being one of a horde of brothers and sisters with whom to share his life. He saw it as a lost privilege that no amount of money could buy. It was little wonder to him that Mary Emma had grown so attached to the Brook family.

The picture of a domestic paradise was fractured by the loud squall that Noah emitted to the accompaniment of a pervading and most unpleasant smell. Tom escaped, saddled and bridled Mulderrig, who seemed pleased to see his master, and took himself off to explore the area. . . And that was as much as he had been able to recall in any detail.

Friday morning passed in a blur of geese, meals, inspecting the small-holding and chopping firewood for the kitchen fire which was never allowed to go out. Somehow, he lived through the dragging hours that preceded Mary Emma's expected arrival; and when an approaching carriage-and-pair clattered, clopped and rattled over the hardened clay ruts of the road, Tom went out into the front garden to be ready to greet his love. He opened the carriage door and offered her his hand.

★

Chapter Twenty

Their fingers touched and a current flashed between them. The coach departed in the direction of Passendean as their eyes met. "I thought I'd lost you, Tom," Mary Emma said with a sweet gravity that made his heart beat faster. In both face and form she surpassed anything that he had imagined. Tall and graceful, with a becoming modesty that left him in no doubt as to her virtue, her slender rounded form in its narrow, clinging frock enchanted him. He could do nothing but gaze into eyes that had first captivated him when they had met as children in the flower garden of Lyndon Manor, eyes that he now saw deepen to a violet-blue as they gazed back into his own.

Mary Emma, dimly aware of the effect she'd had on him, made to withdraw her hand; not only was it firmly retained but she also found herself indecorously crushed to his breast in a fierce embrace. When at last she was able to breathe again, she stood on tip-toe and gave him a swift, welcoming peck on the cheek. In her innocence she was unprepared for Tom's reaction. To her embarrassment, he clasped her in his strong arms once again, this time kissing her full on the lips in a public place and in broad daylight.

"Oh, my darling, darling girl," he murmured against her hair. "It's been so desperately long. I thought I should never find you again; it seems like a miracle."

"Miracle or not, Tom, I think perhaps we should go into the house," Mary Emma said, softening her admonition with a mischievous smile. "We're drawing attention to ourselves."

"Eh?" Tom looked back and forth along the highway. "Oh! I'd completely forgotten — But let me look at you, Mary Emma." Her hands in his, he held her at arms' length. She appeared to endure his scrutiny with innocent pleasure. Her most arresting feature, Tom decided, was the loveliness of her head. He adored the soft curve of her neck, which fashionable upswept curls revealed as an intoxicating white column, above her firm, fichu-draped bosom. Dark curls fringing her high brow stirred in the evening breeze. He searched for traces of the pretty girl he'd left in the cornfield three years earlier. In the sweet and utterly feminine face before him Tom recognized only the shapely nose and the extraordinarily beautiful, dark-lashed blue eyes. The lips and cheeks were fuller than he remembered, the chin more determined. His pretty girl had grown into a beautiful woman who possessed the additional allure of purity and who was as yet, he guessed, unaware of the potency of her effect on the opposite sex. So much for her appearance, thought Tom; as to her personality. . .

Little Dovey Brook ran out of the front door, shouting excitedly: "Mary Emma's here!" Seeing Tom holding her favourite's hands, the little girl grew shy and came to a stop halfway between door and gate.

Wrenching her hands from Tom's grasp, Mary Emma slipped through the gate, crouched down and held her arms wide. Dovey hurtled along the few feet of pathway and threw herself into Mary Emma's waiting arms. Soon, both were whirling around in a twister, Dovey shrieking with delight and Mary Emma laughing in response.

How lovely she is, thought Tom. What a wonderful mother she'll make.

"Now run along, Dovey, and tell Mama that I'm home," Mary Emma said. "She's a little darling," she added, smiling up at him. "They're all such lovely children, Tom. And each one an individual with special qualities—"

"I'm glad you're fond of children, sweetheart," Tom said softly, kissing her on the cheek just before he stooped to enter the front door. "Pray God we'll be blessed with a brood of our own before long, Mary Emma," he whispered.

"Your face is all red," young John Brook proclaimed as they came in, and to Mary Emma's mortification all eyes turned to verify his comment.

Dulcie Brook understood it all in an instant. "Yew just keep a still tongue in yor head, young mester John," she said. "Folks 'ave eyes an don't need yew to point things out fer 'em. Take no notice of 'im, m' dear. Come along in an sit yerself down. I've made a pot 'o tea an it's just ready to pour. You'll 'ave a cup, Mr Challiss, sir?"

At this, Mary Emma looked so surprised that Tom had to explain himself all over again. "And so I'll not be Mrs Thomas Roberts, after all," she said wistfully. "I've practised writing it, over and over." She sighed. "What a dreadful waste of time, paper and ink. But I daresay I shall enjoy writing Mrs Thomas Challiss just as much."

"There's a sight more to marriage, young miss, than finnickin' wi' pen an' ink," Adam Brook said sternly.

"For 'Eaven's sake, Adie Brook!" his wife chided playfully as she folded freshly-dried laundry and placed it in a large wicker basket. "We all find that out soon enough and Miss Mary Emma won't be no diff'rent from the rest on us. Oh, no!" she continued without pausing to draw breath, "that Noah's stinkin' the place out agin. Yew'll 'ave ter fergive us, Mr Challiss. But we don't seem to 'ave no jurisdiction over our youngist. I dew beg yore pardon, sir. I'll take 'im out ter the barn an clean 'im up." But the frightful smell lingered long after Noah had been whisked away.

Mary Emma caught Tom's eye and smiled roguishly and they both knew she was recalling his remark about a large brood.

"Aye; an that's jist one o' the inconveniences young'uns bring with 'em," Adam said darkly. "Damned 'ard work, it is, rearin' young'uns; gimme clean 'ealthy animals any day. There aint no 'orrible smells wi' animals; jist good 'olesome manure."

Tom did his best to keep a straight face; but, in spite of his efforts, a huge guffaw loosed itself, to the consternation of Brook. "I beg your pardon, Adam," Tom said as he wiped away tears of mirth. "When did you last clean out a pig sty?"

Discomforted, Brook mumbled: "Well. . . ter be honest, I never did. Yew know what I mean though, Tom; cow's muck's an 'ealthy smell, natural-like—"

"—And baby Noah is nothing but a little animal, Mr Brook," Mary Emma surprised Tom by saying. "As soon as he's able to take care of himself—"

"—That's jest it! Over a year, 'e is, the young pup, an no sign of him takin' 'imself in 'and."

The subject of their conversation was brought in, all smiles and sweet-smelling once more. Mary Emma took him from his mother, gathered him to her and kissed his chubby face. "Are they being unkind to you, my darling," she said. The boy responded by clutching at her curls while dancing up and down on her lap.

"'Tis bedtime fer yew, my lovely," Dulcie Brook said, whisking her youngest from Mary Emma's arms. "And yew John, an' Ann; see ter Zeb an' Dovey. There's bread-an' milk in the kitchen, then orf ter bed wi' the lot o' yer."

Peace and quiet reigned when Burt Brook came in a short while later. His eyes lit up when they rested on Mary Emma. But when the youth noted her proximity to Mr Challiss his eyes clouded over, and after bidding them good-evening he took himself out to the kitchen to wash and eat and they saw no more of him that day.

Adam Brook bathed himself in the kitchen every Friday night without fail. While he scrubbed away a week's accumulation of dirt, Tom, Mary Emma and Mrs Dulcie Brook sat in the spacious all-purpose living room. Mrs Brook had a basket full of mending beside her chair and was busy repairing the ravages made among their scant wardrobe by her active brood. "Don't yew mind me, m' dears," she said as she stitched up rents and darned holes in socks. "I was young once meself and can be quite deaf when I choose to." Blind an all, if it comes to that, she thought, stitching away contentedly. To see a young couple so besotted with one another was as good as a play and she wouldn't have missed the opportunity for the world.

Seated a distance away from their hostess, Tom and Mary Emma expressed their thanks for her tolerance. Merely to be in each other's presence gave them unspeakable joy. That they might feel themselves free to flout convention into the bargain, with their chaperone's blessing, was tantamount to locking a greedy child into a sweetshop. At first, they observed strict decorum, keeping to a staid conversation carried on from opposite corners of the large settle on which they were seated.

From time to time Mrs Brook flicked a glance at the handsome young couple and was amused to see that the gap that had separated them had narrowed a good deal so that they now were close enough to hold hands. That's right, m' dears, she thought, with a quiet smile.

"You haven't told me why Miss Peters left you," Tom said. "Did she go to another post?" He was alarmed to see tears well up into Mary Emma's eyes, spill over and run unchecked down her cheeks. "Whatever have I said?"

"Nothing, nothing," she assured him. "It's nothing you've said or done, Tom." Still the tears streamed from her eyes. "I'm sorry," she said, as she dabbed at her eyes and nose. "I had thought I was over it; but the pain of losing dear Miss Peters is still so hard to bear." He waited for her to compose herself. "She's dead, Tom. Miss Peters, who was just like my own mother – as are you, Mrs Brook – died over a year ago."

Shocked, Tom said: "Dead? How?"

"Last summer she and I took a trip to the Yorkshire Dales," Mary Emma began. "It had been a cold spring and as soon as the weather grew milder Miss Peters suggested we needed a change. The air here at Welthrop is famous for its purity; but this part of Lincolnshire can become so dreary and monotonous in miserable weather. I'd had no word from you, Tom, and Miss Peters had urged me to prepare myself for the worst should news of your fortunes eventually find its way to us. Although we did our best to keep up our spirits we became despondent, myself especially so. Weeks of grey, damp and windy weather added to our depression. Miss Peters grew worried and feared for my health because I'd become so thin and pale. My employer, Lady Vyvyan, agreed with Miss Peters that the holiday would be beneficial to us both and I was immediately given a fortnight's leave from my duties. Lord Vyvyan, one of the kindest and most considerate of gentlemen whom one could wish to meet, would hear of no objection to his offer to meet all expenses, and bade us go and have as good a time as might be had with propriety by two single ladies."

As the tale unfolded, Tom had experienced a growing alarm at the disclosure of the threat to his beloved's physical well-being. "Why didn't you tell me before this that your health had been undermined?" he said with more severity than was intended.

"It would have served no purpose," Mary Emma returned. "There's scarcely been time for discussing the past, until now; apart from which I am, as you can see, fully recovered from my illness."

Another stab of fear. "What illness?"

She smiled and patted his hand. "Patience, dear Tom. Shall I go on?" Having been given leave to proceed by a curt nod, she continued: "We stayed at the seaside resort of Scarborough, chosen for us by Lord Vyvyan because of its good repute as being beneficial to invalids on account of its medicinal waters. He had taken a suite of rooms for us with a Mrs Todd, whose famous and comfortable boarding-house is situated a little way out of the town of Scarborough.

"When we arrived we were delighted with everything we saw and soon the sunshine and the bracing air began to work miracles on us both. We took carriage rides out onto the open moors and spent large parts of each day picnicking and walking, and sketching anything that took our fancy. We took early morning walks along the beach and I gathered specimens of marine life to show my little charges back at Passendean. The weather was mild; but scarcely warm enough for sea bathing, and soon a week of our little holiday had flown before we were aware of it."

Tom had relaxed a little yet was uncomfortably aware that there was something of a darker nature still to be told. "It sounds idyllic," he said. "And the second week?"

A frown marred Mary Emma's smooth forehead and her eyes became moist. "If only we had returned to Passendean at the end of that first week everything would have been perfect," she said, ending with a sigh. "We had no idea that our holiday was so soon to be cut short by life-threatening illness within a few days."

"Life-threatening?" Now he was thoroughly alarmed, and just as suddenly relieved when his eyes reiterated what she herself had told him: that she was fully recovered from whatever ordeal she had undergone. In his agitation he had moved dangerously near to Mary Emma so that there was no gap between them at all.

"Excuse me, m'dears," Mrs Brook said in the lull in the conversation; "I must be orf ter bed or I'll be fit fer nothin come mornin." Gathering her mending together she piled it into her basket. "I'll leave yew tew ter see yerselves to yer beds. I know I can trust yew, Mr Challiss, ter mind that nothin untoward occurs under Mr Brook's roof." Her eyes left him in no doubt as to what she meant; but to make doubly sure she added in a confidential whisper: "I daresay yew an Miss Kay'll want ter discuss the callin o' the sibbits so that yer can be married as quickly as time allows when yer git back ter yer place in Norfolk, sir. Good-night ter yer both, an Gord Bless."

"Sibbits?"

Mrs Brook had reached the door and turned around with a smile. "The marriage banns, sir."

"Oh, yes; the marriage banns. Good-night to you, Mrs Brook. Sleep well."

"That I always dew, Mr Challiss, sir. Yew'll not be long follerin me Miss Kay?"

"No, no," Mary Emma assured her. "Good-night, Dulcie."

When they were alone Tom took a folded paper from his breast pocket and unfolding it, held it out for Mary Emma to examine in the light shed from a nearby lamp.

"Tom! A special licence!" she exclaimed, to his delight throwing herself into his arms and recoiling in confusion as soon as she realised what she'd done. "How did you get it so soon?"

"Very simply. I stopped off at Lincoln on my way to Welthrop and was fortunate enough to gain access to the Bishop's Palace where I met the bishop himself in the garden. He had the goodness to hear me and granted me the licence within a few hours."

"So there'll be no need to wait three weeks for the calling of the banns?"

"No, sweetheart. We might be married tomorrow, if we chose to." Tom appeared to be becoming agitated as he produced a small leather-covered box. He surprised her further by leaving his seat and sinking to one knee directly in front of her before clearing his throat. "Dearest Mary Emma, first and most importantly, I hope you can find it in your heart to overlook the difference in our station."

"Oh, Tom," she said impatiently, seizing his free hand and covering it with kisses while her mischievous eyes met his. "Do get on with it, dear."

Encouraged, he smiled up at her, cleared his throat once more and, suddenly becoming grave, folded her left hand between both his own. "My dear Miss Kay, will you do me the honour – the very great honour – of accepting this ring as a token of my esteem and affection and with it the sincere hope that you will, at some time in the very near future, consent to become my wife."

Mary Emma preserved her decorum while Tom made his little speech; but with the best will in the world a smile lit up her face at its conclusion. "Yes, yes, yes!" she cried, jumping to her feet. "A thousand times yes, dearest Tom." He opened the box, took out a ring and slid it onto the fourth finger of her left hand. She stretched her left arm its full length and held the yellowish cluster of stones beneath the lamp's beam. "What a beautiful little flower, Tom," she said, pulling his head down to kiss him on the mouth. "You must have had it made especially for me," she said as they drew apart. "I love it; it's like a little lime flower. What kind of stones are they?"

He seized her in his arms and cupped her chin in is hand. "Yellow diamonds, Mary Emma, darling." And that's all you need to know, he thought, as his mouth fastened on hers with such a searching ferocity that she swooned against him just as, after a prolonged rattling of the handle, the door opened.

"–Ah! me dears! I thought yew was a long time comin' upstairs." Mrs Brook playfully wagged a finger at them. "So – 'ave yer talked it all over? When's the 'appy day ter be?"

Tom smiled broadly. "Miss Kay has graciously consented to become my wife, Mrs Brook. But there'll be no need of sibbits because I have a special licence with me that I applied for and obtained at Lincoln. We are to be married within the week."

"Well, I congracherlate yer both with all me heart; but yer must git orf ter yer beds at once or Brook'll be down 'ere in 'is nightgown and a bad temper ter see what the rumpus's all about."

As if she had returned from a distant planet, Mary Emma murmured: "In one short week I shall be Mrs Thomas Roberts Challiss – and mistress of Uppham House. I can hardly believe it. It doesn't seem real."

Yew'll be brought down t'earth before long, me girl; time'll take care o' that, thought Dulcie Brook with a twinge of pity as she lowered the wick of the lamp before blowing it out.

Tom had trouble sleeping and could scarcely endure the imprint Mary Emma's soft pliant body had left on his own. Only after he had been lying awake for an hour or more did it occur to him that he'd not yet learned the fate of Jane Peters. The tête-a-tête had shot off on a tangent completely beyond their control once Mrs Brook and her mending basket had left them. Thankfully, no more than a week divided him from his eager bride-to-be and there was much to be seen to in the interval.

★

Saturday and Sunday passed in a flurry of excited talk in which Tom had learned that Miss Peters had succumbed to complications arising from scarlatina. She and Mary Emma had developed a fever, followed by sore throats and furred tongues. Initially the doctor had diagnosed tonsillitis: but when an outbreak of scarlatina in the area became public knowledge the physician revised his opinion even though, he told their worried hostess Mrs Todd, scarlatina was a rarity among adults. After the disease had run its course and both women were pronounced out of danger, Miss Peters had relapsed; she had developed rheumatic fever followed by pneumonia, which had proved fatal. Tears had been shed in the telling and Tom realised, as never before, how closely linked the lives of the governess and her charge had been. He found himself wondering whether there had been any truth in Lambert Jardine's sneering comments about Mary Emma being the offspring of a liaison between the plain-faced governess and old Josiah Kay. And then, impatiently, he told himself that none of it mattered now; for it didn't explain, to his satisfaction, Mary Emma's beauty of form and face, her innate grace and well-bred yet high-spirited demeanour.

All too soon, it seemed to the lovers, Monday morning came and with it a dense fog. Nevertheless, the Passendean carriage arrived on time; but, unusually, the coachman alighted and, bearing a note in his hand, came up to the door of the house. Mary Emma, seeing that the note was addressed to herself, looked her surprise as she thanked the man and broke the seal. "If you'll step inside, Jenks, I'm sure Mrs Brook will see that you're given something hot to drink after your drive through this fen fog. Agnes," she called, "please take Jenks through to the scullery and ask your mother if he might be given a hot drink. I need to speak to Mr Challiss before I leave for Passendean. I don't suppose it'll take me more than ten minutes."

Tom was hunched over the kitchen table writing as Mary Emma came in and planted a swift kiss on the nape of his neck. "Read that," she said complacently, dropping the note and skipping out of his reach as he made to grab her around the waist.

He did as he was bid and, having read its contents, looked up in amazement. "What? Lord and Lady Vyvyan want us to be married from Passendean?" He threw the note onto the scrubbed tabletop, scraped back his chair and faced her. "Impossible!"

"But I don't see why?"

"You must see that we cannot offend the Brooks by complying," Tom said. "It will look as if we prefer the grand Vyvyans to them! I, for one, can't – won't do it."

"What's this?" Mrs Brook came in carrying Noah. "Hot words so soon, m'dears?"

Scenting the aroma of milkiness and boiled nether garments that Noah exuded wherever he happened to alight, Tom wondered if he himself would ever become inured to that peculiar blend of nursery smells; and whether it made any difference to the unwary recipient if those horrendous stenches, which Noah seemed to produce with startling regularity, were emitted by one's own offspring. Would they, could they possibly be more bearable then?

Mary Emma had shown Mrs Brook the note without offering her a word of explanation. Dulcie settled Noah into his cot, stood up and took Mary Emma's hands in hers. "Why, of course, yew must go, my lovey. Yew'm always said 'ow kind 'is lordship is, an 'ow pleasant her ladyship can be. Why! 'Tis wonderful, really. A great honour they're doin' yer. My, though! I'm glad 'tis yew 'avin ter sit down an eat wi' sich fine folk. 'Twouldn't do fer me; I wouldn' be able ter swaller so much as a crumb fer fear o' chokin'. Think no more about it, m'dear. O' course yer must go!"

"What will Adam have to say about it, Mrs Brook?" Tom asked.

"Yew leave Mr Brook ter me, Mr Challiss. 'E won't like it, I don't deny; but 'e shall be brought ter see sense by persuasion an' argument. That's a battle 'e knows 'e can never win. And, when it comes down tew it, he'll come to agree wi' me that it's too fine a chance ter miss – one that comes ter folk but once in a lifetime."

All objections to the project apparently removed, Mary Emma kissed Dulcie Brook on her unlined cheek and said: "I don't know what I've ever done to deserve such kindness, Dulcie. But, didn't you understand? We're to ask any friends we like to the wedding breakfast. Do say you'll come. It won't be anything without you and Mr Brook and the children—"

"Perhaps a neighbour could be found to look after Noah for the few hours that—"

"Tom! How could you suggest such a thing?" Blue sparks seemed to fly from Mary Emma's eyes. "Of course: the whole Brook family must be present. It just wouldn't be the same without little Noah."

Mrs Brook was laughing uncontrollably. "Lor' bless yer, Miss Kay," she managed at last. "Jist imagine those grand lofty rooms at Passendean that I've 'eard about echoin' with Noah's blarrin, not ter mention worse tricks 'e 'as 'idden. Don't yew fret yerself, Mr Challiss, sir. Me sister Alice jist loves 'im ter bits. She'll 'ave 'im fer the day, no worry. That is," she glanced from one to the other, "if you're really serious about the whole family, barrin' Noah, blightin the gates o' Passendean?"

Much relieved by the knowledge that the sleeping sulphur bomb would be excluded, Tom expressed his hope that Mr and Mrs Brook would give them the pleasure of helping to make their wedding day additionally memorable.

"We shall 'ave ter see what Mr Brook 'as ter say about it. Our Burt will let yer know first thing termorrer." Mrs Brook had started to collect the ingredients and utensils for breadmaking as her four young ones trooped in to take their places around the large table in readiness for their lessons with Agnes.

"I shall be late!" Mary Emma exclaimed, having completely forgotten that Jenks was waiting to take her to Passendean. Snatching a wrap and bonnet from the pegs just inside the front door, she kissed Mrs Brook, allowed Tom a peck on the cheek, and ran out to the waiting carriage.

Tom heard it rumble away, picked up his list and took himself out into the garden to try to order his thoughts.

★

Adam Brook had hummed and hah-ed but had finally given in, as Dulcie Brook had expected he would. He had accepted the invitation to Passendean with the proviso that Burton obtain permission to show his father around the garden and grounds.

There had been no time in which to order a newly-tailored suit of clothes for himself so Tom had purchased an unclaimed outfit which was sufficiently fashionable not to disgrace himself or his bride; but he had insisted that Mary Emma's trousseau should be of the finest Lincolnshire had to offer. That being of a fairly modest nature, Lady Vyvyan had insisted that her *protegé* accept some of her own unworn finery until proper provision could be made to provide the items essential to a lady's wardrobe. Perhaps a visit to London or Paris in the weeks following the marriage could supply any deficiency, the noble lady suggested. When Tom heard this it alarmed him. Once they were settled at Uppham he had no plans to travel anywhere for a very long time, if ever. "I suppose a trip to London might be managed during the winter months," he murmured to himself, doubtfully; but such an excursion had not figured in his immediate plans. Further cogitation soon brought the unpleasant realisation that his own wishes and desires would have to take their turn – even give way – to those of Mary Emma's; no longer would he be free to please himself but must discuss everything. Defer? He frowned as this idea sank in. Not very likely. No! Never! He would be master in his own house. What a huge step marriage is, he thought; my life will be altered irrevocably once we are wed. That Mary Emma truly loves me and will be a warm and generous wife I have no doubt; but to give up the freedom to please myself in all matters is truly sobering. Chafing at the thought of the matrimonial bond and what it represented – himself as a willing victim, his loss of a liberty that seemed to him all the more precious now that it would soon be lost for ever, reminded him of his brother's attitude to dealings with the opposite sex: his lack of emotional involvement. Yet, hadn't George confessed that he did love Garnet Brown? Why, at this very moment he was seeking her out with a view to marriage! Of course, his brother was more experienced with women, more mature . . .

Tom wondered if he were not too young to be hobbled for life with a wife to support . . . and babies would surely come! Ah, dear God! Noah. The stink of that child – for over a year his home had been filled with the stench of rotten eggs; and he the *eighth* of Adam Brook's brood. As for his bawling, it was enough to send any sane man mad. Would he himself be able to stand it, day in day out, year after year? Had he made a terrible mistake in having agreed to resign himself to the huge responsibilties the marriage vows would demand of him?

★

Chapter Twenty-one

The days leading to the wedding ceremony had passed in a frenzy of activity that had left everybody exhausted. Mary Emma, Agnes and her sisters had seemed to be smothered by silks, satins and lace on the few occasions Tom had glimpsed them and a parade of dressmakers, seamstresses and shoemakers came and went at all hours. Yet once everything had been made ready for the great day tiredness had vanished and spirits soared. Tom's sole contribution to the proceedings had been accomplished in a single day's ride to Gainsborough and back to select and purchase their wedding rings. Increasingly feeling something of a spare cog in an efficiently whirling machine, he had saddled Mulderrig and escaped from the frenetic activity that appeared to fill even the vastness of Passendean and had ridden over to Welthrop to the comparative calm to be found among the Brook family.

They had been conversing a little while when Tom's innocent remark concerning the lavish kindess bestowed on himself and Mary Emma by Lord and Lady Vyvyan seemed to react on Brook's temper as if salt had been rubbed into an open wound. His eyes flashed and he growled: "'Tis easy enough fer folks wi' cartloads o' money ter whip everybody inter doin' their biddin' in double-quick time." Dulcie had replied calmly: " 'Tain only the money, Adie; Lord an Lady Vyvyan know how to pull the right strings, an all. I won't 'ave yew criticizin' 'em. Why, they could'na done more fer Miss Kay if she was their own child." Adam had flung himself sulkily into a chair and allowed himself a grudging: "Aye. S'pose so."

As he jogged Mulderrig back to Passendean through the hazy golden afternoon Tom had to admit that Adam Brook was right. The possession of a fortune brought privilege, deference and servility in its wake; but Tom would rather do without those appendages. He firmly believed that wealth carried obligation towards the needy. The trick to using a fortune wisely was to try to treat others as one would wish to be treated; to use it to do good by stealth while leaving the capital untouched.

Absence from Mary Emma's company during the day was irksome; but it had the effect of putting into perspective his urgent need to be joined to her in marriage. To sit down in her presence and dine formally in the august company of Lord and Lady Vyvyan was an exquisite form of torture and when the wedding day dawned he went into the chapel not only an eager bridegroom but also a willing victim.

The ceremony over, Tom slid the little gold ring onto the fourth finger of Mary Emma's left hand, so supple and white, and seeming to him no bigger than a child's. The minister blessed them, reminded them of the solemnity of the vows they had taken and declared them man and wife. She lifted back the Honiton lace veil and the radiance that shone from her face was like the sun coming out from behind a cloud. Their eyes met in mingled joy as Tom stooped to kiss her lips. He stepped back, smiled at her and the love that blazed from her eyes took his breath away.

Agnes Brook, conscious of her responsibilities as chief bridesmaid, gravely stood by in readiness to restore the bride's posy to her as the newly-weds turned to leave Passendean's private chapel. The three younger Brook sisters, ten-year-old Ann, seven-year-old Fanny and five-year-old Dovey, also bridesmaids, were transformed by their apparel: cream silk frocks tied with blue satin sashes with blue satin slippers on their feet. Though of less importance than their older sister they enhanced the procession from altar to chapel door and drew from the assembled guests appreciative glances and kind remarks as they followed the bridal pair along the aisle. Tom seemed to be floating on air; everything seemed unreal. He had the odd sensation of watching himself and Mary Emma, her hand resting lightly upon the crook of his arm, progressing along the length of blue carpet. All doubts about the rightness of their marriage had flown; he felt that with Mary Emma to share his life all difficulties would be overcome somehow. Proud of his lovely young wife, he vowed never to forget the solemn moment when he had placed the gold band on her finger and made her his own.

As the procession emerged from the chapel porch a peal of bells rang out from the small cat's-eared tower that rose beside the chapel. Ann, Fanny and Dovey Brook, themselves once more, ran ahead of the bridal couple in boisterous enjoyment as they strewed flower petals along the gravel path that led from chapel to mansion. Laughing, cavorting, they tossed up handfuls of petals into the autumn sunshine.

Lord and Lady Vyvyan had spared no expense in their efforts to make Mary Emma's wedding day a happy and memorable one and, although the number of guests was modest by comparison with the thronged celebrations usually held under Passendean's vast roof, by using the second dining-room and only one or two of the smaller salons the guests were less overawed than they would have been had the most splendid reception rooms been used.

The wedding breakfast had been set in the yellow dining-room, and the lofty walls picked out in white and gold filigree gave the guests, who were used to taking their meals in humbler and less formal conditions, a feeling of breaking their fast in a cathedral on Sunday rather than at a wedding feast. The meal was served by impressively bewigged footmen dressed in a livery of yellow satin and lace ruffles, half-hose white silk stockings and black patent pumps. However ordinary and well-disposed to their fellow men the tall, handsome young men might be when in their bath tubs, they struck Tom and Mr and Mrs Brook and their family as alien and disdainful. Their intimidating presence, as they haughtily glided about serving the awestruck guests, ensured an oppressive silence. Lord and Lady Vyvyan, dismayed, saw that the villagers were subdued by this unaccustomed formality. That hadn't been their intention at all. The host beckoned his head footman over and quietly dismissed him and his team from the room. When the last manservant had left, and after the massive doors had been closed in oiled silence by him, Lord Vyvyan spoke.

"Welcome, friends, on this happiest of days," he said in a pleasantly unaffected voice, which came as a surprise to Tom after the mangled vowels of Lord Belmaine and his even less intelligible son. "Everything we need is before us so we'll manage well enough by serving ourselves. I believe," he said, his eyes twinkling as he looked around the table, "that our glasses are suitably charged—" by which he meant that the children had been served pink lemonade. "Therefore, I propose a toast." He raised his wineglass and inclined his head in the direction of Mary Emma and Tom and waited for his guests to follow suit. "To the bride and bridegroom: long life, health and happiness!" The atmosphere thawed noticeably as a cheerful chorus of voices – high, shrill, low and soft – echoed the toast. The children guzzled their lemonade until the crystal goblets were drained and then broke into natural and animated chatter. Mary Emma smiled and whispered to Tom: "You see? Aren't they lovely people?"

Seeing that Lady Vyvyan's eye was upon them Tom merely said: "Yes; indeed they are," and raised his glass in salute. "Might I return the toast, my lord?" Receiving a smile followed by a nod of assent, Tom waited while the goblets were refilled and then said: "To our most generous hosts, Lord and Lady Vyvyan, who have made this day such a splendid success. Three cheers!" Each cheer was louder than the one before and as the last died away young

Zeb complained in his penetrating treble: "Ma, I'm hungry. Are we allowed tew eat any of this food; or ain it fer us?" Which destroyed the very last particle of reserve as everybody laughed good-naturedly and Lord Vyvyan implored them to help themselves before the covered dishes cooled. When he was an old man, Zebulun Brook would earn himself many a free pint of ale by recounting the tale, which his contemporaries never tired of hearing, of the wedding feast that took place at the great house of Passendean in the autumn of 1815 where he and his family had sat down with a real lord and his lady and dined off the best bone china and eaten indescribable but delicious vittles with solid silver cutlery and drunk from the finest crystal goblets.

It seemed like a dream to the Brook family when they heard musicians tuning up in the adjacent room and, after a short silence, wonderful harmonies and sweet melodies wafting their way. Begging to be allowed to leave the table, the Brook children stole up to listen at the closed door of the room in which the men were playing. Lady Vyvyan had followed them with her own children in tow and whispered: "Open the door and go in: they're playing for you." Their eyes huge at such an idea, they looked up at Lady Vyvyan with suppressed excitement. When John pushed the door inwards, looked round at his siblings decisively and crept into the music salon, they followed him. Everything was so beautiful; it was if they were living in one of Agnes's fairy tales. The other adults drifted in as the musicians struck up a country dance simple enough to allow even three-year-old Zeb to join in. The hours whirled away. Dovey disappeared and was discovered sound asleep on a brocaded sofa; which prompted Mrs Brook to announce that "'twas time they was orf 'ome to their beds."

When the Brook family left they took much of the celebratory sparkle with them and only politeness prevented Tom from spiriting Mary Emma away to the suite of rooms that had been allocated to them for the consummation of their marriage. It seemed to Tom that, well-meaning though Lord and Lady Vyvyan indubitably were, they were constrained to conduct each and every detail of everyday life with undue ceremony. It simply would not occur to them to leave Tom and his bride to themselves; but they must see to it that servants were on hand to pander to every whim.

"I shall send you Woodruff. She will prepare you for your marriage bed, Mary Emma," Lady Vyvyan told her. "She is very experienced in such matters and attended me on my own first night." They were seated together at one end of the music salon out of earshot of their husbands. She lowered her voice, nevertheless, and taking Mary Emma's hand in hers, said kindly: "Forgive my speaking to you on such an intimate subject, my dear; but, as you have no mother to advise you, I feel it incumbent upon me." She avoided the girl's eyes. "I just want to say that you have absolutely nothing to fear, you know. Everything that is to take place tonight is perfectly natural. But you mustn't appear too eager; your husband would deem such behaviour coarse and unseemly. Er – Be guided entirely by his wishes. That really is all there is to it. One soon becomes accustomed to a husband's demands, my dear, and learns to obey almost willingly after a while." She patted Mary Emma's hand, looked the length of the room to where Lord Vyvyan was in deep conversation with Tom and lapsed into silence, for which Mary Emma was profoundly grateful.

"Thank you, Lady Vyvyan," Mary Emma said softly, her face scarlet, recalling that Dulcie Brook had given her quite different advice one evening the week before.

"I've seen 'ow yew are with yer Mr Challiss and yew an 'e 'ave nothing ter worry about, lovey. Yew'm both that eager ter mate that yewm certain to be a mother nine months later, mark my words." They had been engaged in folding bedsheets in the time-honoured fashion and as they folded the sheet into ever smaller rectangles drew nearer one another. "An don' yew 'av no truck wi' them wet-nurses; yew feed yer own babby at the breast until his first teeth begins ter nip; then 'tis time enough ter wean him. Reckon yew'll 'ave a parcel of 'em, or I'm no judge; yew both bein so besotted an Mr Challiss such a fine, lusty specimen of a man." As she'd been about to place the neatly-folded sheet in the wicker laundry basket, she'd paused, wrapped her bare brown forearms in the sweet-smelling snowy linen, and her expression had softened. "Yew an me're both lucky, Miss Kay; a lovin' and regular man in a woman's bed's worth all the drudgin' that young'uns bring. Not that yew'll 'ave ter worry about that – I dessay," Dulcie had sniffed. "Yew'll 'ave some other woman ter do the rough work, yew bein' born an brung up a lady."

Woodruff appeared in the music salon. "Everything's been made ready, as you directed, Lady Vyvyan," the servant said deferentially. "Is Mrs Challiss ready to come up, ma'am?"

"Yes, thank you, Woodruff." Lady Vyvyan squeezed Mary Emma's hand. "Now. Off with you to bed. I shall pray for you, my dear," were her hardly comforting words.

Mary Emma was conscious of Tom's head turned in her direction as she and Lady Vyvyan's personal maid left the room and wished herself miles away from the formalities of Passendean.

★

The luxuriously-curtained four-poster was enormous. Mary Emma had climbed aboard by means of a small flight of stairs and now sat with her arms clasped about her knees waiting for Tom. By pretending to herself that the indignities inflicted on her person were being performed upon somebody else she had weathered the ordeal of a ritual preparation for marriage as deemed necessary by the edicts of some women in high society, especially those drawn to the exotic, as was Lady Vyvyan. First her perfectly clean body had been immersed in a bath of warm water perfumed with attar of roses. Mercifully, she had been asked to lie face down on a dais in the commodious dressing room that adjoined the main bedchamber, and had burrowed her flaming face into the Turkish towel on which she lay completely naked. A wonderful sensation had pervaded her body as something warm and emollient had been massaged into her skin and she hadn't suffered the slightest embarrassment by the time Woodruff asked her to turn over so that the rest of her body could be anointed in the same way. A loose garment made of finest white silk had caressed her satin skin, her waist-length black hair had been brushed until it crackled, her finger- and toenails had been filed, prodded and polished and finally Woodruff had stood back to survey the effect her arts had had on Mary Emma's appearance.

All reserve banished, Mary Emma asked with a mischievous smile: "Will I do?"

For answer, Woodruff led her over to a pier glass and said: "See for yourself, ma'am." Mary Emma was astonished at her own reflection; she looked, while not painted in any way, enhanced, quite unlike her everyday self. "Thank you, Woodruff," she murmured. "I think you have done wonders."

Usually staid to the point of unapproachability to any but her aristocratic mistress, Woodruff remarked: "One does not create wonders, Mrs Challiss, ma'am. One works from the material one is given and you are of the finest. You are, indeed, the loveliest bride I have ever prepared in this way," she added effusively. Recollecting herself, she added: "Will there be anything else, ma'am?"

"Thank you, no, Woodruff. That will be all."

"Oh! One more thing, Mrs Challiss, ma'am. Her ladyship has given instructions that you and Mr Challiss are to have breakfast sent up tomorrow morning."

"How very kind of Lady Vyvyan."

"Her ladyship gave me instructions to ask if there was anything special you or Mr Challiss would wish to be prepared."

"No, no," Mary Emma said, wishing the woman would leave her, "nothing."

"Very good, ma'am. At what time would you care for breakfast to be brought, ma'am?" Woodruff asked impassively.

Mary Emma's patience was becoming strained. And yet... "I should think nine o'clock would be suitable, Woodruff. Please convey my thanks to Lady Vyvyan for her many kindnesses. Thank you."

"I shall, ma'am. Good-night." The two doors closed as Woodruff made her way out of the suite and Mary Emma relaxed... Tom! Tom! Where are you, my love?

The door opened and he entered. The door closed. The robe Uncle d'Escalles had given him slid to the floor and he stood naked before her in the lamplight. "My dearest, darling love!" he said as he threw himself onto the bed and kissed her with a passion that ignited her own. Her shift was off, he in bed, she in his arms and married – at ten o'clock – at one o'clock – at four o'clock. By dawn they were well and truly married and fell asleep in each other's arms.

★

When Tom and Mary Emma made their appearance next morning Lady Vyvyan was shocked to observe the new Mrs Challiss's incandescence. "Positively unseemly," she whispered to her lord. "And have you noticed how often they touch one another?"

"I see no wrong in her. She's a fine-looking young woman in love with her husband, Eleanor," he said. "One must make allowances, my dear. It takes some women that way on their marriage night." At which implied criticism of herself his affronted wife shot him a reproachful look.

By the time luncheon was served, Lady Vyvyan had regained her good humour and said to Mary Emma: "We are all going to miss you so much, my dear. It really is too bad of you to have taken such a hold on our hearts only to abandon us in favour of Mr Challiss. You do realise that now I shall be put to the dreadful inconvenience of advertising for a new governess?"

"I'm sorry, Lady Vyvyan," Mary Emma said. "But I have given the matter some thought. What did you think of Agnes Brook? Although she isn't a lady by birth, she's softly-spoken, has very nice manners and is a born teacher of young children."

Lord Vyvyan interrupted them. "I'm sure she is a very amiable young girl; but I'm afraid that I could not consider a farmer's daughter a suitable person, one to whom I could entrust the care of my children."

Mary Emma staved off Tom's evident wrath with a look. "Well, my lord," she said gravely, "I sincerely hope you will be as fortunate in your eventual choice; for in dismissing Agnes Brook on account of her birth you are depriving your children of a wonderful, loving girl who would bring them nothing but happiness as well as a love of learning."

Lady Vyvyan was not pleased at the turn the conversation had taken and said to her husband: "I should not have raised the subject while we are at luncheon. I beg your pardon, my lord."

Tom held his tongue, with difficulty.

"There is no need for an apology, my dear," Lord Vyvyan said to his wife. "I meant no disrespect to Miss Brook; she is not responsible for her station in life. It is an unfortunate fact." He addressed Mary Emma. "I have no doubt that Miss Brook possesses all the admirable qualities that you attribute to her, my dear; but you must surely agree that she just won't do as a governess for my children."

To Lady Vyvyan's surprise, Mary Emma said quietly: "But I cannnot agree with you, Lord Vyvyan. I'm sorry to contradict you; but if you were only willing to give Agnes a trial—"

"Now, that will do!" Lady Vyvyan said to her sharply. "You forget yourself, Mrs Challiss."

As Tom was about to speak in defence of his wife as well as of Agnes Brook, Lord Vyvyan forestalled him. "The very fact that you hold the young lady in such high esteem is a recommendation in itself, my dear Mrs Challiss." He toyed with a piece of cheese before abruptly pushing it aside. "What do you think, Eleanor?"

"I? It has nothing to do with me, has it, Charles?" Lady Vyvyan was visibly displeased at being drawn into the discussion of the suitablility of Agnes Brook for the post of governess to her husband's children. Her part in the hiring of governesses ended with the writing of the advertisements.

"You misunderstand me, my dear," Vyvyan said, his voice laden with forebearance. "Do you agree with me that we should give this girl – Miss Brook – a trial?"

"Oh! Is that what you meant? It hardly matters to me one way or the other, my lord. The final word in these matters is yours, of course; but the girl did impress me as possessing a natural fastidiousness and good taste. Of course, her speech—"

"—is grammatical and melodious," Tom heard himself say. "Naturally, she will be bound to utter the occasional word or phrase in her native dialect; but where's the harm in that?"

Lady Vyvyan bestowed on him a pitying look. "The harm, my dear sir, is that our children will begin to sound like village hobbledehoys, and that is unthinkable."

Furious with her, Tom threw down his napkin and stood up. "If you will excuse me, madam" he said, "I feel in need of fresh air. Might I take a turn in your flower garden, sir?"

Lord Vyvyan was on his feet. "By all means, sir; I'll accompany you if I may. Please excuse us, ladies."

To say that Lady Vyvyan was discomposed by the turn of events would not be too strong a word. "Well!" she said. "I cannot think what has got into Charles."

"I think he is inclined to give Agnes Brook a trial as governess, dear Lady Vyvyan, and that he looks to you to support him in his experiment."

Eleanor Vyvyan looked astonished. "Do you, really? Of course, it really is none of my affair; but if you think I can do any good—"

Mary Emma jumped up, ran round the table and caught hold of Lady Vyvyan's bejewelled hand. "Oh! But you can, my dear friend. I promise you. You will be assisting Lord Vyvyan to make a wise decision. There are naturally refined females in all classes and Agnes Brook is one of them. She is a sweet, intelligent girl and just at the age to be moulded for a position in higher society. With your help she would be the governess you desire her to be in no time. Oh! Lady Vyvyan; do say you'll give Agnes a chance to prove herself."

It was soon settled. Agnes Brook took Mary Emma's place as governess at Passendean and after a somewhat shaky start became a permanent fixture there.

The last day of the young couple's sojourn at Passendean arrived and it had been arranged by their hosts that a carriage should convey them and their belongings, which included a number of expensive wedding gifts from Lord and Lady Vyvyan, to Welthrop. Tom had arranged through Burton Brook for a covered carriage and driver to be hired on his behalf and had given Adam Brook's address as the starting point for the long journey back to Uppham. Tom and Mary Emma made their farewells to Lord and Lady Vyvyan who begged them to write often, all differences between the four having been forgotten, and they set off on the short drive to Welthrop.

It was a relief to see the hired carriage waiting for them as they drew up outside the Brook's rambling house and their boxes and packages were unloaded. As the splendid carriage departed to return to Passendean, the driver of the workaday clarence turned from adjusting his team's feeding bags to introduce himself. He was a strong-looking man of perhaps thirty-five years and about Tom's height, who wore an open-faced expression. "Name of Ollander, sir," he said, touching the rosette which adorned his low-crowned beaver before holding out his hand to Tom.

Surprised by the forward gesture, Tom, nevertheless, shook the man's hand and said: "Thomas Challiss. Glad to meet you, Mr Ollander. I trust you and your team are in good fettle for the journey?"

"We are, Mr Challiss, sir," Ollander affirmed cheerfully, "and raring to be off."

"My wife and I have to make our farewells to the family within and we'll be as much as half-an-hour. I hope that'll not inconvenience you?"

"Not at all, Mr Challiss. I charge by the hour. After all, you're the one who's paying for my time so who am I to grumble? If you don't mind, sir, madam," he acknowledged Mary Emma with a slight bow from the waist, "I'll sit myself down and eat my picnic while you're within; then I shall be as fit for the job as my horses are."

Now here's an unusual man, thought Tom, as he made an elbow for Mary Emma. She was obviously of the same opinion for, once out of earshot, she remarked: "What a very pleasant man Mr Ollander seems, Tom; not at all what I should have expected a carriage-driver to be. For one thing, there's nothing servile in his manner, for which I'm thankful. And another thing: I liked the way he offered his hand to you just as if he were your equal."

"You noticed that? I must confess that after being deferred to at Passendean I was momentarily affronted by his audacity," Tom laughed. "To think that I, who am most likely from a humbler background that Ollander's, should have so soon forgotten that all men are created equal and that it's usually only a question of money or property that sets some of us apart." They had been spotted by Fanny Brook who came running out of the front door to greet them. The little girl placed her hand in Mary Emma's and dragged her into the house. "Come and see!" she cried. "Spindle's had kittens. There's five and Ma says I can have one for me own." She picked up one of the blind kittens and stroked it. "They were born while we were at Passendean and Pa says Spindle's a sly old puss."

"Have you thought of a name for it, Fanny?" queried Mary Emma as she stroked the kitten very gently. Before the girl had time to reply the whole of the Brook family, except Burton and Agnes, were upon them and Mrs Brook had difficulty in making herself heard.

"Oh! Be quiet, all of yew, dew! I can't hear meself think!" The children were quelled and the only voices to be heard now were those of Tom and Adam, who were so deeply engaged in their own conversation that they hadn't heard Dulcie's protest.

Though Tom tried to persuade Adam Brook to give him the answer he desired concerning the position of Head Gardener and Farm Manager at Uppham the older man remained obdurate. Brook merely repeated his promise to give the matter some thought and to let Tom know his decision within a month, as previously agreed.

Dulcie plied them with refreshments for the journey and fitted in as much gossip as time allowed, ending with: "Now that Agnes is gorn, I've made arrangements fer all the young-uns to attend the Methody Sundey School so that they don't fall be'ind wi' their book-larnin," while following Tom and Mary Emma up the garden path. As the two women exchanged kisses, Mary Emma whispered: "I think you're an excellent judge of newly-married couples, Dulcie." And Adam and Tom wondered what on earth could have been said between their respective wives that had sent Mrs Brook into such a paroxysm of laughter. Wiping her streaming eyes she called after them: "I'll keep me eyes open fer the stork near the end o' June next year, then."

All their good-byes said and the last kisses exchanged between Mary Emma and Ann, Fanny and Dovey, the closed carriage rolled away with Mary Emma inside it and their belongings safely deposited on the seat opposite her, with Tom riding alongside on Mulderrig. They had travelled less than ten miles and were passing through desolate fenland when a screaming blustery wind sprang up out of nowhere. It tore the yellow autumn leaves from their twigs and whirled them up into the air; it battered the grasses and sedges and it buffetted the clarence so that the horses grew restless as they lowered their heads to battle their way across the flat landscape. Ollander reined them in, climbed down from the box and spoke to Tom. "We're in for a blow," he told him, eyeing the horizon anxiously. "In the fens it's serious. We must make for cover."

"A blow?"

Wondering why the carriage had stopped, Mary Emma poked her head out of the window, got a speck in her eye and with the other eye saw that the sky had darkened alarmingly. "What is it?" she cried into the fierce wind and a mouthful of grit and dust was blown into her open mouth which caused her to splutter and choke.

"See that?" Ollander's indicated a dark cloud that was sweeping towards them. "We'll be caught up in the middle of it unless we can find shelter at once."

"This way!" Tom shouted, pointing with an outstretched arm to a lane as his hat was torn off his head, swept over a hedge into the turbulence and carried away out of sight. "It looks as if it leads to a farm. I'll go on ahead." His hair tousled by playful airy fingers, he galloped off as the late autumn day darkened further until it seemed more like a bad day in midwinter. They heard Tom galloping back, watched him turn Mulderrig to face the way he'd just come and saw that he was gesturing for them to follow. Ollander, a scarf now wound about his nose and mouth, his eyes screwed into slits, climbed back onto the box, turned the skittish horses into the lane with consummate skill and set them galloping after Mulderrig, forgetful of Mary Emma's being rattled about inside the carriage like a single pill in a vast pillbox.

In the increasing gloom they made out the figure of a woman waving her arms about to attract their attention as she stood beside the open doors of a large threshing barn; she too had her head well wrapped-up against the wind and the increasing amount of detritus borne on it. The carriage and pair followed Mulderrig under cover and a dazed Mary Emma staggered out as, with Tom's assistance, the woman dragged the heavy barn doors across the opening, fastened them securely and, gesturing to them to follow her, was the first to brave the gale.

Heads down, they struggled in darkness through the swirling black soup, Tom attempting to shield his wife from the worst of the fierce, screeching turmoil and the vegetable missiles that were flying around them. Only by clinging to the woman's fluttering skirts could Ollander find his way and Tom, in turn, clung to the driver's coat for fear of becoming lost while binding Mary Emma to his side with his free arm. With a slam of the door they were inside the farmhouse where silence, earthiness and a low fire replaced the noise, chaos and darkness which reigned outside. Their saviour held a spill to a glowing ember in the grate and lighted the lamp then applied the bellows to the fire to cheer everybody up. Once their eyes had adjusted to their soft beams the travellers were appalled to see the havoc wreaked on their persons by the blow. Any one of them could have been mistaken for a scarecrow that had been dragged up from the depths of a coalmine: they were covered in fine black peat dust from head to toe. Mary Emma's bonnet hung backwards on its sooty ribbons and the colour of her pretty travelling frock was unrecognizable.

Objects whizzed horizontally past the window, that could have been diminutive witches riding broomsticks out on a nightmarish spree. The farmwoman unwrapped her head and spoke. "Well," she said, shaking the wrap, "I've seen some blows in me time but this do beat all. Me man's out there somewhere. I just 'ope ter Gawd he found cover before it struck. See that?" She pointed to the latticed window. "Those're the last of the sugar beet flyin' past, ripped outa the ground; all 'is hard work gone fer naught – blown away, an 'alf the field with it, I shouldn't wonder. I dunno what we've ever done to deserve it." She shook her fist at the unseen enemy beyond the window. "I 'ates this fen country at times like this. Tch!" She ran her forefinger along the inside sill and held it up to show them. "Just look at that, the filthy stuff. Everything in the place will be in the same state – covered in black peat dust. It's enough ter make a weaker woman weep. But I'm fergittin meself. Sit yerselves down while I get yer something ter drink."

"We're so very grateful to you for saving us from the worst of the storm, ma'am," Mary Emma croaked, her throat still dry from the dust she'd swallowed. "Would it help if I were to dust some cups?"

"Aye, lass; and thank you; but you won't find no cups, only beakers," the woman said, struck by the young woman's pretty speech and kind manner. "You could all do with an 'ot drink and I'll 'ave it ready in a jiffy. The betsy's almost boilin'."

While remarking on the phenomenon, and the furious speed at which it had overtaken them, the two men had been employed in dusting one another off and were making a fine smother in the small room. Tom had a sudden recollection of his pale-faced, battered-looking wife emerging from the carriage. "Mary Emma," he said, looking anxiously into her now blackened face, "you must have been knocked about a bit as we dashed to the barn. Are you all right, my love?"

"Thank you, Tom. I'm fine now," she said, placing her hand on his sleeve," but I'm afraid the Sèvres porcelain and the Waterford crystal will be in pieces when we come to unwrap them. No; I'm a little bruised but none of my bones are broken, thank heaven."

"I'm sorry to hear about your misfortune, Mrs Challiss," Ollander broke in, quite as though he were their equal, thought Tom pettishly, "I should have given thought and driven with greater care; but there was something of urgency about the situation that overrode all other thoughts. Please accept my apology, ma'am."

"Not at all, Mr Ollander. Pray don't mention it." Mary Emma smiled, her sooty face making a bizarre contrast with her shining teeth and eyes. "It is for me to thank you for your expert handling of the horses under such circumstances."

A flame of jealousy leapt through Tom. He knew he was being unreasonable but was unable to control the emotion. "I think it is this good woman we have to thank for getting us to shelter so promptly and efficiently," he said, crossing the small room in one stride and shaking the farmwoman's roughened hand.

Ollander saw he'd unintentionally offended Challiss and said: "We do indeed, sir. Thank you for your good sense, ma'am. It is greatly appreciated."

The woman poured boiling water into three beakers and handed them to her guests. "Oh, go along wi' you!" she cried in mock rebuke. "If I don't know what ter do when a blow springs up outa nowhere by my time o' life then I'm not much use to anybody." Good breeding prevented any of the three visitors from exclaiming their surprise at discovering that the beakers contained nothing more than Adam's Ale. Each of the men dutifully emptied his quota and Mary Emma was especially grateful for the scalding liquid which soothed her raw throat.

The farmwoman was looking out of the window and observed: "The leaves're quietin down now. 'Tis blowin itself out. You'll be able to git along again in a few minutes." Tom offered her half a guinea which she politely refused. "I need nothing from you, sir," she said with simple dignity. "'Twas my pleasure ter be able ter do something for the quality. My man'll be sorry to 'ave missed such grand company. If yer 'appen ter be in these parts agin, please ter do us the honour of callin in, sirs and madam. 'E'd love ter meet yer." Tom saw she'd mistaken Ollander for a gentleman.

The wind had almost died down, the air was clearing and they decided to be on their way. As they drove back along the lane they met a chimney-sweep making his way to the farm they'd just left. He looked as surprised as they did; it wasn't often closed carriages used the lane. He tipped his hat, which was secured by a scarf tied under his chin and Tom, having no hat to raise in response, acknowledged him with an inclined head. Only when they had passed on did he realise that this must be the farmer; for the implement Tom had thought from a distance to be a sweep's brush had resolved itself into a rake and a hoe carried at shoulder height. He laughed to himself as he jogged on beside the carriage for the unfortunate farmer had been as black as the inside of a pocket; but it was sobering to think that he and Mary Emma, Ollander and the horses might have ended up even blacker than they already had.

They had intended to spend one night at the *Golden Lion* in Lincoln and had travelled only a few miles out of The Isle of Axholme when the blow had overtaken them. Surprised to discover that no more than three-quarters of an hour had elapsed during their imposed shelter, they decided to press on to the cathedral city. But first it was imperative to find somewhere to rid themselves of peat dust.

The sun came out again turning night into day, and after travelling a few miles along the mail road they came to Scotton where they were able to find rooms in an inn where Tom and his wife bathed and swiftly conjoined again before changing into clean clothes. Ollander remained with his horses and after making them comfortable sluiced himself under the pump in the yard, donned a fresh shirt and was ready to continue the journey when the Challisses, recognizable once more, rejoined him.

The route to Lincoln was covered in good time and without further mishap. Ollander was greeted effusively at the *Golden Lion* as if he were well-known there and Mulderrig and the carriage-and-pair were given over to the care of an ostler while Ollander started off on foot on a private errand. Tom and Mary Emma were busying themselves in overseeing the transferrence of their belongings from the carriage to their room when they were distracted from their task by a shout made after Ollander's departing figure. "By God! *Ingleby*! Is it really you?" A brightly-uniformed officer had caught up with Ollander and was staring into his face as if he couldn't believe his own eyes. Glancing at Tom, Ollander took the man by the elbow and led him back into the stables out of earshot.

"What did he call him?" Mary Emma said, wide blue eyes meeting Tom's.

"Ingleby, as clear as day."

"What do you make of that, Tom?" she asked, as they entered the inn.

He stopped, and looked back the way they had come as if he were reviewing the encounter between Ollander and the military man. "Something about Ollander has been nagging me ever since I first clapped eyes on him. He struck me as being out of his class – come down in the world, I suppose I mean. He has the manners and bearing of an officer and a gentleman, don't you think? Well. . . no doubt he'll enlighten us in his own good time."

"I think you're right, Tom. He is a gentleman and, if I'm not mistaken, high born. How extraordinary! What a fascinating mystery that he should have hidden his identity behind an assumed name."

"And he handles horses with great expertise," Tom pondered as they washed preparatory to dining. Addressing Mary Emma as he dried his hands, he said: "I shouldn't wonder if it comes out that he served in some capacity in the Allied Army's Horse Artillery." All thoughts of war were swept away as he met his charming young wife's enquiring eyes. He took her in his arms and a lingering kiss followed; but, there being no time at present to take matters further, they went down to dine.

They had reached the stage of trying to decide which fruit to select as a dessert when, across the room, they saw Ollander returning in the company of the military gentleman and sitting down to dine with him in a private booth. The men were soon deep in animated conversation and appeared to pick at their food in an absentminded fashion. They were still locked in dialogue when Tom escorted his wife up to bed.

The following morning, as they made ready to continue their journey to Norfolk and, ultimately, to Uppham, the man they had until now thought of as Ollander spoke directly to them. "I suppose you must have wondered what all the fuss was about last evening," he began. "It was not my intention to deceive you, Mr Challiss; I give you my word as one gentleman to another. My name is Giles Ingleby and I've assumed the name Ollander for reasons that we needn't go into now. It would take too long in the telling and I think it best if we get on our way while the weather is fair." He studied the clear blue sky before meeting Tom's eye. "That is, sir, unless you demand an explanation here and now."

"I will accept your word – as a gentleman, sir," Tom assured him as he mounted Mulderrig. "It's high time we were on our way. We've many miles to travel before dark."

★

Chapter Twenty-two

"When, after the Battle of Salamanca, I read my own name among those listed as missing in an old copy of *The London Gazette* in the summer of 1812 it seemed a heaven-sent opportunity for me to disappear for ever." Giles Ingleby, alias Ollander, began. The three travellers were seated before a cheerful fire in one of the private rooms of the *King's Head* at Holbeach. Although they had hoped to complete their journey on the day in question the team were spent and Ingleby had refused to tax them further. Moreover, dusk was approaching and it had grown chilly so Tom, recalling the comforts of the inn on his outward journey had suggested they made their way there. A splendid dinner, consisting of a roast sirloin of beef with all the usual accompaniments, followed by a light suet pudding over which the waiter had poured hot golden syrup, had seemed a perfect end to the day and now they sat toasting their toes and sipping mulled wine listening as Ingleby unfolded his history.

"That must have been an eerie experience – to see oneself written off, so to speak," Mary Emma remarked.

"How were you able to escape detection?" Tom asked.

"It was easy enough during the confusion that always reigns in the aftermath of a battle and night fell before the orderlies had managed to identify all the bodies. I had sustained a sabre cut to my arm and must have fainted through loss of blood. When I regained consciousness, at first I wondered where I was; then the pain in my arm jogged my memory. Some well-meaning person had tied a tourniquet around my arm but had gone away and left me without releasing it."

"That could have been nasty," Tom said. He'd spoken of his own experiences as one of His Majesty's Imperial Foot Guard in Wellington's campaigns in France and Belgium. He'd been correct in his assumption about Ingleby; he'd been a captain in the British Horse Artillery; the Second Hussars attached to the 5th Division of the 5th British Hanoverian Brigade. Tom registered that last fact as being very precise.

"Yes. But fortunately for me, I couldn't have been left unattended for very long and I was soon able to see to the regulation of the tourniquet myself. Without wishing to distress Mrs Challiss, sir; you and I know how soon even a simple wound can cost a man a damaged limb if it isn't cleaned and dressed regularly. As it happened, I was very lucky and stumbled into a field hospital run by a young doctor who was dedicated to trying to mend young men's limbs rather than hacking them off indiscriminately; but it was his angel of a sister who pulled many a man through who would have been snuffed out without her dedicated nursing."

"I suppose the doctor's name wouldn't have been Brown, by any chance?" Tom asked, thinking of Garnet and her brother, for the coincidence seemed too great.

"Hadn't time to find out," Ingleby said. "We walking wounded were soon sent on our way to make way for the really serious cases."

"And how was it you came to be listed with the missing?" Mary Emma queried.

"It hadn't been my intention to desert; but as a few of us were attempting to return to our regiment we were cut off by the enemy. It was then that the idea came to me to disappear for, you see, I have a very good reason for wishing to be thought dead." He ceased talking and stood up. "That's all I'm prepared to say: so I'll wish you both a good night's sleep and will be ready to start immediately after breakfast."

Tom laughed at such an anticlimax. "Well, Ingleby, you don't think we'll let you get away with leaving us in suspense, like this: do you? You'll have to tell us why you thought your disappearance was necessary, now that you've decided to take us into your confidence this far."

"'Fraid not, Mr Challiss," he said adamantly. "I've already revealed more than was prudent as it is by divulging my name. I know I can trust to your discretion: however, I'd be greatly obliged to you if you'd continue to use my assumed name for the remainder of the time I'm at your service."

"Well, I don't know about that," Tom said doubtfully. "Isn't the cat out of the bag already, now that your military friend has seen that you're alive and kicking?"

"Oh, he's as safe as houses," Ingleby replied confidently. "I do realise it's asking a great deal after so slight an acquaintance; but I really am not at liberty to reveal anything more. So – if you'll forgive me – I really must bid you good-night, sir. Mrs Challiss, ma'am." He bowed politely and was gone, leaving them open-mouthed at such an unsatisfactory solution to the mystery.

"What can he mean by such mysterious behaviour?" Mary Emma said as soon as Ingleby-Ollander had left them.

With sudden insight, Tom said, "I think I have a very good idea, my love. I, too, am sorry he left the whole thing up in the air like that; but if what I suspect is true, disclosure will have to wait until we reach home and nobody else is around. Now, my darling," he kissed her eyes, nose and lips. "You must dismiss all thoughts of Mr Ingleby from your pretty little head for you and I have some unfinished business."

★

They arrived on the outskirts of Downham late in the afternoon of the following day. Groups of men lined the streets, as before, and the unusual sight of a closed carriage accompanied by a horseman had heads turning. Tom couldn't help noticing that he was the chief object of their attention. All along the High Street men drew attention to him by nods in his direction as he approached, nudged their neighbours as he drew level. Once he was past them he looked back and saw that they continued to follow him with their eyes, their lean faces turned towards him wearing expressions he was unable to read – except he saw that no man smiled. Wondering what such behaviour could mean, he hoped to God that no mishap had befallen his house or lands just as his bride was to see her home for the first time. A cloud obscured the sun as they rode up to the gates and he was disconcerted further when Joseph Aldrich rushed out with an anxious look on his dark face.

"Welcome home, Mr Challiss, sir," he puffed. "I'm enormously glad to see you returned safely. I'm sorry to say that I have bad news with which to greet you, sir; an accident—"

"Accident? Who's had an accident? Is it bad?"

Aldrich's unhappy brown eyes met his and his voice reached sepulchral depths as he said softly: "The Honourable Percival Belmaine is dead, Mr Challiss; he was killed instantly while out hunting; thrown at a jump, fell on his head and was found dead seconds later by two following huntsmen who, fortunately, witnessed it all."

Relieved to hear that nobody at Uppham had been involved, Tom thought: is that all! Of course, it's sad for the old boy, left alone. Most unfortunate – and damned bad luck for Belmaine; but these things happen all the time—

Mary Emma leaned out of the lowered window of the carriage. "What is it, Tom? Why have we stopped?" Reading its name, she gasped: "We're at Uppham House!" Her face lit up so that it fairly dazzled Aldrich with its youthful beauty. "Oh, Tom! I can hardly wait to see it."

"Mary Emma," Tom said absentmindedly by way of introduction, preoccupied as he was with Aldrich's news. "Er – My dear, may I introduce

Mr Joseph Aldrich, my steward and right arm at Uppham."

"Enchanted, Mrs Challiss, ma'am," Aldrich said, his dazed eyes looking as if he really were, before taking her gloved hand in his, bowing over it and straightening up. His eyes on her face, he said: "Might I be allowed to say what a delight it is to welcome you to Uppham, Mrs Challiss, and how happy I shall be to serve you in any way I can, ma'am. If I'd known you were to arrive today arrangements could have—"

"Thank you, Mr Aldrich," Mary Emma replied gravely, acutely conscious that her position as mistress of Uppham dictated that she should maintain a discreet distance between herself and the voluble, warm-hearted little man.

The driver of the carriage – Giles Ingleby in his assumed role – had watched the encounter from his elevated position and speculated about the possibility of problems arising from the steward's fascination with the beautiful Mrs Challiss. So, thinking to help Tom by cutting the interview short, he enquired: "Shall we drive on, Mr Challiss?"

Tom also had noticed the effect Mary Emma had had on Aldrich. "Yes. By all means, Ollander, drive on." He eyed the sky. "Looks as if it could rain at any moment and I'd prefer Mrs Challiss to have her first glimpse of the house in sunshine, if possible."

As he flapped the reins lightly across the backs of the horses Ingleby noted the steward's exasperated expression. "Wait! "Aldrich shouted; but the carriage had already entered the tree-enclosed drive to the house with Tom on Mulderrig accompanying it. Thunder rolled across the darkening sky as they entered the tunnel, large drops pattered on the thin ochre leaves of the trees and it began to rain heavily. Ingleby pulled on a waterproof cape and the horses shied as lightning zig-zagged overhead and was reflected in rivulets of rainwater that ran into the ditches on either side of the once-gravelled, now rutted, drive. By the time they emerged into the park all colour had drained from sky and landscape, and Uppham House was no more than a monochrome blur on a rainswept rise. His heart heavy with disappointment, Tom dug his heels into Mulderrig's flanks and galloped ahead of the carriage to the stables.

Bob was nowhere to be seen. Tom cursed him under his breath as he tended to his mount and heard the carriage roll into the cobbled yard. He'd wanted everything to be perfect for Mary Emma's arrival. The old mansion looked ten times better on a sunny day and one's first impressions of a place meant a good deal if it was to become one's permanent home. Thunder growled overhead. Damn and blast the rain! It was too bad, he thought as he vented his bad mood by vigorously currying Mulderrig's matted hide. Hearing the carriage come to rest under the projecting roof and aware that Ingleby would be about to uncouple the team, Tom ran out into the downpour before Mary Emma had time to alight. "No!" he called out. "Drive up to the front of the house. No; wait. I'll join you."

Mary Emma drew her skirt to one side as he jumped in beside her. "You poor boy," she said, observing his woebegone expression, "you're positively soaked."

He smiled to hide his disappointment. He'd imagined a very different arrival: the sun shining on a joyous reception with all the servants ranged before the steps to honour their new mistress. Now the dreary aspect presented in the gloomy light by the bedraggled trees and untended gardens before the house was utterly depressing.

"Oh…" Mary Emma expelled a long sigh. "Oh, Tom!" He turned to her and his heart lifted as, impulsively, she kissed his rainwashed cheek and then laughed gaily. "What a treasure, Tom; I had no idea from your workaday description of it that it would be such a beautiful old house. And to think I am to be mistress of all this." She threw her arms around his neck, lifted her face to his and murmured: "Thank you, darling, darling Tom."

Ingleby, lashed by the howling wind and almost drowned by the deluge, stood impassively beside the coach in readiness to open the door for the amorous young couple within – once they came down to earth – as if he were idling away a glorious summer day.

Rudge had spied them from the house and came hurrying down the wet steps with such speed that his neck was in danger. He carried with him two umbrellas; one, under which he struggled to shelter himself as best he could in the gusty wind, was already open; the other, still furled, he opened with difficulty, in readiness for Mary Emma – who was lightly clad in a summery travelling coat, straw bonnet and satin slippers – to step beneath as she alighted from the carriage. Thanking him for his thoughtfulness, the new Mrs Challiss took the umbrella from Rudge and waited for Tom to join her. Already soaked to the skin, Tom assumed a dignity he didn't feel as he squelched up the steps bearing Mary Emma on his arm, leaving Rudge to struggle with his own umbrella which had inconveniently blown inside out. From his place beside the carriage Ingleby looked on with amusement as the odd procession mounted the flight of steps. Mary Emma, battling with the wind for possession of her umbrella, collapsed on the top step with a peal of laughter as it was tugged from her grasp. She watched it bowl away across the ruined garden as Tom, infected by her laughter, scooped her up off her sodden feet and into his arms, kicked open the door, carried her over the threshold and into Uppham House.

The drenched figure of a furious Rudge followed them in. He banged the door shut with an uncharacteristic violence that somewhat relieved his anger against the forces that had conspired to make him – albeit temporarily – lose his dignity.

Thinking himself forgotten, Ingleby shrugged his shoulders. Rain that had collected in his hat's brim trickled forward past his nose as he climbed onto the box of the carriage. It wouldn't be the first time he'd used the carriage as a bedroom; in his line of work he'd spent many nights in far less comfortable conditions than that.

"Hold hard, Ollander!" Tom called from the shelter of the open front door. "I thought you were following us in. Lord knows where the stable lad's got to; can't be found. If you'll see to the carriage and stall the horses first, I'd be obliged. Of course, once that's been seen to, you'll join us as our guest." Ingleby saluted him and turned the horses. At the sound of the vehicle a gangly, sleepy-looking stable boy came running out to assist the stranger. After a quick rub down the horses were accommodated in clean dry stalls, their muzzles soon buried in the full mangers. Ingleby, meanwhile, had drawn the clarence under the shelter of a projecting roof provided for the purpose and, having witnessed the care which had been taken of his team, he handed the startled youth a half guinea before walking up to the house. Already in a cheerful mood at the splendid way things had turned out, Ingleby's spirits rose even further when the sky lightened to a discernable blue, the heavy clouds parted and the sinking sun appeared. For a moment he envied young Challiss his lovely young bride and the picturesque old mansion which glowed in the glorious sunset; but common sense told him that such domestic anchors were not practical for a man in his line of business.

★

A pacified Rudge, comfortable and neat again and wearing his Sunday clothes while his aunt steamed his working outfit before the wide kitchen fire, had ordered pitchers of hot water to be carried up to the bedchamber of his master and mistress.

Looking backward at Mary Emma as he turned the handle for her to precede him into the room, Tom wondered what could have caused her face to show such pleasure and turned to follow her gaze. Was he dreaming? The room into which they passed was immaculate and tastefully decorated in the latest style.

"What a beautiful room, Tom," she cried enthusiatically. "From what you'd told me about the state of the interior decoration of the house I was prepared for stained walls and dingy fabrics. But I call this absolutely splendid!"

Dazed by the transformation of his former bedchamber, something that had wonderfully been accomplished in the short period of his absence, Tom turned full circle before saying: "I left this room almost a wreck and was feeling ashamed to have to bring you into it, love. Aldrich is behind this miracle, unless I'm mistaken. There's a lot more to that man than meets the eye."

"I love it," Mary Emma declared. "Chinoiserie's the very latest thing, you know, Tom," she said catching hold of his hand and pulling him towards a decorated panel. "Isn't this exquisite, Tom?" Involuntarily, she shivered.

Alarmed, Tom began peeling off her wet clothing. "What on earth was I thinking of? Kick off those silly slippers, Mary Emma," he directed. "The last thing we want is for you to catch a cold." She'd no sooner removed her damp stockings than he was kneeling before her chair and chafing her cold feet between his warm hands. Worried by the intense cold that gripped her feet, he wrapped them in a Turkish towel, poured hot water into a bowl, unwrapped them again and commanded: "You must warm them, my love; cold feet can lead to all kinds of maladies."

She dipped in a toe, found the water too hot by contrast with her gelid flesh and bone, and withdrew it. Annoyed by her supposed obstinacy, Tom gripped her feet by the ankles and plunged them deep into the water. "Oh! Oh!" she cried, trying to draw her feet up, "please don't; you're scalding me, Tom." Stubbornly, he kept them submerged. Watching the flesh turn from white to pink to red, she sobbed: "Why did you do that?" Tears spilled down her cheeks and she looked so unhappy that Tom began to wonder if he hadn't treated her cruelly after all.

"I didn't mean to hurt you, darling," he said, kneeling before her and patting her feet dry. He stood up and pulled her to him. "Oh, my sweet love," he shuddered. "I couldn't bear it – if you became seriously ill." He'd been about to say "to lose you" but hadn't wanted to tempt fate. "There, there," he soothed as her sobs subsided. "You really are a silly little thing to even think of wearing such flimsy footwear when abroad, darling. Promise me that you'll be more sensible in future."

"How could I tell that it was going to rain?" she said pettishly, pulling away and looking at him with a spark of anger in her eye. "You really are most unjust. My one concern when we got ready at Holbeach was not to disgrace you by my appearance when we arrived at Uppham."

Full of remorse, he asked: "How are your feet now, sweetheart?"

A dazzling smile lit up her face. "Warm as toast, thanks to you, you great bully."

Once more master of the situation, he looked down his nose at her and said with mock severity: "So; you concede that I was right to do what I did?"

Her face suddenly grave, Mary Emma caught hold of his hand and kissed it. "I do, sir – just this once; but I warn you now, Tom: I'm not one of those wives who will allow themselves to be bullied without complaint, even if I do worship my husband."

Uncertain whether she was in earnest or merely jesting, he cupped her face in his long hands so that she had no option but to meet his eyes. "My darling," he said, "it was never my intention to bully you, believe me; I was truly concerned for your health. Prompt action was necessary, my love. I've seen men die from neglecting feet as icy as yours were, especially if the feet are also wet."

Fully contrite, Mary Emma said: "What a silly little fool you must think me, Tom. I beg your pardon for accusing you unjustly and making such a fuss."

"We'll say no more about it," he murmured as he bent to kiss her; and the neglected pitchers of hot water, so thoughtfully provided by Rudge, grew cool as they took their pleasure of one another for the first time under Uppham's roof.

Insisting his wife stay in bed, Tom went down to dine without her. Expecting to find only Ingleby waiting for him in the library, he was surprised to hear voices and, as he got nearer, recognised Aldrich's bass as one of them. His hand on the doorknob, he heard the steward say: "–and it will be my unpleasant duty to tell him so."

"Good-evening, gentlemen. Tell me what, Joseph?" Tom enquired. He seated himself and said to Ingleby, who had remained standing: "You've introduced yourselves? Make yourself at home, Ollander. Help yourselves to a glass of madeira, gentlemen, but nothing for me."

Taking Tom at his word, Aldrich poured two glasses, saying, as he handed one to Ingleby: "Good-evening, Mr Challiss, sir. You dashed off in such a hurry that I hadn't time to tell you everything concerning the accident. I trust I may speak freely in front of this gentleman?"

"Certainly, Joseph: I hope you're free to join us at dinner? Good. Well? Go on, man. What have you to tell me that's so unpleasant?"

Bravely, Aldrich plunged in. "There's no doubt that young Belmaine's death was caused by his own negligence, sir. He took the jump too early, according to those who witnessed it."

"Then I should have thought that was the end of the matter," said Tom. "Am I to understand that there's more to it?"

"I'm afraid so, Mr Challiss, sir. He was thrown by Saladin, that Arab stallion you sold him, sir." He moistened his dry lips and swallowed hard. "And Sir Everard Belmaine is content to allow it be thought that the horse was to blame, sir."

Consumed with anger, Tom jumped up. "Is he, by Jove. Well, he shall have me to deal with, face to face. I'll pay him a visit first thing tomorrow morning."

Ingleby, who had been observing the way the two men interacted while silently sipping his wine, quietly set down his half-empty glass on the small wine table beside his chair. "Pray excuse me, Mr Challiss," he began. The others were surprised by the interruption. "While I'm conscious of the fact that I have absolutely no right to offer you the benefit of my advice, I beg you to listen to me, sir."

"Let's hear it, then," Tom said without a moment's hesitation.

"After all," Aldrich interpolated, "you are not compelled to follow it, sir."

Ingleby spared him a calculating glance before saying to Tom: "While your anger at this aristocrat's unjust behaviour towards you is perfectly justified, sir, it might be as well – as you must continue to live in proximity with him – to treat the gentleman with the contempt he so richly deserves."

Now, Tom noticed, it was Aldrich's turn to study the carriage driver whom he assumed to be named Ollander, and saw that Ingleby had gone up in the steward's opinion of him. Interested, while still incensed, Tom said: "What d'you suggest I do?"

"Nothing," Ingleby replied, taking up his glass and continuing to sip his wine.

Joseph Aldrich could not contain himself. "Admirable advice, if I might make so bold as to say so, sir," he said, raising his glass to Ingleby in a toast.

"Let him get away with it, you mean?" Tom thundered, still in the mood for revenge.

"Believe me, my dear sir," Ingleby said calmly, "it is the soundest revenge one can offer when wrongly accused; to quench the flame of malicious and idle gossip by ceasing to feed it."

"I see your point," Tom conceded: "but wouldn't that be perceived as cowardice; a slur on one's name, a slight to one's honour?"

"Belmaine would like nothing better than a public quarrel, my dear sir. For one thing, it would give some credence to his lie along the lines of no smoke without fire. It takes moral courage to face down calumny. Show yourself the better man, sir, and ignore him."

While Tom pondered Ingleby's advice, Aldrich warned him: "Be careful, Mr Challiss. To appear to gain ascendancy over Sir Everard will make a powerful enemy of him, sir. He's not only a patrician and sinfully proud, but is also a magistrate and has shown that, given the opportunity, he'll deal harshly with anyone who upsets him."

"Of course," Ingleby observed, "there is always danger for lesser mortals when dealing with that class of people. But to be drawn into a public argument when you have right on your side would, if I might suggest it, be foolhardy."

Aldrich had noticed, with a jolt, that Ollander had finished his cautionary remark without observing due deference and that Challiss hadn't turned a hair at the omission. Why, he thought, the man's nothing but a damned Radical, I'll be bound.

"Hmm," Tom said. "Well, Ollander; much as it goes against my natural inclination, I do see the wisdom of your counsel." He shrugged. "Seems I'm damned if I demand an apology from the wretched man and damned if I do nothing. According to you and Joseph, I'll offend Sir Everard Belmaine whatever course I pursue."

"Then I strongly advise you to let sleeping dogs lie, sir," Ingleby offered as the gong sounded, summoning them to dinner.

As they made their way to the dining room, Tom waylaid Peckover and explained that, though his mistress was a trifle indisposed she was not seriously ill, and that the footman was to instruct Maddy to take up her mistress's dinner on a tray without further delay.

★

As they seated themselves and soup was being served, Tom turned to Aldrich and said warmly: "I believe I have to thank you, Joseph, for the astonishing transformation to our bedchamber. Mrs Challiss was transported at finding herself ensconced in such a fashionable and exquisitely furnished room. It's truly marvellous." Aldrich allowed himself one of his rare smiles and Ingleby was amazed by the transformation it made. The little man might even be called handsome by some women who were drawn to that kind of hirsute swarthiness. "No thanks are necessary, Mr Challiss, sir," Aldrich said, his brown eyes sparkling. "Beginning the restoration of the mansion with your bedchamber gave me the greatest pleasure you can imagine, sir. I sincerely hope that you'll not think me presumptuous if I ask you and Mrs Challiss to do me the very great honour of accepting the newly-appointed room as my wedding gift."

"That's very generous of you, Joseph," Tom said, his face beaming, "I shall convey the news of your great kindness to Mrs Challiss. I'm only sorry she isn't here to thank you for herself; but she's in danger of contracting a chill from the dowsing she experienced on our arrival and so I thought it best if she kept to her bed."

Over dinner, Aldrich took the opportunity of bringing his master up to date with events that had occurred during his absence; such as his and Jem Webster's ideas for purchasing a pair of oxen for ploughing, cows for the dairying, pigs for fattening and hens for their eggs, so that, should lean times befall — as it was apparently predicted they would, as the economy grew shakier with plummeting prices — the estate would be self-sufficient. "We see eye to eye on most things," Aldrich finished enthusiastically, "and Jem was surprised at my knowledge of animal husbandry. I don't have practical experience, you understand, sir; but I do have a good memory of how Uppham was stocked in its heyday."

Tom was astonished that the two men had found it possible to form a working partnership following their initial hostility to one another. "Well done, Joseph. Was anything discussed about clearing the beggared land?"

"Naturally, we assumed that it would be prudent to clear as much as we could as soon as possible so that crops could be sown; but nothing can be started without draught animals, sir."

Ingleby stifled a yawn.

Tom laughed at his blatant nudge to neglected hospitality and suggested they move back to the library, it being one of the more habitable rooms in the house. As they settled themselves with tankards of ale before the fire Aldrich drew from his breast pocket three letters which he handed to his master. Tom glanced at the handwriting and was overjoyed to see among them one from George. The others were of less interest, one being from Tom's bankers, Bagg and Bacon, and the other bore no identifying information. Though impatient to read what his brother had to tell him, politeness forbade reading his letters whilst entertaining so they were laid aside.

After a comfortable silence in which Ingleby had asked permission to smoke his churchwarden, the enigmatic coach driver said: "There is a matter I wish to lay before you, Mr Challiss, that could be of benefit to you while assisting me."

"Oh?"

"I find that I must continue my journey on horseback."

Tom and Aldrich looked at each other and back at Ingleby. Tom said: "That's dashed odd; and what do you propose to do with the clarence, sir?"

"That's just it," Ingleby said, leaning forward and tapping his clay pipe gently against the side of the fireplace to dislodge the dottle. "I suppose you wouldn't be interested in becoming the proud owner of a carriage-and-pair, Mr Challiss? She's in tip top working order, sir, and the horses're in fine fettle, to boot."

Intrigued, Aldrich enquired: "And how do you propose to acquire a horse for your own purposes, Mr Ollander?"

"Yes," Tom said, thinking how delighted Mary Emma would be to have her own carriage. "Do you intend hanging on to one of the pair?"

"Oh, that would never do," Ingleby said, refilling the bowl of his pipe and drawing air through the long stem until the freshly-lighted tobacco glowed a healthy red. "No. I was rather hoping that you would have a nag in your stable that I could take in part exchange. The clarence and matched pair are worth a pretty penny, sir."

"I wish I could accommodate you, Ollander," Tom said, seeing, in his mind's eye, the prize about to slip from his grasp.

Aldrich said tentatively: "I have been thinking of changing my own mount, Barbary, for something heavier, more suited to my calling. He's a strawberry roan gelding, if that's the kind of thing you're looking for. I could let you have him for a fair sum. Perhaps we could come to some agreement?" Before the three men parted that night a compromise had been reached that satisfied all parties. Ingleby had purchased Aldrich's roan out of the money given him by Tom when he became the owner of the carriage-and-pair; and the steward had a generous sum, given him by Ingleby in exchange for the roan, with which to purchase the horse of his dreams.

★

Mary Emma awoke next morning to sun filtering through the window of her bedchamber and with a sense of happiness and well-being; in fact, never in her life before had she experienced such utter contentment. She stretched herself out in the bed with the gratitude of a temporarily beached starfish sucked back into the life-giving sea. For, thanks to Tom's care, she'd suffered not the slightest ill-effect from her exposure to yesterday's elements. Apparently loath to disturb her, he'd kept to his side of the bed for the first night since their marriage and hadn't so much as touched her. Later, when she had turned towards his back, she'd found him fast asleep and her disappointment had been complete. This morning, grown even hungrier for his attentions, she'd been frustrated again when she'd awoken to find his side of their bed unoccupied and cold. She hopped out of bed, washed her face in the cupful of water that was left in the pitcher and, without waiting for Maddy to appear, began dressing. In the act of brushing her hair she saw that the face that looked back at her from the glass was not the same as that to which she was accustomed. Yes, her face was different; it had something to do with a mysterious change that had occurred within her body; something more than the emptiness she'd felt within herself when in bed her languorous body had pulsated with longing for Tom to meet its primaeval demand. Without knowing what it was, or when it had happened, she knew that she was no longer an inexperienced girl; realised that her body had started to ripen into fruition as surely as she'd observed the ovary of a buttercup begin to swell with seeds once its petals had fallen. It was a ridiculous analogy, but apt; she had no doubt at all that after less than a week of marriage she was with child. It was another week before she expected to deal with the menses. Dulcie Brook had talked to her about conception and had said that, to be sure, a woman had to wait until at least two monthlies had failed to appear before she could be sure that she'd conceived and that there would be other signs that would leave her in no doubt. Other signs? Oh, why hadn't outspoken Dulcie been more explicit? Now she had nobody to ask… but there might be a surgeon's book in the library…

"Ah, good. You're up, my love, and looking well." Tom took her in his arms and kissed her lips. "There's something I want to show you." He searched her face as if he, too, saw a change in her. "Are you really quite well, Mary Emma?"

"Quite well, my lord," she smiled, making him a low curtsey while wondering how she would be able to keep her secret? It would be too silly to tell him of what, as yet, she only suspected. "What is it you want me to see, dear?"

"Come with me, my lady," he said, taking her by the hand and leading her down the stairs to the front hall. "Now, close your eyes – and no peeping." She heard Tom ask softly: "Ready?" Felt his strong hands cover her eyes, heard the faint squeak from unoiled hinges as the front door swung open, before he said: "You may open them now."

Her eyes adjusted to the light, Mary Emma looked down the front steps. She saw the bright filly then laughed as she saw Bob's face split into the broadest of smiles. Turning to her husband, she breathed: "For me?" and at his smiling assent seemed to glide down the flight of steps to where Bob stood holding the horse. Throwing her arms around the grey's neck she whispered into her ear: "You and I are going to be great friends, you pretty little thing." Tom would remember the peal of Mary Emma's laughter as the filly nodded her head up and down as if she understood.

Now that each had a horse for the purpose, Tom suggested there could be no better time to show her around the estate. Immediately after breakfast they set out, Mary Emma being compelled to wear her travelling cloak as she had no riding habit to cover her legs which, no matter how hard she tried to conceal them, would poke from beneath her narrow-skirted dress as she rode side-saddle and the skirt worked its way up around her waist. Once away from the house she was less conscious of it and soon forgot her inadequate attire as the excitement of discovering the diversity of the Uppham estate absorbed her interest. Her heart was full of love: for Tom, for the coming child – for she was convinced of it as a fact – and for this lovely place to which her husband had brought her. Her rapt expression told Tom everything he wanted to know: Mary Emma was captivated by Uppham as much as he.

They entered a neglected orchard whose gnarled trees had become almost lost among encroaching undergrowth and she reined in her horse and slid to the ground. He needed no explanation and, for the first time, they coupled under the open sky. The tumult ebbed and, spent, he rolled off her. "Oh, Mary Emma, my sweet love," he whispered, "what have I done to deserve such happiness?" She attempted to speak; but he silenced her with a kiss so passionate that it left her lips bruised and swollen. "I'm sorry," he said, "but this privilege I have with you is beyond anything I imagined." Before he turned his head away she saw the sparkle of tears on his lashes. They had lain alongside one another for some minutes, their mounts quietly pulling at the long damp grass that clambered up the trunks of the trees, when a bearded collie bounded up to them. Somebody came crashing through the undergrowth closely upon the dog's heels and they hadn't had time to haul themselves up and fully adjust their clothing before the young shepherd, Clem Rix, was upon them.

"'Zooks!" Rix squawked, almost tumbling over himself in surprise. "Saw summat white among the weeds an thought it were one o' me sheep got tangled up." Abashed, he touched the brim of his hat, stammered: "'Mornin' ma'am, mornin' Mr Challiss," whirled about and was gone.

Following the fast-disappearing figure with his eyes, Tom laughed ruefully and said: "Now it'll be all over Downham. We'll be the laughing stock of the place."

Mary Emma, brushing twigs and moss off her cloak, gave him a roguish smile: "What else would the inhabitants of Downham, or anywhere else for that matter, expect a young newly-married couple who are madly in love with one another to be doing, sir," she said. At which he caught her in his arms, kissed her lightly on her tender lips and made a step of his hands for her to mount the filly.

"Thought of a name for her?" he said, as he swung himself into the saddle and they started to canter away from the orchard.

"Genty – because her coat's like snow and she's sweet-tempered," Mary Emma said, her face rosy with the afterglow of lovemaking. As they galloped across the open parkland she slackened the filly's pace first to a canter then to a walk. Tom looked round to see where she had got to and rode back to join her. He might not have been present for all the notice she took of him as, stilled, she stared intently at something ahead of her. After a while she turned to him with shining eyes and said: "That would be the perfect place for it, Tom. D'you see?" Pointing with her crop to the west of the mansion, to where a stretch of land had been allowed to revert to nature, she asked: "What distance d'you think it is from the western courtyard to those mature Scots pines?"

Humouring her, he said: "Hard to tell from here; but I should estimate a couple of hundred yards. Why? What's going on in that head of yours?"

"Oh, Tom! Don't you think it would be perfect?"

"I dare say I would, my love, if I had the least idea of what you're talking about. Are you going to let me into your secret?"

"Why, I'm talking about having a lime walk planted, of course," she said as if he ought to have known. "Please say you think it's the perfect place."

Puzzled, he said: "I was not aware that we had discussed any such thing, Mary Emma."

"Oh, don't be so stuffy," she said, poking him playfully in the chest with her crop. "You must remember how we've said since we were children that we'd make our own lime walk if ever we got the chance."

"Darling – I've been out of the country for three years."

"That's no excuse," she said, her eyes dancing. "Please promise you'll say yes, Tom."

He disliked the way she was harassing him. "I cannot promise anything of the kind, Mary Emma, without first consulting Joseph Aldrich and Jem Webster. We've made rough plans for the planting of next year's crops—"

"If they're nothing but rough plans what's there to prevent your changing them?" she demanded.

He frowned. "It isn't as easy as that, my dear. I've got to set about making this place self-sufficient. Once Aldrich, Webster and I have a fair idea of what we're to plant and where – that will be the time to begin discussing the ornamental layout of the park."

"We shall have wasted a whole year's growth if you stick to that plan," she argued.

He looked at her as if he were seeing her for the first time. "Mary Emma," he said sternly, "I must ask you not to interfere with the management of the land. You will have quite enough to occupy you when it comes to overseeing the restoration of the house. Furthermore—"

She didn't wait to hear any more; his suggestion that the role of captive housekeeper was to be her lot in life so angered her that she dug her heels into Genty's flanks and streaked across the park towards the stables.

Bob was currying the mare when Tom trotted Mulderrig into the stable yard but of Mary Emma there was no sign. Tethering his horse, he made a few remarks to Bob before striding towards the house in high dudgeon.

After questioning Rudge, he found his wife in the library making her way along the shelves in search of a particular book. Seething, he said: "You'll find the volumes on household management on the other side of the room."

Maddeningly, she said in her sweetest voice: "Thank you, Tom," but, other than that, ignored his remark and continued to search among the books in front of her.

In two strides he was beside her. "Stop this nonsense, Mary Emma," he said, catching hold of her hands. "You're behaving like a spoilt child."

It wasn't the wisest remark to make under the circumstances. "Is that how you perceive me?" she said coldly. "Then it's no wonder that you treat me as if I were."

"This silly behaviour is because I will not allow you to have your own way, isn't it." When she remained silent he ordered: "Answer me, Mary Emma." He expelled a sigh of exasperation. "Can't you understand that it's vital that we clear and plant the land as soon as humanly possible? This is no time to think about planting trees!"

"Sit down, please, Tom," she surprised him by saying. "I've been meaning to mention the legacy left me by my guardian. You must remember Mr Josiah Kay?" she said, ironically, raising her eyes to his.

"Well?" He wouldn't forgive her too easily.

"I haven't come to you a pauper, Tom: in fact, you have married a wealthy heiress. Part of my fortune comes to me for my sole use and so I hope you won't object to my spending some of my own money on the construction of the lime walk."

★

Chapter Twenty-three

This seems to be the day for revelations, Tom thought, realising how little he knew of his wife's recent history. That he loved her was indisputable; but he had to admit to himself that the adult Mary Emma possessed some disconcertingly unfeminine traits as well as an imperiousness of manner that he found hard to accept. And now the distasteful subject of money threatened to prove yet another bone of contention. "I do remember Josiah Kay very well indeed," he said. " I haven't forgotten that I was employed at Lyndon Manor as his gardener's boy and that it was there that we first met. I was foolish to imagine that the gulf in our stations would be eradicated by marriage."

Swiftly, she moved from the library steps on which she'd been sitting and came and perched on the arm of his chair. "Promise me, Tom, that you'll never again refer to the supposed inequality in our rank. Promise me!"

The unpredictability of her behaviour made him dizzy. "You're very eager to elicit my promises, Mary Emma; have you so soon forgotten your own?"

"What promises?"

"Why, that you would love, honour and obey your husband. You've shown ample proof of the first, Mary Emma. Perhaps deference and obedience are qualities that are more difficult to demonstrate – and for you to accept."

She hung her head at the accusation before lifting it again and staring at him as if he had struck her. "You haven't given me an answer, Tom. When you have, I'll gladly discuss our marriage vows, if you like."

"What?

"I want you to promise me that you will, from this moment on, agree that we are equals. It's so silly; at least you know for certain who were your parents. I have no idea who mine were or even where I came into the world. I only know that, from my earliest memories, Miss Peters was there to love me and take care of me. So, according to the rules of society, my background is even more obscure than yours."

He pulled her onto his lap and held her in a tight embrace before kissing her. "You have my promise that the subject will never arise between us again, my dearest." He kissed her again before saying: "But what of this legacy? I had, of course, heard of it on the day I had the argument with Jardine, but had quite forgotten about it."

She kissed him and said: "Good! That proves that you didn't marry me for my money, doesn't it." Suddenly serious, she settled herself more comfortably on his lap, and gazed up at him. "I apologise, Tom, for behaving so selfishly and without consulting your wishes concerning the lime walk. But you know what a creature of impulse I am and always have been; I spotted the site and, as far as I was concerned, the only thing remaining was for the work to begin on the project right away."

He'd been only half-listening to her, his mind preoccupied with her legacy. "I was, perhaps, too severe upon you. After all, we have a lifetime in which to learn to tread the difficult path of matrimony, Mary Emma, and I, too, am a novice." Just as he had smoothed away their current differences, he ruined all his good work by adding: "So you'll agree that the work of getting the farm in working order must take precedence over your plans for a lime walk."

She jumped off his lap and faced him. "Oh, Tom!" she cried, her voice full of exasperation. "You haven't listened to a thing I've said. If we are to be considered equals, it doesn't only apply to social station, in my view. If we are to have real equality then I, too, must be consulted, must be concerned with everything concerning Uppham. That means that I wish to have a say in what happens outside the house as well as within it. No; don't speak. I refuse to be nothing more to you than a woman who sleeps in your bed by night and creeps about the house by day—"

"That is enough!" he thundered, jumping to his feet and towering over her. "I will be master here—"

"And what am I, pray?"

"Mistress of Uppham, of course. But you knew that."

"And what do you consider that means, Tom?"

"Must we go over and over it? It's enough to drive a man to drink. But I'll spell it out for you once again: you are my wife. You are to be, I hope, the mother of my children. You will ensure the smooth and efficient running of this house and see to it that the servants know their duties and carry them out discreetly."

She plumped herself down on the nearest chair. "And just where did you get the idea that I would be content with such a role?"

"What on earth do you mean? It's your duty—"

"Duty? Who says so? Not I! Dear Tom; you talk as if we're living in the last century. Women may seem to be content with the lot that generations of men have accorded them; but, believe me, there are many of us who mean to *live* in the world: who are *not* content to sit at home making a comfortable nest while the other half of the population go out into the world and live exciting lives and are, many of them, financially rewarded for doing so while their wives remain at home and penniless after a lifetime of servitude."

My God! He'd married a bluestocking! "A fine speech, my dear; and one that you didn't dream up in the schoolroom, I'd guess. I cannot say that I'm not shocked, because I am – deeply. And there was I, thinking that Uppham meant as much to you as it does to me."

"It does."

"And who is to run the house if you are to be out of it – what was it – living?"

"You said you intended to engage a housekeeper," she reminded him. "One doesn't keep a dog and bark oneself, Tom."

"Providing it's the right kind of dog," he observed sourly. "And what do you suppose you will you be doing while a stranger takes care of our home?"

"Sometimes, I shall be overseeing the housekeeper and attending to other matters concerning the running of the house. But I hope I shall be allowed to go out when I so desire, to go among the villagers, helping them where I am able."

"And you'd neglect your children in order to pursue your own interests?"

Why was he being so difficult? "If, and when, I have children, Tom, I shall always put their needs before anybody else's – including yours, my dear."

"I see," he said, as far from seeing as a blindfold man would be on a sunny day at noon.

"Well… It seems that I've taken a stranger for a wife; for I simply do not recognise you as the sweet girl I knew before I went away."

She sighed heavily. "How much does any of us ever know one another, Tom? I mean, really know. We're attracted to the outside shell of a person which gives away little of what goes on inside. Living as man and wife can become little more than a dreary habit in the end." She appeared to be thinking deeply, and then said: "Perhaps the freedom I was accorded at Lyndon Manor has made me what I am and I'm sorry if you're disappointed in me, Tom. But the little girl you left waving you good-bye in the cornfield in the autumn of 1812 is gone for ever. I am a woman now. I have independent thoughts and ideas. . . . Have you heard of Mary Wollstonecraft?"

"Should I have? Is she somebody you have in mind for the position of housekeeper?"

Mary Emma laughed at the bizarre idea. "No; the lady's been dead for almost twenty years but she wrote a marvellous book, *Vindication of the Rights of Woman*, and any woman who's read it is never the same again. I read it last year."

Not deigning to comment and silently cursing Mary Wollstonecraft, Tom changed the subject: "About this housekeeper business. You'd better have a word with Joseph when you're ready to engage her. Up until now it's been his responsibility to engage staff and we mustn't offend him. I suggest you speak to him about it soon."

Tenacious as a bull terrier, she said: "And the lime walk?"

He marched away two strides and the same number back in order to maintain his self-control. "Saints preserve us, Mary Emma! What would you have me do?"

"Would it carry any weight if I were to tell you that the fortune left me by my guardian is to the tune of thirty thousand pounds per annum?" Tom's eyes opened wide as the figure penetrated his brain. "And that I have inherited, for my sole use, the annual profits proceeding from a sugar plantation in Barbados, along with a considerable quantity of jewellery?" Overwhelmed, Tom sank onto a chair. "Well, Mr Challiss, sir? Am I to have my lime walk?"

"Well... I think it might just be possible to squeeze a little out of our annual budget to allow you to proceed with your plan, my dear. But you must observe strict protocol and speak to Joseph and Jem as to the choice of site." Seeing her ready to protest, he forestalled her: "However, I think you might rely on me to throw in a good word." Until now he had thought himself adept at managing women and he wondered why nobody had ever told him how difficult some women could be.

"Thank you, darling," Mary Emma said, giving him a kiss. "I thought you might be pleased about the legacy. Oh! Tapp, Tapp and Cummins – a firm of solicitors at Cromer – were appointed by my guardian to look after his interests, Miss Peters told me, and wrote down their names unless I should forget it. As if I could! It's so droll." Their tempers restored, they laughed together before Tom said: "How is it that firms entrusted with managing the affairs of others so often bear comical names?"

"More memorable, I suppose," Mary Emma laughed. "Now, Tom; we must be deadly serious."

"Eh?"

"I'm off to the kitchen to make myself known to the servants in my capacity of Mistress of Uppham. I've already made the acquaintance of Maddy, Bob, Peckover and Rudge; but I feel dignity requires of me that I make a formal visit to the kitchen. I'll see you at luncheon."

He took himself upstairs to read the letters Aldrich had given him the night before and smiled as he imagined his wife's chagrin at finding but one more servant to queen it over in the person of the cook, Mrs Rudge.

★

George's letter was the first to be opened. It was dated a week earlier. As soon as Tom's eyes had devoured the spikily-written lines he shouted: "Well done, George!"

Dear Tom,

> *I expected to hear from you before this but I suppose it's a case of out of sight out of mind, you lazy dog. It will not surprise you to learn that I have found Garnet and our daughter, Aurora. The saucy little wench winds her Papa round her little finger and he can deny her nothing. I have to thank you, brother, for reuniting me with my womenfolk. You will be pleased to hear that Garnet and I were married by Special Licence a few days since and that I have booked passage to Canada. We sail on the Fifteenth of September & hope to reach Lower Canada in about six weeks. Once settled I will forward an address. I trust I can rely on you to write. Hope you have been as lucky as I & have found your Miss Kay. Should we never meet again in this life I take this opportunity to tell you that stumbling across you in the army was one of the best things that could have happened to me. I am glad & honoured to have known you.*

> *Good luck with the old place & don't let it kill you off before your time.*

> > *Your Brother, George Wretham Challiss.*

> *P.S. Making you a Present of Quicksilver. Will arrive by special messenger.*
> > *G. W. C.*

So they've already sailed, Tom thought, experiencing a pang as he realised he might never see his brother again. The second letter Tom opened was from his bankers, Bagg and Bacon, requesting him to call in person at his earliest convenience to discuss a very important matter with regard to his financial situation. Puzzled as to what it could mean, he laid the stiff parchment aside to re-read. The gong sounded. The third, grubby-looking letter would keep until after luncheon.

He'd attained his majority on the fourth of July, while searching for Mary

Emma. The anniversary of his birthday had passed unheeded by him on his last visit to Felixton. Only now did he realise that he'd unwittingly celebrated the event by coupling with wall-eyed Mrs Roberts in the spring room of Moat Farm. Just a week ago his future had seemed so bright, his world full of happiness. The dream he'd had on the battlefield at Waterloo was well on the way to becoming reality; and yet the thought of it gave him little comfort. At twenty-one he was Master of Uppham and in the possession of a fortune that would enable him to restore it to its former glory; he had found Mary Emma transformed into a beautiful woman, an ardent lover; and, with the knowledge of the immense fortune she'd brought to the marriage as her dowry, he should have been delighted with the way everything had fallen into his lap. Why wasn't he? Many men would consider themselves extremely fortunate. Yet, at this moment he was depressed. He was unhappy. He'd not enjoyed the quarrel with his wife, his head throbbed, he was devilish hot and now he'd developed a damned tickle in his throat. Must be a cold on the way.

As he mechanically swallowed untasted food he was conscious of Mary Emma's chatter while hearing nothing she said until he was jolted out of his reverie. "What?"

" ...dear Mrs Rudge... Why, Tom! Are you feeling unwell, my dear?"

"What are you talking about?" He spoke sharply. "Why do you ask?"

Jumping up and running round the end of the table to where he was seated she laid her hand on his forehead. "Mercy! Your head's on fire. And your eyes – We must send for a doctor at once." Her voice was distorted, as if it came from the bottom of the black well into which he slipped headlong.

★

"I suspect pneumonitis," the young doctor said gravely as he took Tom's pulse. "How long has your husband been unwell, ma'am?" he asked, as they stood beside Mary Emma's and Tom's bed and gazed down at Tom's stricken figure.

Reminded of Miss Peters' fatal illness, fear clutched at her heart. Oh, God!

"Mrs Challiss, ma'am?"

"Forgive me, Dr Barnes. I'm sorry. How long? I can't say. Except that he's been soaked through twice in the last few days." She was suddenly unable to speak.

"His lungs are inflamed – we don't want it to develop into full-blown pneumonia. But he's young and strong – two powerful aids to recovery. Keep the steam-kettle going night and day to help his breathing; there's not much else I can do. We shall have to wait and see." He was concerned for the young woman, now so deathly pale. "He must be nursed night and day and you'll need all the sleep you can get. You'd better hire a reliable night nurse." He scribbled down a name and address.

Hardly daring to put the question into words, Mary Emma whispered: "Is there nothing more you can do to help him, doctor?"

He shook his head. "No, I'm sorry; but, you must take care of yourself, Mrs Challiss." She followed him downstairs and Peckover returned to him his hat and coat. "Good-day to you," Dr Barnes said, shaking her hand. "Try not to worry too much. I'll look in again tomorrow morning."

News that the master was seriously ill was soon spread by servants' gossip and it wasn't long before word reached the ears of Joseph Aldrich. He arrived at the house at sunset and left his newly-purchased horse with Bob. The youth took the bridle with an approving grin after sizing up the strong-looking black stallion's indeterminate pedigree. That first evening of Tom's illness, Joseph Aldrich established himself as one of the cornerstones of the new régime and indicated to a worried Mary Emma just how valuable and indispensable a friend he hoped to become to them.

★

Falling. Bottomless well; spiralling down, smells − fresh blood, mud and ripe corn... Land lightly as feather on moss. Tom Roberts part of the cacophany. Clash of sabres, bugles blare, horses whinney, cannon thunder, muskets explode, oaths uttered in many tongues, men scream... Tom's head pounds. Mylotte's lips move... Irishman's words drowned by noise of battle... Tom drifting above the carnage − Hougoumont − trampled cornfield. There! Corpses of Tom's friends, the almost-dead, strewn limbs, stretcher-bearers, writhing horses − entrails − eyes − crows, scavengers wrench teeth, draggled women search corpses − horrible! horrible! − Tom voiceless... four peasants stare at him, point fingers of accusation... Tom looks away... still, they point... faces change − to those Tom saw lining the streets of Downham... "Try to swallow some soup, Tom dear." *Mary Emma? ... Must must find her! Dead? Scarlatina... pneumonia... No! Not dead... There she is! Whirling away from Tom in the fens blow... The ring! Reville's stolen her ring... silver spurs. Tumbled from Genty... Scent? Lime blossom...* "What's that, Tom darling?" *Mary Emma?* "He's delirious ma'am." *Falling... falling ... falling... Noah?* "It's all right sir; just lie still." *Floating... Who's that? Tom looks down on a woman in a blue dress.* "Mary Emma!" *Tom's found her, sees the top of her head... she's wearing a strange white cap... long white apron... Not my wife... watch her bathing Tom's forehead.* "My head." *Angelic face... bends over Tom... Mr Challiss? Water cool.* "Thank you." *Falling... drifting... falling... black, black night...*

"He's breathing more freely," Dr Barnes said. "With care, he should recover."

★

As weak as a new-born kitten, Tom lay in bed propped up on pillows. "How long?" he said, in disbelief.

"Almost three weeks, love," Mary Emma said as she busied herself arranging a fresh bouquet of hothouse lilies sent up to the house by Joseph Aldrich. "Aren't they glorious? Joe's been just wonderful, Tom! Why, the first night you were taken ill I was at my wit's end. But everyone was so kind."

"But — *Three* weeks! There must have been a good deal of unpleasant nursing".

"Oh, Nurse Vale took care of that side of things; she's been absolutely splendid, Tom. And I do so like Dr Barnes! He inspires one with such confidence and yet he doesn't try to pull the wool over one's eyes. Oh, dear! He expressly told me not to tire you and here am I prattling on."

Himself drained of energy, he smiled at her youthful vigour. "I love to lie here and watch you; and I'm delighted to listen to you prattling on, my darling. And what's all this about Joseph? When did my old sobersides of a steward become your Joe?"

"When he insisted on taking the first night's watch," Mary Emma said, perching herself on the edge of the bed. "Nurse Vale wasn't free at such short notice and Joe offered to sit with you and to fetch me if necessary. He is a truly good man, Tom."

Lassitude seeped through his body and he closed his eyes. Mary Emma said: "You must rest now, dearest," and brushed his brow with her lips.

The nurse had entered the room unobserved and stood just inside the open bedroom door watching the young couple. *It wasn't so long ago,* she thought, *that I too had a man of my own to love and care for.*

Mary Emma turned away from the bed and was startled to find the nurse in the room. Finger to her lips, she opened the door wider and held it for the young woman to pass through before her. Once out on the landing, she said softly: "He's resting now, Nurse Vale."

"Splendid, ma'am; he'll soon grow strong again now that the worst is over.

Peace and quiet, plenty of sleep and good food can work miracles in such cases; in fact, it's one of the best cures I know for a great many ailments and minor illnesses."

"I'm sure you know best, Mrs Vale. I can't thank you enough for all that you've done for my husband. It was a privilege to be present and observe you at work; I've learned a lot."

A fleeting smile crossed the nurse's face. "Good; I'm glad. But no thanks are necessary, Mrs Challiss; it's my profession. When things go well, I think it must be the most rewarding occupation in the world for a single woman to follow."

Sobered by the implication of what hadn't been said, Mary Emma observed: "You must have seen your fair share of disease and death, Nurse Vale?"

"I have, madam. Now. I think I should sit with Mr Challiss. It's early days yet and one can't be too careful in cases like this. If you'll excuse me, madam."

Mary Emma watched the slender figure of the nurse enter their bedchamber and close the door. She thought again of what she had learned of the nurse's recent past: how, having been married for less than a year, she had been widowed in the final moments of the Battle of Waterloo. Nurse Vale was still only twenty-four. So young, thought Mary Emma; and fear touched her heart at the thought that she might have lost Tom had it not been for the devoted care of Nurse Vale and Dr Barnes. Life without Tom was unthinkable; had he died, her reason for living would have been removed. How petty the silly squabble over the lime walk seemed to her now, by comparison. She saw herself as an immature and spoilt young woman who had been indulged and fussed over from her earliest years. But she had prayed for Tom's deliverance and had made a bargain with God that, if only Tom were spared, she would try to be a better, less selfish person. Now she had no option but to live up to her bargain.

Dr Barnes had advised her to get plenty of fresh air and exercise or, he said, he'd soon have another case on his hands. It being a fine autumn morning, she decided to give Genty a gallop. Still minus a riding habit, she adopted the same dress as before, hoping she wouldn't meet anybody of consequence during her ride. To her chagrin, she had no sooner set out to explore the site she'd proposed to Tom as being suitable for the setting out of the lime walk when she saw Joseph Aldrich approaching. There was no way of avoiding him and, riding sidesaddle as she always did, she made sure that her cloak was well-wrapped about her legs.

"Good-day to you, Mrs Challiss," he said, doffing his hat, as he drew level.

"It is a very great pleasure to see you abroad on such a splendid day, though, as is often the case, the wind is gathering strength and I'd be surprised if we're not in for a gale before nightfall. How does Mr Challiss seem today?"

"Good-morning, Joe," Mary Emma said. "Better, but very weak still. I left Nurse Vale sitting with him. How d'you find the horse? He looks in fine fettle."

His face lit up at her praise of his animal. "Splendid, splendid. It's as if we were made for each other; he's a tractable beast, aren't you Dimon, old fellow?" he said, patting the horse's neck affectionately. "It's good to hear that Mr Challiss is on the mend; he was very ill and we must thank God for his mercy. As for Nurse Vale; that young woman is most unusual in the devotion she gives to the afflicted – an absolute treasure."

Mary Emma found Aldrich's praise of the nurse too effusive for her taste.

"Are you off anywhere in particular, Mrs Challiss, or might I impose my company upon you? 'Twould give me infinite pleasure, ma'am."

Loath to offend him, she divulged her plan, adding that if he were interested enough to assist her in the pacing out of the area she'd be much obliged. That he was delighted to be of immediate service to her was obvious. Always looking his best in the saddle, he'd appeared to grow an inch taller at her cordial answer.

"I can lay my hand on a Gunter's chain, if you can wait a bit," he said, all efficiency. "It'll prove an invaluable aid to measuring the land with some accuracy."

"Oh." She recalled that a chain had something to do with mensuration but, never having had occasion to put theory into practice, was vague as to its use. "I must return to the house in time to take luncheon at one," she said, controlling Genty who was becoming impatient at inaction.

"Fortunately, it's on our way," he said, urging his horse towards some dilapidated outbuildings. "If you would like to give your restive filly a canter I'll meet you on site in a trice."

It became obvious, as Mary Emma approached her chosen tract of land, that it would be physically impossible to measure the site. Now that she was actually upon it, it seemed a desolate place. The whole area was a tangle of brambles and bindweed, ash saplings and decaying wild flowers. As she gazed at the uncultivated land, bundles of silken filaments were wrenched from the seedpods of rosebay willowherb and flung up into the air as if by an unseen hand; a meandering chain of white stars was carried away from the intertwined mass of thorns, to lodge among the stunted wild trees and bushes. Fancifully she thought: those could be lost dreams. She shivered and refused to believe that the phenomenon portended anything other than perfectly natural and normal seed dispersal by windpower.

Aldrich joined her, glumly surveyed the beggared land before them and turned to her questioningly. "This is the spot you've chosen, ma'am?"

Defensively, she said: "When I first spotted it, it seemed ideal; but, now–"

"Well. It certainly won't be wanted for pasture at the moment; a devil of a job getting it cleared, begging your pardon, Mrs Challiss. And, as far as I'm aware, there are no other plans for its use." He looked away from her and gave a short, awkward cough. "To have this cleared in time to plant saplings this autumn – and we're a bit late for that already – would cost a fortune even if we could find somebody to oversee the project. Something on this scale is beyond my province, you see, ma'am."

To his surprise, Mary Emma smiled. Looking him straight in the eye, she said: "Oh, Joe! You are clever. I know of just such a person." In a rush of excitement, she told him of Adam Brook and the possibility of his moving to Uppham as Head Gardener and Farm Manager. "I think all he needs is a little persuasion. The prospect of such a project as this might just do it. He has a large family to think about; so Tom promised him a house to go with the position. Do you know of anything on the estate that would house them and is also fit for immediate habitation, Joe?"

He'd been taken aback by the sudden news that his own position as steward was in jeopardy. Speaking slowly, he asked: "Is there room for such a post as has been promised to Mr Brook as well as that of steward? Our work would be bound to overlap. I hope his appointment won't mean I'm about to be made redundant."

Horrified at the idea that she had wounded him by her thoughtlessness, she exclaimed: "Oh, Joe! I'm so sorry. Of course not. Your position is secure for life; that's understood. Oh, dear. I shouldn't have meddled – it's not only for myself, though; a lime walk also has special associations for Mr Challiss. It's bad enough to have to wait for the trees to reach maturity; but I cannot rest until work on the lime walk begins. My husband was right to urge patience; I shouldn't have meddled with things that I know nothing about–"

"Please, please, my dear Mrs Challiss! Do not reproach yourself like this." Aldrich was all concern for his mistress, himself forgotten. "I'll discuss the construction of the lime walk with Jem Webster; he is the epitome of good sense and prudence and, ten to one, he'll come up with a solution that will suit everybody."

"Thank you, Joe. I'm very grateful."

His face had fallen into sombre lines: "As to the matter of a house for Mr Brook and his family, nothing comes to mind at present – nothing fit to take young children into, that is." He cogitated. "But I think I see a way out, that is, if Brook agrees to take the position. Leave it with me, ma'am." He gave her a rueful smile. "I think we must abandon the plan for the present, Mrs Challiss. But, I promise you, I'll see what Jem can suggest and let you know soon." They rode back the way they had come, the measuring chain lying unused in Aldrich's pannier.

★

"Excuse me, Mrs Challiss." Nurse Vale had reached the bottom of the staircase just as Mary Emma came through the front door. She held out a sealed letter. "This has lain on the dressing table in your room since I first came, ma'am. It's addresssed to Mr Challiss and, I thought, might need an answer."

Mystified, Mary Emma turned the letter over in her hands and said: "I hadn't noticed it; since I took to sleeping on the truckle bed I've not used the dressing table for fear of disturbing my husband." What should she do? She'd interfered enough with Tom's affairs for one day. "Do you think I should ask my husband to open it?"

"No. It might contain something that would agitate him," the nurse replied at once. "To be safe, I rather thought you would read it yourself before giving it to him." With trembling fingers Mary Emma opened out the stiff folds of the letter and looked first to the foot of the page for the signature. From Adam Brook! Oh . . . Why hadn't she found this before the silly quarrel with Tom? "Thank you, Nurse Vale. I'm most grateful to you. I must deal with this immediately."

. . . **canot see my way to make enuf outa gese ●   Therefor I am holding you to your ofer of Head Gardiner at Upam • It will be so much beter for us all • Acourse I canot come less there is an ouse to be thrown in •**

The qestion of wages is <u>most important</u> • •
You agreed to pay me the 1st a the month reglar so that I can see my way clear and stay out of det • I hope that will be so as money

seems to run through Mrs Brook's fingers just like walter • •
Pleas reply at your earlyest convenence Mr Chalis sir •
Things are geting very ~~anx dif~~ • • • ard this end •
  Yours obedently,
                              Adam Brook

The poor man. He must have been looking for an answer every day since posting his letter weeks ago. Perhaps he thought he'd forfeited the chance of the position! It was too bad, and she blamed herself for not finding the letter sooner. Poor Dulcie; she must be at her wits' end with worry. That an answer must be sent at once by express messenger she was certain; but dare she take it upon herself to act on Tom's behalf? If only she knew what to do for the best. Of course. Joe would know how to act and would advise her sensibly. The thought of sharing the responsibility emboldened her. Adam and Dulcie and all the little Brooks must be sent for at once.

In the dining room, Maddy was surprised to see her mistress snatch up a slice of ham and place it between two lettuce leaves. She was even more astonished when Mrs Challiss wrapped the unusual sandwich into a napkin and crammed it into the pocket of her cloak. Maddy had never seen her mistress acting so strangely. When Mary Emma poured herself a glass of wine, drained it in one draught and – without a word to Maddy – ran out of the room again, the girl shook her head in disbelief.

Bob was surprised in the middle of a yawn when he saw his mistress throw the saddle onto Genty's back, adjust the stirrups, snatch up the reins, gallop out of the stable yard and into the park in the direction of the drive.

He was at home! As she sped out of the tunnel she caught sight of him in his garden. Pulling on the reins so hard that Genty's hooves skidded on the grass as they came to a stop, Mary Emma dropped to the ground and ran up to the astonished steward. He'd scarcely been able to believe his eyes when he'd beheld Mrs Challiss galloping towards him riding sidesaddle at breakneck speed, her cloak flapping as if she were a giant bat and her white stockinged legs displayed up to their blue garters!

"What is it, ma'am?" he said, his face a map of concern. "Mr Challiss is not worse?"

"No, no, Joe; but I need your advice urgently. Can you spare me a moment of your time?" He'd soon heard the whole story and concurred with her instinct that the Brook family should be sent for at once. He would himself write the letter to Mr Brook and despatch it by special courier this very afternoon. "There's one other matter that concerns me, rather, ma'am. Where to put the family when they take up residence at Uppham." He studied her reaction.

Her eyes widened at the implication. "There's no house?"

"Not on the estate. However," his eyes sparkled as he waited to spring his surprise; "there is a most suitable house in the village, at Church End. The former occupant, old Mr Bebb the sexton, last in the line of a family even larger than the Brooks, recently died. It's a fine house and I've kept it in reasonably good repair: the odd lick of paint, you know, and the roof is absolutely sound. Bebb's been rattling around in the place for the last ten years since his youngest sister died—"

"But that's splendid!" Mary Emma said, tightly clasping her hands together against her breast. "What about the furniture? They'll want to bring their own things, of course."

"I'll enclose money to pay for cartage and the whole family can travel with their goods." Looking enormously pleased with himself, Aldrich added: "I think that should suffice, Mrs Challiss, ma'am."

"Thank you, Joe. Oh, thank you!" Without thinking, Mary Emma kissed him on the cheek. "You are the nicest, kindest man I know – next to my Tom, of course," she added hastily. At which pronouncement each of them blushed; but for different reasons.

★

It should have been a glorious sunny day, thought Mary Emma as, from one of the upstairs drawing rooms she looked out over the park which was now largely hidden in fog. While she wanted the weather to match her buoyant mood, she refused to be down in the dumps, for the Brook family was expected to arrive in the early part of the afternoon. But there was even greater cause for her happiness: Tom had come downstairs fully-dressed for the first time since his illness. Although signs of the ordeal he'd undergone were still obvious, he was gaining strength daily, though he still needed to put on weight in Mary Emma's opinion. He wasn't quite yet the splendid man she'd married. And that was another thing! Two months had elapsed without a show and she could hardly contain the wonderful news that they were to expect a child in seven months' time. He would be a May baby, just as Dulcie Brook had predicted. He. Mary Emma was as certain that her first child would be a boy as she had been about his conception. It was all too wonderful.

Last week she had returned to their shared bed and had longed to mate with her husband. But Nurse Vale had warned Mary Emma that Tom must be given time to recover his strength: the resumption of conjugal relations must be left to his discretion. Mary Emma realised that she was being given sound, though unwelcome, advice. Over the recent weeks she had grown to depend on Ruth Vale's sound common sense and had begun to wonder how she would manage once the nurse had departed. Not that Tom needed her services any longer; but the calm, sweet-faced woman had become a staunch friend and Mary Emma would be sad to see her go.

She glanced out of the window. The fog had thickened and was swirling among the tops of the trees where tattered brown and yellow leaves hung glistening and dripping with moisture. They *must* come soon; darkness would be upon them in a few more hours and the children should not be exposed to this damp air. As if in answer to her thoughts, she caught a faint sound, the hooves of several horses, clip-clopping slowly out of the tree-tunneled drive, which grew louder by the second. Shrill excited voices provided a descant to the jingle and clatter of the team of horses and the roll and creak of the pantechnicon. The lumbering vehicle, swaying precariously from side to side, emerged from the fog. It reminded Mary Emma of one of the black tugs she'd seen at Scarborough rolling about in a swell at sea; and because the cart's enormous wheels were hidden by ground mist the nautical illusion was realistic. The long-suffering carter, so well-wrapped up that he himself seemed to be an especially large parcel, hauled on the reins and brought the noisy contraption to a halt in front of the steps. As if wakened from a daydream, Mary Emma jumped off the window seat and hurried down the stairs to greet the Brooks. On her way past the library she banged on the door without pause and called: "They're here, Tom."

He was beside her in a moment, ready to escort her down the steps; but she turned to him and said: "No, Tom. You're not quite well, yet, dear. You must stay in the warm. This damp air is treacherous." He looked so disappointed that she stood on tiptoe and kissed him and her spontaneous demonstration of affection had the desired effect.

"Of course, you're quite right, my love," he said, and a sigh of exasperation escaped him. "Nurse Vale has forbidden me to set foot outside the door until next week at the earliest and only then if the weather's fine. Damn this fog! You go ahead and welcome Adie and Dulcie and make my excuses – but don't make too much of a fuss about it!" he called after her as she wrapped a shawl around her shoulders and descended the steps. John Brook was first to emerge from the back of the covered cart and the boy stood gazing about him. He was soon joined by Ann, Fanny and Dovey. Mr and Mrs Brook next appeared, Dulcie with Noah struggling in her arms and shrieking: "Det down! Det down!"; of which she took not the slightest notice.

Young Zeb was the last to leave the cart and made his appearance tousle-headed and rubbing sleep from his eyes. While the children, except John, who considered himself superior by virtue of age from the rest of his siblings, surged around Mary Emma and told them a tangled version of the trials and tribulations of their protracted journey out of the Isle of Axholme, Adam and Dulcie waited for the moment when Mary Emma would be free to welcome them. "Run up the steps to the front door and push it open – it isn't fastened – and you'll find Mr Challiss waiting to welcome you just inside the door. He's been ill –" she spared the Brooks an eloquent look– "and so he mustn't come out in the fog."

Bob had come running at the sound of horses and catching Mary Emma's signal shouted up to the carter to turn his team and vehicle and follow him.

As her last words had trailed up the steps behind the departing children, Mary Emma had turned and held out her hands to Adam and Dulcie. "Welcome to Uppham, Mr and Mrs Brook! Tom and I are so glad that you decided to come—"

Her words were cut short by Dulcie who had thrust Noah into her husband's arms as Mary Emma had begun her speech and now clasped the young matron in a firm embrace. They drew apart and, her eyes sparkling, Dulcie Brook said: "Bless yew, yew darling girl; bless yew and yer husband both." She smiled at Adam. "Here, Adie, give 'im ter me."

"Det down!" urged the wriggling bundle; and this time his mother allowed Noah his freedom, watched him fondly as he climbed the stone mountain in the wake of his brothers and sisters to find out where they'd gone, and followed watchfully behind him.

"It's so good to see you, Adam," Mary Emma said, shaking his hand. "Tom has been looking forward to your coming immensely. Indeed, both of us are overjoyed that you've agreed to take the position."

"Dunno bout that, Mary Emma . . . ma'am," he said as they followed Dulcie up the steps. "Nasty ole daggly day, innit? Ter tell yer the truth, we was more or less on our beam ends when that messenger rode up as if Beelzebub were after 'im. We'd almost give up 'ope, yer see; thought the letter'd gorn astray. But Mrs Brook kep' on sayin' as 'ow yew an Mr Challiss wouldn't let us down. That there 'ad ter be a reason fer us gettin no answer. An she was right. She usually is." They'd reached the top step; but Brook wanted to finish. "Acourse, I aint no letter writer. Thatten were the first I ever wrote in me life," he added proudly. "But Dulcie's 'ad some schoolin' an she 'elped me with the spellin so we got along that way, yer see. Anyways, here we are, an right glad ter be 'ere after sich a wearyin' time of it." He stood at the top of the flight of steps and turned about with the intention of surveying his new kingdom. "Nothin' ter see save a few daggly trees on a day like this; fair mecks yer all of a dudder," he said, shaking his shoulders in an exaggerated shiver.

Mary Emma laughed at his clowning. "Then you'd better come into the warm at once, Adam," she said, as she pushed open the door.

After the sick-room silence that had reigned throughout the house for weeks, the noise made by the liberated and excited children running in and out of rooms and up and down the stairs was deafening by contrast; but Tom was smiling.

"Come in! Come in out of the damp, Adam," he said, clasping Brook's hand. "Welcome to Uppham." He looked about him distractedly. "Mary Emma," he called, spying her standing behind Noah as the yearling ascended the staircase at breakneck speed, "shall we take tea, and perhaps something a little more warming, in the dining room, my dear?"

"Of course, Mr Challiss," she answered, careful to see that Tom be accorded the dignity of his position before his presumed subordinates. "I'll be down directly." Catching Noah around his middle, she hugged him to her and whispered: "How would Noah like some lovely cake?" and made him her slave – temporarily.

After their marathon journey – for it had taken them several days to accomplish – the Brook family were grateful to be grounded and beneath the roof of a house. They had slept under the canvas covering of the pantechnicon for the last four nights and made do with food that Dulcie had scrabbled together for the duration of the ride. Water had been their only drink, apart from a quart of milk that had been carried for Noah. That had turned sour by the end of the second day so the boy had had to put up with the same drink as the rest of them; but he'd not seemed any the worse for it. "Pore Zeb'd began tew suffer from the swayin of the cart right away," Dulcie was saying as the tea-things were in the process of being removed by Peckover, assisted by Maddy. "Couldn't keep a morsel down, the pore lamb. But nature's a funny thing; he began ter sleep fer much o' the time the cart was on the move. Then, when we got tew our resting place for the night, he'd become as bright as a button again, pruggin about with the others as if nothing'd ailed 'im." . . . And so the afternoon wore away into a murky dusk and the younger children began to flag. At six-o'clock, after a good meal which had included plenty of milk and fresh fruit, Dulcie and Ann gave each of the little ones a quick wash to remove the worst of the dust of travelling. The two youngest were worn out and made no protest when carried up to beds which had been moved into Tom's former bedchamber.

John, Ann and Fanny, feeling very grown up, were permitted to stay up until eight o'clock. Dovey's eyes had begun to droop a good hour before the appointed time; but she stubbornly refused to be shown her bed until Ann and John left the charmed circle of which they formed a part. All five children had been crammed into two beds, which was nothing new to them: John and Zeb in one, Ann, Fanny and Dovey in the other. Noah was to sleep in the adjoining dressing room with his parents. This arrangement suited everybody; for the Brooks were together in their own unit yet well away from Tom and Mary Emma's room in the west wing. Within a few days the Brooks would move into the house at Church End, which was in the final stages of a complete spring-cleaning and redecoration under the joint supervision of Ruth Vale and Joseph Aldrich. The scheme had given paid employment to many grateful villagers and, in addition, Aldrich had set himself the task of tidying up the large garden during the few hours of light remaining after his long day's work.

"It's another part of the dream falling into place," Tom said to Mary Emma as they climbed into bed. "How lucky the Brooks are to have such a fine, sturdy brood. It's time we gave serious thought to starting our own dynasty, my love," he murmured, as his hand found her breast. She melted at his touch and thanked God for her deliverance from celibacy before revealing to him her astonishing secret.

★

Chapter Twenty-four

On a dark and dismal day in late November, Mary Emma found herself in the unusual position of being at a loose end. The constant upheaval arising from weeks of reparation and decoration of the mansion were driving her to distraction. The mess and dust made by the workmen was frightful and she had given up insisting that the rooms they had formerly occupied be cleaned daily. Once their home had been commandeered by the army of builders, plumbers, carpenters, plasterers and painters, attempting to live among such chaos had become impossible. How could Joe Aldrich have even contemplated the idea of beginning the restoration of Uppham House at such a miserable time of year? She knew how. His usually sharp mind had become preoccupied. His involvement with Nurse Ruth Vale had begun with an exchange of ideas for improving the property as they'd laboured together on improving the house and garden at Church End, and Mr and Mrs Brook and their six younger children had moved into their comfortable home three days after their arrival at Uppham.

Their work completed, Aldrich had returned to his lodge and Nurse Vale to her cottage in Downham. Yet, there had been reports of the two being seen together in close conversation not only in the High Street of Downham but also among the cottages and farms of Uppham St Mary. It seemed that a warm friendship had developed between the widower steward and the widowed nurse and that friendship had, in turn, ripened into deeper feelings on both sides. Now the two, whom Mary Emma would have categorized as being among the most level-headed creatures on the face of the earth, were seldom out of one another's company and 'definitely moony-eyed' — Maddy's description of their current state. In daily expectation of hearing the announcement of their betrothal, Mary Emma had grown impatient when no such news had been forthcoming.

Worst of all had been Tom's and her own removal to a shabby suite of rooms in the east wing of the mansion while the rest of the west wing was being fully restored to match the high standard of their private rooms. The light at the east end of the house was cheerless at any time of year after mid-morning; but as the year died it became so gloomy that she couldn't settle happily to any of the pastimes she generally enjoyed when at leisure. Today, the only occupation that recommended itself to her was to lose herself in the reading of a really good book. If only Downham were not such a sleepyheaded kind of place the bookseller would have had in stock plenty of copies of the book whose title – among the educated classes, at least – was on everybody's lips and she would have been, at this very minute, occupied and happy.

A month before, on a rare visit to the draper's shop in Downham, Mary Emma had overheard two gentlewomen discussing, with great animation, the plot of Miss Austen's *Pride and Prejudice*. It had sounded so amusing: just the kind of enchanting, romantic story in which she delighted – so thoroughly modern – that, her business at the draper's concluded, she had hurried straight from the premises to the nearest bookseller to buy a copy, only to be told that he was sold out. It wasn't until after she'd placed the order at Downham, weeks ago now, that she'd read in Tom's *Gazette* that the book had actually been published two years earlier. Had she been aware of that fact before placing her order with a provincial bookseller, she would have sent immediately to *Hatchard's* in London's Piccadilly, for a copy and would have been, at this very moment, lost among its pages. It really was too bad!

Oh… Why had Tom had to go to Lynn again today? To be fair, he'd invited her to accompany him but she'd declined. Now she'd give anything to be released from the topsy-turvy house and the consuming boredom brought about by the unusual circumstance of being at a loose end. It would be hours until Tom returned from Lynn…

Remembering that, as yet, nothing had been done towards clearing the library, she thought that there must be something of interest among so many volumes, foxed and dilapidated though many of them were, and she decided to try her luck there. It was quite a trek from the east wing and along the passage to the centre of the house where the library was situated. The room had been unoccupied for a good while and smelled of the damp whose brown stains mapped the walls and ceiling. That should have been cured, now that the roof had been re-slated, thought Mary Emma, and she made a mental note to give Rudge instructions to have the library fire lighted twice a week throughout the winter months.

Quite why the day of their quarrel over the planting of the lime walk should have entered her mind at that precise moment, Mary Emma couldn't have said. She'd been into the library on several occasions since then without arousing memories of that unpleasant time. As she recalled her behaviour on that day and her part in the argument, she felt herself blush with shame, and saw re-enacted in her mind's eye how Tom had angrily directed her attention to the books on Household Management.

She sighed as she sauntered over to the shelves which he had indicated, and she had pointedly ignored, and ran her hand along the leatherbound spines. She'd had enough experience of household management in these last weeks to last her a lifetime, she thought with irony, as she idly removed the slimmest volume she could find from among those shelved in front of her. Unable to stop herself thinking about the delights to be had if only she could have been curled up before a roaring fire, devouring with her eyes the pages of *Pride and Prejudice*, she stifled a yawn, took the slim library volume over to the window to make the most of the poor daylight, opened it at the first page and was spellbound by the precise and delicate copperplate which covered the page. Before Mary Emma had completed reading the first entry she realised that she had stumbled upon a treasure and turned it over in order to read its title. Stamped into the leather of the spine in gold lettering she read: *The Commonplace Book of Lavinia Wretham Challis, June 1780.* George Challiss's mother? So absorbed had Mary Emma become in the intricacies of household management, much of which was totally new to her, that she was startled as the door was thrust inwards. She peered across the darkened room towards the doorway.

"What on earth are you doing, sitting here in the cold and dark?" Tom asked her crossly. Flinging down the book, she ran into his arms.

★

Surrounded by the smell of fresh paint and the paraphernalia of decorating, they reclined upon a dust-sheeted sofa in front of a huge log fire. They felt at home in the dining room and returned there each evening in order to save the servants extra work on their account. The meal over, they sat in companionable silence: Mary Emma happy to have Tom's arm about her shoulders and Tom happy to feel her body close to his. He broke the long and congenial silence by saying: "What a frustrating time it's been, this last few weeks. I had hoped that the men would've made swifter progress; now it seems doubtful if everything will be in place before the end of the year. You would be better away from all this upheaval, my love"

She pulled away from his embracing arm and faced him. "Are you saying that you want me out of the way?" she asked in surprise.

"It's not what I want at all, Mary Emma. But you must admit that, with the place in such a confounded mess, in addition to my being out of the house for the greater part of each day, it would be pleasanter – more beneficial – for you to be elsewhere in your delicate condition, my dear," he said. "There's the child to consider." He was discomforted by her peal of laughter. "Oh, Tom! You sound like an old married man. We're not quite Darby and Joan yet, dearest. What nonsense you do talk! Ruth Vale says I must live a perfectly normal life, eat well and take plenty of gentle exercise—"

"–And that's another thing! Whatever Nurse Vale says, I won't have you galloping about at top speed on Genty. Now that cannot be sensible for somebody in your condition. Suppose you took a tumble?"

"Did I hear my lord actually say 'won't have' ? But you're right, Tom; I must take care of myself; but I feel so well. And I refuse to be banished from my husband's affections."

"Good; that's as it should be. But I don't like to find you sitting alone in dark, cold rooms when I come home. That cannot be good for you, Mary Emma. I couldn't believe my eyes when I realised it was you seated by the library window. You looked so. . . so lonely."

"Well, I wasn't lonely in the least," she lied. "As a matter of fact, Tom, I was following your advice. I've found the dearest little book on housekeeping."

He caught up her hand and held it briefly to his lips. "I wish you wouldn't rake that up, darling. I had hoped it was long forgotten."

Kneeling up and pecking him on his cheek, she smiled. "I didn't mean to be unpleasant, Tom." Anxious to demonstrate to each other that the quarrel was truly forgotten, they embraced warmly and, after a few moments fell to discussing all that had occurred since the foggy arrival of the Brook family...

Once Tom had been pronounced out of danger, Joseph Aldrich and Ruth Vale had taken charge of much of the organisation involved in temporary removal to the east wing of Tom's and Mary Emma's belongings. For two days and two nights before their installation blazing fires were lighted in every room, floors swept, aired bedding carried into the best of a poor selection of bedchambers and the windows were opened on dry, sunny days – in short, the place had been made as comfortable as possible.

The day after he and his family had removed to the refurbished house at Uppham St Mary, it being fine and sunny, Adam Brook had walked the considerable distance to the site Mary Emma had chosen for the laying out of the long avenue of limes. He'd fully understood her eagerness to get the saplings established and, with the aid of an army of day labourers engaged – at two shillings a day – from the superfluity of men idling about Uppham St

Mary and Downham, the huge area had been cleared within three days. Aromatic blue smoke from great bonfires composed of scrub, bushes and scraggy trees had drifted over the park and the vista that had been opened up, once the scrub had been removed, vindicated Mary Emma's choice of site. Adam visualised the lime walk in its maturity and approved the project with his whole heart. It reminded him of his early days as a young gardener at Lyndon Manor; and he marvelled that nobody could have foreseen that little Miss Kay, who had played under the great limes there, would one day be the instrument of his change of fortune.

Head Gardener, Mr Adam Brook, had convened a meeting in his comfortable front parlour to discuss the distribution of labour between himself, Jem Webster and Joseph Aldrich in order to avoid the overlapping of areas of authority. He'd said adamantly that he wanted no part in the management of the farm. This had surprised the other two, who had assumed the position filled. "Much as I'd like tew offer meself," Jem had said, "I han't got the necessary knowledge. But I dew know of a farmer whose bin turned orf 'is land; a sound man, honest an trustworthy. Shall I put it tew 'im first, or should we let Mr Challiss know, even though he aint properly mended yet?" Tom, still suffering from the early stage of pneumonitis, had not learned of the appointment of Kit Warrender until a fortnight later, after Joseph Aldrich's consultation with Mary Emma and Ruth Vale. He had met Warrender very briefly since and had approved his appointment as farm bailiff.

Once restored to health, Tom put into practice a scheme he'd had in his head almost as soon as he'd won Uppham from his brother. The terrible plight of the unemployed labourers, their numbers grossly swelled by former soldiers and sailors made redundant by the cessation of the war with France, had continued to haunt him. Wanting to do what he could to alleviate the plight of these men who, through no fault of their own, found themselves in the position of landless serfs, Tom had devised a plan that would give some of them the means of growing their own food. If the men were to work small strips of his land and grow upon it potatoes, turnips, cabbages and other means of nourishment, they would not only be enabled to feed themselves and their dependents, but also their time would be spent in useful labour. This in turn would restore to the men the dignity without which they perceived themselves as no better than the lowliest animal. By making space on his land to provide allotments to the starving agricultural labourers he hoped to be able to help them and their families survive the long winter.

While it was too late to do much more than designate the area to be given over to the allotments, which would number fifty to begin with, and to mark out the plots – each one chain in length by half a chain in width – Tom and Adam were all too aware that they would produce nothing much for the coming winter. Added to that, was the knowledge that no crops had been produced on Uppham lands within the last few years. There would be no grain to spare and moreover, there would be no winter threshing in consequence: work that had, in former years, been a means of sheltered employment throughout the long winter months. Added to that, the hay crop was of such a poor quality that Tom had had to buy in three wainloads of hay from a neighouring farmer who had produced more than he needed and it seemed to him that he was spending money hand over fist with nothing to show for it in the way of profit. One evening Mary Emma, finding him in an unusually quiet and thoughtful mood, discovered that he was worrying that his fortune, that had once seemed so vast that it was apparently inexhaustible, might be running through his fingers.

"Surely not, Tom," Mary Emma said, worried in turn at seeing him so obviously upset. "What have Bagg and Bacon to say about it?"

"That I have nothing to worry about. That it's far too soon for any interest to have accrued from the investments made in my behalf... and yet I'm uneasy—"

"Have you spoken about this to anyone else, dear? Joe; or that friend of yours at Fakenham?"

"Daniel Jones. No, I haven't." In his agitation, he'd begun to stride up and down. He halted in front of her. "Perhaps I should. I'm not much use here at the moment," he murmured. "Plenty of others to oversee everything." Suddenly: "Mary Emma! How does a short trip to Fakenham strike you?"

She cried: "Why, I should love it above all things, Tom. I can think of nothing better than getting away from Uppham in its present state at the moment."

★

The clarence was proving too useful at Uppham at present, having been pressed into service to transport Ruth Vale to and from Aldrich's lodge to the mansion where she slept each night. Presently unemployed in her professional capacity, the nurse had agreed to take on joint responsibility with the steward for seeing that, during their absence, Tom's and Mary Emma's wishes were carried out to the letter.

The weather had turned bitterly cold and the sky was filled with that unique light that presages a fall of snow. Mary Emma looked up as the first flakes fell; she peered out from the window of the covered coach that Tom had hired and the snowflakes appeared almost black against the light. "Mmm. That smell! How lovely fresh snow is, Tom," she said as the carriage drew into a space beside a handsome house bordering the High Street. "That first soft downy fall, that settles on even the tiniest ledge and picks out the bare twigs and the textures of the trunks of the trees – it's so beautiful. Is this it? What an impressive *façade*. Oh! I'm so glad we came away."

The front door had been flung back and Daniel Jones came out with a muffler wound about his neck whose fringed ends reached almost to his feet. Lodged among his black curls, snowflakes glittered in the glow that came from the illuminated windows of the house. "Welcome, welcome," he said warmly, while shaking Tom's hand. "So good to see you, Tom. Won't you introduce me to your charming wife?"

Clad in a claret-coloured full-length woollen cape, its fur lining complementing a saucy beaver bonnet, Mary Emma was a credit to her proud husband. The attorney's close scrutiny of her face combined with the icy air on her warm cheeks caused her to blush furiously. She smiled as much from the sheer exhilaration of her release from the confines of the musty coach as at Daniel, and he understood only too well what all the fuss had been about on Tom's part. He thought of the near-tragedy of the stolen limeflower ring and experienced a glow of satisfaction as he recalled that it was he who had been the means of restoring the trinket to the young lady's hand.

The introductions over, the attorney said: "Well, come in out of the cold. This is a delightful surprise, Tom. Delightful!"

"We simply had to escape the interminable chaos," Tom explained as they followed their host up the narrow staircase. "We've been living in dust and dirt for – well. . . it seems like for ever!"

Mary Emma laughed. "Looked at from this distance, I cannot imagine how we stood it for so long. Drying paint is the most awful smell imaginable; and just to be able to breathe air that is not full of plaster dust is wonderful."

Looking at her, the attorney was almost reconciled to the idea of matrimony as he replied: "Well, my dear lady, please make yourself at home for as long as you deem it necessary for the recovery of your health! I'm only sorry I hadn't more notice of your coming so as to rearrange my professional commitments."

Embarrasssed by the breach of etiquette implicit in Daniel's last remark,

Tom said: "Yes. My apologies, Dan; but it was decided on the spur of the moment."

"I understand how it was and meant no criticism, Tom; please, forgive my clumsiness of expression. What I intended to say was that I would have made enquiries about entertainment in the locality; but I seldom indulge in such things myself. I'm afraid you will be thrown upon your own devices during the day. Still, here's the local rag ; it might be of some help." He gave Tom a single news sheet.

Daniel's manservant materialised. "Some tea and toast, as soon as you can manage it, Frith, if you please," the man's master commanded and, after a deferential bow, the etiolated wraith retired to do his master's bidding. "Should warm you up," the attorney said cheerfully as with small steps he crossed the room to the windows. "Snow's beginning to settle, I see. Now. Draw your chairs up to the fire and we'll make ourselves cosy," he said, energetically closing the window curtains with noisy swishes of brass rings across brass poles.

Tom began: "I'll come straight to the point of our visit—"

"Ah! I suspected there might be an ulterior motive that brought you away from your little paradise," the attorney smiled; "something other, that is, than the repainting of the rainbows."

Mary Emma didn't quite know what to make of him. That he admired and respected her husband was clear to her. That he respected her, as Tom's wife, was evident. Yet she sensed there was a quality in Daniel Jones that defied analysis so far.

"I'm not happy with the management of my finances." Tom stopped short as Frith glided in with a laden tray, deposited it on a small table beside the fire and withdrew.

"No need to worry about Frith," Daniel assured him. "Go on."

"Well… that's everything in a nutshell," Tom said, feeling slightly foolish.

"Hmm." The attorney stood up and began to distribute napery and plates of buttered toast.

"Would you like me to pour?" Mary Emma asked, and proceeded to do so after Daniel had assented.

After a further hiatus, in which cups of tea were handed round, the attorney said: "I shall have to ask you to be a little more explicit, Tom. Just what is it that is unsettling you?"

"Nothing I can put a finger on," Tom said miserably. "But – well – on my last visit to my bankers—"

"Who are?"

"Bagg and Bacon, of Lynn—" The attorney emitted a soft, "Ah!" but motioned with a rotating hand that Tom was to continue: "—I was astonished to discover that the statement of my account showed a figure far short of what I had thought I actually had deposited with them."

"Tom!" Mary Emma exclaimed. "Why on earth have you not mentioned this to me?"

Jones registered surprise at her interruption. "And how do you think I might be of assistance to you?" he asked Tom.

"I thought that you might be able to get to the bottom of it," Tom said, lamely.

His hands beneath his coat tails, his handsome head bowed in thought, the lawyer began to pace the carpet while Tom and Mary Emma nibbled toast and sipped tea. "That might not be an easy thing to accomplish, Tom," was his disappointing conclusion. "They are a large and well-respected banking house. To my knowledge, they are utterly trustworthy in any financial dealings with their regular clients… at least, I never heard of anything untoward connected with the bank's name. Are you certain you have grounds for suspicion?"

Tom moved uneasily in is chair. "No. Well… not exactly. I mean – I understand the basic figures… It's just that I thought I had so much more money than they tell me I have." He tried to avoid his wife's expression of astonishment.

Puzzled, Daniel sighed and shook his head from side to side then looked at Mary Emma. "Mrs Challiss. Do forgive us for discussing dull financial matters in your presence "

"Not at all, Mr Jones," Mary Emma said firmly, responding to his patronising air with hauteur. "I find the subject absolutely fascinating. I can't think when I was last so pleasantly diverted. I'm only too happy to sit here and listen."

"Oh." He was plainly discomforted by the young woman, scarcely more than a girl out of the schoolroom. "In that case—" he said coolly, turning to Tom. "Suppose we start at the beginning. How much was your fortune worth when you deposited with Bagg and Bacon initially?"

"Three hundred thousand pounds."

The attorney's supercilious expression underwent a dramatic change. "You're certain of that figure, Tom? Would you mind very much writing it down?" He fetched pen and paper.

Tom took the pen, dipped the quill into the inkpot and wrote down a chain of numbers. "There," he said, handing the sheet of paper to Jones.

"The figure you have written here," he said, "is thirty thousand pounds. Is that what you meant to write?"

Tom jumped up and towered over his friend. "But that's what Bagg led me to believe," he said, in some distress. "And on my last visit to the bank I found it has dwindled to less than twenty-two thousand. Are you saying that they are right?"

"I don't know. What made you think that it should be ten times as much as you actually had?"

He felt sick. Why had he imagined that figure? Tom asked himself. *Had* he imagined it? Desperately, he closed his eyes and tried to transfer himself back to the diamond merchant's premises in Calais. He watched as Monsieur Fleury held the yellow diamond up to his eyeglass for minute inspection; saw the merchant scribble a row of figures on the receipt as he rapidly recited the amount in francs. Tom's comprehension of the French tongue had never been one of his strengths. Inside his head he vainly tried to slow down the Frenchman's pronunciation of the sum – and failed in the attempt.

"Tom?" Mary Emma's hand was on his arm.

He opened his eyes and said slowly: "I believe I've been a damned fool. I beg your pardon, my dear. Either I misunderstood the Frenchman to whom I sold the diamond or he cheated me."

"You *sold* the diamond?" Daniel said, allowing a note of excitement to creep into his voice. "Tell me all about it." The lawyer and Mary Emma were enthralled by the tale he related. "Then there was a receipt," Daniel said, as Tom finished.

"Yes."

"Can you put your hand on it?" Daniel asked urgently.

Tom thought hard. So much had happened since the sale of the diamond that he was no longer sure where to look for the receipt, even supposing he hadn't already lost it. "I'm not certain. I've a suspicion that it was stolen from me on the Dover Road... Yes. I'm certain now. It was in my pocket book. I lost everything when I was attacked by a pack of ruffians: except Mary Emma's ring, that is, which I'd sewn into my hat. It's no use going over it. I've lost a fortune." His shoulders slumped.

"Oh, dear Tom!" She was beside him. "Pray, don't distress yourself. Things might be a great deal worse, my love."

Daniel Jones threw her a sardonic look. How could anybody, even a woman, be so sanguine about the loss of so much money? "You say you have something of the order of twenty-two thousand pounds in your account at this moment?"

"Give or take a few hundred for unpaid accounts," Tom said gloomily.

"Then you are a very fortunate man, Tom. Much might be made of even half such a sum by judicious investment."

Mary Emma spoke up. "Tom. I've been thinking. Are you sure that Monsieur Fleury quoted you the price for the diamond in pounds sterling?"

"By Gad, madam!" Daniel Jones said, in his enthusiasm clasping her hand between both his own and removing them at once. "That's it! Were you paid in coin?"

"Most of it was in gold louis," he said, visualising the heavy panniers, "but there was also a bundle of notes—"

"That's dashed odd!" the attorney said, frowning. "Tell you what I'll do," he said, jumping up and going to his desk. "I'll write to Spector's bank at Dover and see if old Spector has kept a copy of the banker's draft he sent to Bagg and Bacon. It'll take some time to get to the bottom of this, Tom; but, as far as I can tell, there are no grounds for thinking you've been swindled. Leave everything to me, old chap."

Relieved to have the mystery explained, even though the explanation had reduced his fortune by such a vast amount, Tom said: "I can never thank you enough, Dan. You have set my mind at rest as far as you were able."

"Nonense! It was Mrs Challiss who solved the mystery for us. I congratulate you, madam." He bowed from the waist.

It was too much for Mary Emma, who smiled and said: "I do wish you would call me either Mrs Challiss or, even more to my liking, Mary Emma. As yet, sir, I am but seventeen and being addressed as *madam* – though technically correct according to the rules of etiquette – makes me sound too much like one of my own grandmothers – except that I have no idea just who my grandmothers were."

Taken aback by this saucy speech, Daniel was at a loss as to how to respond; but Tom burst out laughing. "Really, my love," he spluttered, "have you any idea how absurd you sound? But I agree; you don't deserve to be adressed as madam for some months yet and I think we all know each other well enough now to address each other by our Christian names. What say you, Dan?"

He inclined his head and smiled his most charming smile: "By all means. I shall be delighted to be accorded that familiarity – Mary Emma."

She was annoyed to find herself blushing. "Good. And may I call you Daniel in return?"

Again, he dipped his head and, this time placed his right hand on his heart. "I am flattered and honoured to be the object of the friendship of such a charming lady."

"Well, don't over do it, old fellah!" Tom chided him, only half in jest.

Frith was in the room, his presence announced by the most delicate of coughs.

"Yes, yes, Frith," Daniel said without turning round to acknowledge him, "you may serve dinner in half an hour. Meanwhile, be so good as to bring us a fresh bottle of claret, will you." The servant left as silently as his own shadow while his master busied himself at a side table with a decanter. "You'll have a sherry before we dine? Tom? Mary Emma?"

Altogether, it was a very pleasant evening. The dinner of roast pheasant was superbly cooked and when the Challisses complimented Daniel on his cook, he laughed. "At times like the present, I send Frith out to the *Crown* which is but a few steps from here. He'll have ordered it soon after you arrived. Now. About tomorrow. I have to pay a visit to Cromer and you, I'm afraid, will be left to your own devices."

Mary Emma clapped her hands and cried excitedly: "Tom. Cromer!"

"Eh?"

"Oh, *dearest* – you cannot have forgotten so soon," she said, as Tom still wore a puzzled look and Daniel, eyebrows raised, awaited enlightenment.

"Really, Tom! *Tapp, Tapp and Cummins*!" she said, enunciating the three names slowly and clearly, as if he were a dunce.

Tom was as mystified as ever; but Daniel said at once: "The solicitors? Am I to understand that you have business with them?"

"Oh . . . them," Tom said, as though waking from a dream. "Why, yes; as a matter of fact, we have. Am I at liberty to divulge in what capacity, my dear?"

"Of course, Tom; it's no secret – at least, not from Daniel."

The story of Mary Emma's vast fortune and the income to be expected from the sugar plantation – whose name, she suddenly recalled, was Eden – was told in a few words. ". . . and Tapp, Tapp and Cummins are the solicitors who dealt with my late uncle's affairs. They have his papers. So, I was wondering–"

Anticipating her request, Daniel said; "But of course, dear lady: we'll travel to Cromer as a threesome. That is, if you have no objection to starting at first light? The snow will, I fear, make it something of a tedious journey; but if you are content I, for one, shall certainly enjoy the company."

"That's very good of you, Dan," Tom said, wondering if his wife had not placed his friend in a position from which he'd been unable to escape without appearing discourteous. "To have my wife's affairs fully explained before transferring everything to Lynn will set our minds at rest."

"I've no wish to interfere in your private affairs, Tom; but have you any objection to my presence at the meeting with Tapp? I expect it's the senior partner with whom you'll deal. You've had one scare, old chap, and perhaps I'll be able to spare you further financial worry."

To Daniel's astonishment, Tom asked: "Is that agreeable to you, Mary Emma, my dear?"

"Thank you for asking me, Tom," she replied. "Yes, most agreeable."

The premises belonging to Tapp, Tapp and Cummins were situated above a funeral director's in the High Street and Mr and Mrs Challiss and Daniel Jones called on the solicitors to explain their business at the earliest opportunity. They were seen in the first instance by Toby Cummins, the junior partner. Prematurely bald and pasty-faced, with strands of black lank hair, the elderly young man seemed to derive a perverse pleasure from telling them that they couldn't possibly see either of the senior partners. Mr Silas Tapp was engaged for the whole of the morning and Mr Jonas Tapp was indisposed; the victim of a vicious wisdom tooth that was averse to cold weather. "But I should be only too delighted to be of service to you, Mr Challiss."

Jones took it upon himself to intervene. "Thank you, Mr Cummins. You'll forgive my speaking out of turn; but I'm here in the interest of Mr and Mrs Challiss." He gave the man his card.

Cummins came down from his high horse as soon as he'd had time to read the piece of pasteboard: *Mr Daniel Jones, LL.D.* "Good heavens! This *is* an honour, my dear sir. Er — Of course. I'll see what I can do to get you an appointment before luncheon; though I know how pressed Mr Silas is, what with all Mr Jonas Tapp's work to handle as well as his own." A door had opened while Cummins was speaking and a man of middle years with a fresh-coloured face topped by a thatch of silver hair stood in the opening and peered at the prospective clients over the top of wire-framed spectacles.

"Did I hear — ? Daniel! It *is* you. This is a very great pleasure." The two men, obviously well-acquainted, shook hands. "Do forgive me, my dear sir,"

Tapp said to Tom. "And madam. Please. If you'll be so good as to go into my office, I'll be with you directly." He said something *sotto voce* to Cummins before following them in. The door closed behind him and he asked them to be seated. "Now." He rubbed his hands together. "I take it, these good people are prospective clients. How can I be of service to you, sir?"

Tom became flustered. "Well, sir; it's actually my wife who has some business with you – But I forget myself. Thomas Challiss; and this lady is my wife, Mary Emma Challiss, born Kay."

As soon as he heard the name of Mary Emma's guardian, Silas Tapp's eyes sparkled with recognition. "Ah! To be sure. Allow me to congratulate you on your marriage, Mrs Challiss. Though it's sad that we should meet for the first time because of the demise of your late uncle, Mr Josiah Kay. He is much missed. Such a splendid gentleman. And you are here, I take it, to look at his will and your inheritance. Quite so, quite so."

Mary Emma nodded. "Yes, Mr Tapp, thank you for sparing me some of your precious time; I know how busy you must be."

"Pray, don't mention it, madam," Silas Tapp beamed. "Here was I feeling down in the dumps with the gloomy weather, with nothing to look forward to all day but a pile of dull, dusty, dreary work. Then you appear and it's as if the sun had walked right into my office." So wrapped up was the solicitor in the youthful vision of Mary Emma in her claret-coloured cloak and stylish beaver bonnet that he missed the amused glances that passed between Tom and Daniel. "It won't take me a minute to put my hand on your late uncle's boxes. I keep all such important items in my safe. Pray excuse me, Mrs Challiss – gentlemen. I shan't be a moment."

Nor was he. He re-emerged from an inner room that was hardly bigger than a cook's pantry carrying three large japanned metal boxes clamped between his arms and chin. Using his raised knee, he swept aside some papers to make room for the boxes and lowered them onto his desk. The visitors noticed that the boxes were of different depths: the bottom box was deepest, the middle of the three less deep and the topmost box might almost be called shallow. Silas Tapp seated himself at his desk, cleared his throat and removed the shallow box from the pile. From a massive bunch of keys on a large ring he separated a smaller ring on which hung three small keys and selecting one of them inserted it into the keyhole of the shallow box. In the expectant silence of the office a burning coal settled and a clock ticked ponderously.

Mary Emma leaned forward in anticipation. Daniel inspected the heel of his boot and Tom, feeling detached from the whole business, stared out of the upper window at the buildings opposite and read the name of **THOMAS HORNER Secret Spring Maker** and wondered what odd business went on under that roof.

"The will is quite straightforward, Mrs Challiss," Tapp said. "Do you wish me to go through it with you?"

"If you would, Mr Tapp."

"Ahem!" Silas Tapp rushed through the preliminaries. "This is the last will and testament of me, Josiah Hobart Kay, of the parish of Felixton in the county of Norfolk, bachelor.'" Here the solicitor paused to regard Mary Emma over the top of his spectacles. Tom and Daniel exchanged looks at this and Dan raised his right eyebrow. "'First, I desire to be decently buried at the discretion of my excecutors hereinafter named; and after all payments of my just debts, funeral and testamentary expenses, I give and bequeath unto my nephew Lambert Jardine, former resident of Hobart, Van Dieman's Land in the Antipodes, Lyndon Manor, its lands and properties thereon and an annual income of two thousand pounds per annum for the upkeep of Lyndon Manor and its estate as long as he resides on the said estate. Should he predecease me, his share of my will is to be included in the bequest to Mary Emma Kay.' "

"But that's extraordinary!" Tom burst out. "Why should Jardine have thrown up such a lucrative property to return to Australia? Unless—"

"If you don't mind, Mr Challiss," Tapp said, "I would rather we didn't go into that at present."

"Forgive my interruption, sir. Please to continue."

"'. . . to be included in the bequest to Mary Emma Kay. To my aforesaid beloved daughter, Mary Emma Kay—" The solicitor paused at a slight interruption. "'. . . to my aforesaid beloved daughter, Mary Emma Kay, until this time known as my niece, I bequeath the whole of my remaining properties on the condition that she attain the age of twenty-five years or, alternatively, that she be married, before she may accede to the said properties.'"

"Daughter!" Mary Emma and Tom had cried out in unison at the revelation, and had fallen silent at the reprimanding look fired from Mr Tapp's grey eyes over the top of his spectacles as he had continued to read after the hiatus.

"'To my friend and companion, Miss Jane Ann Peters, I bequeath an annuity of ten thousand pounds.'" He looked up from the will to say: "I have been unable to contact this Miss Peters—"

"She's dead," Mary Emma said flatly, her eyes filling with tears.

"Oh? I'm sorry to hear that, Mrs Challiss; she was obviously a friend of yours."

Unable to speak, Mary Emma nodded while she sought her handkerchief.

"My sincere condolences, madam," Tapp murmured. He tapped the will. "Do you wish me to proceed?"

"Please."

"The remainder of the will consists of various minor bequests… a small annuity to a former slave in Barbados who goes by the odd single name of Mardi; three thousand pounds to a Mr Wade Southwood, Esquire – again, I have no address for him – nor have I for a certain Adam Brook, to whom Mr Kay bequeathed one thousand pounds." He muttered to himself: "Mrs Esther Mawby, one thousand pounds… et cetera, et cetera… The will was duly executed by Peter Smith, landlord of the *King's Head* at Felixton, the Reverend Arthur Daly and Dr Simon Fitch, both of Felixton, and was proved on the eighth day of December, in the year of our Lord, one thousand eight hundred and eleven. That's the meat of it." He sat back in his chair. "I believe you wanted to say something, Mr Challiss?"

"I am able to tell you the whereabouts of both Mr Southwood and Mr Brook, Mr Tapp, sir."

"Ah. Splendid! Splendid," the solicitor said, rubbing his hands together as if he were a satisfied grasshopper. "Mr Cummins will take down their addresses before you leave." He smiled and his eyes twinkled through his lenses. "Anything else?"

"If I may," Daniel said, uncrossing his legs and leaning forward. "This fellow, Lambert Jardine – Has anything been heard of him since quitting Lyndon Manor?"

Tapp threw him a shrewd look. "Since you mention it… it's widely believed that he perished in the fire–"

"That's not the case, sir," Tom said. "To my certain knowledge, he stayed for a while in the lodge at Lyndon… *after* the fire."

"Really? Thank you for that. I had no idea that he'd been seen again after the night of the fire. My informant was adamant that Mr Jardine never left the premises. So, naturally, I had assumed that he was deceased."

"Was there any investigation? I mean, did anyone examine, thoroughly, the site of the destroyed manor?" Daniel persisted.

The solicitor looked alarmed. "Do I understand you correctly, Mr Jones? Are you implying that there might have been skulduggery?"

"I don't wish to imply any such thing; I asked you if there had been an investigation after the fire?"

Tapp said slowly: "I'm unable to say; but I had no reason – until now – to question the veracity of my informant's testimony."

Daniel leaned nearer Tapp's desk. "The name of your informant, sir?"

Without hesitation, the solicitor replied: "Mrs Esther Mawby."

★

Chapter Twenty-five

Once the will had been read, matters were arranged between Daniel Jones and Silas Tapp to oversee the transfer of the three japanned boxes to Bagg and Bacon's bank at Lynn. The contents of the boxes, when laid out on a baize-covered table in the solicitor's office, had been both a surprise and a revelation.

The middle of the three boxes had contained, among several official-looking documents, three *aquarelles* of what appeared to be the tropics and also a carefully-executed drawing of a beautiful black girl.

When Mr Tapp had lifted the lid of the third and deepest box, the eyes of the onlookers had been dazzled by silent explosions of colour as each item was placed on the green baize: fiery gleams shot from rubies, sapphires, emeralds and opals; scintillating points of light darted from multi-faceted diamonds, peridots, aquamarines and citrines; the quieter, lustrous sheen of ropes of pearls, both white and black, seduced the eye with their flawless loveliness; and, twined together in a glittering tangle, numerous gold bracelets, rings and earrings glistened and twinkled in the November sunlight that briefly found its way into the solicitor's office between the chimney pots. "A pirate's hoard," Mr Tapp had explained. "When the foundations of Mr Kay's new bungalow were being dug in the grounds of his sugar plantation in Barbados an old chest had been unearthed," he'd said, "which, when prised open, was found to hold the treasures you see here." Daniel Jones had remarked that such immense wealth brought with it great responsibility.

After some discussion, they'd thought it best to return the boxes temporarily to Mr Tapp's safe and Mary Emma had agreed to Daniel's arranging for the conveyance of the boxes, as soon as possible to Lynn, by coach and under armed guard.

Tom was stunned by the fact that his young wife was so wealthy. He'd known that she would inherit a fortune from her guardian: but of such magnitude! In his mind's eye he saw the bent and withered owner of Lyndon Manor, but could scarcely connect the crabbed-looking old man with the contents of the japanned boxes. In a rare insight, he thought: every person in the world has a story to tell and we'd be astonished if we knew only half the secrets of those closest to us. Tom shook his head from side to side in amazement, unaware that he did so: *that* old man? While Tom had worked as Gardener's Boy for Josiah Kay at Lyndon Manor it hadn't occurred to him that the gnarled old gentleman might once have been young, had most likely laughed and loved and – most surprising of all – had been something of an adventurer.

After they'd all enjoyed a splendidly-prepared luncheon with Mr Silas Tapp at the solicitor's invitation, Daniel had been left behind in the town to attend to his own affairs. When Tom and Mary Emma had left the inn one of the first things she'd wanted to do while they were in Cromer was to visit Josiah Kay's grave and Tom had decided they must pay another visit to Hannah Mawby at Felixton: the conflicting reports of the fire at Lyndon Manor had unsettled him. What if Lambert Jardine had not gone back to Australia? What if he hadn't perished in the fire? The old dread of Jardine seeking him out had returned and he pinned his hopes on the possibility that Mrs Mawby would be able to enlighten him further on the subject.

★

It didn't take them long to pick out the ornate granite edifice surrounded by arrow-tipped railings: besides which, the newly carved monument was ostentatious and glittered in the sun. Mary Emma carried a cheerful bouquet of dried cape goosberries and honesty – the only plants that had appealed to her in the florist's shop. Close enough to the grave to read the inscription, which had been set into the carved lettering in lead, they read:
Sacred to the Memory of

Josiah Hobart Kay
Born 25th December 1745
at "Eden", Barbados.
Died at Lyndon Manor, Felixton
in the County of Norfolk
3 August 1811
in his 66th year
Requiescat in pace

Mary Emma stretched her arm through the railings guarding the tomb and placed the orange and silver bouquet on the melting snow among the birds' footprints. She sniffed and said: "I didn't know he'd been born on Christmas Day," and dabbing at her moist eyes, "or that he'd been born in Barbados."

"No reason that you should have known, is there?" Tom said as they negotiated the slushy paths on their way out of the cemetery. "But, now you mention it, his skin did have a yellowish cast to it – you know – such as pale-skinned people are left with after living in the tropics. Damnation!" He looked down at his feet and saw that he'd landed himself in a pothole filled with melted snow. This led him to inspect his wife's footwear and he was relieved to see that she was sensibly shod in a pair of highlows made of strong brown leather.

"I hope you approve, sir?" Mary Emma smiled, holding up her right boot for his inspection. "My husband was very severe upon me for getting my feet wet not long ago. You see, Tom, I am capable of taking good advice, my love." Anxious, in turn, for her husband's health, after his recent brush with mortality, Mary Emma said: "We must return to our lodgings at once, Tom, and get you out of those damp boots."

"No need, my love," he said as, arms linked, they slipped and slithered towards the cemetery gates, "these were George's old army boots; absolutely waterproof. I must say, I thought the bent Mr Kay I remember looked older than his actual years."

And with similar small talk they had made their way out of the cemetery.

★

Expecting Esther Mawby's head to appear at the top window of Lyndon Manor lodge in response to his loud "Hullo, there, Mrs Mawby," Tom's spirits plummeted when no sign of life was forthcoming. On further inspection he discovered that the small side gate was locked. As he was walking away in disappointment, Mary Emma bent down and picked up a scrap of paper from the melting snow. "Look, Tom," she said. "It looks like – Yes! It's a note." She gave it to him to decipher.

The ink had run from the effects of moisture and Tom had difficulty in making sense of the blurred, badly-formed handwriting. "As far as I can see," he said, "she's quitted the lodge and gone to live... Here... What does this say?" He pointed to a string of smudged letters and Mary Emma scrutinised them. To make matters worse, the sun had become obscured by clouds and the light had dimmed.

"It looks like... could it be 'pasty'?" Mary Emma asked doubtfully.

"Patsy! ... As-is-Mrs-Frith!" Tom shouted. "Give it to me." He screwed up his eyes as he tried to read by the fading light. "By George, I've got it!" he cried excitedly. "Look." They bent their heads over the sodden scrap which bore the diluted legend:

EMAWBY

GONTERLIV

NICEPASTY

Mary Emma following his index finger as he made out each word. 'E. Mawby' that's Esther 'g-o-n-t-e-r-' ... is that an l? Ah! 'Gone to live nice'? – she means *niece* – Patsy.' That's it! 'E. Mawby. Gone to live' – she's left out *with* – niece Patsy'."

"Where does this Patsy live," asked Mary Emma. "Do you know?"

"No idea," Tom said gloomily as they returned to the coach that had brought them from Cromer to Felixton. "Well I suppose that's that; I don't see what else we can do. It's already starting to get dark."

"Beggin yer pardon, sir," the coachman called down, touching the brim of his hat with his whip handle, "did I 'ear yew rightly? Be yew a-lookin fer Patsy Frith?"

Astonished that help should come from such an unexpected source, Tom looked up to where the coachman was seated on his box. "Do you happen to know where Mrs Frith–" *Mrs Frith!* – "lives, my good fellow?"

"Aye, I dew, sir. She be barmaid at the *Queen's Arms*, Fakenham. That is, if 'tis the same Patsy Frith. 'Tain likely there be tew o' the same name round these parts, is it?"

Fakenham! "No, at least, not very. Thank you – what's your name?" Tom liked the look of the cheerful young coachman.

"Fuller, sir. Glad ter be of 'elp. Shall we be a-goin' on ter Fakenham, then?"

"It's on our way, Fuller." Tom eyed the gathering sable clouds. "How soon can we be there?"

"Time fer dinner, I reckon, sir, all bein well. That do yer?"

Now, seated in the coach they had hired at Cromer, with Fuller at the reins, Tom and Mary Emma bowled along, with fast-approaching night above and mud and freezing slush below, on their way to Fakenham in quest of Mrs Patsy Frith and her aunt, Mrs Esther Mawby. Tom had several questions he wanted to put and, between them, he was certain that those two women had some of the answers.

★

Although Tom had not noticed her behind the public bar of the *Queen's Arms*, Patsy saw the young couple come in and, recognizing Tom, her heart lurched. Tom requested a private dining room, if there was one to be had –

which there was, the landlord told him and, having ordered dinner, asked if he and his wife might have a room for the night. Their host left them while he went about his business and they closed the door of the dining room, which was really little more than a cubicle, and embraced. Mary Emma, eyes dark with desire, looked up at Tom and said petulantly: "So we're going to spend the night here. Couldn't we have gone home, however late?"

He sighed in mock exasperation and kissed the tip of her nose. "Is there no pleasing you, woman? Yes; we could have travelled through the night on dangerously icy roads and we might have reached Uppham in one piece; but I have business here and it won't be concluded until, perhaps, a very late hour." She tried to speak and he silenced her with a kiss before continuing. "Besides which, we are supposed to be taking a break from the chaos at home. Yet, it seems now, you cannot wait to get back to it."

"It's true," she said, tracing the outline of his lips with her finger. "Much as I longed to be quit of the mess and worry, I have a hankering to be back by our own fireside," here she dropped her voice to a whisper, "and in our own bed with you, dear man, beside me."

He laughed. "You are absolutely shameless, Mary Emma – thank heavens."

A knock on the door was followed by their host bearing a tray… An hour had passed and they had removed to the private saloon, Tom taking his brandy with him. A log shifted, flared and settled into the embers and grey ash as they toasted their toes on the iron rail before the hearth. The red, barebricked room was cosy. Candles and firelight flickered on the brick-and-timbered walls, the chairs were upholstered in red plush, and mulberry velvet curtains had been drawn across to shut out the winter night. The landlord poked his head around the door to enquire if they had everything they needed.

"Since you mention it, sir," Tom said drowsily, "I would like a word with one of your servants, Mrs Frith, if I may. Is that possible?"

"'S a busy time, just at present, sir," the man said; "but I'll mention it tew 'er an' let her orf when trade slackens. It usually dew about ten o'clock, if that aint tew late fer yer."

"Thank you. I'm obliged to you," Tom said, suppressing a yawn. "No matter what the hour, I would appreciate a word with Mrs Frith tonight. Tell her I'll make it worth her while." The innkeeper looked at him with increased respect and said that he would see to it that she would "git orf as soon as her gits the chance."

"I'm sorry, dearest," Mary Emma said, following a prolonged yawn, "I simply cannot keep my eyes open a moment longer."

Concerned, Tom said: "How could I be such a fool? Of course, my love: you must get to bed at once. Because you're almost as willowy as ever I keep forgetting your delicate condition. Take care that the bed has been properly aired, Mary Emma, and that a good fire has been lit in our room. See that the sheets are not stained—"

"Tom! You're worse than a mother hen," she laughed. "And, anyway, it is I who have been studying household management. You may safely leave it to me to see that our bedchamber is fit for habitation. Oh... I must go up, Tom." She went.

Left to himself, Tom began to fit together fragments of the puzzle that had been floating about in his head all day. That Mrs Patsy Frith was in some way connected to Daniel's shadowy manservant, Tom was convinced; for it had turned out that not only did both reside at Fakenham but also within a short distance of one another. And that business of Lambert Jardine and the fire—

"You wished tew speak ter me Mr Challiss, sir?" Mrs Frith was in the room.

"Ah! Thank you for coming so soon, Mrs Frith. It's very good of you to spare the time, especially at this late hour—"

"If we could get on with whatever it is yew 'ave ter say," the woman said dully.

Tom was irritated by her sullen attitude. "Of course," he said, shortly. "Please sit down, Mrs Frith." He paused while she seated herself in a chair opposite him. "I have one or two questions I wish to put to you and I would be grateful if you would do your best to answer them." She kept her silence. This was going to be more difficult than he'd anticipated. "I don't wish to appear impertinent or to pry, you understand."

She gave him a cynical smile. "Does that mean I c'n go, then, sir?"

He'd just have to plunge in. "I'm intrigued by your surname: Frith. It's not common in these parts, I believe?" She said nothing; just sat there impassively. "No. Well, it struck me that you might have some family connection to the manservant of a friend of mine. Unfortunately, I have no idea of the fellow's Christian name—"

"Luke," she said in a toneless voice. "'E's me father-in-law. Works fer that attorney, Daniel Jones as lives in the 'Igh Street. Will that be all, sir?"

"By no means," Tom said, bridling at her insolent tone. "So you are married—"

"Was," she corrected.

"—you were married to…?"

"'Is son, Young Luke Frith, 'e were known by. Can I go now, sir? We're awful busy—" Patsy Frith started to rise from her chair.

"Sit still!" Tom said, growing angry. "Am I to understand that your husband is dead, Mrs Frith?"

Tossing her head, she said: "How dew I know what yew unnerstan? If yer mean: am I a widder, then I s'pose I am."

Tom leaned forward and asked: "You mean, you don't know for certain?"

"No. Not fer certin," she said, sulkily. It was obvious she was going to give nothing away voluntarily.

"Would you care to explain how that has come about? Is your husband lost?" he prompted.

Appearing to deliberate, she nodded. "I suppose that would be one way o' puttin it."

Disgusted with himself for using a form of bribery, he placed two golden guineas on the table that separated them. "I really do need more information than you seem to be willing to divulge," he said. "Perhaps these will help to jog your memory." To his dismay she leaned towards him and with her fingertips flicked the coins onto the floor.

"I'll remember what I choose ter remember, sir;" she said, looking him straight in the eye, adding defiantly: "Yew'm mistaken if yew think I c'n be bought!"

Damn the obstinate woman. "About the fire at Lyndon Manor—" He saw that his words had her attention at last. "Your aunt, Mrs Mawby, gave me an account of what had apparently happened that night and the following day; but, it appears, she gave a different version of events to Mr Silas Tapp."

Mrs Frith appeared to sag and became less defiant. "How so? What's she bin sayin?" Tom told her. She shrugged her shoulders. "Hmm! Auntie be gittin sorft in the 'ead," she said, bluffing it out.

"Not when I spoke with her last," Tom contradicted her. He said coaxingly: "Why not tell me what really happened, Mrs Frith? It will not go beyond these four walls, I give you my word. It's simply that, until I get to the bottom of what happened, I am in danger – perhaps my life will be forfeit – from the threat of Mr Jardine's vicious revenge for something I did unintentionally."

A transformation washed over the barmaid's face, which became all smiles and rosy dimples. "Why didden yew say that in the beginnin, sir! Why, Mr

Challiss, yew c'n set your mind at rest on that score, sir. Yew won't be 'earin no more from that blackhearted varmint. Oh, no, sir: he be gone Down Under, as 'e useter say."

Relieved, yet still puzzled, Tom said: "Well, that's good to know; but how do you account for Mrs Mawby's two versions of his disappearance?"

Patsy looked around the room as if the walls might have sprouted several pairs of ears. "Lean closer, Mr Challiss, sir," she said in a hoarse whisper. "I ain bin quite straight with yer, sir; beggin your pardon. 'Tweren't on me own account – the lives of others is at stake, sir." Wide-eyed, she whispered: "Yew swear nothin I say will go beyond this room?" He swore on his mother's grave. "Well, sir, 'twere like this. . ."

The story Mrs Patsy Frith had to tell was not altogether to Tom's liking: it seemed to him that, merely by listening to her he was, in some way, condoning what had taken place on the night Lyndon Manor had been destroyed. But he had given his sworn promise that whatever he learned should remain a secret. Only as the history of that night unfolded did he begin to realise to what he had committed himself.

★

Their errands in East Norfolk accomplished, by first light the following morning the Challisses were ensconced in the hired coach, their feet invisible amongst the fresh straw that filled the bottom of the vehicle where they rested upon heated bricks wrapped in flannel. Outside in the frosty air, a well-wrapped Fuller sat on his box, whip in hand ready to depart. The whip cracked, Fuller cried: "Gee-up!" and the four sturdy horses stamped their hooves to gain purchase in the residue of frozen slush. Slowly the wheels began to roll over the ashy, cobbled yard of the *Queen's Arms* and Tom and Mary Emma were on their way home to Uppham, a distance of some thirty-four miles. Once they had joined the mail road they made good progress and hoped to reach home in time for luncheon. Now, at last, they were at liberty to talk over the events of the last two days without the fear of their conversation being overheard.

Tom, who had been speaking for some time, went on: " . . . and then she swore me to secrecy and of course, I, being anxious to get to the bottom of things, readily agreed. But she'd barely begun her tale when I realised I'd been too hasty. I trust I won't live to regret my lack of prudence."

"Oh, Tom! You should have taken more care," Mary Emma said, her eyes full of anxiety. "You'd better tell me all about it so that I can judge for myself."

"Mrs Frith," he began, already heartily sick of the name, "began by saying that her husband – who goes, or did, by the name of Young Luke – had always been too fond of strong drink and it was because of that they came to meet. He was a customer in the *Queen's Head* several years ago, got drunk and Patsy put him to bed for the night. As she said: things went on 'natural-like' of their own accord from there and within a few months, her being in the family way by that time, they married. The child did not survive more than a few hours and the midwife told Mrs Frith that it was unlikely she'd have another."

"Poor woman," Mary Emma murmured, instinctively placing a protective hand on her own abdomen. "Go on."

"Some weeks before the night of the fire, Luke – who was a wheelwright by trade and who had been at Lyndon Manor from the age of ten years old – was given a week's notice to quit by Wade Southwood on the orders of Lambert Jardine."

"How old was he when that happened?"

"I can't say – I don't think I was told – but under thirty I think. Anyway… Luke took the usual remedy for ill-luck and got blinding drunk on two jugs of strong ale which he stole from the kitchen and which was supposed to be for the live-in servants' supper that same evening. The loss of the ale was soon discovered by Esther Mawby – you'll remember her, she was at that time cook at Lyndon Manor – so, ignorant as to the thief's identity and unwilling to have blame cast upon herself for the missing jugs of ale, she went straight to Mr Jardine who was, as you know, a wealthy master who, if he chose to exercise it, had the power of life and death over his servants."

"It's wrong! No man should have such a hold over another's destiny, no matter how rich," Mary Emma cried in a burst of indignation. "It's like playing at being God."

"Yes, m'dear, I quite agree," Tom said, patting her gloved hand. "Well… as you can imagine, Jardine was none too pleased. He marched over to the bothy used by the live-in labourers and demanded that Young Luke be brought outside. If he was angry before, he flew into a towering rage when he was told that Luke had disappeared during the afternoon. According to Mrs Frith, Jardine ranted and raved until the men hoped he would die of an apoplexy, and he threatened those still in his employ that their jobs would be forfeit unless the wheelwright was found before nightfall and brought to him, Jardine. The threat of hunger and want and – as a result of those two spectres – death even, are powerful weapons wielded by rich masters over poor men. To cut a long story short: Luke was found and, barely sober, dragged up to the manor. In the interest of seeing fair play, Wade Southwood insisted on remaining behind after the lower orders had been dismissed. It was his account of that night's happenings, which Mrs Mawby learned about in the letter Wade wrote her from Cornwall, and which Patsy Frith read out to her aunt."

Mary Emma said: "So far I think you have nothing to fear, Tom dear."

He sighed. "You'd do well to hear me out before you come to any conclusions, Mary Emma. Wade Southwood wrote that Jardine, a powerfully-built man, laid about Young Luke Frith so savagely with a horsewhip that he seemed likely to kill him if allowed to continue. So Wade, himself a tall, strong man, stepped in and wrested the whip from Jardine's hand, cautioning him to be careful he didn't commit murder and that he, Southwood, was a witness to what the master had done that night."

Mary Emma's face was hidden in her hands. "How horrible," she said. Lowering her hands, she looked at him. "I can't help thinking of what might have happened to you, Tom, had Mr Jardine managed to get you into his power. Oh... he was such a terrible, wicked man."

"Hush, now," Tom soothed, kissing her pale cheek. "Mercifully, that's all over and done with. Shall I go on? . . . Meanwhile, as it's inclined to do in these parts, a blow had sprung up out of nowhere, and debris was soon crashing about in the violence of the wind. According to Patsy Frith's memory of Wade's letter to her aunt, Jardine returned to the house and left Young Luke lying unconscious and bleeding profusely on the lawn outside the long windows of the library. Wade wrote of seeing Jardine slumped in a chair, a balloon of brandy in his hand while he sat apparently reading by lamplight. Even as Southwood watched to satisfy himself that Lambert Jardine had calmed down sufficiently to be left, a stone was hurled from the darkness of the shrubbery that surrounded the lawn. It crashed through the window, leaving a great hole and shattered the glass reservoir of the oil lamp; the whale oil splashed over Jardine and the chair in which he sat and the fluid exploded into flames as the lamp's wick, which still burned, touched it. Before Wade could cry out or move a step, man, book and chair were one flaring torch fanned by the draught from the broken window and Jardine's mouth was stretched into a scream which was out-howled by the shrieking wind as, frantically, he tried to fight the flames that engulfed him."

"How dreadful," Mary Emma exclaimed. "Wicked as he was, I wouldn't have wished his end to be such a violent one."

"As Wade stood, transfixed, gazing in at the scene of horror, the door from the house opened into the library and he saw Old Luke Frith – Daniel's manservant – rush into the room and attempt to reach Jardine. Wade swore that Frith's intention was clear: that he meant to try to save his master's life. Old Luke snatched up a woollen rug from the floor and threw it over the blackened scarecrow that, moments before, had been Lambert Jardine. He started towards the writhing, hairless thing more than once but was beaten back by the heat engendered by the fine old books and furniture that had caught alight. Acrid smoke filled the room as shelves full of leatherbound volumes shrivelled and were reduced to charred animal skins – What is it, my love?"

"Stop the coach, please, Tom," Mary Emma gasped. "I feel sick!"

Tom lowered the window and stuck out his head, shouting: "Fuller! Stop the coach at once. My wife is unwell."

As soon as Mary Emma had retched up a quantity of thin vomit the spasms in her stomach abated. "I'm so sorry, Tom," she said as, handkerchief to her lips, she climbed back into the warmth of the coach. "It was nothing; I'm perfectly well again now."

"You're quite sure? Poor little thing. It's I that should be apologising to you, my love. My only excuse is that I'm still a novice at this marriage business and haven't learned to keep quiet when speaking to ladies on subjects that might give offence."

"Nonsense, Tom. It wasn't that," Mary Emma said. "I think the motion of the coach was as much to blame as anything you said. Perhaps we could ask Fuller to go at a slower pace, dear?" They had travelled some miles and, now that the sun had risen above the winter horizon, Tom agreed that they could afford to proceed at a less frantic speed. He conveyed this idea to Fuller who had no doubt that they would "be seeing the black stalks o' Downham afore long."

"Where had I got to?" Tom asked as the coachman, riding his team at a more sedate pace, set off once more.

"Old Luke Frith was attempting to save Mr Jardine but, from what you've told me so far, the poor man must surely have perished. Am I right?"

"Yes, I'm happy to say you are, my love." He expelled a long breath. "I've nothing to fear from that man any longer and the relief is so tremendous you couldn't possibly imagine it."

"Did Mr Southwood have anything more to add?"

Tom turned to her. "Something of great significance to Patsy Frith; I understood at once why I had been sworn to secrecy before she'd say a word about it. Old Luke was overcome by the smoke and fumes that were soon so thick that it became difficult for Wade Southwood to see clearly into the room. By that time, flames had been spotted by others and a hullabaloo spread from the bothy to the burning house. Men carrying buckets and other receptacles came running and, as had been drilled into them, formed a chain from the lake to the seat of the fire. Amid the confusion Wade, who was about to seek help to try to rescue Old Luke, saw a man fight his way from within the house into the blazing library, grab the insensible man by his armpits and drag him from the room."

"And you think the man who rescued him was Old Luke's son?"

"That was never said to me in so many words," Tom said; "but why else should Patsy Frith be so fearful?"

"But… if it really was Young Luke who saved his father's life, he was a hero, surely? I don't see —"

"Wait. Old Luke Frith was discovered by another of the men where he'd been laid out on the grass well away from the worst of the fire. Nobody could remember seeing anybody with the unconscious man or how he'd come to be there. Given water to sip, and more water splashed on his burned hands and face, Old Luke revived; for, despite his nickname, he was not a very old man. It was only when he was questioned, some time afterwards, that it was discovered that his voice had gone, damaged beyond repair by the heat and smoke he'd inhaled."

"That explains his eerie silence as he waits on Daniel," Mary Emma murmured. "How terrible for him! But, Tom… What is Daniel Jones's part in all this? Why did he keep quiet about it when he must have known all along of the connection between Old Luke Frith, Mrs Mawby and her niece's part in the conspiracy of silence concerning the destruction of Lyndon Manor? Oh, Tom! When I think of the all the beautiful paintings, *objets d'art* and lovely old furniture which would have looked so well at Uppham – everything that was destroyed that night – things I grew up with and took for granted would be part of my life for ever, it makes me so sad."

He drew her to him. "Don't be sad for things that are gone, darling. Fortunately, we are rich enough to replace most of them; and think what a fine time we shall have seeking them out!" Her anguished face was a window to her thoughts. "Oh, my little love. I know how attached you were to your beautiful home; but things can be replaced. What would I have done with my life if you had perished in that fire? I should have had no reason to live." His mawkish words restored her spirits at once; which had, perhaps, been his intention.

"For heaven's sake, Tom! *What would you have done with your life?* You would have moped about for a few weeks, I expect, caught the eye of another pretty maid and, being the lusty young man that you are, would have bedded her and, perhaps wedded her before six months had elapsed from the date of my funeral."

He laughed, that she had so easily detected his ruse. "Perhaps you're right, madam. You had better take care not to wither too soon or I'll divorce you on the grounds of your becoming stale." At that, she committed the unladylike act of removing her left glove and using it as a feeble weapon with which to chastise him.

Once he had recovered from a fit of laughter at her antics, Tom imprisoned the offending hand and said: "Allow me to finish my tale, woman. The mystery remained of what had become of Lambert Jardine's charred body. It's never been found by anyone in authority. When I learned that, all my old fears returned that perhaps, after all, Jardine had somehow survived the ordeal. But – and here is the strangest part of her story – Mrs Frith was adamant that the man was dead, adding the phrase, *to her certain knowledge.* When I questioned her further on that point, she replied that she had seen his last resting place and his blackened corpse lying in it." They became aware of the coach slowing and saw that Fuller's 'black stalks' – the chimney pots of Downham – were to be seen in the distance.

"So where is Mr Jardine's body hidden, Tom?" Mary Emma asked with a touch of impatience.

"When Patsy Frith said that he'd gone Down Under, I missed the implication. Apparently, the floorboards of the library, like the rest of the manor, had burned through and everything, including Jardine's body, hurtled into the wine cellar. Everything above the library had toppled onto it; but the wine cellar had a vaulted roof to it you remember? Built with a diagonal pattern of bricks that made it especially strong. Charred debris falling from the floors above had demolished only part of it and Jardine's body had lodged on the roof of that part of the cellar. Before the next morning, the body had been removed from its exposed position and had tumbled into the depths of the vault. It didn't take much effort to loosen the heated brickwork so that the unsound roof was weakened further, to the stage where more of it was induced to collapse and so entomb the body. Mrs Frith helped her husband in these dangerous undertakings: the removal of the body from its ledge and the demolition of the roof of the wine cellar; hence her claim to the irrefutable evidence of Lambert Jardine's death and the explanation of his supposed disappearance."

"What was that phrase she used?" Mary Emma asked.

"'To her certain knowledge'," Tom reminded her as the team trotted past Martlets. The sight of the long wall that enclosed the estate recalled to Tom the unpleasantness of Percival Belmaine's riding accident and the part he himself had unwittingly played in it by selling him Saladin. "She finished her account with the assertion that she'd no idea where her husband, Young Luke Frith, had gone after that last act and assumed he had left the district. How true that is, I can't say."

"Was he much damaged by the effects of the fire when he rescued his father?" she asked him as they turned into the lane that led to Uppham House.

"His hair, eyebrows and hands were burned; she mentioned nothing else," Tom said disinterestedly, as they swept through the gates of Uppham and the burden of responsibility for his little kingdom mantled his shoulders. Why were the gates open?

★

Chapter Twenty-six

Tom supposed Joseph Aldrich to be out on business to do with the estate. Yes, he thought, that would account for his absence as Fuller, with consummate skill, drove his team through the leafless tunnel of trees. Glimpses of the park flashed between mature trunks and Mary Emma's thoughts immediately flew to the lime walk. She longed to see how the work on its layout and planting was getting on. Seated beside her, Tom had lapsed into silence once they had passed through the gates and she stole a look at his profile in an attempt at gauging his mood. Conscious of her scrutiny, he turned his head and said: "I was wondering why the gates had been left open."

She laughed at his serious expression. "Does it matter? Obviously, somebody has called by carriage to visit us. After all, nothing much bigger than a horse, dog or pedestrian can get through the side gate."

Fuller, who had been well briefed by Tom at the outset of their journey, drove the team into the stable courtyard, reined his horses to a standstill, jumped down from his box and was opening the door of the carriage before Tom and Mary Emma had had time to collect themselves. "Right yew are, Mr Challiss, sir, ... Mrs Challiss, ma'am," he said cheerfully, as he assisted them out of the vehicle. "Reckon that be a fine run we 'ad; mail road clear an no 'old-ups or bad weather ter speak of."

"We're most obliged to you, Fuller," Tom said, glad to be able to stretch his legs. "We were in luck when we hired you as our driver. First class handling of the team; well done. Now; if you'll – Ah! There you are, Bob. Help Fuller with his team, will you? And after that, take him up to the kitchen and ask Mrs Rudge to give him a good hot dinner." Bob set about his tasks. "You'll spend the night, Fuller?"

"Kind o' yer, sir; but no, I won't, if it's all the same ter yew. Once we're fed an rested I'll be on me way back ter Fakenham. After all, time's money, as they say."

"Speaking of which," Tom said, bringing out his purse, "this should cover our fare and your expenses."

Fuller looked at the gold coins as they lay in the palm of his hand. "That's mighty generous of yer, Mr Challiss, sir." He saluted Tom by tipping his beaver as a mark of respect. "Good luck ter yew an your missis, sir, if I don't see yer afore I go," he called, as he began to unhitch his team.

Bob had been loitering in the background and, seeing that his master had finished with the coachman, hesitantly stepped forward. "Mr Challiss, sir! Afore yer go there's summat yew oughta see, sir, if yew'll foller me."

Mystified, Tom asked Mary Emma to wait a moment while he followed the stable lad into the stalls. He followed Bob along the row of stalls until he came to one that had previously been unoccupied and, to his astonishment, saw the noble head of George's Quicksilver hanging over the door. "Hullo, Quicksilver, old boy!" Tom said, stroking the animal's nose as he asked: "Who brought him, Bob?"

"'Twere a little fella — but bout me own age, I reckon," the lanky youth said with a grin. "Right spark, he were. Name o' Mark Runciman — Said 'e were a jockey at Newmarkit, an that Mr George Challiss ax 'im ter bring 'is 'orse back tew Uppham. I reckon that were all, sir." Tom turned to go. "Oh... sir! Quicksilver were brung in 'is own 'orse box fixed tew a cart, all proper like."

Ah! That accounted for the large gates being left open. "Thank you, Bob. Anything else?"

The lad scratched his head. "What was it, 'e said? Oh-Ah! Said 'e 'oped ter see yew at Newmarkit one o' these days and tew tell yer that 'jockeyin is gettin paid good money fer 'avin a good time'. I think I got that right."

Recalling Mark's cheeky face, Tom laughed. "I'm sure you have, Bob. Thank you for telling me. And it's good to have Quicksilver back home with us. Take good care of him, won't you, and see that he's exercised regularly. We shall have to buy in more winter feed with so much livestock about the place," he said, as he walked away from the stalls to rejoin his wife.

★

More good news awaited them at the mansion: the builders had vacated the west wing and had begun work on restoration of the east wing. Mrs Rudge had prepared them a wonderful meal of roast partridges, baked and steamed vegetables and delicious sauces followed by a suet pudding over which they poured rich cream and raspberry syrup. Mary Emma sighed with contentment. "Oh, Tom; it's so good to be back in our own dining room." She surveyed the newly-appointed room. "I simply adore it," she said. "It's so elegant. Don't you agree, dear?"

Tom nodded, his thoughts elsewhere. "Eh? Why, yes. It's absolutely splendid, my love," he said without looking about him. "I wonder why it took young

Runciman so long to deliver Quicksilver," he mused. "It's some months since George left us."

Endeavouring not to allow herself to be piqued by his lack of interest in the new décor that surrounded them, Mary Emma said: "I don't suppose a jockey is at liberty to go wandering about the country at the drop of a hat, Tom; he would have had to wait for the opportunity to arise."

"You might be right," he said doubtfully. "Though I'll wager he's been running the Thoroughbred at the Newmarket races and making himself a small fortune on the side." He smiled in the smug certainty that he had the right of it as, following a knock on the door, Rudge entered. "What is it, Ned?"

"I was asked to keep an eye open for your return, Mr Challiss," he said, and to Mary Emma, "Good-afternoon, madam. Mrs Vale is waiting to see you both, sir. She's in the withdrawing room overlooking the park and has been here for some time."

"Then we'd better see her at once, my dear," Tom said, glancing at his wife who nodded enthusiastically. "Has she been offered luncheon, Ned?" he asked, throwing down his napkin and draining his glass of claret in one draught.

"She was, sir; but declined. Shall I tell her you'll be up, sir?"

"No, don't bother. Mrs Challiss and I will go to her at once."

Ruth Vale rose from her chair by the window as they came into the beautiful room. Mary Emma went to her open-armed and embraced her with genuine affection. "Ruth," she said, as they drew apart. "It's so good to see you and looking so well, dear."

The nurse smiled and said: "I can't remember ever feeling better, Mary Emma. You see—"

Mary Emma clapped her hands and cried: "You and Joe are getting married! Am I right?"

Mrs Vale looked surprised. "Well… yes, we are… But that isn't the reason for my visit."

Tom, who had been a willing spectator to the demonstration of affection between his wife and the woman who had been largely responsible for his recovery, said: "What is it, Mrs Vale? Not Joseph?"

"No, no. It has to do with Agnes Brook. She has come home to live with her parents."

"Please, let us be seated," Mary Emma said in a rush, then: "Agnes? What can have happened? Tell us at once."

Tom's brain leapt ahead. In his mind's eye, he saw sweet Agnes, fresh and vibrant, and alongside her faded Lady Vyvyan; imagined handsome Lord Vyvyan comparing them both – and choosing Agnes.

"It's the worst possible news where a young woman's honour is concerned, Mary Emma," Ruth said gravely. "Girls are such easy prey, so defenceless against seduction by a charming and determined man."

"Oh, no!" Mary Emma cried, her eyes filling with tears as she looked at Tom. "Oh, Ruth; how terrible. Who would do such a thing?"

"Agnes names Lord Vyvyan as the father of her expected child."

Prepared for such news, Tom said: "What do Adie and Dulcie say? They must be heartbroken."

"You know how practical Mr and Mrs Brook are; of course, they see that any prospects of a good marriage for Agnes are ruined now. Yet, to them, it's not the end of the world. Good parents that they are, they're prepared to take their daughter back into the family and to look after her child as their own when it is born. In that respect, she is very fortunate; not all parents would be so willing to take on a burden of shame."

Mary Emma bridled. "Shame? I blame Lord Vyvyan. He is a married man and a gentleman; he should have had greater command over his feelings—"

Recalling the irresistible charms of Ghislaine that he himself had been powerless to resist, Tom said gently: "Mary Emma, my love, the damage is done. And you are rather too harsh in your judgement of Lord Vyvyan. It is possible, you know, for a forward girl to sweep the steadiest of men off their feet merely by a provocative smile, the allure of a slender figure, a pretty laugh or other seemingly innocent antics. In such cases it is unfair to place the blame solely on a man's weakness."

"Tom!" Mary Emma looked positively shocked. "How can you be in sympathy with such a villain? Poor Agnes is but fifteen years old! Fifteen! Hardly more than a child herself. Do I take it you condone his lordship's behaviour?"

Ruth Vale raised a dark eyebrow. "There is a flaw in your argument, Mr Challiss. Lord Vyvyan is a married man in his thirties. He has a wife and children and has no business looking elsewhere to assuage his appetites, especially if his victim is an innocent young girl entrusted to his care. There is such a thing as chivalry, sir."

Annoyed by the united attack the women had launched against him when his sole intention had been to put the affair into perspective by getting them to view the misfortune from the male point of view, Tom said in reply to Mary Emma: "Of course not! He has lowered himself in my estimation by taking advantage of the girl. But have you considered the fact that he might have a reluctant wife? All I wished to imply was, that young women should be discreet in their relations with the opposite sex. Nature has designed the male of the species to propagate, whether it be cat, dog, horse or man. The desire for man to replicate his own image is a driving force that must find release in the female of the species – or elsewhere." He threw up his hands, "Or what are men doing by tying themselves to a female for life in order to breed?"

Mary Emma had been staring at him wide-eyed and open-mouthed as his diatribe had proceeded. "Good God! Is this my husband speaking? Is that all I mean to you, Tom? An animal on hand to assuage your lust and accidentally bear you a litter of pups?" He shook his head at her wilful misinterpretation of his argument.

"Your husband is remarkably discerning – and frank, Mary Emma," Ruth Vale said, smiling with obvious admiration at Tom for his outburst. "And, I feel sure, meant no such thing as you seem to imagine. We don't know the whole story, it's true. And until we learn what part Agnes had to play in the affair it is uncharitable of us to set ourselves up as judges." She opened her reticule and withdrew a card. "This is an invitation to our wedding," she said, giving it to Tom. "Joseph and I would not be entirely happy unless you were both there to wish us joy. Do say you'll come."

Mary Emma, still smouldering at Tom's assessment of the position of women in respect to their husbands, had difficulty in summoning a suitable response to Mrs Vale's pretty speech. "How lovely," she managed to get out. "When is it to be, Ruth?"

Tom had read the card. "Christmas Eve. Felicitations, Mrs Vale—"

"I do wish you could bring yourself to call me Ruth, Mr Challiss," she said.

"Delighted to," Tom said, inclining his head, "as long as you return the compliment."

"Thank you, Tom. It will be a quiet wedding in St Mary's; neither Joe nor I want a fuss, just our friends. You've not met the new vicar, I think. Old John Wood has gone into retirement at last and this new man, Fieldgate, is like a breath of fresh air."

"But you *will* be having bridesmaids, Ruth?" Mary Emma implored.

"Not one," Ruth said, laughing at her friend's woebegone expression.

"Oh, but it won't be a proper wedding," Mary Emma protested. "Who will hold your bouquet during the performance of the rites?"

"I rather hope you will, my dear," Ruth said, returning Mary Emma's happy smile.

"Oh, Ruth! I never knew you to be a tease before. Oh, thank you. I shall look forward to it tremendously – if you don't think I shall be too large by then," she added doubtfully.

This time Ruth laughed outright. "Oh, my dear; don't be such a goose. One can do wonders with lace and veiling, even when dressing a matron, you know."

Unnoticed by them, Tom got up and walked to the door, where he lingered just long enough to say: "I see that there is much you ladies have to discuss to which I could contribute little or nothing. If you'll excuse me, I'll pay a visit to Church House and see how the Brook family are getting on." Mary Emma and Ruth scarcely heard him and were unaware of his departure.

★

"Oo is it, Agnes?" Tom recognised Dulcie Brook's voice as Agnes Brook answered the door in response to his knock. The girl met his eyes defiantly with her own. "It's Mr Challiss, Mother," she called into the back of the house. "Come in, won't you, sir. Mother will be so pleased that you've called." Tom was struck by her innate dignity as he followed her through the house into the large cheerful kitchen.

"How are you, Mrs Brook?" Tom said, his hand extended in friendship. He looked around the bright, newly-painted kitchen as, wiping her floury hands on her clean white apron, Dulcie came towards him and grasped his hand.

"Why, Mr Challiss! This is a nice surprise." She looked past him and her face clouded over. "Ah! Mrs Challiss will be busy up at the big house, I dessay."

Noting her disappointment, Tom made a point of again looking around the kitchen and asked her: "How do you and Adam find the house, Mrs Brook? Is everything to your liking? You must let us know if you find anything lacking."

"Oh, sir! 'Tis wonderful, ter be sure. Did yew know that Mr Aldrich had an earth closet built inside the old washus so we don't 'ave ter go outside in the dark? An that there pump's built inter the sink." Her face now was alight with happiness. "We 'ave every comfort a body could wish for, Mr Challiss. Adie an me, we're that grateful tew yew–"

"That's enough of that," Tom said sternly. "I had no intention of coming here so that you could thank me for something that is yours by right, Mrs Brook. As Head Gardener your husband has a position to uphold. Where's that young rascal, Noah?"

Dulcie dimpled at the mention of her youngest. "Why, 'e were in the parlour – which Agnes tells me I should call 'the withdrawin room' – a minute or tew ago. I'm sorry to disoblige yer, sir, but I'm preparin our supper an I'll be in 'ot water if it aint on time when Brook comes 'ome from work. P'raps you wouldn't mind takin yerself along the passage to the front o' the 'ouse; it's the room on the right. I 'spect the door's open; Noah'll soon make 'imself 'eard."

Following her instructions, as he approached the room he was arrested by a conversation. "Once more, Noah, dear," he heard Agnes say; and had the delight of hearing the tiny boy recite quite clearly: "One, tew, buckaw-my-shew. Sree, four, knock-at-ter-door. Five, six, pick-up-sicks. Seben, eight, lay-'em-straight. Nine, ten, a BIG-FAT-HEN!" Agnes laughed, and said: "And that's *you*, you pickle!" Shrieks of laughter followed and, walking into the room he saw that Agnes had her brother by his middle and was whirling him round just as he'd seen Mary Emma do with Fanny. It saddened him to think of Agnes's plight, and he sighed heavily as he thought of the waste of such a wonderful person. For what could her life be now?

"Oh! Mr Challiss! You startled me. Isn't our Noah a clever little boy?" she said, kissing the infant without waiting for a response from Tom.

"I couldn't help overhearing him recite his nursery rhyme; it was quite delightful," Tom said to her, suddenly shy of the boy's blue-eyed stare.

"Tell Noah himself, then!" she said, surprised at his coldness towards her brother.

Tom cleared his throat and bent down to the child and realised he hadn't the first idea of how to address someone so young.

To cover Tom's embarrassment, Agnes picked up her plump baby brother and gave him another whizz. The boy laughed so much that Tom was fearful he would make himself sick. Instead, Noah freed a loud report from his nethermost part and shrieked even louder until he was almost hysterical and his sister, laughing, said: "Oh, dear," and looked at her hand. "He's wet himself. It's my fault for getting him over-excited, poor little boy. I think you might find the kitchen a safer place, Mr Challiss. If you'll excuse us, I'll go and make him comfortable. Come along, Noah," she said, stifling her giggles against the chortling child's chest as they left the room together.

Tom watched her go and was full of admiration for the easy and natural way she had handled an embarrassing situation. He cursed himself for an inept fool when it came to making contact with the very young; but, he asked himself, was he really to blame? He'd had little childhood himself and no siblings from whom he might have learned the art of baby talk. Depressed by his failure to understand babies, he anticipated his impending parenthood with apprehension. He was roused from his gloomy introspection by the sound of Adam Brook's voice coming from the direction of the kitchen and he made his way back there by way of the twilit passage.

"Ah! There yew are, bor," was Adam's greeting as Tom came through the door, "I were just sayin ter Mrs Brook that I hadn't clapped eyes on yer for some days. Where yew bin, then? Jauntin abroad with yer missus, Joseph Aldrich said."

"Now, where's that Noah got tew? Time fer bed, Dumpling," Dulcie called.

The two men shook hands as Dulcie poured Tom a cup of tea. "Take it inter the parlour, sir; yew'll be more comfortable in there, an yew an Adie will be able ter 'ear yerself speak!"

"Thank you, Mrs Brook." In response to Adam's enquiry Tom said: "Yes. Mrs Challiss and I took a short holiday over on the east side of the county."

"Funny time o' year fer that," Brook said disapprovingly, for the moment forgetting that Tom was his master. "Weren't it bitter cold, that near the German Ocean? I well mind that ole east wind sharmin round Lyndon Manor each winter… 'twere enough ter fleer yer, an I'm right happy to be in sorfter parts."

Tom smiled. "I'm glad to hear it, Adam; but even here it can be cold enough."

The two men had been talking over estate matters for barely a quarter of an hour when young voices were heard as the family appeared from various directions and each hungry mouth made its way to the kitchen. "That's that, then!" said Brook with resignation. "You'll join us, Mr Challiss, for a slice of Mrs Brook's game pie?"

"Oh, Pa!" Young John Brook scowled at his father as if he were a traitor.

"Don't yew be so sillybold, young John," his mother said, by way of reprimand, as Adam Brook divided the huge golden-crusted pie into portions. "There's plenny ter go round; an even if there weren't, it aint no 'xcuse for bad manners terwards a guest."

Tom couldn't remember when he had smelled such a rich savoury game pie and could easily have eaten a generous portion; but said: "It looks and smells most appetising, thank you, Adam; but my wife will be expecting me to join her for dinner shortly. I must be going."

At John's unmannerly outburst Agnes had looked at her young brother reprovingly. The boy knew what was expected of him but couldn't bring himself to make a direct apology. "Mr Challiss, sir," he said, as Tom was preparing to leave the Brook family to their supper, "did yew know that a gravedigger used ter live in this 'ouse?"

"Why, yes, John, I did. Old Mr Bebb, the last of a large family. What of it?"

"Well, sir; when I 'eard that, I said to Agnes: 'then there weren't nobody to dig a grave fer 'im, were there; so what 'appened when 'e had ter be buried?'"

"I know! I know," shouted Zeb. "Vicar 'ad t'ax fer a... fer a..."

"Volunteer," Ann supplied. "An so, one o' the men who'd bin hangin about in the High Street said he'd have a go at it—"

" — an he dug the grave so perfickly that the vicar axed him if he wanted to be the new grave-digger," added Fanny.

Not to be outdone, Dovey took a deep breath and said shyly: "An he *did*... So now he *is*."

Everybody laughed at her neat summing-up of the story and, under cover of the merriment and chatter, John Brook made his apology. Tom accepted the boy's mumbled words with an affable nod accompanied by a wink; which subtle handling of John's display of greed raised that young man's estimation of Tom considerably.

"We'll discuss the front terrace tomorrow, Adam," Tom said, his hand on the kitchen door knob. "I'll expect you about nine o'clock. Good-evening to you all." As he let himself out and jogged back towards his home astride Mulderrig, he contrasted the boisterous warmth of the Brook's home with the silent magnificence of his own. He resolved there and then to endure any unpleasantness or noise that a string of babies would inevitably bring in their wake if, in the end, he could find himself head of such a lively tribe of children as those Adam and Dulcie Brook had produced.

He found his wife, lamp in hand, exploring titles in the unheated library. "Mary Emma! What are you up to now? Haven't I told you that you must take better care of yourself. Tch! You've nothing on your feet but a pair of those thin-soled kid pumps again. This room is damp. It's cold. It's a positive ice well!"

"Now, Tom, please don't fuss!" she said, as lifting the hem of her linsey frock she displayed her right ankle. "Look! I'm wearing woollen hose; so, you see, you've nothing to worry about, my love. I do know how to take care of myself and I wish you would stop treating me as if I were a child!"

He hadn't sought a quarrel and was astonished by how quickly a domestic storm could blow up out of nowhere. "Do I? I really don't mean to, my dear. It's just that—" Placing the lamp on a table, Mary Emma ran to him and threw herself on his chest. "I didn't mean to snap at you, either, Tom. Please forgive me, dearest."

The dinner gong sounded. There being no time to dress, Tom kissed his wife who kissed him back. After a while he extinguished the lamp, made an elbow on which Mary Emma laid her hand and, reconciled, they took themselves into dinner.

After they'd waited on their master and mistress Rudge and Peckover discussed the Challiss's gracious entry into the dining room and pronounced them the most dignified young couple they'd ever known.

★

The following morning Tom and Adam Brook were seated in the front withdrawing room, for Tom a necessary evil until a more appropriate venue was decided. As he was wearing work clothes, Brook had been overawed by the splendour of the room and apprehensive of setting foot in it. Tom had dismissed his offer to remove his boots and so the gardener had gingerly stepped onto the new Persian carpet and, as he related to Dulcie afterwards, "pampled acrorst the plushness of it in me muddy boots like an ox over cat's ice," and she had laughed heartily at the image evoked by his words. Ideas had been tossed to and fro, respecting the renovation of the garden fronting the mansion, and Tom acknowledged to himself that his decision to take on Adam Brook as his Head Gardener had been a wise one. But now they'd hit a stumbling block. "I agree with what you're saying, in principle, Adie," he said; "but it must be drawn up on a plan before we go any further. D'you reckon you're up to it? Can I leave that to you?"

Brook sucked in his breath and shook his head doubtfully. "Don't reckon yew better do that, Mr Challiss, sir," he said dolefully. "I aint 'ad much schoolin, see. I never bin one for pen an paper. What I dew know's all in me 'ead. I 'ardly got any sleep last night fer worryin about it. What we gonna dew, Tom? I was 'opin, like, that yew would take care o' that side o' things."

"I don't think that would do either," Tom said ruefully. Why Joe Aldrich's lush conservatory should suddenly flash upon his inner eye, he couldn't have explained. "I have it!"

Adam scratched his head. "'Ave yer? What yew got in mind?"

"We'll bring in the steward, Joseph Aldrich. You've met him. It was he who was chiefly responsible for the refurbishment. . . repairs and redecoration of Church House. Joe's a sensible man. I'm sure he'll be able to suggest something; he might even agree to take on the task of drawing up the working plan himself."

Brook looked discomposed at hearing this. "I was 'opin I'd be me own boss, Mr Challiss, sir. I tell yer straight: I don't take ter the idea o' playin second fiddle to the steward."

"No such thing!" Tom assured him. "You're in charge and, as far as the garden goes, your word is law, Adam. I haven't made myself clear: Joe's sure to be able to suggest something helpful, that's all I meant."

The gardener brightened. "Ah. . . well, that's different. Where dew I git 'old of 'im?"

"I've a meeting with him at ten o'clock this morning. Good heavens! Where does the time go? He'll be here any moment." Tom walked over to a smart new bell-pull and gave it a tug. "I'll get Peckover to bring us something to eat and a hot drink before we go outside. I think it'll be best to look at what we have to do on site. D'you agree?"

"Oh-ah," Brook replied. "No good talkin wi'out seein what's ter be done."

Peckover appeared, took instructions and departed to act upon them. Soon afterwards, Rudge opened the door and Joe was shown in. Aldrich bade Tom and the gardener good-day and Brook and Tom returned the greeting. Peckover reappeared carrying a tray of victuals and Maddy followed him with a pot of hot chocolate and cups on a second tray. The servants retired and Tom poured a measure of whiskey into each cup, added the steaming chocolate and handed them to Adam and Joseph.

"Now. Let's get down to business," Tom said, motioning to the others to help themselves to plates of food before taking one himself. The problem of getting the plan of the proposed garden drawn onto paper was discussed. Joseph Aldrich immediately offered his services as draughtsman if Mr Brook would be so good as to describe what it was he, Joseph, was required to do. The fortifying refreshments finished, they were about to take themselves outside when the door opened and they were confronted by the mistress of the house.

"Good morning, gentlemen," she said, entering and closing the door behind her. "I was looking everywhere for you, Mr Challiss, and here you are. Have I missed something important?"

All three men wished Mary Emma a good morning, in return. "No, no," Tom said airily. "We're just on our way out to discuss the planning of the front terrace—"

"Oh?" His wife's tone of voice put Tom on his guard. "Am I allowed to accompany you?" She wasn't smiling.

Tom raised his eyebrows in the form of a silent question to Adam and Joseph.

"If I may?" Joseph said to Tom and Adam. "I'm sure another pair of eyes will prove invaluable, Mrs Challiss; but I should warn you that a bitter wind is blowing."

"Then I shall dress myself accordingly," Mary Emma said. "I'll join you on the terrace in a few moments." As soon as she'd left the room, the three men gave vent to their thoughts on this unlooked-for turn of events.

Tom said: "I don't suppose another opinion can do any harm? After all, women see things differently – or so I've been led to believe."

"Dunno why women 'ave ter stick their oars inter a man's work at all," grumbled Brook. " 'Tain as if we'd be likely ter meddle wi' their housekeepin. 'Ow would they like that, I wonder?"

Joseph looked up to the windows of the room they had recently vacated, as if he imagined Mary Emma still there, gazing down on them. "I, for one, value Mrs Challiss's opinion highly. She showed unusual discernment in the selection of the site for the lime walk, for instance," he added, pointedly addressing Adam Brook.

Brook humphed his disapproval of Aldrich's encomium and said grudgingly, "Aye; I'll grant yer that. But she got the idea for it from Lyndon Manor; 'tweren't 'er own. I don't 'old with petticoat rule, any'ow, no matter how comely or high-larned the wench wearin' the petticoat mebbe, beggin yer pardon, Mr Challiss."

Mary Emma had overheard this last remark. "You're right, Joseph," she said with a shiver, "it is a bitter wind; but one can get used to anything in time – even the strange idea that a woman might have a mind of her own and might be able to contribute something to what truly is a man's world." Her eyes flashed sparks.

"I see you have read Mrs Godwin's memoir," Joe said with obvious approval.

"Well, yew've lorst me," Adam Brook said, looking at Tom. "But I dew know I'm gettin frawn, 'owin an mowin in this wind; cuts clean through yer."

Mary Emma came up to Brook and took one of his red, raw-boned hands between her gloved ones. "Oh, dear Adam; let's not fall out over this," she implored. "If I promise to keep quiet, that is, unless I really can't help myself, do say I may play a small part in planning what is to be my own garden."

Immune to her blandishments, he said huffily: "Well. . . Acourse, I'm only the gardener, after all's said an done, an must foller instructions, ooever gives 'em."

Unable to stand by in silence any longer, Tom said: "Mrs Challiss will, of course, be guided by you, Adam; just listen to any suggestions she might have and try to reach agreement. But, as I said before: you are in charge and I won't have your authority undermined by anybody." His grey eyes challenged Mary Emma's. She thought it best to hold her tongue for the present; but had no intention of giving in as easily as Tom seemed to imagine she would.

His dignity restored, Brook said: "Well, since it be agreed that I am in charge," he threw Mary Emma a look that was half triumphant, half appeasing, "I suggest we start by clearin all this rubbidge." He swept his arm to include the whole of the area under discussion. "What d'ye say, Mr Challiss, sir?"

"An admirable suggestion, Mr Brook," Tom said. "Take on as many labourers as you think necessary to do the job in a reasonable time, at a shilling a day, and consult Joe or me concerning anything you're uncertain about." Purposefully, and without another word, he took his wife by the elbow and led her away into the house. Once inside the front door, he kicked it shut with the heel of his boot and turned her round about to face him.

★

Chapter Twenty-seven

They stood inside the front door glaring at one another, the house abnormally quiet in contrast to the whistling winter wind outside. Mary Emma waited for her husband to explain his high-handed behaviour, her lips sealed in a mutinous line, her bosom heaving with suppressed anger. Tom was breathing hard after the furious speed at which he'd frog-marched his wife away from Brook and Aldrich into the house.

"Don't you ever do such a thing again!" he thundered, his face an angry red mask. "Never put me in such an impossible position in the presence of others, Mary Emma, whereby I am forced to choose between insulting you in public or disagreeing with my staff." That said, Tom continued to breathe heavily through dilated nostrils.

He so reminded Mary Emma of an angry bull that, before she was able to stop herself, she burst out laughing. At her reaction, the surprised look on Tom's face only made her laugh the harder. She tried to speak, but could only point her finger at his now stricken face, while tears of hysterical laughter ran down her cheeks and she held her side to assuage the pain in her diaphragm.

"Mary Emma!" He meant to say it sternly; but her uncontrollable fit of laughter had infected him and her second name ended unsteadily.

Now she was doubled over and almost out of control. An hysterical rag doll, she staggered against him; he steadied her and it turned into a passionate embrace. "Let's go upstairs to the withdrawing room," he said softly, his arm about her waist.

Maddy's curiosity had drawn her towards the commotion coming from the front hall and she had reached the cellar door in time to witness her master and mistress's embrace and Tom's whispered invitation. When she returned to the kitchen she said to her Aunt Bee: "'Twere like something out of a story book, Auntie. Made me come over all of a dudder." To which Mrs Rudge replied tartly as she rolled out pastry: "Don't yew get the idea that marriage is a bed o' roses, young Maddy. It won't last. They'll 'ave their ups and downs, same as anybody else, yew mark my words." The cook briskly rotated the pastry, floured her pin and continued rolling. "A lot goes on be'ind closed doors that yew wouldn't believe, even if I was ter tell yer."

That night, as they lay together in bed, Tom said: "It's time we inspected the new vicar, my dear. After all, we should be setting a good example to our servants, both in and out of the house. So tomorrow morning to church we will go, whatever the weather." Supported on one elbow, he leaned over her, tenderly kissed her on the lips and murmured: "I hope that meets with madam's approval?"

From her prone position, Mary Emma sat up and nipped his ear with her sharp white teeth. "I won't have you making me out to be a silly, unreasonable female!" she said, after he'd protested at the nip and stopped further damage with a lingering kiss. "No, Tom: be still for a moment," she said, as his hands roamed her body. "I do beg your pardon for belittling you before the servants, dear; but I don't think I was wrong to want to play a part in the making of the new garden. You yourself said it was to be my garden. Suppose I dislike what you and the others come up with? After all the work, will you be willing to have it altered to suit my taste?"

He expelled a heavy sigh. "Must we discuss this now, my love? Can't it wait until the morning?" His hands were busily at their work again.

"Oh…," she sighed as delicious sensations invaded her body. Suddenly: "No!" She sat up and faced him. "Please, Tom, do let us settle this business of the garden—"

He withdrew his hands as if she were a leper. "By all means, madam," he said coldly. "My love, are you able to tell me how many candles we burn each week? Do you know, at this moment, how many bedsheets are in need of mending? How much is beef per pound? What is spent in purchasing the supply of flour for a month's consumption?"

"No," she mumbled, avoiding his eye. "But I'm not interested in such things, as you well know. Besides, Ned Rudge and his aunt take care of that kind of thing—"

"That kind of thing is called housekeeping, Mary Emma, and, in the absence of a female to whom such duties can be delegated, it is a wife's duty to see to 'that kind of thing'." Her rejection of his marital advances had annoyed him and recalled Adam Brook's remark about petticoat rule. "How do you think Dulcie Brook has managed to feed her family and run her home so efficiently all the years they've been wed?"

"That's an invidious comparison!" snapped Mary Emma. "Having no servants, Dulcie has no option but to look after everything herself and to perform, *singlehanded*, Tom, every menial task that has to do with the running of the house."

"All right. Forget Dulcie for the moment. Whose responsibility was it for the tasks I mentioned when you resided at Lyndon Manor? Or Passendean?"

"Again, you are making comparisons with establishments that do not match our circumstances at Uppham," she said.

"How so?"

"Oh, Tom, how can you ask? Those were two very grand establishments; not so grand as Martlets, to be sure; but vastly superior to Uppham." With dismay, she saw that her thoughtless words had wounded her husband. "I apologise. I had no intention of demeaning Uppham, my dear. All I meant to say was that both Lyndon and Passendean had a vast army of servants which had to be overseen, whereas—"

" — *whereas* our poor little mansion is run by a handful of insignificant, docile peasants!" Tom said, growing angry.

Mary Emma was truly contrite. "Oh, Tom, my love!" Tears glistened. "Please forgive me. If it sounded as if I slighted Uppham…"

"You did."

How could she make amends for her clumsy blunder? "Tom. Don't be angry, darling. I have a suggestion to put to you. Is it quite out of the question for us to employ a housekeeper? Somebody of good breeding and education who could fulfil such a position? That would leave me free to turn Uppham into the kind of home we have both dreamed of: a house, while not as large as they, that would rival Martlets and the others – hush! – not in grandeur or pomposity – but by becoming a place of intimate beauty; the kind of place people of intellect and people of interest will want to visit because of its reputation – for its laughter, warmth and hospitality."

While she had been speaking, Tom had thought: but she might be describing the Brook family and homely, cosy Church House! Taking her, unprotesting, into his arms he kissed her tenderly. She could have no doubt of his love for her, as he said softly: "My darling, rich, spoilt, little wife: once you have learned to obey your husband's wishes and commands, you may have anybody or anything you desire."

★

They entered the church porch while the two summoning bells were ringing. Once his eyes had become accustomed to the interior gloom Tom, aware that he was the object of scrutiny and that the eyes belonged to somebody on his right who was seated at the back of the church, glanced in that direction and met the dead-eyed frosty gaze of Sir Everard Belmaine.

The elderly aristocrat sat in solitary magnificence beside a glowing open fire to the right of his elevated pew and reminded Tom of a badly weathered stone effigy with orange lichen growing down its right side. As he was about to turn away, Belmaine's manservant handed him a paper *pochette* containing an enclosure, before taking himself off to the pews reserved for the lower orders of Martlets.

"What did he want?" Mary Emma whispered as they took their places.

Tom saw that the reverse of the *pochette* bore the Belmaine crest on a triangular flap which he lifted, disclosing a card. Printed on the card beneath the familiar crest he read:

Sir Percival Belmaine
Requests the Pleasure of the Company of
Mr and Mrs Thomas Challiss
to a Nuncheon at Martlets
One O'clock on December 1st. 1815
R.S.V.P.

An invitation to Martlets! The bells stilled, the organ swelled and the congregation rose to their feet to sing the first hymn. While those around them raised their voices in unison and sang: "O come, O come, E-mma-a-a-nu-el..." Tom held the invitation for Mary Emma to read, fascinated by seeing his own name written on it in an unknown hand. What on earth could be the meaning of this belated acknowledgement of his existence? He returned the card to its wrapper, tucked both into the pocket of his waistcost and attempted to join in the singing, though his patched attendance at any place of worship ensured his ignorance of both words and tune. During the final verse of the hymn, the recently-appointed vicar ascended the pulpit steps with decorous and measured pace and, sermon in left hand, waited for the hymn to finish. His name had already replaced old John Wood's on the blue painted board in front of the church entrance. Tom had noticed the shiny gilt lettering: *The Reverend Edward Fieldgate, M.A. (Oxon).* He judged the handsome, fresh-faced vicar to be in his middle thirties and recalled Ruth Vale's high praise of him.

"He uses his voice as a beautiful, powerful tool which he manipulates with such skill as to rival that of Edmund Kean's – I heard *him* at Drury Lane. After old John Wood's mumblings, the Reverend Fieldgate is a joy, Tom. His voice rises and falls in all the right places and rebounds off St Mary's ancient walls so that even old Mr Meadows, who is profoundly deaf, catches some of his words." She had warmed to her subject. "Edward Fieldgate makes the scriptures sing with poetry, and his flashing-eyed curses and threats of damnation make the young and the faint-hearted quail. Nobody sleeps through *his* sermons! It's even said that one or two parishioners have actually admitted to enjoying them."

The Reverend Fieldgate stood in his pulpit waiting for the hymn to finish and allowed a long pause to elapse after the last note had died away. When he was satisfied that he had the congregation's undivided attention, Fieldgate stated his text: "'The fear of the Lord is the beginning of knowledge: but fools despise wisdom and instruction.'" He leaned forward and rested his clasped hands on the front of the pulpit. "Who among us have not, at one time or another, set themselves up as knowing better than anybody else how a thing should be done?" he asked. "My friends, I fear each one of us is guilty in that respect. None of us has had the wisdom of Solomon bestowed upon him. . . "

As he developed his theme, he appeared to be looking directly at Mary Emma who shrank beneath his candid gaze and kept her eyes lowered for the remainder of the sermon.

"I should like you to turn to Psalm 40, which you will find in your bibles – those of you who have them – and to follow the words as I read them. Verse 10." He paused to allow his largely untutored flock to find the place. The rustling pages ceased.

"'In the volume of the book it is written of me,
that I should fulfil thy will, O my God:
I am content to do it;
yea, thy law is within my heart.'

Wonderful words, which we must take to our hearts, everyone of us, from the youngest to the oldest; not to learn them unthinkingly, as does the scholar who recites his alphabet, but to abide by them... to make that verse a rock, a foundation stone, for the way in which we mean to live our daily lives..."

Another hymn was sung, and the reading of the lessons followed – one of which was read by young Dr Barnes in his pleasing baritone – and then the singing of the final hymn brought the service to a close. As the organ played a lively voluntary, with no sign of its bellows failing as on the last occasion Tom had attended church, and the churchgoers drifted out into the grey light of a winter's midday, Tom apprehended his wife's subdued mood and asked: "Are you quite well, my dear?"

She replied: "...Quite well, Tom, thank you; I was merely digesting the sermon. Mr Fieldgate has given me food for thought; especially after my behaviour to you – and Adam and Joe – yesterday. Oh, there he is . . . " Her solemn mood gave way to her usual high spirits as she left Tom and went to shake the Reverend Fieldgate's hand. Following in her wake, Tom smiled, and thought that his wife would have great trouble in harnessing her impetuosity for a while to come. Used to pleasing herself, it wouldn't have entered Mary Emma's head, he thought, to restrain her indecorous impulse, to subdue her own will, in deference to her husband's position.

"Good day to you, Mr Fieldgate," Tom said, offering his hand. "Thomas Challiss of Uppham House. I see you have already made the acquaintance of my wife."

Mr Fieldgate inclined his head. "I have had that pleasure, Mr Challiss. Good to find you both among us this morning, sir. Might I look forward to the pleasure of your company at evensong?"

"I think not, on this occasion, Mr Fieldgate," Tom said, thinking that two visits to church in one day was rather too much of a good thing.

"Ah! Mrs Challiss indicated that you would be joining us. We are usually rather thinner on the ground at second service and I had hoped— However, let me say what a pleasure it is to have made your acquaintance, my dear sir, especially as we are such near neighbours." A striking-looking woman approached. "Catherine, my dear; this is Mr Challiss of Uppham House. My wife, sir." Tom beheld a statuesque blonde.

"This is indeed a pleasure, madam," Tom said, bowing from the waist and raising his hat. "And these are your children?" A handsome boy of about ten years and a pale-faced, plain little girl, possibly five years the boy's junior, had come to stand by their mother's side.

Mrs Fieldgate smiled without showing her teeth. "Yes. Robert and Frances. Bid Mr Challiss good-day, children." Mary Emma chose that moment to join the group. Ignoring Mrs Fieldgate, she burst out: "Oh, Mr Fieldgate! These must be your children. How very like you your son is!"

"May I present my wife, Mrs Challiss," Fieldgate said, glossing over Mary Emma's breach of etiquette. The two women bowed politely, each having taken the measure of the other in the space of time it had taken them to complete the action. "I beg your pardon, ma'am," Mary Emma said, blushing furiously: "I hadn't realised—"

"And our children: Robert and Frances." The children bade Mr and Mrs Challiss good-day so beautifully that Mary Emma found herself gushing:

"What delightful children, Mrs Fieldgate; they are a credit to you, ma'am."

"Mr Fieldgate has a large share in the credit, Mrs Challiss, if there be any," the vicar's remarkable wife replied tartly.

Tom had watched the by-play and said to himself: Aha! Mary Emma has met her match at last. Mrs Fieldgate is not one to countenance frivolity, I think. "It has been a pleasure, Mr Fieldgate," Tom said. "You preach a memorable sermon, sir."

"You can have given him no greater praise, Mr Challiss," Mrs Fieldgate said, smiling broadly and revealing pretty, very white teeth. The transformation to her face, severe in repose, was astonishing and Tom's heart missed a beat. "Come, children," she said, her arms about them, "we must see that Papa's refreshment is ready for him." She bid the Challisses good-afternoon and her husband followed soon after.

Mary Emma saw at once that the vicar's wife ruled him by stealth. She'd rather die than allow herself to bind her husband to her in that underhand way, she thought.

Giles Ingleby's pair of carriage horses had been named on a whim by Mary Emma one day while on a drive into Downham to enquire if *Pride and Prejudice* had arrived from London. She had again been disappointed and on the way home she had decided that the animals should be called Castor and Pollux because the perfectly-matched animals were so alike they might be mistaken for twins. Now, as the Challisses made their way back through the churchyard to the clarence, the horses whinnied and Mary Emma went to them and rubbed their noses.

Tom's attention had been attracted by the unusual sight of Bob, the stable lad – who, he saw, was fast becoming a young man – bending over an older man whom at first Tom failed to recognise. The stranger was seated upon a slablike tomb – his shoulders bowed, his head in his hands – the epitome of despair. It appeared to Tom, as he paused to watch the pair, that young Bob's hand rested on the man's shoulder because he sought to comfort him. Mary Emma had entered the coach thinking Tom to be following and leaned out of the door to ask him what he was doing. He begged her to wait a moment and continued to observe Bob and the unknown man who, since Tom had turned to speak to Mary Emma, had risen to his feet and, Tom saw, was above average height. Although he had his back to him, Tom realised at once that he had seen the man before yet, irritatingly, was unable to place him. He got into the coach, slammed the door and Peckover urged Castor and Pollux on their way.

"Isn't the Reverend Fieldgate a charming man," his wife began, and went on without waiting for his opinion: "What did you make of Mrs Fieldgate?"

"Mm? Mrs Fieldgate? Why... I thought her a very handsome woman," Tom said vaguely, his mind preoccupied with Bob and the mysterious man in the churchyard.

It wasn't at all the answer Mary Emma had wanted him to give. "Oh, Tom! I didn't mean her appearance. What did you make of her as a woman?"

"I haven't the faintest notion what you expect me to say, my love," Tom said, truly baffled.

"Why, I hoped your opinion of her would be similar to mine," Mary Emma said. "I think her a cold fish who is able to wind her husband round her little finger. "

"Oh-ho! Do I detect a note of rivalry in your criticism of the lady?" said Tom.

"What nonsense! Did you not notice how she scorned my compliment in praise of her children?" Mary Emma said as they drove past the wall that enclosed Martlets.

"'Fraid not, my dear," he answered abstractedly, his mind haunted by images of Bob and the stranger in the bleak wintry churchyard.

"Oh! You can be so exasperating, Tom! It isn't worth talking to you when you're in one of your distracted moods," Mary Emma said, gazing out of the window.

As they approached the gates of Uppham House a worried Joseph Aldrich waylaid them. He waved his arms about to stop the horses and brought down on his head a string of oaths from Peckover as the young footman wrestled with the startled animals. Once he deemed himself safe from being trampled to death, the steward sprinted to the door of the vehicle and banged on the window. "Mr Challiss!" Winded, Aldrich bent double to recover his breathing. Tom was out of the coach immediately, his first thought that the mansion had gone up in flames while he'd been at church trying to sing hymns.

"Sir! Terrible news! The hay barn's been fired! Every last wisp has gone up in smoke... and the barn is destroyed! Kit Warrender did his best to save it, in vain."

A short-lived relief followed the implications of what Aldrich had said. The house was safe! Then the seriousness of the steward's words penetrated his brain. "The *hay*? Gone, you say?" It seemed incredible. "You're certain, Joe?" Winded, Aldrich nodded silently but vigorously. "My God!" said Tom, appalled. "The winter feed – lost. What can we do about it? We've grown nothing ourselves this year and it's not been too good a harvest for those who did."

"Aye; that is so, sir; it's been a bad year for arable farmers one way and another. Because of the government's restrictions on imported grain, some of the smaller farmers are ruined. Why, the price of wheat has fallen to nine shillings a bushel! That's a fall of five shillings and sixpence since the bumper price in 1812." His face betrayed his agitation. "What's to be done, Mr Challiss? Everybody will be in the same boat, with no feed to spare." He threw up his hands. "It's a disaster."

Mary Emma had joined them. "What about the horses?" she cried. "Oh, Tom. How shall we feed them? Of all times, it had to be winter, when the grazing is poor."

"Or non-existent," added Tom. "How can it have happened? It's confounded bad luck all round. What do you know about conditions in the rest of the country, Joe? Is the yield as bad everywhere?"

"I can't answer that. Bad as it is for horseflesh, I fear it is the human population we should be worrying about at this time. It's this wretched Corn Law that's causing widespread unrest, Mr Challiss. Because British corn has not exceeded the so-called famine level of eighty shillings per quarter... almost eight bushels – ye Gods! *eighty shillings*... when did corn ever reach that low figure? – and widespread unemployment has reduced demand because the poorest cannot *afford* to buy their bread at such a price! And the government refuses to allow foreign wheat to enter the country duty-free. I tell you, Mr Challiss, sir; thousands will starve this winter, unless something is done to feed the unemployed and dispossessed." Aldrich's dark face had become suffused and angry.

"We can't stand talking here, we shall all freeze to death," Tom said. "Hop in Joseph and we'll all go and look at the damage. Then perhaps you'll dine with us, we usually eat at two on a Sunday... Where's Ruth?"

"I've seen the damage and have no wish to see it again so soon, Mr Challiss; so I'll decline your offer and forego your kind invitation to dine with you. Ruth has been at the scene of the conflagration all morning; she insisted on doing what she could to help." Tom had observed that, in his agitation, Aldrich had become verbose. "I stayed until noon and had been here but a short while when you returned from church."

"I cannot persuade you?" Tom said. "Then we'll be on our way. And thank you for your thoughtfulness, Joe. It is appreciated." He and Mary Emma returned to the coach and directed Peckover to drive to the stable block.

An exhausted-looking Ruth Vale came up as the clarence rolled into the yard. "It was hopeless from the start, apparently," were her first words. "Warrender has no idea what could have caused it; but the hay being tinder dry the whole of it more or less went up in a few minutes. He fought valiantly, Tom, and his hands are badly burned. It was all I could do to hold him back when he would certainly have perished had he returned to the blaze. Since I've had time to think, his behaviour has been puzzling me. If there had been anything living in there I could have seen the point of his trying to rescue it. But, as far as I am aware, the barn was empty. I saw young Bob walking down the drive as Joe and I came up.

"Where is Warrender now?" asked Tom. "It's time he and I met."

"He is unmarried and homeless," said Ruth. "He lodges with the Brook family in Church House."

Mary Emma had stood by, shocked at the sight of Ruth's dishevelment, wondering how she could bear to be seen in public in such a state. Mention that the Brooks had given shelter to their Farm Manager was humiliating. Why had Dulcie, or Ruth herself, said nothing? Resolved to hold her tongue on this occasion, she remained mute.

"Has he gone there, then?" Tom asked, holding his temper in check: the news that his Farm Manager had been reduced to the expedient of lodging with his Head Gardener and his large family had both surprised and irritated Tom. Why hadn't Brook or Aldrich said anything to him about it?

"I don't know; I expect so," Ruth said wearily, in response to Tom's query. All three stood staring at the smoking ruins of the barn in silence. After a while, the nurse said: "I must return to the lodge. Joe's expecting me and there's nothing more I can do here."

Unable to maintain her silence, Mary Emma urged: "Tom! Ruth cannot be expected to return on foot in this bitter wind."

"Of course not, I wouldn't hear of such a thing," said Tom, ensuring that Peckover understood what was being said. "You must take the clarence, Ruth. Thank you for what you have done this day. It was a mercy we weren't all at church as, it seems, were most of the occupants of Martlets," he added, as Ruth entered the coach.

They watched the team roll away until it was out of sight. Mary Emma shivered and Tom drew her to his side. "Come, my dear. Let's get in out of this wind. "Well... it looks as if the honeymoon is over for good and all, my love," he said, as they trudged up the steps to the front door. "And it's about time we settled down. I've lost touch with what's been going on here and things are starting to get out of hand. Why did nobody say anything to me about Warrender's lack of accommodation?" he said, opening the front door for her to precede him before following her.

"Or Ruth or Joe to me?" Mary Emma said peevishly, as Maddy appeared to take her mistress's hat and coat.

"Perhaps we are perceived as a pair of gadabouts," Tom said, thoughtfully, as they made their way upstairs to the back withdrawing room. "After all, I have been absent for much of the time since I became master of Uppham. But all that is about to change! Starting tomorrow, I shall ride the rounds of the estate every morning and, once the men see that I mean business, they'll have no excuses for slacking."

Surprised by his determined look, Mary Emma stopped halfway upstairs and said: "Oh, dear; life is going to be awfully dull for me from now on, Tom."

"Nonsense! It's time you, too, settled yourself. There remains much that requires attention in the mansion; the nursery, for instance. You will not lack company, my love; Ruth will be pleased to visit... and Dulcie... when she can spare the time."

"Hmm! Once in a blue moon," his wife grumbled as they recommenced their climb. She sighed. "But you're right, of course, Tom. And it isn't long until Ruth and Joe's wedding. There'll be lots to do." They reached the landing. "Oh, darling!" She clasped her hands on her bosom. "Do say we may have the wedding breakfast here!"

Indulgently, Tom kissed her forehead. "Hadn't we better ask Ruth and Joe what they have to say about it first?"

"You are right, of course, Tom. Oh! One of us should reply to Sir Everard's kind invitation. It's less than a week to December the first. Shall I do it?"

"Thank you, Mary Emma; but I think the reply must come from me, even if my handwriting is inferior to yours." Tom penned their acceptance and had just dusted the wet ink with chalk when they were summoned. He laid the quill on its rest. "There goes the gong. Once we've eaten, I think we should pay the Brooks a visit."

"Good! I look forward to it; and I'm dying to meet Warrender. Aren't you?"

★

Chapter Twenty-eight

Barty Peckover was none too pleased at having to turn out again so soon. He'd barely had time to swallow his dinner and had been looking forward to a lazy afternoon only to be disappointed when his master ordered the clarence again. "I'm fair sick o' these goin's on of a Sundey," he grumbled.

Mrs Rudge sat before a bright fire, a cup of tea in her hands, toasting her slippered feet on the polished steel hearthrail. "Oh, go along wi' yew! All yew youngun's is the same when your'e axed to do anythin outa the ordin'ry. 'Taint as if the master makes a habit of it now, is it?"

"But it's Sundey!" Barty protested. "Ain a fella allowed no time orf? Ain no better than a slave, I ain. 'Tain so bad drivin 'em down to Brook's, but I 'as tew hang about until they wants ter come back, an that's me Sundey gorn." And so on and so forth as he bundled himself back into his layers and made for the stables.

Acrid smoke lingered in the vicinity of the yard and Barty was sensible to the fact that the fire could have done much more damage had it spread to the stable block. With relief, he saw that Bob had not driven the clarence under cover and that all he himself had to do was put in the horses.

★

Kit Warrender was not surprised to hear the team draw up outside the house: he'd been expecting it. What a damned mess he'd landed himself in just as he'd found his feet again. Yet he couldn't have acted differently if he'd wanted to. Philosophically, he made up his mind to stick by Evritt Pawl – whatever the outcome of Mr Challiss's visit. He took a deep breath as he heard the Challisses being welcomed and got to his feet in order not to be found at a disadvantage when they came into the room. The door opened inward and he was face to face with his employer for only the second time since his appointment as Farm Manager. He stepped forward and offered his hand: it was warmly grasped by his master, who topped him by an inch.

"We meet again, Mr Warrender," Tom said affably. "Settling in? May I introduce you to my wife?" Mary Emma shook hands with the large, shockheaded man, to whom she took an immediate liking as soon as their two pairs of blue eyes met.

"That's right, yew make yourselves at 'ome," Dulcie said as they seated themselves in Mrs Brook's parlour. "Let me know when you're done an we'll 'ave a cup o' tea together. Oh, Mary Emma! It's that good ter see yer – an lookin so well."

"If you'll excuse me, Tom – Mr Warrender – I'll leave you to your business discussion," Mary Emma said, "Mrs Brook and I have much gossip to catch up on."

Pleasantly surprised by his wife's desire to absent herself, Tom rose briefly from his chair as she left the room. Once they found themselves alone, Tom asked Warrender what he knew about the fire.

"'Twas that sudden, sir; the barn went up like a torch."

It was obvious to Tom that the man was feeling his way and he said: "How do you account for it? Had somebody been careless? A lighted candle, perhaps, or...?

It was no use shilly-shallying. Warrender made up his mind to tell Challiss everything. "You're right, sir, ... in a way, I mean. Though 'twere an accident, no doubt about that. No malicious intent, you understand. You might say I'm partly to blame; 'cause, if I hadn't brought the man to Uppham in the first place–"

"What? You had better tell me everything you know," Tom said, "from the beginning."

"It might seem like an excuse, blaming this latest Corn Law for everything," the Farm Manager began, "but if it hadn't been for that I'd still be my own master. 'Twas impossible to make ends meet. I'd laid off one labourer after another, until there was only me and Evritt Pawl left to manage everything. I hated to do it, Mr Challiss, sir. I knew I was throwing those good men on the street. 'Cause there's no work to be had, not for the likes o' them. They're proud men, sir, and would rather starve themselves than go to the Poor House. So, each week they sell one thing to buy food for their families, then the next, and so on, 'til there's naught left to sell. Then they can't find the rent money for their cottages and so the landlord throws 'em out to live as best they may. 'Tis bad enough in summer when they might get a day's harvesting; but they've no chance in winter, now that the threshing's being done by machines. Whole families are without shelter, without food for their stomachs and people are dying, Mr Challiss. Dying of starvation! In England. And the gentry don't give a damn!" Warrender had worked himself up into such a rage that he'd brought himself to a stop.

Tom said: "I knew things were bad—"

"Bad, you call it? Disastrous, is the word I'd use." He bowed his head. "Still, ranting and raving at you are not going to change matters. I'm forgetting myself, sir."

"Understandably," Tom said, unsure of what the man was getting at. "I fail to understand… What has all this to do with the fire?"

Warrender expelled a bitter laugh. "Everything! If it hadn't been for the Corn Law I'd still have my farm and you'd still have your barn full of hay."

Tom shook his head. "You're not making sense, man. I have no idea what you're talking about. I've been out of the country for years, fighting the French."

"Ah, now I begin to see," Warrender said. "You didn't strike me as an unsympathetic individual, sir. I'll try to be more plain and go easy on the politics."

"If you would."

"Well, sir. . . Things got to the point where I had to let Evritt Pawl go – you might have come across him: he's taken on the job of gravedigger here – and I couldn't see to everything myself, however many hours I worked. My cows went dry and…" he swallowed hard and batted the air. "You don't want to hear about all that," he said dolefully. "'Tis a common enough story in these parts as well as abroad. Well, sir; Sir Everard Belmaine'd had his eye on my farm for years. He hated it, because my few acres made inroads into what would otherwise be the neat edges of the Martlet estate. I could see that the way things were going they could only get worse for me, so I sold up to him in order to have something behind me in case I decided to emigrate to one of the colonies. It was then that I met Jem Webster at the *Queen's Head* and he told me of the vacancy at Uppham for Farm Manager. I don't think I've had the opportunity to express my gratitude to you, Mr Challiss, for taking me on on Jem's say-so. After all, you know nothing about me, sir, except what he told you."

Tom smiled. "I have a pair of eyes in my head, Warrender," he said. "Besides which, you have a reputation among Downham folk as a competent farmer. But anybody praised by Jem Webster comes highly recommended. Go on with what you were saying."

Kit Warrender warmed to his employer at these words. "You can depend on me, Mr Challiss," he said. "I know farming. I come from generations of farmers and I'd never willingly let you down."

"Good," said Tom, growing impatient. "Glad to hear it."

"I felt bound to say that, in my own defence," Warrender said. "I hope you'll remember it later on, sir."

"I'll bear it in mind."

"Well… with my farm sold – six generations of Warrenders had it, sir, – I had next to nothing and nowhere to go. 'Twas then Jem said he'd speak to the new Head Gardener to see if he could give me lodging in return for a small rent – course, I didn't know at the time that Adie had such a parcel of bairns – anyway, they tucked me into a little room that came off the attic – right snug it is – I couldn't have done better if I'd asked Belmaine to take me in. So it's all turned out for the best."

Donkeys minus hind legs sprang into Tom's mind. He said: "Get to the point, man. The fire!"

"Well… Before I come to that I must confess to something, sir."

Tom heaved a heavy sigh. "Well? For heaven's sake, get on with it!"

"I'm doing my best," Warrender said, "I can't be rushed, Mr Challiss. I have to tell it as it happened, in the right order, or I tend to lose the thread."

"I apologise, Mr Warrender. Please, in your own time."

"Well… Mrs Pawl'd been ailing for many years, ever since their boy was born, really; and when Evritt lost his place and then their cottage they had nowhere to go. 'Twas then young Bob suggested they come and shelter in the hay loft—"

"At Uppham?"

"Well… of course, sir. Where else would they have gone? So that's what they did. But Mrs Pawl was already very weak, Mr Challiss. She was unable to walk unaided. By that time I'd already started working here and it wasn't long before I had my suspicions that young Bob was up to something. To cut a long story short, sir, I found out what was going on at the stables; but Evritt begged me not to give them away. His wife was nigh to dying, you see, sir, what with her being already so weak and the business of them losing their home. I just hadn't the heart to turn them out. So I turned a blind eye, as you might say. I even went so far as to take Mrs Rudge into my confidence and she promised to save scraps of food to feed them."

"My God!" Tom said. "Why on earth didn't somebody tell me that all this was going on under my nose?"

Warrender looked Tom steadily in the eye. "You hardly seemed to be here, most of the time, sir. I knew that what I was doing would appear wrong in

your eyes and I suppose it was wrong; but if you had seen that poor woman –
nothing but skin and bone..."

"You have nothing to reproach yourself for, Warrender, and I'm sorry if I
seem to have been negligent of my responsibilities. However, that is about to
change. Now. Are you able to finish your account?"

"I am. Young Bob was so happy to see his parents—"

"His parents—?" Tom echoed incredulously.

"Didn't I say? Well. . . they all have the same surname so naturally I
thought..."

To his shame, Tom realised that he'd never known Bob's last name. "I... I
didn't know Bob had any parents," he stammered. "Go on."

"Bob was so happy to see his parents warm and well fed that he asked
Evritt if there was anything he hankered after that wouldn't cost a fortune.
Evritt said he missed his pipe more than anything and Bob said he should have
one before the day was out."

Suddenly, Bob's frequent absences took on a new meaning. "I think I
begin to see where this is leading," Tom said.

"I daresay you do, sir," the Farm Manager said, nodding his head. "Well . . .
young Bob goes off into Downham and brings Evritt back a churchwarden
and a twist of tobacco. Mrs Pawl almost smiled when she smelled the familiar
aroma of Evritt's pipe, said it reminded her of happier times. But digging
graves in winter is hard, sir, and poor old Evritt hadn't got his strength back
after being without proper food for so many weeks that he came back to the
loft tired out. Well. . . He was lying snug in the hayloft with Mrs Pawl nearby
she was growing weaker by the hour – I doubt she would have lasted the night
– and he fell asleep with his pipe in his mouth. According to what he said
afterwards, though I know he was in shock, the next thing he remembered was
finding himself awake with his wife kneeling over him trying to beat out his
flaming coat with her bare hands."

"Oh, My God!"

". . .with her bare hands. Her sleeve caught fire, then her hair; she let out a
shriek and fell back. Dead. As Evritt carried her body out of the blazing loft
the floor collapsed and they fell into the stables below. Wisps of burning hay
drifted down with him and lighted the fodder. Young Bob ran in and dragged
his father away. But Mrs Pawl's body was burned to ashes in the fierce blaze.
'Twas horrible, Mr Challiss."

Subdued by the knowledge that he had been partly to blame for the tragedy, Tom said: "Must've been an inferno, Warrender. My thanks for your clear account. Where is Pawl now? Ah! Was it he I saw with Bob in the churchyard this morning?"

"Quite likely. He did run off in that direction with young Bob following soon after. If there's anything I can do to help, sir—"

But something else was bothering Tom. "I have the feeling that I've seen Evritt Pawl before somewhere, and yet his name is unknown to me. What do you know of his history, apart from what you've already told me?"

Warrender pulled a wry face. "Well... I can only tell you what he told me himself. His mother was a servant at Martlets and, as so often happens, was seduced by one of the sons of the house. Bessie Pawl, her name was and she vowed that he should never forget who his father was. Evritt told me more than once how his mother made him repeat his name over and over when he was a little boy."

A chord was struck in Tom's memory by Warrender's words: he could hear his own mother patiently teaching him to say his own name: Thomas Roberts *Challiss*. But his Grandfather Roberts had driven that name from his mind until his meeting with his half-brother George at Waterloo had resurrected the seed that his mother had carefully planted, that he might never forget his father's name entirely. Now here was history repeating itself. "What's his full name? Do you know?"

"Funny you should say that," Warrender said. "It struck me as a strange sort of name to saddle a newborn child with. It's Everett Bellman Pawl; but everybody calls him Evritt and few know his middle name. Well... It seems his mother never married but neither did she want for anything. Money was never short and she was given a cottage to live in rent free for the term of her natural life. Evritt was sent first to a dame school; then, when he'd outgrown that, to study with the Reverend Wood, the vicar that was. Evritt became quite a scholar. His mother had hoped that he would escape working on the land and study for the church – which old Mr Wood said he was quite capable of doing – but it wasn't to be. Evritt had just reached the age of fifteen when his mother, who was still only a youngish woman of thirty or so, died of smallpox. You can see her gravestone in the churchyard: a great slab of a thing fashioned out of polished black marble full of shining blue fossils. Evritt said that on the day of his mother's funeral somebody sat watching it from inside a plain black carriage but he couldn't say who it was. So . . . his mother dead, the cottage was no longer his home and the money that had come as regular as clockwork stopped. That was when Evritt first came to my father looking for work and would have been with me still, but for the Corn Law."

"Thank you, Mr Warrender," Tom said; "I'm obliged to you. You have an excellent memory for detail, to be sure. I want you to know that I am here to help in any way I can. Please do not hesitate to come to the house – that is, until I am able to make other arrangements – should you have any problems that cannot be solved by yourself, Adam Brook or Joseph Aldrich. You should have confided in one of us concerning the Pawls' plight; but I appreciate the difficulties involved. After all, we had hardly got to know one another and that was not your fault but mine. Mrs Brook must be gasping for her cup of tea! Let's join the family." The two young men, having got to know one another a good deal better than before they had sat down to talk, decided that the other wasn't nearly as reserved as he'd first thought him.

Darkness was falling as Barty rode his team through the leafless tunnel of trees that led to Uppham House. Frost was in the air and the evening star glittered in a cobalt sky. The young footman-factotum drove with his neck well down inside his muffler, his hat pulled low over his face. He was mulling over his trip to Church House which had turned out to be much pleasanter than his anticipation of it. . .

Mrs Brook had insisted that he join the family in the vast kitchen. He'd balked at the sight of so many children milling about but it didn't take him long to discover that each child was intent on his or her own business. Soon, a glass of warm punch in one hand and a slice of plum cake in the other, he'd begun to think that it wasn't such a bad way to spend a Sunday afternoon after all. When his eyes had accustomed themselves to the shadowy corners of the room he had discovered a lovely girl seated on a low chair with a young boy on her lap. He had soon decided that she must be Brook's disgraced daughter who had been sent home for falling foul of someone's lust. Well, he thought, staring at her as he demolished the cake and washed it down with punch, a feller might do a lot worse... The fire had been under discussion while Peckover had been ogling the girl and now he pricked up his ears.

"Of course," Tom was saying, "as there's been a death in the case the magistrate must be notified."

"Oh, Tom!" Mary Emma protested, "is that really necessary? Who would be any the wiser? No murder has been done. As Mr Warrender told you, Mrs Pawl was already dead before the fire got out of hand. And Mr Pawl did his best to save her."

"Nevertheless," Tom said firmly, "he would find himself in a difficult position should his part in the fire and his wife's death become known outside the estate."

Warrender cleared his throat. "I'm with you, Mr Challiss. Best to be above board. Though I'm sorry it'll give Evritt more aggravation. Bad luck seems to stalk him, poor fellow."

"Yew'm best see tew it first thing termorrer," Adam Brook advised. "It'll only go agin 'im if Sir Everard finds out 'e were laggardly in ownin' up tew it."

"Sir Everard Belmaine is the magistrate?" Mary Emma said, her blue eyes distressed. "Oh, dear! He's a most severe-looking old man."

"But fair, ma'am," Warrender said. "He's not vindictive, like some. Evritt will get a fair hearing, you may be sure of that."

"Hmm," Tom said sceptically. "I have heard varying reports of his dealings with those he deems his inferiors – and that's all of us in this room."

"Well, if bein' one o' the quality means havin' ter look like 'im I'd rather be meself!" said Adam, causing a shout of laughter. After which Barty had driven them home.

★

Bob Pawl emerged from the shadows as the team pulled into the stable yard. Barty looked at him in a new light after what he'd overheard at Church House. He'd thought of the stable boy as a clumperton who was a bit touched in the head and had been inclined to look down on him because he'd slept in the hay loft and had to wash in the horse trough. As if scales had dropped from his eyes he saw that Bob, though still emerging from the gangling stage, was well-made and, if he could have been given a good wash and some decent togs, might not be a bad looking cove. "All right, Bob?" he said affably as he jumped down from the box and the two of them started unhitching the team. "What yer gonna do 'bout feedin' Castor an Pollux? Poor devils 've bin up an down that drive like a bandylore terday. They're blown."

"Load o' hay come, compliments o' Belmaine," Bob told him, surprised at Barty's friendly tone. "Must've 'eard about the fire – or seen the smoke, more like."

"Well, strike me dumb! What's got into 'im? Dried up ole dandy. Never thought he'd 'elp anybody out. Did yew?"

"Never give it a thought," Bob said, leading the horses out of the shafts. "But I ain arf glad 'e thought of it. Dunno what we'd a done wi' this lot to feed an no hay."

Barty cleared his throat. "I 'eard about yer ma," he said. "Bad business. 'Ow's yer dad took it?"

"It's 'it 'im 'ard," Bob said, "even though 'e knew ma wasn't long fer this world. 'E feels responsible-like fer not gettin' 'er out. But I told 'im: I'm as much ter blame fer the 'ole thing as 'e is. 'Twere me give 'im the pipe in the first place."

"Good luck ter yer, then," Peckover said, suddenly embarrassed. "Leave yer tew it." Wouldn't like ter be in 'is shoes, he thought, as he jogged on foot back to the warmth of the kitchen and something hot to eat. 'E'll be up before the beak. Rather 'im than me!

★

Mr and Mrs Challiss were seated before a flaming coal fire in the back withdrawing room. The window curtains had been drawn across, the candelabra lighted and they stared drowsily into the fire, replete after a light supper of roast duck.

Mary Emma sighed and said: "Poor Agnes."

"Why, 'poor' Agnes?" Tom said through a yawn. "She seemed perfectly happy to me."

"What she seems and what she feels are two different things," Mary Emma said reprovingly. "While you and Kit Warrender were shut away I had a long talk with her. Tom, it's far worse than we thought. She loves Lord Vyvyan and is actually *glad* – her word – to be carrying his child. Though she knows a marriage is hopeless."

Tom sat up straight. Another ghost from the past! "She confessed to that? Then, indeed, I pity her. My own mother found herself in the same predicament."

"Oh, Tom, dear. I had forgotten," Mary Emma said, rising and kissing him before settling herself on his lap. "I cannot imagine what it must be like: to be unmarried and carrying a child out of wedlock. I don't think I could be as brave as Agnes. Oh, it's all right at present, because she hasn't begun to swell. Once she does, she'll be an object of shame, and unkind people will point her out or call her vile names. Yet she takes it all so calmly. I don't understand her – and I thought I did."

"We must be able to do something to help," Tom said, "if she's willing to be helped, that is. It's a delicate subject to broach, darling. It would be better coming from you. . . or Ruth, perhaps."

"Ruth would think less of it; she's a nurse," Mary Emma said, brightening and dismissing the problem from her mind as settled. "But, Tom, what about the horses? I cannnot bear to think of my poor little Genty with nothing to eat! And you must have Mulderrig fit to carry you about the estate. What's to be done?"

Before he was able to reply, there came a double rap on the door and, invited to enter, Peckover came in.

Mary Emma, who hadn't had time to remove herself from her husband's lap, got up as decorously as she could and sat down on a nearby chair.

At the same time, Tom, startled at the sight of his footman, whom he'd imagined off duty, said more sharply than he intended: "Well, Peckover, what is it?"

His face arranged in a dutiful footman expression – sightless, so to speak, Barty said: "I think you oughta know, Mr Challiss, sir, that a load of *hay has* bin delivered, courtesy of Sir Everard Belmaine. So the 'orses is fed fer ternight, at least, sir."

Tom jumped up. "That's grand news, Peckover! Thank you for coming up to tell me. How much hay did Sir Everard send?"

"Can't say, sir. But Bob can prob'ly tell yer."

"Right! Ask him to come up at once, will you. I want to see him anyway."

Downstairs once more, Barty threw on his coat, took a lantern and went out to the stables. He reasoned that, now that the hay loft had been destroyed, the stables would be the only place left for the lad to bed down on such a cold night. So he was surprised to discover no sign of Bob's having slept there at all, so far as he could tell. "That's peculiar," Barty said, biting his lip in puzzlement. "Wonder where 'es gorn?" He thought it best to report back to his master.

His reappearance, minus Bob, caused Tom concern. "He must be about somewhere," he said to Peckover. "Forgive me, my dear," he said to his wife, "I shall have to go in search of him myself." Thanking Peckover, he dismissed him.

Dismayed, Mary Emma said: "But it's freezing out there, as well as pitch dark, Tom! At least, call at the lodge and get Joe to help."

"If it is freezing out there, Mary Emma," Tom said, summoning Rudge, "it's even more imperative that Bob is found as soon as possible – and his father. I suspect where I find one, I'll find the other. Don't wait up for me, my dear. I'll be back as soon as I can." Rudge was directed to fill two flasks with brandy and to have Tom's riding clothes ready at once.

After searching the stables, the clarence and the site of the razed hay barn, he saddled Mulderrig and, a pair of small dark lanterns fixed to either side of the horse's girth, rode at once to Aldrich's lodge. On being shown by Joe into the comfortable sitting-room he realised, with great relief, that his search was over. Evritt Pawl and his son, blankets over their shoulders, were seated before the fire drinking mulled wine.

As Joe left them, father and son rose to their feet and faced the visitor.

Tom was struck by the resemblance between the two: Evritt, a fine-made man who held himself erect and, despite his drapery, had a refined air; Bob, a slighter version of the older man, although dirty and unkempt in appearance, bore the same stamp of refined breeding. The three of them stared at one another in silence for a split second and in that instant recognition flashed upon Tom. From a distance, he'd mistaken Everett Pawl for his half-brother: the late Honourable Percival Belmaine! "How do you do, Mr Pawl," he said, offering the man his hand.

A look of surprise crossed Pawl's drawn face as he held up his bandaged hands. "I've been better, sir," he replied, his eyes frosty below singed eyebrows.

"Forgive me," Tom said. "That was clumsy of me. I was sorry to hear of your sad loss. My condolences."

Pawl inclined his head. "Misfortune and I are no strangers, Mr Challiss," he said. "I was born to it." Young Bob Pawl looked at his father with anguished eyes.

"You have my sympathy, Mr Pawl. Now. About immediate arrangements. I think it best that you face Sir Everard Belmaine, the local magistrate, tomorrow morning. Were it merely the loss of the hay nothing need have been mentioned. But there's the question of the body—What are your sleeping arrangements for tonight?"

"Mr Aldrich and I were discussing that very thing at the moment of your arrival, Mr Challiss, but had not reached a decision. You know we are homeless?"

"I knew you were," Tom began.

"My son, too, has nowhere to lay his head, sir. Now that the hay loft, which was all he could call home, has burned to the ground I think most people would reckon him to be homeless."

This was an undisguised rebuke and Tom had difficulty in keeping his temper. "I have to admit that I have been remiss in ensuring that Bob had decent quarters. It hadn't been drawn to my attention. . . You see, my brother—"

"I understand, Mr Challiss. You've been master of Uppham for only a short while. It's common knowledge in Downham." He spoke to Tom on equal terms.

"Wait here," Tom said, "I'll fetch Mr Aldrich. Please. Be seated. I won't be a moment." He returned with the steward almost at once. "Mr Aldrich. Have any plans been made for the sleeping arrangements for tonight for Mr Pawl and his son?"

"They may stay with me, Mr Challiss, sir, for as long as is necessary. There's ample room and I am glad of the company."

"That's good of you, Joe," Tom said, "but it cannot be a permanent arrangement. One of my priorities must be to build some cottages for the farm servants to live in. For now, I shall be very grateful to take up your offer. I'll be down at nine tomorrow morning to collect Mr Pawl and Bob. We must make a clean breast of what has happened here today."

"Very well, Mr Challiss," Aldrich said, "we shall be ready in good time."

"Is that agreeable to you, Mr Pawl?"

"It is, Mr Challiss; you have shown yourself to be a most humane man, sir."

Tom laid his hand on the man's shoulder. "Good. Then I'll wish you all good night and let's hope for a happy outcome tomorrow."

★

Chapter Twenty-nine

When Mary Emma awoke next morning it was to find Tom's place in the bed empty and cold. Though she had tried to keep awake until his return the previous night, she had fallen asleep amid the coral glow of the flickering fire. Apart from Tom's illness, last night had been the first time since their marriage that she and Tom had not lain together and the thought saddened her. The honeymoon was over, she decided dolefully, as she snuggled down in the bed and wondered if he had already tired of her. Later, as she ate a solitary breakfast, Rudge imparted the news that her husband had taken Peckover and the carriage to call first at Aldrich's lodge, to collect Mr Pawl and his son, and then to accompany them to Martlets to request an audience with Sir Everard Belmaine in his capacity as magistrate. The mistress of the house was greatly displeased at being abandoned without a single word, never mind a *billet doux*, from her absent husband. This is how it will be from now on, she supposed; Tom abroad on estate business while I'm expected to stay at home twiddling my thumbs. "Well," she said to the dining-room walls, before jumping up and tugging the bell-pull, "we shall see about that!"

Rudge reappeared. "You rang, madam?"

"Of course I rang," Mary Emma said crossly, "otherwise you wouldn't be here, would you."

Rudge appeared to be unperturbed by his mistress's rudeness.

Imperiously, she said: "Please see that my mare is saddled, Rudge. I mean to ride over to visit Mrs Brook. Genty needs the exercise as much as I do."

"I beg your pardon, Mrs Challiss," Rudge said deferentially, "but I have strict orders from Mr Challiss to see that you do not go riding in your – ahem! – delicate condition, madam."

"What?"

"Mr Challiss instructed me, madam, to tell you that, should you require outdoor exercise he suggests you walk about the park in the vicinity of the mansion."

By a huge effort of self-control, Mary Emma said, "Thank you, Rudge. That will be all." As soon as he had closed the door silently behind him she ground her teeth, let out a howl of rage and dashed the milk jug to the floor.

To her consternation, Rudge returned to enquire if she had called him back. Her cheeks hot with embarrassment, Mary Emma assured him that she had not, and he departed for the second time. What I need is a companion, she decided, and I intend to do something about it this very minute! Not waiting to summon Maddy, she dressed herself warmly, taking care to wear woollen hose and stout boots, and sought out Rudge. She ran him to ground in the kitchen where she caught him seated beside a roaring fire, drinking a tankard of ale. He spluttered an apology for being found in idleness. Counting on his mistress's ignorance of the fact that he should have been polishing the silver, he asked if there was anything she wished him to do. "Yes, Mr Rudge, there is," she said with great self-possession. "Please to inform Mr Challiss, should he wonder at my absence, that I have decided to follow his excellent suggestion. I am going to take a walk and hope to be back in time to take luncheon."

"Very good, Mrs Challiss. Should I say in which direction madam has decided to ramble?" Rudge enquired.

"Tell him I've gone to Timbuctoo!" she said, sweeping out of the house by the servants' door. At which Mrs Rudge folded her brawny arms across her bosom, pursed her lips and nodded meaningfully at Maddy to indicate to the girl that their master and mistress were definitely having one of their 'downs' – which she had predicted not so long ago.

The half dozen casual labourers engaged in clearing the horticultural muddle in front of the house stole covert glances at the red-mantled young woman who set off at a smart pace towards the drive and murmured that she must be the missus.

*

Tom and the Pawls, accompanied by Kit Warrender, sat in a small, cold, plainly-furnished room into which they'd been shown by a disdainful footman on their arrival at Martlets. Yes, Sir Everard Belmaine would see them; but he was presently engaged in taking breakfast and would not be at liberty to hear what they had to say until ten o'clock at the earliest.

Kit Warrender had agreed to accompany the others as an eyewitness to the fire and, more importantly, as an accomplice in sheltering vagrants on his master's property without his prior knowledge or permission. The four Uppham men sat in the dreary room on hard chairs, listening to the ticking of the clock on the mantelpiece whose hands appeared to be made of lead, so tardily did they move. . .

The tenth chime died away, the door was opened by a bewigged footman and, as the servant stood aside to allow his master to pass, Sir Everard Belmaine entered the room. After bidding them a crusty "Good mornin'," he dismissed the footman who closed the door behind him. The four Uppham men rose to their feet and Sir Everard walked with military erectness – though he had never served his country in that capacity – to a rickety table and seated himself behind the improvised barrier. His voice issued from a throat that was dry from lack of conversation and gave to his first words an unintentional severity that made Bob quake in his boots.

"Please be seated. Who among you is to act as mouthpiece?"

Tom rose. "I shall lay the case before you, sir," he said, ruffled by the old gentleman's seeming hostility.

"If you would rather be seated, Mr Challiss, please do so." Tom sat. "Proceed."

"Thank you, sir," Tom said, grateful that he would not have to look down on the magistrate. By the time he had laid the facts before Sir Everard he saw that the hands of the clock had unaccountably whizzed round to ten minutes to eleven.

The magistrate's face had betrayed nothing as Tom had unfolded the story of the fire; but now he said: "Does anyone wish to add anything to what has been said?"

Kit Warrender, who was well-acquainted with Belmaine, raised a bandaged hand and said: "If you please, sir. I'd just like to say that I also was guilty in the business of concealing Mr and Mrs Pawl in the hay loft. I kept quiet out of common humanity. Mr Pawl and his wife had lost everything of value and Mrs Pawl was so weak and ill that she was near death's door. They had nowhere to go, Sir Everard, and I wouldn't expect a dog to have to sleep under a hedge in this weather. I see now that I should've taken Mr Challiss into my confidence at the start; but . . . I didn't." He'd been about to say that his master had hardly been around at the time, but had thought better of it.

"Any one else?" The old man's lined face with its high-bridged nose scanned the faces of the men seated opposite him beneath a high window, their backs to the light.

"If I might add something," Evritt Pawl said, Tom and Warrender painfully aware of his omission. "I hold myself entirely to blame for the accidental destruction of the hay and the barn. Nobody else is culpable, Sir Everard. If there is any punishment to be meted out it should be to me."

Tom wondered if any of the others had noticed the startled blink that the magistrate had been powerless to conrol at the sound of Pawl's educated voice. Or had it been more than that? Before anybody could stop him, Bob said: "But 'twere me as give 'im the pipe in the first place... sir. If I 'adn't done that there wouldna bin no fire."

"Hmm," Sir Everard pouted his withered lips while he considered what had been said. "You have been refreshin'ly candid," he said. "Nevertherless, I cannot condone the behaviour to which you have admitted. The law must be upheld. Were landowners, such as myself and Mr Challiss, to find themselves subject to hordes of vagrants occupyin' their outbuildin's willy-nilly, it is impossible to foresee where such an invasion of private property would end. If I were to ignore what has been said I should be advocatin' that Great Britain turn itself into a democracy." At this Evritt Pawl's eyes burned with repressed fury. Belmaine went on: "As to the death of your wife, Pawl: it is a very serious matter and I offer you my sincere condolences. I have no wish to inflict unnecessary pain, but must ask if any evidence has been found of her remains?"

Kit Warrender said: "I was at the scene of the fire this morning, Sir Everard, before we came to Martlets. The debris was still smouldering – half-burnt fallen beams too hot to touch; as you can see, I got burned yesterday and wouldn't risk it."

"Some hours have passed since then: the ashes will have cooled," Belmaine said. "I suggest we adjourn and meet at the site of the fire at two o'clock. You agree, Challiss?"

"Of course, sir," Tom said, adding hastily as the others trooped out: "Before we leave this room I wish to state here and now that I shall not press charges for trespass or any other misdemeanour against Mr Pawl, or his son. Nor shall I lend support to any ruling that brands Mr Warrender a criminal."

Before replying, the magistrate recorded something in a black-covered ledger, carefully replaced his quill pen, sprinkled the wet ink with chalkdust and blew it off into the empty fireplace, during the execution of which the Pawls and Warrender had made their way out to the waiting coach.

Once they were alone, Belmaine laid a restraining hand on Tom's forearm and observed: "A moment, sir. You have declared your intention not to press charges and no one can compel you to do so. It is your prerogative. However, young man, I must tell you that I view such misguided leniency with dismay. Word will soon spread among the workforce that you are a soft master. It won't do, sir. Advantage will be taken of your good nature. You will be robbed blind by your own servants. Also, you have a duty to others among the landed gentry when exercisin' the method in which you choose to deal with those who take the law into their own hands. I tell you plainly, sir: the method you have chosen is unorthodox. It is incumbent upon every one of us who belong to the rulin' classes to demonstrate a united front, to present to the lower orders an impregnable bastion of solidarity when dealin' with lawlessness of any kind."

Tom laughed. "Sir, you've mistaken my status. I'm not one of the landed gentry. Though I can lay claim to a father who was of that class, my mother's people were honest yeoman farmers, and it's to that class I consider I belong. My earlier life hasn't fitted me to consider myself superior to my fellow men. Nor do I consider myself inferior to those supposedly above me. I am of the people, sir! It's true, I enjoy the trappings of the gentry; but that doesn't make me blind or deaf to the plight of those less fortunate. I'd rather try to help those poor devils, who some might mistakenly consider beneath me in rank, than tread on them when they are down, sir."

Sir Everard Belmaine surveyed him from hooded eyes. "Then you're a demned fool, sir!" he said robustly, "and have chosen a difficult path to follow. Still, I admire you for sticking to your guns, Challiss. It makes a change to encounter such frankness, though your talk smacks of radicalism. I'll be equally frank. I mistook you for one of Percival's racin' cronies and cold-shouldered you on the day he brought you here to choose a nag. Glad to find I was wrong. All that folly's over, thank heaven."

"Forgive me, sir: please accept my belated condolences on the untimely death of your son," Tom said. "Ah! And my thanks to you for the load of hay you sent to Uppham yesterday. It was very good of you, sir; I won't offend you by offering payment. But if ever there's anything I can do for you—"

"Quite, quite," the old aristocrat said dismissively, as if he were shooing away a troublesome fly. "More than enough hay and to spare. Good yield this year. If you find you need more, let me know. I have no more need of it as horse-feed. I've sold off the string; no need of the animals now... Until two, then."

Wonder who bought Saladin? Tom thought, before saying: "Mustn't keep my friends and servant waiting in this bitter weather, sir. Good day to you, Sir Everard."

Peckover's face was invisible, apart from watering eyes and a scarlet nose, the latter protruding above the coils of his muffler. As Tom climbed into the waiting clarence he realised, too late, that he'd mentioned nothing of Belmaine's invitation to nuncheon which was due to take place in a few days' time.

Tom was not too surprised by his wife's absence when he reached home and assumed her to be enjoying her walk. He ate luncheon alone and hardly missed her company, occupied as he was with the morning's events. Belmaine's involuntary start of recognition of something to do with Evritt Pawl nagged him. Obviously, Sir Everard had not known Pawl as an acquaintance. Had Belmaine detected the family likeness, despite Pawl's face and form being in shadow? If he had, he'd concealed the fact behind an impassive façade. Neglectful of the passage of time, it seemed to Tom he'd no sooner sat down to eat than it was time for him to walk over to the hay yard.

To his consternation, the others were there before him. Sir Everard Belmaine had chosen to remain in his coach out of the wind that screamed across the blackened wasteland where the haybarn had once stood. Mischievously, the whirling wind sucked powdery ashes into a helix, a ghostly gyrating form that hovered briefly near them before flying up and disappearing with a thin wail into the upper air.

"What were that?" Bob whispered in terror, his words snatched away by the wind. "'Twere a haunt!" His eyes enormous, his head shrank down inside the collar of his worn coat. Addressing his father shakily, he asked him: "Were it mother?"

"It might have been," Pawl replied, "for her bodily remains must have been at least partly-cremated by the ferocity of the blaze and would have mingled with the wood ash."

"It looked like what my grandma used to call a highsprite, a kind of ghost. She swore she could see 'em," Kit Warrender added, thoughtfully biting his lip and frowning up to the point above them where the thing had vanished.

Tom, too, had been shaken by the strangely apt phenomenon but said: "It's nothing but the wind stirring up the ashes. Sh! Here comes Sir Everard. Pull yourselves together for much depends on what happens in the next few minutes."

"Good afternoon, Chall–" He was staring at Evritt Pawl. "Who is this man?" he demanded in his unfortunately imperious delivery.

"I am Everett Bellman Pawl, Sir Everard; a blood relative of yours."

Belmaine turned ashen. When he was able to find his voice, Belmaine asked severely: "Why did you not make yourself known this mornin', sir?"

Perfectly collected, Pawl replied with a degree of inherited hauteur: "The time and the circumstances were not appropriate, sir."

"You've put me in a demned embarrassin' position, sir!" Sir Everard snapped. He became aware of Tom, Bob and Warrender standing silently by, listening with avid interest to every word. "We will discuss this more fully later," he said wrapping his dignity around him like a second cloak. "I have no wish to catch my death by standin' about in this demned gale a moment longer than is absolutely necessary. Let us get on with the business in hand."

Warrender offered to investigate the charred debris and sifting ash but Tom, indicating the Farm Manager's bound hands, would not hear of it. He advised Sir Everard to return to the shelter of his coach; but the old gentleman steadfastly refused to budge and said that it was his duty as a magistrate to observe proceedings closely.

Tom began to sort through the few solid-looking humps, all that remained of the former building, though he had little hope of finding anything of evidential value that would point to Mrs Pawl ever having existed. A ferocious, steady wind had turned the blazing barn into a furnace that had, in turn, become a perfect cremator. No vestige of the woman's corpse remained. As Tom raked through the ashes one last time in order to demonstrate his thoroughness to Sir Everard Belmaine – who, a quizzing glass held to his left eye, stood as near as he dared – he moved aside a half-buried flint. He gave a triumphant cry as he dislodged something that he'd found in the cavity left by the flint's removal from the baked earth below the warm ashes. Holding it in the palm of his filthy hand he walked up to Belmaine and showed him his discovery. Taking out his handkerchief, Tom rubbed the ash and soil from what they all saw was a ring. When the last traces of detritus had been removed a beautiful, probably valuable, ring was revealed; it was of gold with a band of five alternating red and white stones forming the top half of the hoop.

Sir Everard Belmaine asked Tom to draw closer, examined the ring closely through his glass and said: "Good Lord! This ring belonged to my own mother. It adorned her hand throughout my childhood. How it comes to be here I cannot imagine." He wore an expression of great severity before which many felons had quailed as they awaited sentence. "Has anybody present an explanation?"

"More recently it belonged to my own mother," the startled listeners heard Evritt Pawl say. "She told me it had been given to her by my father on the occasion of my birth."

Sir Everard gave Evritt a searching look before saying: "Our business here is finished. But I am not yet sufficiently satisfied to bring these proceedin's to a close. I shall require your attendance at Martlets at eleven o'clock tomorrow mornin', Mr Challiss; bring only Pawl – Mr Warrender and young Pawl need not accompany you." He stretched forth his open hand. " I had better take care of the ring for the present."

★

Long shadows stretched across the flat windswept landscape as a vermilion sun dipped behind a silhouetted hedgerow. Tom stood looking out of one of the the front withdrawing room windows and was surprised to see how the afternoon had worn away while he had been sitting beside the fire deep in thought. He looked at the clock. Where on earth had Mary Emma got to? He summoned Rudge. The manservant told him as much as he knew of his mistress's whereabouts, while discreetly omitting the reference to Timbuctoo. Tom dismissed him without another word on the subject of his wife's absence, which was beginning to worry him. The silly little thing! he fumed, reluctant to leave the warmth of the fireside to go in search of her. He would give her another quarter of an hour and hope that by that time she would have put in an appearance. The ticking clock seemed abnormally loud in the absence of any sound other than that of coals shifting and settling as they burned through and the wind whistling outside the house. Now he became really anxious. If she were out in the park, perhaps injured in some way, she would soon succumb to the effects of the elements. His agitation grew, until he was impelled to jump up and to pace up and down the room. Glancing every few minutes at the clock, he willed the quarter of an hour away but capitulated before the hand reached the appointed time. He summoned Rudge a second time.

"Has Mrs Challiss returned yet, Rudge?" he asked swiftly. On learning that she had not, he ordered the manservant to lay out again the riding clothes he had worn that afternoon. Rudge was to send Peckover to the stables directly to tell Bob to saddle Mulderrig, and to harness the team in case it was needed later on; but first to feed and water the horses and then cover them while they waited in the yard.

Darkness had descended by the time he was ready to set out and a new moon gave little light. Adopting again his former plan of attaching the two small lanterns to his horse's girth, he made first of all for Aldrich's lodge. As he approached the building he saw that the window curtains had been closed and sent forth a cheery red glow into the bitter night. Joe's surprised face had appeared in the gap of the partially-opened doorway and the few words exchanged between the two men soon told Tom that he'd drawn a blank. He rode out of Uppham's gate into the village of Uppham St Mary and to Church House where he prayed that he would find Mary Emma with the Brooks. He pulled the bell and waited. Mary Emma answered it.

Drawing him into the hall, she jumped up and kissed his frozen cheek. "I said to Dulcie not to worry, that you'd soon work out that I'd be here," she said happily. "Come into the warm, Tom." It was neither the place nor the time to tell his wife what he thought of her inconsiderate behaviour. That could wait. Swallowing his rage, he said with assumed affability: "Glad to find you safe and sound, my pet," as they entered the Brooks' kitchen.

A scene of homely comfort greeted Tom. Dulcie was busying herself with making supper and Adam was home and seated beside the fire with his youngest son on his lap and a stumpy pipe in his mouth. "Evenin', Tom," Adam said drowsily. "Gits late earlier this time o' year, don' it. Yew come ter fetch the missus? Why, yer look frawn, bor," he said, placing Noah on the rag rug before getting up. "Yew could dew with a drop o' somethin' 'ot inside yer," he said, suiting words to actions. The kettle was already steaming away on the trivet before the fire and Adam had made Tom a hot toddy in seconds, urging him to: "Git that down yer."

Mary Emma swept up Noah from the floor and held him above her head one moment and the next swooped him towards her cherry lips for a kiss. This game thrilled the little boy who exercised his powerful lungs in ear-splitting laughter. "Now, that's enough, Mary Emma. The young varmint!" Dulcie said, complacently regarding the apple of her eye. "We can't 'ear ourselves think! 'E'll 'ave an accident next, an supper's near ready." And to Ann and Fanny: "Come on, girls; set the table, dew."

Agnes came and took Noah from Mary Emma. The little boy didn't mind which pretty lady spoiled him and sighed happily as he settled down on his big sister's lap, nestled up to her with his thumb in his mouth and begun to suck it noisily. Agnes was astonished to see Tom actually smiling as he followed Noah's antics.

Suddenly serious, Tom said quietly to Mary Emma: "Now I must ride back to the house, drag Peckover out into the cold and give Bob the additional trouble of stalling the horses for the night once we get back. I hope you are satisfied with your little escapade." He fastened his cape and picked up his hat.

"You're not goin' already, bor?" Adam said, obviously disappointed.

"I must go to fetch the clarence; Mary Emma may not ride in her condition."

"What?" Mary Emma cried. "Are you saying that my going out has *inconvenienced the servants*? I never heard of such a thing!"

Agnes lifted Noah from her lap and handed him to John who, in turn, dumped him on Dovey's lap. "If I might make a suggestion, Mr Challiss?" she said quietly. "Mary Emma is welcome to stay here overnight. My bed is large enough to take two, sir."

Seeing that this plan would solve all his problems at a stroke, Tom asked his wife: "What do you think of Agnes's suggestion, my dear?"

Reluctantly, Mary Emma admitted: "I suppose it would save you a lot of time and trouble, Tom. Thank you, Agnes. What do your parents say to the suggestion?"

"'Tain our bed you'm gonna be sleepin' in!" Dulcie said. "Agnes is old enough and sensible enough to 'ave her own jurisdiction when it comes to sharin' 'er bed. Eh, Adie?"

"Acourse, she is. Our mawther's got 'er 'ead screwed on, right enough, jist like 'er ma," Brook said, smiling fondly first at Agnes then at Dulcie, adding: "both of 'em 're treasures."

Privately, Tom concurred with Adie's assessment and couldn't help comparing the Brook women to Mary Emma who, in his opinion, seemed deficient in feminine qualities by comparison. "So? Is it settled? You'll spend the night here?" he asked.

How easily he can spare my company, thought Mary Emma. "I shall look on it as an adventure," she said, smiling with false gaiety. "Do I walk home tomorrow?" she asked Tom.

"Don't you think you've done enough walking for the moment, my dear?" he said with an ironic smile. "No, Mary Emma. I have to visit Martlets again tomorrow morning. I imagine my business will be concluded by mid-day. Look for me to collect you in the clarence some time between eleven o'clock and noon. Good-evening, my dear," he said kissing her on the cheek. "Thank you, Agnes, for your thoughtfulness. Good-evening, Dulcie and Adam." He tapped his topper firmly on his head. "And sweet dreams, all you young Brooks." He was warmed by their chorus of response; but had been chilled by the cold fury he'd observed in his wife's eyes.

As he galloped along the frosty, rutted lane he carried with him images of the well-ordered harmonious household that the Brook family enjoyed. He asked himself how it was that two seemingly simple people had created such a domestic paradise? What had been their plan? Had they had a plan at all?

Mulderrig's hooves clattered rhythmically past Aldrich's lodge and into the tree-arched drive. That Adam and Dulcie themselves were the key to the harmony that reigned at Church House he had no doubt. He analysed the reasons for the family's placidity and could find no other explanation for their happiness than that they were content with their lot in life.

It seemed to Tom that, provided they had sufficient to their needs, they were unaspiring. He had no doubt at all that the Brooks were settled in Church House for life; that Adam Brook would be content to fill the position of Head Gardener at Uppham until he was carried to the churchyard to enrich the consecrated ground with his decomposing remains. The former Miss Dulcibella Burton's children were her riches: she craved nothing the material world had to offer. She, too, was content with the life fate had decreed for her. To have been granted a parcel of healthy children with the wherewithal to nurture them and to provide for their bodily wants, and the desire to give to them unstinted time and love until they were old enough to fend for themselves, was to her a kind of heaven. To have her love for her family reciprocated by each and every one in it was all that she desired in her lifetime. Tom saw that some might perceive the Brooks' life as narrow; but the seam of their marriage went deep and was inexhaustible and one of its by-products was wisdom. Agnes Brook was living proof of that, thought Tom, as he trotted Mulderrig into the stable yard.

Bob, a sack across the shoulders of his thin coat, showed up at once and Tom, wrapped in his own thoughts, found his being there nothing unusual. The lad's relief was evident when Tom told him that the team would not be needed again that night.

Peckover's face became wreathed in smiles at the news that he wouldn't be required until tomorrow morning and, once Tom had left the servants' basement, celebrated his escape from a Norfolk winter night in the open by settling himself in Mr Rudge's chair beside the fire, the manservant having retired to his room for the night. Mrs Rudge and Maddy made a small party of it. They drank mulled ale, ate cold cuts of meat left over from the previous day's joint and finished off with large slices of a new seed cake Mrs Rudge had baked that afternoon.

A door banged, feet stamped on the doormat and Bob Pawl came in looking frozen. Having no other place to lay his head, he'd been invited by the cook to spend the night on the hearthrug in front of the huge open fire in the kitchen. Bob anticipated with enormous pleasure the luxury of dropping off to sleep feeling really warm once more. For although he'd been comfortable enough at Aldrich's, he hadn't found the steward's lodge convenient to his job and Aldrich had offered to speak to the master about providing the youth with a permanent berth for him that was nearer to the stables. The thought of his sleeping with the horses again, buried in straw in an empty stable with only mice for company, had been a doleful prospect for the stable lad, after experiencing the comfort of a real bed in a room with a coal fire at Aldrich's. He'd confided his predicament to Peckover who had mentioned it to Mrs Rudge.

"Doan seem right that a growin' lad should bed down wi' the beasts, dew it?" the sympathetic cook had said to the footman. "Pore dardledumdew, the way 'e yarms 'is vittles! Fair makes me 'eart bleed ter see the lad ser clemmed."

So now, as he came into the kitchen he was made welcome, and was helped to thaw out by downing two mugs of warmed ale one after the other; after which Mrs Rudge steadily plied him with broken meats, hunks of bread and seed cake and more ale until, eventually, his gargantuan appetite was appeased.

★

Tom and Evritt Pawl once more sat waiting for Sir Everard Belmaine. To their surprise, they had been shown into an elegant room which was cheered by a good fire. "What d'you make of the change of venue?" Tom asked Evritt in a subdued voice.

Pawl's eyes crinkled at the corners. "I'd say our dignified host has remembered his manners," he replied quietly. The fire crackled and roared spurts of blue flame, a pretty clock fussily ticked off the seconds until Belmaine walked in on the dot of ten.

"Good mornin', gentlemen," the old man said, turning a chair in their direction before seating himself beside the fire. "Thank you for comin' promptly."

Tom and Evritt made their 'Good mornings' and waited.

Sir Everard said: "I have called you here under false pretences. There can be no reasonable doubt that the burnin' of the hay barn and Mrs Pawl's subsequent death were accidental. I have recorded a verdict of 'Accidental Death Caused by Fire in a Hay Barn' and that is exactly how Mrs Pawl's death will be shown in the burial record." He waited for them to comment. Their silence led him to raise his eyebrows: "I take it that the verdict meets with your approval?"

Tom and Evritt signified that it did and waited for him to continue.

"My true reason for wishin' to see you together this mornin' will soon be made plain," Belmaine said enigmatically. "First," he said, addressing Evritt, "I would like to find out more about how my mother's ruby and diamond ring came into your possession."

"I thought that had been fully explained yesterday afternoon," Evritt Pawl said.

"And so it had," Belmaine agreed affably. "What I really want to get at has to do with the identity of the man who you say was your father."

Evritt Pawl's face took on a forbidding expression that did his Belmaine forebears credit. "If you have any doubts on that head, Sir Everard," he said severely, "I suggest you consult the baptismal records in St Mary's vestry."

Unruffled by the younger man's angry outburst, Belmaine said: "Suppose we dispense with that for the moment. Tell me your history in your own words."

Mollified by Belmaine's calm response, Evritt began: "My mother, Elizabeth Pawl, known as Bessie, was a servant who worked for a time at Martlets, Sir Everard; though it's unlikely you knew of her existence. While little more than a girl, she was seduced by your brother, Robin Belmaine, then a young man of twenty. The pair fell in love but, once my mother told him she was carrying his child he was unable to face the disgrace he'd brought on his illustrious family by a liaison with a lower class female. So he deserted my pregnant mother in order to join the British Navy. Before leaving Downham to join the Arctic Expedition of 1773 as a naval lieutenant, he purchased a cottage which was to be hers for the term of her natural life. In addition, he ordered a sum of money, sufficient for her needs and for those of the expected child, to be paid to her on a quarterly basis. As well as that, he left a sum of money with his lawyer to be used in the education of his baseborn child – namely, myself – should the expected child be a boy. If a girl was the fruit of their illicit union no such sum was to be paid out... I trust I am not tiring you, sir?"

Tom was glad that Mary Emma was safely at home out of earshot.

"Eh? Tirin' me? Not in the least, Mr Pawl," Sir Everard said, his face engraved in sombre lines. "But you're openin' cupboards and settin' skeletons rattlin'. Go on with your story."

"While engaged on the Arctic expedition, my father struck up a friendship with another lieutenant, namely, Horatio Nelson. It was a friendship that was to flourish until Nelson's death at Trafalgar in 1805... But I'm getting ahead of myself."

Before he was able to continue, Tom broke in: "While this is a fascinating tale, Sir Everard, I fail to understand why you considered my presence necessary."

"Be patient, sir," was all the reply Tom got for his interruption. "Please go on, Mr Pawl."

"I'll be as brief as possible," said Evritt, "the early years of my life sped by in a succession of happy days with my young mother until it was time for me to begin my education. Always prudent in financial matters, my mother realised that the bulk of the money set aside for my education would be needed when I reached the higher echelons of learning. On hearing of an excellent school run by a widow in the front parlour of her own cottage, who lived a few doors from where we ourselves were living, my mother enrolled me as a pupil at the early age of four years old. From being a solitary child I suddenly had a family of playmates. I thrived on learning and grew strong in the rough games played in the fresh air on the green in front of our row of cottages. Before long I had learned as much as the widow was able to teach me and she herself suggested that my mother approach the Reverend John Wood, who was a Latin and Greek scholar, as she had always supposed these languages to be necessary for any student aspiring to enter a university. My mother called on John Wood, at that time a man in his prime, who, after putting me through my paces, agreed to see what he could make of me. I was by that time nine years old. Then followed some of the happiest years of my life. Book-learning was as meat and drink to me and I took it in and digested it as easily as I did my daily bread. By the time I had reached my fourteenth year I was well-prepared to try for a scholarship to Oxford. John Wood was himself a master of arts who had graduated from Oxford University. He expressed high hopes for my success and it had just been agreed that I should try for the entrance examination when my mother was struck down with smallpox." He stopped abruptly and bowed his head. "Forgive me..."

Ignoring Evritt Pawl's access of emotion, Belmaine said to Tom: "Would you mind givin' the rope a tug, Challiss. Save me the effort of risin'."

Tom obeyed and, as if he'd been stationed just outside the door, before two seconds had elapsed a powdered flunky appeared. Belmaine ordered hot chocolate to be brought immediately. That accomplished, he said to Pawl, "Do you feel able to continue now?"

"I apologise for my weakness, sir. Had you had the pleasure of knowing my sweet mother you would scarcely be surprised that such a painful memory should re-open the deepest of wounds. The ring found buried in the earthen floor of the barn had been put there by Bob on my instructions."

"You knew it had been buried there?" said Tom incredulously. "Why did you say nothing of it before this?"

"I was far from certain that it had survived the fire; I had not been present when my son hid it and was ignorant of the protective flint."

"But why bury it in the first place?" Tom asked.

"My poor wife had become so emaciated that it was obvious that the ring, with all its powerful associations with my mother, would be lost. It was continually slipping from her fleshless finger and she and I agreed that it should be saved to be passed on to Bob's future bride. Though we had been next to starving more than once, it had never entered our heads to exchange the ring for money or food."

Belmaine, who had been silently listening to their dialogue, now said: "I have no reason to doubt all that you have said, Mr Pawl, but I need to satisfy my curiosity as to why you and your son speak with such disparate tongues. If it isn't an indelicate enquiry, might I venture to ask how and when you met your wife?"

Pawl smiled grimly to himself. "I haven't yet told how, my hopes for a better life having been dashed by my mother's early death – for I was turned out of the cottage a month after her burial and the quarterly allowances ceased at the same time – I followed my father's footsteps and enlisted in the navy. Unlike him, I had no fortune with which to buy myself into the officer class. I enlisted as a common seaman. By dint of studying all the books on seamanship I could lay my hands on, and with the assistance of interested superiors I succeeded, albeit by quarter inches, to elevate myself until I was made bosun. I was, at that time, sailing with a fair-minded captain who saw in me the potential for the transition from the uncommissioned ranks to the officer class. By the time I had reached my majority in 1793 I had risen to the rank of sub-lieutenant and we had become embroiled in the fight against Bonaparte. It was during one of the skirmishes with the French at the blockade of Toulon in 1804 that I was gravely wounded. For months I was not expected to live. I, and others who had sustained wounds, were rowed ashore by night to a smaller island off the north coast of the Ile de Porquerolles and there, against all odds, and thanks to the nursing of a French nun, I recovered.

It took me many months to find my way back to England. There I received a small pension, sufficient to keep only myself. When eventually I returned to Downham it was to discover that I had fathered a son out of wedlock some years before. You know him as Bob. He was born in 1799. I married his mother to legitimise my son, for I was determined that he should not bear the stigma of bastardy for the rest of his life as I have done. By that time he had been reared as a rustic and had survived under the harshest conditions. I knew no trade and had no option but to take up work as a common farm labourer living away from home. Kit Warrender's father took me on out of pity, I think; but I learned quickly and, until the implementation of this oppressive Corn Law made me redundant, was a useful member of society."

Tom, who had been intrigued by Evritt's deliberate omission of the circumstances under which he and his wife had met, said: "Where did you say you first made your wife's acquaintance?"

Again, Evritt evaded the question. "We didn't live together until this autumn," he said slowly, "and then her... illness... was such that we... did not resume marital relations. We are all of us grown men and know the ways of the world, do we not? To speak plainly, I had lain with Sally for only one night before leaving to join my ship."

The truth had dawned on Tom long before Evritt had ceased to speak. "You're saying that the late Mrs Pawl was a kittywitch, if I understand you rightly," he said.

"Eh? What's that?" Sir Everard shouted. "What're y' *sayin'* – ? D'ye expect me to believe that young Bob's mother – *the dam of me own grandson* – was a – a – ... You're *certain*?" Eyes agog, his monocle fell as he recollected Bob's image. "'Zounds!'"

Evritt said wryly: "There are all kinds of skeletons, Sir Everard, and not a few of them have been hidden in cupboards belonging to the quality." To Tom, he said: "Your assumption was correct, Mr Challiss. My late wife – if I may use that hallowed term for such a poor lost creature – was a whore, though more by default than design. I unwittingly exacerbated her downfall by fathering upon her my child. Not that she was an innocent, even then; but her body at that time was free of the French crown. The woman had no other means of earning her bread. To her credit, she put our son away from her before her plunge into utter degradation. I called him Robin, after the father I never knew – except through my mother's words – but his mother's diminutive for it, Bob, has stuck to him to this day."

The old man had slumped back in his chair and Tom was reminded of a deflated toad clad in the latest fashion. He shook his head slowly from side to side. "To think that the Belmaines have sunk so low."

"Nobody need be any the wiser, sir," Tom said with false jollity.

"What was it you said about the parish records, Mr Pawl? What is it I shall find in them?"

"You will find my baptism in St Mary's Church records for 1772. It names my mother as 'Elizabeth Pawl, singlewoman of this parish.' She was a beautiful and healthy girl whose family had been settled in these parts for two hundred years before the first Belmaine was heard of. Her introduction into the Belmaine line has enriched it immeasurably. Comparisons are said to be odious; but I invite you to compare my physique and intellect with that of your legitimate son, the late Percival Belmaine. As to the record of my baptism: examine the margin closely and you will see in minute writing a later addition. It says: 'Beloved son of Robin Belmaine of Martlets in the parish of Downham.' And, should you contemplate having that record removed I would remind you that the bishop of this diocese has transcribed copies of all records to the year 1810. Even were you tempted to try to wipe the record from your family's history there will always be those who know of it, among them God himself, sir."

"If what you say is true, and you give me no reason to doubt it," said Belmaine, "then you are my nephew – of a sort. My only son has perished and since his death the handin' over of this place has preyed much on me mind."

Unaware that he did so, Tom leaned toward the old man in expectation of his next words.

"You seem to be admirably fitted to take my place as the owner of Martlets when the time comes for me to meet my Maker," Sir Everard said to his nephew.

Evritt Pawl stiffened. "Do I understand that you propose to make me your heir, Sir Everard? I find that quite incredible, if so."

"I realise that it might have come as a bit of a shock to you," Belmaine said eagerly. "But, don't y' see? You have a son! I slept none too well last night, thinkin' it all through. Why, you're the image of me brother. Robin reincarnated. Oh, I know that old story of Nelson," he said with a touch of impatience. "But Robin died at sea *after* Trafalgar in 1807, at Copenhagen. Percival was m' last hope, and now he's gorn. But you and Bob are here! Robin's *line* – unknown to me all these years. It's a miracle!" He grew excited. "'Tis easy enough to change y' name by Deed Poll—"

"Fate decreed that I was born a Pawl and that is the name I shall bear until my dying day, sir," Evritt said severely. "I cannot speak for my son, of course. Bob's life is his own. You Belmaines have treated neither my mother nor me well. But at least your brother did his best to make amends when he learned of my mother's death."

"Made amends?" the old man queried haughtily.

"There is a remarkable tombstone in the churchyard of St Mary's. Anybody in the village will point it out to you," Evritt said solemnly. "Next time you're there, leave the comfort of your crested coach, walk a few steps and read its inscription."

★

They left Sir Everard Belmaine soon after mid-day after promising to send Bob to have a talk with him, at a time to suit his and their convenience. He had urged them not to leave it too long. "And get the boy a proper suit of clothes!" had been his parting shot.

On their way to collect Mary Emma from Church House, Tom said to Evritt: "I did quite a bit of thinking while you and your uncle were unravelling the past. Time flies, and if we're not careful all we have left are regrets for what we might have done, or might have done better. Please tell me to mind my own business if you think I'm taking a liberty. I shall be sorry not to get my own way; but I shall quite understand if you don't wish to bind yourself into another man's service. Unless you are content to continue in your present post as the parish gravedigger I should like you to consider making a change to a more comfortable way of earning your living."

Evritt's eyes sparkled. "Somehow I feel that digging graves, while necessary and useful, might come more easily to a man whose thoughts are less troubled by the thought of the time wasted in shifting piles of earth from pillar to post, when swift and cleansing fire can achieve the same end, and that without the necessity of filling our churchyards with bones and stones," he said.

Tom stared at him. "You don't mean that you actually advocate the burning of the dead as a matter of course?"

"Why not?" Pawl asked in surprise. "Surely ash takes up less space on the face of a globe whose population is increasing at an alarming rate in every country?"

"It's a radical idea," said Tom meditatively. "But I doubt whether it would ever become popular in England. I mean... In the past, burning's been reserved for heretics and witches... and victims of terrible diseases. No. I cannot agree with you, Evritt. But aren't you curious to find out what it is I am offering you?"

"I apologise, Mr Challiss. I'm afraid I'm inclined to go off on these hobby horses from time to time! Forgive me. It was the idea that I might be rid of an occupation that distresses me more than I can say that caused that outburst. It occurred to me after my wife's death: the cremation of her disease-ridden body had been so quick, so clean – Tell me, sir; what is it that you wish to put to me?"

"I need somebody of education and an ordered mind to sort out my library—"

"My dear sir!" Pawl exclaimed, his whole demeanour undergoing a transformation, years seeming to drop away from his face before Tom's eyes. "I would happily undertake such a fascinating occupation without a salary... er... as long as I was fed, of course," he added cautiously.

At that, Tom laughed immoderately. "Forgive me, Evritt, but I can't remember when I gave a man so much pleasure merely by uttering a single sentence – and that left unfinished. Do I take it that you accept my proposal?"

"Oh, Mr Challiss, sir; I do, I do with all my heart." He held his bandaged hands palm upwards and looked down at them. "These will rejoice to be back in their true element. Too long, far too long, they have been used as tools to grub among the soil. When these bandages are removed, sir, they will reveal scarred, roughened hands that might seem to have belonged to a felon doomed to work in a stonebreaker's yard. But they still remember how to caress a calfskin volume, Mr Challiss, how to draw a book forth without damage to its spine and how to create order out of chaos." He closed his eyes and opened them again as if a prayer had been answered and Tom saw that his lashes were moist when he asked: "How soon may I begin?"

"As soon as you can find a gravedigger to fill your vacancy," Tom answered, amazed at how simple the negotiation had been. "And, of course, you will live in."

"Look for me before dark today, then," Pawl said, full of excitement. "If you'll stop the coach I'll get out and walk back into Downham. Unless he himself has been gathered by the reaper, I know the very man for the job."

★

Every member of the Brook family, except Burton, was seated around the large table in the kitchen and about to say grace. Seated between Dovey and Zeb, Mary Emma had her eyes closed and her head bowed over her clasped hands as Tom waited by the open door for the solemn moment to pass. The sight of his wife in an attitude of humility charged his whole being with so powerful a love for her that it was a physical blow. Noah, peeping through his fingers, spotted him and cried out: "Tom!" as those about to dine raised their heads and added their own greetings.

A restrained buzz broke out as dishes were passed to and fro and the carefully prepared meal began to be demolished. "Dovey, make room an shuft nearer ter Fanny so that Mr Tom c'n sit next tew 'is wife," Dulcie said, not pausing, as with a steady rhythm she dished out helpings of shepherd's pie one after the other and passed them down the long table. "Don't yew be shy, now, Mr Challiss – unless yew think my pie's not good enough fer yew," she said saucily while fluttering her eyelashes at him.

Laughing at her mock flirtation, Tom corkscrewed himself into the tight space and found his thigh touching his wife's. Reaching for her hand, he pressed his lips to her inner wrist. "I'm sorry to be so late, my love," he murmured, "but it was a very busy morning. I have much to tell you." The Brook children, except Agnes who averted her eyes and John who ate without pause, stared wide-eyed at their guests' open love-making, surreptitiously nudging each other under cover of the tablecloth. Belatedly, Tom said to Dulcie: "I don't intend to be robbed of a sample of your excellent cooking a second time, Mrs Brook. One might almost survive on the delicious smell of this pie alone."

"Dew that fancy speech mean yew don't want none, then?" she teased, her laden spoon poised mid-air. "Well... I s'pose yew'd better pass 'im a plateful, Mary Emma, or I'll never 'ear the last of it!"

Everyone was busily consuming the savoury pie amid a general clatter of cutlery on crockery, bursts of conversation and other mealtime activity when Mary Emma said to him: "You have much to tell me? Good. Then we're even: for I, too have had a busy morning and have much to tell you, Tom." How good his hard, warm thigh felt pressed against her own! Try as she might to deny it, she had missed him terribly and ached to be alone with him. The midday meal over, the Challisses praised Dulcie's excellent cooking and said their farewells. Mary Emma kissed Agnes and Noah, who was sitting on his sister's lap and wouldn't be denied, and at last they were free to go home.

Once inside the coach with Barty perched on its box, they fell into each other's arms without a word. When under their own roof together again, after being apart for so long, Tom gave Rudge instructions that, as Mrs Challiss was fatigued she was going to lie down until dinnertime, and on no account was she to be disturbed. What he omitted to say was that he himself would be joining his wife in bed.

★

Chapter Thirty

Tom looked across the expanse of table at his wife and thought that she had never looked lovelier. Her choice of a blue velvet gown had set off the blue of her eyes and sent blue lights shimmering among the black curls which had been swept upwards to reveal the contours of her face. That Sir Everard had been bowled over by his neighbour's elegant wife had been evident from the moment he set eyes on her and Tom saw that the old man would be as putty in her hands. Their host sat at the head of the long table, his young guests either side of him. They were approaching the end of what had been a series of delicious but exotic dishes. When Mary Emma had exclaimed at their dazzling presentation, Sir Everard had inclined his head and told her that his chef had worked in the same kitchen as the renowned French chef Antonin Carème, whose fame had crossed the Channel to the epicurean wasteland that was Britain. "Indeed," the old man said, after downing a large glass of madeira in one, "it's said he has caught the eye of the Prince Regent and he's anglin' to poach the virtuoso from Tsar Aleksandr. It's rumoured that Prinny's offered Carème a salary so fabulous that he will find it difficult to refuse."

The old fellow has certainly come out of his shell, thought Tom, as he followed his host's example by swallowing his wine at a single gulp. During the meal he had been wondering to what purpose he and Mary Emma had been invited to nuncheon.

As if he had divined Tom's thoughts, Belmaine said: "You must be wonderin' why I asked you here today. Well, I'll tell you. Since Percival's death I've grown sick of me own company, not that he was at home all that much but we did manage to dine together most days. Eatin' in a room this size on one's own is a demned lonely business, Challiss. Now. If I had your delightful wife sittin' opposite me each time I came to table that would be a different matter. You are to be envied, sir."

Mary Emma smiled at the old man's flattery. "Oh, Sir Everard," she said, "we are such an old married couple now that my husband scarcely notices whether I'm present or not. Why, only the other day, he abandoned me in order to sample the delights of Martlets. Indeed, he was so charmed by everything he saw here that he forgot all about collecting his wife from

Church House until past noon. Isn't that so, Tom, dear?"

Taking her embroidered version of the truth as an attempt at small talk, Tom replied: "Quite, my dear."

"Let's adjourn to the small salon for coffee and brandy – and whatever takes y' fancy, Mrs Challiss, ma'am," Belmaine said, bowing in her direction. Rising with difficulty and shuffling towards an adjoining door, Belmaine led them into a room that Tom recognised as the one in which their second meeting had been held. "Please to make yourselves comfortable," Sir Everard said, down from his high horse. He pulled the bellrope, a footman appeared, coffee was ordered and soon brought.

As before, a splendid fire warmed the room which, despite its title, was large and lofty. "Glad you brought up that subject, Mrs Challiss; it's jogged my memory." said Belmaine. "I've had a visit from young Bob Pawl. I should think you'd be ashamed, sir, to see one of your household goin' about dressed like a scarecrow," he said, scowling at Tom from beneath bushy white brows. "Well, never mind that: I've had that remedied. I want to discuss the runnin' down of me stables. I keep a team of four for the carriage and a few nags for the men's use. The oxen have their own supply and I've more hay left than I know what to do with. Can you use it, Challiss?"

"It'd be a godsend!" Tom said.

"Wonderful!" said Mary Emma, and before Tom could get another word in:"That is so good of you, Sir Everard. We were getting desperate, as the load you sent us after the fire is well down and we had no idea where to look for more. Oh, thank you."

Her gratitude has been shown with more grace and warmth than I could have managed, thought Tom, but decided to add: "We are, indeed, most grateful, sir."

"And before you say any more, I'm makin' you a present of it," Belmaine said. "Now. As the string's bin sold – purchased by the Earl of Ballycoigne's factor on his master's behalf as a lot and shipped off to County Tyrone – that leaves me with an Under Groom and a Stable Lad on me hands. That's where you come in, Challiss. It's likely – very likely, I should say, that Bob will be leaving your employ shortly and you'll require someone to care for the nags. How d'ye feel about givin' work to me Under Groom or the Stable Boy – or both, if you can find enough work for 'em to do?"

Mary Emma's eyes lit up as they met Tom's. He smiled at her repressed enthusiasm and nodded confirmation and she clapped her hands for joy. Tom left his seat and strode over to Belmaine, whose hand he grasped. "They are the very servants we lack, Sir Everard. Thank you for thinking of us," he said. "You have met our most urgent needs. Unfortunately, there's a snag to the plan."

Belmaine looked displeased at the idea of finding his generous offer thwarted. "Eh? What snag's that?"

"The hay barn that burned down included the sleeping quarters for those caring for the horses. At present, I have no other accommodation to offer them."

"Where's young Bob sleepin', then?" Belmaine asked, watching him closely.

"At my steward's house; but that is a temporary measure," Tom explained.

"Was, sir! *Was* a temporary measure. Bob's bin sleepin' on the hearthrug in the kitchen for a week or more now," he said severely. "And you none the wiser. Your estate's a shambles, sir. Always was, come to think of it; at least, since your grandfather's time. Gone to the dogs, has Uppham. Used to be a grand old place when I was a boy. But runnin' a large estate is hard work, Challiss. If *you* don't want to do it, then for heaven's sake delegate your responsibilities! Manage the place, m' dear fellah, by employin' men you can trust to carry out your orders, whether you're at home or abroad."

Mary Emma had bridled at the old man's hectoring tone. She drew in her breath to express her disapproval; but Tom motioned her to silence, and said: "I apologise for not taking adequate care of your nephew, Sir Everard—"

"You miss the point, sir!" the old man thundered. "If you're goin' to give yourself airs and keep a parcel of servants, do so! But let the world see that you know what you are about, man. Treat your servants with an iron fist in a velvet glove. That'll earn you their respect. And one of the first things a responsible master should do is look to his servants' welfare: good clothes, if you aint goin' in for a livery, regular vittles and decent lodgin's, sir. And when you've seen to all that, you might consider payin' 'em somethin' a year. Good servants are an investment, Mr Challiss, and you'll reap dividends commensurate to your initial input only if that input is sufficiently good. I'm not sayin' you have to *talk* to the beggars, or even like 'em. But treat them with respect and some of it will rub off on you." He sat back in his chair and poured himself a second brandy.

For a few seconds nobody spoke. Belmaine stared gloomily into the fire and Mary Emma and Tom looked at each other in a state of mild shock at the magistrate's tirade; but Tom realised that what he had said so forcefully was full of wisdom and good advice. He said: "I thank you, Sir Everard, for your guidance to one who is, as must be obvious to you, a complete novice at handling servants—"

"Whereas *I* am not!" Mary Emma said, a touch imperiously, Tom thought. "You must know, Sir Everard, that I grew up in an establishment which, though nowhere near as grand as is Martlets, was the grandest manor house in that part of East Norfolk. My late uncle, who was also my guardian, kept a full complement of servants, in and out of the house, and the whole place ran on oiled wheels."

Sir Everard had put up his quizzing glass at the onset of her outburst and now lowered it. "Indeed, madam," was all he said, coldly.

"As we are being so candid," Tom said, "in addition to being base-born, you might as well know that I, myself, was formerly one of the full complement of servants employed by my wife's guardian."

" *Really?*" Belmaine said in a tone of interested surprise. "Well, sir, you seem to have done remarkably well for yourself under the circumstances," the old man said approvingly. "To have had the great good fortune to have inherited Uppham at so early an age and to have made such an advantageous match, as you appear to have done, has set you on the road to fortune without a doubt. I congratulate you, sir."

★

Mary Emma had quitted Martlets in a huff at the old man's treatment of her.

"You have nobody to blame but yourself, my dear," Tom said in answer to Mary Emma's complaint of Sir Everard's dismissal of her contribution to the conversation. "He is of an earlier generation: one in which women knew their place and were not invited to express their opinions on matters that had not been addressed to them."

Piqued by Tom's remark, his wife said: "He's nothing but a silly old man! And as for his patronising remarks about you 'appear to have' made an advantageous match, it was a deliberate slight on me. You should have defended me, Tom. Moreover, I thought he was very rude to you and I admire the way you kept your temper under such trying circumstances, dear."

"It wasn't so difficult," Tom said, his voice trembling as the coach bumped and jiggled over Downham's rutted High Road. "He spoke good sense and showed me up for what I am: a gardener masquerading as a gentleman."

"I will not countenance that. You, my dear husband, are one of nature's gentlemen: you were born one, my love. As for Sir Everard — *he's* no gentleman, for all his wealth." She tossed her head. "I consider Martlets a prime example of what those wanting in good taste can do to what could be a perfectly lovely establishment in the hands of somebody of true refinement."

Tom laughed. "And I suppose you think that's yourself? What conceit!"

Mary Emma didn't deign to reply and they lapsed into silence for a while.

"I'll call a meeting of the men tomorrow morning and see what they have to say on the subject of delegation," he said, decisively.

"Oh, and I suppose your resolution will last just as long as your previous idea," she said scornfully.

"What idea?"

"How soon you forget! Why, your determination to ride around the estate every morning. You've had no time for it, but have taken yourself back and forth to Martlets ever since as if you were mesmerised by the wretched place."

"You're hardly being fair, Mary Emma," Tom said, wondering what he had done to deserve her acid tone. "The fire and its aftermath had to be sorted out, you must see that."

"Oh… I do, Tom. I don't know what gets into me at times. One minute I'm as happy as a lark, the next I'm cross and being unkind to everybody. I'm sorry, dear. Can you forgive me?"

"But of course." To change the subject, he said: "How soon did Agnes say she would be free to take up residence with us, my love?" For Mary Emma's 'great news' on the day they had dined on shepherd's pie with the Brooks had been that she had persuaded Agnes Brook to become her companion, arguing that Agnes would enjoy greater privacy during her pregnancy by moving into the mansion. Tom had approved the scheme wholeheartedly, telling his wife that since Miss Peters' death she'd lacked a sympathetic female companion and confidante. "After all, my dear," he'd said lightly, "a wife needs somebody to whom she can relate her husband's faults and injustices." At which remark, Mary Emma had dimpled and said: "I see you are getting to know all about females, my lord." So it had been agreed that Agnes was to become one of the family.

"I'd like to have her here at once, of course," his wife said. "But she feels she would like to spend Christmas with her family and I can understand that. Just imagine how jolly they will be, all together. Burton's coming home as well: it'll be his first visit to Church House."

"So not until after Christmas," Tom said. "By that time, Joe and Ruth will be married. Everything's changing so quickly. And now it looks as if we're to lose Bob. I feel so guilty at having allowed him to live here in such terrible conditions."

"That's Joe's fault!" Mary Emma snapped. "You cannot be expected to know what is going on everywhere at every minute of the day, Tom."

"Which is more or less what Belmaine said, in so many words, wasn't it. Of course, he was right. I *must* call that meeting – don't allow anything to steer me away from it, my dear," he appealed, unwittingly causing her heart to flutter by admitting his need of her help in the management of the estate. "I must try to sort out this business of delegating responsibility."

"My dear," Mary Emma said, firmly, "once you have done that you will begin to enjoy your position as master. You will have time to plan what you want done and you'll have time to oversee things occasionally – when you want to. You must learn to *govern*, Tom; and that's quite a different matter from poking into minor affairs that might perfectly well be dealt with by your upper servants. Darling. . . Please let me help you," she implored. "It's no slight on your manhood to defer to me in matters of the running of the house, or, dare I say it, planning parts of the grounds and I have so many ideas for the improvement of Uppham. I *promise* that I'll try to be discreet and not to belittle you in the presence of others – as Sir Everard was quick to perceive that I did. I acknowledge that he was quite right to put me in my place. I see that now."

Had the carriage not been rolling into the stableyard and Bob appearing at once, Tom would have taken her in his arms. As it was, the impulse passed and was replaced by astonishment as he caught sight of Bob's transformation. He was dressed in a stout suit of clothes made from a knobbly woollen material which he told them was called tweel, or tweed or something, and that it came from Scotland. Leather gaiters covered his legs from knee to ankle and on his feet he wore a pair of strong leather boots. What struck Tom immediately was that the tall youth might be taken for one of the landed gentry dressed for a shoot. His hair had been washed and cut professionally and his clean skin revealed a healthy glow that Tom had never seen before.

"Why, Bob," Mary Emma cried, as she alighted from the clarence, "I hardly recognised you! I had no idea that your hair was blond: you look positively handsome. Beau Brummell had better look to his laurels."

Tom felt for the lad, who blushed to the roots of his hair; after all, he reasoned, he was more or less the same age as his wife. Somehow her badinage was unseemly and he made up his mind to tell her so at an appropriate moment.

"Sir Ev'rard 'ad 'em made fer me," Bob explained. "'E says I'm 'is nephew; though I don't see as 'ow I can be. D'you? 'E talks ser lah-di-dah, I c'n 'ardly understand 'im. Mr Challiss, sir! 'E wants ter go an' live with 'im at Martlits. Says 'e'll make me into a gennelman. But I dunno. Wot d'ye think I oughta dew?"

"It's a great chance, Bob," Tom said. "And you need have no doubts: Sir Everard Belmaine is your relative, right enough – to be absolutley correct he's your grand uncle, which means that you have Belmaine blood in your veins. Sir Everard is a lonely old man and I think you would like him once you really got to know him: he isn't nearly as severe as he looks. Your father has turned down the opportunity to inherit Martlets. That makes you Sir Everard's heir. He has none other."

Mary Emma had held her peace, aware that Tom was doing his best to explain the situation to Bob while at the same time trying to persuade him to accept it.

"Mr Challiss is right, Bob," she said, after silently seeking Tom's approval to speak on the matter. "Such a great chance for advancement will never come your way again. I don't know if you're aware of it but, if you doubt your relationship to the Belmaines, you have inherited the family's high-bridged nose!" she said with a smile.

Bob hung his head and shook it from side to side. "I dunno." He looked up at them, his candid grey eyes troubled. "What's folks gonna say? I mean – if I start ridin' about in *kerridges* and talkin' funny-like. An' I know me father won't like it."

Tom said: "This isn't about your father, Bob: it's about you and your future. As a matter of fact, your father has decided to take no part in your decision. He has said publicly that it's your own life. You're wasting it here. Don't you see that? But you must make up your mind soon because I need to know where I stand. When do you think you will be able to give me an answer?"

Confused, Bob bit his lip. "If I could talk to pa about it first—"

"Come to dinner at seven-o'clock, Bob," Mary Emma said warmly. "We expect your father to be dining with us this evening. You can talk to him afterwards."

"Wot? Me 'ave a proper dinner at the big 'ouse? I dunno – I can't take it all in."

"If you don't turn up by a quarter-to-seven I shall come and fetch you myself!" his young mistress said. "Think how that would look," she added.

"I wouldn't risk it, old fellow," Tom said, laughing. "We'll expect you any time from six-thirty onwards. How do you like your beef? Rare, medium or well-done?"

That persuaded him. "I ain' fussy, Mr Challiss," he replied with a shy and engaging grin. "I ain' 'ad ser much of it ter bother about the way it's cooked, sir. I'll take it as it comes."

★

The Challisses persuasiveness and his father's blessing had worn away all Bob's doubts and objections and a week later he had left the stables at Uppham to take up his new life at Martlets.

During that final dinner at which both Bob and Evritt Pawl had been guests, it had emerged that Sir Everard had poached Evritt from Tom to serve as tutor in the first stage of Bob's transition to a gentleman. Father and son were to spend four hours each morning shut away among the literary treasures to be found in the library at Martlets. As well as book learning, Bob would be compelled to undergo the tortures of speech-training until all traces of his Norfolk accent had been eradicated. Sir Everard was canny enough to realise that his own dangerous affinity to Bob's delivery was little more than a difference in pronunciation; whereas Evritt Pawl's speech patterns had been caught early enough to provide him with the Reverend John Wood's accent: the refined tones of an Oxford graduate. Initially, Pawl had protested at Belmaine's imposition. He had looked forward with joy to a secluded life among books, shut away from a world that since reaching manhood he had not, until now, found very congenial. But Belmaine had prevailed by using reasoned argument and eventually had brought Pawl round to his point of view: he pointed out that the former gravedigger would not only have the use of two well-stocked libraries but would, in the process of tutoring his own son, come to know him.

All had gone well in supplying the parish with a substitute to take Pawl's place as parish gravedigger. Among the surly groups of unemployed men, Pawl had made the acquaintance of a strong young man, formerly a soldier. Hardened to death and burial as a commonplace of war, the idea of being paid to dig pits and fill them in again, as a means of livlihood, was attractive to penniless Eli Lowe and he had accepted the position with alacrity. Where he slept each night nobody thought to enquire.

Evritt Pawl's work pattern had started immediately and the change in him was startling. In his element, he warmed to teaching his son all that John

Wood had taught him and in doing so relived those happier days when the world had seemed his oyster. Nothing could have delighted him more than to be responsible for sorting and ordering the muddled library at Uppham. It was as if his tortuous path through the thorny garden of life had led him to Paradise. Everett Pawl, as he came to be known from this time on, his self-esteem restored, actually began to look happy. His hazel eyes gleamed with contentment as he crated and labelled the contents of Uppham's library in order that they might be removed to one of the restored rooms in the east wing of the mansion. Each afternoon, having eaten a light luncheon in the company of his master and mistress, he would retire to work among the interesting though sadly dilapidated volumes. The task would take him years to accomplish and that secret knowledge was a large part of the source of his contentment. He was secure.

★

"May I, Tom?" Mary Emma implored. She had raised the question of the repair and redecoration of the library which, since becoming empty of books, had been revealed to be a place of crumbling squalor. Never a handsome room, without the floor to ceiling volumes, which had concealed much of the ruin caused by decades of seeping damp, its unadorned walls proved as unlovely as a whore who after a strenuous night's employment removes her cosmetic mask to reveal a ravaged face.

On his way to a meeting with his senior servants to discuss the subject of delegation of responsibility, Tom had no time for such frivolities as paints, fabrics and carpeting. "My darling, you may do what you like with the place," he replied without considering that she would take him literally. "You'll have months to accomplish whatever scheme is rattling around in that pretty head of yours, Mary Emma. Just make sure that you don't turn the place into another private boudoir. See that it remains the library, whatever you do with it. And on no account are you to tire yourself. Use Peckover to shift things about. No, my love. Do not involve me in more decorating, I implore you. Now, I really must leave you. I hope to be finished my business in time to take luncheon with you and Everett."

And he's the very man I want to see, thought Mary Emma as Tom took himself off.

"I do apologise for disturbing you, Everett," she said in her most honeyed tones, "but I'm in need of your advice concerning the library."

Pawl looked up from perusing a stained volume. "If you think I might be of help, Mrs Challiss, then of course I shall be only too happy to see in what way I can be of assistance to you," he said, following his mistress out of the pleasant room in which he had been engaged in sorting through a box of musty volumes. Everett had been mildly annoyed by his mistress's tearing him away from a rare volume of Virgil's *Eclogues* printed in the original Latin. He had just reached the part in the absorbing preface to the main work in which the editor of the volume, in his brief sketch of Virgil's life, had mentioned the confiscation of the poet's lands when Mrs Challiss had interrupted his reading. However, his irritation was soon forgotten as they entered the damp, barren space that had been the library and she outlined her plans before asking him to comment upon them. He was astonished by her grandiose and thoroughly modern ideas for the new library.

"Really, Mrs Challiss, I hardly know what to say," he said. "You seem to have thought of everything, and on such a grand scale. It will be the finest library in West Norfolk. There is just one thing I ought to mention."

Eagerly, Mary Emma said: "Good! I hoped you would have something to contribute; after all, it will be your domain. What is it that I have omitted, Mr Pawl?"

"Well, ma'am, many of the volumes – which incidentally are quite rare and some of which are very valuable – have sustained water damage. Rows of them placed upon your beautiful new shelves in their present state will, I fear, resemble sets of bad teeth framed by beautiful mouths."

"Oh, dear! Of course they will! You are right, Mr Pawl. They must be rebound in new calf and tooled in gold leaf with the Uppham crest on every single volume."

Everett was aghast when he contemplated the vast sum of money needed to be found for such an undertaking. It was not his place to mention such a thing but he sincerely hoped that his master had the wherewithal to carry out his mistress's scheme. He envisioned the new library in which he hoped to spend the rest of his working life and silently praised the gods for smiling on him after so many years of his enduring their frowns of displeasure. But the long, testing wait made the reward all the sweeter.

★

On the first Sunday in December the whole Brook tribe – minus Burt, who was to remain at Passendean until Christmas Eve – sat together in one long pew with Everett Pawl, Tom and Mary Emma. Joseph Aldrich and Ruth Vale were seated in separate pews in different parts of the beautifully decorated church. Looking painfully self-conscious in a splendid set of new clothes, the young man formerly known as Bob Pawl endeavoured to get used to his new identity: Robin Belmaine. He thought everybody in the congregation must be thinking him a fraud. The cheval looking-glass in his bedchamber had shown him that he looked the part; he even looked a Belmaine. Yet inside his head he was painfully aware that he had but to open his mouth to return to being Bob Pawl, the bumble-footed Stable Boy. Seated now beside his grand uncle, Sir Everard Belmaine, in the elevated pew with its lockable door and glowing fireplace, he held himself erect in unconscious emulation of the old man.

"Doan that Bob Pawl give 'isself airs, now that 'e's come into 'is fortune," Mary Emma heard one villager whisper to another. She turned her head, looked directly at Bob and inclined her head in acknowledgement. In reponse, Sir Everard, mistaking her intention, frostily dipped his nose by a millimetre. It was all Mary Emma could do not to disgrace herself by laughing in church; for Belmaine had reminded her of a startled woodpecker who had blunted his beak in trying to peck an iron post.

While stragglers crept in after the cessation of the bells the organist softly began to play Purcell's *Voluntary on the 100th Psalm*. Edward Fieldgate mounted the pulpit steps during the singing of the first hymn and the service was underway. Mrs Fieldgate sat in the front pew directly below her husband and, consciously or unconsciously, lent an air of genuine piety to the atmosphere by the beatific expression that shone from her uplifted face. On either side of their mother sat her children, handsome Robert and wheyfaced Frances.

The reading of the banns of marriage took longer than usual, as several couples had decided to take advantage of the waived fees for those marrying on Christmas Eve. Among those named were Joseph Aldrich and Ruth Vale, whose eyes sought each other out at the mention of themselves. The little church seemed fuller than usual, which was usual as the Christmas festival approached, and the Reverend Fieldgate noticed among his flock several parishioners whom he did not recall having seen in church before; but was glad to see them drawn to worship by whatever means. The advent hymn drew to a close and after Fieldgate had delivered his blessing and walked down the side aisle to the church door Sir Everard and his nephew were the first to follow him out. Having learned of the young man's good fortune, Fieldgate delivered a few kind words to him, shook hands with both Belmaines and watched them wander off into the churchyard instead of returning to their coach.

★

"And you say this stone has lain here for almost as long as you have lived, Rob?" the old man said, incredulously. "Well, I'm blessed! Not that the name would have meant anythin' to me, of course. It's a foreign-lookin' thing, aint it? Whoever heard of black marble bein' used to stand over an English grave?"

"S'pose I've always liked it," Rob said, looking at the inscription which he was unable to read. "Seemed like Grandma were still 'ere, though she died afore I was born. Even when I was old enough ter know better, I useter be comforted by sittin' on the stone. It's pretty, innit? Those blue lights – like stars twinklin' in a black sky."

"What's does it say?" Sir Everard drew nearer to the inscription, his quizzing glass held to his right eye and read:

Time is
Too Slow for those who Wait
Too Swift for those who Fear
Too Long for those who Grieve
Too Short for those who Rejoice
But for those who Love,
Time is not.

and beneath the description of how aspects of time are affected by different emotions:

Sacred to the Memory of
Elizabeth (Bessie) Pawl
Dearly Beloved
1755-1787

Robin, never before having heard the words spoken, said: "What dew it mean, uncle? 'Ow can time be not?" He turned his head and, embarrassed by seeing tears standing in Sir Everard's eyes, mumbled: "Sorry." Belmaine patted the young man on the shoulder. "Nothin' you did, me boy. I'm just a foolish old man. Come on, there's a fine dinner of roast pork spoilin' and it's demned chilly standin' about among the gravestones. Time we went home."

★

Chapter Thirty-one

Tom's meeting with Adam Brook, Joseph Aldrich, Kit Warrender, Jem Webster and Clem Rix, while stimulating, had been as painful as if he'd thrust his bare hand into a hornets' nest. Reticent at the outset of the discussion, the men had soon become heated in voicing their own concerns, each egging on the others to the point where their grievances had poured forth thick and fast until Tom had held up his hand and demanded silence. Pulled up sharp, the men had turned sullen until they were made to understand that their master would consent to hear each of them in turn. If anyone else had anything to add, he should wait until the chosen person had had his say: only then, Tom had said, quietly but forcefully, might the men speak out of turn providing they spoke one at a time. He had invited Joe to speak first.

"The men are quite right in saying that they are doing their best, as far as they can tell, but are uncertain as to how much leeway they have in taking responsibility for the multitude of decisions they have to make throughout each and every day. I've told them to come to me, in the first instance, and have tried to do my best but my best, it seems, is simply not good enough, Mr Challiss, sir." He paused and waited for Tom to comment but his master merely said: "Go on."

"If I might digress," Aldrich said hesitantly. "It seems to me, sir, our priority must be to rebuild the hay barn." He'd begun to show signs of agitation: licked his lips and swallowed audibly before saying: "I might go so far as to say that a parallel priority is to provide proper accommodation to house the outside servants; indeed, it is a matter of the utmost urgency. I'm talking about a substantial financial outlay, Mr Challiss, sir." Here again he paused, obviously anticipating an outburst of some kind from Tom who, to his relief, nodded his assent and expressed his encouragement by a smile. "What I propose, sir, is that a row of cottages be built—" The others, who until now had adhered strictly to Tom's edict of silence unless invited by him to speak, broke out in enthusiastic agreement.

"Decent accommodation for the estate workers is something that's long overdue, I agree," the men were delighted to hear Tom say. It had the effect of regaining their attention and they waited in leashed silence to hear what he would say further.

"Whatever other grievances you might have," he began, "and you have many, it seems, the building of these cottages must come before anything else – I agree with Mr Aldrich about that. The stacks can be sheeted for now. The cottages are of urgent necessity as estate staff numbers continue to grow – two-storey buildings that will provide ample space for married men and their growing families. Single men must share in the first instance. And the cottages must be substantial, brick-built places of generous dimensions on their own plots. That raises the question of an architect, a reputable builder, and an army of builder's labourers to begin work on them at once."

Jem Webster had raised a hand. "If I might make ser bold, Mr Challiss."

"Go ahead, Jem."

"Well, sir; me bein' a wood-worker since I were a lad I got plenty o' contacts, yer see. I can give yer the names o' three or four reliable builders and any number of brickies and plasterers, tilers, roofers, thatchers, plumbers – you name 'im an' ten ter one I knows 'im. On the subject of architects, I ain ser knowledgeable. But dew yew really need one o' them, sir?"

"But, of course!" Tom had said, astonished by Jem's ignorance. "I can't afford to throw good money away on a row of hovels that will fall down as soon as the first gale blows across the fields."

Joe raised his hand. "If I may, Jem? Mr Challiss, sir. It's well-known in these parts that homes of uncomplicated design, based upon a modest number of rectangular rooms designed for living in on a daily basis – as opposed to grand rooms intended as expressions of wealth or to exhibit fancy decoration, rather than serviceability, you understand – have been… indeed, continue to be, built without the skills of a professional architect being required or even thought necessary."

Tom frowned at him. He had not liked Aldrich's veiled references to the recent expensive refurbishment of his own mansion, whether his remarks had been unintentional or not. "What exactly are you suggesting, Joe?"

Aldrich indicated that Jem should expand on the subject. With a grateful nod at the steward, Jem had said: "Any one o' the builders I know are quite capable o' drawin' up plans for a cottage, sir. After all, they've 'ad practical experience an' know their business inside out. They're practical men, sir, an' can put their 'ands tew any skill that goes inter the makin' of an 'ouse with as much attention ter detail as the best apprentice or articled artisan he might employ. Downham builders know how ter build, Mr Challiss, an' build ter last. I could 'elp with the carpentry side, sir."

Kit Warrender nodded his agreement before requesting permission to speak. "Aye, Mr Challiss, Jem's right. Of course, sir, you must do as you think best; but there's no point in throwing away good money. Anyway, an architect might well hold back the start of building and you said yourself it was urgent."

"Hmm. There is that side to it."

"If I might mention it," Warrender continued, "I noticed a disused marl pit way out on our north boundary, up by Carrpit Farm. Carr stone's a useful dressing and would give a nice finish to the cottages, Mr Challiss; but, o' course, sir, that's up to you."

Joe was acknowledged. "There's also the question of a Stable Boy to fill the vacancy left by Bob," he said.

Another headache! "That's in hand, Mr Aldrich. Again, it's a question of accommodation since the upper rooms in the barn burned down."

Clem leaned forward, his green eyes bright from being out of doors night and day. "Sir! Old Mr Plumb is orf ter Norwich ter live with 'is dotter. 'Is cottage'll be goin' beggin' by Christmas, if that's any 'elp."

"That's just the time when the newly wed will be seeking to set up home," Tom said, thoughtfully and almost to himself. "But — much as I hate to put Uppham's needs above those of the villagers, I shall have to take advantage of it, I suppose. Unless anyone here has any alternative to offer?" Nobody had. "Thank you, Clem." As an afterthought he added: "How's the flock faring?"

"Ah… I was gonna tell yew about it, Mr Challiss. Some've gorn missing."

"Missing? D'ye mean stolen?"

"I wouldn't go so far as that, sir. More like . . . wandered orf, like." He's avoiding my eyes, Tom noticed.

"How many animals are missing?"

Clem swallowed; but his voice still came out as a squawk: "Seven, sir." The men looked towards the shepherd with expressions of open-mouthed disbelief.

Tom thundered: "*Seven!* Where were you when they strayed?"

His Adam's Apple dancing, the sandy-headed shepherd swallowed again. "Well, sir… The first time one went missin' I were asleep. Not that I meant ter be asleep, I jist… was. When I counted 'em that night, as I penned 'em up, I coulda sworn there was an 'undred, sir, same as always. I always count 'em in tens, see. Then, bugger me, when I counted 'em out agin next mornin' one were gorn."

"When was this?"

Clem's gooseberry eyes swivelled up into his head to seek an answer and found none. "I can't rightly say, Mr Challiss." He chewed his bottom lip between yellowed teeth.

Now Tom was angry. "You must do better than that, Rix."

"Er... Ah! I know. It were that mornin' I stumbled on yew an your missus among the bushes. Yew remember, Mr Challiss." Clem's eyes narrowed. "Yew'd jist finished an 'ard ride." He leered at the four older men "Reckon we both had a surprise that mornin', sir!"

"Remember where you are!" Joseph Aldrich admonished the young man.

Good God! So the young varmint *had* seen everything, thought Tom. "That accounts for only one of the seven. Get on with it! What about the others?"

"I can't tell yer, sir," the shepherd mumbled. "I gits ser tired that no matter 'ow 'ard I try, I can't keep me eyes open all night long, Mr Challiss; 'tis agin nature. All I can say is that I lorst three in one night a coupla weeks ago an then a couple more last week."

"That accounts for only six animals," Tom said wearily. "How do you account for the seventh?

"Ah! That's easy, sir. That' un vanished last night." His inquisition over, Clem sat back.

"Beg pardon, Mr Challiss, sir," Kit Warrender chimed in. "It seems to me that what the lad needs is a page. He can't be expected to watch his flock for every one of the twenty-four hours, day after day, sir. He must have a page, sir."

"Of course, Warrender's right, Mr Challiss," Aldrich said. "It's obvious that whoever is doing the poaching has monitored Rix's habit of falling asleep for most of the night and sees no risk at all in helping himself to your flock."

"Damnation!" Tom said. "This has to stop. By thunder, we're down to a measly ninety-three sheep in only five months! It won't do. Check the fences, Warrender. D'ye know of a reliable lad who would be willing to be taken on as shepherd's page?"

"I do not, I'm afraid, Mr Challiss," the Farm Manager replied, his voice full of regret. "I can ask 'round in Downham, sir; plenty of young boys looking for a place there."

"No need to dew that, sir," said Clem Rix. "Me brother Ben's thirteen an out of place. Should I set 'im on, then?"

Ickeny young whipper-snapper, thought Tom. "Is he also in the habit of falling asleep on the job? Don't bother to answer. I'd like to speak to him first, Rix."

Clem eyed him sullenly. "When might that be, then, Mr Challiss?"

"That doesn't concern you," Aldrich intervened. "I'd advise you to show your master more respect, Rix, or we might be looking for a shepherd as well as a page!"

The annoying lad pointedly ignored the steward and stared out of the window.

Adam Brook had sat in a shadowed corner of the room without uttering a word. Now he got up and brought his chair forward into the light. "Suppose yew tell Mr Challiss about your Uncle's shop, young Rix," he said quietly.

The shepherd sat up as if galvanized. "I ain got no uncle," he protested feebly.

"Are yew willin' ter swear on the Bible that the grocer, William Harris, is not your mother's brother?" Brook persisted.

"Oh! *That* uncle," Rix said, realising he'd been found out. "What of it?"

"I think you know what of it," Joseph Aldrich said smartly. To Tom, the steward said: "Might I advise you, sir, to dismiss this person with a month's wages in lieu of notice. It will prove cheaper in the long run than keeping him on."

Clem Rix's freckled face was contorted into a very ugly mask. "Yew dew, an' yew'll be sorry yew was born," he snarled at Tom. "There ain no 'ouse yet that can't be fired! No matter 'ow big. Try me, an you'll soon find out."

Tom got up without a word and walked to the bell rope. He gave it two tugs.

His silence unnerved the shepherd, who blustered: "'Ere, what yew doin'? Yew don't think I'm gonna wait 'ere ter be carted orf ter gaol, dew yer?" He ran to the door and reached it at the very moment the invariably dignified Rudge opened it. The startled man was confronted by an unknown ruffian, who shouted in his face: "Out o' me way!"

Rudge found himself unceremoniously tumbled backwards out onto the upstairs landing. Dimly aware of a besmocked, gingery blur as Clem Rix streaked past him down the stairs and out of the front door, the dazed manservant picked himself up off the floor, calmly adjusted his rumpled clothing, swept into place his sparse strands of disarranged hair and staggered into the room. "You rang, sir?"

Rix having made his escape, Tom ordered Rudge to send up hot chocolate. Next, he put into practice his new regime by delegating to Warrender the job of acquiring a replacement shepherd, and also a page, so that twenty-four hour watch could be kept over the flock, adding: "Oh, and Kit; purchase another ten impregnated ewes from a reputable farmer, to make up for those that have been stolen."

Joe Aldrich and Jem Webster were to report back to Tom once the builder and his men had been engaged so that the building of the cottages could be started immediately, despite the awful weather. The cottages were to be sited in an area of land that had lain fallow for as long as Aldrich could remember, but which appeared to be fertile and well-drained, and had a brook running along is southern boundary. He would check that the site was suitable and, if it proved fit, would see to it that the footings were marked out and dug before Christmas. It would be hard work for the labourers as, below the snow, the ground was frostbound. "The men will need feeding well, Mr Challiss," Aldrich advised. "Many of them are enfeebled through lack of proper food, particularly butchered meat; they live on turnips and the like, and the odd trapped rabbit or poached fish or fowl. I don't know where it's going to end, with the worst of the winter still to come. It would help to speed the work if tents could be provided near the site so that the men were on hand from dawn to dusk. Have you objections to them working on the sabbbath, sir?" Tom said he hadn't, that it must be left to the men's consciences, with no pressure on them to labour on the Lord's day; but there could be no financial reward for idleness: they would lose a day's money.

The new garden before the front of the house had been cleared and marked out though Tom thought it different in design from what he remembered of the plan Adam had drawn up for him to approve. Thinking himself mistaken, he hadn't mentioned it to Brook. It had occurred to him as he and Mary Emma prepared to retire that evening and he had brought up the subject.

"Oh, yes, Tom," she'd said lightly, as she sat up in bed hugging her knees and watching him undress. "Didn't I mention it? The night I spent with the Brooks, Adam and I discussed the layout and I suggested a few minor adjustments. You did say I might, my dear. You do remember? Adam agreed with most of my ideas and we decided not to bother you with it as you had so much on your mind – the fire and where to obtain hay..." Acknowledging defeat, Tom had climbed into bed beside his wife and blown out the candle. His wife had taken his hand and placed it on her abdomen. With a mixture of awe and delight he had felt his child moving about within his wife's womb and his love for her had overwhelmed him. They had created a life.

★

The weeks leading up to the celebration of Christmas flew by in preparation of the wedding of Joseph Aldrich and Ruth Vale. The staid couple had politely refused Mary Emma's offer of them holding their nuptial feast amid the splendour of Uppham's grander withdrawing room, the one that overlooked the park. Thwarted in the carrying out of her original plan, Mary Emma had begged to be allowed to help redecorate the large parlour at the lodge and to assist in any dressmaking that Ruth thought necessary. The widow had laughed at her enthusiasm, answering that her personal needs were of a modest nature and that the parlour would do very well as it was. Whereupon Mary Emma had pestered her into accepting the gift of two bolts of fine velvet, one black, the other orange-rust, to be made up into evening gowns. Ruth had capitulated and had resigned herself to just the kind of feminine flummery she despised, rather than give offence to her young friend. But she had remained adamant where the parlour was concerned, gently employing the argument that, as she was the bride-to-be, she must be allowed to have the last word. So Mary Emma had had to content herself with having prevailed in the matter of the frocks which, when she saw how well Ruth looked in them, she had.

Tom had been relieved to receive a letter from Daniel Jones. He wrote that Mary Emma's inheritance had been transferred to Bagg and Bacon's bank and that the directors looked forward to the pleasure of meeting Mrs Challiss whenever she might be in the vicinity. Included in the letter was an account of Daniel's investigations into the disappearance or otherwise of Lambert Jardine and the lawyer wrote that he 'had it on the very best authority that nothing further would be heard from the former owner of Lynford Manor.' Tom had allowed himself a cynical smile on reading that: Daniel Jones must have known all about Jardine's death during the fire from the beginning, might even have had a hand in the disappearance of Young Luke Frith. The fact that the vanished man's father, the almost voiceless Frith, by becoming Daniel's manservant must have thrown himself on the lawyer's mercy, shook Tom's faith in Jones' integrity; on the other hand, it revealed a hitherto unsuspected soft spot in the lawyer's steely character. "Wonder what Dan would say if he knew that we had discovered the truth of the matter for ourselves?" he muttered, tucking the letter away in the bureau. As far as he was concerned, it was over and done with. Best forgotten. Odd, that he'd mentioned nothing about the amount of gold deposited with Fector. He would drop Dan a line in the hope of enlightenment.

★

Robin Belmaine had taken to living with his grand uncle as the proverbial duck to water and the effect on his outward appearance was startling. His residence at Martlets and the eating of regular meals of the best quality had enlarged him outwards and upwards. New clothes had been commissioned and he was splendid indeed.

Everett Pawl considered it unlikely that his son's original accent would ever be entirely eradicated; but Robin was assiduous in his efforts to emulate his father's delivery and would pass now for the son of a prosperous yeoman. "You must attune your ear, my dear boy," Everett said to him one morning towards the end of the third week in December.

"If I knew what it meant, sir, I'd willin'ly foller your advice," Robin laughed.

"Tch! I must have told you a thousand times, Rob: I-N-G is pronounced ing!" his father cried. "Try it again: in-ing-in-ing. Tip and sides of tongue on the hard palette for the en. Raise the base and sides of the tongue and bring down the soft palette to get a crisp ng sound."

The young man tried the exercise and did better.

"Hmm. Improved. And it's follOW, not follER," Everett said grudgingly.

"Yes, sir," Robin said, a twinkle in his eye. "Are we goin' on with readin' *Tom Jones*, pa? I can't wait to find out what *happens* next."

Everett allowed his eyes to crinkle. "You manage to sort out the endings of your -ing words and if you are able to recite the whole list without dropping a gee or missing an aitch we will read a whole chapter of Fielding together. *Tom Jones* was written by Henry Fielding – Fielding, with a gee. I am addressed as father, or papa."

Robin Belmaine had much work to do to repair the deficiency in his formal education, which had been non-existent until a fortnight ago. Possessing a quick brain that had been deprived of systematic teaching for sixteen years, he revelled now in the acquisition of knowledge for its own sake and learned at a prodigious rate. His father had been astonished by his son's thirst for learning. Robin had memorised the alphabet in a single morning and had learned to read an early primer before the end of the first session. As if he had been a desert plant deprived of water for years and the drought had been ended by a deluge that made the dehydrated plant burst into bloom overnight, Robin's intellect expanded beyond his father's imaginings. Everett Pawl had anticipated that the imposed tutoring of his son would be little more than an onerous labour of love: instead, he looked forward to his mornings with increased pleasure as he witnessed the blossoming of Robin's mind. Perhaps the greatest surprise of all was Pawl's discovery that his son possessed a wicked sense of humour and, since his being rested and well-nourished, knew how to laugh and be happy.

Despite the snow and slush, the razor-edged wind that scoured his face and the discomfort of walking over frozen rutted roads, one of the greatest delights that had befallen Everett Pawl since his change of fortune was the freedom to walk the two-and-a-half miles each way between Uppham and Martlets every morning. The idea of receiving payment for wandering about the countryside seemed to him nothing short of a miracle. Yet he perceived that, no matter how early he started out for his tutoring at Martlets, no matter how smartly he covered the distance, valuable time was being squandered; in particular, the walk back from Martlets to Uppham followed by luncheon, though most welcome, took a large slice out of the middle of the day. Pawl had compensated for this lacuna in the labour for which he was financially rewarded by continuing to sort and arrange for batches of books to be crated and sent off to James Annis, bookbinder. Situated in London Lane in the city of Norwich, the bookbinder's premises had been visited by Everett to judge their suitability, together with the quality of Annis's finished work, before handing over the important task of binding every volume that was to furnish the restored library of Uppham House. His zeal had not gone unnoticed by Mary Emma and she had mentioned it to Tom.

"He's wearing himself out, Tom," she said. "He insists on walking back and forth to tutor his son but seems to feel guilty that he is allowed so much unsupervised freedom of movement. So he makes up the time spent out of doors by working before breakfast and again after dinner until midnight. It's ridiculous! I've tried reasoning with him but he refuses to change his ways. What can we do?"

"What he needs is a horse," Tom mumbled. He'd been only half listening as he studied the plans for the cottages that had been drawn up by the builder he'd engaged.

Mary Emma ran over to his chair, for despite her condition she was not yet very heavy, and kissed him. "Oh, you're so clever, my love! Why didn't I think of such a simple solution? Shall I see to it, my dear?"

Engrossed, Tom looked at her without seeing her. "Eh? What?"

She whipped the plan away from him. "Tom! You're not listening. May I tell Everett that he may purchase himself a horse? To save him walking and so to save time."

"Oh! A horse for Pawl. Good idea! Well done, my love." He retrieved his plans and, becoming absorbed once more, murmured abstractedly: "Yes, of course. You go ahead with it, my dear."

Mary Emma waited impatiently for Pawl's return from Martlets at one o'clock to tell him the good news. His face fell. It seemed he had never learned to ride. Refusing to be outdone, Mary Emma suggested that Robin could teach him.

"It's most kind of you, Mrs Challiss, ma'am," he said miserably, "but it really isn't necessary. I'm quite happy with the way things are."

His mistress refused to listen to his protest. "I suggest we drive to Martlets this afternoon and see what Robin has to say about it, Mr Pawl. The possession of a horse for your own use will allow you much more freedom as well as saving you time." She smiled at him, her blue eyes fastening themselves on his hazel orbs.

Afterwards, he told himself that he must have been mesmerised; for he had willingly agreed to everything she had suggested and, like a fool, had laid himself open to injury or death. A horse had been purchased that very afternoon and after luncheon the next day a delighted Robin had started to teach his nervous father to ride. An hour's riding lesson had followed, the first of several that it would take to calm the reluctant horseman's fears. Until he was able to ride well, it was agreed that Everett should take his midday repast at Martlets and after his lesson would return to Uppham House in one of Sir Everard's carriages. Once he had learned to control his mount he had begun to enjoy his new accomplishment. While he regretted the loss of his daily walks he had to agree that, taken all round, the change was probably for the best.

★

Chapter Thirty-two

On the morning of the twenty-third of December 1815 Tom, Mary Emma and Everett were finishing breakfast. Through the windows the dark day was turning rosy and the sight of the faint tinge of colour in a monochrome landscape gave Mary Emma the urge to be outside. Tom had his nose in an old copy of the *London Times*. Mary Emma replaced her cup carefully in its saucer and said: "Tom, dear," smiling up at Everett Pawl as he silently mimed his "Please, excuse me" and left the table to set off for Martlets.

"Mm?"

"Tom! Put down that paper and listen to me, please."

"What is it!" he said, rattling the paper angrily and peering over the top. "Good God, Mary Emma; can't a man enjoy his breakfast in peace?"

His remark annoyed her. "I have sat here in silence while you and Everett Pawl gloomed your way through the meal. I call it unsociable, as well as the height of bad manners, to sit there, your head hidden behind a news sheet, ignoring the wife of your bosom." She assumed a sulking pout.

Laughing at her antics, he put down the paper. "What an antiquated expression. Well, 'wife of my bosom', what is it that you have to say to your husband that is of such urgency that his early morning peace must be destroyed?"

"Oh, Tom!" she threw down her napkin and moved around the table to perch herself on his lap, ignoring his mock protest at her increased weight on his stomach. "Let's go out! I want to walk in the park and, especially, to take a look at the lime walk. I've not been over there since you forbade me to ride Genty. Do say you'll come, love."

"Mary Emma, I can't," he protested. "There are a thousand and one things that need my attention—"

"Well, Tom, you must just leave the odd one unattended. I have my rights as a married woman and I demand that you accompany me in my perambulation. If you have no care for me, think of our unborn child, who, at this very moment," she seized his hand and held it against her body, "is demanding an airing. Or would you rather I went alone and perhaps fell over on the ice?"

"You saucy baggage! Is that any way for a matronly married woman – with child, to boot – to address her lord? Threaten me, would you?" He took her in his arms and kissed her until she was breathless. When he considered she'd been thoroughly reprimanded he said: "I can spare you an hour... but only if you can be ready in ten minutes. And don't forget to put on your pattens." ...

"Oh, Tom! It's so good to be out and the wind on my face," she cried, her eyes bright. "Do you realise? I haven't had a ramble for days, if not weeks. Cooped up in that musty old library, first with Everett then with Peckover, then with Jem Webster – No sooner was that sorted out than I was at the lodge helping Ruth with her trousseau."

"You have only yourself to blame for that last, my love," Tom said, as they tramped across the snow-laden park leaving a double trail of footprints. "You will thrust your oar into things that are no concern of yours, instead of waiting to be asked."

"Am I really that awful?" she asked, genuinely ignorant of the fact.

"My dear Mary Emma, you are: but I wouldn't change you for the most pious, well-behaved wife in the parish. I love you just the way you are: spoilt, difficult and over-familiar with members of the opposite sex, to their confusion."

"Why, Tom! Whatever can you mean? Are you saying that I have committed an indiscretion?"

"Many, I'm afraid, my love. But people seem to get over the shock of it quite quickly." He stopped dead. "Well... I hope you're satisfied, madam. There's nothing much to see. What did you expect? The saplings barely had time to establish themselves before the ground was gripped by frost."

"Oh... How very disappointing. How desolate it is here; and the poor little trees poking through the snowdrifts like thin arms pleading for rescue. Oh, I can't tell you how sad it makes me, Tom."

He hugged her to him. "You silly little goose. I can't think what you expected to find. It will be years and years before it will look anything like a mature lime walk."

"I know. But... Oh, let's go back. I've seen enough," she said. "I can't remember when I was last so dreadfully disappointed. Now isn't that odd! I could fancy eating a piece of coal this very minute, Tom. What do you make of that?"

Tom shook his head at her, and said: "Whatever will you come out with next? Just don't go trying it, woman!"

As they trudged back the way they had come, their faces into the biting wind, Mary Emma's spirits rose. "Oh, Tom!" she gushed, hanging onto his arm with both hands, trying to match his stride and looking up into his face. "Just think, dear. By this time tomorrow Ruth and Joe will have been made man and wife. I can't think how I shall get through the next few hours. I'm sure I shan't sleep a wink tonight."

"But you will," Tom said indulgently, "and probably snuffle and snore the way you usually do. It isn't as if neither had been married before, my love. Unlike us, they know what to expect."

"Unlike us—? Why, Thomas Roberts Challiss! I hope you're not pretending that you'd never had a woman before you bedded me?"

"You know what I mean, you little witch," he said laughing. Bending down he scooped up a handful of snow.

"Don't you dare!" She shrieked, ran, tripped and fell.

Tom reached her side and sank onto one knee, his face stricken. "Mary Emma!" He helped her to her feet and brushed the snow from her coat. "You little fool! We must get you indoors and to bed at once." He swept her up into his arms and hurried towards the house with his precious bundle.

"I didn't hurt myself," she said mildly, in self-defence. "And I didn't fall on my front; I rolled onto my back in the soft snow, Tom. 'Twas not unlike being in bed."

"Stop talking. We must get you to lie down," he said angrily, kicking open the front door, closing it with a backward thrust from his boot and bearing her upstairs two at a time to their bedchamber. Only after removing her coat, hat and shoes, and lifting her onto the bed while still in her frock, did he pull the bell rope.

Mary Emma was in bed by the time Rudge appeared but the manservant made no sign that he thought it anything out of the ordinary. "You rang, sir?"

"See that Peckover gets himself down to Aldrich's lodge as quickly as possible, Rudge. Mrs Vale is sure to be there. Mrs Challiss has had a fall. Tell Peckover to ask the nurse to come as soon as she is able. It's urgent! Quick as you can, man!"

"Very good, sir," Rudge said, leaving the room at his usual decorous pace.

★

Ruth came into the front withdrawing room after examining Mary Emma. "No harm done," she said, reaching for her bonnet. "But you were quite right to send for me, Tom. Best to be sure. Fortunately, your wife has a strong constitution and is in excellent health. From what I gather, she unconsciously minimalised any danger by rolling over onto her back. That she fell onto soft snow helped, too."

"This damned weather," Tom cursed. "If it hadn't been for that – I beg your pardon, Ruth. Forgive me." He sighed. "To be honest, it was my stupid behaviour that caused her to trip. My God! When I think I might have murdered my own child."

"Nonsense, Mr Challiss," the nurse reassured him. "You musn't torture yourself by thinking such things. Healthily pregnant women are surprisingly robust creatures. After all, the species would soon die out if every mother succumbed to the hazards of daily life. Just think how many pregnant women labour in the fields at harvest time from dawn until dusk, then go home to care for their large, robust families, with no ill-effect. No, sir. If anything, it is those of a different class of society, who are cosseted and who lie about on day beds for hours on end, taking no exercise and eating too much: it is those whose pregnancies are in danger of premature termination, sir. And it is those same women who, when they do carry to full term, quite often produce offspring that are sickly and unlikely to survive childhood. But Mary Emma is young and strong and eminently sensible about her responsibilities to herself as an expectant mother."

"Thank God it was not serious," Tom said, as he followed Ruth downstairs.

"Indeed," she said, smiling. "We shall look for you in church tomorrow, Tom. And don't fret about your wife. Keep her in bed for the rest of today and she'll be herself by the morning." Tom watched the clarence bear her away, thankful that such a good friend would soon be living at the lodge on a permanent basis.

Upstairs, Mary Emma lay propped up in bed eating a crisp apple while a roaring fire lent tropical heat to the large bedchamber. She was lost in the pages of Miss Austen's *Pride and Prejudice* which had been sent from the bookseller's by express messenger that very morning just about the time they had visited the lime walk.

★

It was a very quiet wedding. A handful of friends sat in the front pews as the Reverend Edward Fieldgate presided over the marriage ritual. Mary Emma was sorry that Ruth had dressed herself in the dullest, plainest coat and bonnet of pearl grey. There was not even a red or pink rose peeping from the bonnet's brim to redeem the severity of the bridal outfit. Beside the straight, slim figure of his bride, who was of medium height, Joseph Aldrich's shortcomings were accentuated. He was impeccably turned out in funereal black tailcoat and breeches, a dove grey brocaded waistcoat and a white stock that looked as if it should have been wound around the neck of somebody of greater height. As it was, too little of Joseph's neck seemed to separate his large head from his mismatched body and the effect was to make him appear even more ungainly than usual. His nervousness was obvious.

Mary Emma had not been paying attention to the service and was abruptly brought out of her critical meanderings by Ruth's suddenly turning and handing over her flowers for her matron-of-honour to hold while the register was being signed. Dull, dull dull! thought Mary Emma, as she looked down at the insignificant posy of forced lily-of-the-valley. Yet, she reluctantly admitted that their scent belied their puny little creamy-white bells. Mmm… divine…" – wife." Oh! Was it all over so soon? Collecting her wits, Mary Emma returned Ruth's almost colourless bridal bouquet to her and became fascinated as Joe lifted back Ruth's veil and the two sealed their marriage with a kiss. Please God, let them be happy, she prayed. No music played them out of the wintry church, no rose petals rose into the air… Ah. The child somersaulted in her womb and exercised its limbs against its prison wall. How glad she was to have been married in the autumn…

Mary Emma thought the wedding breakfast a very tame affair. Whilst she admitted that the floral decorations were superb, she deplored the absence of music and found the restrained atmosphere oppressive. Should anybody be provoked to laughter, it was of that polite kind that inclines those who notice it to the conclusion that the person emitting such niggardly appreciation of whatever had been said, by producing such a feeble response, either had not understood the joke or had not found it in the least amusing. Yet Tom seemed to be enjoying himself, though she couldn't think why. As for the bridal couple, they annoyed her intensely as they stood about first with this dull guest then with that, exchanging polite nothings in carefully modulated tones. It was more like the aftermath of a funeral, she thought, as the child within her quickened. She sat looking out of the window at the darkening day and wished herself back at home with her book.

Oh! If only handsome Mr Darcy would come striding into the room! He would stir things up. Of course, it was wicked to think such things, but she'd even be prepared to put up with George Wickham's flirting: at least he would banish her ennui with his flashing eyes and witty remarks…

"You're awfully quiet, Mary Emma," Ruth Aldrich said seating herself beside her young guest. "I trust you're not experiencing any unpleasantness after yesterday's tumble, my dear."

The sudden arrival of her hostess at a crucial point in her daydream, in which Mr Wickham had made, the moment before Ruth sat down – the most improper suggestion to a pre-enceinte Mary Emma – jolted her back to reality. Turning from the window, she said, collectedly: "No, none at all. In fact I am very well, thank you, Ruth. My child is very active, that is all."

"And something for which you should be very grateful, my dear," the bride observed solemnly. "Not every woman is as fortunate."

Mary Emma said defensively: "I was not complaining, Ruth. Would you care to feel it move?"

The nurse's face froze. "Perhaps in a less public place, my dear," she said. "Excuse me, I must speak to Edward Fieldgate. He seems to have been abandoned by his wife — temporarily, of course."

Mary Emma stood up and looked around to see what had become of her husband, for he was no longer in the room with the other guests. How tedious the afternoon was, she thought, as she sauntered into the adjoining conservatory. The humidity, the heavily-scented tropical blooms added to her lethargy and she sank onto a handy chair. Is it possible to will myself to sleep? she wondered, closing her heavy eyelids and imagining nothing but black velvet; but what had worked on many occasions when she was a child failed her now and her eyes flew open. An oppressive quiet replaced the steady drone of muted cross-conversations that were taking place in the parlour and she became aware that she was not alone. Nobody had spoken so much as a whisper, there had been no rustle of a garment, yet she was certain that among the hothouse blooms and gigantic ferns another being breathed steadily, rhythmically. As she resumed her promenade among the false jungle, she froze at the sight of a woman's leg. No mere flirtatious ankle peeped from a screen of glossy-leaved camellias, but the whole of the shapely long limb as far as she dared to let her eyes explore. Worse! The exposed leg, in its gartered stocking, was at the angle of abandonment, the knee turned outwards to allow an uninterrupted view of those parts to which only one's husband's gaze should be privileged. Mary Emma coughed and the breathing stopped abruptly. Turning her back on her lewd discovery she made much noise in walking back the way she had come so that the woman should be left in no doubt that she had been left alone. Her face scarlet with embarrassment,

Mary Emma sought out Ruth and asked if she might have a little wine.

"My dear! What has happened?" Ruth said, all concern, fetching the decanter.

"The conservatory... was very hot," Mary Emma whispered before falling into a faint.

★

"I will not be made into an invalid, Tom," Mary Emma said, once they had reached home. "I simply fainted because of the heat in that wretched hothouse!" she lied. Should she tell him of her bizarre experience while in the conservatory? Would he think her indelicate in even mentioning such a thing to him? He was her husband! They were one in the sight of God. Surely that meant in every way, not only as one flesh? She believed that husband and wife should have no secrets from one another. They should be able to discuss, on equal terms, anything under the sun. Good heavens! She was flesh and blood, not one of those delightful fictional heroines to be found among the pages of one of Miss Austen's novels. Oh, the Misses Bennet were a joy to read about; but they lived in a fictional world. They inhabited a utopia where there were no bad smells or sights, in which the poor scarcely appeared, where most of those within their circle spoke divine English scarcely ever above a muted murmur; and the most improper thing an unmarried young woman could do was to take an unaccompanied walk through the fields in a downpour. She envied the Bennet girls.

As they dressed for dinner, she made up her mind to broach the subject. "Tom, dear," she said, "please help me with my lacing. I can't think where Maddy has got to."

He came up behind her and was immediately bewitched by the sight of a dark tendril of hair that stirred as his breath met her white neck. His lips touched the spot below the waving curl and, in turn, each vertebra that was visible above her corset.

Angrily, she twisted around to face him. "Now, Tom, stop it! This isn't the time." She turned back. "Please lace me up, but not too tightly! I don't want to faint again. That was half the trouble this morning: I let my vanity get in the way of prudence."

He sighed at her rebuff, promising himelf to take his full reward later on. "There, madam," he said, tying a bow at the top of the laced stays. He whirled her about to face him again and ravened her lips. "Did ever a man have a sweeter bundle to tie?" he murmured, seductively.

Refusing to allow herself to be distracted from her purpose, she looked him in the eye and said very seriously: "Sit down for a minute, my dear," and pulled him onto the side of the bed where she seated herself beside him. "I haven't told you all that occurred in the conservatory this afternoon, Tom."

My God! The unknown woman who'd stumbled upon his accidental meeting with Catherine Fieldgate in the conservatory had been Mary Emma? What rotten luck. "Before you say anything, my dear, there is something I must explain," he began.

"I like that!" she cried, her blue eyes flashing. "I wanted to speak to you first, Tom Challiss." She was about to go on with her tirade; but something in his eyes stopped her and a cold hand seemed to clutch at her heart. "It was *you*," she whispered, looking at him as though she'd never really seen him before. She shook her head in disbelief and moaned: "Oh, Tom, how could you?"

"Please let me explain, Mary Emma," he said, his face altered by misery. "It wasn't as bad as you seem to think."

They ignored the dinner gong.

"Am I so ugly now that you must seek solace from another woman?" she said, deathly white.

He attempted to take her in his arms but she shook him off. "I can't say I blame you, my love," he said, his voice flat. "I am so sorry, Mary Emma. But you've got hold of the wrong end of the stick. Won't you give me a chance to explain?"

"Of all people, it had to be that odious, sanctimonious—"

"Now, listen to me, Mary Emma. I don't know what you imagine was going on — If this is what reading silly romantic novels leads to… putting all kinds of wicked nonsense into your head… I shall forbid your reading the damned things!"

They ignored the dinner gong.

"You—will—for—bid? *Forbid!*"

He was beside himself with anger. "You *will* listen," he shouted into her face. "Remember your marriage vows—"

She laughed hysterically. "I?"

He waited for her to regain her composure and strove to calm himself. Fearful of doing her some physical injury, he walked over to the bell pull and gave it an angry tug. It came away in his hand. "Damnation!"

"You rang, sir?" Rudge caught sight of the damaged pull: "Oh! Dear me!"

"Ask Mrs Rudge to delay dinner," Tom commanded in a voice unlike his own. "Say, for half an hour, or so."

"Very well, Mr Challiss, sir," Rudge said, keeping his eyes averted from his mistress where she lay in a crumpled heap on the edge of the bed. "Very good, sir."

The door closed behind the manservant and Tom said grimly: "Stop snivelling and sit up!" Silently, she obeyed. "And now, you will hear what I have to say, Mary Emma. No! Don't say another word until I have finished. Thank you, my dear. That wedding breakfast! I can't remember when I was last at so dreary a gathering. I looked for you to accompany me; but you seemed to be having such a good gossip with Ruth that I wandered off into the conservatory alone for a change of scene. Hush! Now hear what I have to say before judging me too harshly, my love.

"I'd just made up my mind to enjoy a quiet cigar out of sight among the ferns when I heard a moan coming from among the potted camellias. I went to investigate and, to my surprise, discovered Mrs Fieldgate lying on the floor staunching blood that oozed from a deeply cut leg. Apparently, she had tripped and fallen heavily against a wrought iron jardinière. The wretched thing had been fashioned to resemble lilies, without a thought being given to the fact that the iron leaves were as lethal as unsheathed sabres. I asked her permission to bind the leg with my handkerchief and she reasoned that there could be no impropriety in my doing so, as we were both sensible married people, and that nobody need ever know of it anyway. I had just finished binding up her leg when we heard the tapping of a woman's heels as she crossed the tiled floor. I know now that it must have been you, my love. At the time, I had to consider Mrs Fieldgate's honour and was loath to reveal her in apparently compromising circumstances. The cut was to the outside of her right thigh and she behaved very bravely, though she must have been in great pain. That's the truth, Mary Emma: make of it what you will."

"Am I allowed to speak, my lord?" she asked in mock humility. "It sounds plausible enough, though some might think it rather too glibly recited," she said, unwilling to let him off too lightly, though in her heart she believed his explanation. "I can't understand why on earth you didn't go and fetch Ruth."

"On her wedding day? Oh, sweetheart, the wedding breakfast was a dull enough affair as it was, without calling on the bride's services as a nurse, to boot. I suppose she'll give all that up, now that she has remarried?"

"Never mind that just now, Tom. I'm sorry I was such a virago, dear; I simply don't understand myself any more. How you put up with me, I don't know. I suppose our dinner is quite ruined by this time, but I don't care if it is for I could eat a horse!"

★

Two mornings after Christmas Day the sound of a one-horsed conveyance was heard approaching the house. A constant flow of traffic drays carting timber, bricks, pipes and tiles as well as domestic vehicles and horseriders, had reduced the snow to slush and the slush to mud which in turn had frozen hard overnight. Mary Emma, who was in the gutted library discussing details of shelving with Jem Webster, was drawn to the window by the unaccustomed sound and was delighted to see Burton Brook holding the reins of a cob who drew behind him a canary yellow, small-scale phaeton. Seated beside Burt was his sister Agnes and behind Agnes was her box. "Oh! Excuse me, Jem," she said, leaving the carpenter open-mouthed in mid-sentence as she hurried out of the room. Snatching up a shawl as she passed the cloak cupboard, she threw it around her shoulders and went out to meet her friends.

Mary Emma called down to them from the top step, "Welcome to Uppham House," descended the flight and held out her arms. "Agnes!" The two young women embraced. "Are you here to stay?" She shook hands with Burt and was surprised by his firm, masculine grip. "My, how you've grown: I would hardly have recognised you had it not been for Agnes." He grinned down at her. It was a joyous meeting. "Come in, come in!" she cried, pulling Agnes along by her hand while Burt followed with his sister's box. "Tell me, who is the proud owner of that splendid little phaeton? Is it yours," she asked Burt doubtfully, the light four-wheeler seeming much too dainty to carry his weight very far, though the cob looked strong enough. To Mary Emma's astonishment, Agnes smiled shyly and said: "I am," and awaited her friend's comment.

"Agnes! It really is yours? A moment while I ring for some hot chocolate to be brought," their hostess said, pulling the temporary bell rope and inviting them to seat themselves. "Have you breakfasted? Would you like something hot to eat, Burt?"

"Yew know ma, Mrs Challiss," the fine-looking young man said, staring at his boots before looking up at her with a grin. "If Christmas 'adna jist gorn, I'd o' thought I were bein' fattened for the feast in place o' the goose. Not that I'm grumblin', yew understand; ain nobody c'n cook like ma. Thanks all the same, ma'am, but I couldn' even eat the crumbs left be'ind from a plate o' mince pies, she's stuffed me ser full."

At first, Mary Emma did most of the talking. She was so full of happiness that her tongue hardly stopped wagging long enough for her to be given the answers to her questions. Agnes Brook laughed along with her brother at Mary Emma's high-spirited chatter which, they knew, stemmed from her excitable nature and avid curiosity about themselves since she and they had last met. Though in Agnes's case it had been only the day before yesterday, it had been many months since Burt and Mary Emma had been together long enough for a conversational exchange to take place. Agnes was content to sit and listen while the talk flowed back and forth between them non-stop, until Mary Emma turned to her and asked: ". . . and Lord Vyvyan actually asked you what you would like as a Christmas gift, Agnes? You sly fox! So all through the wedding ceremony, while you sat in the church looking so demure and prim, you were nursing your secret. I should never have been able to keep such a splendid piece of news to myself."

"She wrote to Lord Vyvyan with her idea for a little cart that'd take her up an down this long drive, once she were livin' at Uppham," Burt chipped in.

"You look at life from a different perspective, Mary Emma," Agnes said with a smile. "As to the cob phaeton – isn't it a lovely little thing? I thought long and hard about what would be most useful not only to myself but for the family – and others. Father said I shouldn't have accepted such an expensive gift but mother overruled him. Something I didn't tell you before, Mary Emma. Charles – Lord Vyvyan – offered to divorce his wife and marry me when he knew I was carrying his child; but I wouldn't hear of destroying their family."

Burt, who had been studying his large raw-boned hands as they lay, fingers interlocked and palm upwards on his lap, suddenly cracked his knuckles to relieve his embarrassment at the turn the conversation had taken. "Picked up the cob an phaeton from a coachbuilder's at Wigginhall St Mary's where the mail coach dropped me orf," he said. "Enjoyed drivin' meself the rest o' the way an the mail roads wasn't tew bad. 'Twere jist like drivin' a toy, reelly. An that cob's one o' the sweetest-tempered little 'orses I ever come acrorst. Yew'll 'ave no trouble 'andlin' 'im, Agnes."

His sister noticed he'd changed the subject. "Good. I hated the idea of being so near the family and yet having to face walking so far both ways to get there and back – as it becomes more difficult for me. I feel that mother must be able to call on me if she needs to, which is not very likely," she explained. "And then it occurred to me that it would be useful for us to use in driving about the park, Mary Emma."

Mary Emma got up and kissed her practical-minded friend. "Wonderful!

You're a dear, Agnes," she said. "Always thinking of others. But, do tell me: did Lord Vyvyan say you might have anything you wished? You might have had diamonds!"

"Oh, Mary Emma!" she laughed and Burt, obviously relieved to have left more embarrassing topics, joined her in imagining the absurdity of Agnes dressed up like a duchess. "When would I have occasion to wear diamonds?" she asked. "They would have been perfectly useless, whereas a means of transporting myself from here to home, as and when I wish to, is almost as good as having a magic wand."

Crestfallen that her suggestion had met with so little approval, Mary Emma conceded: "Of course, you are right. Though diamonds do fetch a pretty penny and you might have sold them."

Burt Brook shook his head. "Aye, she might've done that, Mrs Challiss; but money int everythin', is it? Ser long as yew 'ave enough ter git along with I doan see why folks crave tew 'ave more. Money an' riches ain brought Lord an Lady Vyvyan much 'appiness, 'ave they? There's a parcel o' things that'll make yer 'appier than pilin' up money, though I doan say as I won't be savin' up meself ter git married one day afore long. Seems ter 'appen tew everybody in the end, doan it, no matter 'ow 'ard they strives to iscape its snares."

The two young women laughed at his fatalistic view of his future. "You won't even know you've been caught, Burt, until some young maid you've been busily pursuing decides it's time to let you catch her," Mary Emma said.

"It'll be painless," Agnes assured him, wondering if he had anyone in mind.

"Aye, you'm prob'ly right," he said with his engaging grin. "'S all part o' life, I s'pose."

And so the morning wore away and soon it was time for Burt to take his leave of the two young women who promised to see him before his return to Lincolnshire and Passendean. Mrs Brook was expecting her handsome son back for the midday meal so he made his farewells and stepped out smartly to walk back to Church House.

★

Chapter Thirty-three

Tom had been astonished by Lord Vyvyan's gift to Agnes Brook. The fact that so elevated a personage should have thought fit to make such a present to an unmarried woman – though he himself still thought of Agnes as a girl – of humble origin who would, in a few months' time, give birth to a bastard child, compelled Tom to see Miss Brook through new eyes.

His first thought had been that the man must be out of his senses. On second thought, he saw the gesture for what it was: a token of the man's love. That led him next to think of the trouble that had been caused by himself not considering how Mary Emma would be enabled to get about, once she had had to quit riding. How much annoyance to himself and frustration for his wife had arisen by his not thinking of such a simple solution: yet, apparently, the idea of some means of independent transport had come from Agnes herself. Extraordinary! The girl had a good head on her shoulders. Nevertheless, he had forbidden the women to drive the phaeton beyond Uppham's gates. Agnes had looked crestfallen while Mary Emma had protested loudly.

"That is quite ridiculous, Tom," she said, firing up. "The very reason Agnes asked for it was so that she should be able to visit Church House, which, as you know, is in the village outside our gates! Are we supposed to walk, in all weathers, from Aldrich's lodge into Uppham St Mary? Why, it must be all of half a mile! You cannot expect it of us, especially as the months pass. Beside which, it will ruin Agnes's well-devised plan."

"All right. ALL RIGHT!" he snapped, closing his eyes and flapping his hands at her. "Please don't make such a song and dance about it. It is of your safety I'm thinking. The starving, idle men hanging about the streets of Downham are becoming dangerously angry: they're reaching boiling point. Jem Webster says its only a matter of time before they take the law into their own hands. It's their families that are suffering and the men won't allow that to go unchallenged. That brightly-painted little carriage with a well-fed cob pulling it, never mind its two occupants, would be like a red rag to a whole field of bulls. If anything should happen to either of you—"

Aware that he had relented several sentences back, Mary Emma smiled sweetly and said: "Oh, Tom. It is good of you to trouble your head about us, my dear, when you have things of greater importance to occupy your time, but there really is no need. I'm sure Jem's been exaggerating. Anyway, of what use would Agnes's little phaeton be to them? It's unique. Everybody would know it had been stolen from Uppham."

Puzzled by her friend's response Agnes said: "Thank you for your concern, Mr Challiss. According to Burt, what Jem says is true enough. The men are desperate. He was in the *Queen's Head* on Christmas Eve and told us that the men were talking angrily about storming the shops in Downham in order to get bread for their starving children. Others were heard to admit to the poaching of fish, fowl and game from private lands and those assembled agreed that the landed gentry could afford to lose the odd sheep, pig or pheasant without noticing their loss."

"Did they, by God!" Tom said, his initial worry forgotten. "We'll see about that!"

"Now, Tom!" Mary Emma said, a warning in her tone, "please don't do something that you'll live to regret. At least, speak to Jem, Kit and Joseph first."

"I've no intention of going off half cock, my dear," he said. "You may rest assured: I'll call a meeting with them this very day. And Mary Emma, I propose to kill several birds with one stone by inviting the men to dine here every day, starting New Year's Day. My grandfather Roberts hadn't many outdoor servants, but he always had them dine at the farmhouse at noon. That way, he kept his finger on the pulse of what was going on about the farm. I was only a boy, and so forbidden to speak during the meal; but there was nothing wrong with my ears and eyes. I saw that problems were nipped in the bud. It was a good practice and one I intend to resurrect. May I take it that you will instruct Mrs Rudge accordingly, my dear?"

"No, you may not, Mr Challiss!" Mary Emma said. "Don't you think you might have discussed the matter with me before considering it cut and dried? How on earth do you expect Mrs Rudge to cope with such a large number to cook for in the middle of the day?"

Agnes, unwilling to bear witness to their disharmony, made an excuse to leave the room and Tom was sensitive to the fact that their quarrelling had driven her away.

He sat down. "Mary Emma," he said, following her name with a prolonged sigh, "I fear that our squabbling has offended Agnes. I freely admit that I am at least as much at fault in this as you are, my dear. But we must try to respect her feelings."

"Fiddlesticks!" his wife said. "Agnes is no niminy-piminy parson's daughter, Tom. Why, growing up in such an overflowing household as the Brook's, she must have seen and heard everything a hundred times over."

"Not necessarily. Don't make the mistake that I did," he said. "Agnes was only the second born. She knew a few years of real peace and tranquillity with her mother and Burt before the rest of the Brook tribe arrived. From what I've observed, she's a very sensitive young woman and possesses finer feelings than one might suppose."

"Oh, undoubtedly; she does. It hasn't taken you long to get inside her character. Though I must confess to being surprised that you have found out her excellent qualities so soon. You're right, of course; we should make a greater effort to exercise restraint. It was my fault. I'll go after her and make our apologies, Tom."

"Before you go, my dear," he said seriously, "I must ask you – have you ever known Adam and Dulcie Brook to quarrel in public?"

At the door, she paused before turning to face him. "D'you know, Tom, I don't believe I ever have. Now isn't that curious?"

"Is it?" he questioned. "It seems we have much to learn about the give and take of marriage, my dear. Indeed, we must try to do better; or I foresee the years that stretch before us as one long battleground. It isn't a pleasant prospect, is it."

She came back to where he sat and whispered: "But we love each other, Tom. Isn't that enough?" Adding in full voice: "Though, much as I love you, and truly, I do, I doubt whether I'm capable of adaptation. You're stuck with me, dear, warts and all."

He laughed. "I shall keep my eyes and ears open for a cure for warts, then."

"You've already found it. I'm going in search of her now."

★

The groom sat slumped in a chair, his left leg supported by its ankle resting on his right knee, and stared around the empty library. No thanks to Sir Everard for recommendin me to the jumped-up owner of this 'ole, the man thought. He felt contempt for any man who thought an empty, rain-stained, bare-boarded room a fit place to conduct an interview. When he had acquired the position of Under Groom at the beautiful stables at Martlets he had thought himself in clover for life; and had it not been for the bad luck of Percival Belmaine's accident he would have been there still. Who could have foretold that Sir Everard would sell off the string and, as the last of the mounts had left, he would find himself out of a job? The doorknob turned and his prospective employer came into the miserable room. The groom was surprised to find him such a young man; even so, he had the cuddy look of his breed and was red-haired into the bargain. He got to his feet, and stood waiting, hat in hand, for his prospective master to speak.

So this is the man Belmaine recommends so highly, thought Tom, as he entered the room. Hard to know what to make of him; looks a mite cocky. Well . . . we shall see. "Good-morning," he said, affably offering his hand which the other, with some surprise, shook. "You are William Wright, I believe?"

"I am, sir."

"I must apologise for meeting you here. We're in the process of refurbishing the place. I thought it preferable to conducting our business in the stables, which are cold and draughty. You heard about our fire, I suppose? We've plans to rebuild a modern block and with them sleeping quarters for the stableyard staff. "

"I 'eard something about that, sir."

This is going to be damned hard going, Tom thought. "The fact is, Mr Wright—"

Zounds! he called *me* Mister!

"— that things are rather topsy-turvey at the moment. I feel bound to tell you that, should you accept the position of groom here, I have no accommodation ready for you in the stable block at present."

The man's self-assurance left him. "It won't do, Mr Challiss. I was counting on livin' in. I was led to believe, Mr Challiss, sir, that an 'ouse went with the job. Did I get it wrong?"

"No, you're quite right about that," Tom said. "It's just that nothing's ready to move into at the moment; the cottages are going up as we speak. But it's a bad time of year to be building and progress is slower than we expected."

"I dunno, sir," the groom said, studying the dusty floorboards and shaking his head. "I was countin' on it, see?" He looked up and his troubled eyes met Tom's. "I got married the week before young Belmaine broke 'is neck bein' thrown from Saladin. Yew know how long ago that was, Mr Challiss. Well . . . Me an Meg only 'ad the one night tergether. Ever since then I bin at Martlits an' she's bin frettin' at 'ome with her mother. So, yer see, sir, I was countin' on an 'ouse so's we'd be tergether."

"Hmm." Thinking rapidly, Tom suddenly remembered old Plumb's empty cottage. Joe Aldrich should have taken it in hand by this time. But was it ready for occupation? And would Wright accept it after his comfortable berth at Martlets?

"I'm sorry that the new cottage isn't ready, Mr Wright—"

"I'd best be goin' then, 'ad I, sir?"

Tom smiled. "Only if you want to after what I have to say. There is a cottage."

Wright's face altered dramatically as he waited for Tom to go on.

"It's not on the estate. It's in the village of Uppham St Mary. You'd have a fairish walk to and fro each day—"

Wright stepped forward, grasped Tom's hand and shook it firmly. "I doan mind that, sir. Oh! Mr Challiss. Wait 'til I tell Meg the good noos."

"Hold ye horses, man!" Tom said, thoroughly pleased at the way his news had been received. "The cottage is quite run-down. It's last occupant was old Mr Plumb and I imagine, as he lived there alone for several years, that the inside's none too clean."

"Yew wait 'til my Meg gets 'er 'ooks inter it, sir. She'll soon 'ave it shinin' like a noo pin. 'Ow soon before we can move in, Mr Challiss?"

"It'll only be temporary, just until the new place is finished," Tom said. "Have a word with Mr Aldrich at the lodge as you pass by. He'll let you have the key."

As Tom was seeing him off the premises, Wright seemed disinclined to take himself away. "Is there something else?" Tom asked, adding: "You'll be expected to start at eight-o'clock tomorrow morning, unless you hear anything to the contrary. You finish at six. See Mr Aldrich about your wage."

"Right yew are, Mr Challiss." The groom drew in his breath and chewed his lip, then said in a rush: "It's about me brother Ben, sir. Shoulda come with me 'smornin'. 'Es 'avin a tooth pulled by the blacksmith; bin givin' im some clawth."

Clawth? Must mean pain, perhaps discomfort. "Oh?"

"Well, sir; Ben was stable boy at Martlits. Sir Everard lead us ter believe that yew'd take us both on. Meg an me'd give 'im bed an board, sir; that'd be no trouble."

"You can vouch for your brother, Mr Wright?"

"Oh-ah, Mr Challiss, sir, I can. Fair loves tendin' horses, do Ben, an a good grafter. 'E'll pull 'is weight, no need ter worry about that."

"How old is he?"

"Thirteen, sir, and as jannock as they come, Mr Challiss."

Jannock? "I'll take him on, on your say so," Tom said, and was happy to see a look of relief cross Wright's face. "See Mr Aldrich about his wage."

"Thank yew very much, Mr Challiss. Yew won't regret it, sir."

Tom experienced the satisfaction of having been able to provide young Wright with a secure future while acquiring a much-needed groom to take care of the growing string of horses. Supposing him to be about twenty-two years of age, he watched the well-made young man – who resembled the majority of the Downham working men in being neither handsome nor ugly, was of average height, his hair a sunbleached brown above a fresh complexion, with light eyes and an open expression – stride out towards the drive at the end of which lay the key to his future happiness.

★

Joseph Aldrich liked the look of Will Wright. He liked the way the groom met his eye unflinchingly, the firm grasp of his hand and the neatness of his person. His wage was generous at twelve shillings a week, plus Plumb's weatherproofed cottage, the key to which he handed him as they took leave of one another. "It's no palace," the steward warned him, "and I doubt if it's as good as you've been used to; but it's a roof over your heads. If rumours are anything to go by, that's more than a lot of men have at the moment."

"They'm stickin' it out, if they can, Mr Aldrich," Will said, his expression grim. "Their wives and younguns 'ave thrown themselves on the mercy of the Parish. Makes me count me blessin's, I can tell yer. Then there's those who've bin put ter work mendin' roads, ter make 'em earn their bread. Acourse, the men're 'umiliated at findin' themselves forced to foller that callin'. Many of 'em have bin masters an most of 'em are skilled journeymen; or soldiers an sailors who've fought for their country an can't git work because they've lorst an arm or a leg – or worse'n that. It's a rill comedown. I tell yer this, Mr Aldrich, if things doan improve fer the labourers pretty quick ther's gonna be rill trouble. The workin Englishman'll stand only so much before he breaks out."

Aldrich looked alarmed. "You surely don't think that anything will happen in Downham?"

"Unless things alter drastic'lly, I do, sir. Anyway, I've taken up too much of your time as 'tis; so I'll be on me way ter tell Mrs Wright me good noos. Good-day tew yer, Mr Aldrich."

Wright's opinion of the mood of the out-of-work labourers and the men lately returned from the Penisular Wars had unsettled the steward. Silently, he thanked God that he was employed on a large estate, safe and secure from any violence that might erupt from the road gangs formed from the aggrieved men who hung about the streets of Downham. Anyway, they had no need to approach Uppham, for the lane leading to its gates was as yet unmetalled and had been repaired quite recently. Assured that everything would be well in his little enclosed world, he took himself into his office to study the estate diaries.

At luncheon, Ruth Aldrich asked her husband who the visitor had been, not having recognised him when she let him in. On being told who he was and his business with Joe, she observed: "He looks a steady, trustworthy man. Just the kind of man the Challisses need; they are such a pair of lovesick babies. Perhaps things will change for the better once they become parents."

"Well, my dear," Joe said, as he prepared to leave her in order to visit the building site and check progress, "it has been said that a man doesn't become fully a man until he has fathered a son. The main fault is that both Challisses are selfish, Mary Emma particularly so. Each is determined to triumph over the other. It remains to be seen if the child they expect in the spring will make any difference to them."

She smiled at him as she fastened his cloak. "Does the adage about fathering a son hold true if the child should be a girl, sir?"

His eyes glowed like rubbed amber. "Some men become sufficiently mature without the need of offspring, Ruth. I hope I am one. Should we be blessed, I care not of what sex the child is: providing it takes after its mother in looks, of course."

"Dear Joe," Ruth said, kissing him warmly. "We must wait and see. Each of us has lost a child, lives with the piercing heartache left by that wound; it must have been by divine purpose. God knows best, Joe. If we are to be blessed I, for one, should not care which of us it favours, so long as it is perfectly formed and has all its faculties. We are in His hands." His heart full, Joseph embraced his wonderful wife.

★

Tom's plan to have his senior servants to dine at the mansion every day bit the dust. He sought out each man independently and their response to his suggestion had been identical and adamant: a concurrent rejection by the men, on the grounds that it would be an unnecessary interruption in their already busy schedules. As Jem Webster had put it: "Thanks all the same, Mr Challiss;

but workin men're used to a one-journey." The term was new to Tom, who asked him to explain. He'd answered: "Well, we're used ter workin without stoppin fer meals, see. We usually take a pricker bag ter keep us goin." Ah! He means *dockey* bag, different dialect. "Most workin men look forrard ter sittin down tew a proper meal about shutten-up time, see."

"Right. I see your point," Tom had said. "It seemed to me an excellent opportunity to air any grievances or discuss ideas. But there we are!" he'd said, plainly annoyed. "You all seem to be of one mind about it so I'll drop it." Nevertheless, he had made up his mind to discuss an alternative with Mary Emma, for he refused to jettison what was, he was certain, a very good idea.

Jem had raised another matter. "Now that young Clem's vanished inter thin air, there's a lodgin goin beggin at Mrs 'Ignell's place. It's left the poor old dame feelin lonesome all over agin. Said she'd be glad tew 'ave the right kinda person. 'Tis the long, dark evenins is allus the worst fer 'er. Told me she misses young Clem's company somethin awful. Seems 'e were good ter the old woman. 'Elped 'er about the 'ouse, fetchin water an choppin wood. Things like that. Jist thought I'd mention it."

"My thanks, Jem. I'll bear it in mind and let Aldrich know," Tom had said as they parted. The carpenter's comment about Mrs Hignell's late lodger had surprised him. Apparently, there was a soft side to the ickeny young varmint, after all.

★

Nobody was able to say who Mrs Hignell's new lodger was or what exactly he was employed to do about the estate. He lodged with her; but he was no shepherd.

Kit Warrender had filled that gap with a reliable man, already known to him, who had behind him a long and successful career as a shepherd. Despite his blameless reputation, since losing his last place – which was on account of his master's farm being sold to a gentleman requiring more lands over which to hunt – the shepherd had had difficulty in securing another situation. At forty-five, his age was against him. He was looked on by the majority of the *nouveau riche*, many of whom had profited from the long wars against the French, as a poor risk. Longevity was spurned by them when it came to assembling an army of servants for indoor or outdoor labour, on the dubious grounds that older workers were prone to a greater variety of maladies than the young, the most likely of which would be imminent death. Besides, older servants usually grew wrinkled or ugly, or both: and the new landowners disliked their popinjay friends to see such unedifying non-persons stationed among their beautiful possessions. In their estimation, a servant's looks – a pretty face on a maid, a well-turned calf on a six-foot flunkey – far surpassed prime skills such as those possessed by many of the hundreds of ragged, unprepossessing, starving and out-of-work labourers. After all, the upstarts reasoned, worn out nags were sent to the knackers' yard, weren't they?

David Deacon's almost unlined face gave the lie to this generalisation. His blue eyes, deep-set and piercing, centred in triangles of stretched eye-skin, were the legacy of years spent in the open, habitually staring into the distance through all kinds of weather while keeping his flock in view. Black-haired and black-browed, the shepherd's bronzed face and fleeced jerkin resembled pictures of the French-Canadian trappers that veterans of the British-American War of 1812 had brought back with them. Deacon, by choice a celibate, had a constant companion in his crossbred dog, Fly, a Smithfield sheepdog-terrier. His most valuable possession, Fly was an essential tool in the management of Deacon's flock. The shepherd, used to the harshest conditions and, apart from his dog, preferring his own company, had told Warrender that he'd be content to sleep in the lambing shed until after the lambing season had ended, or until the promise of a cottage of his own was honoured, whichever came first.

When Tom learned that the flock was in such capable hands he breathed a sigh of relief. He had never taken to Clem Rix and, if the truth were known, had been glad to see the back of him. He would pay the new shepherd a visit as soon as he had the time. His plans for the resurgence of Uppham, formed months ago in Belgium, were taking shape and he considered he had much of which he could be proud.

The key positions in the staffing of Uppham had almost all been filled, he thought with immense satisfaction. There remained that of Gamekeeper and, he supposed, Housekeeper; though he wondered if that would be necessary now that Mary Emma had the assistance of Agnes Brook. He would consult his wife on that point. That led him to recall her objection to his midday dinner with the men and that led him naturally to reprise their earlier conversation. It had been on Mrs Rudge's behalf that Mary Emma had objected. Of course! She had been right; for the cook was an old woman and could hardly be expected to take on an extra burden at her time of life. He would speak to his wife about hiring an Assistant Cook and see what she had to say about his midday dinners then.

★

In the bedchamber, the manhandled bell pull had not been repaired, Tom noticed. It had been replaced. Where a perfectly serviceable rope had hung, there now gleamed a flimsy-looking sash of exquisitely-embroidered silk, a piece of feminine frippery that, at the first tweak Tom judged, was bound to part company with the mechanism that connected the apparatus to the kitchen bell board. He went in search of his wife and found her ensconced with Agnes in the front withdrawing room.

Before he had time to draw breath, Mary Emma cried: "Oh, Tom; there you are! What do you think, my dear? Agnes says she is able to play the piano. I simply had no idea. It's the very thing we need—"

Brutally overriding his wife's excitable babble, Tom made himself heard by means of his stronger, deeper voice. "My dear Mary Emma," he boomed. "Please be so good as to enlighten me. What is that strip of nonsense that has appeared in our bedchamber, pray?"

Agnes gathered her things into a small basket, rose, her needlework in her hands and murmured to Mary Emma. "Would you prefer me to leave?"

"Please, Miss Brook. I beg you, stay. Pray be seated," Tom said, ashamed of his ungentlemanly behaviour. "That was rude of me. I humbly beg your pardon, ladies."

"You see what a good influence you are on my bear of a husband, Agnes," Mary Emma said tartly. "Had I been alone here, he would have carried on in his usual browbeating way. Am I not right, Mr Challiss?"

"I need to fetch some more silk," Agnes said to Tom. "Please excuse me."

Tom strode to the door and held it open for her to pass. As Agnes left the room, to Mary Emma's astonishment, Tom bowed to her from the waist before closing the door behind her.

"Well! Now I've seen everything," Mary Emma said, obviously highly amused by his courteous behaviour towards her friend.

"Then, what a pity it is, my dear, that you seem to learn nothing from Agnes's example," he said gently. "It's obvious that she finds the atmosphere between us insupportable."

"Nonsense. You make too much of it, Tom. Have we really become so insensitive to one another?" she asked, puzzled that he should think so. "As far as I am aware, I behave exactly as I have always done."

He laughed and caught her in his arms. "What should I do if you were to become a docile little wife, my pet? It's plain that you're never going to change your spots, Mary Emma. It's too late. In which case, it is I who must make the effort." He kissed the tip of her nose. "Unless you think I, too, am a hopeless case?"

Suddenly serious, she looked up into his eyes and he saw that her own were moist. "Tom. Don't ever stop loving me, will you? I will try to think before speaking. Dear Miss Peters perpetually warned me that no husband would tolerate such a giddy wife. I will try . . . I do try, though you may not think it. I can't be Agnes any more than I could be Miss Peters, Tom. I can only be myself and I'm afraid you'll have to put up with me as I am, complete with all my faults."

"You haven't answered my question, wife; was that deliberate?" he said. "Am I, too, beyond redemption?"

"What nonsense you talk at times, Tom Challiss," she mock-scolded him. "No, my dear. You were not fashioned into a selfish ball of clay by the time you were two years old, as was I. Time has not really tested either of us yet, Tom; but if I thought I could become anything like as good a wife and mother as is Dulcibella Burton Brook I would award myself a medal. So there you are!" she laughed, "selfish to the core. At least in that respect I am consistent."

"Have you forgotten all that Miss Peters taught you so soon? I seem to remember her dinning into both of us that goodness is its own reward," said Tom, visually remembering the pleasant schoolroom at Lyndon Manor in which they'd shared lessons. "And Dulcie is good. And so is Adam. That family! What is it about the Brooks that fills me with envy? For I do envy them, my dear, with all my heart."

A tap on the door was followed by Agnes, all smiles, her hands hidden behind her back. "You have an important visitor, Mr and Mrs Challiss!" she cried exuberantly, flinging wide her arms. Freed from captivity, Noah sprang out from behind her skirts. He ran to Mary Emma demanding: "Twizzle Noah," as Dulcie came into the room.

In a dilemma, Mary Emma appealed to Tom who amazed them all by picking up the little boy by his armpits and twizzling him until the room rang with laughter.

★

Chapter Thirty-four

"It's a misunderstanding," Joseph Aldrich said to Tom. "I was under the impression that Thompson had spoken to you, or you to him . . . I don't know! I couldn't have been mistaken, Mr Challiss. He was so convincing that, thinking he had your approval, I – naturally – employed the man. After all, it was you yourself who, only the other day, expressed the wish to hire a gamekeeper. So naturally – "

"Yes, yes," Tom said, annoyed that a key servant had been engaged without his prior approval. "But, in your opinion, Joe, the man is sound? What credentials had he? Did he offer a character reference?"

Aldrich relaxed. "Oh, of course, Mr Challiss! I wouldn't have given him the time of day had he come without good references – for he had no less than two."

"Two? That's a bit unusual, isn't it?"

"Well… yes," Aldrich conceded. "But it wouldn't be the first time I've been offered more than one, especially for one of the more senior positions on the estate."

"I see. Well, I don't suppose any harm's been done, Joe. I'm sorry that I blew up like that," Tom said, aware that he'd over-reacted. "I've every confidence in your judgement, of course. You've done much more of this hiring and firing business than I have, after all."

"It's a great relief, Mr Challiss," Aldrich said, smiling. "If you are quite certain that Thompson has your permission to begin his duties right away, I'll advise him."

"Might as well. How does Mrs Hignell get on with him?"

Aldrich frowned. "At present she seems rather in awe of the man. It's true, he has a certain air of command; he's no Clem Rix and I don't see him chopping wood and drawing water for the old lady."

"Hmm. She'll miss the help. That's a pity."

"He struck me as one used to making decisions for himself who would be punctilious in the execution of any task he set his mind to."

"A paragon, Joe?" Tom said, raising an eyebrow. "Not many of those about."

"Exactly the virtues necessary to gamekeeping, I suggest, sir," the steward said.

Word soon spread that Mrs Hignell's new lodger was that much-despised member of the countryside, a gamekeeper. Until his arrival, poaching the Uppham estate had been as easy as picking buttercups in summer and the out-of-work farm labourers viewed Thompson's appointment as gamekeeper as a black mark against Tom Challiss. Before this affront, the new upstart owner of Uppham House had done little to provoke the Downham men's dislike. His engagement of an armed protector of Uppham's woods and fields, to be pitted against unarmed poachers driven to relieving him of a surfeit of wildlife in order that they and theirs avoided starvation, categorised him in their eyes as one of the detested gentry. Those casual labourers who had earned the wherewithal to purchase a tankard of ale at the *Queen's Head* sat around the corner table bemoaning their lot.

"'E's showed 'isself in 'is trew colours now, right enough," young Ben Rix said. "Clem allus said Challiss were one o' them, though he pretended otherwise."

"Give the man 'is doo, bor," a quiet man in his thirties argued. "'Twere 'e took us on at a fair wage ter work in 'is garden. Ain many o' the rill gentry as'd dew that, now; be fair."

"Fair! Thassa load of ole squit! 'Ow can it be fair, when one man can spend money like water on tricolatin 'is mansion an re-arrangin 'is poncey garden, when better men than 'im's druv ter patch roads? Answer me that, Jacob Coy," Ben said belligerently, his green eyes challenging the older man.

"'E ain done nobody no 'arm, far as I can tell," argued Coy.

"That were trew yisty," chipped in a small mousey-looking man, "but yer can't say that about 'im now. Like young Ben says: blood will out, an Challiss's is blew, or I'm a Dutchman. Wi' that lot, it's on'y a matter o' time afore they shows their trew colours. An 'e 'as," the man said emphatically before draining his tankard.

A man with a face that bore the scars of smallpox leaned forward so that the others were favoured with his ale-laden foul breath. "Yew be careful." He shifted his gaze about the shadowy room and whispered: "Yer doan know oo might be list'nin."

In a dusky corner, away from the firelight, unreached by the beams of lantern or the flames of candles, Gil Thompson sat immobile, his ears alert to every word that was being said around the labourers' table.

Nothing to go on at present, he thought, taking a silent sip from his tankard. But they're up to something, that's for sure. If not tonight, then soon. I'll hang on a while longer, just in case. Pity to miss something important...

"... wi' bread the price it is, there ent no alternative, bor! Even a married man ent able ter stretch 'is foo shillons ter feed 'is liddluns, so wot chance do us singletons 'ave of keepin clear o' the workus?" The speaker sank his voice to a whisper so that Thompson had to strain his ears to catch what was not so much said as breathed. "Scrouge yer 'eads this way. Yew 'eard about these noo poachin laws that're meant ter frighten the likes of us, bors? 'Arsh! 'Arsh, they is. Crewl. 'Tis said yer can git up ter seven years' transportation tew t'other side o' the world, if'n yer gits caught. Downrigh diabolical, I calls it! Back in me native, I mind me ole dad gittin caught, back in 1800. Worst the beak could throw at 'im in them days were one month 'ard labour. That were jannock; transportation ent."

At this, the huddled labourers muttered or mumbled furiously in dense counter-point, each utterance effectively masking the others; but their faces spoke volumes.

"Gotta catch us first!" Ben Rix's broken treble piped up. "I ent afraid o' no ole gamekeeper," the sandy-haired younger brother of former shepherd Clem Rix boasted. "Reckon I knows Uppham woods better'n any noo-come foreigner."

"Pipe down, yer gastless young fule!" the man with the pitted face hissed, his small eyes flicking to the dark corners of the room. "Yew can't keep yer voice down, yer can git!"

"Yew ent my master, Ned Pitts," the youth hissed back.

"I'll 'ave none o' your chelp, Rix," Pitts breathed, so close to the youth's face that the stench of the man's breath must have been insupportable. His already small eyes became slits. "Yew wonna look out, yew dew. Gamekeeper might not know oo yew are, but we dew. Eh, bors? We'm sick o' yore gammarattle, yer sillybold young bugger. Seven years over the sea'd dew yew a power o' good!"

Ben swallowed the dregs of his ale. "I ent stayin 'ere among a lot of raw ole men putterin an runnin on bout things they can't change. Where dew it git yer? I ent no ole sawney. There's them that can poach an those that gits caught, an I'm one o' them that won't never git caught, see." He started to rise.

His huge hand on Rix's thin shoulder, Pitts pressed him back into his seat and spoke in a sepulchral whisper. "Yew ent goin nowhere 'til we says so. Eh, bors?"

"Doan be ser titchy, Ned," Coy said wearily. "Leave the lad alone. 'E gits on my wick, an all; but we was all young once. 'E's all talk an shanny, jist like 'is brother."

"I doan aim ter git transported 'cause some sillybold young 'ack-slaverer can't 'old 'is tongue," Pitts growled, his yellow eyes nailing Ben to the back of the settle by way of his own terrified gooseberry orbs. "Yew ser much as breathe one word of wot's bin said 'ere ternight – or any other night – an yew'll 'ave me ter reckon with, bor. Yew wanna drink like a man, then yew act like a man, see? One word gits out an I'll know oo ter come lookin fer. So yew'd bedder keep it squat. Goddit?"

His voice belying his words, Ben said: "I ent afraid o' yew, Ned Pitts. Yew might come lookin, though I'm surprised yew can see anythin' wi' those little yeller eyes o' yourn; but yew'll 'ave ter ketch me first!" Somehow, he evaded the intended crushing blow from Pitts' gorilla-like arm, dived beneath the table, wormed his way among the muddle of boots, spit and sawdust and rushed out of the inn.

Thompson made his escape undercover of the ensuing turmoil, satisfied that his evening had not been wasted.

★

The reason for Dulcie Brook's visit had been stated once everybody had calmed down after Noah's twizzle. Agnes and Mary Emma had taken the boy off to find him something dry to wear under his long dress. This was most opportune as Dulcie had wanted to see Tom alone.

"I dew 'ope yew won't mind me callin unannounced – which Agnes says is very bad manners – but it's about our John, Mr Challiss."

"He's not ill, Mrs Brooks? Anything I can do?"

Dulcie closed her eyes and batted the air at the foolish idea of one of her children falling ill. "Nothin like that, sir. In some ways, I wish it was somethin that could be ser easily put right. If I thought a dose o' caster oil would dew the trick my troubles with the boy would be over."

"You must tell me all about it presently, ma'am," Tom said solicitously, unaware that he was about to be given a free course in parenting an obstinate child. "First, please allow me to offer you something hot to drink. What do you fancy?"

"Oh! That's very kind of you, sir. If it ent too much trouble, a nice cuppa

Indian would be most welcome, Mr Challiss. I can see why our Agnes is so 'appy to be livin in sich luxury," she said, in a matter a fact way, as if she were discussing the price of flour. "Yew dew 'ave a master lot of wonderful an beautiful things. Must take an awful lot o' lookin after," she added, taking an inventory of the room with a competent housewife's judicious eye.

Tom smiled at her guileless praise as he tugged the bell sash and ordered tea and biscuits for two from Peckover. "Now, Mrs Brook; what is it that's troubling you?"

"Well, Mr Challiss, it's like this..." The gist of her recital was that eleven-year-old John Brook was making a thorough nuisance of himself and upsetting his younger siblings because he refused to accept nine-year-old Ann's 'jurisdiction' over him during their daily lessons. He had reached the stage of flatly refusing to undertake any work Ann prepared for him and had declared to his overtaxed mother that he was too old for book-learning and 'girls' stuff', such as drawing, weaving and studying natural history. When asked by his mother how he intended to spend his idle mornings, the boy's eyes had brightened. He would get a job.

"I ask yew, Mr Challiss, with most every man in Downham thrown on the mercy o' the Parish, where dew 'e think a boy oo knows nothing is goin ter find employment? I've no right tew ask, sir – Agnes would die o' shame if she knew I was even thinkin o' sich a thing – but if you could spare a moment to put yer mind ter the problem... I doan wanna worry Mr Brook with it; 'tis a mother's place to make certin her children keep on the straight an narrow."

"I see," Tom said, finding himself absolutely at a loss by the thorny problem that had tumbled into his lap without warning. "What d'you think he might be capable of doing?"

Dulcie's face fell. "Well... That's why I come ter yer, sir. 'E can't do nothin much, 'cept feedin' chickens or fetchin' water—"

"Capital!" Tom shouted, as Peckover brought in the refreshments before retiring discreetly. "A boy who can fetch water is the very servant we need at Uppham, Mrs Brook."

Dubiously, she said: "Yew *sure*, sir?" Distractedly, she poured two cups of tea.

"Why, it's absolutely providential, ma'am!" Tom said, accepting his tea. "Thank you. Tell me: is he able to chop wood and perhaps run errands?"

She replaced her cup in its saucer, thoughtfully. "'E can run errands, acourse; but I dunno as I would like ter think of 'im usin' an axe, sir. No. I definitely shouldn't like our John ter be usin' an axe, Mr Challiss. I can't agree ter that."

"Oh, that's a pity," Tom said, thinking only of Mrs Hignell's needs.

Aware that a God-given chance of settling her wayward son was slipping away, the anxious woman said: "'E's only a small boy, Mr Challiss. 'E can't be expected ter dew a man's work, not jist yet." She sipped her tea absentmindedly.

Thinking of his own boyhood, Tom respected her cautious, motherly attitude. "No, of course not, ma'am. You're quite right. Well . . . we will have to wait for him to grow a little older before we pile work that's too much for him onto his shoulders."

"Oh! There!" Carefully, she replaced her empty cup in its saucer and continued to stare into its depths as if she saw there a lost opportunity. "Thank yew all the same fer your kind offer, Mr Challiss—"

"Mrs Brook," Tom said gently. "John may fetch water for Mrs Hignell, if he wants to, for three shillings a week. The old lady's finding it hard to fend for herself. Her previous lodger kept her in kindling and fetched water from the pump for her each each morning. Never mind. I'll see that somebody else does that for her."

Dulcie's face lit up with joy. "Oh! But, sir… Our John can chop *kindlin'*. I thought yew meant cuttin' down trees an' the like; I see the labourers at work on the noo garden, an' I thought… Oh, sir! John will be pleased and ole Mrs 'Ignell's place is so 'andy, tew. Oh, 'twill be good fer the boy tew find 'imself useful."

"How will Mr Brook take it?" Tom said, with genuine interest.

"Never mind Adam, sir," she said. "'E'll agree that it's fer the best in the long run."

Young John Brook was overjoyed when he heard that he had been released from petticoat tyranny and was halfway to becoming a working man. Adam Brook had put in his pennyworth, more to show that he was head of the family than for any genuine objection to his young son's desire for independence, but, as Dulcie had forecast, he made no difficulty once he'd seen that John was keen as mustard to start earning his own living.

Everett Pawl and John Brook grew accustomed to encountering each other in the mornings as they made their separate ways to their employment. Before long, Everett was touching his hat, or nodding, to greet the boy and John would respond with a cheery "Good-mornin', sir!" even when it wasn't. In that way they forged an acquaintance which was anticipated each day with mutual warmth and interest.

★

One wet day in January 1816 Tom came home to a new sound in the house. After a hard day of overseeing the various projects that he had set in motion around the estate he was weary indeed; yet as soon as he stepped across the threshold he realised that the atmosphere of his home had changed for the better. He stood in the front hall in his dripping redingote as if bewitched, spellbound. Music! Muffled by distance, a sweet voice rose and fell to the accompaniment of a skilfully played keyboard. He shook his head in an effort to banish the alluring melody to assure himself that he wasn't imagining the phenomenon. No, it was real. Enchantment drifted down to the hall from the front withdrawing room and made him aware that an essential part of himself had, until this moment, been dormant for months.

The charming combination of exquisite harmonies underlying the silver purity of the voice rinsed his grateful ears like a reviving shower upon drought. The charm spread through his tired body and exhausted spirit until it reached and calmed his heart. Not since his sojourn in his uncle's house at Escalles had his spirit been so moved. Harmonious, sweet music – such as the more melodious and beautiful Christian hymns – could stir his sluggish soul, had the power to sooth, to restore his serenity. Some quality within himself had desiccated among a desert of harassing problems. It was as if his body had withered into tasteless dried meat and had been revived by a delicious marinade of oil, wine, vinegar and herbs. This jumble of thoughts and emotions sped through him, reached the extremeties of his mind and body in the seconds that had elapsed between his coming in and the ending of the few bars of the song he'd heard. Merely to say that he had been profoundy moved by the experience would be a travesty of a description of the transformation that he had undergone.

The spell broken, he shivered, discovered that he was wet, cold, dirty and hungry and went in search of dryness, warmth, cleanliness and sustenance. Only then would he allow himself to discover the identity of the person responsible for the introduction of culture into his home: but, of course, he already had a very good idea who that person might be.

He was wrong. As he entered the room the talented musician, her back to the open door, was playing something that Tom guessed was from the previous century. Expecting to find Agnes Brook busy at the keyboard, he was taken aback to discover that, not only was Agnes nowhere to be seen, but the figure that occupied the piano stool belonged to Mrs Aldrich. Unaware of his presence, she performed with bravura the intricate piece which seemed to Tom to consist mainly of fluent and rapid runs up and down the keyboard interspersed with dazzling displays of sparkling showers of notes. After a repeated pattern of notes which were executed in a descending order, Ruth Aldrich finished the piece with two ascending fistfuls of keys, whose rich sound reminded Tom of a trumpet flourish and which were followed by both hands plunging to the lowest notes on the keyboard in the form of a rhythmic full stop. Involuntarily, Tom applauded.

Ruth spun round on the stool, her eyes wide with surprise. "Why, Mr Challiss! How long have you been standing there listening? I thought I had the room to myself."

"Long enough to recognise that you are a great proficient on the keyoard, Mrs Aldrich. That was simply splendid. What was it?"

Though her usually pale cheeks were flushed by the exertion that had been necessary to perform the piece she had just finished, Ruth replied calmly: "The last movement of one of Mozart's sonatas. Did you like it?"

" 'Like' is not the word I would choose, Mrs Aldrich. It was a superb display. Where on earth did you learn to play like that?" As an afterthought, he stared at the smart new instrument. "By Gad! Where did that spring from? It certainly wasn't here last evening."

Ruth Aldrich was provoked to laughter. "Oh, Mr Challiss! What a droll thing to say. You didn't suppose that I was making all that noise without a pianoforte? Isn't it a beauty?"

"D'ye mean to say the thing belongs to us? Must've cost a pretty penny, I'll wager." He had a vague memory of Mary Emma mentioning something about a getting a piano... something to do with Agnes Brook?

"Well, I didn't bring it with me," Ruth said, seating herself on a sofa. "It arrived this morning and your wife invited me to try it out. It's a splendid instrument. One of Erard's latest manufacture. I've never played on anything better."

"I had no idea that you were such an accomplished musician, Mrs Aldrich," Tom said, his eyes sparkling. "We must have a... um... *soirée*. The house hasn't been christened properly yet. Yes! We'll make it into a party, invite our friends."

"Really, Tom?" Mary Emma cried as she wandered into the room followed by Agnes. "Oh, how simply wonderful! When? Oh, Tom! How do you like our new grand pianoforte? Isn't 'grand' the right name for it? And doesn't Ruth perform splendidly?"

Kissing his wife on the cheek, Tom smiled at her fondly. "Which question would you like me to answer first, my dear?" Even Agnes managed to smile at that. Before they had time to discuss the wonderful new acquisition further, the dinner gong reverberated up the stairwell and Tom escorted his bevy into dinner where, to his great delight he found that Joe Aldrich and Everett Pawl had joined them.

★

From his viewpoint behind a mature oak that stood in the area of thicket outside the newly demarcated lime walk, Clem Rix had watched the comings and goings of the inhabitants of the mansion all afternoon. For his vigil he'd donned a sheepskin jacket and tied a muffler over his felt hat and the lower half of his face, hoping to keep out the deathly cold that gripped him in his immobility, and that the muffler would also help to mask his identity.

In his deep pockets he carried, besides part of a loaf and a hunk of cheese, various components of an incendiary nature. He stamped his feet and blew on his fingers to get his chilled blood back into circulation and began to feel more cheerful as daylight faded and lights appeard in various windows of the watched house. His awareness that a fortune had been spent on the mansion's refurbishment added relish to the deed that Clem Rix planned. He'd heard from Jem Webster that water closets had been installed about the interior of the mansion: fancy affairs, with prettily patterned porcelain bowls, that had a special bend so that they didn't stink in the rooms. Finnickin lot! Resentment against the jumped-up Challisses and those he considered their toadies had its origin in several slights, real or imagined, and burned fiercely within his breast. Since his dismissal from the post of Uppham's shepherd, and the discovery of his involvement in the poaching of several animals from the flock he had been hired to guard, while he waited to take his revenge he had hidden in the roof of his uncle's shop, emerging only by night – until this dark January day.

The fools! Rix thought contemptuosly, as he began to assemble his crude incendiary device. Think themselves safe from the troubles affectin us oo live beyond Upham's gates, dew they. Fair sickens me ter think o' the money that's bin poured inter tricolatin yon 'ouse, an better folks than them starvin all over the country for the want of money ter buy bread. Need a lesson, that lot dew.

Undercover of the moonless night, he crept towards the west wing of the house, the front room of which had been lighted until a short while ago and was now in darkness. That Jem had been engaged in some sort of carpentry in the room Rix was approaching had been clearly obvious from his observations of the afternoon. He was under no illusion that his simple apparatus was capable of burning down the entire mansion; his intention was to frighten the Challisses. He cursed the rain, and snarled at the absence of wind, both of which would work against his scheme. His device ready, he crept up to one of the sectioned windows and picked up a rock that glinted wetly in the light thrown down from an upper window. Wrapping one end of his muffler around the hand that held the rock, he waited for a sound to mask the breaking of glass. It came in the form of a roomful of men and women's laughter.

By the time the laughter had died away one small pane had been smashed. So far so good. Rix had trouble igniting the flint he'd borrowed from his uncle without the latter's knowledge. He knelt down over the tin box, made a screen out of his coat front, produced a spark among the lint and stood up with the glowing firetin sheltered inside his coat. Fishing in his right pocket for a small glass bottle stuffed with an oil-soaked rag, from which hung a tongue of cotton that had been previously drenched in whale oil, with a couple of swift movements Rix dropped the burning tinder onto the crude wick and flung the flaming bottle into the library. He didn't wait to see the effect of his act but sped away into the black night, over the rainsoftened earth of the new garden, across the rough grass to the west of the house, down between the two lines of spindly lime saplings, through a hole in the perimeter fence and out into the lane, as if his green eyes could penetrate the darkness with the skill of a cat's.

★

"... but, supposing we were to meet up for dinner at the end of the day, Adam? What then?" Tom asked, as the men downed their claret in one and Peckover replenished their empty glasses.

Adam Brook, Jem Webster and Kit Warrender – who had arrived at the house soon after the end of dinner when the ladies had withdrawn to leave Tom, Joe and Everett to their drinks and cigars – had been prevailed upon to take a glass of wine as they talked business. The gardener shook his head in response to Tom's suggestion. "Dulcie wou'n't wear it, bor. Come ter that, nor would I want 'er tew. My place is wi' me fam'ly of an evenin at the end of an 'ard workin' day, come summer or winter. Any'ow, I don't 'old wi' mixin' bus'niss an pleasure – an me dinner is one of me chiefest pleasures these days, 'specially if my Dulcie's made it. Sorry, Tom... beggin' yer pardon, sir... Mr Challiss; yew'll 'ave ter dew wi'out me."

This was a great disappointment to Tom. "I understand, Adie. You're a family man; wife and family must come before any other consideration. Still, I won't pretend I'm overjoyed at your decision. What do the rest of you have to say?"

Nobody wanted to be the first to speak. To fill the embarrassing silence Everett said: "I'm afraid I shall be present for the foreseeable future, Mr Challiss."

"Your presence is taken for granted, Everett," Tom said impatiently. "I meant my question to be directed at the estate servants." His full grey eyes searched the faces of Joe, Jem and Kit, who evaded his gaze by various means.

"Forgive me, Mr Challiss," Joe Aldrich's bass voice broke the awkward silence. "Speaking entirely for myself, you understand: Mr Brook's sentiments mirror my own. At the close of a long day one begins to anticipate a few hours relaxation in one's own home which, especially in the summer months, are sadly all too few. We have our women-folk to consider, sir. You wouldn't wish us to neglect our wives and..." Here he yelped and seemed to be taken with a choking fit as he bent down to rub his ankle.

"Is there something I should know about?" Tom asked, his irritation rising as the meeting veered away from the direction he wished it to follow.

Nobody enlightened him. Instead, Kit Warrender reddened and blurted out: "'Tis very good of you, sir, to have thought out this plan, but... pleasant as it would be to take our dinner in this spanking new dining room, I mean – " He broke off and mutely appealed to the others to help him out.

"I think what Kit's tryin' ter spit out," Jem Webster said quietly, "is that we all appreciate the sentiments be'ind your idea, Mr Challiss; but there ain one of us thinks it'll 'elp ter run the estate any better than if we was ter continew ter take our suppers at' ome, like always."

Seeing his master's face take on the aspect of a particularly dark thundercloud, Aldrich attempted to throw oil on troubled waters. "You see, sir," he said tentatively, "the estate is not so vast that we won't see one another during the day – "

"You mean," Tom said, beside himself with repressed anger, "that you're prepared to carry on in the old hit-and-miss way! Well, gentlemen, understand this: should I discover that any man here is attempting to pull the wool over my eyes he'll find himself looking for other employment pretty damned quick."

Jem was affronted by his bullying tone. "I dunno why yew should take on so, Mr Challiss," he said. "There's none but honest men in this room. Yew doan know when yew'm well orf, sir. Why not leave us ter git on with the jobs you're payin us ter dew? When we 'ave anythin ter discuss, we'll come ter yer an discuss it at the time."

Joseph Aldrich relaxed and leaned his back against his dining chair. "Jem's right, Mr Challiss, sir. The present system works pretty well, although I'm bound to agree with you that it is – er – flexible, even... as you say yourself, of a hit-and-miss nature. Nevertheless, the work gets done fairly efficiently, I think you'll find, Mr Challiss, sir. Might I be so bold as to enquire, sir, if you have had occasion for complaint, in the way of progress or quality of work, concerning any of the projects you have given us to complete?"

Tom was dumfounded. Here was a new Aldrich indeed; one who had the confidence to challenge his master's rule! "Well, sir; you don't mince your words. Since you ask, I am bound to admit that everything seems to be going on as well as can be expected, considering the time of the year –"

For an instant everyone froze at the urgent clanging of the recently installed fire bell; the dinner gong's brassy shiver was added to the bell's busy metal tongue a second later. The men, immediately alert, scrambled up from their seats and followed Tom who reached the door as it opened and Rudge's face loomed in the aperture. His usual calm ruffled, the manservant – who, it seemed, had sprinted upstairs – puffed out his message: "Fire in the library, sir. Maddy's run to the stables... to see if Will and Ben Wright are still there... get them to start the bucket chain."

Mary Emma, Ruth and Agnes leaned over the balustrade and watched wide-eyed as the men ran towards the library and Tom called up to the women to remain where they were. They heard Jem Webster shout: "DON'T OPEN THE LIBRARY DOOR!", and watched as the men turned in a body to follow the carpenter out of the front door and into the wet night.

★

Chapter Thirty-five

Soon after the end of dinner the ladies had withdrawn to leave Tom, Joe and Everett to their drinks and cigars. They were now in the front withdrawing room and Mary Emma rang for tea to be brought. A decanter of wine stood on a three-legged table, within easy reach of the women's chairs, along with a jug of water and another of lemon cordial. The three friends made themselves comfortable near enough to the fire to feel its warmth without the danger of its spoiling their complexions and, after a few inconsequential remarks had been tossed back and forth, Mary Emma decided it was time to pluck up the courage to enable her to broach a delicate subject.

While the others continued to sip their tea from dainty bone china cups, she replaced her own cup in its saucer without a sound and said: "Ruth, there's something I've been meaning to ask you for some time, dear." She looked at Agnes as if a question had occurred to her but then seemed to decide against asking it. "It's of rather a delicate nature, Agnes. I should hate to embarrass you, my dear."

Smiling at her friend over the rim of her cup, the young woman said: "I daresay I shall be able to stand it, Mary Emma. Pretend I'm not here."

Ruth's sweet face had looked all concern at her young friend's opening statement. "Tell me at once what it is that's worrying you, Mary Emma," she said. "Has it to do with your condition? You're not losing blood?"

"How perceptive you are, dear Ruth," Mary Emma said. "It does have something to do with my condition. But... perhaps not in the way you imagine. Oh, dear! I am finding this most awkward. So embarrassing –"

"There is nothing you can say to me – or ask me – that will embarrass me, my dear; put that out of your mind. We are all women here, a sisterhood; two of you are about to become mothers. Let us speak unashamedly and frankly to one another and help each other in those matters that I've known doctors sometimes find it difficult to put into plain English."

"Oh, Ruth," Mary Emma said, "you are such a comfort. And yet I hardly know..."

"Has it to do with your husband's attentions, my dear?" the former nurse asked gently.

"I don't believe it! How could you possibly know that?" Mary Emma asked, her eyes wide with surprise.

"I am a nurse, Mary Emma, and have nursed women – and men – in all sorts of conditions. Women have confided in me, aware that I would respect any confidences they divulged. Such trust has provided me with a store of useful knowledge. It is more than likely that yours will reveal itself to be a problem common among pregnant women with demanding husbands. Am not I right?"

"You are a marvel, Ruth! It is that very problem that –" her face became suffused with a rosy blush but she stumbled on "Tom... that I... Forgive me. I cannot bring myself to utter the necessary words."

Ruth smiled understandingly. "Shall I try, my dear? It is plain to all who come into contact with you that you and Mr Challiss are very much in love with one another. It is only natural that you should both wish to express that love in its most intimate, God-given form. You have an urgent need to become one, to copulate, which is the purpose of marriage, after all. Being so lately married, your desire for one another is insatiable. Am I right thus far?"

"It's incredible!" Mary Emma cried, her cheeks aflame as she glanced at Agnes who, she noticed, seemed to be accepting everything she heard with aplomb. "Please go on, Ruth. We haven't reached the point that troubles me... us."

"I'm coming to that, my dear. I want you to understand that all that you have experienced so far is perfectly natural and almost universal," the nurse said in her low voice. "I should perhaps observe that we human beings are of a higher order than the beasts of the field. Copulation for its own sake is nothing more than lust in action. Lust, as you are aware I think, is the fourth of the seven deadly sins. Animals have the need to propagate their species, to breed, just as we have. We cannot know what an animal experiences during its mating process. However, human beings have been given divine knowledge of what men in their wisdom have called love."

Agnes surprised the other two by interrupting. "Yet, Mrs Aldrich, men and women may experience deep and moving emotions for one another before... copulation, may they not?"

Ruth bestowed a warm smile upon the young expectant mother. "For many innocent women, that is the purest, loveliest form of love between men and women, my dear. Sadly, the physical side of marriage comes as a dreadful shock to them, particularly if their wedding night is the first intimation of it."

"How terrible that must be!" Mary Emma exclaimed.

"Indeed it must," said Ruth. "When such innocent women – or ignorant girls, if you will – come by carnal knowledge for the first time and realise that this violation – for that is what some ignorant virgins consider their husband's demands upon them to be – will be perpetrated upon them, night after night, into that inescapable, interminable future called marriage, they are driven to commit the ultimate crime."

"The ultimate crime?" questioned Mary Emma.

"Why, self-murder, suicide," Ruth said solemnly. "Goodness! This will never do!" she said brightly. "We must not get onto morbid subjects, my dears. To return to your original question, Mary Emma. You are, perhaps, wondering for how much longer you should continue conjugal relations whilst in your present condition. Is that it?"

"Exactly, Ruth," Mary Emma said, happy that the problem was out in the open at last. Tom... and I... is... are worried that we might harm the unborn child."

"Nature would not be so careless," Ruth said, with a twinkle in her eye. "You have probably begun to experience some discomfort now that the child is enlarging within the womb. Now might be the time to adopt a different position for the reception of your husband's member. His weight on your abdomen is worrying you both. So, adopt another position, my dear. Try lying on your side. Penetration will not be so deep; but you still will be able to afford your husband comfort in his need. There is no necessity to deny him. And his closeness to you at this time is a wonderful way of sharing the advent of birth that involves both parents."

"Good heavens, Ruth," Mary Emma said, her eyes shining with gratitude, "you have absolutely no difficulty in putting delicate matters into plain words, have you! I should be absolutely ashamed to utter such intimate physical terms out loud – "

For an instant everyone froze at the urgent clanging of the fire bell, followed almost at once by the reverberations of the dinner gong and shouts of "Fire!"

Mary Emma, Ruth and Agnes ran out onto the landing, leaned over the balustrade and saw the men rush from the dining room towards the library. "Stay where you are, ladies!" Tom called up to them. Somebody shouted a warning not to open the library door, before the men turned back and ran out of the front door.

"Do you think we shall be safe up here?" Mary Emma asked anxiously. "Suppose the fire should spread and we were to find ourselves cut off from rescue?"

"I can smell smoke," Agnes said, leaning out over the balustrade; "but I can't see any flames at all. It's probably best to do as Mr Challiss said."

"I think you are right, Miss Brook," Ruth Aldrich agreed calmly before leading the way back to the withdrawing room to continue the absorbing subject of married love, pregnancy and childbirth.

Mary Emma drew their attention to the drinks table and the three women filled their glasses with cordial and sat down again to await developments.

★

An hour passed. At the end of that period Rudge appeared, once more restored to his customary stately demeanour, to inform them that the fire had been extinguished and that the library, though badly damaged, had been saved.

"Oh, no!" Mary Emma wailed. "My beautiful library! Jem had all but finished the fitting of the shelves."

"Was anyone injured in trying to put out the fire, Mr Rudge?" Agnes asked.

"Yes," Ruth said, "I was about to ask the same thing. Does anybody down there need my help, Rudge?"

The man pushed his lips forward and shook his head dismissively. "Nothing untoward, madam. Mr Aldrich and Webster have sustained minor burns to their hands, I believe. That is all, madam. If I may, Mrs Challiss: Mr Challiss wishes you to go to him. He is waiting for you in the dining room."

"Of course, Rudge. I'll come directly."

"I will accompany you, Mrs Challiss," Ruth said. "I'd like to take a look at those burns. Please excuse me, Agnes."

"Oh, may I not come with you, Mrs Aldrich?" Miss Brook pleaded. "There must be something I can do to help."

Too late, it was borne upon Mary Emma's conscience that, while her friends' thoughts had immediately been for others' needs, hers had been for something materialistic that concerned mainly herself and she felt ashamed of her selfishness. "Of course," she said. "By all means. Let us all go and see in what way we can make ourselves useful. Though I imagine that Rudge, Peckover and Maddy will have got there before us."

As soon as the three women made their appearance at the door of the damaged library, Tom strode up to them. "What are you doing here?" he asked.

"There is nothing for you to do and you will be in the way of the men."

Ignoring his rebuff, and holding out her right hand, Ruth Aldrich demanded calmly: "Your hands, please. Mr Challiss."

As if he were a small boy, he obediently held out his hands, palms upwards while at the same time protesting: "All this fuss! I tell you it's nothing, Ruth."

She examined first one hand and then the other. "These are badly blistered. They need attention, sir. Please come with me and I'll attend to them directly. Rudge mentioned that Mr Webster's hands are burned also."

"Damn the man for a meddling fool," Tom said peevishly. "There remains much to do here, madam, and I'd be obliged if you and my wife would take your selves out of the way."

"Tom! Please keep a civil tongue in your head!" Mary Emma said sharply. "You have absolutely no right to speak to Mrs Aldrich so rudely. She is a guest in our house, sir."

"I beg your pardon, Mrs Aldrich," Tom said, "but, for your own good, will you please go! And take Mrs Challiss with you."

"Very well, Mr Challiss," Ruth said with a sweet smile. "I am happy to do as you request, for I see that my services are no longer needed."

Mystified by her sudden change of demeanour, Tom turned to speak to Joe and saw that Agnes Brook, as she had passed the linen press upstairs, had snatched up a pillowcase and was busily tearing it into bandages. Worse, Jem Webster was meekly standing before the pretty young woman waiting to have his burns dressed.

Seeing that Mr Challiss was looking at her rather irately, Agnes said: "I hate to ask you, sir, when you are already so busy here; but might I prevail upon your good nature? I would be most obliged if you would have the goodness to go to the kitchen and fetch a quantity of flour. A basinful should be sufficient, Mr Challiss. Thank you, sir."

Dumbfounded by the girl's audacity – he persisted in thinking of Agnes Brook as a girl – Tom clamped his lips together and swallowed the oath that threatened to break forth, turned on his heel and strode from the room.

The remaining men eyed each other with amusement and Mr Brook said to his daughter: "That told him. But it aint your place ter tell the master of Uppham tew run yer errands, me girl. Still, he'll thank yer fer it termorrer. If he doan, 'e's less of a gennelman than I give 'im credit fer."

Jem was tongue-tied. But Kit Warrender championed Agnes. "You're a proper managing little woman, Miss Brook. You'll make some young man a good wife one o' these days, I shouldn't wonder. Wish my hands weren't burnt and bandaged already, just so that I could have the pleasure of havin' 'em treated by such a pretty nurse."

To Agnes's relief, Tom chose that moment to return bringing with him an enormous mixing bowl full of flour. Somehow she managed to keep a straight face and, taking the bowl from him, said: "I am obliged to you, Mr Challiss. Thank you, sir. I'll be as quick as I can and then I'll be out of your way."

Having had time to review the matter, Tom had admitted to himself that the women had deserved better treatment than he had meted out. "It's very good of you, Agnes. I see now that the three of you intended only to be kind and I humbly apologise for my rudeness." To Aldrich, he observed: "Your charming wife was absolutely right, Joe; it's only sensible to take precautions. Please convey my apologies to her for my ungentlemanly behaviour."

"That will not be necessary, Mr Challiss, I assure you," the little steward said with winning grace.

While the carpenter's heart thudded in his broad chest, Agnes floured his blackened and blistered hands with the cool and dry powdered grain, and finished by bandaging them neatly with linen strips. Tom saw that the girl knew what she was about and consented without a fuss to undergo the same treatment which, after all, was no hardship; on the contrary, he found that the simple remedy soothed his burned hands amazingly. Such a small quantity of flour had been used, after all, that he wondered why on earth Miss Brook had asked for a bowlful. Strange creatures, women, he thought as he joined the others in putting the library to rights.

★

The damage to the library at Uppham House paled into insignificance as news found its way to Uppham St Mary over the following days. It consisted of reports of countrywide machine-breaking, tales of millers being injured by starving mobs who robbed them of their grain and flour, stories nearer to home of the plunder of potato cleats and other food stores and, perhaps the most frightening news of all, widespread rick burning. It was a salutary lesson. For without fodder how would the valuable animals on the gentry's farms survive the winter? The idea that the gentry considered animals of greater value than human beings and that beasts were better fed than themselves or their wives and children drove the starving men to desperation. Desperate men take desperate measures. The starving labourers, a term that included redundant soldiers and sailors who continued to swell – and to their consternation found themselves among – the evergrowing numbers of the unemployed, were beginning to organise and to take into their own hands the matter of their right to exist as *men* – as opposed to some species seen by those in every class above them as on a par with the beasts of the field but who might be treated with less consideration than their dumb friends. For the majority of animals had winter shelter, which was more than could be said for many of the homeless labourers. The Poor House beckoned and was resisted until there was no alternative but to enter its hated doors.

But these desperate measures were viewed by those in power as lawless pursuits and the gentry stiffened their resolve to repress the men further. Laws became more stringent and penalties became unduly severe, in proportion to the lightness of the offences committed, with the intention of making examples of the 'criminals' who got caught because of bad luck or their own carelessness. Poachers and rioters were considered some of the worst offenders and severe punishments were meted out to them.

★

As if the conditions of the poor were not already bad enough, the south-easterly wind changed direction overnight to be replaced by a strong north-easterly which soon made its unwelcome presence felt among those without proper food or shelter. The savage wind scoured the flat landscape, whipping topsoil from farmland and shredding any tender plants that had had the temerity to show their heads. For its final test of strength against the starving labourers the wind drove before its icy breath rain, sleet and snow. At first, the snow floated prettily down in large soft flakes. The whey-faced children of the poor were reminded of happier times and played with the beautiful but potentially deadly snowflakes. With their bare hands the labourers' children formed into balls handfuls of the treacherous white substance that would take many lives that winter. Snowmen stood on the green in Uppham St Mary.

It grew colder. The east wind was relentless as it screamed around the cottages, hovels and makeshift shacks of the poor, silently covering every surface with a white pall. Soon, the labourers' families had almost nothing to eat, nothing to burn, little to wear. Eventually, every stick of furniture had been burned or sold or bartered for food.

Ill-health, starvation, death and a sense of utter hopelessness of improving their lot, had the beaten labourers and their families clamouring to be taken into the detested Poor House. Lines of thinly-clad and emaciated people, their few belongings long gone could, with truth, demonstrate that they were destitute. That they had been reduced to this shameful state by circumstances beyond their control was humiliating enough. But it was this very state of having been reduced to abject poverty that provided them with the only passport for entry into the workhouse.

Clem and Ben Rix, Ned Pitt, and others who met regularly at the *Queen's Head*, were determined to avoid such a fate and laid their plans accordingly.

★

Their reasoning was simple: Sir Everard Belmaine had too much and they had too little and it was their intention to even things up. The rich provided an example: take what you want. To that end, they huddled around their chosen table in the *Queen's Head* on the Friday night of the week following the burning of the library at Uppham House. His piggy eyes having probed the dusky corners of the room, Ned Pitts was satisfied that nobody of a suspicious nature lurked among the shadows.

"Remember ter keep yer voices down," Pitts whispered. He had appointed himself the men's leader though he was, perhaps, the one among them with the dullest brain. A blacksmith by trade, Pitts had gained ascendancy over the group because he possessed not only the greatest strength, but also the skill to fashion out of metal ingenious and delicate traps and springs like nobody else in the vicinity. Moreover, his livelihood was secure in that anybody who used a horse required his services and that included almost everybody above the class of labourer. Pitts had a gargantuan appetite for food and was in the unusual situation of being able to satisfy it. Had anybody taken the trouble to question his Friday night drinking cronies they would have discovered that not one among them liked the massive bully. He was tolerated only because he was wealthy and useful to them: he paid for their drinks and made the devices that were necessary for poaching. As the men were, for the most part, penniless, he was paid in kind. Food being to him a passion, Pitts was content to take the fruits of their poaching as payment for his labours on their behalf.

"Sat'dey night at bull's moon, it is, then," Clem Rix mumbled. "I'll take the 'Ome Wood, as agreed. An I doan wanna see any o' yew lot nowhere near it, see?"

"Why would we?" Ben Rix said, forgetting to whisper, whereupon he felt a painful blow to his shin and received a baleful stare from the yellow-eyed blacksmith. "Give over!" the lad complained in a pained whisper. "I ent goin' nowhere near 'Ome Wood 'cause I got bedder pickins waitin' fer me somewhere else." He looked smug.

His brother leaned closer. "Yew'd bedder tell us where, Ben; we doan wanna be doublin' up, does us."

Ben said defiantly: "I reckon Belmaine's keepers're gonna be on the lookout all over Martlits. I ent no ole sawney; I ent goin' there."

"Stop skywannickin' an spit it out, or I'll lam inter yer with this," whispered Pitts, flourishing a huge fist. "Yew're jist the kinda ickeny young bugger to land us all in gaol. Ent got no more sense than a rainbird."

"All I know is," Ben whispered back, "that I ent agoin' nowhere near *yew* – yer fumble-fisted dardledumdew. *Yore* the one's gonna git us inter bother wi' the magistrates, Pitts. If yew went poachin', yew 'd be 'eard pruggin' about fer miles around."

"Fer Gawd's sake stop yer branglin' an answer me this," Jacob Coy whispered to Ben. "Is yew gonna be roamin' about Belmaine's istate, or int yer?"

"No, I ent," Ben whispered back.

"Reckon that's all we need ter know, bors," Coy mumbled. "Ser long as the young varmint ent nowhere near us, we'm safe enough, I reckon." He picked up his tankard and, draining it, looked hopefully at Ned Pitts.

"Termorrer night, bull's moon, it is, then," Clem Rix affirmed softly; and in an aside to his young brother muttered: "An if'n yew'm plannin' ter lift a ewe from Uppham istate yew'd best fergit it, bor. 'Eard Challiss took on a noo shepherd – one oo doan sleep night nor day, keeps a silent dawg wi' 'im. Yew'd best look out, Ben"

"That ent nowt but a roment," the lad scoffed. "Stands ter reason: everyone's gotta fall asleep sometime, Clem, even a dawg. Any'ow, I got me own ways o' geddin' dawgs ter sleep. I'll jist bide me time, see?"

★

"It was indeed a mercy that the library was empty of books, Mrs Challiss," Everett Pawl agreed as he and Mary Emma sat over the breakfast table after Tom had excused himself. "Annis has made a beautiful job of rebinding the volumes on archeology, ma'am. Superb craftsmanship and a joy to handle. Daily, I count my blessings. Daily! I cannot thank you and Mr Challiss enough for rescuing me from what might have been my lot in life. I refer, of course, to the digging of graves until I was beyond digging my own, Mrs Challiss, ma'am."

"You have more than proved our choice a wise one, Mr Pawl," Mary Emma said, sipping a third cup of tea. "But I can't help wishing that there hadn't been that setback with returning the books to their proper home. I am impatient to see the library restored to a glory it cannot have had for decades, if the state of the books and the shabby state of the room itself were anything to go by. I do wish there was some way of facilitating the repairs and the decorating. It all goes on so slowly. If only Jem were not such a perfectionist."

"I cannot believe you would be content with anything less, ma'am," Pawl smiled, as he helped himself to another slice of wafer thin wheaten loaf and pared a sliver of cheese. "If I might make a suggestion?"

"Anything – as long as it has to do with speeding the work on the library."

"I've had my eye on young John Brook, Mrs Challiss. From what I have observed, he's a bright lad and would benefit from being apprenticed to a trade. If not, I fear he will drift into an insecure life as a itinerant casual agricultural labourer."

Surprised to discover that Pawl even knew of the boy's existence, Mary Emma asked: "Do you mean Miss Brook's young brother?"

"The same. He and I exchange a greeting each morning as we take ourselves to our employment –"

"Employment? Young John?" Mary Emma exclaimed. "Why, he can't be more than eleven years old! Do you mean to tell me he's earning his own living already?"

"Hardly that, ma'am; though many boys – and girls – four years, or more, younger than he, are put to work in the cotton mills of the north. No. John's work consists of supplying Mrs Hignell, who has sadly become incapacitated, with water and wood each morning as well as running a few errands for the old lady. To return to my suggestion, Mrs Challiss, if I may?"

"Of course, go on. What is it you have in mind?" Mary Emma's brain raced ahead. "Apprentice him to Jem Webster!" Doubtfully, she shook her head. "More time would be wasted by Jem's explaining to the boy what to do. It would drag things out even longer, I'm sure."

"The boy is observant, Mrs Challiss, as well as bright. While it's true that Mr Webster would be compelled to explain the art of carpentry to John eventually, that wouldn't be his immediate concern. The boy could assist him in many ways, lighten his load, so to speak, and thus leave Mr Webster to concentrate on the practical work."

"I begin to see," Mary Emma said, her enthusiasm for the idea growing. "We must consult Mr Challiss on the subject and also see what Jem has to say about it. It seems a good chance for John." She delicately dabbed her lips and laid aside her napkin. "Leave it with me, Mr Pawl, and I'll put your suggestion to Mr Challiss at the first opportunity."

★

A sickle moon glimmered feebly on the wintry landscape as Thompson left behind him the stale warmth and comfort that had been provided by the inn. He had heard all he needed to know long before the whispering group in the *Queen's Head* had broken up for the night and had made his escape as soon as he'd overheard Ben Rix's boast. As he trudged briskly through the newly-fallen snow, lighting his way to his lodgings in Uppham St Mary by means of his small lantern, he congratulated himself on the fact that such a piece of luck had fallen into his lap. He supposed that Mrs Hignell would have been in bed for some hours, as was her custom in the dark days of winter, and the man – whose true following was not strictly that of a gamekeeper yet similar to it in a way – let himself in as quietly as he could so as not to disturb her. In fact, he'd made the generous offer to oil the squeaking lock to the front door with such secrecy in mind, giving as the reason his assumed occupation, which necessitated the comings and goings at night in particular. Once he had one of the poachers in custody, it was Gil Thompson's intention to bag the rest of the gang. Not wanting to count his chickens too soon, he was elated, nevertheless, that his investigation had come to fruition so speedily and with his having had to expend so little effort. He couldn't remember when a case had given him so much ease or pleasure in its solution. Couldn't have been cosier at such a nasty time of the year, particularly in this God-forsaken part of the country, he thought. He chuckled to himself softly as he removed first his gaiters, then his stout boots, before throwing himself otherwise fully-dressed onto the narrow bed and dropping immediately into undisturbed slumber.

★

Tom had thought Everett Pawl's suggestion for the apprenticing of John Brook to Jem Webster a first-rate idea. "Though Jem can be touchy," he said to Mary Emma as they prepared to retire for the night. "I shall have to choose my words very carefully, especially as he's already under pressure to finish the restoration."

"That's my doing," Mary Emma said, presenting her back to him in order that he might unlace her stays. "I shall make Jem understand that it is our wish that he take on John but that he will find himself under no increased pressure if he agrees to do so." She removed her stays and laid them by. "Indeed, Tom, I shall request him to try to complete the shelving and painting in sections, so

428

that the newly bound volumes may be returned to the library as soon as they arrive from the bookbinder."

Tom had scarcely been paying attention to her. His eyes had settled on the discarded pair of stays and his face had taken on an expression of distaste.

Annoyed by his lack of response, Mary Emma faced him and asked: "What have I said that has so obviously caused your displeasure?"

"Eh? Oh, no; it's nothing you've said, my dear. Those." He pointed at her stays. "It surely cannot be good for the child you are carrying to constrict yourself. What has Ruth to say about it?"

"What should she have to say about it?" Mary Emma said peevishly. "It's none of her concern. You don't really expect me to go about unlaced, Tom?" She looked shocked.

He drew her into his arms. "I can think of nothing that would please me more, madam," he murmured against her hair as he held her softness against him. "You, Mary Emma are a bewitching little minx at any time of the day. But without those damned imprisoning stays you send my senses reeling with desire. Come to bed, love."

★

"Nobody axed *me* what *I* thought about it!" John Brook protested on having been told that he was to start as apprentice carpenter at Uppham House on the following Monday morning at eight o'clock. "I doan wanna be no carpenter."

As Dulcie wound a muffler about his neck and head prior to his going to see to Mrs Hignell's wants, she said: "Nobody axed yer 'cos yew'll dew as yore told, John Brook. Tain every day sich an oppertunity drops from the sky." And that was that.

★

As chance would have it, Tom Challiss decided to exercise Quicksilver through Home Wood at first light on the very Saturday fixed by Ben Rix for his poaching exploit at midnight, or bull's moon as he'd put it.

On entering the wood he found it unrecognisable: transformed into an enchanted otherplace. Drifting snow had filled hollows and every dark trunk bore a badgerlike white stripe on its north-facing side. Individual twigs brushed against the grey sky as white plumes, their undersides delicate charcoal lines. Stillness enveloped the hushed wood. No bird sang. Tom marvelled at the sense of tranquillity, the utter peace of it.

As he trotted Quicksilver into a tablesmooth, snowfilled glade he was confronted by the figure of Giles Ingleby as he broke through the far trees at speed. Quicksilver, startled by the sudden appearance of the man running straight at him across the glade, reared onto his back legs, neighed with terror and pawed the air. Showers of clodded snow rained from his hoofs and Tom had some difficulty in calming his excited mount. "What the devil are you doing here, frightening my horse?" Tom shouted angrily at Ingleby, as he struggled to settle the nervous Quicksilver.

"'Twas not my intention, Mr Challiss, I assure you," Ingleby laughed as he propped himself against the trunk of an oak and attempted to regain his breath. "I might as well accuse your damned great horse of frightening me, sir." His calm response took the wind out of Tom's sails.

"I suppose you are aware that you're trespassing, Ingleby, or Ollander – or whatever you're calling yourself today?" Tom said, still shaken by the shock of the encounter combined with wrestling to regain control of Quicksilver. "We've had trouble with poachers lately. Is that what you were up to?" he demanded, not for one minute supposing it to be the case.

Ignoring Tom's query, Ingleby said: "I apologise for making myself free of your woods, Mr Challiss. It might sound a lame one; but my excuse is that I fancied a ramble among the fresh fall of snow before it became sullied." He inhaled deeply. "Such a clean, unique smell newfallen snow has, don't you think?"

Must take me for a damned fool, Tom fumed. "Very plausible. However, I'll thank you for a more explicit account of your reason for making free of my wood when, as far as I was aware, you had taken yourself out of this area long ago."

Not at liberty to divulge the true reason for his presence in Home Wood, Ingleby thought rapidly and decided to bluff it out. "I agree," he smiled. "It sounds too silly for words, sir. But as a Londoner, a fresh fall of snow has a peculiar charm for me. Perhaps you've not seen what happens to snow in London, Mr Challiss? No sooner is the customary filth and soot obliterated by a clean, fresh fall than the London streets are as mucky as ever, with horse manure along every highway; and under pulverising hooves and wheels the snow soon becomes a stew of slush, mud, excrement, cabbage leaves – I leave it to your imagination, sir. Even the macadamised main thoroughfares are little better."

"Hmm," Tom said, as he patted Quicksilver's strong neck and detected the nervous thrill that continued to run along the beast's veins. "You don't strike me as a poor man's Wordsworth but you do appear to appreciate beauty; so I suppose I've no option but to take your word as a gentleman."

"Oh, Mr Challiss, sir," Ingleby laughed, "I'd rather you didn't. I don't think anybody could accuse me of belonging to that class of society. Oh, no, sir. You'd be nearer the mark if you left out the gentle bit."

"That smacks of radicalism, Ingleby," Tom said with a smile, warming to the man in spite of himself. "But how long have you been in Uppham St Mary? You should have called at the house and we could have shown you hospitality."

"Will you take my word for it, Mr Challiss, if I tell you I'm sworn to secrecy? I'm unable to answer your questions, sir," Ingleby said, trusting that his long coat effectively covered his gaiters.

"I see no reason not to," Tom said without hesitation. "You've earned my trust, Ingleby; though I'd give much to know how and why you come to be running about my wood. Perhaps we'll meet again under easier circumstances?"

"Doubtful, sir," the enigmatic man said. "But you never can tell. Now, if you'll excuse me, Mr Challiss, I'll be on my way. I have a busy day ahead of me. Good-bye to you, sir." And touching the brim of his hat Ingleby walked off among the trees.

Thanking his lucky stars that he'd avoided a very close shave, Ingleby-Ollander made his way out of Home Wood and took the nearest way back to his lodgings in Uppham St Mary. As he approached the cottage on the snow-covered green he saw that the boy who fetched Mrs Higden's water, surrounded by various receptacles, was shovelling snow into an empty cauldron. He asked him what he was doing.

His face scarlet from the combined effects of exertion and the muffler that his mother had wound tightly about his head and throat against the raw weather, John Brook paused in his labours just long enough to say: "Pump's frozen," before continuing to pile snow into the large black pot until it was full to the brim.

Ingleby observed that other cottagers were bent on the same activity. "I'll take hold of that, boy," the man John knew as Thompson surprised him by saying. "You start on the preserving pan while I get this lot melted."

John gave the usually taciturn gamekeeper a cheery grin. "Thanks very much, Mr Thompson. Me arms was beginnin' tew ache. I've already got Mrs 'Ignell's betsy on the boil fer 'er mornin' tea."

"You're a good lad, John," the fraudulent gamekeeper said approvingly.

"You've done enough here for one morning. Go home. I'll see to it that the old lady has plenty of water and kindling to keep her going before I set off on my rounds."

"I split plenty o' kindlin' yisty, Mr Thompson, an there's a good fire goin'."

"Well done, lad; you're a credit to your mother," the Londoner said. "You can get along now and leave this to me. I'll make sure that Mrs Higden's comfortable."

Content, in the knowledge that he'd be paid for the work being done by the changeable Mr Thompson, mercenary John Brook set out happily to walk back home. Thompson's compliment concerning Mrs Brook revised the boy's opinion of him. He thought now that the severe-looking man couldn't be such a bad cove after all.

Ingleby-Ollander-Thompson finished John's chores and congratulated himself on a job well done. He wasn't thinking of the number of containers he'd filled with melted snow, in order that his landlady had plenty of water to hand, but of the valuable knowledge he'd gained from his early morning walk through Home Wood.

★

Chapter Thirty-six

Following a less than bountiful harvest, the price of corn had continued to rise and talk of the intention to issue paper money added to the unemployed labourers' list of grievances. The price of bread was beyond the means of many agricultural labourers' families, depressed wages saw to that. Resentment and anger against those who 'had' by those who were condemned by the law makers to 'have not' goaded the likes of the Downham unemployed to take matters into their own hands. If their starving families were to survive the long winter months then it seemed only right and fair that the rich should be made to relinquish a share of the abundant quantities of provender that covered the acres which had deprived the labourers of their common land.

Shortly after midnight on Saturday, or as Clem Rix had called it, bull's moon, he and those of a like mind who frequented the *Queen's Head* of a Friday night to drink Ned Pitt's health – as long as the blacksmith footed the bill – made their separate ways to different parts of Sir Everard Belmaine's estate. Martlets had been selected because its owner was guilty of two crimes against the poor, according to the band of poachers: he not only belonged to the gentry but was also a magistrate.

No moon to speak of. Clad in dark clothes, which were all they possessed, little more than moving shadows themselves, the men slunk from shadow to shadow. Each had sworn to himself to return home with deep pockets full of meat of some kind.

"Doan care if it's nothin' bedder'n hollow meat," Clem Rix had said to the others after Thompson had left the inn the night before. "I ent finickin'. A wild rabbit wi' onions is fit fer a king's dinner, ter my mind."

"Nah!" Ned Pitts had objected. "Rabbit can be got any day. I could fancy lamb, now; or, as yew're goin' to a place as 'as a deer park, venison. Now *that's* worth riskin gaol fer, venison is." His piggy eyes gleamed at the prospect.

"'Cept yew ent the one oo'll be riskin gaol fer it, o' course," Ben Rix mocked.

"Yew'll take me shillins fast enough, yer young varmint," Pitts glowered back.

"Me an my missus and the youngun's ent had roast pheasant for a hage,"

Coy said dreamily. "Pheasants is ser daft they'll walk inter yer net an almos' thank yer fer the privilege. Eh, bors?"

"Thing is, doan git caught, bors," Pitts cautioned. "Leddit go, if yer finds yerself in bother. No sense in geddin yerselves in gaol. Liddlun's can addle on turnips fer a few days wi'out meat an not come to no harm. Live ter fight another day, says I," the enormous blacksmith said with a swagger at his grand phrase.

"Mine 've addled on turnips tew many days already," Jacob Coy said softly, looking into a desperate future. "I ent goin' 'ome ternight wi'out a brace o' pheasants, at least."

The men had separated and gone to their homes and those with hungry children had closed their ears to their wives' complaints about lack of food, yet had given no hint of their intentions for the following night. By the time Saturday night, bull's moon, arrived each man had slipped silently away to his chosen hunting ground.

★

Robin Belmaine, formerly known as Bob Pawl, had begun to flourish in all directions once the manure of good food, warmth and a sympathetic intellectual environment had been applied to the starved soil of his neglected brain. In a few weeks he had grown into a graceful and good-looking young man. Having caught him on the cusp of manhood, nature had colluded with nurture in bringing forth a finished specimen of his sex that, though it had been retarded by the winter of his earlier existence, had flourished all the more vigorously because of its deprivations.

That Sir Everard Belmaine doted on his grand-nephew was evident and, had Robin been an inferior specimen, his uncle would no doubt have ruined the young man by overfeeding him with all the luxuries that money and position could supply without his nephew having striven to earn them. If Sir Everard had only known it, Robin's greatest gift had been supplied by the young man's own father, Everett Bellman Pawl. The librarian's respect and love for his recently-restored son, and his gift for teaching him all that he had himself been taught, had been the chief ingredient in Robin's metamorphosis from a gangling, insalubrious dullard into a young man whom any father would have been proud to acknowledge.

Everett Pawl was, by no means, any father. His undoubted intellectual and natural gifts had been stifled and stunted since his life had been damaged by his mother's early death and were, it had seemed to him, doomed to be buried with him in the Uppham St Mary graveyard. Since being given the opportunity to use his unique gifts in the education of his own son his talents had found an outlet and had gushed forth and given him relief as great as a beneficial blood-letting. For to impart to his son all that John Wood had fed into the young Everett's receptive brain was to reinhabit that earlier, happier time of his life. The mornings spent with his son in the pursuit of knowledge amid the graceful setting of Martlets had healed Everett spiritually, emotionally, mentally and physically so that he, too, had suffered a sea-change. Apart from the daily boon of watching his son's intellect develop, Everett's residence and employment as librarian at Uppham House possessed the quality of a magical dream. He still had difficulty in accepting that his life looked set fair until he finally sailed off into the sunset. Unable to believe that his luck had changed so drastically, he sometimes dreaded that he might yet wake and find himself back with the shivering, unemployed men who thronged the streets of Downham.

Sir Everard perceived that father and son had grown close and generously kept as much out of their way as he could during their studies together. He looked forward enormously to the quarter hour's break for refreshment at ten forty-five each morning when he allowed himself to join their company. He could afford to be generous to Pawl as, until recently, he'd had the companionship of Robin for most of the day.

The comfortable pattern of their daily lives gradually became disarranged as more of Sir Everard's time was taken up with his magisterial duties. Petty larceny, damage to private property, attacks upon millers and storekeepers, poaching and general unrest in town and countryside, all ate into the magistrate's private hours until he began to resent the causes of his impoverishment. He had always prided himself on his ability to conduct a fair hearing; yet the surly, filthy and ragged wretches that had been brought before him lately had hardened his heart against themselves by their obvious lack of respect for his office. No longer a young man, he resented these stinking, starving beggars who seemed to want to deprive him of what little time he had left to savour a new-found happiness in life that had begun with the miracle of the discovery of his dead brother's son and grandson when he himself had been at his lowest ebb. His sentences for infringements of the law grew more severe almost without his noticing. More men were sent to Norwich to await the next assizes. Their wives and children, left without providers, were invariably thrown onto the mercy of the parish and had no alternative but to apply for admission to the workhouse. And more gangs of unemployed men, who replaced the imprisoned labourers, hung about the streets with nothing to do but seeth at the injustices meted out to them and mutter among themselves that there would have to be a change, that they themselves would bring it about. The gentry whispered dreadful words among themselves, such as sedition, anarchy, radicalism and revolution as they nervously armed their servants and prepared to fortify their properties as best they could against the coming troubles.

★

Forewarned is forearmed, David Deacon thought as he and his dog Fly sat watching the penned herd, from a place well away from the lambing shed and screened by a hurdle. Thompson had assured him that nothing untoward would happen until midnight at the earliest so Deacon had dozed on and off during the day in the certain knowledge that Fly would rouse him if necessary. Though they were sheltered from the worst of the bitter wind, the night was still marrow-chillingly cold. Alert now to every slight sound – the cracking of an icy twig, the scurry of a rabbit – shepherd and dog waited for the expected thief. They hadn't long to wait.

As the soft squidge of feet compacting snow at each step grew nearer, Deacon motioned Fly into the open and the clever dog laid himself across the hurdle gate as if he were there to guard the sleeping flock.

A dark shadow moved across the clearing to where Fly lay, silently alert while feigning sleep. From his pocket Ben Rix extracted a poisoned rat and laid it where the dog could not fail to see it on opening his eyes. Meanwhile, Deacon had crept from his hiding place and, before the young poacher had so much as lifted the pen's retaining hurdle, had stunned him with a blow to the back of the head from a stout branch.

Ben sank to his knees without uttering a sound and fell unconscious onto his face in the snow. It was an easy task for the shepherd to bind the lad hand and foot with rope and fasten a sack over his head, things he'd prepared beforehand.

Fly had stood as soon as he had perceived his master's hand signal and now looked down at the rat that lay, dimly perceptible against the snow, at his feet and sniffed at it. Before he could get his teeth into the rodent, an agonised cry rent the air. The dog looked towards the trees in the direction from which noise had come but stood panting, tongue lolling, obediently awaiting instructions from his master.

"Go, Fly!" Deacon commanded and the dog was away like an arrow, snow flying from his back paws as he skimmed across the woodland floor.

Testing his handiwork to ensure that the would-be poacher hadn't a chance of freeing himself, Deacon, the branch still in his hand in case the crude weapon should be needed again, ran to the lambing shed and snatched up the lighted lantern that hung inside, before following Fly's footprints.

Deacon's lantern picked out Fly who was standing beside a writhing, moaning figure. The man lay fastened by his leg to a man-trap and spreading dark stains in the snow showed that he was bleeding profusely from the wounds made by the trap's vicious iron teeth.

Stifling an oath, Deacon said: "Try ter keep still, bor. Whoever set this trap needs a dose of his own medicine! Down, Fly! Good dog. Tell us yer name, lad?"

"I'll be damned if I will!" Clem Rix got out between teeth clenched with pain.

"That's all right, bor," the shepherd said calmly. "Now listen carefully ter what I'm gonna say."

Clem, his eyes screwed shut, his lips pursed in obvious agony, nodded.

"I'm gonna try ter pull the jaws apart, bor. It'll give yer some clawth; but if yew want ter save yer leg you'll stick it like the man I take yer ter be, see."

Clem nodded.

Deacon placed the lantern on the snow and, by the beams it cast across the injured man, studied the fiendish contraption and saw that its long tines were sunk deep into the man's leg above the ankle. He was sickened by the sight of it. Despite the intense cold, he began to run with sweat, the product of the fear that ran through his body at the thought that he might lack the strength to free the man and injure himself into the bargain. Should he fail, the poacher would die from loss of blood or exposure to the cold, or a mixture of both. In which case, he wouldn't allow himself to fail – God willin'. "Ready, bor?"

Clem nodded.

It soon became clear to Deacon that he would have to release the spring somewhat before he would be able to use the branch as a substitute for the man's ankle bone. God help me! he thought, as it dawned upon him that he would have to pull the jaws of the trap apart with his bare hands. He couldn't do it! Cold sweat streamed from every pore in his body. He had to do it. "Open yer eyes, bor. No! Doan eye yer leg. Listen ter me. I ent no 'ero, I'll tell yer that fer nothin'. But I can see only one way of gittin' yer out of this mess, bor, an I'm gonna need yer help."

"What d'yer want me ter dew, bor?"

David Deacon told him, pulled the injured man into a sitting position, which elicited another agonised moan, and gave him the branch to hold. "We've only the one chance, bor. Understand? If we fluff it–"

"Git on wi' it!"

As Deacon's hands took hold of the ugly handles of the trap the slight vibration caused by the touch of his hands on the iron spring provoked a scream of agony from Clem. Tears sprang to Deacon's eyes at the realisation of the additional suffering he had unwittingly caused. He tried to put out of his mind that he had the young man's life in his hands, that his effort to release the trapped leg depended on his puny strength. Not a religious man, he nevertheless prayed with fervour for God's help as, with a tremendous effort and shaking arms, he began to pull the handles of the trap apart.

As soon as the blooded tines gleamed in the lantern light, Clem jerked himself forward and thrust the stout branch into the the angle of the opening.

But the precaution was unnecssary. A strength that he had not known he possessed flowed into Deacon's arms and quivered along each length through muscle, sinew, blood and bone until the evil engine lay, something akin to a shark's wide open mouth, a spiteful blacker oval on the blood-drenched dark snow. Deacon picked up a fallen branch and touched the spring of the mantrap. Its jaws snapped shut and shivered the oak with such force that splinters from it exploded high into the air.

Clem, who had been busy tying a makeshift tourniquet fashioned from a muffler about his injured leg, looked up at the sound of the loud metallic snap in time to see tiny daggers of wood falling perpendicularly into the snow where only minutes before he had lain, trapped. He froze at the sight. "'Twould've bin useless, bor!" he said, his voice hoarse with the horror of his imaginings at what would have happened to himself and his rescuer. "I owe yew me life, shepherd," he said humbly.

By means of a combination of Clem leaning on Deacon and hopping clumsily in the soft snow, and the shepherd dragging the injured man backwards by his armpits over places that were impossible for them to negotiate in any other way, they returned at last to the fold. Ben Rix lay where Deacon had left him bound hand and foot with his head in a sack and, by all appearences, he hadn't stirred since the blow to his head had been delivered by the shepherd an hour earlier.

★

It was all over Downham, all over Uppham St Mary and, for a few hours, was the reigning topic at the manor house: poachers had been caught redhanded at Martlets, Sir Everard Belmaine's estate. The gossip flew back and forth. 'How many?' 'Man I spoke to said 'twere a gang o' twenny or more.' 'Anyone we know?' 'Taken inter custody, so no-one's the wiser'... and so on...

Wide-eyed with a mixture of excitement and terror as she heard the news, Mary Emma said: "Thank heavens it was Martlets they chose and not us, Mr Challiss."

Tom drained his teacup. "I don't suppose Belmaine would agree with you, my dear," he said as he buttered a slice of toast. "But the poachers would have known that we're not stocked with game in the same numbers as Belmaine. We have no deer, for one thing, nor are we likely to have."

Agnes had said nothing for some time but had been content to sit and listen. During a lull in the conversation she said: "John came back from Mrs Hignell's early yesterday morning."

Everett Pawl laid down his knife. "So I understand, Miss Brook. Apparently your brother decided to call here on the advice of your mother after his noonday fare, in order to make the acquaintance of Mr Webster."

Agnes smiled at the scholarly librarian. "He did, sir. And he told Jem Webster a strange tale."

Mary Emma, who had been bored by their dull breakfast conversation, coming after the exciting news of a band of poachers being apprehended so near to her own home, pricked up her ears. "That sounds intriguing, Agnes. May we hear it?"

Agnes Brook related John's account of the unusually kind behaviour of Mr Thompson. "... and then he said John might go home and that he'd see that Mrs Hignell was made comfortable."

"From what I hear of the man," Tom said, reaching for an orange, digging his thumbnail into the zesty peel and starting to remove the skin, "that doesn't sound like his usual behaviour at all. I still haven't had the pleasure of the man's acquaintance. I must make it my business to catch him tomorrow, as I've never seen him in church."

Stifling a yawn, Mary Emma said: "I can't see what you find so unusual about this Thompson's behaviour, Agnes. Or you, Mr Challiss. Mightn't a person have a sudden impulse to do something unselfish? It has been known, my dear."

"It's time I got myself ready for church," Tom said, "If you'll excuse me, Miss Brook; Mr Pawl." Mary Emma also excused herself and followed him out though a further heavy fall of snow around dawn had decided her against joining her husband in Sunday worship.

"I'll be along directly," Agnes called after her friend as she removed her napkin.

But as she was about to rise and to follow the Challisses, Everett Pawl said: "Might I crave the indulgence of a moment of your time, Miss Brook?"

She sat down at the dishevelled table again. "Of course, Mr Pawl. What is it?"

"This business about that odd gamekeeper, Thompson," Pawl said. "I do find his behaviour most peculiar, Miss Brook."

"In what way peculiar? Have you met the man, sir?" Agnes asked.

"I cannot say that I have actually met him to speak to," Pawl admitted, "but I have observed him on more than one occasion and a less likely gamekeeper I have yet to set eyes on."

"Oh?"

"His clothes and boots are far too new and far too neat, for one thing," the librarian said as he pared a sliver of cheese, spiked it with the snake's tongue two-pronged cheese knife and laid it on his side plate.

"It's possible he bought himself a new wardrobe in order to make a good impression upon his new employer, Mr Pawl," Agnes offered as an explanation.

"Yes, I do see that," Pawl conceded. "Yet, I understood Mr Challiss to say that he and Thompson have yet to meet." He popped the cheese into his mouth.

"Ah! Yes, you are right, Mr Pawl. It doesn't seem to add up, does it."

Pawl swallowed the last of his cheese. "As you are no doubt aware, Miss Brook, young John and I have struck up a nodding acquaintance. In fact, I'm happy to say that he and I have become very good friends."

"John has mentioned it," Agnes said, smiling. "He has you down as a hero, sir."

Unusually for him, Pawl beamed. "Very good friends indeed, I might go so far as to say," he said. "Your brother has confided to me that he, too, has his doubts as to the veracity of Thompson's claims of eligibility for the post he currently fills."

Agnes grew alarmed at this disclosure. "Doubts? What can a small boy know about the duties of a gamekeeper?" she said, convinced in her own mind that there must be some mistake.

"John, as I am sure you are aware, Miss Brook, is a very bright boy, a very observant boy. He has noticed that Mr Thompson follows no regular beat, for one thing; that he doesn't know the difference between a hen pheasant and a partridge for another; and that he hasn't the first idea of the best kind of gun to carry when he does pretend to make his rounds of the estate."

"You're quite certain of all this, Mr Pawl?" Agnes said, her misgivings roused anew at the idea of John's being thrown into the company of such an underhand man.

Everett Pawl allowed his eyes to crinkle. "I think we both know that John is utterly trustworthy, Miss Brook."

Agnes smiled. "Yes, that's true. But he has a mind of his own, too," she said, "as well as an imaginative streak that sometimes gets him into trouble."

Everett Pawl dabbed at his lips with his napkin and laid it aside. "It might be as well to say something of John's and my misgivings on the subject of Mr Thompson to Mr Challiss, Miss Brook. Something is definitely not quite right about the man and Mr Challiss should be alerted to the fact so that he may act accordingly."

★

Tom and Everett were the only churchgoers from Uppham House that morn- ing owing to the heavy snowfall. Their individual horses were able to negotiate the journey to St Mary's with reasonable ease, compared to a team dragging a coach, so it had been deemed prudent that Mary Emma and Agnes, each in a delicate condition, should remain at home.

The meagre congregation sat dotted about the gloomy, unheated church amid a cacophany of coughs and sniffles and shuffling damp, cold feet. Though Edward Fieldgate did his best to enliven the dismal gathering, his usually mellifluous voice was disadvantaged by a sore throat. The singing was thin and poor and the organist's mittened fingers were so frozen that he accidentally, and frequently, produced harmonies that were more than a century ahead of their time as sounds acceptable to the human ear as comprehensible music. Fieldgate, obviously unwell himself, shortened his sermon and earned the gratitude of his flock by doing so.

As the straggle of worshippers made their way out of the inhospitable house of God into the equally unfriendly temperature that greeted them in the churchyard, Tom heard Everett say behind him: "Good morning, Mr Thompson." Turning to satisfy himself that at long last he was to meet his gamekeeper, he was astonished to discover himself face to face with Giles Ingleby.

For a second, Tom was thrown off guard; then, recalling that Ingleby was engaged in some sort of undercover business, he said: "Mr Thompson, I believe. We meet at last, sir."

Without batting an eyelid, Ingleby responded: "You must be Mr Challiss, sir. Good to meet you, sir. You'll have to excuse me, sir, I'm due at Martlets by noon. This poaching business. You've heard about it, I suppose? Good-bye to you, sir."

"He seemed friendly enough, Mr Pawl," Tom remarked as they found their mounts and swung up into the saddles. "Don't know about you, sir, but I'm fairly frozen. I must do something about getting some kind of heating into the church before the whole congregation is carried off to the churchyard having died of pneumonia. That place in winter is like sitting in an open grave for an hour. Care for a little something to warm you before we set out?" He proffered his hip flask which was full of brandy.

"Thank you, Mr Challiss, it's very good of you, but not for me," Pawl said. "So you took to Thompson, did you? I must say, he struck me as a very slippery individual."

Tom wondered what had occasioned that remark. "Oh, one of these so-called busy men; always rushing off to something they want the world to know is of the greatest importance, that cannot take place until they themselves are present."

Everett grinned sourly at Challiss's observation before setting his horse at a smart trot along the snowy roads. Tom stowed away his flask and caught him up and the two men rode the rest of the way back to Uppham in silent companionship.

Because the sermon had been curtailed, Sunday dinner was a good two hours away and Tom decided to take a look at the state of the stables and the string of horses. He had left the new groom, Will Wright, to his own devices until now and had no occasion, so far, to find fault at the way the animals had been cared for. Will was nowhere about but Tom was aware of small sounds that seemed at odds with the movements made by horses. As he made his way from one loose-box to the next the unusual sounds stopped and he distinctly hear somebody whisper: "Sh!"

Tom noticed that the stalls were spotlessly clean, the mangers full, and the horses well-tended: everything in good order. He continued along the line of boxes until he came to one that appeared to be empty. He opened the door and saw a small booted foot sticking out of a pile of straw. Maddy! He closed the door again and walked away. Mary Emma could deal with this situation, he decided, as he walked back to the house, and idly wondered which of the brothers was fondling the girl.

The pleasant sound of the pianoforte wafted downstairs from the withdrawing room and he guessed that it must be Agnes playing it; for the thin, simple melody suited the girl's apparently uncomplicated nature, though it lacked the technical brilliance that had marked Mrs Aldrich's performance. Tom stood in the hall listening and allowed the simple sweet sounds to permeate his thirsty soul. A miracle was taking place: Uppham House was beginning to feel like a home at last. He decided then and there that his children would be given the opportunity to study music as an accomplishment, so that the whole family's lives might be enriched by the civilising influence of soothing music for as long as the children remained at home. So enraptured had he become by Agnes's performance that, when he joined them, he quite forgot to mention to his wife that he had seen young Maddy almost hidden in a pile of clean straw and apparently up to no good.

★

Before first light on Sunday morning Ben Rix, who had suffered no lasting ill-effects from Deacon's knock-out blow apart from a sizeable bump on the back of his head, slunk through the hushed wood to the back door of Aldrich's lodge. After his hammering on the door for some minutes, a sleepy Joseph Aldrich shuffled in lint slippers through the conservatory and peered through the back window into the darkness. In the light cast from his candle, the wild figure of a strange youth pantomiming to be let in was vaguely alarming. While he stood there wondering what he should do in these uncertain times, Ruth, who had followed him downstairs, went and opened the door. Ben described his brother's injuries, where he was hidden, and how he and the shepherd were worried that Clem might lose his leg, or worse, if it didn't receive attention immediately.

"He must be brought here at once," said Ruth, astonishing her sleepy-headed husband into wakefulness. "Is your brother able to walk at all?"

"'E can 'op, missus," Ben said. "But it's a fair way; 'e couldn't make it."

"Joe, dear," Ruth said, speaking urgently. "Get dressed at once. Take your horse; the lad can ride double with you. When you get to the fold, use one of the hurdles as a stretcher. You and Ben will have to carry Clem back here. You'll have to hurry, Mr Aldrich; it will be light soon. Off you go!" To Ben Rix's amazement, the steward went without a word of protest. He soon discovered it was his turn to be ordered about. "Ben. When you and Mr Aldrich have brought Clem here, you must run back to the fold and fetch back Mr Aldrich's stallion at once. . . . Do you ride?"

"No, missus," the youth said, his green eyes agog. "Dunno nothin' 'bout 'orses, 'specially not a stallion!"

"Oh, dear!" Ruth clapped her hand to her forehead. "Never mind. I'll follow on the roan and bring both horses back together. Now hurry, Ben! Your brother's life may depend upon it!" As soon as he'd gone, she rushed upstairs to put on her riding habit.

★

"A letter?" Tom said to Rudge. "When was it delivered, Rudge?"

"While you were at morning service, sir," the manservant said, "shortly before noon, sir. Somebody brought it to the house on foot, sir."

"Thank you, Rudge. That will be all," Tom had his attention on the folded but unsealed communication. Intrigued, he unfolded it and straightened it out. "Good God!" he said softly to himself, as he took in the seriousness of the first few lines.

"Did you say something, Tom?" Mary Emma murmured from her seat beside the fire where she was engrossed in a second reading of *Pride and Prejudice*.

He hadn't heard her. "Dear Challiss," he read. "Many thanks for your tact this morning. A word to you. Poachers were in your woods last night, the same woods where we stumbled across each other the other morning. I caught one but somebody freed him. He will not get far. He is badly injured and has lost a lot of blood. He must be in hiding on your estate. A word of warning. It is your duty as a citizen to turn the man in when you find him or you will be found guilty of aiding and abetting a known criminal. Yours, I." Stunned, he re-read the few lines, dwelling on the threat implicit in the last. Anger thrilled through him. Impudent, lying scoundrel! So he had been up to something yesterday morning. And what's this about loss of blood? Shot? He shook his head, puzzled. Who *was* Giles Ingleby, Ollander or Gil Thompson, and how many other aliases had the man? He's a clever rogue, no doubt about that, thought Tom. Must be some kind of spy. In whose pay? ... Stalking poachers. Why?

Following his usual discreet knock, Rudge opened the door and announced: "Mr Aldrich, sir."

What Joseph had to tell him sent a chill through Tom's blood. For a moment he thought about the implications for himself, for Mary Emma and Agnes – everybody reliant on him – and made his decision. He would do his best to hide the Rix brothers until the time came for them to leave Uppham. "As soon as Clem is fit to be moved he must be brought up to the house," he said. "Now that the workmen have finished most of the rooms in the east wing the brothers will be able to lie low here." He would hear no protestations from his steward as to the folly of such action and sent Aldrich away a very troubled man.

★

Chapter Thirty-seven

Jem Webster's patience was running out. Whether it was his mistress's child-carrying state that was making her such a thorn in his flesh he was unable to say: though, remembering the wild mood swings that had affected his usually placid-natured woman, Nell, at such times, he guessed that young Mrs Challiss was suffering from a similar affliction. Women! If only they could learn not to interfere with a man's work they'd earn their place in heaven. Fair git on yer wick they do at times, he thought, as he made his way from Uppham St Mary towards Downham and the *Queen's Head*. A smile lit up his face as he thought of warm-hearted Nell. Worth all the straight-laced besoms in Norfolk, was generous-spirited Nell. And it didn't seem to worry her that they'd never got round to having the sibbits called that would have made an honest woman of her.

The sight of a squad of tatterdemalion ex-servicemen marching up and down a slushy side street and carrying spades, picks and an odd assortment of farm implements, in place of firearms, brought him up short. Seeking out a corner of a shop where he could observe their actions without himself being conspicuous, Jem watched their drill. The precision with which the band marched, wheeled, halted and manipulated their arms was very impressive, despite the motley crew's unkempt appearance and their ludicrous miscellany of arms. Among the company of drilling men he recognised many who had worked solely as agriculural labourers all their lives. That the squad was being trained to respond to military command and were being prepared for impending action left nobody who observed them in doubt that the desperate, skeletal men had reached the end of their tether.

It came as a relief to Jem to push open the door of the inn, to enter its smelly warmth and to shut out the sight of the desperate men. He shook his worried head at the thought of the fate that awaited many of them and secretly and selfishly was glad not to have to account himself one of their number any more. What he had witnessed put into true perspective his irritation with the missus up at the mansion and he resolved to count his blessings instead of dwelling on the young woman's minor, and probably temporary, shortcomings. He ordered a pint of ale and took a seat near the fire.

It had been some weeks since he had found the time to take himself off to the inn for a quiet drink away from the womenfolk and their chivvying ways. He wouldn't call it naggin, 'zackly; but he come over all fingers an thumbs whenever a female entered his work space, particularly his young mistress and her decidedly fancy ideas for tricolatin' the library.

Unsettlin, spose you'd call it, he thought. Thank God for my Nell! If there's a mawther in Uppham S'Mary knows when tew 'old 'er tongue, it's me lover.

From being wrapped deep in thoughts of the puzzling nature of the opposite sex that he found exasperating, yet mysteriously alluring, Jem gradually became aware of the conversation taking place between the ex-sailor innkeeper and a customer.

"…use ter meet at that very table over there. I noo they was up ter somethin' but they allus paid cash fer their grog and caused no trouble so I let 'em git on wi' it. 'Ow was I ter know they was plannin ter do ole Sir Everard Belmaine's over? Like I tole the Bow Street officer, I got me livin' ter make same as anybody else." He wiped over his counter with a filthy cloth in order to advertise the fact that his work was never done.

His customer, who had listened sympathetically, avoided the innkeeper's face while puffing his pipe and said: "I ent never seen one o' them. What they like?"

"I only met the one I tole yer about," replied the innkeeper, resting his folded arms on the bar, dirty cloth dangling from his hand. "Right crimblin' man, he were. Use tew 'ide 'imself away in the darkist corner he could find and sit there, still as a bleedin statew, an make half-a-pint last all night, the mean bugger. From Lunnon, he said. I coulda told 'im that! 'E were a right cockney. I met plenny o' them aboard ship".

"But what's 'e look like?" the customer persisted. "Did 'e wear a yewniform, or suthin' like that?"

The innkeeper ceased to demonstrate his industriousness and leaned his folded arms on the bar as before. "No! That woulda give the game away wouldnit, bor! No. 'E dressed 'isself as a gamekeeper, though I thought ter meself 'twere a funny kind o' disguise to chewse fer these 'ere parts, them gennelmen bein' more unpop'ler than most. Crewl bugger, an all. Tole me 'ow he set one 'o them mantraps in Challissis wood."

"'E never!"

"An 'e caught one of 'em, an all."

"Dead?"

"No. The bugger iscaped; though 'ow 'e coulda done's a myst'ry"

"I never 'eard of any man gettin' free o' one o' them crewl injuns afore," the customer said as he drained his tankard and pushed it forward for a refill. "They dew say as 'ow a man's likely ter bleed ter death from his injuries, bor. I doan see 'ow any one could git away wi' it, when 'e must've 'ad 'oles in 'is leg as big as them made be a fold-pritch. Dew yew? Yew tell me 'ow."

The landlord lowered his voice. "Only one man in these parts capable o' releasin a sprung mantrap. 'Twas 'e that sat wi' 'em an paid fer their drinks."

"Oh-ah? Oo'm that be, then?" ... His mind caught up. "Lessen yew mean–"

"SH-sh-sh! Keep yer voice down, bor," the alarmed innkeeper said, surveying the room, "yer niver know oo's list'nin."

The customer sniffed. "Thought yew said they was all caught and sent orf ter Norridge?"

"Most of 'em was," the innkeeper agreed. He dropped his voice to a hoarse whisper that was louder than many a person's normal voice. "*Tew* of 'em iscaped, see? An, if yew was thinkin of a certin blacksmith jist now, yew'm right. 'E is the only man I knows of that would have the super-yewman strength needed ter pull open a sprung trap." He nodded sagely.

Agog at what he'd just learned, the drinker said: "Oo was them tew got orf, then?"

The innkeeper tapped the side of his nose. "Now, that'd be tellin, wouldnit, bor." He sank his voice to a whisper approaching the sound that is commonly considered a whisper and leaned over the bar: "Wot if I was ter tell yer they was closely related an 'ad sandy 'air an eyes like gooseberries?" He nodded as he watched recognition dawn in his customer's eyes, and silenced him with: "Belay that yarn, bor."

★

At first, Kit Warrender refused to believe his eyes, hoping that the dismal light was playing tricks with his unusually good eyesight. He crunched a few steps nearer the humps. They were barely distinguishable from the low bushes and brambles that had been transformed by the frosting of snow carpeting the beggared area next to the lime walk. The thud of his heart told him that he'd not been mistaken: bodies. Their rounded forms belied the fact that those who had found their last resting place on Uppham land had been slowly starved to death. Kit saw two sticklike arms protruding from the blanket of snow. "Ah, no!" the young Farm Manager moaned, his voice thick with tears at the pitiful sight. He dashed at his blue eyes with an angry gesture. Banished tears were replaced by a dangerous gleam. "Somebody's gonna pay fer this!" he resolved, as he began to dig away the snow that covered the bodies.

The crust of frozen snow did not yield up its horrible secret easily. Kit had trouble breaking the icy shield that imprisoned the small arms in sleeves of glass, carefully prizing it off the marbled flesh in fragments with the knife he always carried with him. He persevered in his grisly task until he was able to free the mantle of ice and snow that hid the child's body and heave the canopy aside as if it were the lid of a sarcophogus.

"Sweet Jesus!" the young man cried as the full horror of his reluctant discovery was laid bare by feeble morning sunshine that slid from behind a cloud and spotlighted the scene. Now his tears fell hot and fast as his stunned senses fully realised the tragedy that he had excavated.

An emaciated woman lay on her back with her eyes open, her beautiful face as fine as any of the carved effigies Kit had seen in St Mary's church. Her fleshless arms encompassed the bodies of two children, a boy who might have been six years old and a baby, sex and age indeterminate, whose hollow-eyed, pinched little face would never have been allowed to grace any tomb as a carved cherub. No coats? In this weather? Kit was puzzled by the terrible omission. His heart full of compassion for the little family and their cruel end, he bent down to try to close the lids of the woman's eyes. His hot tears splashed onto the corpse's face; but defeated by death, he was quite unable to veil the frozen orbs and they stared up at him in hazel-eyed reproach.

Once he had alerted Joseph Aldrich to his grisly discovery Kit, badly shaken by the incident, took himself off to walk through Home Wood and to the clearing beyond it where the flock was penned. He needed to talk to one of his own kind and knew of nobody more likely to be a sympathetic listener than shepherd Deacon.

*

The ordinarily reserved shepherd had welcomed the sight of someone to talk to after the harrowing events that he had endured over recent hours. His isolation had provided him with too much time to dwell on the hideous images that had bludgeoned his usually tranquil mind. Repeatedly, he relived those extraordinary minutes, when he had called upon a God, in whom he professed he had no faith, to aid him in releasing Clem from the trap, and had been shaken by the subsequent miracle of the immediate empowering of his arms and hands that had enabled him to do so. Scenes of the events that had happened in the wood haunted him: Fly tearing away into the dark wood over the snowchanged landscape; feeble lamplight throwing distorted shapes and images across the trapped man's body; the blood draining from the injured leg and spreading its dark monochrome stain on the shimmering snow; the young poacher's incredible bravery; the seemingly endless journey of getting Clem back to the sheepfold; the terror of discovery by the gamekeeper; the felling of Ben Rix and the fear that he'd murdered the youth; the poisoned rat that could have cost Fly his life; the transfer of Clem Rix to the lodge; the wonderful Mrs Aldrich; the hurdle stretcher... And the sequence would repeat itself, over and over, until he thought that he must end up a madman.

As David Deacon had related the list of the night's happenings and added to them those that had followed it shortly after dawn, Kit began to understand the toll it must have taken of the shepherd's nerves. The man couldn't stop shaking; though he protested vigorously that he didn't feel the cold. "You could do with something strong to drink, man," Warrender said, "I've nothing with me. Anything in the the lambing hut?"

Deacon's shoulders lifted in a silent laugh: "On'y sheep dip, an I doan fancy swiggin' that! But that's enough about me. What brings yew this way, Kit?"

Deacon's tale had taken away a little of the rawness of the horror of Warrender's discovery. Kit's one idea had been to unburden himself by unfolding the story of the tragedy that had befallen one family belonging to the agricultural labouring class. He'd thought to discuss with him how successive injustices had reduced the unemployed, penniless men until they were driven to poaching, to stealing bread; how their women and children were dying from starvation and exposure to the elements; how recent changes in the law had brought about the degradation and humiliation of a whole class of society whose last refuge was the stigmatising workhouse.

Warrender decided that this was not the time to pile more misery on the shepherd and steered their talk towards the state of the ewes and lambing. "I'll get back to you later on, David, and bring a bottle of something with me," he promised.

After breaking the cat's ice that had covered the water trough anew, since his removal of the thick layer that had formed overnight, and checking that the stock had sufficient feed, he made his way back to Aldrich's lodge. As he swung along with a comfortable stride he thought over what he'd been told by Deacon. It tallied well with Clem Rix's account; except that the poacher had made the shepherd out to be some kind of hero. Kit had had his doubts about the poacher's release from the mantrap: he'd seen what the devilish things could do and had privately discounted the idea of the wiry, mild shepherd's having sufficient strength to free Clem from a set of those vicious iron jaws. Now he was certain that the young man had told the truth. No wonder David Deacon was Clem's hero; the modest shepherd deserved the accolade.

A pale-faced Clem Rix, reclining on a sofa among the exotic blooms of the conservatory, greeted Warrender with: "Thought I 'eard yer voice earlier. Bad start ter the day, findin them bodies, bor. Pore li'l devils! Wot'n end, eh?"

Kit sighed and seated himself on the end of the sofa. "Probably for the best, the way things're going for people like them. I don't know where it's going to end, Clem. How did the country get into this state? We've always had the poor in our parish; but I can't recall things ever before being as bad as they are now. Since the slump after the war the huge numbers of labourers thrown out of work have become much more noticeable. The poor stand out like a breed apart. This is supposed to be a Christian country. The gentry seem to think that by going to church in a carriage twice every Sunday they'll save their souls. Maybe. But what of their consciences? I'd like to see some of those fat matrons getting down on their knees to feed the children of the poor. Can't they see the people starving before their eyes? Are they blind?"

"My ole dad use ter say: 'There's none ser blind as them as won't see.' I reckon he were right, an all; folks on'y see wot they wanna see. An starvin beggars ent a pretty sight."

"How's the leg, Clem?" Kit asked.

"Still there, thank Gawd, bor, though 'tis early days. Reckon I'll be 'orfling fer the rest of me nat'ral; but nothin ser bad as'll stop me gittin about, once it's mended."

"When're they moving you up to the mansion?"

"Yew tell me, bor! Ain 'eard another word 'bout it since Mrs Aldrich tole me 'twould 'appen." Clem's green eyes lit up. "That woman's a wonder. I'd o' lost me leg without 'er elp, fer sure."

"Your lucky day, Clem," Kit agreed, "to have had a nurse on hand after such a nasty accident."

Clem's face slipped from that of a pleasant young man to that of the disgruntled individual who had accosted Tom Challiss in Downham High Street the previous summer. "'Tweren't no accident! Somebody set that damned contraption delib'rately. 'E noo what 'e were up tew, the bastard! I only wanted a rabbit or tew."

Kit thought to change the subject. "I've been wondering who the mother and her two children were that I found this morning," he said. "What could have brought them onto Uppham land and how did they get past this lodge?"

"That ain no myst'ry," Clem scoffed. "The bound'ry fence leadin inter the lane is full of 'oles. They must've got in that way. We'll find out oo they was afore long."

The bad state of the boundary fence had escaped Warrender's memory. He would set men onto repairing the worst areas this afternoon. "You said Mrs Aldrich poured something over your leg, Clem. Seems to have done the trick."

"Gawd! That were almos' worse'n the trap! Mrs Aldrich said it would 'urt an, my Gawd, she were right 'bout that," the young man said, able to smile now at the memory. "Didn' 'alf give me some clawth. Niver bin in sich agony in all me life. 'Twere like fire an brimstone in one. I know it 'ad whiskey, lemon an vinegar in it; but there was other things, an all; 'ealin 'erbs o' some sort."

"Must've done the trick, anyway," said Kit, smiling at the young man's colourful language and glad to have banished the disfiguring look of revenge Clem's face had worn as he'd mentioned the trapper.

As Clem's face cleared, he shook his head from side to side as if to clear it, too. "I use ter think that folks as talked diff'rent ter me was la-di-da. Since livin' with the Aldriches in their own 'ome I see that they can't 'elp the way they sound, pore buggers, no more'n me. I mean, it's what people *does* as matters, ain it, bor. I niver 'ad no ma; but I can see 'ow a good one can make all the diff'rence, now that I've got ter know Mrs Aldrich. ... ... 'E ent ser bad neether, once yer git ter know 'im proper," he added, as a tardy afterthought.

★

Joseph Aldrich would have counted Clem's assessment of him a victory over prejudice. If the steward were honest, it had taken him just as long in his acceptance of the rough young man. Somehow, Ruth had skilfully averted downright unpleasantness between the two by her gentle voice and calm demeanour. But the injured poacher was far from Aldrich's thoughts at the present moment as he related to Tom the unpleasant details of Warrender's discovery earlier that day.

"Have you managed to discover their identities?" Tom asked, his face showing plainly his distress at learning of the gruesome and pitiful discovery.

"The finding of the bodies caused a minor sensation, of course, Mr Challiss," Aldrich said. "The men downed tools at once fearing, I suppose, that the corpses might belong to one of them. Happily, that was not the case, sir. But one of the gardening labourers said he recognised them as Mrs Coy and her children. Apparently, the husband and father, Jacob Coy, one of our garden labourers, has just been arrested for poaching and sent to Norwich to await trial."

"This is terrible, Joe!" Tom said. "Imagine that poor woman's feelings— Oh, my God! It doesn't bear thinking about. For heaven's sake, Joe, don't let Mary Emma get to hear of this, or who knows what might happen to her in her delicate state."

Aldrich nodded assent. "Shall I ride over to Martlets, Mr Challiss? There are formalities to be observed. Sir Everard Belmaine, as magistrate, must be informed of the circumstances under which the three bodies were found on Uppham land, sir. Then, I suppose, I should call at the workhouse to arrange for a pauper burial."

"You'll do no such thing!" Tom shouted. "It was no fault of theirs that they died as they did. The poor woman had brought her children here for a purpose, Joe. We can only guess at what it was. It's possible that she thought she might get help from us." He looked very grave as he said softly: "And so she shall." He looked Aldrich directly in the eye: "I shall approach Mr Fieldgate about arranging for the Coy family to be buried in consecrated ground. Moreover, I shall see that a headstone is erected to their memory. By God! I'll see to it that they didn't suffer in vain and what's more, the whole parish shall share in it, too."

★

For a few days the subject of the Coy funeral was the chief topic of conversation in the parish. Mr Fieldgate had, at first, demurred when Tom had put forth his request that the family be buried in consecrated ground. When he realised that Mr Challis would not yield over the matter, to salve his conscience, the minister made a swift search of the parish registers and discovered, to his immense satisfaction, that the deceased Mrs Coy came from decent yeoman stock going back for several generations. It seemed that her union with agricultural labourer Jacob Coy had led to her eventual downfall. Of course, Mr Fieldgate in no way blamed the enclosures that had led to the disappearance of the common land on which the Coys had once grown their vegetables and kept a pig and a cow; nor did he blame the gentleman farmer who had turned off Jacob Coy when times became hard, or the government for its repressive laws that had worsened the family's plight. No. As far as he could see, Jacob Coy had been the architect of his own misfortune by belonging to the labouring classes – and hadn't he heard that the man was no more than a common thief and even now languished in gaol? Still, if Mr Challiss was willing to foot the bill, and was content to give a generous donation to the church into the bargain, the reverend gentleman could see no real harm in it. In this way the minister, aided and abetted by Mrs Fieldgate, brought himself to believe that, all in all, to bury the Coys in consecrated ground was no more than was their due as parishioners of Uppham St Mary.

Mary Emma did hear something of the funeral and was mildly surprised to learn that her husband insisted on attending it; but as she had just had word from her bookseller that Miss Austen was shortly to bring out a new novel entitled *Emma*, the event passed almost unnoticed by her. What with the excitement and anticipation of the forthcoming publication, together with the daily improvements to the library, she was so well that she scarcely had time to notice that her child was growing larger and becoming increasingly active. Then there was the joy of Agnes's music and games of chess and cards to brighten the tediously long winter evenings; but these, too, were drawing out, so that life seemed to her to be full of hopeful expectation amid a daily round of quiet pleasure.

★

Towards the end of February 1816 a temporary thaw made the roads passable enough for Agnes Brook and Mary Emma to visit Agnes's family at Church House. The anticipated journey would be an easy one lasting, at the most, fifteen minutes each way if they drove the cob and yellow carriage at a sedate pace. Tom had reluctantly given his permission for his pregnant wife to accompany Agnes, on the condition that they drove sensibly, and both young women had looked forward to the outing with a sense of liberation from the household and its irksome demands upon their time. Well wrapped up against the cold and full of excitement at the prospect of feeling the wind on their faces again, they waited for the stable boy to bring the team to the front of the house. Young Ben Wright brought the pretty little contraption to a halt below the mansion steps, ran up the flight, pulled the bellhandle and waited.

The ladies emerged dressed as elegantly as two fashion plates in their furlined velvets and high-crowned silk bonnets. Ben was overwhelmed by the obvious wealth advertised by their clothes and wondered what the ragged unemployed would make of their colourful display; but he knew his place and it wasn't up to him to point out the dangers to which the women exposed themselves. He watched them as they drove away and wondered, too late, if he should have gone with them.

"Oh! It's so good to be out in the air again!" Mary Emma exclaimed. "Isn't everything beautiful, Agnes? How well the cob-phaeton runs, even over the uneven patches. I wish we might have our drive paved, as Tom says the roads of the great cities are beginning to be. It'd be like riding over velvet."

Agnes laughed softly. "The air is wonderful Mary Emma; a tonic after so many weeks spent indoors." She inhaled deeply. "If only the sun would shine the day would be perfect," she declared as she manoeuvred the cob and the canary yellow carriage out of Uppham's gates.

When the sun deigned to appear, the increase in its warmth was noticeable. Its pale golden light shining over dazzling whiteness transformed the monochrome scene. Hollows were identifiable by subtle shades of lilac and mauve, puddles trapped liquid turquoise and aquamarine in their icy depths, and last autumn's bracken shook its tattered papery fronds of pale amber in the wind. Dark evergreens glowed in the gardens and distant views between the houses revealed defoliated trees showing off their beautiful winter forms against a huge skyscape of everchanging clouds.

Their route took them into Downham High Street for a few yards before they took the turning off it into the village of Uppham St Mary. As they bowled along Mary Emma and Agnes became engrossed in exuberant conversation, feasting their eyes on the pretty houses whose warm coloured carrstone bricks showed to advantage in the winter sunshine, and so failed to notice a knot of raggedly-dressed out-of-work labourers until they found themselves brought to a halt as the cadaverous men ringed their phaeton. Although fear thrilled through her and the child in her abdomen turned a somersault, Mary Emma remained outwardly calm as she said: "What is it you want of us?"

One of the men spoke for all. "'Ow about a little o' what yew've got, me fine lady?" he said menacingly, and looking around the circle of faces at his friends for approval which they silently returned. "Them mantles'd keep us all in food fer a month, I don't doubt. Eh, bors? Fetch a pretty penny at Lynn, I shouldn't wonder."

A second man said facetiously: "I could eat an 'orse, meself. Plump little cob, int 'e."

Agnes held up her reticule. "You are welcome to all that I have here," she said.

Mary Emma looked at her in astonishment and her eyes flashed as she addressed the men. "You have no business waylaying defenceless women going about their own business," she scolded. "Kindly stand aside." She raised her whip, intending to urge the horse on its way.

The first speaker had grabbed Agnes's small bag and after rummaging in it had brought out a few copper and silver coins and jingled them in his palm. He looked up as Mary Emma raised the whip. "See that!" he cried. "Threaten us with your toy whip, wouldja, m'lady?" Before Mary Emma knew what was happening the man had snatched the whip out of her hand and was brandishing it before her frightened face. "You'd not be quite ser 'igh an mighty with a scar on yer cheek, now, wouldja?" he sneered. "First orf, yer can give us them fancy mantels you'm wearin'. My missus could dew with sumpin ter warm 'er up; I ent no good fer it no more. Come on, bors, 'elp the ladies orf wi' their fine togs like the gennelmen yew are."

"Leave 'em alone," a third man said quietly.

The two women stared at the speaker and saw that his face was largely concealed by a floppy-brimmed felt hat. His mouth and teeth appeared young.

The third man retrieved the whip from the menacing man – the men took care not to use names – and as he handed it back to Mary Emma she noticed that his hand was grotesquely disfigured; it reminded her of a roast rack of lamb minus its paper frills. The man became conscious of her scrutiny, thrust both hands out of sight and said: "We mean yer no 'arm, ma'am; but many of us 'aven't eaten in days an it makes us fergit our manners. If yer could spare us something we'd be more'n grateful."

His respectful appeal softened Mary Emma's resolve to give the ruffians nothing. Realising that her fine clothes would be too easily identified she took out her purse, turned it upside down onto her lap and immediately saw that there were enough golden guineas there to satisfy each of the men surrounding them.

The starving men were mesmerised by the glimmering heap of gold. They took their coins with a mixture of stunned humility and smouldering anger at the obvious inequality of their lot in life compared to that of the wealthy young woman's.

They drove away without looking back with Mary Emma keeping the reins in her left hand where she'd taken hold of them as Agnes gave up her purse to the men.

"Are you all right, Mary Emma?" Agnes asked solicitously.

"I'm all right," she replied angrily. "Are you?"

"How terrible!" Agnes said, and before she could go on:

"Just wait until I tell Tom about this outrage," Mary Emma fumed. "I can't think what things are coming to when a pair of respectable women cannot drive about their own streets in safety. You're absolutely right, Agnes; it is terrible."

"You misunderstand me, dear," Agnes said. "I was referring to the awful plight of those men. Why, it was obvious that they spoke only the truth when they said they were starving, poor things."

Mary Emma glanced at her friend's profile and grudgingly admitted that she was right though she refused to say so. "Did you notice the badly burned hand of the man in the floppy hat?" she said divertingly as they turned into the road that would take them to Uppham St Mary.

"No. But he seemed superior to the others who spoke. Don't you think so?" Agnes said. "I was looking at the horn that hung from a cord about his neck. Did you notice it?"

"A horn? How very odd!" Mary Emma said. "No; I didn't notice it, my dear. Ah, here we are," she added, as they came to a halt outside Church House.

Agnes laid a hand on her friend's arm. "I think it would be best to say nothing to mother about what happened in Downham, Mary Emma. It would only alarm her."

"You're right," Mary Emma agreed. "After all, we have to pass that way again to get home. Let's hope those awful men will have gone by then."

After alighting from the phaeton, the two young women adjusted their bonnets and straightened their apparel, using each other's guidance in lieu of a looking-glass. Satisfied that their fashionable appearance would provoke the desired response from Mrs Brook, they walked up to the door and pulled the bell. Overhead, a window was flung up and Ann's head poked out. The girl was overjoyed to see her sister and, after pulling down the window, she flew downstairs and opened the front door. Ann's gasp of ecstatic delight and the clasped hands on her chest gave them the very response which they had hoped their fashionable clothes would provoke.

They smiled at one another, kissed Ann in turn, and walked into the peculiar atmosphere that made Church House such a desirable place in which to spend the day.

★

Chapter Thirty-eight

Mary Emma and Agnes conspired to keep their alarming experience from everybody rather than cause further upset and after a few days other matters helped to push the unpleasant episode to the backs of their minds. Both young women now exhibited signs of their maternal expectations. Fortunately fashion was on their side and the loose fall of their highwaisted dresses helped to disguise the fact that their formerly virginal and slender bodies no longer bore scrutiny when undressed. The clever use of a pad of wool worn at the back immediately above the elevated waistline prevented the dress from falling in at the waist and the new style Mary Emma had adopted two months earlier Agnes copied now that she, too, had begun to swell to ripeness.

"Listen to this, my dear," Tom said one blustery March morning as they sat over their breakfast table. They were alone for once, their usual companions having taken themselves off early. He held a newly opened letter in his left hand. "It's from Daniel Jones." He fell silent as he read the letter to himself.

"Is that the whole of it?" Mary Emma said with a mischievous smile, "or am I to be privileged to hear more, sir?"

"Eh?" As her words sank in Tom laughed. "I beg your pardon, Mary Emma. It's the most extraordinary thing... '*My Dear Mr Challiss*, de-da, de-da, de-da... He goes on with pleasantries... Ah! Now, listen to this—"

"I have been all ears for the last two minutes, Tom," Mary Emma said, biting into another grape and swallowing the morsel. "Do get on with it, dear."

"'*I hope to see you at Lynn Regis on the Twenty-First Day of March. I have business with Bagg & Bacon's Bank on that Day that might be of interest to you and Mrs Challiss. It has to do with a Mutual Acquaintance – the erstwhile Owner of L.M. Do your utmost to be there, my dear sir, as you will undoubtedly hear Something to your Advantage.*' And that's all! Apart from the usual formal ending. What d'ye make of it?"

"Well," Mary Emma returned to her plate the twig and stalks of the few grapes she had been nibbling. "It's the family ghost rearing his ugly head again, I'm afraid, Tom. He's dead but he refuses to lie down. Lambert Jardine has never meant anything in my life but trouble."

"*Your* life!" Tom exclaimed. "It was me he wanted hanged or transported. But we have nothing to worry about from the man himself, my love. He really is dead. This must have something to do with his fortune."

"Bother his fortune, Tom!" his wife said energetically. "We don't need it. Why not leave things as they are, dear?"

"It's plain you've never been short of money, Mary Emma. Anybody who has will tell you never to look a gift horse in the mouth." He stretched his long arms above his head and brought them down abruptly when he felt her tickling him under his arm. "Now stop that! Suppose one of the servants were to come in?" he said crossly.

"Stuff! You're becoming an old married man, Thomas Roberts Challiss," she taunted; "and if you turn sour and grumpy on me before you're seventy I shall sue for divorce on the grounds of lack of a sense of humour."

"Mary Emma!" he said, with a laugh at her outrageous nonsense. "Please remember your condition. It ill becomes you to clown about in your present physical state."

"Oh, I don't know," she smiled, running her hands down her swollen abdomen and holding her dress tightly over the bulge so that her ripening figure left nothing to his imagination. "I consider I'm exactly the right shape for a clown. Don't you?"

"You are incorrigible, wife," Tom said, planting a kiss on her forehead. "I've made up my mind: I shall go to Lynn on the twenty-first and find out what Daniel's cryptic message is all about." He removed his napkin and threw it onto the table. "Now I must go over to Mrs Hignell's to see how things are there now that Ing – Thompson's vanished. What an extraordinary fellow! As well as leaving me in the lurch he didn't hang about long enough to collect his wages. Where on earth am I supposed to find another gamekeeper?"

"He's no loss, from what Ruth said," Mary Emma remarked. "As to where you'll find another gamekeeper; why not engage a reformed poacher, Tom? You could do worse; there are plenty of them hanging about the streets of Downham. Anyway, it isn't your problem; Joe Aldrich should be the one to sort it out, shouldn't he."

He looked at his girlish wife. "You're quite right: it's Aldrich's job. I'll get him to look for a replacement at once. As to your idea of employing a poacher turned gamekeeper to catch the beggars – Where do you get these strange ideas from, my love?" he said, his eyes smiling into hers. "It's no good: I shall never understand women and you least of all, Mary Emma." Yet as he walked to the stables to collect his horse he wondered if she might not have had a very good idea indeed.

Maddy came in to clear the breakfast table and was surprised to find her mistress still seated. The girl made a clumsy bob and apologised before turning to go.

"Stay a moment, Maddy," Mary Emma said. "I have a bone to pick with you, my girl."

The maidservant turned to her mistress and her scarlet face was a study as conflicting emotions played across her features. "Yes, Mrs Challiss, ma'am?"

"Come over here, my dear," Mary Emma said kindly, aware that she had frightened the girl. "Did you think I wouldn't notice the number of times you have neglected your duties of late, Maddy?" To her consternation the maidservant burst into tears and started to dab at her eyes with a corner of her apron. Mary Emma got up and took the sobbing girl in her arms. "There, there, Maddy," she said, gently patting the girl's back. "I'm not cross with you, my dear. Pray don't upset yourself."

"Oh, Mrs Challiss, ma'am," the girl said, taking a step backwards and gulping down her sobs, "I am so sorry. I know I've been a bad girl but I reelly couldn't 'elp meself."

Oh, dear, thought Mary Emma, it is worse than I imagined. "Suppose you tell me all about it, my dear. What is it that you think you have done that is so bad?" As it turned out it was something and nothing, after all. The gist of Maddy's tale was this: she and Ben Wright being of an age, they had become good friends and had taken to escaping from the monotony of servitude whenever they thought they could safely escape notice. "Mostly, I've run over ter see Ben when you and Miss Brook or Auntie Bee don't need me. Ben an me like skywannickin' in the stables. Oh, Mrs Challiss, ma'am! We 'ave such larks! Ben knows a master lot about 'orses an other animals; 'e tells me all sorts o' stories about nature." Her recently tear-filled eyes shone with excitement now. "Ben Wright dew know the names of all the birds an insects an wild flowers, ma'am, an 'e's promised ter teach me all about 'em soon as the snow forgives an we can go out inter the park."

Mary Emma laughed. "You're a saucy young baggage, Madeleine Smith! How dare you stand there and tell your mistress that you intend to run off to play in the meadows as soon as spring arrives!"

Maddy gasped and her hand flew to cover her mouth as she realised that she'd let the cat out of the bag in her excitement. "Oh, Mrs Challiss, ma'am," she took hold of the corners of her apron and curtseyed. "I dew beg your pardon, ma'am. I dew 'ope you'll fergive me. Auntie Bee said me tongue would get me inter trouble one day an she were right."

Mary Emma seated herself on a settle and patted the space next to her, saying: "Come and sit down by me, Maddy."

"Oh, ma'am," the girl said fearfully, "I daresn't! If uncle Rudge was ter catch me I'd be in reel trouble."

"Leave Mr Rudge to me," Mary Emma said. "Now, Maddy. I think you are happy here at Uppham, are you not?"

"Yes'm," the girl whispered, obviously fearful of what was coming next.

"I'm glad to hear it. But you really cannot expect to run away from your duties in the mansion. There's a lot to do here, Maddy, and you surely don't want to give the other servants more work while you go off to play with Ben?"

"Oh, they don't mind, Mrs Challiss," the girl said blithely. "'Tis only a bit o' dustin', an settin' the tables an such like that I bunks arf from."

"I wish that were all, Maddy," Mary Emma said, a little more severely now that the girl had pulled herself together. "But there have been times recently when I have needed your assistance with my toilette and none of the other servants have been able to find you. That is not only discourteous to me as your mistress but it is also a waste of the other servants' time. So we'll have no more of it, my girl. D'you understand?"

Maddy curtseyed again and whispered: "Yes, Mrs Challiss." Her face crumpled and she wailed: "I am so very sorry, ma'am. If I promise not tew dew it again, will I be able ter keep me place?"

"You silly little goose!" Mary Emma laughed. "There's no question of your dismissal. But mind what I say, there's a good girl. And you had better keep away from the stables Maddy. You're growing up, you know and Ben, even William, will be bound to get ideas about you that might get you into serious trouble if you allow them too much freedom with your person. Do you understand my meaning?"

Maddy stared at her mistress's swollen figure, bit her lips and hung her head in embarrassment. "Yes, Mrs Challiss, ma'am."

The servant's blushing face in its frilled white bonnet reminded Mary Emma of a ripe pippin wrapped about with a kerchief. She kissed the girl on her hot cheek. "Good! I'm glad we understand one another. Now get along with you and go about your duties without any more nonsense." Once Maddy had gone Mary Emma raised her eyes to the ceiling in despair before coming to a decision. She walked upstairs and, having reached the back withdrawing room, went straight to the escritoire, seated herself before it and took out a sheet of writing paper.

Half an hour later she had a letter written to a domestic agency asking them to place an advertisement in several newspapers requesting eligible persons to apply, in writing, for the position of Housekeeper at Uppham House, Uppham St Mary, near Downham in the County of Norfolk; she gave her own name as the correspondent.

Later that morning, she gave the advertisement to Agnes to read and asked her if she thought she needed to add anything further. "It's perfectly well, so far as it goes, Mary Emma" her friend said, handing the sheet of paper back to her. "But might it not save time and notepaper, dear, if you were to ask the agency to advertise for an Assistant Cook at the same time?"

Mary Emma was annoyed with herself for not having thought of it first. "Oh, d'you think I should?" she said, feigning doubt.

"I only thought… Poor Mrs Rudge is over sixty and looks so very tired at the end of the day."

"Does she? I hadn't noticed. But then, I have no occasion to visit the kitchen after dinner. As far as one can tell, everything appears to go on perfectly well without my interference."

Agnes rejected the imputation. "I had no intention of interfering, Mary Emma. It's just that Mrs Rudge appreciates having somebody to talk to in the evenings, other than Mr Rudge or Barty Peckover, both of whom seem to prefer to be anywhere else but the kitchen after a hard day on their feet, fetching and carrying."

"Hoity-toity, Agnes Brook!" Mary Emma laughed. "What a stern speech to your friend. I stand – or, rather, sit – before you and consider myself duly rebuked."

Agnes smiled. "That was not my intention, Mary Emma, nor is it my place to be so presumptious. After all, you are the mistress of the house, not I."

"You sly fox!" Mary Emma said, her eyes smiling. "That's teaching me my place while implying that I am mistress in name only. You are right, I suppose. I am neglectful of my duties; though I did see fit to reprimand young Maddy this morning. But your cruel criticism, though justified, brings us back to my letter. Perhaps now you begin to see the necessity for engaging a professional housekeeper. I am too spoiled and lazy to keep traipsing up and down stairs, checking that the grates have been swept or running my forefinger along surfaces to detect whether they are really free of dust. I would far rather listen to you singing and playing the piano, or lose myself among the pages of one of Miss Austen's earlier novels while I wait for *Emma* to arrive, or drive about the park in the cob-phaeton with you by my side, my friend."

At the close of this diatribe on housekeeping Agnes burst into laughter. "Oh, Mary Emma! You make it sound as if preserving and maintaining one's home is to be deplored. I cannot understand your disinterest in domestic matters. A job of work well done can be so rewarding."

"Yes, and lasts for all of five minutes if one is lucky!" Mary Emma said crossly. "Why, no sooner have Rudge and Peckover waxed the hall floor than Tom is bound to walk across it in his muddy boots without a thought for those who keep it bright and gleaming."

"Well... Of course, such inconsiderate behaviour towards one's servants might perhaps be gently brought to the attention of the offender," Agnes said. "Which brings me to another related subject, Mary Emma. I hope you will not be offended if I speak perfectly frankly?"

"Oh, dear! I don't like the sound of that at all. But I suppose it will do me good to hear what you have to say: it usually does, my dear watchdog."

"Well... Since the refurbishing of the house the number of rooms to be cleaned and cared for has doubled. It's true, few of the rooms in the east wing are out of dustcovers. Even so, the housework is now beyond the three house servants who were already here when you arrived, leaving aside Mrs Rudge. I respectfully suggest, Mary Emma, that you need to engage at least two more housemaids."

Mary Emma smiled. "As usual, Agnes, you see everything so clearly. Why, you're more than qualified to take on the post of housekeeper yourself."

"I would never consent to that, Mary Emma," Agnes said gravely. "At fifteen, I do not consider my life quite over, simply because I have committed an indiscretion. I intend to be mistress of my own home one day, with or without a husband. And when that day comes, I shall run my home in exactly the same way that my mother runs hers."

"Do you mean to say that you would willingly sacrifice yourself to a life of drudgery: to child-rearing – without a staffed nursery – and to constantly supplying meals with no cook or scullery maid?" Mary Emma was shocked by the very idea.

"You left contentment out of your list, Mary Emma. You've seen how happy my parents' home is. If I'm fortunate enough to meet a man who will forgive my fall, one who can love me and my child in spite of it, that's what I want for myself and my husband – and for our children. That's my idea of a life of pleasure, not drudgery."

Mary Emma raised an eyebrow. "Scandalous! You're building castles – or rather, ruined cottages – in the air, my dear. It wouldn't do for me, I'm afraid."

Agnes smiled indulgently. "No, Mary Emma, it wouldn't do for you at all. You were meant for quite a different kind of life – the one you and Tom are building here. It wouldn't do for me any more than my ideal would befit you. Nevertheless, we each have a great deal to be thankful for, even now, compared to many women."

★

Tom saw at once that John Brook was doing a grand job at Mrs Hignell's cottage. Split kindling was stacked high against a sheltered wall near her front door. She told Mr Challiss that the boy filled her containers every morning without fail so that she was able to keep herself and her little home clean, as well as having plenty of water with which to make tea and do her bit of cooking. The few errands she wanted John to run were usually finished by about ten o'clock each morning. John had told Tom that once he'd completed his chores for his mother he was free until the afternoon when he walked up to join Mr Webster in finishing the library. He'd taken to his new life and, despite his initial misgivings, was eager to begin his long apprenticeship into the mysteries of carpentry. Tom, satisfied that the boy looked after the old woman, noted that she had a room free once more, since Thompson had taken himself off, and cantered Mulderrig back towards the Uppham estate.

Downham High Street was an uncomfortable place for anyone who might be mistaken for one of the despised gentry. Tom was glad that he was mounted and that his journey through the streets thronged with disgruntled men, bitter women and their abnormally quiet, docile and feeble-looking children was soon accomplished. The mood in Downham was that of a powder keg about to explode and he was glad to have reached the quiet lane that led to his own gates without any mishap having befallen him. He dismounted at the lodge and left his hack to crop the grass verge.

Fortunately, Joseph Aldrich was at home and the business of taking on a new gamekeeper was soon concluded. Next Tom suggested that Warrender might prefer to move out of his lodgings at Church House in favour of more privacy at Mrs Hignell's cottage. Joe was eager to get off to the building site, as work was pressing ahead now that the weather had yielded a little, but to his annoyance Tom detained him further.

His hand in his breast pocket he said: "There's something I think you ought to see, Joe," and drew forth a crumpled handbill which he smoothed out on the table. "I had a letter from Daniel Jones, my attorney at Fakenham, which will take me to Lynn on the twenty-first – make a note of that – and he enclosed this. I'd rather we kept its contents between ourselves at present, old fellow. With both the women in my house in delicate conditions it wouldn't do to frighten them unnecessarily."

Aldrich looked from Tom's face with its anxious expression to the printed bill, picked up the paper, took it over to the window and silently began to read.

'To the Gentlemen of Ashill'*

This is to inform you that you have by this time brought us under the heaviest burden and under the hardest yoke we ever knowed; it is too hard for us to bear; you have often times blinded us by saying that the fault was all in the Place-men of Parliament: but now you have opened our eyes, we know they have a great power, but they have nothing to do with the regulation of the parish.

You do as you like, you rob the poor of their commons right, plough the grass up that God send to grow, that a poor man may feed a cow, Pig, Horse, nor Ass; lay muck and stones on the road to prevent the grass growing. If a poor man is out of work and wants a day or two's work you will give him 6d per week, and then a little man that does not employ a labourer at all, must help pay for your work doing, which will bring them chargeable to the parish. There is 5 or 6 of you have gotten all the whole of the land in this parish in your own hands and you would wish to be rich and starve all the other part of the poor of the parish. If any poor man wanted anything, then you will call a Town meeting about it, to hear which could continue to hiss him the most, which have caused us to have a county meeting, to see if we cannot gain some redress.

Gentlemen, these few lines are to inform you that God Almighty have brought our blood to a proper circulation, that have been in a very bad state a long time, and now without an alteration of the foresaid, we mean to circulate your blood with the leave of God. And we do not intend to give you but a very short time to consider about it, as we have gotten one or two of the head, on our side. There was 2 cows and an Ass feeding on the road last Saturday, and there was 2 farmers went to the keepers and said they would pound them, if they did not drive them away, one of them candidly went home, got a plough and horses, and ploughed the grass up that growed on the road.

We deem the miller to be full as big a rogue as you farmers for the wheat raise 1s per Comb. He will then raise 2d per stone; so we drive the whole before us and knock down the Mill and set fire to all houses and stacks as we go along: we shall begin in the Night.

And the first Man that refuses to join the Combination shall suffer death in a moment, or the first person that is catched saying anything against the same, shall suffer death. We have had private ambushes around us for some time, and by this time you will find it is coming to a point.

Take notice that this is a private letter wrote at this time, but we fear it will be too public for your profits; so we wish to prepare yourselves ready for action; for we intend to have things as we like; you have had a good long time. We have counted up that we have gotten about 60 of us to 1 of you: therefore should you govern, so many to one? No: we will fight for it and if you win the day, so be it.

Swines, Fokelee, Moocher

* Quoted in *Bread or Blood* by A.J.Peacock. Reproduced by kind permission of Gollancz.

Aldrich flung down the paper, rushed out through the conservatory and Tom heard him retching up his breakfast. After a short interval the steward returned, his handkerchief to his lips, his face drained of colour. He tried to speak. No voice came at first; then he said in appalled accents, in which his deep voice was reduced to a sepulchral whisper: "They surely wouldn't think of doing such terrible things as this," he took up the the handbill and struck it with the back of his hand, "in our own parish, Mr Challiss? They can have no quarrel with you, sir; you have been fairness itself in your dealings with the poor."

"I hoped to be, Joe," Tom said. "Lately, I've thought that I should be doing a lot more instead of hiding myself away from reality. Mrs Coy and her children brought that home to me. How could such a dreadful thing have happened in today's England? Ashill's less than twenty miles from Downham – a morning's ride."

"You don't really think we shall be attacked in our own homes, Mr Challiss," Aldrich said, aghast at the prospect. "We must lock the side gate from now on, sir. Fix up a bell—"

Tom shrugged his shoulders. "I see no point in locking gates, Joe. The starving French couldn't be kept out of the Bastille; their rage was so great against the injustices they'd suffered at the hands of the aristocracy and the bourgoisie that the mob tore at its walls with their bare hands. Hunger is a powerful incentive to anarchy; and driven, desperate men – even Englishmen – will unite in revolt against repeated oppression; it's the only weapon they have. Rioting is the lighted touchpaper of revolution, Joe, and there have been riots all over the country."

"You talk like a radical, sir!" Aldrich said, firing up, eyes flashing.

"I've heard that term bandied about quite a lot since I came home; but I'm not quite certain of its meaning," Tom said, surprised by Aldrich's vehement attack. "If to be termed a radical is to acknowledge that this country is in turmoil, that changes must – and will – be made to the existing social and economic conditions of the poor, then, yes, I suppose that is what I am."

"Mr Challiss, sir!" Aldrich said in great agitation. "Are you aware that you could find yourself in trouble for voicing such views? Should Sir Everard Belmaine get to hear of your. . ." the nervous steward couldn't bring himself to utter the word a second time, ". . . socialistic leanings, he has the power to clap you in gaol, sir."

To Aldrich's chagrin, Tom laughed outright. "Sir Everard is quite aware of my views, Joe. He might not subscribe to 'em but he hasn't a closed mind on the subject." He snatched up the copy of the 'private' letter addressed to the Gentlemen of Ashill – which one of the rioting radicals had made public by printing off a stack of handbills from the original – and stuffed the notice back into his breast pocket. Seeing that his views and action had caused the man's face to crease with anxiety, he added: "Don't worry, Joe; I'll keep any thoughts on the subject to myself. But I will say this: those men have right on their side and there's bound to be trouble." Master and servant parted amicably enough, their mutual respect intact.

The first flakes of a snow shower began to fall as Tom unhitched Mulderrig. "Won't lie for long, this time of the year," he said to the horse as they covered the distance between the lodge and the mansion. But by the time Wright had walked the hack to its stall a white mantle had blotted out every hesitant sign of spring. "Damnation!" Tom growled to himself. "No wonder the men are muttering about '1800 and frozen to death'. They're right about that. Deacon's in for a hard time with the lambing."

"Is that you, Tom?" Mary Emma called from the open door of the library. "Oh! Is it snowing?"

As she had complained to Agnes, Tom walked straight across the polished floor to her in his snowy boots leaving a watery trail in his wake. "It is, my dear. And it's a damned nuisance, just as the building project was surging ahead."

"Oo!" She shivered as he kissed her warm cheek with his cold lips and she returned the salutation. She looked through the window and out over the whitened park. "Oh...," she wailed. "Only yesterday Agnes saw her first celandine this spring, and that was late enough, and the hawthorn buds were teetering on the brink of bursting. I don't blame the leaves for refusing to show themselves in this chilly climate."

Despite the problems occupying his mind, Tom smiled at her nonsense. "Another setback," he said, shrugging himself out of his full length coat with his wife's assistance. "As if things aren't bad enough for those poor devils."

"Who?"

Holding his exasperation in check, he strove to keep his voice even. "I'm sorry, my dear. I'm talking about the hundreds of people who are starving on our doorstep. Those who have had to try to survive the winter months with insufficient food in their bellies–"

"Tom Challiss! I won't listen to such coarse language–"

"You can't shut your eyes and ears to what's going on for ever, Mary Emma," he said, his voice rising.

"I will not be shouted at, Tom," Mary Emma said quietly.

He made an effort at controlling himself. "I beg your pardon, Mary Emma. Forgive me. But we can no longer go on as if we inhabit a separate little world of our own, as if what is happening to the poor of Uppham St Mary and Downham – all over the country! – has nothing to do with us."

"Dear me! Whom have you been with who has put you in such a passion that you come home ranting politics like one of those fiery radicals?"

He stared at her in disbelief. "And what would you happen to know about such things, madam? 'Tis scarcely a fitting subject for such a pretty head to bother with."

She smiled enigmatically and said: "Aha! That's my secret, sir. I have been receiving a political education from somebody who has experienced, at first hand, the very hardships of which you speak."

"Now, Mary Emma! What nonsense is this? Unless Agnes—"

"And what first hand experience of hardship has Agnes Brook ever had to endure, may I ask? You will have to do better than that, sir," she teased.

He shook his head. "I'm in no mood for guessing games, wife. I don't believe that you've been in the company of any such person! Why, these days you hardly leave the house."

"Pray, do go on, sir."

"With what?" he snapped. He glanced at the grand-daughter clock that stood opposite the front door and saw that the mealtime was still several minutes away. "I've had enough of this," he grumbled, striding towards the library to check progress.

"Getting warmer," Mary Emma said, smiling mischievously.

"For heaven's sake, Mary Emma! ... You surely can't mean Jem Webster?"

A peal of laughter escaped her such as Tom hadn't heard for many weeks, he realised. "There!" She clapped her hands. "Well done, sir! You got there in the end."

He stepped back and embraced her, saying: "If I have behaved like a bear with a sore head the only excuse I have to offer is the press of business, my dear."

She raised herself on tip-toe and kissed him on the lips. "I'm so sorry, Tom. I'm no help to you, am I. But, truly; Jem has been doing his best to make me understand that burying our heads in the sand like ostriches will not prevent angry men from turning on those in more comfortable circumstances than themselves. He says we should read the newspapers every day to find out what's really going on."

Tom's brow darkened. "Does he, by Gad! I had no idea that a quiet revolution was being plotted under my own roof. I'll have a word with Webster myself after we've dined. Ah! Good," he cried, as the dinner gong sounded. "I'm simply ravenous."

"But you will have your hunger satisfied, Tom, unlike some," she said, archly.

Jem Webster preferred to eat his dockey alone wherever he happened to be working rather than to join his master and the others at the formal dining table. As he alternately bit into his wedge of cheese and hunk of bread, stopping now and then to wash them down with ale, he surveyed his workmanship with a critical eye, goading himself to spot an imperfection. It gave him enormous pleasure to allow his eyes to travel over each skilful moulding, the alignment of each shelf, the position of the knobs on the cupboards, the perfectly-fitted brass hinges on each of the book rests, the library chair that became a set of steps in one hand's turn, the sliding ladder on its overhead rail, myriad details of skilled carpentry that would go unnoticed by one less practised in discerning such precise work – and then to find not the least fault.

Many of the innovations had been made according to Mrs Challiss's instructions and, as she had come up with new ideas almost every day since the fire, he'd been at his wits' end to cope with the quantity of intricate work. He'd disliked going behind his mistress's back; but he'd had no alternative. For a single carpenter to marry her clever ideas with the tight timescale she'd demanded would have been an impossibility. He'd been compelled to farm out most of the smaller jobs to three redundant men: a cabinet maker, a joiner and a journeyman carpenter, who possessed the tools of their trades. For, since the postwar depression many woodworkers had been reduced to selling their tool chests, each containing up to two hundred cherished tools that had been handed down from father to son for generations. Without their chests the men were useless. Once he'd been asked to take on young Brook as an apprentice deception had become harder. Fortunately, by the time the boy appeared most of the large work had been accomplished. Before John Brook's arrival it had been comparatively easy to smuggle in and out of the mansion hinged book rests, lengths of beading awaiting carving and drawers and chests in sections for his team of eager craftsmen to work on. The outworkers had agreed to work for two shillings each per week, all that Jem could afford, and had suffered the indignity of such a low wage in order to follow their crafts. That the work began in the short dark days of winter aided his deception: he'd arrived early with finished panels, before the household was astir, and had left in the dark evenings to deliver new pieces of work.

Mrs Challiss had agreed to his hiring two professional decorators to finish the ceiling, walls and ornamental plastering and, finally, a french polisher. He'd been able to dissuade her from carrying out her crazy idea of having the library finished in sections so that the newly bound books could be returned to the shelves.

Seated on a box, Jem rubbed his hands over his thighs, which were covered by a full-length holland apron, to remove any grease that might be lingering from his snack and had just picked up his steel rule to resume work when his master tapped on the door and strode into the room.

"Good-afternoon, Jem," he began briskly.

Jem rose from his temporary seat. "Arternoon, Mr Challiss."

"You've finished your snack?" Noting the crumbs and the replaced stopper in the ale jug, he said: "Good. Well, I won't beat about the bush, Jem. I hear that you've thought fit to instruct Mrs Challiss in matters that she has no business worrying her head about, especially in her condition."

"Oh-ah? What's she bin sayin?"

"That you've thought fit to acquaint her with the various causes of the present unrest among the poor."

"Did I now? Put that way, it sounds as if I might've done somethin wrong. Is that what you're geddin at?"

"Be that as it may," Tom said, his anger rising at Jem's self-possession, "you have absolutely no right to discuss such unpleasant subjects with your mistress."

"What dew she say?"

"What d'you mean, man? I've just told you!"

"No yew aint; you've told me what yew've 'eard an follered it wi' a lot o' fancy words that I wouldn't think o' usin 'cause I dunno what 'alf of 'em mean."

His calm rebuttal took Tom by surprise and he came down from his high horse at once. "Do you deny that you've been filling Mrs Challiss's head with tales about the troubles in Downham."

"I dew."

The man was tying him in knots! "Then suppose you tell me what you and she have been discussing – apart from library fittings and the like," Tom said, more calmly.

"Ah! I'd be 'appy ter dew that, Mr Challiss." He seated himself back on his box. "Pity yew didn't ask me that in the beginnin."

Damn his impertinence! "Suppose you get on with it," Tom said, perching his left buttock on the edge of a large mahogany table whose satin smooth surface was ready for french polishing.

"Young Brook's liable to turn up any minute," Jem said, glancing out of the window towards the snow covered drive. "Still, 'e'll prob'ly be late, on account o' the snow," he added. "As ter what I said ter Mrs Challiss . . . Well, 'twere her as axed me about it in the first place, not t'other way round, as yew seem ter think. 'Twere that jaunt she an Miss Brook took in the liddle yeller coach t'other day an the drive through Downham set 'er thinking about things, Mr Challiss. She's got a good 'ead on her shoulders 'as your missus – fer a female, I mean."

"Yes, yes. Get on with it; and keep your opinions about Mrs Challiss to yourself!" Tom said, annoyed that he hadn't fully considered the dangers posed to the two vulnerable women on their short drive to Church House.

"Well… they run intew a spot o' bother wi' some poor starvin devils who pressed 'em fer money."

"Good God! I had no idea, Jem. Were they threatened?"

"Not 'zackly threatened, only frightened at first, though accordin ter Mrs Challiss, they dint show it. It were all over in minutes an no 'arm done."

Tom frowned. "You mean to say that the men allowed them to continue their journey without further trouble?"

"Oh-ah; once the ladies give 'em some money the men let 'em go. 'Twere after she got 'ome that Mrs Challiss told me about it and axed me about the men, women an youngun's 'anging about the streets in silence. Seems tew 'ave noticed 'em at last."

"And what did you tell her?"

"Yew aint gonna be offended if I speak out, Mr Challiss?"

"I'd like to know what you said, Jem. You may speak freely."

"Well, I told yer 'tweren't no use people like yew an yer missus tryin ter 'ide away from the troubles an' thinkin they 'adn't anything ter do wi' 'em. Jist because yew've got a lot o' little things that take up your time, an fill your days, it makes yer sneerfroys terwards the likes of us. I said tew Mrs Challiss: most o' what the gentry think's important an necessary aint nothin but a lot o' time wastin; piddlin liddle time fillers that aint got a lot ter do with real livin." He held up his hand in defence. "Hold yew hard, Mr Challiss; hear me out afore yew blow me 'ead orf. Yew aint gentry, yew told me that when we first met; but, it seems ter me that you're goin on fair ter try an ape those as are." He waved his hand around the library. "All this, fer instance: the money that's bin spent on tricolatin this one room could've saved 'undreds from near-starvation this winter. I point it out as one example an doan mean ter cast 'spersions on what yew think fit ter dew wi' yer own money. An I doan lose sight o' the fact that yew've bin good ter me in givin me work, neether.

"By 'idin' away on your istate, yew can try ter blot out what's 'appenin' outside your gates. But a man don't choose ter be born poor or ugly, Mr Challiss, any more'n the aristos and the gentry can choose oo's soft bed the stork drops 'em in. I might've mentioned ter Mrs Challiss that the bone o' contention atween them an' us is: they've got money an security an we aint. It's the unfairness of it as sticks in a man's craw when all 'e asks fer is the right ter work and ter be rewarded fairly fer it."

Tom was surprised to find that many of Jem's opinions and ideas corresponded to his own. "I've known both worlds, Jem," he said. "It's true, I've never known starvation — thank God! — but my life hasn't always been a bed of roses; still, I don't want to go into that now. I agree with you that those in power have mismanaged affairs disgracefully. It cannot be right to force up the cost of provisions in order to make profits from the needs of the poorest in our society."

A spark of approval gleamed in Jem's eye. "Well, Mr Challiss, I will say this: yew aint entirely a larst cause."

Tom laughed. "Glad to hear it! But talk's cheap and, even if it weren't, I don't know what's to be done for the mass of the unemployed to improve their conditions," he finished lamely.

"You could give 'em back some of their land, Mr Challiss," Webster suggested.

This was too radical an idea for Tom to accept. "As far as I'm aware, nobody on this estate has appropriated commons land; its location wouldn't allow for that."

Jem pulled a wry face. "'Urts, doan it; ter think of somebody takin away what's rightfully yours. Bit be bit, they've stolen every last thing away from those men yer see 'angin' about Downham, short of a dogged pride in their independence. Many of 'em would rather starve than give in and slink orf ter the workus. But it's comin' tew an end, Mr Challiss. Yew mark my words. Afore long the 'orns o' Downham'll sound all over the town, an when they dew they'll be blowin' in the wind o' change."

Tom didn't know quite what to make of the carpenter's last remark and put it down to his attempt at a colourful prediction of additional local unrest.

The appearance of Peckover at the door with worrying news brought his conversation with Jem to an abrupt end and drove the carpenter's pronouncement from his mind.

"Mr Pawl's compliments, Mr Challiss, sir. There's bin trouble at Martlits an 'e says would you please spare 'im the time to come an talk to 'im about it, sir. 'E's in the 'all."

★

". . . but you must have heard the term bandied about, Mr Challiss; it's on everybody's lips. Those who had sympathy with the Luddite movement a few years ago have banded together and are stirring up trouble again. They must have a ringleader. It's a natural development of the general feeling of disgruntlement and despair that has hung over the whole country since the end of the war."

"What have Luddites to do with this trouble at Martlets? Peckover said something about arson?"

"Quite true. Arson, machine-breaking, destruction of private property – every window in his conservatory smashed, the roofs of his stables robbed of their slates – it was only a matter of time before an attack against Sir Everard's place; there have been a number in the county. I regret to say that his increasingly harsh sentences, on poachers in particular, have had a great deal to do with the rise in resentment against him in his official capacity as magistrate."

The seriousness of the assault on his wealthy neighbour's estate alarmed Tom. "Was anybody hurt in the attack?" he asked, thinking particularly of elderly Belmaine and young Robin.

"A footman has been seriously injured," said Pawl. "Should he die it will, of course, become a hanging matter for the culprit, should he be caught. But the raiders had vanished by the time the militia arrived; they were too late to catch anybody redhanded. It was a carefully planned attack, sir. No doubt about that."

"So that's why you were absent from luncheon," Tom remarked. "We wondered what'd kept you."

"I couldn't just walk away and leave Sir Everard and Robin to face their troubles alone. The devastation is appalling, Mr Challiss. The damage must run into many hundreds of pounds," Pawl continued, as he appeared to look inwards at something in particular. "Of course, the haystacks went up in no time. The beautiful stable block is a terrible sight. I was reminded of the burning of your own hayloft and my unwitting part in it and what followed."

"I'm sorry you were reminded of that, Everett. When did the raid take place?" Tom asked, wondering why none of the dogs had, apparently, barked a warning.

"The servants raised the alarm soon after four-thirty this morning, Mr Challiss. Apparently, the threat of trouble having died down, or so it was thought, Sir Everard had relaxed his defences. It was the first night in months that the footmen had been relieved of night guard duty and, as luck would have it, his gamekeeper happened to be following poachers in Raven Wood, which is the farthest point on the estate from the house and its adjacent buildings. It's a terrrible tragedy, sir. Terrible."

Tom was appalled by what he'd heard. "As you say, it was very carefully planned; with military precision, I should say. The dogs must've been silenced and the poachers in Raven Wood were obviously a divertionary tactic; no doubt about it."

"My opinion, exactly," Pawl said. "Pray extend my apologies to Mrs Challiss for missing luncheon without prior notice, sir. I have eaten at Martlets. Now, it's quite time I got on with my work among my library volumes. If you'll excuse me, sir."

Watching him go, Tom wished he too was able to lose himself in some absorbing pastime, only to realise that he was unable to name one that would blot out of his mind all that he had heard in the last few hours. He went to find Mary Emma, to ask her about the trouble she and Agnes had had with the unemployed men. After a lengthy search, he found his wife sleeping on a day bed in the back withdrawing room. Her face was lovely in repose and he longed to stretch out beside her and take comfort from the nearness of her ripening body. Banishing the selfish urge, he sighed heavily, crept to the door and closed it quietly with the intention of seeking Agnes Brook. Her soothing company was just what he needed to dispel the hive of unpleasant topics that swarmed in his troubled head.

★

Voices in quiet conversation alerted him to the fact that Agnes was not alone. He opened the door into the front withdrawing room and was surprised to find Adam Brook and one of his younger daughters, Ann, chatting happily to Agnes.

The head gardener stood up at Tom's entrance. "Arternoon, Mr Challiss," he said. "I 'ad ter come up ter the 'ouse tew tell yer that young John's got a cold so 'e won't be up this arternoon tew 'is work."

"Good afternoon, Adam. Miss Ann. I'm sorry to hear that John's unwell. I'll let Jem know."

"I already done that on the way in," Adam said. "Jem's made yer libr'ry inter a rill masterpiece, Mr Challiss. Jist like one o' the gentry might envy, eh." His eyes twinkled as he made his little dig at Mary Emma's pretensions to grandeur. "Ann 'ere, 'eard I was on me way up an begged tew ride pillion on ole Dobbin's broad back. She's bin dyin ter see Agnes; but Dulcie wouldn't let her out after it snew agin."

"I hope yew don't mind me coming without an invitation, Mr Challiss, sir," the young girl said doubtfully. "But I were that desperate tew get out of the house tew have a talk with our Agnes that I just had ter come when I saw the chance."

"I'm very pleased to see you any time you care to pay us a visit, Ann," Tom said. "Mrs Challiss and I are always happy to see any of the Brook family, you know that."

Agnes smiled warmly at him for his kind words to her sister. "And I was so pleased when Peckover showed Ann in," she said. "I do miss them all when I am sitting here quietly by myself. It isn't that I crave company; but I do feel the lack of others moving about these vast empty rooms when Mary Emma's resting."

Tom smiled. "We are doing our best to remedy that, Agnes, but nature won't be hurried."

"Yew make the most o' your freedom, bor," Brook advised, halting as he intercepted Agnes's admonishing glance, "... Mr Challis. Yew'll have precious liddle peace once them babbies start coming thick an fast."

"What nonsense you talk, Father!" Agnes remonstrated. "Why, you know you love every one of us to distraction and wouldn't wish yourself master of a deadly quiet home that resembled a nunnery full of a silent order of nuns, not for a pot of gold."

Brook laughed, revealing that he'd lost another molar. "Right ole schoolma'am, aint she. Pity the pore devil oo takes yew on fer life," he said, smiling at his own wit. As the two sisters began to gossip about home matters, including Noah's latest developments, Brook's manner changed abruptly and he subdued his voice. "I'd like a word wi' yew in private, Tom. Is there somewhere we can talk wi'out interruption?"

"I was going to inspect the progress on the building work, Adam," Tom said, wondering what could be of such secrecy that Brook's own daughters were barred from hearing it. "Would you mind if we killed two birds with one stone?"

"'S all right by me. Let's go. Left me 'at an coat downstairs."

They cut across the park to the building site and Adam Brook unburdened himself as they tramped through the snow.

There had been further trouble at Martlets. "'Twas Kit Warrender oo tole me," Adam continued. "Bad trouble up in Raven Wood. Seems Belmaine's gamekeeper set a couple o' spring guns as a warnin ter poachers. Young Ben Rix comes acrorst one, points it in the opposite direction, then goes an 'ides in an 'olly grove ter keep watch. Sure 'nough, along comes the 'ead keeper. Jist then two hen pheasants come rattlin along like a coupla dice boxes and distract Ben. He leaves 'is cover, the keeper starts terwards 'im an steps on the spring. Gun goes orf, straight at the keeper's 'ead. Killed outright."

Tom stopped in his tracks. "What a murderous thing to have planned! My God, Adie! What kind of evil man dreams up these terrible, inhuman traps to set on men who, in the main, are only after something to put in their children's empty bellies?" Deep creases lined his forehead. "And what of Ben Rix?"

"That'un leads a charmed life, bor. Got clean away. But not afore one or tew of 'is mates went ter see oo'd gorn ter meet 'is Maker, an see Ben Rix still alive. Nat'rally, none of 'em wanted tew 'ang fer somethin they dint dew. So they give 'emselves up ter the militia, who was at a dead end, so ter speak, 'angin about the forecourt o' Martlits. But their time weren't zackly wasted, as it turned out, 'cause they took the poachers inter custody. The men'd rather face a spell in gaol, even transportation, than be wrongly accused o' murder. That's 'ow the story goes, any'ow."

Tom shook his head in dismay. "And Sir Everard? How has he taken it?"

"Well, now you're axin! 'Twere the last straw as far as 'e were concerned. Warrender says 'e collapsed after some kind o' fit an is confined ter bed in a dark room after a bloodlettin, or leeches, or somethin in that line."

"This is terrible! The whole thing's a tragedy, Adie," Tom said, greatly alarmed.

"An that aint all," Brook continued in a confidential tone as the bitter wind scoured their faces. "Seems that the fancy doctor Belmaine 'as tew attend 'im – what's 'is name? Somethin Dutch-soundin. Yew must know it, bor," he said accusingly.

"Dr Peter Vandernoot?"

"That's 'im! 'Is lot come over with them Adventurers way back, though 'e's as English as roast beef – when yer can geddit! – even talks proper. A right sneerfroys bugger. Where was I?"

Despite the grave topic of conversation, Tom found himself smiling at Brook's robust use of his native tongue. "Something about Dr Vandernoot, was it?"

"Oh-ah! He's tole Belmaine ter rest in bed fer a week, an then, if the ole man's strong enough ter travel, Vandernoot recommends 'im ter go abroad wi' that chap oo useter be Bob Pawl. What's 'is name?"

"Robin Belmaine."

"Right yew are! An there's more, Tom: Belmaine's ter give up sittin on the bench and his somethin-startin-with-em dooties immediately. I reckon that's the lot."

They'd arrived at their destination some minutes before the end of Adam's recital. Now the gardener took his leave and, as Tom watched him trek back to the house, he realised that life as a civilian and landowner, even a wealthy one, was far from being the carefree dream of domestic bliss he'd imagined it when he'd first heard that he was to become master of Uppham House. Nightmares were threatening the peace of his little world with increasing frequency as the year 'Eighteen hundred and frozen to death' approached its vernal equinox.

★

Chapter Thirty-nine

Tom Challiss reckoned to make the trip to Lynn and back in one day, despite the miserable weather and the bad condition of the highways. Against Mary Emma's advice, he chose to ride Quicksilver, reasoning that the thoroughbred would shorten the time it took to cover the dozen miles each way and allow him plenty of time for his meeting with Daniel Jones.

He arrived on foot at Bagg & Bacon's bank well before noon, having left Quicksilver in the capable hands of a groom at the livery stables a short distance away. A deferential young clerk showed Tom into a room at the rear of the premises, which, Tom noticed, was several degrees warmer than that which housed the clerks.

Mr Bagg and Daniel Jones, who were seated in comfortable chairs, looked up and got to their feet on his arrival and the clerk erased his own insignificant presence as the three gentlemen shook hands and exchanged polite greetings.

Once the door had closed, the corpulant banker seated himself behind his imposing mahogany desk, smiled and rubbed his palms together briskly. "Well, gentlemen," he said, his oily voice suggestive of the regular quantities of rich food and nourishing liquids that had rushed over his vocal cords since birth, "this is a very great pleasure. Let us get down to business." His smile vanished as the door reopened and the same obsequious young clerk who had shown Tom into Bagg's office crept in with squeaking boots. He deposited on a side table a tray which bore a pot of steaming hot chocolate and three cups and saucers. Carefully keeping his eyes averted from the three wealthy-looking gentlemen, attending only to what he should be doing, the narrow-shouldered clerk poured chocolate into each of the three cups and, timidly making eye contact with the great man, received Bagg's silent signal that he might serve the drinks to his master and his guests. The clerk did so and the door closed for a second time. Bagg glared at the closed door as if the planks of wood had been guilty of some misdemeanour. "Yes. Hrrmph! Well, gentlemen. With your permission, I shall invite Mr Jones to open the proceedings." The professional smile, that didn't reach his wary eyes, was in place. He relaxed into the depths of his imposing chair, latticed his fingers and laid his plump hands on the desktop's tooled skiver.

"Thank you. Mr Bagg. As I intimated in my letter to Mr Challiss, I have rooted out the mislaid fortune of Mr Lambert Jardine, deceased owner of Lyndon Manor. As you are aware, sir, the fortune amounts to a considerable sum: something in the region of one hundred thousand pounds. At least, that is the figure I have to date; for it is by no means certain that I have located all of that gentleman's hidden spoils."

Tom was staggered by the size of the fortune. He thought angrily: such a vast amount of accumulated wealth as the property of one man is an obscenity when contrasted with what has happened to the labouring classes. "You say there's a possibility of there being even more to be found?" Tom said, dazed. "Has anyone any idea where or how Jardine managed to amass this tremendous fortune?"

Daniel peered at Tom over his spectacles. "Does it matter, my dear sir? The fact is that, as no will to his estate has been found – most likely it was destroyed in the fire along with everything else – Mrs Challiss is his sole heir. Your star is in the ascendant, my dear sir! Why, placed alongside the fortune left her by Mr Josiah Kay, Mrs Challiss – and by association yourself – will become one of the richest persons in the county! And, if my guess is accurate – and I see no reason to doubt it – there is indeed more to come. I have instigated searches as far apart as the West Indies and Australasia. But I'll acquaint you further with the relevant facts if or when I am successful."

Mr Bagg sat listening to the lawyer in a happy dream and his seraphic smile almost reached his eyes as he anticipated the greedy percentage of the capital he would accrue merely by guaranteeing to safeguard Mrs Challiss's fortune. It was indeed a happy day, spring or no spring. As he sipped his cooling chocolate he glanced out of the window at the leaden sky and decided there would probably be no spring in this unnaturally cold year.

"Well.. . . . . I'm not quite sure how I should react to such extraordinary news, gentlemen," Tom said, baffled by what he'd heard. "Except to thank you, Daniel, for your diligence on behalf of Mrs Challiss. I – frankly, I'm too astonished to think coherently."

Bagg sniffed and said drily: "I understand, Mr Challiss: the sudden news that you are to become richer by such a staggering sum has naturally overwhelmed you. But believe me, my dear sir, by the time you have digested your luncheon the idea of such a pleasant prospect will have grown upon you. Mr Jones will bear me out, I dare say, when I predict that, by the time you are relating the good news to your lady wife, the idea will no longer seem at all alien to you. By tomorrow evening, the fact that you have become the recipient of such a tidy windfall will be viewed by you both as no more than is your due as people of standing. Am I not right, Mr Jones?"

Daniel laughed. "More or less, sir. But you shouldn't confuse Mr Challiss's reactions with those which are common to the majority of men who would find themselves in a like situation. My esteemed client can be a little unpredictable."

Tom smiled wrily at the lawyer's accurate assessment of his character; but on this occasion he decided that it would be more diplomatic to keep to himself his true opinion of the banker and his jaundiced view of mankind. "I think stunned would be a fair description of my present state, Mr Bagg," he said. "It is for me to thank you both once more, gentlemen, for your industry in this matter." He glanced at Daniel. "However, might I suggest to Mr Bagg that he be so kind as to write to Mrs Challiss concerning the matters discussed here today?" And to Bagg: "My wife was unable to accompany me due to her delicate state of health; but I am certain that she would appreciate the courtesy of a summary as, technically, the fortune belongs to her."

The banker's eyes opened fully for the first time since Tom had entered his presence. "My dear sir!" he remonstrated, "your wife has promised to obey you, has she not? What is hers is, of right, yours, Mr Challiss."

Somehow, Tom managed to keep his temper. "That is for my wife to decide, sir; I claim no jurisdiction over her material possessions. Some people marry for love."

"And most of 'em live to rue the day, sir!" Bagg snapped back, met the lawyer's admonishing eye and immediately softened his manner. "But, of course, it is not my place to tell my valued clients how to run their affairs: I seek merely to advise, sir. I apologise if I have given offence – quite unintentionally, let me hasten to add."

Business concluded, Tom and Daniel left the bank in search of refreshment.

★

Extraordinary! Tom thought, as he made ready for bed, that so much had happened when he'd been absent from home for just a few hours. All he had wanted to do was to eat his dinner and relax in front of a good fire with a bottle of madeira and the two newspapers he'd picked up on his way through Lynn; but destiny had decreed otherwise. By comparison with what he'd learned on his return, the astounding news of his wife's recent legacy had dwindled into relative unimportance as, in retrospect, material gain so often does to those who already possess a fortune. Hence Midas's error, thought Tom irrelevantly, recalling Miss Peters' lively readings of the Greek myths in the schoolroom at Lyndon Manor. He stifled a yawn. An exhausted Mary Emma slept peacefully on her side of the bed. He wouldn't wake her; instead, he slipped in quietly beside his wife, snuffed out the candle, lay on his back in the fireglow and reviewed his day to the soft sound of her breathing.

After a splendid luncheon, whose main dish had consisted of poached salmon, he and Daniel had parted company shortly after three o'clock: the lawyer had further work which detained him at Lynn and Tom was anxious to make an early start on his return journey to Uppham.

Some miles along the London Road, Quicksilver cast a shoe. Tom jumped down and scrutinized the hoof. No option: walk his horse back to town, find a smithy. He finally located a working farrier as night fell. Several riders waited, their mounts requiring the farrier's skills. By the time Quicksilver had been shod it was late. *The Three Tuns* beckoned. Supper! A chance to recuperate, spend a night at the inn and return home after luncheon the following afternoon.

★

After a non-stop journey lasting more than three hours he was feeling saddle sore and was thankful to enter his own gates. As he passed the lodge he was surprised to see it in darkness and assumed that the Aldriches must be up at the mansion; but that took no account of Clem Rix who was usually at home. No doubt an explanation would be forthcoming he thought as, wearily, he surrendered Quicksilver to Ben Wright's care.

As soon as he entered his front door he sensed that the house was a hive of unrest. The appearance of his agitated wife confirmed his suspicions and he suppressed a weary groan as she made her way downstairs closely followed by Agnes.

"Oh, Tom!" she cried, on seeing him, "thank heavens you're back! We've had *such* a dreadful day! You cannot imagine how our lives have been disrupted–"

"Now, calm down, Mary Emma," he said patiently. "Come into the dining room and sit down. Good-evening, Agnes; please, join us."

"Oh, Tom! I'm sorry, my dear," Mary Emma began as soon as they had settled themselves. "Did you have a good journey? How did you get on at Lynn? Did you see Daniel? What was the business concerning Lambert Jardine?"

Fighting off his exhaustion, Tom replied to each of her rapid questions in turn, then asked her if he should reveal the figure of her legacy in Agnes's presence.

"But of course! What is there to hide? Dear Agnes is the soul of discretion, unlike her giddy friend." The two friends exchanged affectionate smiles.

He named the sum. Agnes evinced astonishment but said nothing.

Mary Emma clapped her hands for joy. "Oh, Tom! How wonderful! There will be absolutely no holding me back now, my dear. Oh, ... I have such wonderful plans for the garden and the park... that is, if you agree to my suggestions?"

"My love, as I told Mr Bagg: the fortune is yours – to do with as you will. I appreciate your consideration in inviting me to approve your pipe dreams, my dear. Might I suggest you follow the advice of the experts in each field? There's little point in employing a steward, farm manager and head gardener if you ride roughshod over their long-term plans for the gardens and the estate."

Mary Emma smiled. "All right, sir. I freely admit that I was wrong to try to get my own way over the garden without consulting you and Mr Brook. There! Does that make you happy?" Seeing that she had provoked a smile, she added: "But I think you must admit that the layout has been considerably improved by my suggestions. There! That's enough about that for the moment. What do you think has happened while you were away?"

"Mary Emma, I'm too desperately weary to play guessing games," Tom said; "you'll have to enlighten me."

"I, too, have had a tiring day, you great bear!" she said. "You tell him, Agnes."

Mary Emma had not exaggerated when she said she'd had a dreadful day; in fact, as Agnes unfolded the day's events, the term fitted the circumstances exactly.

"It began about three-o'clock this morning," Agnes began, "with the blowing of horns pitched in every key and making enough noise to reach the house. We were roused immediately; but unsure of the cause, thinking it but a temporary interruption to our rest, nobody except Mr Rudge thought it necessary to dress."

We shall begin in the Night...

Tom's fatigue was banished in an instant by his recollection of the threats contained in the Ashill handbill. "Good God! What next?"

"Fear, chaos, and confusion," were the next startling words that Agnes spoke. "Rudge came up to report that several fires could be clearly seen across the fields in all directions, including Martlets. That Sir Everard's property had been marked for further attack was soon made clear. One of his footmen managed to slip out from the back of the house under cover of darkness and made his way to us. He told us that a mob of rioters had used ladders to climb over the perimeter wall into Martlets and were even as he spoke rampaging about destroying the outbuildings. That the boathouse had been torched after the rioters had stove in the canoes and punts—"

"And, Tom, that dear little summerhouse by the lake has been burned to the ground. Imagine our fears when we learned that the mob was so close to our own home! Our ruined fence," Mary Emma said, angry-eyed, as she relived the experience.

"You must have been frightened out of your wits," Tom said anxiously.

"The anticipation of violence was almost more fearful than coming face to face with the men themselves," Agnes said. "Rudge advised us to dress warmly but to remain upstairs out of sight. He showed tremendous courage, Mr Challiss, and set us all a wonderful example by remaining calm.

"Barty Peckover and Will and Ben Wright had also been roused by the sound of horns in the dead silence of the night and, having dressed, joined us at the house. It seemed very odd and eerily quiet. We all sat about listening and waiting – for what we didn't know and, when we talked it over afterwards, discovered that we had imagined all sorts of terrible things. The footman from Martlets advised us to arm ourselves. "

Tom was growing impatient and said: "And did the mob come here?"

"Rudge sent Barty and the Wright brothers to the kitchen to wake Maddy and Mrs Rudge so that they could begin to prepare food and drink for us all; but the cook and Maddy were already up and busying themselves with mending the fire and setting water to boil. We sat about, eating and drinking, waiting for the blow – whatever it was – to fall and an hour passed and we had had no disturbance.

"At about a quarter past four there came a loud pounding on the front door and we said afterwards that our hearts leapt into our throats with fright. Mr Rudge told us to stay where we were and he and Barty went to the door. 'Who is it and what do you want here?' Rudge shouted through the closed door. And we were astonished to hear Mr Aldrich's deep voice urgently demanding to be let in.

"By the light of Mr Rudge's candle we could see a number of people crowded about the doorway and, at first, thought the rioters had come at last. But it was nothing of the sort–"

"Poor Joe Aldrich looked at the end of his tether," Mary Emma interjected, "he practically leapt into the hall with Ruth hurrying in after him. It soon became clear what had disturbed Joe when Kit Warrender helped Clem Rix to hop inside—"

"And just as we thought that we might close the door, David Deacon and Will Wright, carrying somebody on a hurdle litter, followed on their heels. We saw all this from upstairs, of course," Agnes explained. "Anyway... The horns had alerted everybody at the lodge, Joe had looked out and seen the fires and, quite naturally, assumed it was only a matter of time before Uppham was attacked. Clem being still unable to walk unaided, they had no means of removing him to safety except on horseback.

"While they were getting him ready to leave they were struck rigid with fear by somebody pounding on their door. Assuming it to be the rioters come to sack the place Joe fainted from fright. Ruth's complete attention was on her husband when a man walked in through the conservatory and, she told us, she almost swooned herself. But it was David Deacon, the shepherd. He made her understand that he and Kit had a very sick boy lying outside and must bring him into shelter. Once she had satisfied herself that her husband was recovering from his swoon Ruth took charge at once. On her instructions, Deacon went outside and he and Kit carried in the boy on a hurdle.

"The shepherd said the lad was Clem Rix's brother, Ben, who'd been hiding in the lambing shed since the night following the capture of the poachers in Raven Wood at Martlets. The boy himself had been in Home Wood at Uppham at the time. After the accident with the spring gun and fearing he'd be accused of the murder of the gamekeeper, young Ben had taken refuge with the shepherd; but not before he'd spent a night in the cold and damp of the wood. He caught a chill that had worsened and so David went and got Kit to help him carry him to Ruth at the lodge."

"And, Tom! While all this was going on we were turned to stone by the sound of horns approaching and Rudge looked out and said: 'They're coming! One or two bold men are carrying flares and they've just entered the drive.' Well! Imagine our panic, my dear," Mary Emma said, her hand to her throat, as she recalled her sensation at the time. "Our hall cluttered with muddy-booted men and a groaning boy on a litter, Rudge and Peckover doing their best to appear fearless, and everybody wondering if they were to be burned to death where they stood."

"Mary Emma! You always had a propensity to hyperbole. You haven't forgotten Miss Peters' teachings so quickly? Do try to keep a sense of proportion, my dear."

"Oh, don't be so stuffy, Mr Challiss! I'm merely describing what happened and the way it affected us all. You should think yourself lucky that you weren't here!"

Tom smiled and inclined his head. "I stand corrected. Please go on, Agnes."

Agnes said: "We may smile about it now, Mr Challiss, but I assure you it was no laughing matter at the time. Well... Before we'd had time to think what to do there was a great thumping on the door and we knew by the noise that it must be the rioters. Mr Rudge bravely opened the door and confronted the shouting men."

"About how many?" asked Tom.

"We estimated the mob to consist of between fifty and sixty, apparently all men," Agnes answered.

"Apparently?" Tom looked his astonishment.

"I was certain I detected at least one female voice among the shrieking mob," Agnes said, "and I tried to think myself into her place, to wonder what it might be like to be her—"

"You wouldn't like it one bit, Agnes dear, I can assure you," Mary Emma cut in. "The fact that she sees fit to roam the streets with a howling mob of men is telling enough. Such a person has lost all sense of her own dignity."

"I'm aware that some might object to that," Agnes said, "but suppose she hadn't had the opportunity to develop that sense? No. I meant: what was it that had stirred her to such anger that she felt compelled to join the disadvantaged men of Downham in their dangerous quest for justice?"

"Oh," Mary Emma said, suppressing a yawn. Not quite certain of her friend's meaning, she decided to say no more on the subject. "Do get on with it, Agnes."

Tom looked from his wife to Agnes and, his eyes smiling, said: "It doesn't take the brain of a Newton to fathom that the outcome is to be a happy one; otherwise, you'd not be sitting here to tell the tale at all."

"Tom! Don't be such a marplot," Mary Emma chided him at the moment Agnes opened her mouth to speak. Recognising her error, Mary Emma apologised and begged her friend to continue.

"The men seemed to have a leader and as soon as he stepped into the light Mary Emma and I recognised him as the fellow with the burned hands."

"Oh, do go on, Agnes," Mary Emma said impatiently: "Jem Webster let that cat out of the bag days ago, thinking that Tom knew of it already."

Agnes looked relieved. "Well... It was the same man, without a doubt, for although he kept his hat pulled well down he still wore the tell-tale horn and the coat we'd seen before. Of course, he heard us talking, looked up and recognised us. To our astonishment, he removed his hat and made a theatrical bow that would not have disgraced the stage at Drury Lane, Mary Emma said afterwards. Then he turned and addressed the mob, who had suddenly gone quiet. 'Turn about, men!' he commanded. "We have no business with these people tonight. They're sheltering friends of ours and can do without further disturbance by the look of it. Let's leave 'em to it: they'll not tip the wink to the militia.' The men mumbled and grumbled a bit and, before anybody could stop him, a huge, ugly man ran up to the door and pushed his way into the hall. He looked straight up at us as we leaned over the balustrade – he had the most horrible little yellow eyes and a badly pock-marked face – and shouted up at us: ' "I seen yer! I seen yer, me fine ladies, an doan yew fergit it! Yew split on us an I'll land yer a teller as'll spoil yer pretty phizogs so's yer own mas won't know yer. Yew keep it squat, see?"

Mary Emma applauded Agnes's performance and, suddenly conscious of her unladylike mimicking of the scoundrel, Agnes blushed furiously.

"Isn't she a marvel, Tom? You should be on the stage, my dear Agnes. Why, I could almost see that dreadful villain all over again, you had him so accurately."

"Then, somehow the awful man was bundled out of the house," Agnes continued, "the mob's leader – who was really quite a handsome man in his way and not at all rough – shouted an order and the hungry-looking men silently formed themselves into a column and marched away across the park and down the drive."

"From the front windows we watched the flares dwindling away down the drive until they were out of sight," Mary Emma added as a postscript.

"For a few moments we were unable to believe that it was over," Agnes said, "and Mary Emma and I couldn't stop trembling for quite a while."

"Things seemed to turn in our favour when they spotted the Rix brothers," Mary Emma said. "I'm sure, had it not been for their presence in the hall, the mob would have overrun the house. I dread to think what the consequences of that would have been after all the restoration work that's been done."

Tom, who had listened without further interruption until now, said: "One cannot assume that they would have behaved in that way, Mary Emma. Oh, bullies, such as the pock-marked man — but that kind of man will behave in a threatening, cowardly manner at any time. As far as I am able to grasp the gist of the men's grievances, they seek not only to awaken the landed gentry to their responsibilities to those they have cheated of land and possessions, but also to swell their numbers in order to intimidate those in power who have ground them down for so many years."

"Father said that it was the arrest of the poachers by the militia that provoked the men to storm the gaols," said Agnes, "to free some of the men who had stolen meat only because they'd been driven to it by their own and their families' hunger."

"I can't say that I blame their actions," Tom said. "I agree with you Agnes. How would one react to one's family starving, to watching one's children dying, but with outrage and anger at the terrible, needless sacrifice. I'd be rampaging with the others for my rights under such circumstances. It's all too easy for people in our situation to condemn the so-called violence, Mary Emma. We can have no real idea of their sufferings from our comfortable point of view."

"Oh, I dare say you're right, Tom," his wife conceded. "But that's enough about them. That wasn't the end of our trials and tribulations by any means, my dear."

"Oh?"

"Lord, no!" Mary Emma said forcefully. "You might recall that we had the Rix brothers cluttering up our hall, apart from Ruth and Joe Aldrich, Kit Warrender and Will Wright? And Maddy and Mrs Rudge were hanging about the kitchen stairs, all agog with a mixture of fright for the probable loss of their honour and the sensationalism of the drama being played out before their eyes. Though what cook had to fear, I can't imagine," she murmured to herself.

"Where are Ben and Clem Rix now?"

"Installed in the east wing," Mary Emma told him, "and God help us if the magistrates get wind of it!"

"And the Aldriches?"

"They'll stay the night, I suppose," Mary Emma said. "I do like Will

Wright. Such a dependable young man." She yawned extensively behind her hand. "Oh, Tom. Sir Everard's footman returned the way he came once the mob left. But before he went he said that his master was on the mend – though this night's work might have caused him a setback, I suppose – and that he and Robin are to leave for Tuscany as soon as Sir Everard is pronounced fit to undertake the journey. Now, if you'll both excuse me I will take myself off to bed at once for I cannot keep my eyes open a moment longer. Agnes, dear: please send up Maddy, will you?"

Agnes had taken herself off to bed soon afterwards, leaving Tom free at last to settle himself down in comfort to read the papers...

Beside him, Mary Emma stirred in her sleep and flung an arm across his chest. He leaned over her and brushed her rounded cheek with a kiss before gently replacing her arm beneath the covers.

He was unable to sleep. His frenzied mind was a kaleidoscope of images and echoing words: his long ride to Lynn and back, the legacy, the reckless mood of the Downham men, the cottages half built, the newspapers – Stupid, to read them just before retiring. No wonder his brain was still over-excited. Jem Webster had been right, though; he should read them every day if he wished to remain in touch with the world beyond Uppham. Even news a day late was better than no news at all. Yesterday's edition of the *London Times* had been so full of interest that it had brought home to him how narrow his horizons had become.

At last he had an explanation for the bad weather they were having. Britain wasn't alone, it seemed, in experiencing lower temperatures and less sunshine than usual: many of the world's temperate zones had been similarly affected. The cause of the unusually cold spell was attributed to dust in the atmosphere following a volcanic eruption in the East Indies last year. Extraordinary! How could they know that?

The quadrille – some kind of dance, he supposed – was the latest thing in fashionable ballrooms; and the Luddite movement, suppressed in 1813, had been resurrected. Since one agricultural machine could now do the work formerly done by a team of men, widespread mechanisation had spread across the country with alarming speed. As each machine carried the threat of depriving the furious men of their livelihood the recombined Luddites were once more rampaging over the countryside with the intention of smashing the diabolical new labour-saving inventions.

One of the most astonishing things he'd read was that Britain boasted two and a quarter million tons of merchant shipping of which one thousand tons were in steam. Steam power? Good God! What miracle would they think of next in this age of invention?

He smiled as he recalled the item about Leigh Hunt's unkind phrase describing Prinny as 'a fat Adonis of fifty' which, when published in his brother's paper, the *Examiner,* had so enraged the Prince Regent that he'd had him imprisoned. And Prinny's friend and fashion adviser, George 'Beau' Brummel, had fled to Calais to escape his gambling debts... As for that poet George Byron and his antics...

What was to be done about those wretched Rixes? It would only take a careless word in Downham by one of the household to bring the law down on them. He must talk to Joe about it first thing. ... The monument to Mrs Coy and her children: he'd heard nothing about its progress for days... Poor old Belmaine. He must visit him some time tomorrow to offer such help as he was capable of giv–

★

A satisfying number of letters were brought back by Barty Peckover from the post office in Downham. Among them no less than fourteen were addressed to Mary Emma and, after begging Agnes to accompany her, they took themselves upstairs to the back withdrawing room to read them. Miss Brook needed no urging as it was obvious that the majority of the communications were in response to the advertisements for domestic staff that had been placed on Mary Emma's behalf by the domestic agency. It took no great skill on the friends' part to separate those letters from women applying for the post of housekeeper and those of the applicants for more menial domestic duties. The quality of the writing paper, the beauty or otherwise of the handwriting and the various devices used to seal the string told much before the seals were broken.

"We'll sort them into three piles, Agnes: housekeeper, assistant cook and housemaids, shall we?" Mary Emma said, acting upon her suggestion before Agnes had time to answer her. "This one must be from a prospective housemaid," she decided, "why, the writing is so ill-formed that it is barely legible and the paper looks as if it might once have been an outer wrapper for meat. What do you think, my dear?"

"I think it might save time if we were to open them all rather than to waste time trying to detect who might have written them," Agnes said.

"Spoil-sport!" Mary Emma said cheerfully. "I pride myself on being able to judge a person's character from their calligraphy, Agnes. Please indulge me in my whim, love."

It was soon done. Four well-written applications made one pile, seven more, bearing less well-formed characters, another and the three remaining barely legible missives, written on what appeared to be secondhand paper that had been ironed, the third.

"Oh! Isn't this fun!" Mary Emma cried. "Now. As I've been allowed to guess who has written them I invite you to open the first."

"Oh! Mary Emma!" Agnes cried in such excited accents that Mary Emma thought it a rather excessive response to her generous impulse, "he moved!"

"Oh, darling!" cried Mary Emma, taking hold of her friend's hand and squeezing it. "May I?"

Agnes's face shone with happiness as she took hold of Mary Emma's hand and placed it on her own abdomen. "Can you feel him? There! He turned right over."

Mary Emma embraced her friend and kissed her soft cheek. "I'm so happy for you, Agnes," she said, and as she pulled away she saw tears of joy sparkling in the young woman's eyes. "It's so wonderful to know that all is well, my dear."

"I was beginning to worry," confessed Agnes. "Oh! It's so exciting, Mary Emma. I shall break my promise to Charles and write him the good news."

Mary Emma looked extremely grave. "I beg you not to be too hasty, my dear," she cautioned. "To remind Lord Vyvyan of your lapse would not be the action of a lady, Agnes."

"Then it's just as well I do not profess to be one," Agnes replied defiantly. "I think Charles deserves to know – would wish to be told – that his son thrives."

"You seem very certain that the child will be a boy," Mary Emma said tartly.

"I am." Agnes laughed, placed her hand on the active child in her womb and said happily: "Mother says that boys begin to fight as soon as they're ready to move."

"Seriously, Agnes," Mary Emma pleaded. "Do not be over hasty. Of course, it's natural that you wish to share your joy with the man responsible for it; but you must think of Lord Vyvyan's position, not to mention the feelings of his wife and children."

"You're right, of course, Mary Emma," Agnes said sadly. "I will do as you say. It is reward enough to know that my child is active and that he continues to thrive."

They returned their attention to the three piles of applications and began to break the seals and open out the letters. Mary Emma smiled ruefully at having misjudged some of them from their outward appearance. The letter written on butcher's wrapping paper came from a cook. But she had correctly surmised that the three crudely-penned offerings written on ironed paper had come from three young girls – sisters – applying for positions as housemaids. Mary Emma and Agnes spent the whole morning in reading and re-reading the applications before coming to the conclusion that none of the applicants for the position of housekeeper was suitable.

"Oh, dear!" Mary Emma sighed. "I can manage without the others if necessary; but I feel that life without a housekeeper is going to be quite chaotic once my child is born. I shall want to devote most of my time to caring for it."

"There might be more applications in tomorrow's post," suggested Agnes. "Don't you think that the very fact that the three sisters took the trouble to iron their secondhand paper showed enterprise and the importance of good presentation?"

"You may be right," Mary Emma conceded. "Let me see them again."

"The fact that they cannot spell or can barely form their letters doesn't necessarily mean that the girls themselves are coarse," Agnes said, secretly wishing the three sisters good luck.

"No… No," Mary Emma said abstractedly as she struggled to decipher the letters. "You know, Agnes, I think you might be right!" she said. "Look at this one again." She passed Agnes the sheet of thin paper, its smoothed creases still apparent:

dear mad am
      i seekwork in a good hom ma die a munth a go + pa last yeer i will do n e thing in a hows to keep it cleen can wash cloes and no how to cleer starh   do not eat a lot and no how to mend
      i am cleen and ty d with no fles in hair   do not care wot werk i do   i wil werk hard
    yors respecful e   faith looret
    plees anser to rev richd white at aveley in essex

"I like the sound of her," Agnes said with enthusiasm. "What about the others?"

"I think Faith must be the youngest of the three," Mary Emma said. "The others are more to the point and slightly better as to spelling and execution. I think the fact that they give the Reverend Richard White as their referee a very good sign."

"I agree, Mary Emma," Agnes said. "I have an idea. Would you like me to go to Aveley and see the Looret sisters? I could give you a much better idea of their suitability if I spoke to them."

Mary Emma's eyes lit up. "Would you, my dear? Yet ... I do not think that it would do for you to be travelling about unaccompanied in your condition."

Agnes said: "I wonder if Ruth Aldrich would be free to accompany me?"

Ruth was. The mission was soon accomplished and the three Looret sisters – Hope, Charity and Faith, aged thirteen, eleven and nine years respectively – were soon installed in one of the large attic bedrooms at Uppham. The three orphaned sisters were of a cheerful, hardworking disposition and thought nothing of rising at six o'clock each morning, working hard all day and going to bed at nine, as long as their needs were met and their master and mistress treated them with kindness.

Agnes had been correct in her supposition that further applications would arrive. Among them had been two of an outstanding superiority to the rest.

The first came from a single young man of eighteen who was applying for the position of assistant cook to Mrs Rudge. His sex, in relation to the position in a predominantly female sphere, had intrigued Mary Emma. That had singled him out at first. Subsequent perusal of his references – he had worked in various kitchens since the age of twelve and had left each to better himself – seemed to her to proclaim his superiority over all other applicants and she had made up her mind to engage him.

"Have you considered Mrs Rudge's feelings in the matter, Mary Emma?" Agnes asked. "She might not take kindly to a young man cluttering up her kitchen."

"It's up to Mrs Rudge to make the best of it," declared Mary Emma. "If nothing else, Martin Harris will save her poor old legs," she added. "Anyway, I like the idea of another young man in the household. I only hope he will prove a permanent fixture. Seeking, interviewing and employing staff is a wearying business."

The second satisfactory application came from Abigail Nevett, a native of Hertford. Unlike other applicants for the post of housekeeper, she began by writing that the only experience she had of running a home was that of her father's, a retired auctioneer and estate agent. At Mary Emma's request, Agnes read the letter aloud to her friend, paraphrasing what appeared to be a long letter.

"Miss Nevett is seeking to engage herself as housekeeper after finding herself practically destitute," Agnes began, "on the discovery of enormous debts owed by her father to various people, that he had hidden from her and that had necessitated the sale of their home and its entire belongings shortly before his death: circumstances which, she says, probably hastened his demise. She goes on to say that she is a gentlewoman by birth and well-acquainted with what is required in the keeping of a gentleman's home. In happier times, she writes, her parents had maintained ten servants and two gardeners. She is the only offspring of her parents' marriage and her mother died young so that she herself has, from the age of eighteen, taken on the responsibility of ensuring the smooth running of her father's house. Although they had, at that time she mentions, employed a housekeeper, Miss Nevett's father had insisted that she act as his hostess at the frequent dinner parties and other entertainments that he enjoyed. Oh! Gracious heaven! Mary Emma, listen to this," Agnes said, "'I think it only fair to tell you,' she writes with admirable candour, 'that from the time of my mother's death my father made a habit of using me in a way no father should approach his daughter. He made the idea of marriage so abhorrent to me that I have abjured all thoughts of matrimony for myself. If it assists my application, I can assure you that it is my intention never to marry.' Poor woman."

"Lord!" Mary Emma said, in shock, "if she means what I think she means it doesn't bear thinking about."

Agnes slowly shook her head from side to side, and observed: "For some women the world is a very wicked place, as it is for orphans and other children, as well as young men, Mary Emma. Shall I continue?" Mary Emma silently assented.

"'My application must be further prejudiced by the fact that, following my father's death I contracted smallpox' – Oh! The poor unfortunate thing," Agnes said as tears sprang to her eyes. "'I was very ill indeed, for some weeks I hung between life and death and was so miserable that I was indifferent to my fate. While I was in the infirmary, the nurses kept looking glasses away from victims of the smallpox. It was not until I took a room with a glass in it in a lodging house in my home town that I saw my ruined face for the first time. I stared at my horrible reflection and wondered what I could have done that was so wicked that God had thought to afflict me so. Then I reasoned that it must have been because of my complicity in my father's criminal act that God had branded me for all to see. I bitterly regretted having survived my illness and wicked thoughts of taking my own life entered my head.' I don't think I can bear to read any more of this, Mary Emma," Agnes said, handing back the letter. "You must read it yourself, if you can bear to know more. It is too sad."

"I'm sorry, Agnes," Mary Emma said. "Of course, dear. I'll go on. Do you want to hear what she has to say, or shall I read it to myself?"

"I suppose I'm a fool to mind it so much," Agnes said. "Read it aloud. If Miss Nevett could live it I must be thankful that I only have to hear about her terrible life."

"You're sure, Agnes? I don't want you getting too upset, my dear."

"No. I'll be all right, Mary Emma," Agnes said stoically. "Carry on."

"Very well, dear. Let me see, where did you... Ah! Here we are: 'entered my head. One day I was so desperately low in spirits that I went to the churchyard in which my poor mother lies buried. Almost without thinking, my steps led me to her grave and so abject with misery had I become that I prostrated myself on her grassy tomb covered in early primroses and gave expression to my sorrow. It was raining, I remember: that soft spring rain that falls as silently as mist; but I cared for nothing and wished myself beneath the earth with my dear mother, and that all my troubles were at an end.'" Mary Emma fumbled for her handkerchief and blew her nose.

She glanced at Agnes as she dabbed at her own eyes and saw that her friend had silent tears coursing down her rosy cheeks. "Would you rather I stopped, dear?" she croaked.

Agnes sniffed inelegantly. "No. Go on, Mary Emma. We might learn what it was that prevented the poor thing from taking her own life. Because she obviously didn't. Did she? Or she wouldn't have been able to pen the letter," Agnes said, her practical mind repressing sentiment.

Mary Emma raised a watery smile. "Of course, you're absolutely right, my dear. She goes on: 'As I lay there, my tears mingling with the rain that watered my mother's grave, I became conscious of a hand laid gently on my shoulder followed by a man's voice asking me: was I ill? How could I raise my head and frighten him with a killing glance from my basilisk face? I became conscious that the man had crouched down beside me and I heard his calm voice close to my ear asking what troubled me. His voice was so gentle that its kindness stirred my heart which I had, for a long time, thought dead as stone. I told him that I wished I was dead. He replied that that was a wicked thing to say and asked me to get up. I told him why I could not and he said that, as he had been blinded, my face would not offend him. Upon hearing that, I drew myself up and turned to look at my comforter. He was quite an ordinary man to look at and it was hard to think of him as blind for he had the clearest, mildest blue eyes I had ever seen. As we talked I experienced a great calm. Strength seemed to flow from the man into me. He made me see that life was worth living if only I could bring myself to care more for others than for myself: that all was not lost and that I must not shut myself away but return to the world and everyday life. While he was speaking to me I felt as though anything were possible. I asked what he thought I might do with my life and he said I must use it in the service of others. When he saw that he had raised my spirits and also my self-esteem he bade me farewell and left the churchyard. After I had said a prayer over my mother's grave, I walked back into Hertford town to the news-seller's. My idea was to buy a news-sheet, though I could ill afford the price of it, and to scour the advertisements to see if anything offered itself for my consideration. Your advertisement for the position of housekeeper was the only one to which I felt I could honestly feel able to offer my service.

"'You should know that when I venture out in public I habitually wear a veil: I feel less self-conscious if my affliction is hidden. Should I be offered the position of housekeeper to Uppham House I would respectfully request to be allowed to wear my veil at all times when on duty. I realise that these impediments must prejudice you against considering me a fit person for engagement in your household; but I beg you not to judge me without seeing me. In the unlikely event that I am deemed fit to be considered for interview I feel that, in fairness to you as my prospective mistress, these flaws in my person and character must be made known to you beforehand.

'I must apologise, Mrs Challiss, Madam, for the unconscionable length of this petition but, having deliberated on the subject for some days, I considered it best that you should be apprised of my more obvious faults at this stage of our acquaintance.

I remain, Madam,

yours Faithfully,

Amelia Nevett.

P.S.

Please to find enclosed with this letter the names and addresses of two reliable referees who have agreed to stand as witnesses to my character. A.N.' "

"Well! What an extraordinary baring of the soul!" Mary Emma said. "What do you make of it, Agnes?"

"It struck me from the very beginning that it was a carefully written and well-crafted letter," Agnes said thoughfully. "She played on our heartstrings unmercifully in order to gain our sympathy. Next, she dazzled us with mysticism – the mysterious man with the remarkable blue eyes part of the letter – and then… that business about wearing the veil at all times. Do you really want such an unusual person presiding over your household, Mary Emma? Imagine the shock to visitors if she got to the door before Rudge!"

Mary Emma ran her tongue across her top lip. "In other words, Agnes, you think she will not do. Well, I'm not so sure. Nobody would string together such a list of reasons why one shouldn't employ her, surely? 'Twould be madness."

"I didn't like to mention it," Agnes said, "but, yes, it would. It's hardly the kind of letter one would write to a prospective employer. Is it? And yet I don't know. I feel out of my depth. I'd hate to do the poor woman an injustice; half of me believes her dreadful history. Of course, you might interview her. After all, nobody can compel you to engage her. And even if you did take her on, it could be on a trial basis: say one month."

"An excellent suggestion, Agnes," Mary Emma said. "But before we do anything else, I'd like Ruth Aldrich to read the letter and tell me what she thinks of it. She has experienced all kinds of unsavoury things during her time as a nurse and has great commonsense into the bargain. Her opinion would be most valuable. And we must take into account the fact that Miss Nevett gives as her referees a clergyman and a doctor, both professional men of some standing in the community. I shall make it my business to consult Ruth before coming to a decision." She rang for Rudge.

When asked, Rudge informed Mary Emma that Mrs Aldrich happened to be in the east wing of the house with the Rix lads, having recently completed attending to Clem's leg after treating Ben's respiratory condition. An hour remained to luncheon and Ruth agreed to read the letter and give her honest opinion of its contents.

To Mary Emma's and Agnes's surprise, Ruth advised Mary Emma to reply at once and invite Miss Nevett to Uppham for an interview. She could bring her references with her, said Ruth, and Mary Emma would be able to judge for herself if the woman was the kind of person she could imagine an acceptable part of her household. "Oh, and Mary Emma, don't forget to enclose money enough for her outward and return journey – and a little to spare!" Ruth advised.

They needn't have worried: Miss Amelia Nevett, when she arrived, was undoubtedly a gentlewoman in reduced circumstances. The veil she wore was not all-enveloping, as were the weeds some widows chose to wear in an attempt to spare the public gaze their superfluous presence. Miss Nevett's device was simple and effective and resembled an Arab yashmak. Enough of her person was visible to make her personal tragedy more poignant. Still under thirty, her luxuriant, waving black hair, which she wore piled high above a pair of large and luminous dark grey eyes, was dramatic in itself. Her forehead was lofty and pale with well-marked brows and bore little sign of the horrible disease that had spoiled her complexion. The gossamer half fall was so fine that Miss Nevett's profile, when turned against the light, was as clearcut as the monarch's head on a penny and Mary Emma observed that its proportions were as refined and as delicately formed as an Italian cameo. Indeed, the wisp of silk was no more than a translucent barrier: it did little more than blur the woman's obviously pretty features and even teeth, while effectively screening the ruin of her once flawless skin. This diaphanous veil was suspended from a device that hooked onto Miss Nevett's ears and under her hair. Though at first a distraction to Mary Emma, she soon grew accustomed to the silken mask as she listened to the woman's low-pitched voice. Mary Emma watched in fascination the silken fall shiver and shimmer at every word Miss Nevett spoke and was reminded of a cloud of breath made visible on a cold day. The noticeably pregnant Mrs Challiss had also noted, with a twinge of envy, Miss Nevett's graceful deportment and slender form and thought that before smallpox had scarred her she must have been a woman of rare beauty. Mary Emma's heart went out to the blighted creature and she soon made up her own mind that, indisputably, Miss Amelia Nevett would do.

It had taken the young Challisses many months to staff Uppham. Now, with the appointment of Miss Amelia Nevett as Housekeeper, Mary Emma considered that their establishment was on the way to becoming as grand a residence as Lyndon Manor had been. Her child turned. "Just let me get you born, infant," she apostrophised, "and then I shall begin on the gardens!"

★

"You shouldn't count your chickens before they're hatched, my dear Mary Emma," Tom said in the manner of a hectoring schoolmaster. They were at luncheon in the company of Agnes, Ruth and Joseph Aldrich. Everett Pawl, habitually one of their number, was absent on account of his having remained at Martlets to dine.

Aware of the company, Mary Emma refrained from sulking. Instead, she gave vent to her frustration by taking Tom to task. "You should have forbidden his going," she said with thinly veiled anger while the others ate in silence. "Sir Everard will have young Robin to look after him. Why must we be deprived of Everett? How am I supposed to get the library finished without his help? Tell me that!"

"It's not exactly the end of the world, Mary Emma," Tom said, munching his way through a scarlet radish. Seeing her about to flare up again, he bolted the rest of the vegetable and, in an attempt at pacifying her, said: "We'll find somebody to replace him easily enough, I feel sure."

"That selfish old man!" seethed his wife. "Why couldn't he simply take along one of his army of footmen in Everett's place? I need Everett here."

"I thought I had explained why," Tom said with an exaggerated sigh that did nothing to ameliorate his wife's temper. "Sir Everard wishes Everett to accompany Robin and himself to Tuscany to make it a party consisting of three generations of the same family. It was Robin's idea, if you must know. He persuaded his grand uncle that his father would be a positive asset, as he has studied the classics. When Everett demurred, on account of his work on our library, Robin pleaded with him and finally persuaded his father that he would be missing the chance of a lifetime. After that, what could I say? Italy is the mecca of classical scholars; besides which, it will be wonderful for father and son to share such an edifying experience."

"He'll never have such an opportunity again," prophesied Joe Aldrich.

"But it really leaves me in the lurch as far as finishing the library's concerned," Mary Emma said dolefully. "Were I clever enough – which I'm not – I'm in no condition to haul piles of books about and run up and down ladders and there's simply nobody else capable of such a task."

Ruth Vale quietly laid down her fork. "Have you asked Miss Nevett if she would be interested in trying?"

"Miss Nevett!" Mary Emma said, her voice full of excitement. "Oh! I wonder? D'you think she might be interested enough to try to help me, Ruth?"

"You can but ask," Ruth said, with an encouraging smile.

It was settled. Everett Bellman Pawl would go to Tuscany with his son

Robin and his ailing uncle, Sir Everard Belmaine, while Miss Amelia Nevett tried her hand, in what little spare time was at her disposal, at compiling a catalogue of the books and other resources to be held in the library at Uppham House.

★

Chapter Forty

April arrived and though a pale haze of green covered the trees in the park the skies remained obstinately grey. A pall of cloud had obscured the sun for days. Wild birds cowered in bare hedges, shrubs or trees, their plumage fluffed out to provide warmth against the miserable cold that continued to grip the land.

Kit Warrender walked Uppham's tilled fields and saw little sign of the promise of a good harvest. The young man's blue eyes were troubled. Everything was late. Looked like farmers would be having another bad year – two in a row; which meant that homegrown corn would be in short supply again. Imported corn would send prices rocketing and the poor would be unable to afford the high prices demanded for their bread, cornmeal and flour. There was bound to be more rioting and now that the labourers had organised themselves into squads of trained men their force of numbers would almost certainly prevail against the relatively few in power wherever the angry men chose to strike. Inevitably, there would be casualties among the agricultural labourers in their clashes with the yeomanry and the militia. The only option left for the dependents of the injured, killed or gaoled labourers was to throw themselves on the mercy of the parish. He could see how a desperate man would not only be willing to sacrifice his own life, if that was demanded of him, but also to put the lives of his loved ones in jeopardy for the common good. Recalling the appalling deaths of Mrs Coy and her two children, which haunted him still and which he would never forget, Kit was behind the men's fight for justice one hundred per cent. The wronged men were determined to effect change for the better and he wondered how he would have acted had he found himself in like circumstances. He shivered as the east wind ferreted its way into every possible gap in his clothing and raised goosepimples on practically every square inch of his skin. In need of a hot drink, he made his way back to Mrs Hignell's cottage where he was certain to find the old lady's kettle on the boil.

He lifted the latch and called a cheerful greeting. No answer. Two steps took him into the only other downstairs room of the cottage. He found her sitting on an old wooden box with her back to the limewashed wall, her head tilted backwards, gazing up at the rafters. Her toothless mouth hung open, slackjawed. Her legs were splayed. Kit touched her gnarled hand and realised that she must have died soon after he'd left for work. As he closed her deepset eyes sadness washed through him at the thought of the old woman's lonely, ignominious death. She had done her best in a harsh world, had remained cheerful in adversity, and had found pleasure in such simple things as the appearance of the first swallows in summer or the surprise of a winter sunset after a dark day. He gulped back his grief and considered the inequity of a person's lot in life and wondered why God allowed such things to be. Gently, as though the corpse of Mrs Hignell merely slept, he gathered the small bundle of sparrow-like bones and its layers of petticoats in his strong young arms and carried them through to the living room where he sat the body in its usual chair beside the fire. He straightened the cap that hid the sparse hair then folded the stilled hands on the narrow lap. Lastly, he arranged the feet symmetrically so that the prominent bunions, which had formed on the old woman's metatarsals after a lifetime of wearing ill-fitting boots, just touched.

The kettle sang on its trivet before a fire which, without its mistress to replenish it, had burned low. There had never been need of a clock in the sparsely furnished cottage, daylight being the measure of the labourer's day; and the absence of ticking, plus the silence left by Mrs Hignell's long-departed and demanding tabby, only served to underline the desolation of the place, now that the bustling old woman's lively spirit had quitted it. Kit poured himself a cup of hot water and sipped it as he wondered what to do next. Let Mr Aldrich know. He'll deal with everything. Aye, that'd be best, he told himself, as he took a last look at Mrs Hignell's earthly remains before setting out on his sad errand.

*

To say that Mrs Rudge had been surprised to learn that not only was she to have an Assistant Cook but also that the position had gone to a young man would be an understatement. "I dew 'ope 'e knows 'ow ter make bread," she said to Maddy, who was plainly excited by learning that there would soon be another young man about the place. "'Tis gettin' ter be a rill drudge, breadmakin' afore breakfast day in an' day out," the stout cook grumbled. "I seem ter get so 'ot an' bothered these days and me legs suffer so, once the 'eat o' summer comes, what with the fire an the ovens, an all. Not that it looks like we'm gonna get much of a summer if this spring's anythin' ter go by. Ent seen so much as a bud burstin', an 'tis April already."

Maddy had stopped listening long before Mrs Rudge had ceased talking, her mind filled with day-dreams in which she and the new assistant had leading roles. With the aid of a damp cloth and silver sand, the girl was supposed to be scouring the inside, as well as the top inch of the outside rim, of each saucepan to a dazzling brightness. Her eyes saw nothing of the work before her and the cloth lay on the side of the sink with her reddened hand resting upon it. Mrs Rudge clicked her tongue and roused her niece to her duties. "Yew'd bedder not let that noo 'ousekeeper catch yer day-dreamin', my girl," she advised. "Miss Nevett's a rill lady an 'er knows what's what! If yew wanter be kep' on yew'd bedder bestir yerself and quit yore shay brained, shammocky ways."

"Yes, Auntie Bee," Maddy said, with a bop to her aunt before setting to and scouring the pots as if her life depended upon it being done properly; which, of course, it did.

The morning arrived when Martin Harris was shown into the kitchen by Barty Peckover. Mrs Rudge was relieved to hear that, although the cheerful youth was too late to make that morning's batch, he liked nothing better than baking bread and was quite happy to relieve her of the daily task. The rumour soon spread through the rest of the household that Mrs Rudge wholeheartedly approved of her new assistant.

The small, wiry young man threw himself into his work with such enthusiasm that the exhibition of his abundant energy made Mrs Rudge feel quite tired; but she was pleased to notice that his good example galvanised her wayward niece into action. While the cook wondered cynically how long Maddy's mended ways would last, she foresaw that her own life was going to be considerably eased by young Martin's willingness to take on much of the daily drudgery that had been her lot for the last four decades. When mid-morning came she made them all a pot of tea as a toast to the new order.

Upstairs, reclining on her daybed, Mary Emma looked back over her first year of marriage and was pleased with the way it was turning out. She loved Tom passionately though she couldn't always bring herself to show it, especially in public. That Tom loved her just as ardently in return he demonstrated in a thousand ways day and night. She was a weary, impatient lump as she awaited the birth of her child. Would she ever again be that carefree girl who had been so deliriously happy in the first few months of their marriage? Oh, that golden time! Raising a foot, she scowled at its swollen ankle and hoped she didn't look as ugly to Tom as she did to herself.

★

"The Reverend Mr Fieldgate is here, sir," Rudge said. "He apologises for the earliness of his visit but says the matter cannot wait."

Tom had not breakfasted and the untimeliness of the clergyman's visit, without invitation or prior notice, was not calculated to put him into a good humour. "Where is he, Rudge?"

"I have put him in the anteroom next to the library, sir. Peckover lighted the fire a while ago, according to Miss Nevett's orders." Had he not been Rudge, he would have followed this statement with a sniff to show what he thought of such profligacy.

"Ah, good!" Tom said, as he adjusted his neckcloth to his liking. "Offer him tea or something and let him know I'll be down directly. And, Rudge, I'd appreciate a slice or two of bread spread with Cambridge butter and clover honey. Immediately. Have it brought up here, if you will. Thank you."

"What's going on, Tom?" Mary Emma said from the depths of the rumpled bed. "Did I hear Fieldgate's name mentioned? What can he want at this ungodly hour?" Peckover brought in the bread and honey. "Oh, is that for me?" she cried, eyeing it greedily. "How thoughtful of you, Tom. I'm ravenous."

"Sorry, my pet," Tom apologised. "I shall have to forego my breakfast. Fieldgate is here on urgent business, though I can't imagine why it couldn't wait until a civilised hour." He brushed her cheek with a kiss and began to eat.

"Tom Challiss!" Mary Emma said, now fully awake and smiling mischievously as she mock-scolded him. "How can you deny your wife sustenance when she is carrying your child?"

"Easily," he said, his mouth full, as he pulled on his boots. He swallowed. "My roly-poly little wife will soon be rivalling Prinny if she continues to eat at such a rate. But I'll have something sent up, my dear. Now, forgive me, but I must go and see what Fieldgate considers to be of such urgency that he must call at cock-crow."

Having expected to find his visitor seated comfortably before the fire, sipping his tea, Tom was surprised to encounter Edward Fieldgate engaged in the process of striding about the small room, head down, hands clasped behind his back and gripping a riding crop. He came to a stop at Tom's entrance, wheeled about and confronted his host, his face suffused with repressed anger.

"Good-morning, sir!" he said, his voice shaking. "Would you care to explain the meaning of that — that monstrosity that seems to have sprung up overnight in St Mary's churchyard?"

"Oh! It's been erected at last, has it? Not before time. Good-morning to you, Mr Fieldgate. Shall we be seated?"

The reverend gentlemen glowered at Tom. "I prefer to stand, sir!"

"As you wish," Tom inclined his head. "What brings you to Uppham at such an early hour?" he said, well aware of the cause of Fieldgate's visit. "You've declined to take tea?" He wandered over to the tea things which had been placed beside the chair in front of the fire. "You'll excuse me if I pour myself a cup, sir; I shall be happy to answer any questions you care to put, once I've wet my whistle."

These dallying tactics had enraged the angry cleric even further but by a tremendous effort of self-control he waited with an assumption of tolerance for Tom to pour himself a cup of tea. "Will you answer my question now, sir?" he barked, as Tom lazily stirred sugar into his tea.

"You won't mind if I sit to drink this?" he asked, raising his cup provocatively at Fieldgate before sipping the hot liquid.

Had Fieldgate been a swearing man, the moment would have been apt. Instead he said in controlled tones: "I have been patient. Oblige me by answering me, sir?"

"With the greatest of pleasure, my dear sir," Tom said, continuing to sip his tea. "Ah! That's better." With studied control, he returned the empty cup to its saucer. "Now, at last, I have bathed my throat and am able to accommodate you. What was your question again?"

Fieldgate breathed hard through dilated nostrils. "No more games, Mr Challiss, if you please! You heard what I said, so let us have no pretence about the matter. I asked if you would care to explain how that ghastly monument, executed in the worst taste imaginable, comes to be sited on consecrated ground."

"Ah. An elaboration on your original theme, if I'm not mistaken," Tom observed. "I understood that I had your agreement, if not exactly your blessing, to bury Mrs Coy and her two children in a designated plot and to erect a monument in their memory. Do correct me, sir, if I am mistaken."

"In a word: no. That was the agreement, after much soul-searching on my part, I feel bound to add, sir. But I had no idea—" The clergyman's beautiful voice took on a harsh and bullying tone that he was careful never to use in church. "There was no indication on your part that you intended to use sacred ground for the purpose of a political statement. A statement, moreover, in the worst possible taste. It will have to be taken down, sir, and that as quickly as possible, which is why I came so early."

Tom said quietly: "The monument will remain exactly as it is and where it is, Mr Fieldgate."

"I beg to differ, sir," the clergyman boomed. "There are higher authorities than I whom you will have to convince as to its propriety. Why, the thing's an utter disgrace and shall not be allowed to stand."

"You have, as yet, omitted to mention exactly what it is about the monument that offends you, Mr Fieldgate," Tom said, eagerly awaiting the clergyman's justification of his objection, which he anticipated would, in turn, arm him with the point he himself desired to make.

"As if you need to ask! The effigies are, to put it mildly, inappropriate, particularly that of the infant, which can only be described as grotesque. As for the inscription—"

"You find it offensive?" Tom said, and shocked Fieldgate by adding: "Good! It was my intention that you should; you and any of those complacent parishioners who are unable to face the brutal truth: that unalleviated poverty inevitably leads to death from slow starvation."

"So it's true," Fieldgate whispered, "you are nothing less than a radical." He raised his voice. "You know that these people can apply to the parish for assistance! There is no need for them to starve. Yet you would rather throw in your lot with that rioting rabble than support your own kind. You amaze me, sir!"

"But 'these people' and 'that rioting rabble' *are* my own kind, my dear sir. I was born into one of the inferior orders of society and see no shame in it. One does not choose one's station in life, be it that of a crazed monarch or a penniless labourer who is so bereft of hope or betterment that he is driven to poaching food for his starving family."

"If you are referring to Jacob Coy, he has met with the fate he deserves! God commands Christians: 'Thou shalt not steal'," the Reverend Fielding said, reverting to his customary mellifluous tones. "He also commands: 'Thou shalt not covet any thing that is thy neighbour's.' Jacob Coy has broken two of the Ten Commandments and he will be punished accordingly."

"And I'd say that he's suffered enough already!" Tom said, raising his voice at what seemed to him Fieldgate's sickening false piety. "Great heaven, man!" he thundered, "where was God when Mrs Coy and her innocent children died of starvation and exposure?"

"You speak blasphemy, sir. Take care," cautioned the clergyman.

"What's the punishment to be for those who look on at such crimes and do nothing?" Tom asked savagely. "Is there a commandment that fits their behaviour as neatly as you have found two with which to condemn Coy?"

"We are all guilty, I fear, Mr Challiss," Fieldgate suggested, his ire suddenly extinguished by Tom's own exhibition of wrath. "Perhaps you would care to furnish me with your own answer to that question when next we meet, sir? You will find the answer in the Old Testament Book of Exodus. But we have strayed from the reason for my visit, Mr Challiss. If I was overhasty in my outright condemnation of the monument you have so generously raised to the memory of the Coys, I humbly apologise. But – my dear sir," he urged with obvious bewilderment, "what on earth possessed you to commission such an ugly thing as a permanent memorial to a mother and her two children? Surely, something of a softer, more aesthetic nature would have fitted the circumstances just as well?"

"As I supposed," Tom said, calmer now that Fieldgate appeared to be genuinely concerned with his reasons for supplying the grim, permanent reminder of the Coys' tragedy, "you have missed the point, Mr Fieldgate, sir. Death in such circumstances *is* ugly. Yet, even in death, Mrs Coy was beautiful; but her boy was not as cherubic as he should have been and her poor baby's skeletal little body and enormous, accusatory eyes will justifiably reproach every one of us who allowed such wickedness to occur in our own parish. I, for one, have no need of effigies. I shall never forget their suffering."

"I see. Your sensibilities do you great credit, Mr Challiss. Most admirable, my dear sir," the Reverend Fieldgate said, thoughtfully. He appeared to be considering their heated exchange. "I owe you a further apology for my ignorant response to something that goes far beyond a crass, blatant political statement – which is what I initially supposed it to be. Your defence of your action, your explanation of what might appear to the uninitiated as merely a gross distortion of what is customarily deemed sensitive, has shown me that it is nothing of the sort. I have to thank you, my dear sir, for enlightening me. Now. As to that inscription." He smiled wryly when he saw Tom's brow darken. "Perhaps you will be so good as to sweep away my objections to your choice of words for that as effectively as you have done with regard to the monument itself."

Pleasantly surprised by the man's sudden reversion to the affable clergyman he had known before their dispute, Tom said: "Do I really need to go into that? It's self-explanatory. I grew to know those words by heart during my short time in the Peninsular Wars. I thought them most appropriate to the Coys' end."

"I see your reasoning, my dear sir. Yes. Indeed I do. I most humbly beg your pardon for my misapprehension of your intention. I was... unprepared for such a stark reminder of the consequences of successive events and their effect upon the lowest orders. I am ashamed to say that I have been biassed in my assessment of these unhappy people and should have paid greater heed to the words of our most gracious Lord."

His penitence struck Tom as true and his opinion of Fieldgate rose in consequence. He held out his hand and said: "I hope we part as friends, sir. It was not my intention to deliberately offend you or the church; I sought merely to draw attention to the repeated injustices that so many of the less fortunate members of society have had to endure for far too long."

As Fieldgate clasped Tom's hand and covered it with his other, he said: "Do you have any remedies to suggest that might effect a beneficial change to this terrible state of affairs, Mr Challiss?"

Tom shrugged. "I'm no politician, sir. I cannot see a permanent end to the difficulties into which our government has led the country; but I have various private plans which might offer some assistance to the destitute of Downham and Uppham St Mary," Tom said, adding: "Of course, I know it isn't nearly enough."

"God bless you, sir," the clergyman said, shaking Tom's hand. "At least you are willing to make a try. And disregard my unfortunate remarks concerning the monument to the Coys. The thing shall stand in its chosen place and shame us all."

They parted amicably, each man experiencing an unaccountable warmth and respect for the other that had been conspicuously absent at the outset of their confrontation.

On the Sunday following the erection of the Coys' startling monument, word spread as quickly as a fanned flame among the churchgoers that their churchyard had been desecrated by the appearance of an unsightly tombstone. "Who put it there?" "Somebody wi' more money than sense!" "But why such an expensive stone for such lowly people?" "What dew them words say?" Tom and Mary Emma kept silent while the majority of the congregation vented their indignation at the use of brash white marble as the material chosen for sculpting the group and the ugliness of the statuary, particularly the figure of the starveling baby. "What dew Mr Fieldgate say?" They soon learned the answer to the last question, for the reverend gentleman spoke to his flock informally on the reason for the placing of the tomb where each and every one of them was compelled to see it as they passed through the churchyard on the way into church. "It is a salutary reminder to us all," he ended, "that we who have allowed this tragedy to happen in our own parish must not allow history to repeat itself."

Some of his flock took his lesson to heart; others had forgotten it by the time they had helped themelves to mustard and horseradish sauce as accompaniments to their roast beef.

★

As Mary Emma grew near the time of her delivery she began to gain extra weight and her ankles started to swell. Ruth Aldrich was concerned and laid the blame for the symptoms at Mary Emma's door. "You're not getting enough fresh air and exercise," the nurse told her. "It's perfectly all right for you to walk in the park, as long as you're well wrapped up against the cold and are accompanied. I notice Miss Brook takes a walk in the park every day without fail. You and she could go together."

"But Agnes isn't as far along as I am," protested Mary Emma. "I'm beginning to feel like a waddling duck! I get out of breath so quickly and if I drop anything I have difficulty in bending down to pick it up again."

"Those excuses are too feeble to be taken seriously, Mary Emma. Now, come along, my dear," Ruth said briskly. "Up off that day bed, on with your coat and bonnet and outside with you! A stroll in the fresh air with Agnes will do you the world of good."

"If I must," Mary Emma grumbled. "Though I don't see what good it will do. I can walk no faster than a tortoise."

Ruth watched the young woman lumbering about as she made herself ready for the outdoors and decided that it was time Dr Barnes gave her a thorough examination. It would do no harm and it would be as well to check that the pregnancy was progressing normally as it approached natural termination.

As Mary Emma and Agnes strolled about the miserable-looking gardens that surrounded the house the younger woman told her friend that Mrs Brook had come back from the Downham shops with the disturbing news that prices had risen again.

"I can't *bear* to think of it," Mary Emma said wearily as she puffed along beside Agnes. "Although it hasn't been exactly quiet in the last few weeks things have simmered down. Now, just when one begins to feel that it's safe to go out into Downham, or even further afield, in your dear little phaeton we shall find ourselves prisoners of the park again. It's too bad!"

Agnes looked at her friend's petulant expression and said: "Too bad for those who will have to find the money for their bread you mean, Mary Emma. You, who have no such cares, cannot imagine what a spectre looms over a good many of the poorer families in Downham and the surrounding villages. Have you any idea what a quartern loaf costs?"

Mary Emma, alive to the air of censure in Agnes's voice, replied: "None whatsoever, I confess, Agnes. It's not anything that concerns me, thank heavens! But there! I can see that you are dying to tell me all about the deprivations of the poor and that I shall have no peace until you have given me my lesson for the day. But, my dear: all we hear on all sides is bread! bread! bread! 'Tis such a tedious subject. Don't you agree?"

Agnes stopped walking and faced Mary Emma. "How *can* you remain so detached from the terrible things that are going on all around you?" She said, her blue eyes blazing. "The price of a quartern loaf has risen to 11½d, almost a shilling! Think about what that means to those with too little money to buy it. Did the monument that Mr Challiss raised to the pitiful Coy family not move you at all?"

"Tom had nothing to do with that monstrosity," Mary Emma said with a smile. An expression flitted across Agnes's face and gave away in an instant everything from which Tom had tried to shield his wife. "Or had he?" she asked sharply.

"Oh, dear," Agnes said. "Tom wanted to spare you, Mary Emma. Forgive me."

"There's nothing to forgive *you* for, my dear," Mary Emma said, her eyes clouding over. "What were those labouring people to Tom? I wonder why he said nothing of it to me?" She shuddered. "Oh! Somebody walked over my grave. Let's go in, Agnes. I'm cold and so very, very weary."

★

Dr Barnes finished his examination and as he drew up the coverlet said: "Splendid! Everything's going very well, Mrs Challiss." He seated himself on the chair placed by the bed. "Tell me: how long have your ankles been swollen?"

"Too long! I'm sick of the sight of them," she said. Then, as if it had only just occurred to her: "I trust they'll return to normal once my child's born?"

"That very much depends on you," the young physician said as he studied her face. He sat back. "Have you had any outlandish cravings, Mrs Challiss? Herrings with jam? Liquorice? Vinegar?" He smiled at her reaction. "Those are just a few of the more bizarre delicacies I've had to forbid some of my patients lately."

"I can think of nothing. Unless you consider it odd to want to sniff wet coal?"

"Ah!" Dr Barnes appeared to be delighted by this disclosure. "Anything else?"

"No, I can't recall–"

"Excuse me, Mary Emma," Agnes said quietly, "but perhaps you should mention the quantity of celery you have consumed these last few weeks."

"What nonsense! It's common knowledge that celery is an excellent vegetable," Mary Emma said with a smile. "But I do admit to an unconscionable partiality for it."

"And you eat it as an uncooked vegetable in combination with other uncooked salad foods, do you?" the doctor asked.

"Why, yes. At least, no. My preference is for the white stalks on their own. I like to keep a jar of prepared celery beside me at all times so that I can nibble it as and when I feel the urge," explained Mary Emma. "Miss Nevett is very good to me, doctor. Look there! A fresh vase of it stands in ice water on my table this very minute."

Dr Barnes studied the cluttered small table that stood beside the day bed.

"Aha!" he said, holding aloft a crystal salt cellar which was almost empty. "How often do you add this to your celery stalks, Mrs Challiss?"

Mary Emma smiled at Agnes and said pityingly to the doctor: "What an odd question. Why, every time I take a bite, of course. 'Tis customary, doctor, is it not? Why, celery without salt would be as unthinkable as coffee without cream!"

"Madam," the young doctor said, his manner suddenly grown very severe, "you will forego any undue intake of this," he flourished the salt cellar before her, "until after the birth of your child. Your habit of coating each bite of the celery stalk in salt has created an excess of saline in your system which will prove dangerous to yourself and to your child if you persist." Shocked into silence, Mary Emma sat bolt upright. Agnes's eyes had widened in alarm at Dr Barnes's diagnosis and he observed, not for the first time, how beautiful they were, sparkling and clear as the purest sapphires.

"There is no undue cause for alarm, Mrs Challiss, provided you follow my advice immediately," the young man said. "I advise you to cleanse your system by taking in quantities of spring water. Boil it first and cool it before drinking.

You may drink the spring water hot, with a slice of lemon added, first thing in the morning. Thereafter, whenever you would take tea, coffee or chocolate, drink water instead. Follow the regime faithfully for ten days. At the end of that period I will call on you again. You should notice a difference in four or five days; but no back-sliding, mind, if you wish to restore your ankles to their former shapeliness. More rest will help to reduce the swelling, but also try to get plenty of fresh air."

Mary Emma's face had grown longer with every sentence Dr Barnes had uttered. "It sounds dreadfully dull, Dr Barnes," she said. "Am I forbidden my celery?"

"Not at all, madam. But I strictly forbid you to touch so much as an unnecessary grain of salt. 'Tis poison, ma'am, in your present state. Perhaps I might presume to enlist the assistance of Miss Brook in the monitoring of the treatment?" he added, abruptly turning to Agnes, his black eyebrows questioning, his dark eyes magnetic.

Confused, both by his unwavering glance and at finding herself so suddenly drawn into the bedside consultation, at which she'd thought herself merely a spectator, Agnes stammered out her consent. Overcome by embarrassment at her own gaucheness, her cheeks flamed and she lowered her eyelids over her troubled eyes.

Young Agnes's artless display of confusion so bewitched Dr Barnes that as Cupid's love-tipped arrow pierced his heart he was oblivious to its fatal wound.

★

Chapter Forty-one

Jem Webster's way to work on the new cottages took him through the corner of Home Wood. On a rare sunny morning in late April 1816 he felt on top of the world. Not only was he one of those fortunate enough to be in paid employment, but he had just learned that he was also the prospective father of his fourth child, two of whom had survived the hazards of modern life so far. His woman, Nell, always generous with her affections, had told him the good news as he ate his breakfast of new bread and cheese.

"'Tis the good Lord's way of fillin' the gap left by our pore li'l Essie, this 'un," Nell said, cutting a wedge of cheese and placing it alongside a hunk of bread and jar of ale for Jem's nooning. "I got yer a special treat terday, lover," she said, producing a withered apple from her apron pocket and setting it beside the rest of his snack. "'Tis dwinged some, but I 'ad'n yisty an the flavour's full o' autumn shine. Take care, my lover," she said, "trouble's not far away in the town." She embraced Jem fondly and broke away. "Go yew through 'Ome Wood fer safety," she advised.

A reluctant spring had finally made up its mind to make itself obvious. Trees appeared to be draped in brilliant green gauze and birdsong echoed through the sunshafted wood. He stopped, to make certain that his eyes were not deceiving him. No! The faintest wash of violet-blue was discernible against the yellow-green foliage of the young hornbeams. Bluebells! He smiled to himself and said aloud: "'Tis over!" By which exclamation he meant that winter had passed. So happy that he thought his heart must burst, he made his way to the building site where he and his apprentice, John Brook, were engaged on supplying and fitting the frames to the windows and doors to the row of cottages. There remained floorboards to cut and plane, doors and cupboards to construct and fit: weeks of work lay ahead of him. Life was good.

★

The welcome sunshine had got Tom Challiss out of bed early and he was on the site and already in discussion with Joe Aldrich as Jem came up. The three men greeted each other cordially and Jem took himself off to supervise John's planing while he himself began to construct a four-panelled door out of seasoned pine.

"A good man, that," said Aldrich, "a true craftsman. Have you seen the work he's done on the frames, Mr Challiss? Absolutely splendid!"

"I have," Tom answered. "It's good to see a man able to use his skills to such good effect. The sad part is that there are as many men of equal skill willing and able to work; but there just aren't sufficient places for them. It's a terrible state of affairs. Were we to take on half a dozen more here, it would only be a drop in the ocean and would also shorten Jem's term of employment."

Surprised by his master's last remark, Aldrich said: "But I understood that Webster was to be employed here on a permanent basis, Mr Challiss."

"Eh? What d'ye mean? Of course, he is. Who said anything different?"

"But—"

"Have you heard that the price of a quartern loaf has risen yet again?" Tom said, his mind distracted. "A farthing, on top of the last rise. Oh, it doesn't seem much to you or me; but to the labourers it'll be the last straw. I can hardly believe it! Almost a shilling a loaf."

Aldrich showed his disgust. "Hm! Eleven pence and three farthings for the staff of life! They dare not make it a round shilling; it would light the powder keg."

"We shall see soon enough," Tom said, his brow creased. "Mary Emma and I had a talk last evening about the plight of the worst off and she came up with an idea to provide employment for a gang of ten men for a period of three months."

"Paid employment?" asked Aldrich, his bushy eyebrows elevated.

"Of course there would be remuneration," Tom said, looking at his steward as if he were a fool. "What would be the point, otherwise?"

"I only wondered," Aldrich said, mildly. "It'll be a great outlay. The men will insist on a fair wage. What do you have in mind?"

"Mary Emma suggested twelve shillings a week per man," Tom said. "I think that's a fair reward for what she has in mind. She thinks we should build a wall to enclose the estate."

"A wall!" Aldrich cried in utter astonishment. "But... Of course, Mr Challiss, I know I have absolutely no say in what is planned for the estate; though it is a real privilege to be consulted. My job is to see that whatever you decide gets done as quickly and as efficiently as is possible in a given time and that the job is well done. But a wall! At this time, when we need new stables and an up-to-date ice house—"

"I know, Joe," Tom said with a rueful smile. "But time hangs heavy for my wife with the child due within the next fortnight. Mrs Challiss needs something of importance with which to occupy her time and this project is dear to her heart."

"I beg your pardon, sir," Aldrich insisted stubbornly, "but has Mrs Challiss any idea of the expense involved, quite apart from the labouring costs?"

"Oh, yes, Joe! To the last farthing," Tom said with a short laugh. "Mary Emma's pretty little head contains a first-class brain, I assure you. She's a great deal brighter than I am but if you tell her I said so, I'll deny it. She intends to feed the men, too."

"Mollycoddling petticoat rule," mumbled Aldrich.

"You'd be amazed at how efficiently she's worked it all out, Joe," Tom said, without trying to conceal the admiration he felt for his wife's acumen. "The wall is to be six feet high – think of that – it'll rival Martlets! And she's written off to the brickfields giving 'em the specifications for the job and ordered 'em to deliver the bricks right away so, once the men have finished digging the foundations, the—"

"Wall of Jericho goes up!" Joe Aldrich shouted, pleased with his own wit and following his remark with a rumble in his throat that might have been a laugh but sounded more like the awakening of a long-dormant volcano.

"And we know what happened to that," Tom hooted, temporarily out of control, as he wiped tears of laughter from his eyes. Suddenly serious, he said: "But let's get it built first, Joe. Eh?" Whereupon both men were afflicted with hysterical laughter again but couldn't have told anybody why. Perhaps it was the thought of a wall in conjunction with the horns that had accompanied the mob who had come in the Night.

★

"But if I *promise* to drive really slowly, Tom," Mary Emma wheedled. "I am so utterly bored, lying on this bed all day. You can have no idea what it's like for me! Even darling Agnes is running out of patience with me. Oh! I so long to visit the Brooks at Church House! Noah must have grown out of all recognition. After all, darling, the worst that could happen would be that our child would be born there, and I can't think of another person I would rather have by me at such a time than dear Dulcie Brook."

"I'm sorry to have to disappoint you, my love," Tom said very firmly, "but Dr Barnes has given strict instructions that, as you are so near the time of your delivery, you must stay near the house." Seeing her face crumple and tears spill down her cheeks, he took her in his arms and kissed her salty eyes. "There, love; don't give in now. You have borne up so well these last tiring weeks." He folded her in his strong arms and rocked her gently back and forth. "I wish there was some way I could spare you, Mary Emma."

She sniffed inelegantly and Tom handed her his silk handkerchief. "Oh, Tom! I don't know how you put up with me. But, if only it was all over and I was in control of my own body once more, I shouldn't mind so much. Agnes is a positive saint and scarcely refers to her condition but goes about the house as if there were nothing the matter with her. Why, I caught her the other day teaching young Maddy to stitch the names of the rooms onto the new linen in scarlet thread."

Tom held her at arms' length. "Perhaps she has the right idea, sweetheart. Keeping busy takes her mind off herself. But, surely, it's Miss Nevett's place to teach Maddy her needlework, is it not?"

"Oh, yes," Mary Emma said. "She was there, too. All three of them were stitching away as if their lives depended upon it," she complained, mouth turned down.

"Why didn't you join them?"

"I? I am the mistress of Uppham House, Tom. Would you have me doing the work of the servants?"

"That's absurd!" he said, leading her to an ottoman and seating himself beside her. "You will lose no dignity by setting a good example to your underlings, my dear."

"Perhaps not," his wife conceded. "But, Tom, you know how I loathe needlework." At that moment Peckover showed Dr Barnes into the room. "Good afternoon, Mr Challiss. Pray, don't get up. You are welcome to stay while I examine Mrs Challiss, sir. My examination will be brief. Good afternoon, Mrs Challiss. And how are the ankles. If I might – Ah! Splendid! I see you have followed my advice and with excellent results. Now, madam. If you will be so good as to lie down on the day bed. Just so. Comfortable? Oh! You're leaving, Mr Challiss? Very well, sir."

"Is everything all right, doctor?" Mary Emma asked timidly.

"Everything is just exactly as it should be, my dear Mrs Challiss," the brisk young man said, removing his ear trumpet from Mary Emma's abdomen. "Now. You are not to worry if you notice less activity from your child, ma'am. The infant's head is engaged."

Mary Emma looked at him in wide-eyed alarm. "What does that mean?"

"It means, ma'am, that your child is ready to dive into the world head first, as is customary for the majority of babes about to be born. One could say, it wants to see where it's going before it braves the outside world. Though I must confess, I never heard of one going back." He replaced his ear trumpet and snapped his bag shut.

Despite his nonsense, Mary Emma laughed as she imagined the picture he'd described. "You consider the birth imminent then, Dr Barnes?" she said, very excited by the idea of setting eyes on her child at long last.

"Any day now, my dear Mrs Challiss," the doctor said cheerfully. "Don't hesitate to call on my services day or night, if you think it necessary, madam. All will be well," he assured her. "You are young and strong; and the birth should cause you no more trouble than the majority of women have to endure."

Totally ignorant of the trouble the majority of women had to endure, Mary Emma thanked him and smiled to herself as she heard the young doctor exchanging pleasantries with Agnes Brook on the landing. "Oh, yes, my darling Agnes," she said softly. "I've seen the way he looks at you as if he could eat you, child and all, my dear. And you – unless I'm much mistaken – will soon be just as besotted with him. That is, if you're not already." Thoroughly contented, she reached for a stick of celery and crunched her way down the length of its blanched stalk in a series of rapid bites.

★

Clem's leg was beginning to mend and he was able to walk about with the aid of a stick. Good food and rest had helped the deep wounds in his leg to heal but it would be months before he would know how much mobility he had lost in the damaged limb. Ruth Aldrich had averted blood poisoning and that other scourge of the wounded, gangrene. Clem was fully aware that he owed his life to the nurse's skill.

Ben Rix, now over the worst of his chest infection, stalked restlessly about the east wing and had more respect for trapped animals than formerly. He peered out of the long windows at the sun shining over the park and could barely restrain himself from throwing up the window, hopping over the low sill and escaping into the fresh air. Mrs Aldrich had forbidden him to leave the house until the weather grew warmer. She observed his restlessness and guessed that she wouldn't be able to confine him for much longer. But, as a known and wanted criminal, what was he to do then?

Ruth discussed the matter with her husband and Joseph said she should talk to Mr Challiss about it. The presence of two young outlaws in proximity to his own home made him distinctly nervous and he would be glad to see the back of the Rix brothers.

When Tom heard that the Rixes were fit to travel he considered where best to send them. If they were sent anywhere in East Anglia, or even further afield, they were bound to be sent back to their place of settlement as soon as it was discovered that they had no business to be elsewhere. He confided his worries to Mary Emma one night as they lay side by side in their four-poster. For a while she said nothing. Suddenly, she sat up, leaned over him with sparkling eyes and asked him: "Had young Ben Rix been caught, what would have happened to him, Tom?"

This was no help at all! "He would have been arrested and held in Wimbotsham gaol to await trial, I suppose. From there he would probably have been taken to Norwich and hanged or, if the magistrates were feeling lenient that day – improbable, as Ben would stand accused of murder – he might have had his sentence commuted to transportation for fourteen years. Where is all this leading, my dear?"

"Exactly!" Mary Emma cried, kissing him. "And he would have been transported to Australia or Van Diemans Land, or some such place in the Antipodes. Would he not, Tom?"

"Yes, almost certainly," he said, wondering what she was getting at.

"Just as I supposed!" she said smugly. "Well then, my dear, why not send them there – only as free men and under assumed names?"

He considered her suggestion. "Hmm. It might work if we can manage to transport them from here to Lynn under cover of darkness. Yes! It could be done. It will be done, thanks to my clever little wife."

"I have an even better idea, Tom," Mary Emma said in growing excitement. "From what one has read in the news sheets, Australia sounds a harsh and undeveloped country with an unkind climate."

"Well?"

"Why not send them to a less populated place? That island to the south–"

"Van Dieman's Land?"

"No. Nearer the Antarctic... You remember: Miss Peters read us all about Captain Cook's explorations! *That* country. It has two main islands. Oh... Cook charted its coastline. Ah! New Zealand, is it not?"

"Yes, I recall her saying that it was a very beautiful, wild country," Tom said, adding: "We must put it to the brothers and let them decide. They might object to leaving England for good."

"Well!" Mary Emma said, flouncing back onto her pillow, "if they stay, they'll probably be hanged." She yawned. "I'm tired of talking about the Rixes, Tom. Good-night, my dear." They kissed, moved apart and eventually drifted off to sleep.

At about three o'clock in the morning on the seventh of May 1816 Mary Emma awoke with backache. Reasoning that, if only she could get off to sleep again the pain would disappear, she carefully supported her abdomen and turned onto her other side. She cried out as giant hands seemed to take hold of her body and try to wrench it apart. Gripped by the worst pain she had ever known, she cried out as again the invisible tormenter gripped her body in a vice and twisted it unmercifully.

Tom was awake. "The child, Mary Emma? Is it time?"

The pain subsided, allowing her to breathe easily again. "Send for Dr Barnes, Tom," she said, amazed by her calm-sounding voice. "And fetch Ruth Aldrich if you can. Hurry, dear. This child appears to take after its mother; it's impatient to be born and doesn't intend to wait. Ah-ah-ah!" Again, the pain held her in thrall and warm water rushed from her wracked body into the bed as the child insisted on its freedom.

A lighted candle appeared and behind it, Agnes's concerned face. "I've directed Miss Nevett to wake Maddy to put more water on to boil, dear. It will soon be over, Mary Emma. Here. Hold my hand and squeeze it as hard as you like."

When she was able to speak again, Mary Emma said: "Thank you. You are so good to me, Agnes. I do wish Dr Barnes would come. Is Ruth here?"

★

Five hours later that morning Mary Emma was delivered of a large boy. He was red-faced and long black hair covered his head.

To Tom, he looked as much like a squashed monkey as anything, but he had the sense to keep quiet about that. Mary Emma's prolonged torment had pierced him to the heart and he vowed never to put her through such an ordeal again, even if it meant remaining celibate for the remainder of his life. Once was more than enough.

Her face flushed from her exertions and exhausted by the laborious birth – which Dr Barnes had the temerity to tell her had been an easy one – Mary Emma took the mewling child into her arms and gazed into the red crumpled face with adoration. The boy opened his eyes and looked up at his mother as she fed him. His suck was strong and gluttonous; he drained her left breast and howled for more. She gave it with love and her womb contracted at each suck, a kind of loving that was quite unlike being with her husband, but equally sensuous. Mary Emma fell in love all over again, this time with her ugly little son. So this was childbirth. Even while the fierceness of the pain was still raw in her memory, she decided, then and there that, if God so ordered it, she and Tom would bring their eight children into the world and create a home for them which was every bit as warm and loving as that enjoyed by the Brooks. With that resolve firmly planted in her mind she fell into a deep sleep.

★

They named the boy Thomas Henry Challiss and arranged for him to be baptised in two months' time. But, just in case anything unforeseen happened to the child, Tom took Edward Fieldgate's advice and had his son's name recorded in the parish register at St Mary's, Uppham.

★

Thomas Henry Challiss was just over a week old when news filtered through to Mary Emma that unemployed spinners and weavers, and others disgruntled with their lot, had massed in the Suffolk town of Bury St Edmunds. According to Miss Nevett – who had it from Rudge who, in turn, had it from Peckover – riots had broken out. The angry mob had marched on a manufacturing hosier and demanded he hand over a diabolical machine that went by the name of a spinning jenny. Damage had been done to property before the West Suffolk Militia had dispersed the tumultuous crowd and a number of the rioters had been arrested.

"When did you say this happened?" Mary Emma asked, thankful, as she looked at her nursing infant, that Bury St Edmunds was such a long way from Downham.

Amelia Nevett said she thought Rudge had given the date as the 14th of May.

"Thank heavens the magistrates had the sense to call out the militia in good time," Mary Emma said, her attention on Thomas as she shifted him from one breast to the other. "Let's hope that's an end to it," she said, meeting Miss Nevett's eyes. "What do they hope to gain by such lawlessness? It will only set the law against them and prejudice their case."

The veiled housekeeper said: "The opinion of sympathisers, Mrs Challiss, is that the people have been patient long enough. Civil appeals to the authorities for a fair deal have yielded no result. Their vast numbers are the only weapon the poor have. What would you have them do?"

Unused to being challenged by a servant, even one as dignified as Amelia Nevett, Mary Emma said tartly: "Fortunately, Miss Nevett, I am able to ignore that question. It is most unlikely that I would ever be called upon by anyone in authority to express my opinion on such a matter."

"Does that mean you have no opinion to express?" the housekeeper persisted.

"Upon my word! You are obstinate, not to say impertinent," Mary Emma said growing angry. Thomas whimpered and she hushed him. "Since you insist: I do think that the poor have had much to bear for a very long time and have borne their deprivations with great fortitude. If it seems to you that I tend to shy away from the discussion of such unpleasant topics, it's because I can offer no solution to the problem. It does *not* mean that I do not care!"

The veil shimmered as a breath was exhaled and Mary Emma saw a smile gleam behind the silken gauze. "It's obvious that you have given the matter some thought, madam." She paused, decided to go on. "It isn't until one has been faced with destitution that one is able to appreciate the hopelessness of these poor people."

"I'm certain you're right," Mary Emma conceded, recalling her houskeeper's recent past. "But you must see that one feels so impotent, however much one wishes to do something, *anything*, that would alleviate their terrible plight."

"You'll forgive me, I'm sure, Mrs Challiss, if I draw attention to your obvious wealth," Miss Nevett said in a respectful tone. "If you are really serious in your intentions, one way in which you could help them would be to set up a soup kitchen. That would ensure that they got bread and at least one hot meal a day, madam."

Mary Emma thoughtfully rubbed her hand up and down Thomas's back and was brought out of her doting reverie by his belch. "A soup kitchen . . . I see. What have you in mind, Miss Nevett? How would it be organised?"

It was the opening that Amelia Nevett had hoped for. Requesting permission and receiving it, she drew up a chair, sat down beside the bed and with shining eyes outlined her plan for feeding the hungry of the parish. . . .

Confined to her day bed, Mary Emma dwelt on how well everything was going. The labourers had almost finished digging the deep footings for the wall; Miss Nevett had recruited women from Uppham St Mary to staff the soup kitchen, which had been set up in a large tent on the green and was running smoothly on a rota system; and her darling Thomas Henry had shed his black mane. She ran a fond finger over his skull with its gently pulsating fontanelle and gasped as a sunbeam slid through the window and revealed a sheen of new growth. The Challiss red hair! Tom had hidden his disappointment. He would be so pleased to find his son had inherited it after all.

★

From an upstairs window Agnes Brook watched Dr Barnes climb into his pony cart and drive away from the house. Dr Barnes... Dear Dr Barnes. Her face became hot and her heart thumped as she recalled their brief exchange after his daily visit to her friend. It had been perfunctory indeed: very professional, very correct – to a casual observer – yet his look and manner towards herself had been full of repressed passion.

Three days ago he had similarly met her on the landing outside the front withdrawing room wherein Mary Emma reclined on her day bed re-reading *Pride and Prejudice* for the third time. Agnes had reached the top of the stairs at the moment Dr Barnes was quietly closing the door on his contented patient and her satisfied sleeping infant and they had come face to face. At first, the surprise encounter had silenced them; but they had no need of words for their eyes conveyed everything, and more, that might have been spoken. He had been the first to collect himself. ...

"Good morning to you, Miss Brook," he said in the delightful baritone whose timbre unaccountably had the power to stir her heart. "And how are you this fine spring morning?"

"Very well indeed, thank you, sir," she said, blushing furiously.

"You take good care of yourself, of course?" he asked, solicitously.

"You mean my – pregnancy, Dr Barnes? Oh, yes. Mrs Aldrich is keeping an eye on things."

"I'm very glad to hear it," he said with a smile, adding: "Mrs Aldrich is an excellent nurse and a fine woman to have for a friend."

"Indeed, she is, sir," Agnes agreed, smiling and revealing her pretty teeth.

Their exchange came to a sudden halt. They stood locked by their eyes as the silence between them lengthened. The young physician took a step towards Agnes and his movement broke the spell.

Recollecting herself, she said: "'Tis very good of you, sir, to ask after my health. Happily, we Brooks come from robust stock and child-bearing is looked upon as a natural part of a woman's maturity."

"More than that, I hope, my dear Miss Brook," the young man said. "Given the right circumstances, a young woman in your condition should be anticipating the tremendous happiness the birth of her child will bring. Yet–"

"Please, Dr Barnes. I beg you to say no more on the subject," Agnes said firmly, determined to bring the conversation to an end. "I fear you are straying into a very private matter and I decline to discuss it with you any further."

"As you wish, Miss Brook," he said, inclining his head, his dark eyes threatening to mesmerise her again. "But, allow me to say that, should you feel at all disposed to raise the subject again, I do have a sympathetic ear."

Agnes acknowledged his well-meant speech with a curt nod. "'Tis kind of you, Dr Barnes; but I do not foresee such an occasion arising. Pray, excuse me." She made him a curtsey, saying as she entered the room he'd just quitted, "Good-morning, sir."

As he'd gone downstairs he'd heard her playing the piano and singing. He had stopped to listen and the sound of her voice had bewitched him into making a proposal of marriage the next time he saw her alone. To his surprise and delight, Agnes had accepted him with a spontaneous kiss, adding: "But first, my dear Dr Barnes, you must ask my parents for their permission. If they agree, I'll wed you soon as you like."

He had stopped by Church House immediately on leaving the mansion and had found himself in luck. Adam Brook had called in for another jug of ale and Agnes's parents had invited the young doctor, whom they knew by sight, into the house. At first, Adam and Dulcie Brook had failed to understand the reason for his visit, but as he made his errand clear they separately raised objections to his request.

"First I 'eard that yew was courtin' our Agnes," Adam said, eyes narrowed. "'Ow long yew known her, then?" When Dr Barnes told him Adam scoffed: "'Taint no time at all! Yew can't be in yer right mind, doctor. Why, me an Dowsabella was walkin' out fer eighteen months afore I so much as asked 'er fer a kiss," he said slyly.

Dulcie laughed at this. "What nonsense yew dew talk at times, Mr Brook," she said. "Don't yew listen to 'is gammarattle, sir. Why, I remember as if 'twere yisty, that Adie seemed ter 'ave as many 'ands as an octerpus, an that I 'ad the devil of a job fightin' 'im orf when 'e wanted 'is way wi' me."

Adie bridled at his wife's disloyal disclosure. "'Twere t'other way round, as I remember it," he said accusingly. "'Twere yew fanged 'old o' me and made me ser duzzy wi' yer kissin' as I dint have enough stren'th left ter fight yew orf!"

Despite the gravity of his mission, Dr Barnes couldn't help himself and laughed out loud. Reminded of their visitor's presence, Adam and Dulcie composed themselves, sat up straight and confronted him.

"Zackly what're your intentions terwards our Agnes, Dr Barnes," Adam said, serious now.

"I want to make her my wife, if she'll have me," Dr Barnes said simply.

"Yew dew know she's a minor, sir?" Dulcie enquired. "An' as if that weren't a bit of a stumblin' block, she'm carryin' a child outa wedlock, inter the bargain."

"I am aware of both those facts, Mrs Brook, and do not consider either one a serious impediment to our eventual union."

"That's master gen'rous o' yer, doctor," Adam said gratefully, grasping the gist of the young man's fancy talk. "Not that I can speak fer Agnes, yew understand? She'm a mind of 'er own an'll dew as well wi'out an 'usband as with'un, make no mistake 'bout that!"

Dulcie stared her husband out of countenance, and said: "'Course, like most young women o' marriageable age, sir, Agnes would like the chance tew give yore offer doo consideration, I'm sure. 'Tis true what Mr Brook says: she 'as a mind of 'er own that nothin' can budge, once 'tis made up. As 'er mother, I fill bound ter say that if she dew agree ter wed yer 'twill be yew gettin the best part o' the bargain, sir."

Doctor Barnes smiled wryly. "As to that, ma'am, I have no doubt at all that you are right. Agnes is a delightful young woman." He coughed politely into his closed fist. "You must have noticed the difference in our ages, sir? I am upwards of twelve years your daughter's senior, Mr Brook."

"'Ardly 'ad the time ter take it all in. Have we? But'n older 'usband is all ter the good, where women's concerned," Adam said. "Besides which, Agnes always did seem older than her years. I doan see no trouble comin' from that. Dew yew, Dulcie?"

"No. But I can't say I dint 'ave me doubts when yew sprung it on us," Dulcie said, "'er bein' 'ardly more'n a girl. As it 'asn't bin mentioned by no-one, answer me this, Dr Barnes: do yew reelly love our Agnes and dew she reelly love yew?"

"Yes, Mrs Brook. It's entirely mutual. You may set your mind at rest on that point," the doctor said showing some emotion. "I would not be sitting here asking for dear Agnes's hand, were it otherwise, I assure you, ma'am."

"Aint no more ter be said, then, far as I'm concerned," Adam Brook said, getting up and shaking the young man's hand.

"That's all right, then," Dulcie said, going up to the startled doctor and saluting him soundly on his right cheek before he had time to resist.

Once free of Dulcie's motherly arms, Dr Barnes said: "As to financial matters—"

"If yew mean money," said Mr Brook, "I've a bit put by fer Agnes's bride portion. 'Taint very much—"

"You mistake my meaning, sir," Dr Barnes said, touched by Brook's lack of mercenary motive. "I want you to know that I am able to provide a good home for your daughter. She will want for nothing, in a material sense. I have private means, in addition to any fees I might earn in the course of my professional duties."

"Bless you, doctor," Dulcie broke in, "we'm 'appy ter know that Agnes'll be comfortable; but 'tis much more important tew us ter know that yew'll love 'er an' treat 'er gentle. That's the way tew win 'er 'eart, sir, same as any other woman. Aint nothin' a woman won't dew fer a man if she knows he loves 'er an will stick by 'er."

The young doctor, catching Adam Brook's shy, smiling glance at his comely wife as she laid down the law, knew that his choice of bride, coming from such wholesome stock, couldn't have been bettered.

★

The Challisses were astonished by the speed with which their physician had wooed Agnes Brook and were even more surprised when they heard that she had accepted him with alacrity. "Do you suppose it's on account of the coming child?" Tom asked his wife.

"Perhaps," she replied absently, as she leaned over Thomas's crib and offered him her finger to grasp. "But I think it would be truer to say that it's a love match, Tom."

"But there's barely been time for them to fall in love or for them to be able to distinguish it — whatever feelings they have for one another — from mere infatuation."

"Oh, Tom! Have you forgotten so soon how it was with us? I loved you from the moment I saw the sun shining on your beautiful coppery hair in the garden at Lyndon Manor," she said, running to him and throwing her body against his so that, instinctively, he folded her in his arms. "Oh, my dear!" Mary Emma murmured against his heart, "I can hardly wait to be with you again; it's been so long."

"What does Dr Barnes say about it?" he said, hungrily searching her eyes as he stroked dark tendrils of hair as fine as smoke away from her face.

"Three more weeks!" she grumbled. "And Ruth says the same. I don't know how I shall be able to bear it, Tom, I want you so *desperately*; and it must be terrible for you."

"I won't deny it," he said, his hand wandering to her breast. "Ugh! What's that?" he said in disgust, as his fingers came away sticky and wet.

Mary Emma laughed at the expression of revulsion on her husband's face. "Milk, of course, you silly! Oh, dear; I wonder how long I shall have to feed my insatiable little guzzler?" They bent over the crib. "Do you realise, Tom, that he's already twelve days old? How the time has flown. Oh! I'm so glad I had a spring baby. Now we shall have all the long sunny days of summer to look forward to."

The perpetual calendar on top of the *escritoire* showed Sunday, May 19 1816.

★

On Tom's instructions, Barty Peckover had been bringing back three newspapers with the Saturday post ever since the disturbances the previous month. They made grim reading and Joseph Aldrich and Tom took a serious view of the upheaval that was taking place all around them. According to the papers, far from dying down, as Tom had hoped the riots would, the trouble seemed to be heading their way. As far as Aldrich was concerned it didn't bear thinking about. The rioters had become emboldened by their successes and had taken to demanding money of those whose farms they attacked. If those threatened refused them actual coins or notes they were forced to allow the mobs credit for beer at local inns where they ran up sizeable bills before moving on, a rowdy, ever-increasing crowd.

Word reached Uppham St Mary that rioters had roamed the village of Feltwell – a few miles south of Downham along the London road – yesterday, and had armed themselves with a variety of farm implements which they had used as weapons and had caused trouble there. Property had been damaged, seemingly for no good reason: fences had been pulled down, and dams had been deliberately breached.

Barty Peckover had seen and heard worrying things in Downham. "Man I was talkin' to said the rioters mean business this time, Mr Challiss. Seems Feltwell's quiet terday; an so I should think, it bein' Sundey an all. Oo knows? P'raps the mob 've 'ad enough riotin' ter satisfy 'em fer a while. But I doubt it. Prob'ly gatherin' stren'th."

"Did you learn anything else, Peckover?" Tom asked the footman. "Anything that might prepare us to defend ourselves, should the crowd decide to head this way?"

"Oh, they'll *definitely* march inter Downham, sir," Peckover said, looking at Tom as if he should have worked that out for himself. "After all, Mr Challiss, the road'll bring 'em straight 'ere, woanit," he said patiently.

"But they'll pass through Southerey on their way," Joe Aldrich protested. "Perhaps they'll stop there," he added hopefully, a worried frown creasing his forehead.

Peckover drew in his breath, pushed out his lips and shook his head from side to side to emphasise his doubt: "'Taint very likely, Mr Aldrich, now is it? Suth'ry's only a little place, innit. No, sir. They'll soon be done *there*. Then prob'ly straight on ter Denver. But that's only another little place," said the Norwicher. "Stands ter reason they'll head fer Downham if they wanna make a big stir, doan it, sir."

"I'm afraid you're right," Tom said. "Thank you, Peckover. Let Mrs Challiss know that I shall miss church today. That'll be all." His next remark alarmed Aldrich.

"'Tis all very well reading about these things secondhand, Joe; but we shall only know what's really being said and done if we witness it for ourselves."

"You're proposing to go and listen to that howling, angry mob, Mr Challiss?" the steward said, aghast. "Forgive me, sir; that would be very foolhardy. The best thing anyone can do in such lawless times is to keep as far away from these unruly elements as possible. Why court danger, Mr Challiss?" he added nervously.

"When I said *we*, Joe, I meant anybody like myself who is curious to see with his own eyes and hear with his own ears what exactly takes place if and when the rioters do descend on Downham. I wasn't implying that you should accompany me; in fact, I'd rather thought that I could rely on you to look after things here in my absence." Tom hoped that his ruse had calmed Aldrich's fears without demeaning him.

"I see," Aldrich said, his black eyes meeting Tom's squarely, showing that he had fully understood that Tom had given him the opportunity to wriggle out of accompanying his master, should the occasion arise. "Of course, sir, if you think it really necessary. But the chance to experience the making of history at firsthand, to be part of it, so to speak—" His eyes glowed. "What a story to be able to tell our children, sir! To be able to say to our sons that we were there and saw history being made."

Tom imagined that Aldrich must have been carried away by the thought of the vicarious glory that would rub off on any casual bystander who happened to witness something extraordinary taking place, without the threat of any personal danger to himself. After all, the man was childless and likely to remain so by the look of things, for Ruth showed no sign that might lead anybody to suspect anything different. He wished he'd kept his intentions to himself, and said: "Well... If anything does happen, I certainly intend to be there. But I meant what I said, Joe: should there be the threat of trouble, you must be here to keep an eye on things. Have Kit Warrender with you at the lodge so that one or other of you can ride for assistance, in the unlikely event of its being necessary. Will you do that?"

The light of excitement in Aldrich's eyes faded at Tom's words. "Of course, sir," he growled. "In the event of the worst happening, would it meet with your approval if I were to send Mrs Aldrich up to the mansion out of harm's way?"

"Oh, indeed! To be on the safe side, Joe, I think you should take her up this afternoon," Tom said, relieved that his steward was not about to contest his decision. "I daresay it'll come to nothing. After all, we're well out of the way here–"

"It hasn't stopped them from paying you a visit before, even so," Aldrich said, triumphantly.

"Well, perhaps lightning will not strike twice in the same place," Tom said, aware that he'd upset the steward. To change the subject, he asked how Ruth was.

Aldrich's eyes widened. "Why? What have you heard that makes you ask after her health so suddenly?" he asked belligerently.

"Why, nothing," Tom replied, wondering what he'd said to upset the man now.

Aldrich studied the pattern on the rug at his feet. "Well, 'twill soon be common knowledge and 'tis only right that you should be one of the first to know: Ruth is with child."

"But that's wonderful news, Joe!" he cried, truly delighted for the man. "Allow me to offer my heartiest congratulations." He caught Aldrich's right hand between both his own and shook it warmly. "Will you have a toast?"

Suddenly alive again, the steward said: "Thank you, Mr Challiss, but I must decline. Too early in the day for me. I almost let the cat out of the bag before," he rumbled, "when I thought I might accompany you into Downham. Ruth is overjoyed, needless to say."

"When is the child expected to make its appearance?"

"Oh, Ruth is precise about that!" said Joe. "She says we shall have our own fireworks on November the Fifth." His delight was expressed in a rumble of mirth.

Infected, Tom joined in the laughter. "Well, at least you know what to expect, Joe, having been through it all before," he said, thoughtlessly. "Damned unnerving experience, I found it. Rather puts a damper on things in that department. Eh?"

"Not at all, sir, not at all!" Aldrich cried enthusiastically, "I find that Ruth is even more eager for my attentions now that the deed is done, so to speak."

Not wishing to elaborate, Tom said that it was time for him to see to the removal of the Rix brothers, which he planned to put into action that night as soon as darkness fell. Aldrich took himself off to Kit Warrender's cottage, the former home of Mrs Hignell, which he'd agreed to rent in its entirety and to which he'd already made several improvements. Aldrich told the farm manager of Tom's suggestion for the removal of Mrs Aldrich to the mansion and the part Kit himself was to play in the protection of Uppham. "You'd better come armed," he told him. "If the rioters do pay us a call it's more than likely they'll have been drinking and there's no saying what they might do if we meet them unarmed."

★

Little Faith Looret had not boasted when she had written that she could wash clothes and knew how to make clear starch. Miss Nevett had examined the freshly laundered small clothes belonging to all three Looret sisters and had been most impressed by the finished articles. Closer inspection revealed to the housekeeper patches of mending so artfully done that only the keenest eye could detect it. Moreover, the fine darns had been artistically shaped into butterflies, flowers or leaves. The work really was exquisite and she made it her business to question the three young housemaids as to the identity of the needlewoman responsible for it.

She found Hope, the eldest of the three sisters, on her knees dry scrubbing the dining room floorboards with a mixture of white sand and Fuller's earth. Hearing herself addressed by the housekeeper, the thirteen-year-old stood up immediately and made a bob. "Yes'm?"

"Which of you girls is responsible for this lovely needlework, Hope?" Miss Nevett asked as she held a mended garment towards the girl.

Hope brushed back a loose strand of hair and tucked it into her linen bonnet, smiling as she did so. "That's our Faith's work, Miss. You can 'ardly tell where the mendin' ends an' the rest of the thing starts, can yer?"

"This needlework is really very fine indeed," said the housekeeper, peering at one of the camouflaging butterflies. "Where did your little sister – how old is she? – learn to do such exquisite work?"

"She's nine, Miss Nevett. We had an old lady lived near us who used ter be a companion to some lady. She took a fancy to our Faith, and me sister started goin' in there nearly every mornin' ter do the old lady's errands, an' other jobs. An' they got more friendly, like, an it just went on from there."

The housekeeper smiled behind her veil. "And it was the old lady who taught Faith to sew," she said, to make sure.

"Didn't I say? Yes'm. 'Twas her that showed Faith 'ow ter make the mendin' inter butterflies and things," Hope said with a smile. "Wish I could do it, but I never 'ad the time ter learn Miss, see."

"You're making a very good job of this floor, Hope," Miss Nevett said approvingly. "Very well. You may carry on." She left the room with the intention of showing her mistress Faith Looret's amazing needlework and hoped that it would lead to something better for the little housemaid.

★

Mary Emma and Agnes were astonished at the beautiful work that young Faith had done and Mary Emma made an immediate decision. "How do you think it would do, Miss Nevett, if we took young Faith off housemaid's duties for half of each day and used her as a fine needlewoman?"

This was most gratifying to the housekeeper who had hoped for just such a result. "It is an excellent idea, Mrs Challiss," she said. "When would you like her to start on the new timetable?"

"Oh, I leave that to you," Mary Emma said with a yawn. Thomas's appetite had demanded assuagement during the night again and she felt very tired in consequence. "Oh, I do beg your pardon, Miss Nevett. Pray excuse me. You must blame my demanding son for my bad manners. I seem to have been up half the night feeding him."

Agnes smiled at the housekeeper and observed saucily: "No peace for the wicked. Eh, Miss Nevett?"

At a complete loss, Amelia Nevett said coolly: "Well. Thank you, Mrs Challiss. I'll see that it's attended to. Excuse me, madam," and glided from their presence.

"Oh, dear!" Agnes whispered to Mary Emma, "I'm very much afraid I've offended Miss Nevett with my nonsense."

Stifling another yawn, Mary Emma said: "Oh, I daresay she'll get over it, dear. She isn't made of glass, you know."

★

Ben and Will Wright were mucking out the fire-damaged stables and getting everything shipshape for Mr Aldrich's inspection later in the day. The young groom was becoming worried by the lack of exercise some of the horses had had since bad weather and his mistress's condition had kept them indoors. Although the climate remained unseasonably cool, now that the sun had shown itself he decided that it was time to turn the animals out to pasture.

"You can give Genty a gallop this afternoon, if yer like," Will told his delighted brother. "She's getting fat around the belly. Won't be long before Mrs Challiss is lookin' ter ride her, I 'spect, an' she won't thank us fer lettin' her mare run ter seed."

"What about Quicksilver, Will?" young Ben said expectantly. "When can I give him a run?"

"Not fer about five years, young'un," Will replied sternly. "He's a headstrong stallion and it takes a strong pair of hands to master 'im. Don't yer go gettin' up on 'im 'til I say yer can, see? I'll take 'im out when he needs a good run."

★

Martin Harris and Barty Peckover had become friends and Maddy sulked because they preferred each other's company to hers. "Wot d'ye expect, girl?" said her Auntie Bee. "They'm young men of an age, int they. Wot would they want wi' the likes o' yew, young Maddy? Why, there's nothin' of yer fer a young man ter fang 'old of yet. Yew got some growin' up ter do, girl. Yew stick wi' young Ben Wright fer the time bein' an' yew wont find yerself gittin' yerself in a fix with one o' them other two."

The assistant cook and the footman had decided to take a brisk walk before the noon snack. Their chosen route took them through the embryo lime walk, up through the edge of Home Wood – where the scent of bluebells was overpowering – and to shepherd Deacon's enclosure.

The shepherd had had a busy spring but, despite the inclement weather, had saved his ewes and their lambs and the evidence wandered contentedly about nibbling the nearby pasture. He'd lost one or two sheep to poachers but reckoned that fair enough in such starving times and kept the knowledge to himself.

The two young servants walked to the perimeter fence to see what progress had been made on the new wall. The footings were dug and the strings in place. The brickwork hadn't been started, but it was obvious from the piles of bricks that were stacked at regular intervals that the labourers intended to start at first light tomorrow morning.

Barty and Martin discussed the latest developments in the nearby towns and villages where riots had already occurred and speculated about the effect it would have on Downham. "Stands ter reason Downham'll be next, doan it," said Peckover, taking a pull from his short clay pipe and puffing out an aromatic cloud of blue smoke at an inoffensive passing bee. "Mr Rudge wants you an' me in the mansion on guard, startin' at three in the mornin'. I ask yer! Bloody three o'clock! Oo'd be goin' around riotin' at that time o' the mornin'? Nobody in 'is right mind! Even bloody rioters've gotta get a bit o' kip, or else 'ow could they keep on goin' about riotin', day after day?"

"I dunno what ter think, Bart," said Middlesex born Harris. "It must be 'ell – no job, no cash, no 'ome and next to nothin' to eat. I'd be riotin', an all! Ain't ser long ago I was destitute meself. It's summink yer ain't likely ter ferget – ever. I made up me mind I would work with food in some way or another. That way I noo whatever else 'appened ter me I'd never starve. An empty belly 'urts, mate."

"Yer done well fer yerself, Mart," Peckover said, his voice conveying his admiration. "You can't do no wrong, s'far as Mrs Rudge is concerned. Good luck ter yer, bor!" He puffed away at his pipe – a thing strictly forbidden in the house under pain of what Barty called 'a right dressin' down' from Mr Rudge – until the tobacco had burned through. He tapped his pipe against the heel of his left boot and stowed it away in an inside pocket to await its next outing. Refreshed, the two young men sauntered back to the comfortable kitchen of the house where they fully expected Mrs Rudge to have done them proud in wedges of chicken giblet pie and quarts of ale.

★

Had anybody been interested enough to set a spy to watch the goings on that took place at Uppham in the dead of night on Sunday, May 19 1816, the spy would have had much to report back concerning an unusual amount of activity taking place on the usually tranquil sabbath. Had anybody been watching closely he would have seen a cartload of turnips, driven by Kit Warrender, leave by the main gate and pass through the sleeping town in the direction of Lynn. Had the watcher lingered, he would have noticed figures on horseback riding up and down the drive that linked the mansion to the lodge. What nobody would have known was that the heaped load of turnips covered the forms of Clem and Ben Rix who, before they reached their destination, would vow never to eat another stinking turnip as long as they lived, if they could possibly help it.

★

Chapter Forty-two

Too early for blowflies, thought Tom in his half awake state. He turned carefully onto his other side, had almost drifted off again, only to become conscious of the persistent buzzing again. This time it was louder. Now fully alert, he strained his ears to clarify the sound as it was borne towards him on the wind. The cloud of blowflies suddenly dispersed into the air and the homogeneous buzz fragmented into myriad distinguishable stridencies: metal on metal, discordant horns, marching feet, gabbling voices, laughter, shouts, cries. The dissonant symphony, in its unique unrehearsed performance given by hundreds of tone-deaf musicians, was approaching Uppham St Mary. Rioters! Out of bed in a flash, Tom leapt towards the window, peered around the outer edge of the curtain and breathed more easily, relieved to see nothing more than the empty park. He padded over to the bedside table and looked at his watch. Too dark to see with the curtains drawn together. Two strides took him back to the window. Eleven-fifteen? Impossible! He should have been wakened hours ago. Where was Peckover? Rudge? Harris? He stretched his ears in an attempt to pinpoint the source of what must be a tremendous crowd. They were passing the mouth of the lane that led to Uppham House, marching along the London Road towards Downham. Tom gauged the vast numbers of rioters by the length of time it took them to pass by the head of the lane. It had come. The rioters were intent on heading for Downham and he doubted whether anybody would be able to control the tumultuous crowd. Silmultaneously with that thought, the cacophony began to die away, reminding Tom of a chattering parrot silenced when a cloth is thrown over its cage, and the marchers to the rear of the column were brought to a straggling halt. He could distinguish nothing more.

"What is it, Tom?" Mary Emma whispered from the bed, fearing to waken their sleeping child. As if sensing his mother's voice, the infant Thomas woke and began to bawl. Wearily, she dragged herself out of bed, went over to the crib and put her baby to her breast. "What is it? What time is it?"

"Very late, my love," he said, pulling on his boots. "Go back to bed, Mary Emma," he said, "you've had a disturbed night. Stay there and rest. I'll send Maddy up with your breakfast."

Mary Emma followed a prolonged yawn with a weary smile. "Thank you, Tom. I'm so sorry if we kept you awake. Thomas hasn't learned to sleep through the night yet, the naughty little darling. Yes, I will stay here, dear, if you'll let Agnes know that I won't be down to breakfast." Tom studied his wife as she reclined among the pillows, her eyes closed, the child's rosy lips clamped to her blue-veined breast, and fleetingly wished he was a painter; for a more lovely madonna and child he thought he'd never seen.

★

Instead of sitting down to his very late breakfast, Tom scandalised Peckover by snatching up a rasher of bacon and sandwiching it between two slices of bread. Eating it as he left the room and speaking with a full mouth, he said he'd probably not be back in time for luncheon but would order something light when he returned.

He was annoyed that his servants had thought it advisable to let him oversleep because Mrs Rudge had informed them all that "a noo baby wants feedin' every four hours on the dot an' it plays 'avoc with everyone's rest". Even Rudge had been persuaded by the cook's advice to countermand Tom's orders and to "let the pore master 'ave a nice lie in."

Tom had wanted very much to be in at the beginning of things and, deciding that Mulderrig would be less conspicuous than Quicksilver, was away on his sturdy chestnut hack within less than half an hour of rising. He flew past the lodge at a swift gallop unaware that a frustrated Joseph Aldrich had been prowling about on the lookout for his master for the past two hours. Slowing Mulderrig to a walk Tom made his way along the lane – which had been transformed by fresh greenery and was starred with stitchwort, primroses, celandines and bluebells – that would bring him into the High Street. He was glad that he'd approached the public highway with caution as the crowd had been halted on the outskirts of Downham and the labourers and others bringing up the rear were only a little past the lane's entrance.

Taking care to remain as unobtrusive as possible, Tom stilled his mount and soon became aware that the crowd was being addressed by somebody in authority.

Nudging his horse a little nearer to the back of the crowd he quietened it and picked up a few enlightening remarks that were being passed among the angry men.

"Me brother's never bin outa work afore this," one said to his neighbour. "Now he's bin thrown on the parish, patchin' roads. Ploughboy lorst 'is place, an' all, an' 'e 'ad nowhere ter go, pore li'l bugger, but the workus."

"Sh!" a third said, trying to raise himself on his toes in order to see and hear what was going on at the front of the crowd. "What's overseer sayin now?"

"Doan matter ter me what he's sayin'," the first speaker said bitterly, "he won't change anybody's mind here. Not terday. Our minds is made up. Eether they gives us bread at a fair price an the wages we're askin' for or, as Mrs Dyer said at Brandon t'other day, it'll be their blood runnin' in the streets as well as ours."

At that moment Tom noticed a group of men tagging on to the back of the crowd behind him who, as they approached, he recognised as the team of labourers who had been hired to build the wall around Uppham. Here was a dilemma! If he confronted them as their employer, he immediately identified himself as one of the gentry. To his intense annoyance he saw that the men had armed themselves with bricks purloined from the stacks waiting to be bonded with mortar. It was all he could do to sit his horse, say nothing and trust that he would not be recognised.

A hand tugged at his stirruped boot. "Please, mister," a youth said to Tom, his eyes raised in entreaty, "I shouldn't be 'ere. It's wrong. They made me come with 'em. I aint one of 'em but they said if I didn't join 'em they'd set fire to me mother's 'ouse."

"Who forced you?" asked Tom, conscious that as soon as he'd opened his mouth he'd suddenly become an object of suspicion and that the belligerent crowd had surreptitiously encircled his horse. The youth, terrified of the reprisals promised in the eyes of the rioters, bit his lip, shook his head then hung it to avoid the men's hostile gaze. Two rioters moved forward and stood guard either side of the frightened youngster and Tom thought it best not to interfere.

During the incident a horseman had ridden away at speed towards Upwell and the words 'Yeomanry' and 'Cavalry' ribboned through the crowd from front to back. "If you'll be so good as to allow me to pass," said Tom to the grim-faced men pressing tightly around Mulderrig, "I'll get out of your way."

"Watch 'im," one of the men said, "we dunno 'oo 'e is. Aint one of us, that's fer sure."

"What's yore business 'ere this day, mister?" a young man asked him.

Tom studied the upturned lean, lined faces that bore the marks of the suffering that the men had undergone. "I mean nobody any harm," he began. "My purpose in coming here is as an independent observer–"

"He's a bloody spy!" a voice shouted, and immediately brought angry murmurs from all those in Tom's vicinity who pressed closer, causing Mulderrig to stamp.

Tom remained calm. "I can assure you, I'm no spy," he said. "On the contrary, I have much sympathy with your cause. Is it wrong for those of us who live in greater prosperity than yourselves to try to understand the cause of your unrest?"

"'E'th all talk," a small bent labourer with few teeth lisped in disgust.

The young man who had asked him his business was fairminded enough to ask: "What did yer expect ter see or 'ear that could be of interest to your sort?"

"I hoped to hear from your own mouths what it is that has brought you to this desperate step," Tom answered, feeling that he'd not expressed himself very clearly.

His remark provoked a number of sceptical exclamations:

"Must o' bin livin' on the moon, the bloody fool!" somebody shouted.

A tall man ravening a stolen loaf paused and shouted up at Tom: "Look at us, bor; doan that tell yer nothin'? We'm starvin', man! Open your damned eyes!"

Another poked Tom's thigh: "Ow'd yew like ter work all the hours God sends and be paid so little on the Fridy that it ent enough to keep yer fam'ly in bread, let alone boots or clo'es?"

As Tom became aware that most of those around him were furtively munching their way through whole loaves, cakes and pies he assumed that the Downham bakers had been looted. He didn't blame the men for assuaging their hunger but foresaw trouble ahead on account of indiscriminate looting when he observed that some of the rioters carried items of goods and furniture that appeared to have been been taken out of malice or greed. Yet, on second thoughts he began to understand why the furious and vengeful men, who had been systematically robbed of everything of value over several years – common land, animals, cottages, household belongings, children lost through starvation and disease, their families divided by the workhouse – had been roused to boiling point by the latest iniquitous rise in the price of bread and should want to redress the balance in whatever way came to hand.

"We aint gonna stand fer the way we've bin treated fer a day longer," the tall man raged. "Are we men, or aint we? What kinda life do we have, bors? 'Tis nothin' but work, fer those of us lucky enough ter 'ave a job, 'ard work an' all, for unfair wages, while the farmers an' the millers grow fat and buy pianners, an such like, fer their daughters to waste their days tinklin'. My daughter, my Phyllis, were sixteen an died of exhaustion so they *said*, in the workus infirmary. Which is one way o' sayin' she were worked ter death in that 'ell 'ole of a laundry there."

A silence fell on the men around them and Tom imagined each one of them recalling similar events in their own lives. "You have just cause to be discontented," Tom said, desperately seeking a way to help them. "Without wishing to appear to tell you your business, I'd like to say that your complaints will be listened to with greater sympathy if you choose a spokesman who is cold sober and who can control his temper long enough to state your grievances politely and in plain terms."

The young man said: "He makes sense, bors. Rantin' an' ravin' haven't got us very far up ter now–"

"We doan need no gennelman ter tell us our bus'ness," a newcomer to the back of the crowd said very quietly. "Our spokesmen is already picked, see? An' you, sir, can keep yer suggestions to yerself!"

Taken aback by the menace contained in the man's voice, Tom sat up straighter in the saddle and, removing his topper, bowed from the waist to the speaker. "I'm much obliged to you, my good fellow, for your timely advice," he said, replacing his hat and tapping the crown to ensure it was firmly in place. "I assure you that I have not the least desire to interfere with any plans you may have. I am but an interested onlooker, I assure you."

"Bloody nothey parker, more like," remarked the lisping man, spitting into the dust.

"Now," Tom said firmly, "please stand clear of my mount's hooves. I shouldn't like to be accused of deliberately causing anyone an injury." Without further discussion, he tapped Mulderrig's flanks with his heels and the roan surged forward, scattering men to right and left as they jumped clear to avoid being trampled. He skirted the surprised mob and trotted his horse smartly past the diverted rioters whose attention had a moment before been riveted on the speaker who had been addressing the assembly. He halted near the improvised platform in the shadow of a large oak. From his vantage point he had a splendid view of the crowd and had also the advantage of being able to overhear what was being said.

Seizing the chance to speak during the distraction caused by Tom and Mulderrig's sudden eruption from the rear, one of the crowd near the speaker shouted: "There are pressed men 'ere who've been threatened at gunpoint inter joinin' the rioters, sir! I'm a cowherd. I'm needed back at my master's farm. You all know that cows need milkin' thrice a day this time o' year!" He glared desperately at the faces of those nearest him. "'Tis past their midday milkin' time."

Another shouted back: "Then yore mistress'll 'ave ter git orf 'er fat backside and lend an 'and. In the end it might dew 'er some good if it learns 'er that milkin' cows is a mucky, 'ard job. She'll 'preciate yer all the more, bor!"

"'Sides which," a fairhaired man who was standing next to the cowman said to him quietly, "'tis fer the good of all that yew bin brought 'ere. Where's yer loyalty ter the combination? 'Tis all well an' good fer the likes o' yew oo 'ave got work. Wot about the likes o' them that aint?"

"Wont 'elp my 'erd," grumbled the cowman. "They ent done nothin', pore dumb critters."

"Quiet," whispered another of the crowd, turning round from in front of the cowman and his neighbours and scowling at them: "the overseer's sayin' somethin'. It's about pressed men. Bugger it! I've 'ad enough o' this. I'm gonna git meself something ter fill me belly." He was as good as his word. Making straight for a bread shop he smashed the handle of the door with a blow from a brick that looked suspiciously like one taken from Uppham's stacks. Once inside, he tore a new loaf to bits with his teeth and bolted hunks of bread as he worked in a steady rhythm, doling out the freshly baked loaves to anybody who held out an empty hand.

From his vantage point, Tom saw satellites start to break away from the main crowd as they quickly followed the first bread rioter's example. He saw several women, among those who forced open a provisions store, run out of it shortly afterwards with assorted pairs of shoes carried in their commodious aprons which they held by the corners to form receptacles. With new hats stuck on top of their own caps, and a variety of similar luxury articles that it was way beyond the means of most of them to purchase, they emerged from the shops with their plunder and melted into the tumultuous crowd which had grown huge as the day wore on. One woman staggered out, her arms laden with a bale of sheeting. Tom glimpsed through the gap in the milling crowd that fought its way in and out of the open doorway a flour sack that had been slashed open. Like snow in summer, the life-giving powder had spilled across and sifted between the newly-scrubbed floorboards. Before anybody could scoop up what remained of the precious cornmeal it was quickly rendered useless as a foodstuff by dirty shoes and unshod feet trekking back and forth through it and grinding it into the now sullied planks. As Tom continued to witness the chaos all about him he saw a woman stagger out of another store with a small sack of flour in her wiry arms.

She carries it as tenderly as if it's an infant, he thought, watching her until she disappeared among the crowd with the precious burden clasped to her narrow chest. For a moment, he contrasted the life of luxury he and his family lived with that which was made plain before his eyes by the orgy of feverish looting that was taking place.

Two men had come to stand beside the mounted gentleman, had stared hard at him and had apparently decided to ignore his presence. One said to the other: "Look at the pore bloody fools diggin' their own graves! 'Tis stealin', pure an simple, an' we know where that'll end."

His companion nodded his head. "So dew they, if they 'ave the ill luck ter git caught! But oo can blame the pore buggers, bor? 'Tis all well an' good fer us oo are in work. But no-one knows 'ow the shoe pinches 'cept 'im oo's wearin' it. They'm desprit." He added that, despite the violent disruption, there had been no physical violence as far as he knew; and to Tom the lawless, frenzied, redistribution of the basic necessities of life was understandable after what he had seen and heard throughout his vigil in the square where the vast crowd had assembled.

Tom continued to look on in a fascinated trance as the looting grew more frenzied. A separate crowd broke into a house one of the labourers told him belonged to a George Thomas and robbed him of about five gallons of beer. A drover forced his way in and to everyone's surprise, instead of joining them in drinking the beer, turned the crowd out, closed the shutters and locked the cellars.

Several labourers, about eight in number, as far as Tom could see, followed into a building a constable whom Tom had noticed stationed outside *The Crown*. Tom asked one of the few passive labourers standing about if he knew what was going on.

"Deputation's puttin' our terms tew the magistrates and overseers, same as they done at Brandon," he said, chewing on a juicy grass stem that waggled as he spoke.

"And that is?" Tom encouraged the man.

The labourer removed the mangled stem from between his teeth and threw it down. "We're askin' fer work, an' two shillin' a day. Aint much tew ask fer, is it?"

Some time later Tom remarked to one of the bystanders: "Look there! The men are coming back and, if their faces are anything to go by, it looks like they've been given a hard time."

"They'll 'ave give as good as they got, an' no mistake," the ruminent labourer said in a confident tone. "'Ere they come now! We'll soon know what was said."

Word spread through the waiting crowd as swiftly as a flame through a dry haystack that 'the Farmers and others could not afford to grant what they wished; but it had been agreed to allow 2s a day and to supply flour at 2s 6d per stone "for those that had large families."

On learning that the men's demands had been refused and that a 'tremendous argument' had broken out between the deputation and the magistrates and that, in consequence, more trouble would be sure to follow, Tom turned his patient mount in the direction of *The Crown* with the intention of finding them both some refreshment there. Changing his mind he dismounted and asked a youth, on the promise of a sixpence, to take his horse to the livery stable and see that he was fed and watered. Curious to witness what was to follow the unsatisfactory outcome, Tom lounged against a tethering rail in front of *The Crown*, arms folded, feet crossed, and waited.

The unsatisfied, boiling crowd refused to disperse and the magistrates, who had followed the deputation into the square, addressed them and asked them to go away. The incensed crowd stood their ground and began shouting not only for their original demands to be met but also added another condition to their peaceful dispersal: the release of a recently imprisoned gang of Southerey poachers who were being held in the town gaol. Tempers shortened and, as if at a signal, a hail of missiles were loosed by the crowd and hurled towards the speakers on the platform.

Unluckily for Tom he'd positioned himself in the line of fire. As he turned in response to the sound of a door opening behind him, a half brick struck him on the back of the head. He sank to his knees. A vague image of magistrates scurrying back into *The Crown* was the last Tom knew before he lost consciousness … *stinking clothes … damp ditch … hoofbeats … running feet … musket shots … neighing horses … Frenchman … Sergeant Mylotte …George Challiss … George? … Mary Emma? … Mary Emma"!' … Mary Emma -a-a-a-a-a-a-a-a-a … … …*

★

a-a-a-a-a ! who? ... head ... blinding pain ... "Head" ... *dark ...*

" ... concussion."

" ... serious?"

unbearable beams ... lanterns two lanterns? where? ... heat ... nausea ... head head ... pain swamping Ugh! bowl ... vomit gushing nightgown wet ... perspiration cold ... "Light!" *... pain ... head head ... head head ...*

★

"... his pulse is stronger but he's still unable to bear the light," Dr Barnes said. "It might not be wise to try to rouse him."

"Oh, no! Do be careful, doctor!" Ruth Aldrich implored. "He's suffered head injuries in the past," the nurse added, as she retreated with the lantern.

As the doctor replaced Tom's arm beneath the sheet, Ruth told him of the patient's injury at Waterloo and of his being robbed on the road between Dover and Canterbury, on his way back to Norfolk, incidents which Mary Emma had regaled Ruth and Agnes with over the teacups.

"Was he badly injured in Belgium then?" Dr Barnes asked, imagining the kind of war injuries sustained from a shell bursting after cannon fire, or similar.

"No, I think not. If I remember rightly Mrs Challiss's account," Ruth said, "neither injury was of a very serious nature. The important thing to remember is that both were to the head and that both caused periods of unconsciousness."

The doctor turned from studying Tom's unconscious form to ask Ruth: "Were there any after effects, ma'am?"

"Not that I heard," Ruth said, feeling bound to add in the interest of the young Challisses: "but one cannot be too careful in cases where the brain has been affected, doctor, however slightly." Suiting actions to words she lowered the wick of the lantern, leaving the already darkened room almost as dark as night though strong afternoon light edged the sides of the curtains and the clock hands pointed to three o'clock. Glancing at the dial, she whispered:"Would it inconvenience you too much, doctor, if I left you now? I must go and see how Joe's getting on, poor man. Though he's out of danger now, I know it would comfort him to have me by his side."

Offended by the nurse's sudden defection, Dr Barnes, said: "If you feel it absolutely necessary, madam, then of course I shall not detain you. On your way downstairs would you be so good as to ask Miss Brook if she could spare the time to attend here? I have other calls to make and somebody should be here to keep watch over Mr Challiss at all times."

Feeling the rebuke implicit in his remarks, Ruth said: "Of course, doctor; I should have said: I asked Miss Brook to make herself available at three o'clock. If I am not mistaken, I hear her approaching."

"Thank you, Mrs Aldrich," the young man said, bowing, and apparently taking no offence at the breach of medical etiquette the nurse had made by speaking on equal terms to her superior. "You have been most helpful. Good-afternoon, ma'am."

The bedroom door opened quietly and Agnes Brook stepped across the threshold, smiled at her departing friend and carefully closed the door after her.

"How is he, Dr Barnes?" she asked softly, drawing near the bed.

"No change, so far," the young doctor answered, his brow creased with anxiety as he studied Tom's closed eyes for signs of animation. "The longer he remains unconscious, the more serious the aftermath is likely to be." Belatedly recollecting his duties as a gentleman and concerned for his fiancée's welfare, he cried: "Oh! Forgive me, Agnes," and placed a chair for her beside the bed. "Pray be seated."

"What day is it?"

The unexpected sound of his voice shocked and delighted them and they saw that Tom had regained consciousness while they had been momentarily distracted.

"Excellent!" Dr Barnes exclaimed, his relief evident. "It's still Monday afternoon, Mr Challiss. Twentieth of May, 1816, to be precise. You were hit on the head by a stone, or something heavier, and it rendered you unconscious, my dear sir."

Agnes took up a candlestick, lighted the candle and handed it to the doctor, who held it before each of Tom's eyes in turn. "I apologise if the light troubles you," he said, "but please try to lie still while I examine your eyes. As I suspected. You have a mild concussion. Nothing to alarm you greatly, sir, but I must confine you to bed. I recommend complete rest for the next forty-eight hours in a darkened room."

His eyes met Agnes's to ensure that she was following his diagnosis and treatment. "Either Miss Brook or Mrs Aldrich will be here to take care of all your needs. If you look forward to a speedy recovery you must give yourself up entirely to their care and do exactly as they tell you. Unless I hear anything to the contrary, I shall be back to see how you fare on Wednesday next. Complete rest, sir. In a darkened room. It is the only remedy. Good afternoon, Mr Challiss." He turned away from his patient and murmured to Agnes: "May I have a word with you outside, Miss Brook?"

"Is it all right to leave Tom by himself, Dr Barnes?" Agnes asked anxiously.

Assuring her that it was, he steered her by the elbow and, leaving the door ajar so that they could keep an eye on Tom, said rapidly: "Yes, it is. But it isn't all right to leave me by myself, dearest Agnes." He spoke earnestly. "For the sake of the child, it's best if we name the day soon," he said. "How important to you is this tedious business of calling the banns, my love?"

Her eyes wide at his impulsive behaviour, Agnes said: "Why, everybody has the banns called. 'Tis expected, Dr Barnes. We should do what is right and proper, sir."

"Of course; and we shall," he said, "but, under the circumstances, I thought we might dispense with that wretched proclamation: a private ceremony would be more appropriate."

Agnes stepped away from him and said gravely: "Dr Barnes, I'm not ashamed of my condition, sir. If you find the calling of the banns an impossibility I must tell you, sir, that I don't. If you still wish to marry me it must be in church and only after the banns have been proclaimed before all who are present on those three Sundays prior to the marriage ceremony."

"If I still wish to marry you?" Dr Barnes looked surprised and took both her hands in his. "What is this? I apologise if I implied that I wished us to enter into a clandestine marriage on account of your condition. Why, nothing could be further from the truth! Why, my dear Miss Brook – dear Agnes – had I to wait a year I would accept it. I can't say that I would be overjoyed at the prospect but I would accept such a condition if it ensured that I could be certain of making you my wife. My desire for a private ceremony is on my own account, I'm ashamed to say."

"Oh!"

"'Tis better you hear it now–" He broke off at the sound of somebody mounting the stairs and Mary Emma came into view. "Later," he whispered to Agnes.

"What are you two whispering about out here on the landing?" she said, walking into the bedroom. Hesitating, she turned to ask: "How is Mr Challiss?"

Dr Barnes followed her into the room. "Resting, Mrs Challiss. He's conscious. But he must not be disturbed or subjected to sudden noise or excitement, ma'am."

"I see," whispered Mary Emma, retreating from the bed in which Tom lay with his eyes closed. "But he has regained consciousness you say, doctor. Oh, I'm so relieved to hear it. I'd better make arrangements to sleep elsewhere until he's pronounced out of danger, don't you think?"

Drawing her even further away from the patient, Dr Barnes placed a finger to his lips and nodded. His voice very low, he said: "To give your husband the best chance of recovery, Mrs Challiss, ma'am, I suggest you remove yourself from his presence for the next few days and visit him for short periods only when he asks to see you. As to your sleeping arrangements: it might be as well for you both, considering the recency of your confinement, to occupy separate bedrooms for one month, at the very least."

About to remonstrate, Mary Emma thought better of it. A month! How vexatious, she thought. And then, remembering her darling baby boy, resigned herself to her banishment and told herself that their reunion would be all the more rewarding after the enforced abstinence.

★

"He was still unconscious when I left," Ruth replied to her husband's enquiry after Tom, as she removed her bonnet and gloves. "How are you feeling now, Joe."

"If you want the truth, my dear, I feel a damned fool! Look at me!" Aldrich cried, indicating his black eye. "What was I thinking of, to do such an idiotic thing?"

Ruth laughed and kissed him. "You're too tenderhearted for your own good, Joe. You'll do exactly the same the next time somebody preys on your good nature."

"But to give the varmint my best coat! What was I thinking of?" he said in an exasperated tone of voice. "And all the while he kept me talking, his accomplice was emptying our larder! If they'd only asked for food I'd have given it and gladly."

Ruth laughed even louder. "But you gave him as good as you got, dearest. He too has his bruises to remind him of his encounter with the fiery steward of Uppham."

Trying his best to assume humility at her praise, Aldrich erupted into hysterical laughter then winced as his laughter wrinkles squeezed his bruised and battered face.

★

As promised, Dr Barnes returned to examine his patient two days after the concussion Tom had sustained while observing Monday's rioting in Downham. To Mary Emma's relief her husband was pronounced out of danger and was expected to suffer no long-lasting effects from the blow to his head. "But you musn't overdo things, especially for the next week or so, Mr Challiss. You are at liberty to get up and dress, to go downstairs even, provided you sit quietly reading or talking. Go on steadily, with no undue exertion or excitement. Certainly, refrain from horse riding, but you might walk slowly in the park towards the end of this week."

"Sounds dreadful dull," Tom said, "still, I will follow your advice to the best of my ability, doctor." His glum expression left him and his face lit up. "What's been happening in Downham?"

Dr Barnes surveyed his patient with a stern eye. "Is this how you intend to follow my advice, sir?" Tom's immediate deflation aroused his pity, enough for him to relent a little and say: "Everything was quiet as I passed through the town. The riots have ceased. That is all I am prepared to say on the matter at this time. Leave it alone, sir. Read no newspapers and raise the subject with nobody; and should anyone bring it up as a topic of conversation, change the subject. 'Tis but a matter of a week or so; that will be time enough for you to acquaint yourself with what took place in the aftermath of Monday's riot."

Tom inclined his head. "I'll do my utmost to submit to your suggestions, doctor, though I can't pretend it will be easy, neither can I guarantee that I'll follow it to the letter."

Affronted by having his professional advice thrown back at him, the young doctor said severely: "Then on your own head be it, sir! I shall bid you good morning."

Aware that he had offended his physician, who was about to leave the room, Tom called him back. "I beg your pardon, Dr Barnes, if it seemed that I took your advice lightly. I promise you, sir, that it will not be for want of endeavour that I flout your instructions. But I know myself too well to be able to give you the assurance you would wish."

"Hmmph! As to that," said the doctor, refusing to be so easily mollified, "I should have thought that an ex-soldier would be able to muster the necessary self-discipline."

Chastened by his rebuke, Tom said: "I've never been one for sitting about with my head buried in a book, Dr Barnes. Now, I enjoy scouring the columns of a newspaper, yet you forbid them. How on earth can I expect to get through the long, tedious hours of each day without some mental or physical exercise, my dear sir?"

"There are many pleasant ways of passing the hours, Mr Challiss," said the doctor, softening his tone. "You may enjoy being read to by any one of the three charming ladies who are constantly in your company. Personally, I can think of no more delightful pastime; for while being entertained one has the added delight of studying the reader's figure, or her face and the light and shade that play across it. Mrs Aldrich and Miss Brook are also proficient musicians. What is it the poet says? Something like: 'Music hath charms to soothe the savage breast'. Is that how it goes?"

Tom smiled. "Is that your diagnosis, that I have 'a savage breast'? Passive ways of getting through a long day. I might learn to play the game of chess, perhaps?"

"On no account! The mental effort involved puts such intellectual exercise beyond the pale at present, Mr Challiss." The doctor considered a moment. "You might take up sketching, or even try your hand at the art of *aquarelle*. Though I'm aware it's deemed a pastime usually thought fit only for young ladies, gentlemen do follow it and some – Mr John Varley for instance – with a degree of success. His manual, *Landscape Design*, is much sought after as a valuable aid to water-colour composition, so I've heard."

"Hmm. Do you dabble yourself, doctor?" Tom asked, eyebrow raised.

"I fear not," smiled Dr Barnes. "I regret to say that my talents do not lie in the direction of the arts; though I do possess a keen appreciation of them in all their forms."

"We'll have to see," Tom said. "If everything else fails to while away the hours satisfactorily then I may find myself induced to request Miss Brook the loan of her paintbox." With that possibilty in mind the two young men parted cordially enough.

As Dr Barnes drove away he noticed Agnes walking purposefully across the park. Though the middle of the month of May was past, by several days, the temperature belonged rather more to winter than late spring. Nature had hibernated as long as she dared, but the increasing brightness of successive, mostly sunless, days had at last tempted into bloom the wild flora that grew about the untended grasslands of the park. As the doctor reined in his pony he observed that Agnes was making for a boggy patch of pasture. Fastening the reins to the rail of the seat of his gig, he jumped down and strode over to intersect her path. As soon as Agnes saw him she waved and waited for him to join her.

He removed his hat and wished her good morning, his eyes meeting hers and finding in them responsive happiness at the chance encounter. "May I have the pleasure of accompanying you in your walk, Agnes?" he said, making an elbow.

Placing her hand on his arm, she smiled up at him and said: "Good morning, Dr Barnes! How very nice. Yes, if you'd like. I'm going to the water meadow to see if the fritillaries have appeared yet. Everything's at least a month behind this year."

"Fritillaries. What are they? Butterflies?" he enquired, recalling the name from his long forgotten boyhood, glancing at her profile as they walked on together.

Agnes was amused. "There is such a species; but I meant one of our most beautiful wild flowers. Mr Aldrich mentioned that they grow somewhere about – Look! Oh, look, Dr Barnes! Did you ever see anything so mysteriously lovely? Over there! Oh! how beautiful! I've never come across a white one before."

Her enthusiasm was infectious, endearing; and the genuine pleasure Agnes obviously took in finding the carpet of strange brownish-purple blooms reminded him that she was really nothing more than a girl, despite her very obvious condition.

"What very peculiar-looking flowers," he remarked. "And are they truly wild?" He stooped to examine one. "That odd pattern on the petals is akin to a snakeskin."

"How clever of you to notice that," she said, smiling up at him as she bent to gather a posy. "Their common name's snake's-head fritillary and they are wild. Phew!"

"Agnes, stop! Your enthusiasm carries you away, my love," Dr Barnes said, taking her by the arm and raising her from her stooping position. "Tell me what you want, my dear, and I'll gather them for you with pleasure." Their eyes met. Powerless to resist the magnetism engendered, they tumbled into each other's arms as naturally as a bee bent on pollen-gathering tumbles into a bluebell. Their first kiss was slow, sweet and infinitely tender.

While not the very first kiss for either of them, it was the first that involved themselves; and for worldly wise Dr Barnes it was the only time he had experienced a kiss that had provoked such a responsive battery of fireworks within his body. "Oh, Agnes! My darling girl," he whispered against her bright hair.

She said nothing, burying her head in his shoulder.

They drew apart and he saw tears standing in her blue eyes. "What is it, my love?" he said, wondering what he had said or done to upset her.

"Nothing's the matter, dear Dr Barnes," she said, smiling. "It's just that… I'm so very happy, so very fortunate to have met you, to have been the beloved of two such kind and gentle men. Yet… There's an impediment to our marriage that must be removed before the banns may be called. I cannot marry you while I am kept in ignorance of something so vital. And, as you know, sir, the banns must be called."

Deflated by her challenge, fearing that her acceptance or rejection of him depended on the answer he gave, he answered her with a question of his own: "What is it that you wish to know, Agnes?"

"Your Christian name, if you please, Doctor Barnes," she said, dimpling.

Gathering her to him, he whispered it into her ear and, holding her away from him again, laughed at the expression of astonishment the revelation brought to her face. Their encounter came to an abrupt end as he suddenly remembered the number of calls to be made before noon; but he kept his promise to pick her flowers. Taking only sufficient fritillaries to make a decent posy without spoiling nature's own display, they quitted the flowery mead, arm in arm, and sauntered back to Dr Barnes's gig.

★

From her vantage point in the front withdrawing room window, with Thomas sleeping in her arms, Mary Emma had watched the love scene with romantic empathy. She brushed her lips against her boy's fuzzy head and thought, with a pang, that the bitter sweetness of unfulfilled love must be one of the most exciting times in a young woman's life. While not exactly envying Agnes the pleasures of marriage that awaited her as the wife of dear Dr Barnes, she felt her own deprivation of Tom's affections acutely. Her breast ached with an accumulation of milk and, guiltily, she kissed the child robustly enough to awaken him and soon found physical relief and comfort in his lusty sucking. Thoroughly contented, she sat on her low chair and stroked one of Thomas's plump little legs with a forefinger as she attempted to analyse the effect nursing her child had upon her as a mother.

Of course, she realised, it was love; but of a kind very different from her love for dear Tom. It wasn't the same thing, at all, as the delicious quivering sensations awakened in her by Tom's conjugal love. Yes, it was quite different from that... She became lost in a dreamy reverie and was restored to the present by the baby banging about with his mouth as he sought to satisfy his hunger. Automatically, she detached angry, unsatisfied Thomas's lips from the nipple of the emptied breast and attached his desperately searching mouth to the plenteous one. The love engendered by her child's drawing sustenance from her own body had just as powerful, as exhilarating an effect upon her as did her husband's love, she decided; but nourishing baby Thomas flooded her with an experience so sensuous, that she thought it would be difficult to find the words to describe the phenomenon to one who was childless that could help them to understand such love.

A knock at the door was followed by Agnes entering with a batch of letters in her hand. "Oh, I'm sorry, Mary Emma," she said. "I didn't mean to disturb you. Shall I come back later, dear?"

"Don't be so silly, you goose," Mary Emma smiled. "'Twill be you in the same state soon, my dear. No need to be shy about it. After all, that's why God saw fit to fashion women's bodies as they are. It's efficient. Feeding one's child is so convenient. What's more, one is rewarded for it by the wonderful sensations created in one's body by the child's sucking. I had no idea. But how did you find your Dr Barnes, my love?"

"Yes, mother says the same," Agnes said. Her eyes sparkling, she confided: "Oh! Mary Emma, Dr Barnes must be the kindest and best man in the world, I think."

"I was watching you play Juliet to his Romeo from up here and was touched by his kind attentions to you, Agnes. Now don't blush! And yet, your lover is capable of great severity, my dear," Mary Emma said, "according to Tom. I should not like to displease him, I must say. But you are of such a sweet and placid nature that I'm sure he will never need to show that side of himself to you. As for his being the best man in the world, I'm afraid I shall have to disagree with you there, dear. For though he is such a paragon, he cannot be the best man in the world because my Tom occupies that position himself."

They were laughing at Mary Emma's nonsense as Maddy brought in a tray bearing hot chocolate and a package wrapped in brown paper which was addressed to Mary Emma.

"How exciting!" she cried, giving drowsy Thomas to Agnes to hold as she took up the parcel and examined it for clues as to its origin. "Oh, Agnes!" she breathed as she read the sender's name and address. "It's my new book. Oh!

How wonderful." She broke the seal, snipped the string and tore off the paper wrapping. "Oh, look," she sighed in ecstasy. "Oh, Agnes, feel the binding: look at the calf leather and its title beautifully tooled in gold leaf. What an absolute treasure! Well worth the guinea."

Agnes's grin had grown broader at Mary Emma's successive exclamations of joy. "It certainly is exquisite. If I might hazard a guess? It couldn't by any chance by Miss Austen's novel, *Emma*, I suppose?"

"But for the fear of damaging my lovely new book I'd bat you over the head with it, you saucy thing!" Mary Emma laughed, full of excitement at the prospect of the hours of entertainment promised by the small leatherbound volume.

"Dr Barnes has recommended that we read to Tom – as long as it's nothing too exciting," Agnes said. "If we were to prepare for it by reading each chapter ourselves before we read it to Tom, we'd be certain that it was fit for him to hear," she added.

"Fiddlesticks!" Mary Emma said defiantly. "Miss Austen is scarcely Shakespeare, is she. I shall begin immediately after dinner this evening and Tom shall judge for himself whether I am a sufficiently good actress or not. Oh, Agnes! I can hardly wait to begin. But I shall be very good and save it for tonight. Why, I won't even give in to the temptation of peeping at the first and last pages!"

Shaking her head and smiling at her incorrigible friend's foibles, Agnes carried sated Thomas away to his crib and left Mary Emma to read her correspondence.

★

Every one of the letters, which had lain neglected on a table while Mary Emma had enthused over the new book, was addressed to Mr & Mrs Thomas R. Challiss. Mary Emma reckoned that the joint title gave her the right to open the correspondence and so spare her husband any sudden shocks they might contain. As it turned out, it was well that she did so.

Taking them in the order they had landed on the table she picked up the topmost and read the sender's name and address, which was:

> *Jno. Danderson, Esq.,*
> *Attorney-at-Law,*
> *King Street,*
> *Lynn Regis,*
> *Norfolk,*

a stranger to her. She opened the folded parchment quite unprepared for the bombshell that what was about to explode before her eyes.

19th May 1816

Dear Mr & Mrs Challiss, it read,

This is to inform you that your bankers, Bagg & Bacon of King Street, Lynn Regis, are at present under investigation concerning the mismanagement of clients' affairs. I regret to say that whilst working on their records I came across your names as investors & savers with the bank. I write in the sincere hope that your deposits with the said bank are not unduly large, as I fear that the bank's losses will turn out to be very heavy indeed & that, consequently, clients' assets will be seized to meet all debts incurred.

You will be happy to learn that while I am powerless to freeze any monetary assets you may have lodged with the bankers, I have made it my personal business to impound a set of boxes belonging to Mrs Challiss, the former Miss MaryEmma Kay, the contents of which I have, as yet, not investigated.

Please forward instructions as to how you wish me to proceed with the boxes I have managed to rescue and which have been conveyed to a place of security.

I remain, Sir, Madam, yr. Ob-t. Serv-t. John Danderson, LL.B.

Mary Emma's first question, after reading the letter from Danderson a second time, was why the letter should have come from him and not from Daniel Jones, for it was the latter who had persuaded Tom to deposit their fortune with Bagg & Bacon. Her heart pounded at the magnitude of the catastrophe as, with trembling fingers, she laid the letter on one side until she could decide how to respond to it calmly. Certainly, all knowledge of its existence must be kept from Tom in his present state.

Reluctantly, she took up the next letter which she saw with some relief was from Tom's brother, George. Heavens! He'd written it at the end of March. No doubt the letter would contain an explanation for the long delay in its arrival.

Dear Tom,

I trust you and your Mary Emma are well and enjoying life. You will be glad to hear that Garnet is with child and is blooming. We expect the child to be born next month and though I would love a son will welcome another daughter if she should turn out to be as wonderful and as beautiful a child as our dear Aurora. Tom, life is so good here that you should consider joining us. The space is amazing and Canadians the salt of the earth. There is plenty of work to be had if one is prepared to get one's hands dirty. We rub along and my old gambling habit is, I trust, a thing of the past as there is little opportunity to indulge it as we are situated many miles from the nearest town. You will laugh when I tell you that I am become a model citizen and have helped to build a church and am working as a common labourer helping to build a school. Garnet, Aurora and I attend church every Sunday. It's the nearest thing in these parts to a club and though I wouldn't say so to any of my former cronies, I must confess to actually looking forward to Sundays.

Take care of yourself, Brother. Perhaps we will meet again one day. My regards to your lady wife.

George Wretham Challiss.

I wish I'd known him, Mary Emma thought. He was good to Tom and sounds as if he's just as good a husband and father. She sighed as she thought of the thousands of miles that separated the Challiss brothers and thought what a pity it was that she would probably never see or know any of the Challiss family that had rooted itself in a distant land.

A glance at the clock informed her that she had time to read one more letter before luncheon. From Italy! How exciting – as long as it wasn't written in Italian.

The letter was dated April 29th 1816 and headed Villa Rosa, Siena.

Dear Mr and Mrs Challiss,

It is with great sadness that I write to tell you of the death of Sir Everard Belmaine. He died in his sleep yesterday afternoon.

He had never recovered fully from his apoplexy and the long journey across Europe by coach was to him a terrible trial.

Despite frequent stops at comfortable hostelries en route to our eventual destination, which you will recall, was Florence, the protracted nature of the travelling necessary to reach that city took its toll of Sir Everard and he was never able to enjoy that which he had set out to explore.

My son, Robin Belmaine, has been much affected by the demise of his grand uncle as the two had become very great friends. We shall remain here for perhaps another week. During that time I must make arrangements for the body to be shipped back to Norfolk. Sir Everard was particularly insistent that he be buried at Martlets in the family vault. It is a sad business. Robin and I are well provided for with monies sufficient to our needs both in Italy and once we return to Downham.

I Remain,
Your Faithful Servant,
Everett Bellman Pawl.

"Oh, dear!" Mary Emma exclaimed. It seemed to be one catastrophe after another. She felt as if all the troubles of the world had descended on her shoulders.

The sound of the dinner gong was her salvation. In an instant, she made up her mind to put all thoughts of wicked bankers, distant Challisses and deceased aristocrats out of her mind, convinced that a good luncheon would fortify her so that she would be able to deal more judiciously with the problems the letters had raised.

★

Chapter Forty-three

During his period of enforced rest Tom had been plagued by a sequence of portentous dreams in which, on waking, he had known himself to have been the central character. These dreams, visions or prophecies, had woven themselves about those closest to him and yet, although Mary Emma's spirit or soul – an essence of her that he failed to define – had been as attached to him as was his own skin, her visible form had been absent from every part of the sequence. Yet he had known it was she.

On waking from the first of the dreams he had assumed that, though vivid, it had been an isolated occurrence brought on by the concussion; but as he had fallen in and out of consciousness the dreams had persisted. Unaware, at first, that each subsequent dream was in some way connected to the one preceding it and that which followed – links in a chain of prospective events that were perceived by him only dimly in the beginning – he began to jot down the elements of each dream as he recalled it on waking.

By the time his convalescence was at an end Tom's notes had produced an extraordinary vision of the future of Uppham. Uncertain as to whether he should divulge these portents he decided to keep them to himself until a time came, if it ever did, for him to reveal them. He rolled up the sheaf of papers, fastened it with a length of pink tape, thrust the bundle to the back of the *escritoire* and forgot about it as soon as he returned to the press of immediate business.

Within three weeks he was as good as new and Dr Barnes allowed him to resume his life as he thought fit. Tom had immediately prevailed upon Mary Emma to let him see all the newspapers that carried reports of the Downham Riots and had read them more than once. That men had been arrested on the second day and sent for trial seemed to him unduly harsh. As yet, he was unaware that two of his own men, Jem Webster and Kit Warrender had joined the marching men and had been arrested along with others before being released without charge. Kit's defection had left Joseph Aldrich to defend the lodge singlehanded and, when trouble had broken out in the form of two drunken rioters who were on their way back to Southerey, Joe had had difficulty in fighting them off. Now all that was forgotten. Fortunately, the steward's injuries had been of a minor nature. Even his bruises had faded to a yellow that merged with his skin.

Downham had returned to an uneasy peace by May 22nd and Mary Emma was among those who had breathed a sigh of relief that life could get back to normal. Now that Tom was up and about again he rejoined her in their four-poster bed, for both husband and wife had decided that their enforced celibacy had continued for long enough.

In the second week of June, 1816, Mary Emma and Agnes were strolling around the new gardens before the house wherein shrubs and flowers had begun to bloom at last. The two friends were, unusually, without baby Thomas who had been left in the care of Ruth Aldrich. Mary Emma, her mind dwelling on their sickroom readings of Emma, said: "I miss our daily readings to Tom. Don't you?" She shivered. "Oh, but Agnes! Didn't you fall just a little bit in love with Mr Knightley? I did!"

"Mary Emma! What nonsense you do talk! He's a mere figment of Miss Austen's imagination," Agnes said good-naturedly. "Oh, 'tis true, one must admire such a well-drawn character. Mr Knightley's portrait is of a handsome, upright gentleman with a steady character who is deliciously severe; but I love a man of flesh and blood, who is just as handsome and highly-principled as Miss Austen's hero."

"Don't be such a dampener, Agnes Brook! You know perfectly well that I was referring to the romance between Knightley and Emma that is hinted at all through the book," Mary Emma said. "My heart was in my boots when it seemed that splendid Mr Knightley might marry beneath him."

Agnes ignored her friend's *faux pas*. Changing the subject, she said innocently: "Will you be in church on Sunday to hear our banns called, Mary Emma?"

"I understood they'd already been called?"

"Oh, they have, twice," Agnes said. "Next Sunday they will be published for the third and last time, dear. 'Tis so strange, to hear one's name proclaimed in church in conjunction with one's prospective husband's. It makes a girl approach the marriage ceremony in a very solemn mood, as if the whole village will be watching to see that she behaves herself beforehand."

"And afterwards!" cautioned Mary Emma. "But you're not really worried about what spiteful people will say of you, are you, dear?"

"No," Agnes said, following the denial with a sigh. "There's bound to be a good deal of talk, Mary Emma, with my being married so near the time of my delivery and then not even to the child's natural father. It's dear Dr Barnes I feel sorry for."

"Well, I'm glad I was married by special licence and spared all that rigmarole," Mary Emma said smugly. "There's much to be said for a private wedding, Agnes. I'm surprised you laid yourself open to censure in this way. As for Dr Barnes, all he has to do is be patient and prepare himself to be an object of pity."

"What can you mean?" Agnes said, wide-eyed. "Why should anybody pity him?"

"Oh, Agnes, my dear! Don't be such a dimwit. Every malicious gossip in Uppham St Mary and Downham will have made up her mind that you bewitched him. For what man in his right mind would consider taking on a woman who is carrying another man's love child?"

"If I didn't know you were supposed to be my friend," Agnes said, her eyes stormy, "I'd suspect that you were thinking the very same thing. How could you be so unfeeling as to say such a thing, Mary Emma?"

Mary Emma turned to Agnes and kissed her. "I was only preparing you for the unpleasantness that awaits you, my dear, believe me. Of course, I think Dr Barnes will be getting the sweetest little wife in the world, Agnes. And that's the truth. And to show you how much I support the marriage, I shall take great pleasure in being in church on Sunday to witness the calling of the banns."

On hearing that, Agnes perked up immediately at the thought that it would be her friend who was in for a surprise.

★

St Mary's Church, Uppham was well attended on the Sunday that would see the final calling of the banns for the marriage of *Miss* Agnes Brook – the self-righteous matrons made much of the fallen woman's title – to young Dr Barnes, whose full name had caused something of a buzz among the congregation when it had first been proclaimed in public.

The Challisses sat in a pew alongside Agnes Brook and Dr Barnes while Mr and Mrs Brook and all the other young Brooks, except Burt, sat in the pew behind. Of course, Agnes and her fiancé were not the only couples to be named that day and the Reverend Edward Fieldgate patiently worked his way down the list of names pronouncing each name as if it were the thing he most loved to do. The prospective bridegroom's name was given first followed by the name of the woman he was to make happy. Fortunately, Dr Barnes's name came early on in the list. The Brook family, having heard the startling name twice before by this time, knew what to expect. Tom and Mary Emma did not; and so it was with astonishment that they heard, in common with the rest of the congregation, the Reverend Fieldgate announce, for the third and last time:

"I publish the Banns of Marriage between Dr Valentine Crieff-Barnes, of Downham and Miss Agnes Brook, of Uppham St Mary. If any of you know cause, or just impediment, why these two persons should not be joined together in holy Matrimony, ye are to declare it. This is for the third time of asking."

Agnes kept her countenance in control and her eyes on Mr Fieldgate but was gratified to hear the gasps of astonishment from the Chalisses in reaction to the doctor's full name. No cause or impediment being forthcoming, the three hurdles of the successive publishing of the banns were cleared and the marriage ceremony could take place as soon as the betrothed couple wished.

The wedding was planned to take place on the 15th June; but Mary Emma's eighteenth birthday was to be celebrated four days earlier and she had decided to throw open the doors of Uppham House in a double celebration which would include a housewarming party. To that end, a large awning against rain was to be raised on the lawn in front of the house so that all the servants and villagers connected to the Uppham estate could be made welcome. It was too much to hope for a fine day in a year of grey skies and low temperatures and so Mary Emma determined to put up with whatever weather was sent and make the occasion as happy as was humanly possible.

"There isn't much time in which to make all the arrangements," she remarked to Tom as they dressed one morning. "I must get the invitations off today, for who knows what plans people have made for the summer."

"Do you think it wise to make such a fuss, my love?" Tom said, his voice strained as he strove to tie his cravat in a Brummel knot.

"Thomas Roberts Challiss! Have you forgotten that I reach my eighteenth birthday on the eleventh? It may not be of great significance to you, sir; but I am determined to make it an occasion of some significance." Noticing his struggles with his neckcloth, she abandoned her own toilette to assist him in tying the bow.

Thomas had been fed earlier and slept soundly. Mary Emma had taken him into his parents' bed and Tom had watched his greedy son guzzling away at his young wife's white breast with such joy in his heart that he thought it would burst. How he had thought he could exist without children of his own seemed ridiculous to him now that Thomas was so much part of their lives. And, if dreams had any meaning, his son would be but the first of many. Mary Emma had grown accustomed to baring her breast to feed her child and now, naked to the waist and uninhibited, stood on tiptoe as she struggled with his cravat.

"Mary Emma!" he said, stepping away from her. "Must you stand there in that provocative way? 'Tis as much as I can do not to ravish you, you deliciously wicked creature. I must say, motherhood has enhanced your charms amazingly and those frilled pantaloons're so damned fetching they're enough to send a fellow dizzy. No! Forgive me. I must restrain myself, my love, until a more fitting time. I have promised to be on site by eight-thirty today to go over the cottages in detail. They're likely to be ready for occupation within a week – that is, if your festivities don't get in the way."

"How glad I shall be when those cottages are finished!" she grumbled. "Then I shall have you all to myself, as I did when we were first married, Tom. You would make any excuse to couple with me in those days."

He kissed her lightly on the nose and tossed her her chemise. "You'd better cover yourself before Maddy comes up, my dear. Pray excuse me, Mary Emma. I really must dash. I barely have time for breakfast. Until luncheon, my love."

Refusing to be put out of humour by her husband's rebuff, she reasoned that it was just as well; for they had made up for lost time since his recovery and, had she told the truth, she would have had to disclose the relief she felt as she heard him clattering downstairs two at a time. With the constant demands made on her body by her son as well as her husband she wondered at times to whom it really belonged. Yet it gave her a warm satisfaction to know that she was indispensable to both and her love for them washed over her in a wave of total wellbeing.

Maddy came in to help Mary Emma finish her toilette; but as the mistress followed the girl's clumsy attempts at dressing her hair by way of the looking glass, she decided that it was time, now that hairstyles were becoming more elaborate, to seriously consider employing a personal maid. "Thank you, Maddy. That will do. Please find Charity Looret and send her to me at once. Tell her to wash her hands first and to be as quick as possible."

Some minutes later, Charity knocked at the door of her mistress's bedchamber. She wondered what possible reason there could be that was so urgent that it called her away from the important business of turning over the carpets with Hope in order that the dust might be banged out of them by their stamping across them in their boots. She remembered the kerchief in which she had tied up her hair just in time to snatch it off and thrust it into her apron pocket as Mrs Challiss bade her enter.

"Ah, Charity. Come in – Where is your cap, girl?"

Charity bobbed a curtsey. "Beggin' your pardon, ma'am, I was trampling the carpets wi' me sister an' 'tis such a dirty, dusty business that we wrapped our heads in kerchiefs. I'm sorry, ma'am, to come before yew without me cap."

"Oh, never mind that," Mary Emma said impatiently. "Tell me, Charity: have you ever had occasion to dress hair?"

Puzzled, the eleven-year-old girl screwed up her freckled face and said: "In what way d' yew mean, ma'am?"

"As in the fashion plates; here, like this." Mary Emma showed the girl a page of the latest hairstyles. "Do you think you could copy any of those?"

Charity Looret studied the page of engravings that showed ladies dressed in the latest fashion with their heads coiffed in the most becoming styles. The girl bit at the side of her thumb. "I don't know, Mrs Challiss, ma'am," she said, doubtfully. "I never tried before. But Ma always let us mess about with her hair, ma'am," she said eagerly. "'Twas red an' curly, like mine an' me sisters'. 'Twas awful pretty. If you're willin' to trust me, I don't mind tryin', ma'am."

Charity Looret is rather a sweet little girl, Mary Emma decided. "Well," she said, smiling at their reflections in the looking glass, "suppose we start this very minute. But first, did you remember to wash your hands?"

"Oh, yes, ma'am!" the cheerful girl said, holding them up for inspection. Using her initiative, she dragged a footstool over and placed it behind her mistress's chair. Smiling back in a conspiratorial way at Mary Emma's image in the glass, she removed the hairpins Maddy had skewered into her mistress's black hair earlier and laid them on the dressing table. "Which style would yew like me ter try, Mrs Challiss?"

No sooner had Mary Emma chosen one of the styles for Charity to copy than the girl set to with determination. First she brushed out her mistress's long hair until it crackled with electricity. Then she calmed the flying strands with her small red hands. With dexterous twists of the naturally curling hair Charity had it tamed into a most becoming style which she miraculously secured with a few strategically placed hairpins which were unnoticeable. Mary Emma's fine features were enhanced by the new high style, with its fluttering ribbon band and elaborate curls cascading down the back and which, in turn, added height and grace to the figure reflected in the glass.

"Excellent, Charity," she cried, "you're a very clever little girl!" Her exuberance woke the baby who began to cry lustily. "There, there, darling," said his mother, going over to his crib and lifting him out.

"Oh, Mrs Challiss, ma'am," Charity said without thinking, "int 'e a little dear."

Mary Emma smiled at the girl. "Do you care much for babies, Charity?" she whispered, as she rocked Thomas back and forth in her arms until his eyelids began to flutter and droop.

"Oh, yes, ma'am," the girl whispered back. "We all dew; but Hope is ever so good with babies, Mrs Challiss. Ma used ter say she 'ad the knack."

Mary Emma laid Thomas back in his crib where he snuffled like a piglet before drifting into deep slumber again. "Did she, dear? I must have a talk with your sister about that some other time. Now," she whispered, "how would you like to keep an eye on Baby for me while I go to my breakfast? Pull the bell if you need any help."

The happy little girl bobbed a curtsey and raised shining and worshipful eyes to her beautiful mistress as she eagerly and silently nodded assent.

★

Ruth Aldrich had not been seen either at the lodge or at Uppham House all morning and, as luncheon was almost ready, Mary Emma and Agnes wondered what could have detained her. They had looked for the nurse to assist them in writing out the invitations that had to be taken to the post office that day before closing. They had all but given her up and were about to go into the dining room when Dr Barnes's gig drew up before the front steps. Rudge, who had spotted them from one of the front windows, went to open the front door while Barty Peckover, on his superior's instructions, sent Maddy to the stables for Ben Wright to take charge of the rig.

Agnes suggested that Valentine Barnes be invited to join them and the young doctor confessed that, after such a night and morning as he and Mrs Aldrich had endured, they were in urgent need of sustenance. Suddenly, what had looked like being a dreary mealtime with only Mary Emma and Agnes to keep each other company – for Everett Pawl, though he'd been in England for a good while, was residing at Martlets to set affairs in order there – had, with the arrival of Ruth and Dr Barnes, been transformed to a sizeable party. Tom, as was his custom these days, would return in his own good time as business allowed.

Once the business of eating was well under way, the reason for Ruth's absence was revealed. "Of course, you both knew that Catherine Fieldgate was expecting a child?" she began.

Mary Emma's knife and fork fell with a clatter. "No. When?"

Agnes said: "I had no idea! She kept it very quiet and nobody would have suspected–"

"Tight-lacing," Ruth said in a condemnatory tone. "Though why she should have felt it necessary, I can't imagine. The Reverend Fieldgate is devastated, poor unhappy man."

Dr Barnes ate his way steadily through the pile of meat and vegetables in front of him and took no part in the conversation, which concerned one of his patients.

"But... You haven't told us what has happened," Agnes said, her blue eyes questioning. "*Why* is Mr Fieldgate devastated?"

Ruth studied her plate before looking up. "I'm sorry, Agnes; it might not be wise to discuss this subject when you are approaching your own *accouchement*."

"Tell me!" Agnes implored. "Nothing you can say will harm me or my child. You'll vouch for that Val, won't you?"

Dr Valentine Crieff-Barnes, knife and fork poised, met Agnes's eyes, judged what he saw there, and said to Ruth: "You might as well tell the whole story. 'Twill be common knowledge by tomorrow, anyway," and continued to assuage his hunger.

"We were called to the vicarage at three this morning," Ruth said. "When we arrived Mrs Fieldgate had been in labour for over an hour. The poor woman was already exhausted. Her travail continued while the night wore itself away but, despite her brave efforts, the child remained fixed. An examination revealed that the child had engaged in the breech position and it was becoming obvious to the doctor and myself that Mrs Fieldgate's constitution could not withstand much more pain. Dr Barnes tried manipulation and was successful. Soon after that the child was born – dead. That fact was concealed from Mrs Fieldgate, whose ordeal had weakened her to such an extent that she had lost consciousness. Edward Fieldgate, alerted by the sudden silence that something had happened, came up to the room to enquire how his wife was progressing and Dr Barnes had the painful duty of telling the poor man of his stillborn child."

"Of what sex was it?" whispered Mary Emma, her eyes full of tears.

"It was a boy, born two months prematurely," Ruth said wearily. "Now it became our chief concern to try to save the life of Catherine Fieldgate. We packed her lower body in ice to try to stem the haemmorrhage but it was hopeless and she died at seven-fifteen this morning. The struggle over, she was at peace and looked as beautiful as a statue of the finest marble." The nurse's voice broke. She hid her tired face in her hands and cried unashamedly. "Those poor sweet children," she sobbed.

Mary Emma left her seat and hurried around the table to comfort her friend. "Come Ruth," she said, "you must be worn out. You need rest. I'll have Miss Nevett prepare one of the spare rooms at once. It's no more than a case of making up the bed and lighting the fire. Please, dear. Do say you'll stay."

Dr Barnes said: "Mrs Challiss is right, Mrs Aldrich. You should go to bed at once for the sake of your own health. Even though you consider yourself strong, you must make this your last case. And you must allow a good interval to elapse before you take on any more cases, once your child is born."

Too weary to make a protest, Ruth nodded and allowed herself to be led upstairs. Miss Nevett later told them she had fallen asleep almost as soon as her head had touched the pillow.

Agnes said: "I'll have Will rig the pony phaeton, Mary Emma. I intend to call on Mr Fieldgate to extend my condolences and ask what he intends to do about young Robert and little Frances."

"Oh, Agnes, dear," said Mary Emma, "it's so like you to think how best to help the poor man. Wait. I'll get my bonnet and gloves and we'll go together. Charity and Miss Nevett will watch Thomas for a while. I'll drive. You musn't tire yourself."

They found Edward Fieldgate in a bewildered state. He seemed utterly lost and physically diminished. When he learned of the two women's concern for his motherless children he shook each of their hands in turn and something of the man they were accustomed to emerged. "Thank you! Thank you!" he said, full of gratitude. "You are most kind; but the children have gone to stay with my sister and her family for the time being. It really is very good of you to have taken the trouble to come. It is greatly appreciated. Everybody has been most kind, most kind. Mr Challiss was here earlier, Mrs Challiss, ma'am, to offer his condolences. Word had got about, you see. Your husband has been a tremendous help to me, ma'am. He'll tell you all about it. You will understand that I am unable to dwell—" His voice broke on a sob which he was powerless to control.

Soon afterwards, Mary Emma and Agnes took their leave. There was nothing more they could do for the bereaved man at present and they left him in the care of his servants. It did not escape Agnes's notice that her friend was unusually subdued as she drove the phaeton towards nearby Church House. To be so near her family home and not to call, for however brief a visit, was unthinkable to Agnes Brook.

"Oh! This *is* a nice surprise, tew be sure!" cried Mrs Brook on opening the door. "My! You do look bonnie, Agnes, wi' that pod on yer! Not long ter wait now, lovey." As if it were a rallying cry, the front hall and passage instantly became clogged with an assortment of Brook offspring all clamouring at once to speak to their big sister and to get hold of her person. When the commotion had died down all the children, except Noah, vanished as silently as moisture evaporating. Then the three women adopted suitably sombre expressions while they discussed the Fieldgate tragedy over tea and scones. All too soon, it was time for Mary Emma to get back to Uppham for Thomas's next feed, with the promise that they should all meet again on the eleventh of June.

Mary Emma's elegant new hairstyle had been noted by everybody with whom she had come into contact throughout the day; but it had hardly seemed fitting to make mention of the trifling fact while news of such awful gravity filled their minds.

★

Tom had been home to dine and had gone out again while Mary Emma and Agnes had been paying their visits. It seemed that, once they had washed and Thomas had been fed, there was no option for them but to return to the pile of invitations that remained to be written, though neither had the inclination for the task.

"Bother!" said Mary Emma, shaking the chalk caster over her wet ink, "I've made a blot on this one," She rummaged about at the back of the *escritoire*. "I know there's an ink eraser in here *somewhere*. What's this?" She drew out a roll of papers tied with pink tape. "How very odd. It wasn't here a few days ago, I'm certain."

"It looks like Tom's writing," Agnes observed, before resuming her task.

The bundle was soon unrolled and Mary Emma, seeing that Agnes was intent on her work, said: "Excuse me, Agnes, while I take this over to the window seat to look at. Will you?"

Agnes was too intent on her work to respond.

★

Mary Emma turned over the bundle and tried to smooth away the curves in the pages before tapping them into place to read. The covering paper bore the title: Recollected Dreams. What? Smiling at Tom's idiosyncratic behaviour she began to read:

Dream Diary

Wed. 22 May 1816. Strange dream. (second time) <u>*Back in mud Waterloo.*</u>
Wednesday eve. 22nd May 1816. <u>*Mrs Rudge gone. Martin Harris Cook.*</u>
Thursday 23 May. <u>*Flew over Upm. S. M. Saw into houses. Dainty (bull)*</u>
<u>*Chdn*</u> : <u>*Brook 8, Barnes 6, Challiss 8, Fieldgate 3 (b. dead), Warrender &*</u>
<u>*Annie B. 4, Aldrich 2*</u>
Friday 24. <u>*Waterloo (third). Will W. gone. Ben W. Groom marr. Maddy. (3)*</u>
Fri. eve. <u>*Mary Emma willing me get well.*</u>

This seemed to be an index to what followed. She looked at the first page of writing and was relieved to see that it corresponded to the index. But... She laid the sheaf of papers down beside her on the cushioned window seat and blankly stared out of the window. Tom's mind had been playing him tricks. The damage to his head had resurrected his injury sustained during the Battle of Waterloo, that was clear . . . and understandable. But the rest? Glimpses into the future? Balderdash! She smiled to herself. Suppose his dream predictions were a true indication of what was to come? Eight children! The very number they'd agreed upon. Reluctantly, she picked up the papers and riffled through them until she came to the page relating to May the twenty-third, the one referring to the families of children, and began to read.

My God! There were eight Challiss children and each one was named in order of birth. Following Thomas Henry 1816 were listed:

Emma & Edward 1819; Patience 1821; Robert Kay 1823; Susannah 1826; Mary 1829; James Uppham 1833.

Her heart thudded with excitement. Twins! How wonderful; obviously named after herself and Edward Fieldgate. But *Patience*; what a nasty, old-maidish sort of name. No. I'd never agree to that! Now, that's a nice touch, Robert *Kay*. This really is exciting, though, of course, it's nonsense! A figment of Tom's imagination. Hmm. Susannah. *Susannah?* Yes, I quite like that. Ah! That's more like it: plain, no-nonsense Mary. Good! And the last of the litter: James but *Uppham?* I think not, Tom, my dear. And, anyway, she thought, it's only a lot of tom-foolery. Who would have thought that dear Tom would have had so much imagination in him as to invent a family for himself? It probably came from his being a ewe lamb and having had a lonely childhood. Should she mention her discovery to him? No. Better to let sleeping dogs lie, she resolved, as she rolled up the papers and retied them.

"Are you finished writing, Mary Emma?" Agnes said, looking at her friend over the top of a finished sheet before folding it and adding it to the growing pile of invitations that littered the table. "Only, there are still very many to do, you know."

"Oh, Agnes! I do apologise, my dear. I got carried away."

"What was it?" Agnes asked, idly curious.

"Oh, something and nothing," Mary Emma said lightly. "Just some scribblings of Tom's." In the act of returning the bundle to the back of the escritoire her fingers stumbled upon the ink eraser and recalled her to her task. "Goodness! Is that the time? We must get these finished within the hour, Agnes, or we'll miss the post!"

★

Barty Peckover brought back two letters addressed to his master that had arrived in Downham by the afternoon mail coach. Dinner over, Tom made his excuses and took himself off to read them in the anteroom adjoining the library.

He'd arranged to have two new doors fitted into the aperture that had always led to the library through an ell in the downstairs corridor and Jem Webster had promised to start work on the double doorway as soon as his work on the cottages was finished. Tom had had his eye on the anteroom without quite knowing what to do with it at first and had drifted into using it as a makeshift study and office. He found sharing the spindly *escritoire* with Mary Emma unsatisfactory and tiresome for, however hard he fought against it, his papers became muddled up with hers and this inevitably led to bickering.

He'd acquired a fine mahogany desk of robust construction and substantial proportions which he found much more to his masculine taste. Mary Emma had driven into Downham and selected a pair of comfortable chairs and a matching sofa, all upholstered in dark green leather. To these stark fitments she had added down cushions made up in gold brocatelle with plain piping for, despite her pleas, Tom had drawn the line at fringing. So far, he'd scooped up his papers and letters into a wickerwork crate to be sorted at leisure. But he discovered, as have many before and since, that one never *is* at leisure for such a tedious task and so the crate and its contents lay in the farthest corner, out of Tom's sight and almost forgotten, gathering dust.

He flung the two unread letters onto his desk, took out his pipe and lighted it, and stretched himself full length on the sofa to mull over the conversation that had taken place during dinner. On coming home he'd found Agnes playing the piano and had learned that Mary Emma was upstairs feeding Thomas...

"And so what have you two been doing all afternoon, shut up indoors?" he'd said.

"We had a very tedious exercise to complete," Agnes replied with a rueful expression. "Ruth had promised to help us but, as you know, she had to rest. I had no idea you had so many servants and villagers on the estate, Tom. You were lucky to have escaped such a thankless task. It kept us both hard at work all afternoon, except for Mary Emma's taking a short break to read something in your hand that she found at the back of the escritoire."

His Dream Diary! "Oh," he said, "I trust my wife found my notes amusing?"

Agnes shrugged. "She said it was 'something and nothing', which I took to mean that, whatever it was, was of little significance to her," she said.

"Ah," was all he had said. So Mary Emma had not taken his jottings seriously. Time would reveal if he had really been granted a true glimpse of their futures...

He laid aside his pipe on its rack and jumped up off the sofa. The letters lay on his desktop accusingly. He was in no mood for correspondence but idly turned them over to read who had sent them. Tch! Lawyers! One was from Daniel Jones.

"About time, too!" he said peevishly. He picked up the second and read the name of the correspondent with a mixture of astonishment and pleasure. What on earth had George's friend, Danderson, to write to him about? Intrigued, he opened Danderson's communication before Daniel's.

8th June 1816

Dear Mr Challiss, he read,

> *I hope this letter finds you in good health. I had looked for a reply to my ult. of the 19th May and can only suppose that illness has prevented you from acknowledging receipt of it. Being anxious to carry out your instructions concerning Mrs Challiss's set of boxes & their contents I looked for an early reply.*
>
> *As I feared, Bagg & Bacon have been declared bankrupt. Consequently, all your investments & holdings with the bank are now declared null & void..*

"What...?" Tom reread the last paragraph. And, thinking he lacked exact comprehension of the words, repeated the exercise. How had such a catastrophe come upon them out of the blue? And what was this about a previous letter? Ah! It must have arrived during his period of convalescence after the concussion. Mary Emma would have kept it from him out of concern for his health. He looked towards the corner in which resided that abominable wicker crate full of jumbled papers and groaned. It must be amongst that lot, he supposed. He took up reading Danderson's letter from where he had left off. Sickened at the thought of what other unpleasant facts were to be disclosed to him, he read:

> However, My Dear Sir, things might have been worse, but for the prudence of Mrs Challiss's former guardian, Mr Josiah Kay of Lyndon Manor, now deceased. Mr Kay left instructions with his solicitors at Cromer, Mssrs. Tapp, Tapp & Cummins, that they were to remove everything from the boxes once Mrs Challiss had seen them if ever she decided to remove them from their safe keeping. The empty boxes were then refilled with old legal papers that were worthless & the weight of the jewel box made up with pebbles.
>
> Bagg & Bacon, finding nothing to interest them among the bogus contents of the set of boxes, allowed me to impound them. The original articles have since been restored to their proper boxes and are in a place of safety of which you will be apprised once you present yourself in person to me at the above premises. I trust these arrangements meet with your full approval and await your further instructions.

> I remain, Sir, yr. Ob^t. Servt. John Danderson, LL.B (dictated).
> *William Clayton, Clerk*
> p.p. John Danderson, Esq. LL.B

So! Mary Emma's vast fortune was lost to them. *Sorsum Deorsum* at work. For what a short time unimaginable riches had been theirs. On the heels of the depressing knowledge that he was no longer, albeit by proxy, the owner of vasts amounts of money came the crushing realisation of the way he and Mary Emma had been spending money hand over fist on the luxurious refurbishment of the Uppham estate. The cottages alone had cost a fortune to build and he, fool that he was, had insisted upon only the finest materials being used in their construction. Thank God, they were virtually finished. With that pigeon-holed in his mind, his next thought was that he must leave for Lynn first thing early tomorrow morning and find out for himself exactly how things stood.

His pipe had gone out. He cleared the bowl of dottle, stuffed in fresh Virginia tobacco, rekindled the comforting weed and after a few puffs he felt calm enough to open Daniel's letter, whatever it might contain.

Dated 7th June 1816, it began:

My Dear Tom,

> *I hope this finds you in good health. You will see, as you read on, that I have been diligent in your behalf and to some profit. It is as I suspected: Mr Jardine had his hands in many pies around the globe. I am happy to tell you that Mrs Challiss, as next of kin, will be the recipient of many large plums, my dear friend. Of one of these you have learned from your visit to Tapp, Tapp & Cummin: I refer to the Eden Sugar Plantation properly titled Le jardin d'Eden which is situated on Barbados Island, East Antilles in the West Indies. It continues to make a steady profit and will provide you with a ready source of income once the paperwork is done.*

> *My investigations into Mr Jardine's affairs revealed another source of income, viz. :- The Eden Sugar Refinery, which is situated in Blackfield Street, Silverdown, East London. This establishment is of recent construction and uses some of the most modern machinery of its kind. I took the trouble to pay a visit to the manufactory and was favourably impressed. Mr Jardine was a shrewd investor and could have hit on nothing more profitable than pandering to the English sweet tooth. The Silverdown refinery will enrich you far more than many a gold mine and, so long as Le jardin d'Eden is well-managed, will never cease production.*

> *Mention of mines brings me to yet another source of income, Tom. Mr Jardine had shares in an opal mine in the Australian hot spring area. That needs further investigation, being in the Antipodes and correspondence slow.*

> *Lastly, he had several shares pertaining to Bethlehem Royal Hospital, commonly known as Bedlam, London. The new asylum building at Lambeth has seen a steady rise in inmates and, consequently the price of shares has risen and looks set fair to continue.*

> *I trust all this is good news to you and will await your instructions as to the management of these important sources of income.*

> *I respectfully advise against depositing any of the above with the banking firm of Bagg & Bacon who have been declared Bankrupt and will not be trading under that name but may well start up again under another. Take great care, my dear friend, with whom you entrust your affairs as I understand from my colleague, John Danderson of Lynn Regis, that you, in the unfortunate company of many, have lost a fortune with Bagg & Bacon.*

My condolences. Please write by return with your instructions.

Yrs. Daniel Jones.

Sorsum Deorsum. Tom wrote at once to Daniel Jones, thanking him for undertaking the investigation into Lambert Jardine's hidden assets; though how the Fakenham lawyer had achieved such positive results in so short a time was beyond Tom's understanding. As to choosing a bank, his dealings with Bagg & Bacon had been a sharp lesson to him in how to lose a fortune in less than six months! The only person he now felt he could trust implicitly was Daniel Jones and he requested him to make a check, on his behalf, on the validity of the deeds of the properties named.

Tom's head was dizzy with the ups and downs of his financial fortunes; but the fright with the Lynn bankers had taught him a valuable lesson: from now on he would keep household accounts faithfully and in minute detail. At the first opportunity that presented itself on his return from Lynn he'd have a meeting with Mary Emma and Miss Nevett about accounting for every farthing, well, perhaps not *every* farthing that was spent. It was impossible for them to continue in the reckless way they had lived since their marriage. They had Thomas Henry's future to consider now and – a very sobering thought! – perhaps those other seven Challiss children he'd dreamt about. It was incumbent upon him to conserve Mary Emma's fortune, to use it sparingly and wisely and make it work for his family's future needs. He found himself burdened with matters of property and realised that youth was a thing of the past.

*

John Danderson had received him coolly; but the explanation of Tom's accident, his lengthy recuperation and Mary Emma's withholding of the lawyer's initial letter soon put the older man in a more cordial frame of mind.

"Demned bad business, Bagg's bank going under," he said, over a glass of madeira. "There was no inkling of the crash, it seems. One day they were doing business as usual, the next the doors were closed. Such scenes in the street outside the premises! Rocks hurled through the plate glass window – that kind of thing. All to no avail. Bagg had already gone into hiding and left Sam Bacon to face the music on his own."

"I can't say I took to Bagg at all, the one and only time I met the man," Tom said, tossing back his wine and banging down the empty glass as he recalled the unpleasant experience in the banker's presence and his bullying treatment of the little clerk with the squeaky boots.

"Then I would say you were a good judge of character, Mr Challiss," said the lawyer, draining his own glass. "Now. Let's get down to business."

It occurred to Tom, as Danderson discussed the ins and outs of owning property, that he had been much happier in the days before he'd had any to call his own. The whole thing was nothing but one big headache, it seemed to him. While it was pleasant to be able to procure on a whim anything one desired, the thought that others had designs on his assets and were prepared to cause him bodily harm in the act of parting him from them rather took the gilt off the gingerbread. He wished he could get up and walk out of Danderson's pleasant office and be done with all matters dealing with finance, property, jewels and sugar. Josiah Kay's bequest had taken on the aspect of not one Pandora's box but a whole set of them, each, when opened up, loosing a host of worries and liabilities that he would – were he single and footloose – gladly forego.

"... might be the preferred option," Danderson finished, looking at him with an expectant smile.

Overcome with embarrassment, Tom asked the lawyer to repeat his proposition.

To Tom's surprise, John Danderson threw back his head and guffawed. When he was able to speak once more, he said, smiling: "My dear Challiss, I have been talking utter nonsense for the last ten minutes. Where your mind was, I should not like to hazard a guess, except to say that it most certainly was not here in this office. Look. May I call you Tom? It's plain that you're out of your depth, Tom. George was equally at sea over this kind of thing and avoided discussing financial matters like the plague. I have a proposal to make that might simplify things."

"I beg your pardon, sir, for my lapse of attention," Tom said, stiffly. "True, I am a novice when it comes to owning property; but do not confuse my ignorance with lack of interest in the method in which you propose to deal with my wife's bequest. You would do me a kindness were you to spell out, in layman's terms, in what way I am best able to safeguard Mrs Challiss's properties. For instance, the treasure chest, now. The contents of that one box alone must be worth a vast fortune."

The flesh around Danderson's eyes crinkled as he smiled at Tom. "I beg your pardon, Tom, in thinking you out of the same mould as George. I see you're a very different animal, though just as interesting, my dear fellow." His attitude changed in a flash. Earnestly, painstakingly, he took Tom through the various options open to him.

The upshot of the meeting was that the boxes were to be removed under discreet armed guard to Uppham House as soon as one of the new patent fireproof strong boxes could be bolted to the floor of one of the basement rooms of the house.

In one month from Tom's meeting with Danderson, Mary Emma's remaining fortune, in the shape of a set of japanned boxes of varying depths, was to be deposited in the impregnable bank vault at Uppham House and Tom and Mary Emma would be the only people who knew where the keys to it were to be kept.

★

Some days after Charity Looret had taken up her post of lady's maid to Mary Emma, Tom looked up at his wife from the paper he was reading and said: "What have you done to your hair?" They were seated in his office after breakfast.

"So you've noticed it at last!" she said sweetly, touching the glossy locks. "I've been sitting opposite you at almost every mealtime for days and yet you haven't mentioned it. Really, Tom! I sometimes wonder if you really look at me at all any more. I might just as well be a new set of cushions that seem to entirely light up a room when they're first in place, but which scarcely merit notice after a period of habitual use. "

He laughed. "I'm sorry, Mary Emma. I have no excuse; except that you are invariably so well-turned out that my eyes are filled with a vision of feminine grace every time I look at you."

"Oh, you flattering fraud, sir!" she cried, dimpling. Raising her eyebrows she added: "But you haven't yet said whether you approve of my new style, Tom."

He made a great show of studying the piles of curls, ribbons and ringlets, asking her to turn this way and that, getting up and walking round her chair, chin in hand, and finally stopping before her, his eyes serious, his face grim, to say: "You do want the complete truth, my love?"

Disappointed, she raised her wide and anxious eyes to his. "Don't you like it?"

"You look perfectly divine, Mary Emma, as always," he murmured, before bending down and fastening his lips on hers.

Freeing herself and jumping up, she cried: "You fiend, Thomas Roberts

Challiss! How could you torment me so?" and began pummelling his broad chest.

Laughing lightly, he stilled her fists and was about to enfold her in an ardent embrace when a discreet rap on the door arrested his intent. The door was opened by Miss Nevett. Veil shimmering with each breath, she informed her master that the Reverend Mr Fieldgate was waiting in the hall to see him in connection with his wife's funeral. "Tell Mr Fieldgate I'll be down directly, Miss Nevett, thank you." The housekeeper left, Tom brushed his lips across his wife's cheek and hurried downstairs.

★

The burial ceremony over, the long line of mourners shuffled past the new plot and saw that the vicar's handsome wife had lived but twenty-nine years.

Catherine Fieldgate and her stillborn child were buried together in the churchyard of St Mary Uppham not far from the monument which had been erected by Tom in remembrance of Mrs Coy and her children. By comparison, Mrs Fielding's headstone was plain, tasteful and modest. Apart from her name and dates, and her child's birth-death date, the stone bore nothing but two short inscriptions: at the top, *Requiescant in Pacem*; and at the foot: *Thy Will Be Done*.

Edward Fieldgate had insisted on performing the burial service himself; by doing so, he ensured the sympathy and earned the undying respect of his parishioners for the remainder of his long tenure as their vicar.

★

Ruth Aldrich had urged Mary Emma to postpone her day of celebration in respect of the recent burial of the vicar's wife and child; but Mary Emma had laid her plans and would not be denied her hour of triumph. She had been overjoyed to learn from Tom that a good part of her fortune had been saved. That fact had put her in a lively mood and she rose early on her eighteenth birthday, pulled back the heavy curtains and with gratitude beheld the beginning of a beautiful day.

At nine, carriages, farm carts, dog carts, drays and wains, riders on horseback, children on ponies or heavy horses and strong-limbed pedestrians poured out of the green leafy tunnel in a constant stream. By ten o'clock the park was thronged with people drawn from every station in society arrived in anticipation of an enjoyable day.

The invitations had been delivered in good time and Mary Emma could detect no absences so far. The June sun shone with a dimmer light than in previous summers, but brightly and warmly enough to gladden the heart. The main rooms of the house were filled with flowers which had been sent over from the gardens of Martlets with the good wishes of its new owner, young Robin Belmaine. Adam Brook had pressed into service all the young servants, male and female, as well as his daughters Ann, Fanny and Dovey, to fill the many vases and to fashion and hang the flowery swags which decorated the long tables under the canopy on the lawn before the house. John and Zeb had been dragooned by Mrs Dulcie Brook, Noah astride her hip, into clearing up the piles of leaves stripped from stems of flowers and other debris resulting from the elaborate floral artwork.

Tom had let it be known that anyone who could lay claim to some connection with the Uppham estate was welcome to stroll about his house and lands. Doors and garden windows stood open, inviting the curious into the refurbished reception rooms of the mansion. The humbler guests wandered freely in and out of the beautifully appointed rooms and feasted their eyes on the splendour. Awed by such unimagined opulence, they contrasted the magnificence of Uppham House with their own sparsely furnished, simple dwellings. Tom had also directed Joseph Aldrich, Jem Webster and Kit Warrender to spread the word among the servants that no wages would be forfeit for the day's holiday allowed the men. On the contrary, every servant – male and female – would receive a gift of five shillings as part of the day's festivities. That had been Mary Emma's idea and she had looked so happy with her plan that Tom's recent resolution regarding the saving of farthings had been temporarily waived.

Agnes Brook had overseen the flower arrangements and now, feeling a little fatigued, was resting in the library. Dr Barnes disovered her there and was pleased to find that they were its only occupants, at least for the time being. Drawing a chair alongside that in which Agnes sat, he flung back his coat tails and sat himself down beside her, fondly imprisoning her idle hands between his own with a gentle pressure.

"This is a glorious day for the double celebration," he began, after stealing a chaste kiss while opportunity presented itself. After studying her face, he said: "You mustn't overdo things, Agnes. I do want my bride to be able to enjoy her own day when it comes. I know how you love Mary Emma and wanted everything to be perfect for her birthday, my dear; but there are plenty of others around to carry out the donkey work as well as yourself."

"But I've loved every minute of it!" Agnes protested. "Oh, Val! The cartload of beautiful cut flowers and shrubs that Mr Belmaine sent was simply incredible: you should have seen it. Not only cut blooms, but rose trees in huge pots to be placed upon the steps and about the park. Somehow, he must have heard that Mary Emma was disappointed with her own garden's offerings this doleful year. His generous gift has made all the difference to the festive look of the tables, too. And Mrs Aldrich came up to the house last evening with several potted palms and other exotics from Joe's conservatory. Doesn't it all look and smell heavenly?"

"It certainly does," Dr Barnes agreed. "But I won't have you tiring yourself out any more today, Agnes. Allow others to wait on you for a change, my dear. Once we are married, I shall see that you take more rest. You might even get to like it."

Mary Emma wandered in through the ell which still lacked the double doors that would afford privacy to both the library and Tom's office. She was carrying Thomas in her arms and the child was turning his eyes this way and that as the sunbeams picked out the gilding on the gleaming leather bindings. "*There* you are, Agnes! I thought I might find you hiding yourself away in here. Good-morning, Dr Barnes. Isn't it a perfect day?" Without waiting for his response, her gaze swept around the shelves, several of which remained empty of volumes. "Oh, dear. What a sad sight. I had hoped all the books would have been catalogued and bound before today. But I refuse to let it depress me! Look, Thomas Henry! See all Mama's and Papa's beautiful books? One day *you* will be able to read all these lovely books, poppet. Just think of that. What a lucky little boy!" She kissed his bonneted head. "Aren't you coming outside, Agnes?"

"A little later on, Mary Emma," she said. "You look a vision of loveliness in that dress, dear. Blue is definitely your colour. I'm so glad it's fine for your birthday."

Dr Barnes, who had risen on Mary Emma's entrance, bowed from the waist and said: "Allow me to congratulate you, Mrs Challiss, ma'am. I wish you joy of the day." He took his fiancée's hand. "If you won't think us too selfish, Agnes and I will spend a little more time together in here. Once she is rested, we'll join you outside."

"Thank you for your good wishes, Dr Barnes," Mary Emma said, smiling mischievously. "I quite understand: I know how precious seclusion is for courting couples, sir! Dear Agnes has worked so hard to make everywhere beautiful; with her time so near she must indeed be quite fatigued. Come along, Thomas," she said, in a mock-petulant voice, rocking her child in her arms. "They don't want us, pet. We'll go and find your Papa, won't we, darling. I know he'll be pleased to see us."

Outside, the sound of an orchestra drifted across the park from beside the lake. Children chased in and out of the trees and bushes, couples strolled beneath the tarnished sunshine, and labourers' wives carried their babies about, a trail of children following in their wake like so many goslings. Mary Emma spied David Deacon wearing a freshly-laundered smock and overheard much speculation as to who had 'got it up so fine'. Old ladies in dresses of black silk, of a style fashionable two decades earlier, with faded funereal feathers fastened to their Grecian headbands, sat in sheltered arbours gossiping, talking scandal and detrimentally criticising the young. In after years they would never tire of reliving the day over the teacups, positive that nothing could compare to 'that day at Uppham House in the awful summer of 1816' and that they hadn't really enjoyed themselves since the famous housewarming party.

Food was fine and plentiful. Ale, wine, cordial and beverages flowed ceaselessly. The orchestra lowered its professional standards to play a couple of rhythmical country dance tunes: "Gathering Peascods" and "Sellenger's Round" for the lower orders to dance to, and repeated the simple, gay dances several times throughout the long day. When the air cooled and bright Venus appeared in the evening sky the lamps were lighted in the park and the musicians struck up the introduction to the quadrille. Those few acquainted with the latest dance craze made up their squares and formed up in couples on the portable dance floor that had been placed handily in front of the refreshment canopy. The dancers attempted its intricate execution to the megaphoned voice of a professional caller, the quadrille being a novelty at Uppham, its five movements and varying rhythms being unlike any dance previously known.

" Look! Isn't that young Belmaine in that set over there? By Gad! I believe he's turned into Prince Charming himself!" Tom said to Mary Emma, unable to believe his own eyes at Robin's transformation. "He's as dainty as a dancing master."

Mary Emma smiled up at her husband, her lovely face vivid in the lamplight. "That's another story that's had a happy ending, Tom," she said. "And he's certainly no newcomer to the quadrille. Look at that footwork! Must've picked it up on his continental travels. I wish I knew the steps. Who's the beauty he's partnering?"

"A stranger to me, my love," Tom said, following the lissome red-head's graceful movements with evident enjoyment. "Though I can't say that I would call the young lady beautiful, exactly." His eyes sought hers. "There's only one woman here that truly fits that description, Mary Emma, and she's standing next to me," he said, with a gallantry that made her face glow and promised an exciting end to the day.

Among the motley throng, now rapidly reducing in number, only a select few had known that Mrs Challiss's eighteenth birthday had been celebrated as well as the housewarming and that was exactly as Mary Emma had wanted it.

The festivities ended when the musicians began to pack away their instruments at eleven o'clock, in consideration of the early hour at which the labourers' families and the majority of house servants must rise on the following morning to begin their long day's work. By the time Tom and Mary Emma climbed into bed shortly before midnight they were weary-eyed and ready for sleep, but not too tired to make love.

★

Chapter Forty-four

"'Tis all very well for them," Kit Warrender grumbled to David Deacon. "If that flashy show yesterd'y was anythin' to go by, Challisses are not feelin' the pinch like a lot o' folks round here. Seem ter be fair made o' money."

The shepherd tapped out his pipe on the heel of his boot before saying: "Tom Challiss's bin a fair master ter yew, int 'e, bor, wouldn't yer say?"

The farm manager wrinkled his weathered brow and scratched the spot beneath his blond pony tail. "Reckon," he conceded. "But it fair makes me wild to see some folks as have so much silver ter chuck about on fripperies when so many poor devils can't even scratch a livin'."

Deacon said mildly: "Yew wanna count your blessin's, bor, 'stead o' belly-achin' 'bout things that won't never be changed: leastways, not in our lifetime. Look where it's got those poor fools who was banged up in gaol fer riotin'. I 'ear them's likely ter be strung up; an all fer allowin' their tempers ter git the better of 'em."

Kit's blue eyes blazed. "Can't yew see the injustice of it, man? Ask yerself why they was riotin' in the first place! 'Twas in the cause o' solidarity. Just 'cause I'm comfortable, don't mean I have the right to let others starve, dew it? Me an' Jem marched with them rioters from Downham that've bin arrested. Did yew know that? And we'll do the same again if things flare up, as is likely. They're fine men, an' honest as the day's long, given the chance."

"I dessay you'm right, Kit. The trouble wi' yew is, you're young, see? Still, that's somethin' time'll take care of, afore long. Yew keep your 'ead down and git on wi' yer work, an' leave riotin' an' troublemakin' tew others. That's my advice ter yew."

"That sort o' talk won't make the troubles go away, shepherd Deacon," Warrender said in a calmer voice. "If we don't act, others will: for it's not ter be borne. A man will only stand so much before he fights back. Things might seem to have gone quiet, but the men are busy, at this very moment, plannin' fer the next uprisin'. It won't be this year, nor the next, mebbe; pr'aps not fer ten or twenty years; but poor, oppressed men discovered something in these bread riots that they didn't know before."

"Oh-ah? What's that then?" Deacon said, as if he were really interested in the answer.

"That they've a weapon that puts the fear o' God inter those in power; that there's hundreds more o' them than there are of their masters! Did yer hear what happened at Ely with the Littleport men on the 24th May, fer instance? That was down ter sheer numbers."

"Well," said the shepherd, puffing at his pipe and bending down to fondle his dog's silken ear as the silent animal lay at his feet, in order to give himself time to think of something more to say, "that's trew enough."

Finding his friend incapable, or unwilling, of sympathising with his cause, Warrender changed the subject somewhat drastically. "Was you aware that an ox is lighter on its feet than a draught horse, Deacon?"

"I hev tew admit that I aint give it much serious thought, Kit, me bein' a shepherd, like, an' not 'avin' much call tew dwell on sich matters," Deacon said, placidly puffing blue smoke into the morning air. "Is that a fact?"

"'Tis an education, to witness such a lumberin' great beast as an ox is, pamplin' across a field at ploughin' time," Kit enthused. "You'd expect it to be bumble-footed now, wouldn't yer? But it's not! 'Tis just like our illustrious Regent, Prinny, teeterin' along on those Louis-hilled shoes that George Brummel introduced his fat friend to."

"Oh-ah," Deacon nodded, crushing a yawn between clenched jaws, "that's a masterpiece, that is." Salvation came in the form of Fly tugging at his coat sleeve. "What's up, boy? *There*! Sorry, Kit, I shall 'ave ter go. Fly's never wrong when it comes ter sheep. After her, Fly!"

Warrender watched his placid friend wander off in the wake of the frantic dog and wondered how the man could stand such a tedious, uneventful and lonely life.

★

With just four days separating the Challisses' housewarming party and the marriage of Dr Barnes to Agnes Brook, Mary Emma found herself in the thick of preparations again early next morning. Before breakfast, while Thomas slept, she went along to Agnes's room and tapped on her door. A sleepy voice invited her in.

"I'm sorry to wake you so early, Agnes dear," Mary Emma whispered, now that the apology was too late to prevent her friend from disturbance, "but I wanted to ask you if it might not be a good idea for you to go home to Church House for a day or two. It's going to be Bedlam here for the next three days while we prepare the feast for the wedding breakfast and organise the reception. We don't want you tiring yourself out, now do we?

Because I know I shan't be able to stop you. What do you think?"

Agnes pulled herself up in the bed and yawned behind her hand. "But – I'm sorry, Mary Emma. I don't know where you got hold of the idea that we were to hold our wedding breakfast and the reception for our guests at Uppham House."

Mrs Challiss stared at her young friend as if she had misheard her. "What do you mean?"

Fully awake now, Agnes chose her words carefully. "Well, we never actually discussed it, did we, Mary Emma? Mother and Father are expecting me to be married from home – from Church House. The whole family's looking forward to it and Burton's arriving on Friday evening so as not to miss it. He's to be best man."

Deflated, Mary Emma sank onto the side of the bed. "It's true; we never actually discussed it, Agnes," she said; "somehow I thought that it would be what you would want. I've had the arrangements in my head for weeks now, along with my birthday and the housewarming. How silly of me." She looked positively dejected.

Agnes stretched out her hand and Mary Emma grasped it. "I can't disappoint my family, dear, now can I?" the younger woman said, her eyes pleading for understanding.

"Of course not," Mary Emma agreed, making a huge effort at sounding more cheerful than she felt. "But... Oh, dear!" She sighed heavily.

"Tell me. What's upsetting you so?"

"Everything's arranged for the wedding breakfast," Mary Emma said. "My birthday flowers will last until then: the servants have carried as many vases as could be accommodated to the spring room. The orchestra–"

Agnes swung her legs slowly over the side of the bed, came up to Mary Emma and put her arms around her. "How kind of you, Mary Emma. How very thoughtful," she said, kissing her cheek. "I am so sorry, dear; but neither Valentine nor I want a big fuss made." She took a step backwards. "Just look at me! Oh, I don't mind my family and friends seeing me in this state at the altar; but we had hoped to make it a modest, quiet affair, dear. Please tell me you understand."

"Of course, I do, Agnes." Mary Emma returned her kiss. "It's just that I did so want everything to be perfect for your special day."

Agnes laughed. "It all depends on what you mean by 'perfect'. Dr Barnes and I – and Mother agrees – think that the Brook family and the Barnes family, together with the Challiss family, Mr and Mrs Aldrich, Miss Nevett, Mr Rudge, the Reverend Fielding, Robin and Everett and all the Uppham servants that would like to witness the ceremony, will be just about the right number to make it a perfect day."

Mary Emma smiled at her. "It does seem as if you have it all worked out. What about the wedding breakfast and reception?"

"Mother has been baking for days. She'd be so disappointed if it all went to waste: not that it would, of course, with so many hungry mouths to feed every day."

Mary Emma took hold of both of Agnes's hands, pulled her down onto the edge of the bed beside herself and said, excitedly: "Would it upset the applecart very much if we were to transport your mother's baking to Uppham House? Then we could have the reception there as I planned, with the Martlet flowers all about us, lights and soft music—"

Agnes laughed. "Oh, Mary Emma! You're incorrigible! But your heart's very much in the right place. I shall have to see what Valentine and Mother have to say. If they agree, you shall have your way. I think I will go home after breakfast this morning and I'll send word by Ann about the decision for the reception as soon as I've talked to Dr Barnes and Mother about it. Will that suit you?"

"You are a perfect dear!" Mary Emma said, her spirits raised considerably...

Young Ann Brook rode up on her father's cob as afternoon tea was being served. She told Mary Emma and Tom, who had been joined by Ruth Aldrich for the afternoon, that: "Dr Barnes and Mother say they think it's a very good idea to hold the wedding breakfast at Uppham," adding to the formal message, "and so do we all. Everybody was cheerin' and golderin' at once and Mother told us to stop because she was in puckaterry with their nonnickin' and couldn't hear herself think. And when Agnes asked Mother if she minded much, Mother said that it was plain as a pikestaff that her eldest daughter preferred a palace to a parlour, so she would give in gracefully. But we all knew she wasn't cross, really, 'cause her eyes were twinkling."

Tom, Mary Emma and Ruth laughed heartily as they imagined the lively scene described by Ann, who didn't need much persuading to help them eat the thin cucumber sandwiches and sponge fingers offered with her cup of tea.

★

Unlike the lovely day that had dawned on Mary Emma's birthday, Agnes Brook's wedding day dawned wet and gloomy. Since that single summer day the weather had deteriorated again and the sun had been once more obscured by the uniform grey cloudcover that had dogged the spring and early summer.

Mary Emma sat on a low chair in her bedroom feeding Thomas and sighed on behalf of her friend. She wouldn't have gone so far as to have wished their special days had been exchanged, yet the sight of the miserable day outside the window was so depressing that she let the heavy curtain drop back into place. The rain dashed against the panes and the drops clung briefly to the glass before trickling downwards like so many tears. Poor Agnes! And she had looked so lovely, too, reminding Mary Emma of a Botticelli painting, at the final fitting of the tentlike dress of sprigged ivory satin brocade that swung loosely from the shoulders. It would be such a pity to see the hem covered in mud. Ruth Aldrich and young Hope Looret had performed most of the needlework; but Mary Emma thought that there couldn't have been a more distinguished gown to be found anywhere that would so effectively disguise Agnes's impending delivery. Agnes had decided to eschew a bonnet in favour of a chaplet of tea roses in bud and that adornment lay ready in the spring room.

Tom turned over in bed and flung out his arm. Immediately conscious of his wife's absence he said sleepily: "Come back to bed, darling; it's scarcely daylight."

"Shh! Thomas is almost done. He's just dropping off to sleep again."

★

Mary Emma awoke two hours later to the sound of Maddy opening the curtains and she was overjoyed to see hesitant sunshine filtering through the rain-spotted windows. As Tom was gone and Thomas slept on, she wriggled down in the bed, lay on her back and went over in her mind the preparations for the wedding breakfast and reception.

"Your tea's on the table, ma'am," Maddy said, with a bob, and Mary Emma saw that the girl was developing a bosom. "Charity's laid out your russet taffeta, Mrs Challiss and I'm just goin' down ter fetch the *h*ot water, ma'am, an' yer lemon-juice is fresh-squeezed. She said she'll wait fer you tew ring when yew want your *h*air done."

So the girl's learned to pronounce her aspirates at last, thanks to Miss Nevett's influence, thought Mary Emma. "Thank you, Maddy; but ask Peckover and Harris to carry up the water. Don't you do it. It's too heavy for you. That will be all for now."

Soon everybody was ready and it was time for them to leave for St Mary's Church. Moist air and sunshine drew forth mingled perfumes of roses, pinks and wallflowers that bloomed sparsely about Mary Emma's garden as Tom and his elegant wife, followed by capable Hope Looret with Thomas in her arms, descended the steps to their carriage. Every means of transport had been pressed into service in order that as many of the servants as could be spared from essential duties might attend the wedding of dear Miss Brook, and the little procession rolled away down the drive at half past eleven. The ceremony was to take place at noon, by which time almost every trace of the earlier rain had disappeared. Villagers stood about the churchyard intent on seeing the dresses worn by 'the gentry', as they thought of the Challisses and their friends, and deriving pleasure from the hour spent beneath the sun-splashed trees.

Late-blooming chestnuts stood about the churchyard in pink and white profusion and red, pink and white hawthorns set the distant hedgerows aglow as Dr Barnes emerged from the flower-swathed arched doorway of St Mary's, Uppham with his bride on his arm. Despite Agnes's wish to have her marriage a subdued affair, the villagers had hung about the churchyard among the grassy mounds, cow parsley and buttercups to cheer the happy couple on their way. For young Dr Barnes had proved himself their friend, and many a mother smiling at the pretty procession made by Agnes, followed by her younger sisters in their white dresses with blue satin sashes, had found in him a good friend in times of need. Even those disposed to censure his girl bride reasoned that such an upright young gentleman as Dr Barnes would not stoop to bind himself for life to a really wicked woman. Though they failed to come up with the reason for his preferring to wed a disgraced girl in her condition, especially as there were plenty of other young, good girls in Uppham St Mary, such as their own Maggie, or Betty, or Phyllis, who were just as pretty as "that Dulcie Brook's girl."

The public part of the day over, the select number invited to do so returned to the mansion in good time to sit down to the wedding breakfast, among which a discerning eye would have been able to distinguish the mouthwatering pies, pasties, moulded jellies and creams that had been made by Dulcie Brook's fair hands.

Burton Brook's prepared speech was full of good fun and was received with appreciative laughter by those who could trace his allusions. Their big brother's words of praise, referring to the prettiness their demure appearance had added to the procession to and from the church, caused the little bridesmaids to blush as he held his glass of claret towards them and paid them his compliments in a deep voice. Toasts were made to the bride, the bride's parents, the groom's parents and to Mr and Mrs Challiss for their generous hospitality, by which time the various wines and heady cordials imbibed in response to each little speech made by Burt had everybody bright-eyed and in convivial mood.

As the breakfast had been arranged for only those closest to the bride and bridegroom, the carpet in the front withdrawing room had been taken up and the furniture pushed back to the walls to allow for dancing. Even as the guests, replete with good food, sat and conversed amid the litter of the feast, the sound of instrumentalists tuning up drifted downstairs. Those keen and able to dance were drawn upstairs by the thoughts of the pleasant exercise to be produced by drifting round the room to the tune of the latest waltz in the company of a congenial partner.

Dr Valentine Crieff-Barnes's parents had not known what to expect when their son had written to tell them of his attachment and proposed marriage to a woman so much younger than himself. When he broke the news to them, in person, that she was about to be delivered of another man's child they had thrown up their hands in despair and had refused to speak to him ever again unless he gave up the idea. Fifteen minutes later, after he had persuaded them that he would never give up the woman he loved – not even to please his parents – they admitted defeat and gave him their blessing.

Today they had made Agnes's acquaintance and, having been prepared to dislike her on sight, had found themselves captivated by her candid nature and the obvious respect and affection she evinced for their son. That he was head over heels in love with his young bride was apparent to all as they watched his eyes follow her every movement about the room. Having decided to bow to the inevitable, it came as something of a shock to the Crieff-Barneses to meet Agnes's parents and the rest of her large family.

Valentine's crusty father, Dr Peregrine Crieff-Barnes, had raised his heavy white eyebrows in astonishment when Dulcibella Brook had swooped down upon him out of nowhere and saluted him warmly on each cheek before he was aware of her intention. His astonishment had soon been replaced by admiration when she had released him and he was able to stand back. Getting her into focus by means of his quizzing glass, he beheld a dazzling country beauty whose handsome smiling face and fine figure had put him in a very good humour directly.

On being introduced to Dr Crieff-Barnes-the-Elder's wife, Letitia, – a small, unremarkable woman in her early fifties – Mrs Brook swooped on her as swiftly as a hawk on an unsuspecting sparrow and narrowly avoided knocking sideways Mrs Crieff-Barnes's elaborate feathered turban. Having witnessed the trouble his wife's elderly maid had experienced earlier in the day in attempting to secure the horribly inappropriate adornment to her mistress's thin hair, Peregrine Crieff-Barnes stood by in an agony of suspense as, following Dulcie's onslaught, the headdress rocked back and forth. The dangerous moment passed. The turban clung to its flimsy perch. Letitia Crieff-Barnes stared at the woman who had greeted so warmly a neglected wife who had not been kissed by her husband for many years, and Dulcie laughed infectiously at the near catastrophe, before apologising profusely. Adam came up to see what all the fuss was about and his amusingly accurate commentary on the dancers soon had the starchy Crieff-Barneses unbending.

Immediately Mrs Crieff-Barnes senior discovered that Adam Brook was Head Gardener to the Uppham estate she struck up a conversation with him concerning the correct way to prune roses, listened carefully to his advice and the two became good friends, unlikely as it had seemed to either of them on first meeting.

The afternoon and evening wore away in the euphoric haze usually induced by excellent food, good wine and other liquid refreshment, congenial company and cheerful music. Suddenly it was time to retire for the night and many of the guests wondered how the oddly-matched newly-married pair would pass the long hours until morning.

★

A week had passed. Valentine's parents had ended their brief sojourn at Uppham House feeling very much happier than when they had set out for their son's wedding. The mansion had returned to its everyday routines and now everything seemed flat and ordinary after the diversion and excitement that had been provided by the housewarming and the wedding.

Agnes – alias Mrs Valentine Crieff-Barnes and known locally as 'Mrs Dr Barnes' – was expecting to be delivered any time now and had grown fretful during the last day or two. She disliked the house her husband had at Downham and wished her child could enter the world surrounded by trees and fields and plenty of fresh air. While it was only natural that Valentine's profession kept him away from home for most of each day and occasionally part of the night, she missed the warmth of her family and most of all she missed Mary Emma's lively company.

It had been her husband's suggestion that she stay with the Challisses for the birth of the child. He had seen that she was discontented. This was so unlike her usually placid nature that it had caused him concern. Two nights ago he had returned from a long and particularly difficult confinement to find his new wife sitting alone in the dark.

Valentine walked over to where the lamp was usually kept, found it by touch but had no means of lighting it with a spill, for the fire had been allowed to go out. He stumbled to the window and pulled the curtains apart: starlight showed the glazing bars of the windows in silhouette and dimly penetrated the room. He turned in the direction of Agnes's chair and sighed. "What are you doing, sitting here in the dark all by yourself, Agnes?" he asked, a weary edge to his voice.

"I have no fear of the dark, Val," she said, her voice devoid of energy, sounding quite unlike her usual self. "As for my being by myself: I'm rapidly getting used to that."

"What do you mean?"

"How do you think I spend my days, Valentine?" she asked him, dully.

"Why... I suppose you read, or sew, or perhaps knit clothes for your child, my dear. That's how most women in your condition spend their days. Isn't it?"

"Then I pity the poor things!" Agnes cried, bursting into tears.

In a moment he was kneeling beside her. "Agnes! Agnes, my love! Stop!" His arms were about her, her head held gently against his chest and he felt the violence of her emotion shaking her body. "Hush, Agnes," he implored. "This isn't good for you; it isn't good for the child. Hush, my sweet girl. Shh." He stroked the hair back off her wet face and kissed her. "Tell me what has upset you so, my darling. Are you afraid?"

She sat up as straight as she was able to within his restraining arms. "If by that you mean: am I afraid of the birth of my child, you know very little about me, Val."

"Then what is it that is depressing you so?" he asked, truly mystified for all his experience of attending women in his wife's condition.

"I am sad," she said. "I don't think I was ever really so sad and lonely in my life before. If only you would share my bed and comfort me."

"We've been through all that. It won't be for much longer, my dear. But sad?" he got to his feet. "What have you to be sad about, Agnes? Don't you have everything a woman could want? Why, if you saw the terrible conditions that some women have to live in you would count yourself blessed."

She gave a bitter laugh that chilled him. "I suppose you think that gilded mirrors, Turkish carpets and brocade curtains are all that a woman needs to make her deliriously happy. Well, let me tell you, sir: they do not! I would far rather live in a tumbledown farmhouse with a sagging roof and have my children sleep three to a bed, as long as that same roof sheltered a loving man whose first priority I was. I mean – I wish I were back among those to whom I matter as a *person* in my own right! I'm lonely, Val. Don't you understand? I'm used to having people who love me about me and I cannot and will not bring my child into the world in such a cold, unfriendly house as this is! I mean it."

"This is foolishness, Agnes," he said, reasoning with her. "Once the child is born you will have plenty to occupy you, believe me. And your lonely nights will be a thing of the past the minute you invite me into your bed so that we may consummate our marriage. I long for that moment as much as you do, my love. But you must see that it's impossible in your present condition? You do understand?"

"I understand that you find me repulsive in my present state! Why can't *you* understand?" she pleaded. "If the child came tonight, I would drag myself outside and bring him into the world in the garden under the stars, among the trees and flowers; anywhere rather than here in this... this miserable *bachelor's* house!"

"Forgive me," he said, wounded by her passionate outburst. "I was not aware that you found my home so abhorrent. It would be best, I think, if you were to return to your father's house – or perhaps you would prefer to go to Uppham House for the birth of your child, Agnes? There is plenty of room there and you would be safe with the Challisses." He kissed her chastely. "Would you like that, my dear?"

"Oh! Do you really mean it, Val?" She kissed him back affectionately. "Oh, you are the best of men, and I don't deserve such kindness after my childish outburst. I feel ashamed of myself for going on at you when you've had such an exhausting day. But it would make me so happy to be with Mary Emma again. May I go?"

He wrapped her tightly in his arms and rocked her as if she were his child and in need of comfort. "You don't have to ask my permission, Agnes," he said softly, kissing her eyes as they gleamed in the starlight. "You must go for both our sakes. Your being in such close proximity is making it very hard for me, you know. I've been selfish and inconsiderate in keeping you here and I'm sorry that you find it such an uncongenial dwelling; but I'm seldom here long enough to notice. We shall choose a house together as soon as it is practicable, my love."

"Really?" She raised her head and met his eyes which she could barely make out in the dim light. "And can it be in Uppham St Mary, Valentine? Do say yes!"

"I wouldn't be so rash as to promise that, Agnes, we shall have to see, my love." He kissed the top of her head. "I still cannot believe that you are my wife; it seems like a miracle. But we shan't have long to wait now and our wedding night will be all the sweeter for this imposed restraint, you'll find. Tomorrow you shall go to Uppham House and I'll call there some time during the afternoon to see how you are, my darling. Now it's late: time to retire. Remember I love you dearly, Agnes; hang on to that fact." They kissed in the manner of brother and sister, bade each other goodnight and borrowed the cook's lamp from the kitchen, where the fire was never allowed to go out, in order to light their way upstairs to their separate beds.

★

"I came up through the lime walk, my dear," Tom said, the following day, as he joined Mary Emma and Agnes in the dining room for afternoon tea. "When were you last there?"

"I don't know. It must be over a week, I should think. Why do you ask?"

"I suggest we all stroll over there after tea, if that will not inconvenience any plans you or Agnes might have made. It really is a little warmer abroad this afternoon and a gentle walk in the fresh air would do you and Agnes good. You are too much in the house, you know. We might take young Thomas with us."

"It's one of the mildest days we've had so far this year," Agnes agreed. "Just the sort of day to give Thomas an airing without his coming to any harm. Providing we go slowly enough, I can think of nothing I'd rather do. Please say you'll come Mary Emma."

Mary Emma laughed and replaced her cup in its saucer. "How can I resist both of you? I'll ask Hope to get Thomas ready at once and we'll make a little excursion of it, just the four of us. I'm so glad you suggested it, Tom, dear." Before anyone could say another word she hurried from the room.

Wondering what his unpredictable wife was up to now, Tom stared at the empty doorway through which his wife had passed and turned to Agnes. "Is anything amiss?"

"Not as far as I'm aware," she replied. "Mary Emma hasn't complained of anything to me."

Minutes later, Mary Emma reappeared carrying Thomas in her arms.

"Here he is, the little darling!" she smiled. "Look, Tom! I do believe he senses that we're taking him outside. He seems so expectant and happy. See how his little fists are waving about as if he can't wait to be off?"

Agnes smiled at her friend's exuberance.

The infant's certainly making minute sounds and movements that could lend themselves to that interpretation, supposed Tom. "Here. Give him to me, my dear," he said, holding out his arms to receive the baby.

Agnes looked anxiously at Mary Emma as she was about to place Thomas in her husband's arms, causing her to hesitate.

"Mother used to carry her new babies abroad in a washing basket lined with something soft," said Agnes. "That way we could carry the baby quite safely between us."

"What a very good idea!" Mary Emma cried, passing her precious bundle to a surprised Tom, now off guard, while she darted away in the direction of the kitchen. She was back almost at once, carrying a wicker laundry basket and some freshly laundered tea towels. Dashing next into Tom's study, she reappeared carrying two of the expensive brocatelle cushions by their corners, placed them in the basket, arranged them to form a comfortable bed and covered them with the clean linen. Snatching up her parasol, in case the reluctant sun should try to catch her out by shining if she left it behind, she announced herself ready to set forth.

Tom laid his son in the impromptu nest and he and Mary Emma, stationing themselves on either side of the basket, took hold of a handle apiece and carefully carried Thomas in the makeshift baby coach down the flight of steps.

They strolled across the grass in the direction of the lime walk with Mary Emma keeping a close eye on her little son who lay on his back staring up at the mottled vault of the sky. "He's watching the clouds moving," she whispered, bending down to baby Thomas Henry and causing the basket to wobble dangerously. "Do you like those big white fluffy things, darling?" she cooed. "They're cumulus clouds."

Tom laughed. "Oh, Mary Emma! Give the poor child a chance. If you were to have your way, you'd be trying to make a meteorologist of him before his first birthday."

Before his wife could respond the sun burned through the cloud and Agnes gasped.

Concerned for her friend's condition, Mary Emma turned to find her staring at something as if transfixed. She followed Agnes's gaze.

"Look, Tom," Mary Emma gasped. "Oh! How lovely!" She moved the parasol away from her son to shield her face from the sun's damaging rays. "My ugly little lime walk is transformed!" They set down the basket in which Thomas Henry lay with his bonnet flopped over one eye.

Thomas Roberts Challiss smiled at the odd picture his son made, bent down, straightened the bonnet, moved the basket into the shade and said: "Well, I hoped it would be, dear. It happens only when the sun shines from the south-west at a given angle. I first noticed it at about this time yesterday. Looked as if we might be unlucky this afternoon; but the sun came up trumps. Isn't it a picture, my love?" he added, standing up and arranging his free arm to encircle her waist which, he noticed with approval, was returning to its eighteen inch span.

Sunshine warming their faces, the young people stood at the entrance to the avenue of spindly saplings and were awed by the spectacle before them.

Pellucid in the afternoon sunlight, agitated by a restless wind, numberless cardioid leaves made moving pictures for their eyes, soft music for their ears. Following many months of arctic temperatures and wintry gloom, the gyrating kaleidoscopic patterns of sunlit green and amber hearts seemed to hypnotize the observers. For Agnes and the young Challisses seemed powerless to tear their attention away from the dazzling display of rustling foliage that constantly fluttered in the strong breeze. They were enthralled by the phenomenon.

Baby Thomas Henry yawned, hiccupped, broke the spell and drew their attention once more to the everyday. Yet the memory of the unique experience lingered and nobody spoke; as if they were reluctant to banish the charm of it.

Mary Emma was the first to speak. "Winter will never seem so long now that we have this miracle to look forward to each year." Still spellbound, Tom and Agnes nodded their agreement.

For the saplings had survived one of the harshest winters and springs in living memory and stood straight and tall in their profusion of new leaf. Adam Brook had done well. While the spaces between the lime saplings made them appear weaker than they actually were, the parallel lines that defined the walk were straight and true.

Even so, Mary Emma grumbled at having to wait so long to see the saplings become trees.

"Have patience my dear," Tom said. "Allow fifteen to twenty years. By that time your lime trees will have grown into a shaded walk of which you will be proud. But even these saplings are something to marvel at on a sunny day, Mary Emma, don't you agree?"

Before anybody was able to comment futher, they heard a shout and turned to see Dr Valentine Crieff-Barnes striding across the park to join them. The young doctor beamed and kissed his girl-wife as Agnes whispered to him that she'd had niggling pains in the small of her back all afternoon.

Overjoyed by the news that his enforced celibacy would soon be at an end, Val suggested they return to the house without delay. Ready to face her travail after months of waiting, Agnes took the arm of her nominal husband and together they strolled back towards the mansion.

Mary Emma shaded her eyes from the sun with her parasol as she watched the couple depart. "If my own experience is anything to go by, Tom," she remarked, "dear Agnes should be delivered of her child within the next few hours. But what if Val refuses to accept Charles Vyvyan's love-child? What is to become of poor Agnes then?" Tom shook his head dolefully. They waited until they saw that Dr Barnes and his wife had safely traversed the uneven ground of the partially landscaped park.

Relieved, Mary Emma suggested that they take a last turn among the lime saplings before the sun changed direction and the natural phenomenon vanished. As his parents bore him into the avenue of shimmering foliage, sedately along its entire length and back, Thomes Henry continued to doze among the tangle of rumpled tea towels, oblivious to the splendour that surrounded him.

It seemed that their child was, at present, as blind to beauty as he was ignorant of the fact that he was next in line to be burdened with the Challiss inheritance. The infant heir slept on while the young Challisses carried him homewards in the wicker basket: over Uppham's park, up the front steps and into Uppham House.

Acknowledgements

To the staff at the National Army Museum Bookshop, Royal Hospital Road, London SW3;

To The French Tourist Board.

To Angela at de Beers.

To Bea at Lilley's Jewellers, Chingford for her description of the cutting of a marquise diamond.

To the staff at The Priory Centre (Local Studies Library) Downham Market, West Norfolk, for their assistance with antique maps and other archive materials.

To Gollancz for their kind permission to quote, without fee, from *Bread or Blood: An Account of the Norfolk Bread Riots.* A.J. Peacock: (Gollancz, London 1965)

Grateful acknowledgement to Keith Skipper, author, for permission to use his glossary *Larn Yarself Norfolk*, without fee. Also to Nostalgic Publications, publishers of the aforementioned glossary, for waiving their copyright fee.

My special thanks are due to Clare Tierque and Dale Noble who spared many hours out of their busy lives in closely reading the manuscript in embryo, who gave unstintingly of their valuable time in correcting earlier versions of the manuscript and for the reading of later drafts.

My sincere thanks to all the staff at Matador, led by publisher Jeremy Thompson, Troubador Publishing Ltd, who assisted in the production of this novel.

For their unlimited patience, unvarying politeness and invaluable professional assistance, special thanks and gratitude are due to Julia Fuller, Jane Rowland and Amy Cooke, without whom *The Lime Walk* would probably not have seen the light of day.

Not least, to the countless others who gave freely of their own time in responding to my unending queries.

Bibliography – Reference only

Every effort has been made to trace all copyright holders.
The author apologises in advance for any omissions.

Bread or Blood: A.J. Peacock (Gollancz, 1965).

The Common People 1746-1946: Coles and Postgate. (Meuthen, 1976).

The Village Labourer 1760-1832: J.L. Hammond & Barbara Hammond. (Allan Sutton Publishing, Glos).

The History of Downham Market: The Downham Market & District Amenity Society, 1999.

Fashion in Costume 1200-1980: Joan Nunn. (The Herbert Press, 1993).

Penguin Dictionary of Historical Slang: Eric Partridge.
(Abridged by Jacqueline Simpson, Penguin Books, 1972).

The Housekeeping Book of Susannah Whatman:
(The National Trust, 2000).

English Social History: G.M. Trevelyan (Longmans. London. 1942).

The People's Chronology: Jame Trager. (Heinemann. London, 1975).

Holden's Annual London and Country Directory 1811: (Michael Winton, Norwich, 1996).

Larn Yarself Norfolk: Keith Skipper. (Nostalgic Publications, Norfolk 1996).

Confessions of a Poacher 1890: (Old House Books. Moretonhampstead, Devon, 2003).

A Thousand Years of Norfolk Carrstone: Claude J. W. Messent, 1967.

A History of Norfolk: Susannah Wade Martins. (Phillimore & Co. Ltd. 1997).